The Sound of Thunder

TAYLOR CALDWELL, an Englishwoman by birth, lived in America since 1906 when her family emigrated to New York State. After many years of research, writing and discouragement her novel *Dynasty of Death* was published in 1938; an immediate bestseller, it launched her on a spectacularly successful writing career.

Since then she has published many more books. Two of her most famous bestsellers, *Captains and the Kings* and *Testimony of Two Men*, were made into successful television series.

Taylor Caldwell died in 1985.

Available in Fontana by the same author

Captains and the Kings
Ceremony of the Innocent
Dynasty of Death
Testimony of Two Men
The Eagles Gather
The Final Hour
The Side of Innocence

TAYLOR CALDWELL

The Sound of Thunder

FONTANA/Collins

First published in Great Britain 1958
First issued in Fontana Paperbacks 1966
Seventh impression July 1986

Made and printed in Great Britain by
William Collins Sons & Co. Ltd, Glasgow

FOR
GEORGE AND HELEN SLOTKIN

"There will always be the sound of thunder, and chaos and ruin and death, in the affairs of men and nations until they achieve God and enter into His tranquillity."

LAO-TSE

EPILOGUE

Dawns always came too soon for Margaret, who loved the night. But this dawn would never come. She was certain of it. Her eyes were so parched that they felt dusty and stiff; she had no tears at all. She had tried to pray, but the terror in her had been a black storm through which no shafts of prayer could penetrate. Could you reach the ear of God if you could not pray, if the agonised tempest of your despair and fear rose between you and Him, a towering, dense pillar of fulminating darkness? There was not even a cry in her; her very brain was mute and cowering; it had no words.

This was grief; this was the very deadness of grief. This was anguish, even if dumb. "Father," she whispered, and her lips were as dusty as her eyes, and the word, she believed, went no farther than her tongue. All she had to offer God was a threat: If—he—dies, then I'll hate You. I'll hate You! But one did not threaten God, the Church said. One did not tempt God. But God was merciless. Are You merciless? her mangled heart demanded. Yes, You've been merciless—all the days of his life.

She leaned her cold forehead against the colder glass of the window, and felt no chill. She was conscious of no exhaustion, no sinking in herself. There was only rigidity, the rigidity of powerful resistance. To God. "The Lord giveth and the Lord taketh away—He gave, but He took away, when it was wrong, when it was unjust, when it was monstrous." She did not think of her children. What did children matter, if he whom you loved more than children, more than God—and yes, she loved Ed more, much more—was dying? Dying, because he had given so much, with faith, with both hands loaded with gifts, asking only that he be accepted and used for the benefit of the receiver! Dying, because flesh and blood could endure only so much work, so much anxiety, so much bewilderment and disillusion and betrayal, so much false accusation and shrill hatred, so much ungrateful grasping and greed!

She was alone. There was no Ed now to put his good arms around her and murmur comfort to her, and draw her head to his shoulder so that she could cry out her frozen tears of anguish. Her children? They were nice children, even thoughtful, even loving, but they were children after all. They would surmount this; they would grieve a while, but youth ran in them like a torrent, and it would take them away, and she would be desolate for ever. Unless, she thought numbly, unless I choose not to live. She challenged God: if Ed dies, then I won't live. I'll follow him, cursing You.

There had never been anything for her, really, but Ed. Neither father nor mother, neither sister nor brother, no children, no other joy, no other fulfilment, no other hope—but her husband. Now a lancelike pain of sheer torture ran through her stumbling mind, through her dimming mind. "Ed, Ed," she whispered. She saw the long dim estate of trees and grass through the window; it was a cemetery, not a home any longer. When had it stopped being either a home or a delight? She could not quite remember. She put her hand to her cheek. Yes, now she remembered. It was when Ed had taken out a mortgage on this big and lovely mansion, and had told her that as co-owner she must sign the papers with him. The mortgage had been necessary, in spite of Ed's vast holdings, because there had been, and still was, a Depression, and there were literally thousands of people dependent on him. Margaret had smiled and nodded encouragingly at her husband while she signed, but upon the signing the house became only a house to her, and not a home. Ed had never known this. Or, had he?

Something quickened in the region of her heart, like a bitter and ruthless fire. It was hatred. Hatred for them all, all of them, Ed's mother, his three brothers, his sister. But the fire could not expand the withered tensity of her body; it raged like a death, but it raged in iron, without heat.

She hurried frantically to placate God. "You won't take him, will You?" She spoke in herself with the voice of a cringing and terrified slave. "You'll be kind, won't You, God? Not Ed, God, not Ed—just anyone else in the world. I, for instance. Take my eyes, my life, give me an awful disease, strike me down, do anything to me, kill me now, give my strength to Ed. He's so strong; it won't hurt him so badly for me to be gone."

Someone was taking her arm urgently; someone had seen

her nodding, had seen her fixed, cunning smile, her silent, moving lips. "Mrs. Enger, you must take that pill Dr. Bullitt gave you; you must! You've got to rest a little. You've stood by this window for hours. Won't you sit down for a minute, please?" It was the nurse. The tiny nightlight on the table near the bed showed her blunt face in large masses of dimness and vague illumination. She was greatly concerned. Margaret stared blankly at her; her mouth retained the fixity of her deathly grimace. She shook her head, and resisted the pull of the nurse's hand. Her voice came faintly through her shrivelled throat. "I can't, I can't. Let me alone, please. How——?" and her voice fainted.

"Mr. Enger is resting comfortably. Look, you can see for yourself."

But Margaret was paralysed. She could not go to the large bed where her husband lay, hardly breathing. Ed was alone on that long and terrible journey, and her voice, her touch, her cry, could not reach him. Her spirit lifted appealing hands to that back but he did not turn.

"There, that's right," said the nurse, in a low and kindly voice. "Let me put this stool under your feet. Now, just swallow this and here's the glass of water. . . . We've got to keep up our strength."

"He's dying; he will soon be dead," Margaret whispered, and the whisper was a rustle. She tried to see the nurse's face through a mist. She grasped the other woman's arm.

"There," said the nurse, comfortingly. "Look, the door of your room is open. We'll lie down and have a little sleep." She was a middle-aged woman and had been a nurse for many years, but it always tore at her heart to see grief. "I'll call you, Mrs. Enger, if there's the slightest change. He's breathing real quiet now. The—the cardiogram wasn't so bad," she added, lying in her compassion. "I've seen worse. I'm sure he'll make it, with the help of God." (She prayed inwardly, Now, dear Blessed Mother, you won't hold that against me, will you, and I'll go to confession Saturday. You've got to lie sometimes, to help people.)

But not Ed, thought Margaret. Ed isn't going to live. God hates me; He'll take Ed, and Ed won't remember, because there won't be Ed any more, no Ed for me any more, because there is no God.

"The doctor wouldn't have left him, if he—well, if he—

was in any real danger," lied the nurse again, and remembered how many times she had told this to so many other piteous wives, or parents, and how many times it had been only a consoling falsehood. " Now, would he?"

She left Margaret in the chair into which she had practically forced her. She had a stethoscope of her own, and she put the plugs in her ears and pressed the disc against the white silk which covered Edward Enger's chest. She listened intently, her lips tight, her eyes sorrowful. The heart fluttered feebly; it wavered, skipped, almost stopped, then took up its weary pulsing again. She glanced at the hypodermic syringe, swathed in cotton, on the bedside table. At six o'clock, Dr. Bullitt had said, sternly. It was only half-past four. Mary took up the syringe, shot a drop or two from the top, then plunged the needle firmly into the arm of the unconscious man. She studied his square, grey face, with the purplish hollows under the eyes, the purplish tints in the furrows about his big mouth and under his chin. She stood there, bent over Edward, watching intently. Then she applied the stethoscope to his chest again. The wavering heart was hardly struggling now. Cold water seeped over Edward's forehead, lay in the hollow between nose and lip, ran from his temples.

Then his stricken heart, rallying, gave a leap, a few running beats, as if in haste; it jumped once or twice. And then it was beating more steadily, more determinedly, as if by an actual act of his submerged will. He moved his head, moaned almost inaudibly. The nurse moved lightly, for all her weight, to Margaret, who was half-lying in the round red chair which matched the red brocade curtains at the windows. The little light in the room evoked twinkling flashes of gold from the draperies, but made Margaret's face ghostly and without substance under the tangled, bright waves of her hair.

"There!" said the nurse proudly. "He's doing fine. Really fine, Mrs. Enger. Why, in a couple of hours he'll be awake and you can speak to him. Now, won't you go to bed and lie down?" she added, coaxingly.

"No," said Margaret. She lifted her arms heavily and ran her slender fingers through the shoulder-length mass of her hair, and it stood about her face in a halo of distraction. "I can't leave, not even for a minute. Thank you," she added, dully, with an automatic politeness.

Margaret dropped her head on her breast. She returned to

her thoughts. What was it that Ed was always saying? "All the days of my life." She had been curious about that phrase, even when she had first met him, over twenty-two years ago, curious about the buoyancy with which he said it, the grim lightness, the casual humour. She had told him, for he did not know, that they came from the 23rd Psalm, and she had repeated the whole Psalm to him.

She turned her head. The dawn was here at last, the reluctant, hidden dawn. She pushed herself to her feet and went to the window again. A magenta slit had vanished, and the cold eastern sky had turned a far and remote green. Its weird light lay over the landscape, revealing it rather than giving it life. Now Margaret could see, very clearly, the long line of the March-bound lawns, the trunks of the immobilised trees, the stiff black branches, the little mounds of corroded snow scattered here and there like the mounds of graves. Like Ed's grave will be soon, she thought. The bells of St. Michael's Church, half a mile away, began to clang, discordantly, to Margaret's ears. That would be the first Mass; two or three of the servants would be leaving by the back door. Would they pray for Ed? Would they remember? Did anyone remember a man except his wife? His children, his brothers, his sisters, his servants, his friends, his associates, his employees or employer, all those he had helped?

Then she saw a yellowish gleam on the crystal-coated arbor vitae near the living-room window. Was it possible that Ed's family were keeping their own vigil, as she had kept hers, all this terrible night? She started away from the window. She did not look at the bed; it was not Ed there, moaning faintly. Ed was far away. Margaret knew that if she went to the bed she would begin to scream beyond her control, that something would break in her and disintegrate and she would fly wildly into a darkness of her own, and without her volition. She brushed by the nurse as she ran from the room.

The broad hall outside was lightless and chill, and the thick carpet hushed Margaret's flying footsteps as she passed closed mahogany doors. Now she was racing down that curved and stately staircase, which seemed to float from floor to floor. The great chandelier hung from the ceiling; it still burned, with its mauve and shadowy pendants and prisms shaking in a slight draught. All the lamps were lit in the long living-room, and exhausted murmurs crept through the dead air.

Margaret, at the foot of the staircase, paused and caught her breath. She ran her hands over her disordered hair, over her slim hips and arms, as if to draw herself together, as if to make of herself a compact and avenging force. She threw back her head with that valiant gesture which Edward had always loved, and her chin became poised again in the position which Gregory had termed "arrogant, without any reason for her being arrogant." Now Margaret's eyes flashed with an almost fiery blue, and her white lips became stern. She went into the living-room in silence. There were Gregory and Sylvia and Ralph and Margo and David. They were weary and silent, Ralph smoking steadily as always, the venetian glass ashtray near his elbow filled to overflowing, the ashes spilling on the polished walnut table.

It had been too much to expect, of course, that Ed's mother would be keeping vigil, too. No doubt she was sleeping snugly, in her big bedroom with the faded chintzes. Margaret had spoken to none of them to-night, except Gregory, who had precipitated Edward's attack; and whom she now hated even more than she hated the others. Even in her numbness Margaret was surprised to see David, who had not been at home when the terror had happened. But Edward despised him more than he despised the others, and accordingly Margaret despised him, too.

Someone had been bringing coffee into this vast living-room which Margaret and Edward had furnished with such pride and satisfaction. The mighty silver service had been placed on the table near the fireplace, in which logs still smouldered. Margaret's best Spode coffee set lay scattered on other tables, the dregs black and cold under the stately silver or crystal lamps. Sylvia, thin and dark as a lifeless twig, but chic as usual, and with her narrow lips painted their usual dark red, was now speaking. "I'm worn out," she murmured. Her face was stark and white as bone, and her tilted black eyes had blurred with fatigue. "I wonder how . . ." She stopped, suddenly, and her white throat revealed a sudden spasm, and she clenched her hands together. She moved her long and narrow body, in its tight-bodiced, wide-skirted black dress, as if trying to find a more comfortable position in the chair. Her black hair, drawn harshly back from her cold bleak temples, was rolled into a big knob on her neck, and, because of the dye used to keep any grey from showing, it had no lights of shadows in it. "Oh, God," she murmured again. "He's our brother, isn't he? Why hasn't someone been down——?"

David, her oldest brother, stood near her, his slender hand on the back of her chair. He was elegant and distinguished as always, and dressed in black, as always, and though more than a year older than his brother, Edward, he had a patrician agelessness. His lean head was bent, his aquiline profile brooding and still. "There's just the nurse," he said to his sister, comfortingly . "And you could hardly expect Margaret to leave him just now. I've been up to the door a dozen times, but it's shut and there's no sound behind it. We've just got to wait, I'm afraid."

Ralph, the youngest, said in his robust voice, "Dr. Bullitt told me it wouldn't necessarily be fatal. Why, millions of people have coronaries every day, and over fifty per cent, now, recover well from such accidents." He was a big and ruddy man with a mass of auburn hair and a round face so vigorous in expression that at times he resembled a strong child.

Margo, Gregory Enger's wife, had been crying strenuously, and her bold face had a crumpled look. Streaks of straight blonde hair were strewn over her wide forehead, and she kept pushing them automatically out of her small blue eyes which were so swollen now. "Jesus!" she exclaimed. "How'd anyone know that he had a bad heart, anyway? You'd never think a man like Ed would drop down—like that." She shivered, and her eyes strayed around the room guiltily.

Gregory, sitting apart from them all, said savagely, "Shut up! For God's sake, shut up! Haven't you done enough, damn you?"

Margo sat upright, in outrage. "Me! I did it?" Now she flushed violently. "It was you! I've been thinking, sitting here. I've been thinking of Dad and Mom, and how they won't even talk to me any more—because of you, and what you taught me. Damn you, yourself! You can bet I've been doing some thinking, old Greg!"

She stared at him furiously, seeing her husband now as a whole, this forty-three-year-old man who was a feebler copy of Edward, this sophisticated man with light-grey eyes that were always dancing maliciously. They were not dancing now. They had a haunted expression, and his big mouth was jerking, and he was deadly pale under the darkness of his complexion.

"You and Margo were with him, and Margaret, when it happened," said Sylvia. Her voice rose sharply, and she turned in her chair to study him the better. "You never did tell us what happened, or why. Tell us now."

"Nothing," he said, sullenly, and again his mouth jerked as if in torment. "He'd just come home from . . ." He stopped, and coloured. "I think it was from New York. Margo and I just happened to pass the library, and he was in there with Margaret, and we talked a little, and then he collapsed."

"I think you're lying," said Sylvia, in a slow and bitter voice. "You were always a liar, Greg. And you won't tell us the truth now."

"Yes," said Margaret, in the arched doorway. "He's a liar. You all are."

They started, then gazed at her with fear and withdrawal, except for David who took a step or two towards her. But she halted him with a fierce motion of her hand. She came into the room, walking silently and gracefully, tall and straight and poised in her severe suit.

"Why do you stay here?" cried Margaret, passionately. "You don't care for Ed. Ed, to you, was always the peasant, the stupid one of the family, the treasury of the family, the dolt, whose only reason for being alive was to service and support you."

"Now, look here," said Ralph, "you don't know what you're saying, Margaret. I know this is awful for you, but you won't let anybody come near you, not even my own wife, Violette, and you always liked her, didn't you? You haven't any right to insult us. Ed's our brother; you've only known him about twenty-two years; we've known him all our lives. He's our flesh and blood——"

"How kind of you to remember that all at once," said Margaret, the passion in her voice rising. "Have you just remembered because you're wondering what Ed has left you in his will?"

"I resent that," said Sylvia, and the slash of her lips stood out in the bony pallor of her face. David, who had returned to her, put his hand firmly on her shoulder. He looked at Margaret with sadness. " I know how you hate us," he said, " and I'm not going to deny you have reason, more reason than you know. But there are things you don't know, too, and this isn't the time or place to tell you. However, please Margaret, I want you to understand, just a little, without exaggeration or too much hate——"

" I understand everything!" exclaimed Margaret, twisting her hands together. Now the haggard eyes sparkled with desperate loathing. " Do you think I'd believe anyone but my husband?"

" Our own brother," said Ralph, " and you won't let any of us go near him."

" Margaret," David pleaded. But she turned and left then and silence followed her. The stairs rose before her endlessly; she climbed for ever into the darkness of the upper hall. She had to lean against the balustrade for a moment, for there was such a constriction in her throat and chest, such a rage of pain. Perhaps I'm going to die too, she thought, and the pain relaxed, as if she had heard a promise of deliverance.

For the first time Margaret came to the bed, no sensation in her feet or legs. She stood beside her husband and looked down at him. His face was faintly coloured, as if with fever, against the white pillows. His eyes were closed and his breath was ragged.

Then she heard a tired whisper. " Margaret?"

She turned her head with a powerful effort. Edward's grey eyes were smiling up at her. She slipped to her knees because she could no longer stand. She let her head fall beside Edward's head. He moved his hand feebly and took her fingers and pressed them against his cheek. " Darling," he murmured, " you're cold."

" Ed," she said. " Oh, Ed."

" It's all right," he replied. " Don't worry, dear. It'll be all right." He moved in his fearful distress and pain. " All the days of my life."

She lifted her head, and she thought, clearly, Yes, he is dying. " You've forgotten the rest of it, sweetheart," she said. " Surely goodness and mercy shall follow me all the days of my life, and I shall dwell in the house of the Lord for ever."

For a long moment or two he regarded her with the

strangest expression, but it was as if he were remembering something, looking far back into the recesses of his spirit. His light eyes darkened and withdrew, pondering, and no longer seemed to see his wife. Even when she took his hand and held it tightly he still did not see.

"For ever," she whispered. "For ever. For ever, my dear, for always. To the end of time."

His darkened eyes closed in soundless peace, and the nurse's compassionate hand touched Margaret's head. "Surely, goodness and mercy," a voice said, but Margaret did not hear.

Her whole life seemed centred in Ed's hand, to which she clung, and all her consciousness was in that hand. Was it becoming a little warmer, or was it that her own hand was turning to ice? She began a groaning litany.

"Father, don't take him. Almighty God, don't take him. Christ, Our Lord, spare him for me. Father, have mercy. Christ, have mercy——"

PART ONE

"Should there be a son or a nephew or a cousin in the family who is capable and courageous enough to do all the work, then the other members need not disturb themselves, or save their money, or labour. For it has been shown by the gods that it is their intention that The Strong One must carry the burden."

—OLD CHINESE SAYING

Chapter One

In a few minutes he would have to go to help his father. Far off, in the hot Sunday quiet of early evening he could hear the Vesper bells ringing, sweet and unearthly against the gold and fiery rose of the western sky. A dusty breeze sang dryly in the trees; the houses, the street, lay entranced in stupefied silence, the cobblestones grey with grime, spattered, here and there, with the brown of horse manure. It was so still that Edward Enger, fourteen-year-old, heard distinctly the distant and languid clop-clop of a horse going home, and the serene rattle of some buggy or carriage filled with a happy family replete from a picnic, a drive along the river, or a visit to relatives. He had never ridden in a buggy or, better, a carriage. But, it was good, sitting this way on the kerb, with no one around, and only the sky and the bells for company. Across the narrow and cobbled streets he could see the quiet porches trailing wistaria, purple in the mauve shadows that filled the air, the Chinese prisms voiceless, the comfortable chairs, cushioned and waiting, the tenantless hammocks. The upper windows of the houses opposite reflected the sky, and seemed to burn with an inner fire. A dog barked, surfeited and content, out of sight, resting after the heat.

Edward thought School Road, where he lived, about the nicest street in the city of Waterford, though it was lower middle class and no home contained any luxuries, such as he had seen elsewhere. On this block, only his own home, behind him on a narrow green lawn, and the Witlock's, boasted a piano. Well, it was something to have a piano! Edward lifted his head, proudly. He pressed his big brown hand against his shirt pocket. Five dollars there! Four of them to-morrow, would go for David's piano. (It was always "David's piano," when the family spoke of it, though Edward was paying "on time" for that glorious instrument. Four dollars a week. Fifteen more weeks. Then it would truly be "David's piano.") Edward sighed, frowned a little. He hated buying "on time." So did his parents. But David had to have that piano.

He leaned his throbbing back against the trunk of the great old elm behind him, and felt the comfort of companionship. Sylvia said it made the house dark and gloomy, and Mr. and Mrs. Enger, who loved the tree, had yet been eager to sacrifice it for the sake of Sylvia's "nerves." She hated shadows and the quiet of serene old branches. Sylvia was all quickness and impatience. But for once Edward had raised his voice, in a house where his voice was seldom permitted to be heard or heeded. ("That dolt!" Sylvia would say.) He, Edward, had said, "If you cut down that tree David don't get more payments on his piano. Hear?" Sylvia had replied with contempt, "The word is 'doesn't,' Stupid."

Edward shook his head, remembering. He had wanted to remind Sylvia, thirteen years old, and in "first year high," that he had had to leave school at the age of fourteen because he was needed. But a quarrel with Sylvia inevitably brought pain to his father's face, and annoyance into his mother's eyes, and cutting remarks from the other children. Edward's parents were sorry that he had had to leave school, even though his marks had not been distinguished. He had, when the decision had been made for him, expressed his awkwardly-spoken wish to be a physicist. "What!" David cried with mirth. "You? Why, you're no good at anything but mathematics!" David, the pianist, had not, of course, understood that mathematics was the most important requisite. But Mrs. Enger had begun to frown and Edward had said no more. His room was crowded with old second-hand books on physics, and he read them and hid them whenever anyone entered. Maybe he was a fool, at that, thinking of being a scientist when there was so much genius in the family: David, the pianist, Sylvia who produced the school play, Gregory who would probably be a famous writer, and Ralph, who would be an artist.

But still, after he had spoken in a loud, firm voice, no one had dared to suggest that the tree be cut down. "I like her," he had said. "I've got a name for her. Margaret. She looks like a Margaret." No one, after he had warned them, had dared to jeer as usual.

Edward, who hated the very scent of power, and who, instinctively, suspected power and the users of power, had been ashamed when he had silenced his family. He had been a bully. He despised bullies. He had wanted to apologise. He looked up at the mighty tree now, and smiled. "If I'd said I was sorry, about Sylvia's nerves, you wouldn't be up there to-day, Margaret. You'd be firewood, for the kitchen stove." The tree, as if in response, bent her lovely green crest, and it glittered with the sunset light, and a bird rose from it, singing. Edward listened. Now birds were SOMETHING! You'd think that David, at least, the pianist who would be famous, would listen to birds, especially at dawn, and at sunset. But David hated the "out-of-doors. So crude." David was fifteen. For an instant, and only for an instant, Edward addressed David in his heart: "You're daffy." Then he hurriedly turned away from the revealing truth, remembering that his father, who had actually shaken Wagner's hand in Germany, and who played the flute, had declared, with an ecstatic clapping of his little fat hands, that David was a genius, with the soul of a musician. Pa ought to know! Besides, Pa had a bad heart and loved serenity and affection in a family. Nothing disturbed him so much as quarrelling and angry voices.

Ed looked at the sunset. God was only for the people who did things, who had missions. "You and I," Mr. Enger had said to Edward in his native German, "we were born to serve. We carry the angels on our backs, humbly. It is a blessing to us, my son."

"I suppose Pa's right," Edward grunted, looking up at his beloved tree.

"Margaret" clamoured in a sudden gust, distressfully. Edward could not interpret, for this was a new voice. He was pondering on the strange and urgent message to him when he heard the brisk flutter of wings and a scrabbling in the dust. A young brown hen flew determinedly on his knee, and he laughed and took her in his hands and cuddled her under his chin. " How'd you get out, Betsy?" he asked, with severity. " Thought I'd penned you in good." The hen pecked feverishly at his lips and cheeks, in her frantic affection. He had bought her at Easter in the local five-and-ten; five cents. " You ain't worth even five cents," he told her lovingly, as she pecked at his ear. " Not five cents, you rascal. Gee, you were cute when you were a kid, just a yellow ball of cotton-batting. Never mind, you're cute now, too." He ruffled the brown feathers on her neck with his mouth and she squirmed with delight. " Why, you're just a kid, anyway. But you got to get back in your pen. Never can tell what'll happen to you out here."

Betsy pushed her head against his neck, then inside his sweat-heavy shirt. She clucked her love. He stroked her gently, eased his back against the tree. Hell of a thing, working all day Sunday, mowing lawns, cleaning out cellars, brushing out furnaces, getting ready for the winter, washing windows, cranking ice-cream freezers, scrubbing down porches, mopping over buggys and carriages, piling up manure in barns, currying horses. But he couldn't complain; he made more on a Sunday than on week days, when he helped his father full time in the store. His father paid him five dollars a week, which was his own. But there was always a call on it before he could buy what he wished for himself. He could keep one dollar of his Sunday earnings. He scratched Betsy's stomach and she held up one claw to give him more room, rolling her eyes in ecstasy. " I'm going to make you a real pen, not just that crate," he told her. He rubbed her against his cheek again, and she yawned with pleasure. He had always wanted a dog, but Betsy was better. She understood everything he said, just as " Margaret " understood. Dogs, now, listened, but they listened with their ears, not " inside " them.

He stood up. Holding his hen he pushed his feet into his shoes. He winced, for his feet had swollen and the blisters hurt. He tossed his dark-brown hair, shaggy and damp with a sweat, off his forehead, so that the new breeze could cool him. Never had been such a hot August like this, in anybody's memory. It kept a fellow dodging under trees, out of the sun, on the way to work or school. School. He had

had to leave school in June, after he had finished the ninth grade. He decided not to think of school; it hurt too bad.

He turned towards his home, a tall, lean clap-boarded house painted light grey with dark-grey trimming, its attic window a slash of scarlet in the sunset. Just then David, in the parlour, began on the "piece" he had been endlessly practising. Edward knew it was a part of the "Moonlight Sonata." Beethoven. His father had told him.

He stopped, Betsy held to his chest, and listened, and his grey eyes, fringed with thick black lashes, opened wide and filled with light. Why, he knew what that music sounded like! Like great white angels moving slowly down golden stairs, with golden shadows on their half-extended wings, their faces grave and majestic, their lips carved like marble, their garments flecked with radiance which shifted and fell like rain. He must have dreamt it, sometime. Even Betsy was motionless, listening.

Then he shuddered, for David had spitefully broken into the very heart of the music with a tinny, syncopated sound, "Meet me at the Fair!—St. Louis, Louis—Meet me at the Fair!" It was the derisive laughter of devils beneath the golden stairs.

"Shut up, shut up," Edward muttered. "That's what I'm paying four dollars a week for. Why can't you play the thing through, when you start it? Just because Pa isn't there. You know he hates that St. Louis thing."

Edward, bending his head, went up the rear wood-planked walk to the yard. Here there was nothing except carefully cropped grass. No tree, no flower, no border. Just grass. Edward had built Betsy a little shelter against the wood garbage shed with its sloping cover. He tenderly placed the protesting bird inside, checked her water and seed, ruffled her feathers.

The hen whimpered through the wire netting. "Don't be afraid," he murmured. "I'm coming home soon. Half-past eight. See?"

He went away, turned his back on the house, and began to trudge the four streets to his father's delicatessen. His big brown neck, his square brown chin, were drawn in, and he had pushed his hands into the pockets of his old trousers. No use feeling gloomy about that damn' David. David was a genius. He, Edward, supposed geniuses must sometimes get tired of their own gifts and " break loose." He forgave David almost at once. Why, hadn't Pa often told him that no one could understand a person who had a gift?

Edward went on, humming. " All the days of my life, all the days, all the days of my life." He had invented the music for the splendour of this phrase; it was noble, like the words. He did not know where he had heard the words, but they had affected him deeply. " All the days, the days, the days of my life!" His voice soared out, pure and strong and masculine, like an angel's voice, and the words he sang were a reverent chant. He lifted his chin, and the last light of the sun illuminated his dark, broad face, with the square nose, the patient, humorous young mouth, the broad, brown forehead, the dimpled chin, the indomitable curve of youthful cheek, and the full grey eyes. His step quickened, as if to a marching song of soldiers bent on a holy war. He forgot he was only fourteen years old and that he had worked since six that morning, and that he was tired. " My life, my life!" he sang, as he bounded up the three wooden steps of his father's delicatessen.

The shop was small, but almost incredibly neat, the two little windows polished to a blazing crystal, the wooden floor whitely scrubbed, the wooden counters without a stain. It was a Lilliputian delicatessen, but very compact, shining and complete. Here hung no twisted lengths of sticky fly-paper from the white ceiling, and no dishes filled with fly-poison on the counters, and no clots of flies hovering over exposed food. Mr. Enger believed in screens; Ralph, his youngest child, had painted a sign on the outer door: Please Close! This so startled customers, drawn as it was in the brightest red, that they hastily obeyed. Even the two barrels of pickles, one dill, one sweet, had been covered with fabric fly-screens over a clean white towel. One could be sure, said the approving housewives, that the cloves one saw in the pungent liquid were really cloves. But the towels, renewed every day, and the screens, did not inhibit the luscious fragrance of the barrels, which mingled with the saliva-evoking scents of smoked ham and corned beef. It was Edward's duty, at six in the morning, to scrub out the little shop, to shine up the meat slicers, to apply suds to the counters, to polish the windows, to align the bottles and tins on the shelves and dust them, to replenish the ice under the counters where galvanised cans held their treasures of vanilla and strawberry and chocolate ice-cream, and bottles of milk. It was his duty to clear away every crumb from the glass case which held doughnuts and loaves of crusty bread, and to polish the glass. The firm cheese, round and resolute as a wheel, had its own glass container, with its own sparkling knife.

Edward was proud of the shop. It would be his, one day, his father had promised him. He took pleasure in the polishing and the scrubbing, whistling between his teeth under the lighted gas lamp flickering away in the dark mornings. He hated dirt of any kind. Until last June, his mother had done most of the labour in this shop before it opened, but now she was too old and too tired. After all, she was thirty-six and her husband was thirty-four and people of that age could not work like a boy. On Fridays, at five o'clock, when the city of Waterford still slept, Edward would accompany his father to the wholesale market three miles away, pulling a large cart behind him. He was already a shrewd bargainer and buyer. Mr. Enger, who was timid and gentle, permitted his son to attend to the business of purchase, but it was he who at the end laid the gold and green dollar bills on the counters. Then they would return in the darkness of pre-dawn, Edward hauling the heaped wagon as if it contained nothing. The bread, wrapped in Mrs. Enger's white towels, was still hot from the bakery, the shrouded hams steamed under their wrappings, the barrels of pickles were sweeter than the morning air.

Once, last spring, Mr. Heinrich Enger had said to his stalwart son, in his guttural Bavarian accent: "It is good, Edward, that the mother does not need to accompany me any longer in these mornings. It is her delicacy. After all, one needs to remember that she was a Von. But I have told you. A Von! From the big *schloss* on the mountain! To condescend to a miserable little burgher like Heinrich Enger, the *gnädige frau*. What a mystery is life. Ah, my parents, God be with them, would not have believed it. A Von."

Edward would murmur appreciatively, but one of his black eyebrows had taken on a sceptical lift lately, in spite of his respect for his parents. His mother was a huge and massive woman, with a shapeless, down-turned mouth fixed in severity, with light-blue eyes and a flashy nose and an amorphous figure, great of breast and hip. Her one claim to comeliness was a mass of hair so pale of colour that it was almost silvery, and the sun brought out dim golden crests on its waves. She spent the evening hours, between mending, combing out that mass for the admiration of her children. She was not Edward's favourite parent, for she domineered over her little fat husband, a head shorter than herself, and told endless tales of the grandeur of her family, the Von Brunners. "The blond Von Brunners," she would say, looking disparagingly at the bald and glittering head of her small and rotund husband, who had only a fringe of black Bavarian hair to embellish his sphere of a skull. Edward hated to see his father bow his head meekly; until he finally understood that Maria's affectionate contempt for Heinrich in some way mysteriously enhanced his stature.

On these journeys to the market, Edward with new curiosity, had discreetly questioned his innocent father. It seemed that Heinrich had played the flute in a tiny cluster of musicians at a *gasthaus*, in the village of Dorfinger, in the shadow of the amethyst Bavarian Alps. The *schloss*, it finally esmerged, was an old but revered ruin, on a foothill, and the Von Brunners had lost most of their money during the Franco-Prussian war. For the last three generations they had made beer, good beer, but not so good as that made in Munich, which the discriminating had preferred. Maria Von Brunner had been only a very poor relation, an orphan of distant connection, and she had come to the *schloss* to teach the family's children. Before that, she had been a "Fräulein" for some Englishers. One day she had accompanied the family graciously to the *gasthaus*, and had admired Heinrich and his flute. "Ah, that day, that day!" Heinrich had said, closing his eyes as if before a dazzling light. "I can see her still, with her hair like silver under her big plumed hat, and her noble smile! I could not look at her; it would have been a desecration."

"But, she married you, Pa," Edward had said, trying to keep his voice dispassionate. "You must not have been so bad." His German was very correct, the family spoke it under the stern tutelage of the mother.

Heinrich shook his head, in wonder. "Ach, it was a miracle. The family was unkind to your mother. She had no money, though they had little more. Her father had been a Herr Professor in Munich and one knows that Herr Professors make no fortunes. The family paid her very little. I was then a man of twenty." He paused. "And she was almost twenty-three," Edward added somewhat grimly to himself. "I dared to speak to her one day," Heinrich went on. "I had saved my money; I was going to America, where the streets were paved with gold, and where even musicians could become rich."

Heinrich laughed with gentle bitterness. He shook his head again. "It was a miracle. Ach, yes. I dared to speak to the Fräulein Von Brunner and tell her my dream, and she smiled at me like the moon itself, and said it was her dream, also. And so, and so, we were married." He paused. At this point, he would invariably become confused. It appeared that the Von Brunners had not been too averse to their Maria's marrying the little fat flautist at the *gasthaus*. "They were very kind, for such unkind people," Heinrich would murmur. "They gave Maria, your mother, a fine trousseau, as the French say. They also gave her five hundred marks. They gave us their blessing. And so, we came to America."

Two months ago Edward, the always kind, had said ironically, "And the five hundred marks helped with the passage money."

"I have told you that their kindness was also a miracle," Heinrich had answered, crossly. He had changed the subject. "There is no room in America for a flautist. But we had no money, I worked for some years in a delicatessen, and your mother was saving and careful, and so we came to this very misbegotten place and opened a delicatessen of our own. Your mother's sensitive soul has never recovered from the shattering of her dreams. However, I make an excellent living, I have five children and a house with only one thousand dollars mortgage, and four of my children are the geniuses. It is the Von Brunner blood. But my children are dark like the Engers and this is a cross; your mother hardly forgives me."

Edward had suddenly pressed his father's small but bulky arm, and Heinrich had smiled that sweet, shy smile of his in gratitude. "It was in March, 1887, when we came to America, and your brother David was born eight months later, in Albany. Your mother was determined to be American, so you have the American names. It is so sad that she must always try to forget her family, who were so unkind. I should have preferred German names, in remembrance. For, are we not Germans?"

"We're Americans," Edward had said, stoutly.

He loved his father, so small, so fat, so innocent and so gentle, with a fierce protectiveness. He stood between his father and his mother, with inexorable partisanship.

Edward was always glad to see his father, to see the smile on the round and chubby features, so flushed and beaming, so kind, so self-deprecating, so eager to please. He had the sweetest temper; he was rarely vexed or impatient. The housewives, sometimes forgetting he was a "foreigner," had a deep affection for him. He never short-changed; he was invariably anxious to oblige. The cookie box was usually open for a child; he had a special cylindrical glass jar filled with striped peppermint drops for the poorer of the children who entered the shop. Sometimes, when things were going very well, he would give a few of these children a one-cent ice-cream cone, generously filled. At Christmas, he had a box of peppermint canes for all children, poor or middle class, wrapped in tinsel paper, or pink suckers in holiday wrappers. At Easter, there were tiny chocolate rabbits. Mrs. Enger did not approve of this waste, but on this her husband, usually so meek and docile and humble, stood firm.

Once he had said: "I remember the Christmas in Dorfinger, the Christmas my father died. We had boots on Christmas, and sometimes an orange and nuts, but this Christmas we had nothing. Nor on the following Christmases. I remember, I looked in the shop windows."

Edward, this evening, saw that his father, perched like a cherub on a stool near the till, seemed depressed. He had his account books spread out before him. He hardly glanced up at his son as he bounded in. He sighed. "It is not doing well, this August," he remarked.

"It never does well in August," said Edward cheerfully. "You always forget, Pa."

"But I hope," said Heinrich. "The mother needs a fine winter coat this year. Thirty-five dollars it is, laid away in the Cohen store. Thirty dollars still owed."

"She'll have it out before the first snow," said Edward in English. He saw a pile of flat tins near his father's elbow. "No sale?"

"Only three, this month," said Heinrich in a lugubrious voice. "What is this, that I cannot sell the English tongue? A fine tongue! A bargain. The Norwegian sardines." And he waved his short arms in despair. "They are twenty-five cents. The tongue is a meal for a family. With the flavour! Smoked like a delicious."

"A delicacy," said Edward. He picked up one of the long flat tins. He frowned. "I forget. What do we sell this for?"

"Twenty-five cents."

"Too cheap—twenty-five cents. You have to *sell* things." Edward considered, then he went behind the counter, found a square of white cardboard and a red pencil. He printed on it: "English smoked tongue, an exclusive import. During August only, thirty-two cents."

He held the card up triumphantly before his father, who was aghast. He fell back into German in his agitation. "That is impossible! That is robbery. The women speak of Enger's. Reasonable. Sensible. Twelve cents profit! Do not be absurd, my optimistic son. No one will pay thirty-two cents. There will be laughter."

"They will pay," said Edward. He took the pile of tins, stacked them in a pyramid. Then he crushed red tissue paper and made a circle about the pile. Against them, he stood his card. "I'll eat every can, myself, and pay you wholesale for them if you don't sell every one before the end of August. That will be in ten days. If you don't give the idea that something is first-rate and exclusive, you don't sell. This'll make the women fight over the tongue. Besides, it *is* an exclusive, by the way. No delicatessen within five miles of here sells it for that price. And are the women going to run there to make comparisons? Even if they do they'll find bigger shops, and bigger prices. We're doing them a favour. You'll see."

"Are you teaching me to see, Edward?" But Heinrich, so worried, smiled.

"I've been reading some new methods of merchandising in the *Retailer's Journal*," said Edward. "People have more money these days. If we don't take advantage of their purses, someone else will. How many tins do we have besides these?"

"Forty," said Heinrich, becoming despondent again. He pointed to a shelf. Edward promptly cleared away the tongue, hid it under the counter on a shelf. "Exclusive," he said. "We've just got these. When we're down to half a dozen, we bring out the others. But only a few at a time."

He went to the rear of the store where the toilet stood in a little closet with a washbowl. He scrubbed his hands, changed a long white shirt he kept there. He combed his thick dark hair. When he emerged there were two women in the store. Each, after examining the tongue, and exclaiming over it, and announcing it was just the thing for the Sunday late supper, bought a tin apiece. Heinrich beamed. He wrapped each tin carefully in a sheet of tissue paper like a jewel and tied it with a coloured string. "Hah, you're learning merchandising yourself, Pa," said Edward teasingly. "You forgot to use the butcher paper or the newspaper or a bag."

"One cannot say that Heinrich Enger does not learn new methods," said his father, with some pompousness. He tapped his tiny fat fingers, which were sprinkled with black hair, on the counter, and thrust out his plump pink lips. His nails were rosy and round. "But we are robbers," he said. "It is not right, it is not Christian. I do not think the Reverend Mr. Yaeger will appreciate it."

"The Reverend Mr. Yaeger will appreciate an extra nickel in the box," said Edward cynically. "From all of us." Then he remembered he had no time for church, nor for the Wednesday Evening Socials. "I never met him. Do you like him?"

"A young man, but so wise!" said his father, with sudden enthusiasm. "Did I not tell you? Your mother's family know his family in Munich. He is new here. He was appointed by the Church Board only six weeks ago, and already he is a success. Such eloquence. It moves the heart. That is why I do not think he will approve."

"He's a Lutheran, not a priest," said Ewward, hardily. "You don't confess to a Protestant minister. He can't even forgive your sins. Why make a fuss? Give him an extra dollar at Christmas." He stretched his arms out with exhilaration. "With the way things are going to go around here, after to-day, you can give him two dollars, and he'll fall on your neck and kiss you."

"Such language," said Heinrich. "Two dollars! The mother will be angry. You must remember she is a gentlewoman, a gracious lady. She will not approve of this already."

"We won't tell her then," said Edward, doubting the righteousness attributed to his mother. "We'll keep our dark and bloody secrets to ourselves. Besides, you're underselling butter. I've struck an average on the market. It's twenty-one cents a pound after to-day."

"No one will buy," said Heinrich, alarmed.

"Yes, they will. Where are the fancy wrappers with the yellow daisies on them? Oh, I've got them. We're going to cut the bulk butter into pounds, and wrap the pounds separately and show a dummy on the counter. We've got to get some extra money for our efforts. Sanitary. Sweet cream. Country-fresh. Give me another card and the red pencil. Who's going to tell the difference between our bulk butter and the nicely-wrapped pounds?"

"Taste," groaned Heinrich, paralysed by this audacity and mendaciousness.

"Taste!" said Edward. "Taste's all in the mind. We'll keep some bulk butter, but push these cut pounds. Pa, you're right in the way of the scale. The women will say they never ate such butter. You'll never sell bulk again, after a few days. They'll be standing in line to get this. You know something? I'm going to cut the pounds into four long quarters. That'll sweep 'em off their feet."

Heinrich watched with complete helplessness. But he took care that Edward weighed scrupulously. He even, after a moment or two, evinced an interest himself. He introduced, with boyish squeals, a new innovation. Each quarter must be wrapped in the daisy-paper. "Pa, you're a genius," said Edward reverently. "I am not so much the fool," said Heinrich, flowing with modesty. He became excited. "Good straight quarters! No cutting and weighing for quarters and half-pounds! We sell cold, golden quarters by themselves! It is worth the extra money, the cutting, the wrapping."

Edward stood and smiled at his father. "A real genius," he said. Somewhere he found a small empty box the size of a pound of butter and covered it with the daisy-paper and wrote another sign: "Quarters, half-pounds, pounds, untouched by human hands. Fresh every day. Daisy Butter, unrivalled."

He looked around for new conquests, but his father said, hastily: "Is it not enough genius for the day? One must not press even genius. Let us consider in quiet and repose."

It was becoming dark, the street outside floated in deep-purple twilight, lit by the moon-like globes of street lamps. A little girl came in. Heinrich, discontentedly checking the money in the till, turned as she slapped the door behind her. He regarded all mankind with maudlin love, but he retained a special love for children. His eye, so perceptive, saw that this child looked too thin, too spindly, and that her cotton frock, a bulky blue-and-white check, was obviously second-hand, its bloused front hanging over the string of faded blue ribbon at the waist, its skirt wide and bunched. Her long black cotton stockings were too big for her, too, wrinkling over her emaciated legs, dropping over the top of her high black button shoes with the scuffed toes. Yet, she was so clean, and even the ugly clothes, even the frill of coarse machine lace around the neck, could not hide her cleanness, her immature beauty.

"Ach, now, little one," said Heinrich, leaning his dimpled elbows on the counter, his small black eyes sparkling. "You are just in time. We are closing. It is eight o'clock." He reached under the counter and decided that this time it was not to be a one-cent store, but a five-cent one, heaped with three flavours. The little girl watched him as he soberly filled the rich cone, and then held it out to her. However, she put her hands behind her back. "There isn't any extra money," she said in a very careful and pretty voice.

"We always give the last customer on Sunday night the big cone, free," said Heinrich. "It is a superstition with us. Here, it is dripping already."

The little girl took the cone eagerly and gazed at Heinrich with thought. "You're such a nice man," she said, and licked. Edward, who had too many brothers and a sister, was bored. He was putting away some cracker boxes, rearranging some cans of soup. There had been eighteen customers to-night, more than on any August Sunday evening he could remember. Ten of them had bought the "Daisy Butter,

Untouched by Human Hands, Sanitary, Country-fresh, Sweet-Cream. Our Speciality." Edward had told the customers, "We are in the business of supplying the neighbourhood with the best." Heinrich, newly distressed, had averted his head at this salesmanship, and had coloured a bright red.

"I haf not seen you before," said Heinrich to the child. "You are new, is it not?"

"I came from the orphanage yesterday," said the child, leaning against the counter to relax herself as she absorbed the delight of the ice-cream. At this, Edward turned abruptly and gave her his full attention. What a homely kid in those sloppy clothes made for an older girl! Then he saw that she was not "homely" at all. She had a small pointed face, the tapering chin cleft by an extraordinarily long deep dimple, the thin nose very dainty, the mouth wide and full and the colour of coral. Her cheek-bones were flushed with the same coral, and were wide and gave delicate strength to her appearance. And she had eyes of the purest, most intense blue Edward had ever seen, set in lashes like fringes of gilt, and a long mass of light-brown hair hanging in waves and rolls over her shoulders and far down her back. Why, she was a pretty kid! Too bad she was only about ten years old; she would be a corker when she was fourteen or sixteen.

"You are living with some people, you haf a new mama and papa?" said Heinrich with loving compassion.

"Well, yes," replied the child, thoughtfully. "But not just that way." She sucked at the strawberry layer, happily. "It's Mr. and Mrs. Baumer."

"Baumer!" said Heinrich sharply, and his smile vanished, and his white-coated, tubby body straightened in shock. "I know those Baumers."

"What did they do with Josie?" asked Edward, coming to the counter.

"She wasn't any good. She didn't wash the floors right, and she didn't polish good," said the child. "They sent her back to the orphanage on Friday. I am much better than Josie." She showed them her little hands. They were sore-knuckled and fragile, and scored with soap and hot water and abrasives. "I'm not afraid of work. I washed all the floors in the orphanage; Mrs. Goetz said I was better than anybody."

"There was Aggie before Josie, and Ellen before Aggie. They've had a whole stream of kids, working them to death and then sending them back," Edward reminded his father under his breath.

Heinrich nodded; his distress became more intense. This child, this little one, this very pretty little one! And those Baumers, mean, middle-aged, tight-fisted, cruel, hated by the whole neighbourhood, and with all that money! But what could one do? There was no law to protect these nameless, exploited children, in the year of Our Lord, 1904. Any monster could secure one of these innocents, under the pretext of adoption, "if satisfactory." The Baumers, childless and sullen-eyed and with hard, malevolent mouths, never had found any of the little girls "satisfactory." They worked them from dawn to night, grudgingly sent them to school as required by law, half-fed them, clothed them poorly from church rummage sales, and then, as the children sickened, they sent them packing back to the orphanage. But the orphanage was overcrowded, badly supported from city and private funds, and eternally looking for "good homes" for the abandoned girls and boys. Who, besides God, cared for them? And perhaps, it seemed, not even God.

"How about a ham sandwich?" asked Edward. "I'm just going to fix myself one."

The little girl looked nervous. "I was supposed to come right back, after getting the milk and the bread and half a pound of butter and six eggs." But her beautiful eyes filled with longing, and she licked her lips. "Haven't had any dinner to-day. Mrs. Baumer doesn't have big dinners on Sundays, just some cold things, and there wasn't anything left over."

"Won't take a second," said Edward, and cut a very thick slice of the pink and fragrant ham, heavily buttered two pieces of bread, and slapped the whole thing together. "Here. And I'm just going to drink half a bottle of milk. You can have the other half. Mustard?"

"No, thank you," she said politely. She had eaten the cone; she sank her even white teeth into the sandwich with gratitude, and looked over the immensity of it with radiant eyes like the sky at noonday. "Um. This is good," she said, her mouth filled. "Best ham I ever tasted. First time we had ham was at Easter. I like ham." She stopped chewing and became nervous again. "This isn't charity, is it? You won't tell Mrs. Baumer?"

"It isn't charity," said Edward. "I just like to have company when I eat. Good ham, isn't it? Hate to eat alone. Here, I'll put the milk in a glass."

Heinrich, so easily moved, was speechless with tears. "You just come in when you feel hungry and eat with me," said Edward. "I'm here every day. If there's a customer you can just go back in that closet and we won't tell a soul. What's your name?"

The child swallowed ravenously before answering. "Meg—Meg Proster. I came in the P's. That's why it's Proster. Mrs. Goetz makes up the names. I came in the P's when I was a baby. But it's really Margaret, not Meg."

"Margaret?" said Edward. "Your name is Margaret?" He put his sandwich down. Yes, she was a "Margaret," with all that beauty and sweetness, with that white forehead broad with serenity and steadfastness. Her hair shone like the crest of a great elm tree in the sun. A sapling of a "Margaret." "I have a tree with that name," he said, impulsively, and out of his tender remembrance, and then blushed.

The little girl nodded solemnly. "There was a tree in the orphanage yard," she said as if all this was quite understandable. "But he was a he. I called him Eddie. He was really an Eddie, big like you; he had leaves like big hands."

"My name's Eddie, too," said Edward. "Ed. That's what they call me."

Her face became luminous with surprise and happiness. She nodded. "Yes, you're an Eddie." Then her small face dimmed sorrowfully, and her gilded eyebrows drew together in pain. "They killed Eddie. One of the boys was climbing him and he fell and broke his head, the boy, I mean, and so they cut Eddie down. I cried and cried. The birds flew away; Eddie took care of them and they cried like me when Eddie fell over on his side. He died." Her eyes filled with tears.

She took another last bite of the sandwich, sniffed, wiped her eyes with the back of her hand.

"Ach, the poor little one," murmured Heinrich, in German. "They have the aching hearts, the little ones, and no one hears. Only the flute can give them a voice, the lonely flute singing all alone."

"Never mind, Margaret," said Edward. "You can have my tree with me. I'll show her to you."

She shook her head. "I can't. I got to work for my keep every day. That's only right, Mrs. Baumer giving me a home, a real home, all to myself, and my own bed. Besides, they're buying a farm. We're going to move next week. A big farm." Her eyes lighted with joy again. "Lots of trees. Maybe I'll find an Eddie there, just for myself!"

"Ach, yes, so I heard," said Heinrich. There was always food on a farm, and even ugly human voracity could not always prevent a child from taking an egg, or sipping milk from a pail, or pulling a peach from a tree, or hiding a handful of nuts. This little one would not starve on a farm, as the others had starved. The misery in Heinrich's heart loosened; he had not known there was such a tightness in his chest until now. He put his hand to it. He must remember what the doctor had told him, no excitement, no emotion, no strain. But what could one do for such a pain, such a drawing-together of hurt flesh? The pain began in the spirit.

"Where is the farm?" asked Edward, already bereaved.

"Oh, it's a long way," replied Margaret, waving one thin arm vaguely. "Millions of miles away."

"Near Albany. I heard already," said Heinrich, in English. "It was the Websters who told me. The Baumers haf enough money; it is always the farm they want, and they saved. Fifty miles."

"I'll come to see you," said Edward. But he knew, he knew. He would never see Margaret again. Margaret Proster. In the P's. He was only fourteen and Margaret was only ten, but he loved her. He wanted to touch her hair, to smooth the back of his hand against her cheek, to rub her dimpled chin. He loved her as man loves a woman. He wanted to shelter her hungry body in his strong arms, and take care of her for ever. For ever. Something nagged at his mind. He whistled dolorously and thought: All the days of my life.

Chapter Two

Heinrich had great terror of and respect for "the law." Edward had once tired to explain that laws were made by men, the mundane laws apart from the natural laws of God, and that foolish laws could be broken, and should be broken. He had even quoted Thomas Jefferson (his hero), to that effect. "But what is this Thomas Jefferson?" Heinrich had asked petulantly. "Law is law; it must be obeyed, not broken, not changed."

"But this is America," Edward had said.

Heinrich had only looked at him reproachfully and anxiously. Laws were immutable. One learned that in the old country.

So, on the very striking of eight o'clock Heinrich resolutely closed his shop on Sundays, and refused to serve any customer hastening in, pleading. "It is the law," Heinrich would say, locking the till. "But my baby needs milk. I forgot until the last minute," the woman might plead. "It is the law," Heinrich would say, with distress, wondering how customers could be so stupid as not to understand.

When his back was turned Edward would sometimes drop a bottle of milk in a bag, thrust it into the customer's hand and whisper that she could pay another time. It had happened to-night; the mother of five children had rushed in for a loaf of bread. Heinrich talked of law and turned his back; Edward gave her the bread.

Father and son, after carefully locking the doors, walked homeward in the warm blue darkness of the summer night. Edward looked up at the moon with alarm, and shook his head. "On the moon, it is blood," he murmured. "For ten years, before the war between France and Germany, there were moons with blood on them. It is an omen."

They walked on, their heels clacking softly on the walks. Edward whistled tonelessly between his teeth. Then he cleared his throat. "Pa, I've been wanting to ask for a long time. Your flute. Could I use your flute once in a while?"

"My flute, you, my son?" Heinrich was astonished. "It is not you who is the musical genius. It is David."

"I'd still like to use the flute, Pa. I can read notes."

Heinrich considered, worried again. He understood these things. The mediocre soul attempting to express itself. But that led to envy and frustration. He winced in himself. Besides, it would disturb the pure genius of his oldest son, David, to hear the shrillness of a flute at the lips of one born only to serve. He shook his head. "Ach, no, Eddie. That would not do. One must think of the sensibilities of David." He relapsed into German. "It is hard to comprehend these things. You would practise in the house. The mother would shiver. It would destroy the harmony, the little harmony that exists in a house blessed by many with the artistic temperament. You would be unhappy; the others, who have delicate souls, would be devastated. I am thinking of your harmonica. You had to give it away, at last, and you paid two dollars for it. It hurt the ears."

I played the harmonica very well, thought Edward, with some anger. I didn't hurt anybody. Miss Johns had me play at Christmas. He shrugged. "All right, Pa, don't worry. Keep your flute. For some grandchild." He patted his father's fat shoulder and Heinrich sighed. "You are so sensible, Eddie. You understand."

A feller sometimes gets tired of understanding, Edward reflected. But understanding was demanded of people who weren't geniuses. It was the least they could do for the gifted ones.

"Genius cannot be acquired," said Heinrch. "All else can, to further that genius." They walked along in mutual silence, then Heinrich, with tears in his voice, said: "I must confess something to you, my son, something I have never confessed to another. I was not a genius; I played the flute only adequately, in spite of many years of prayer and pain and study. What are these, if one is not gifted? For years I did not know the truth."

He turned his head and looked at Edward anxiously; the boy was striding on, his hands in his pockets, his head bent. "You understand, Eddie?"

"Sure, Pa," said Edward, with pity.

"It isn't enough for a man's soul to be moved by music, to adore music, to comprehend it," Heinrich went on, with grief. "I suffered and still suffer, these things. When I listen to Beethoven or Wagner, I am changed, I am illuminated, I am transported to another realm. Yet, on my flute, I was the squeak of a mouse. But I have done very well in the shop," he added, with a pleading note in his voice, an asking note.

"Wonderful," said Edward. "One of these days we'll expand. We'll have a lot of clerks. We'll have the best delicatessen in the whole country! Why, we can do like the Atlantic and Pacific! We can have branch delicatessens. With you supervising and buying."

Heinrich touched his son's sleeve paternally, and with indulgence. "Ach, Eddie, you have the soaring mind. That is because you are young. There must be restraint, prudence."

They were two streets from home now. Heinrich stopped and rubbed his forehead, after removing his stiff straw hat. He coughed. "Eddie," he said. Edward stopped also, and grinned. "A pinochle game, eh? All right, Pa. You go ahead and have your game with Mr. Wolfsohn. I won't snitch."

"Such language. If you cannot speak correctly, in this English, you must learn to do it."

Heinrich rolled the brim of the hat in his little plump hands. "It is, of course, still Sunday," he said uncertainly.

"There's no law against playing pinochle on Sundays," said Edward, with affectionate impatience. "And isn't there something in the Bible about the Sabbath being made for man, and not man for the Sabbath?"

Heinrich rebuked him. "It is very bad, Eddie, that you have no interest in the church."

Edward did not remind his father that the household was so arranged, and all his work, that he did not have time for such an interest. Heinrich went on: "Yes, it is true, the Sabbath for man. Besides," he continued, with more spirit, "when Meyer and I play pinochle on Sunday, I give my winnings to the church plate. It is working for good, *nein*?"

"Sure, Pa, sure. Besides, it isn't Mr. Wolfsohn's Sabbath. His was yesterday."

They stood under a street lamp and gave all their serious attention to this matter. "We can't say a sick friend," said Edward. "We used that three times before. How about me saying that you stayed at the store to do some extra cleaning up?"

Heinrich frowned. "But then the mother would reproach you, asking why you had not stayed." He said this simply, with no thought of all the work his son had done that day.

Heinrich looked up at Edward and saw his face in the lamplight, a suddenly tight and brooding face, for Edward was remembering. "How strange is your expression," said Heinrich, in German. "What is it, Eddie?"

Edward recalled himself. Poor Pa. In some ways, Pa was pretty dumb. But then, most people were dumb. All you had to do was read history, in the books you sometimes got from the library, and sometimes had time to read when everybody else was asleep.

"I'm wondering what kind of excuse we can give," said Edward.

They considered again. "Ma doesn't like Mr. Wolfsohn," said Edward. "And she knows about those pinochle games, though not the Sunday ones. We can't use Mr. Wolfsohn to-night." He rubbed his shaggy hair, distracted. "Oh, I know. You couldn't go to church to-night, so you went to Mr. Yaeger and gave him a dollar. Ma will like that."

"But I went to see Meyer," Heinrich objected. "It is a long way, to Mr. Yaeger. Besides, there would be no dollar given."

Edward hesitated. Five dollars in his pocket, four for the piano, one for himself. Then he hardened himself. He held out his hand. "Give me the dollar," he said. "I'll take it. And you can say you had a long talk with Mr. Yaeger about church affairs. After all, you're on the Board."

"You do not give to the church, my son," said Heinrich, reproachfully.

Edward sighed. "All right, Pa. I'll take the dollar to Mr. Yaeger, my own dollar."

Heinrich beamed. "You are the good son, Eddie." He put on his hat with a flourish. "I am blessed in my children."

Now, all obstacles had been removed. Heinrich marched away, briskly, small and round as a young robin, and as eager. Then, as Edward watched him, he suddenly wheeled on his small feet and came back, his face glistening rotundly under the street lamp. He pushed something into Edward's hand. "My son," he said, in a very singular voice, and hurried off.

Edward looked at the little crumple in his hand. Two dollars. His young eyes moistened. My son. As if Pa had only one son. Edward shrugged. Then he thought, but Pa really has only one son—me. The others are my mother's sons. Poor Pa. Poor Pa, with his flute and his dreams.

The south wind suddenly roared softly to the night, a warm and tropical roar, speaking of the spice islands and the unknown seas and palms against the moon. Edward heard it and listened, entranced.

Then suddenly, he thought, of little Margaret with the gilt lashes and brows. " Now look," he said to God urgently. " That's just a kid, with no parents, and no real home. An awful nice kid. Ten years old, maybe. I don't expect I'll ever see her again. She's going a long way to a farm. Just take care of her, please. You will, please? She understands, about things. Don't let anybody hurt her, will You?"

The wind whooshed again, a great and mystic voice, and Edward's tight features relaxed in a contented smile. He'd never forget Margaret. How could he have believed God would forget such a nice little thing? Trusting, like a bird. Like Betsy.

Edward was now entering a very lonely street, narrow, many of the houses dark though it was only fifteen minutes to nine, some of the houses lighted. He could hear hammocks creaking, the slow rumble of rocking-chairs, the giggling of young girls, the youthful baritones of " admirers," and occasionally, the cry of a wakeful child. I wonder what most people live for, Edward asked himself. What, for instance, am I living for? Well, we have geniuses in the family, and that's something. These people on the porches, behind the trees, are just contented to go on and on, getting nowhere except for a little raise in pay and bringing up kids, and then the kids will bring up kids, and that's all there'll be to it. No end, no beginning. I guess they aren't ambitious. Not to be ambitious, in the Enger house, was to be an animal.

What do I want, me, just myself? Edward demanded silently. Funny, I never thought of that before. Well, I've got to have money, a lot of money, so I can help the rest of them get somewhere. David, Sylvia, Greg, Ralph. They've got to have a chance. There'll never be much money in a delicatessen, not with all those on Pa's neck, and mine.

David, and the rest of them, were already talking loftily of education and opportunities. It takes cash, thought Edward, somewhat grimly. Where do they think it's coming from? They never ask themselves. Just take things for granted. And David talking of New York and music teachers. All for granted. It's a load, thought Edward, confidently, a load I've got to lift.

Ma's just like them. Edward smiled in the darkness. A Von, it seemed, never questioned whether things would be given her, largely. The wind was stirring the Chinese prisms on the porches; the warm air was full of fairy tinkling, a delicate song about strange and unknown places, of lands never to be seen, of voices never to be heard. Edward was suddenly filled with yearning. His brothers and his sister would see and hear, and he supposed that was fine. After all, they were geniuses.

He stopped a moment to watch clouds of witless insects whirling about a corner street light, throwing themselves upon the glass, desperately trying to extinguish themselves, having their little hour before death. Like those people on the porches, thought Edward.

The First Lutheran Church of Waterford was closed and dark. Next to it was the Reverend Mr. Yaeger's house, a little house, small and meek as Heinrich. Edward considered it, standing on the walk leading to the stoop. Well, people sure didn't take care of their ministers, and that was a fact. More Lutherans in this town than of any other sect or religion, and the First Lutheran Church, next to the parsonage, was hardly less mean than the house. And when I was a kid, up to ten when I had to quit Sunday school to work, I thought of being a minister! Edward commented to himself, trying to laugh. People didn't deserve their pastors and their priests. That little old Catholic church, now, near the Enger house—why, the church was neat and clean but cheap looking, and the young priest looked all worn out most of the time, and his coat was visibly patched at the elbows. Edward shook his head. We don't deserve 'em, he said inwardly. He went up the battered steps to the stoop, and pulled at the bell, which tinkled wearily.

One light only was burning in the house, at the window near the door. Edward glanced in. The minister was sitting at his desk with his face in his hands; he lifted his head at the sound of the bell and Edward saw his face. The minister, thin and tall, rose to his feet with an effort and came to the door, the bare gaslight showing his tired and hopeless features and thin brown hair. Then the door opened and he looked out at Edward, puzzled.

"Hallo, Mr. Yaeger," said Edward, speaking cheerily. "I'm Ed Enger, Mr. Heinrich Enger's son. You know, from the delicatessen."

"Oh, yes," said the minister, in a dull voice. "Will you come in, Ed?" He had never seen Edward before. But he had heard of him from members of the Enger family. This would be the lout, the dolt, the stupid boy of the family. How old was he? About seventeen, a big hulk of a youth.

"Thanks, Mr. Yaeger, but I've got to go on home. Pa just wanted you to have some money, for the plate. He couldn't go to church to-night, and he missed this morning. He had a headache." Edward paused. He knew that one of the two dollars his father had given him was meant for himself, a wordless offering of love and helpless perplexity and understanding. Edward hesitated. Then he pushed the two dollars into the minister's hand.

"Why, that's very generous of Mr. Enger," said the minister, with surprise and pleasure. Susan needed another pair of shoes, for school. Two dollars would buy them! One of the minister's most urgent worries suddenly disappeared, and he thanked his God with humility and gratitude. After all, a salary of nine hundred dollars a year did not provide too well for a family of five, even if one had a wife who was an expert at remodelling clothing and making a penny do the work of ten. Then the minister's face saddened. "You said for the plate, Ed?"

Edward gazed at him, and understood with that almost miraculous intuition of his. "No, sir. Not for the plate. It's something for you personally. Pa was talking only to-night, about how ministers have a hard time, specially when they've got families, and he said to me, 'You go and give this to Mr. Yager with my compliments.'"

"Why," said the minister, blinking dryly, "that's very kind of your father." He stood and stared at Edward, whose tanned face was turning red. Edward looked down at his boots. "Mr. Yaeger, I don't come to church often. There's things I have to do, on Sundays. I make five dollars most of the time——"

"On Sundays?" repeated the minister, with some rebuke and sternness. "You work on Sundays, and so can't come to church?"

Edward's colour became deeper. "Well, yes, sir. It's something I've sort of got to do, so I want to make up for it." He thrust his hand into his pocket, and felt the five dollars in bills and silver. Hell, he didn't really need the one dollar which his parents permitted him to keep. What was a bicycle, anyway? Besides, he would make it up in a couple of weeks. He brought out a rumpled bill and gave it to the minister. "That's my own contribution," he said awkwardly.

The minister regarded the bill in his hand. Three dollars altogether! This extra dollar would buy a fine roast for five people, a roast which would last three days. Again he stared at Edward, who was retreating backwards down the steps. "Well," said Edward, "guess I got to say good night, Mr. Yaeger. It's getting late."

"Good night, Ed," said the minister. He watched Edward go down the walk and then down the street. The boy passed under a lamp. Why, thought the minister, he's not a man! He's only a boy, only the age of my own Howard! He has the face of a child. Mr. Yaeger stepped on to the stoop, and, with something aching in his heart, he called to Edward. But Edward had disappeared into the black shadow of some murmurous trees, and was gone. The minister stood on the stoop for a considerable time, the night breeze stirring his thin hair, and when he went inside the house he felt, in some mysterious way, that he had seen with an inner eye, and he was more saddened than before. He smoothed the crushed bills on his desk and looked down at them. Then he put aside one of the bills, gently, and touched it with a tender hand. There would be no roast, after all. This would go to his own personal charity, in the secret name of Edward Enger. His sadness disappeared, and he smiled like a youth. A minister sometimes had his own rich rewards.

Edward, whistling through his teeth, continued on his way. If he went around a few blocks he would pass the Erie Canal. He hurried. He heard a church bell sound the stroke of nine. Ma would be mad.

He was near his home, now. He was trotting very fast and he collided with a silent walker on the street, and jumped back with an exclamation of apology. " Gosh, Father Jahle, I'm sorry!" he said. " I didn't see you."

The slender young priest settled his hat, which Edward had caused to slide to the side of his head. "That's all right, Simon," he answered. "Late to-night, aren't you?" His large brown eyes looked affectionately at Edward, but his expression was grave and still. There were deep hollows under his wide cheek-bones, and his mouth was very pale. He coughed, a long, racking cough, and Edward winced as he always winced at that sound.

" Yes. Had to do something for Pa," replied the boy. He grinned at the priest, and went on. " One of these days, you'll have to tell me why you call me Simon, Father."

" I thought you were going to ask your minister," said the priest, catching his breath and rubbing his concave chest as if it pained him.

" Well, it seems like I never have time to ask him," Edward said. He was embarrassed. He could not explain to the priest that his work devoured so much of his time that there was nothing left. That would be disloyalty to his parents. Then he saw that the priest was gazing at him deeply, and he stepped aside, his embarrassment increasing, and called over his shoulder, " Good night, Father!" He trotted on.

The priest watched him until the night had sucked him in, and he thought: " Yes, Simon. But the cross is not too heavy to bear in God's service, not yet. May the day never come, young Simon, when it will be too heavy, for then your heart will break." He walked down the street, his hands behind his back, and he prayed for the boy whose footsteps he could no longer hear.

Edward was in sight of his own home when he heard the softest and sweetest of music on the warm air, almost a whisper of music, melancholy and meditative, as if some disembodied soul spoke of sorrow. It was one with the night and the rising wind and the black shadows of the trees stretching across the cobbled streets. A Negro boy of Edward's own age was leaning against a tree in the flickering light of the street lamp and he was playing a harmonica, his lanky body bent forward from the tree, his fingers glimmering, his dusky curls trembling.

"Billy!" said Edward, with pleasure. "What're you doing out here so late?"

Billy continued to play and Edward listened. The Negro boy's face was withdrawn, the colour of bronze, and as smooth. His feet were bare, and his blue shirt and black trousers were patched and frayed. It was a fine harmonica, made in Germany, and it had cost two dollars, and Edward had given it to Billy as a gift. As always, when Edward listened to the frail and wailing organ notes of the instrument when Billy played it, he forgot his own regret at having had to part with it and he was grateful and exalted. Billy, his friend, was also a genius. He would be famous some day, Edward would insist. Billy would gaze at him cynically, but he never answered with bitterness. "I guess I'll just be happy if I learn to play it right," he invariably said. "I guess you deserve that, for giving it to me."

The mournful music ended without a flourish; the last notes drifted from the harmonica like a few moonlit moths. Billy said, "You forgot we were going to walk to the Canal to-night, after your old man closed up."

"I'm awfully sorry," said Edward. "But he wanted me to do something for him, and it was kind of important, and I got there late."

Billy shrugged. "It don't matter," he said, and lifted himself away from the tree. "Next Sunday night?"

"Sure, Billy." Edward paused. He thought of his friend's long walk back to the black ghetto where he lived, with the leaning old wooden houses, the dirty street thronged with half-starved children, the cowed old women with the kerchiefs on their heads and the weary men with their dinner pails. "I wish I could walk a ways with you, Billy, but it's awful late."

"Don't matter," said Billy patiently. "You got your own troubles." He wiped the harmonica lovingly with a shred of soiled cloth, wrapped it up, and put it in his pocket. Then he smiled at Edward and his smile was inexpressibly sweet and comprehending, his white teeth glittering in the lamplight. "Sure going to miss you at school, though."

"That's right," said Edward. The two boys stood in silence and looked at each other, and Billy thought, Boy, you got worse troubles than me, even if you eat regular. After a few moments, Billy lifted his hand nonchalantly in farewell, and glided, rather than walked, into the shadows of the trees. Crickets suddenly shrilled to the night, and there was a scent of old hot dust in the air as the wind rose and the dry trees clattered. I wish I could do something for him, really something, Edward said in himself. How does a feller get to be a millionaire?

His home was dark, except for the light of an oil lamp on the kitchen table. Edward opened the back door, and stepped into the kitchen. To his surprise he saw that his mother was sitting at the table, reading quietly, the white oilcloth no paler than her extraordinary hair, which rolled back from her large and flabby face in a high pompadour. Her big and formless body, in its black Sunday silk, was braced with high dignity against the back of the chair, and she held the book as she had been taught as a child—with both hands, one at the side, the other at the bottom. In spite of her bulk and gracelessness, she had a stately air of breeding, not affected, but instinctive.

She rarely, if ever, read in the kitchen, though she worked there. She never served her family any meal, even breakfast, in the kitchen. The family would have preferred to eat here, but they dared not offend the mother's sense of propriety, and permitted themselves to be crowded in the lightless and narrow dining-room, which was too small for so large a family.

Maria Enger lifted her pale and formidable eyes when her son entered the kitchen and put aside her book with measured movements. "You are very late," she said, in her very correct high German. "Where is your father?" Her mouth had no determined outlines, and practically no colour, and it was wide, yet it gave an impression of an unyielding and resolute nature, ponderously strict and hard. Her voice was low and well bred, and she rarely if ever raised it in vehemence or excitement.

"I'm sorry, Mother," replied Edward in German. "I remained to clean and lock up the shop. My father had an appointment with the minister, Mr. Yaeger, and they had matters to discuss."

Maria regarded Edward oddly. She lifted the watch on her massive bosom and looked at the face with significance.

There was something strange about her to-night, a hesitancy. She said, in an abstracted tone: "All the others are in their beds. I, too, should have retired. Yet I waited for you."

"You should not have waited, Mother," said Edward, intimidated and uneasy. He began to sidle towards the door that led into a tiny dank hall. His mother lifted her hand. "I have something to say to you, Edward. You will please sit opposite me in that chair."

Edward seated himself and drew a deep breath and braced himself. He was suddenly conscious of being very tired, and there was a sense of defeat in him. He was wretchedly sure that he was to be kept in this kitchen until his father returned, when both of them would be subjected to a rigorous cross-examination to explain their lateness. It would end, as usual, with his father pretending to be angry with him, and then the anger becoming real out of frustration and fear of Maria, and out of some sick shame. Edward said, hastily: "Please do not be annoyed with my father. There were customers at the last moment, and my father broke his rule for the women with children. Then there was much ordering to be done, with which I helped."

"And there was the Herr Minister," said Maria. "You have said it before." But her voice was not hard, and Edward looked at her in perplexity. "I understand, Edward. I will discuss it no further."

The cuckoo clock ticked loudly in the silence. The wind stirred the curtains at the window. The mirror over the white sink winked and moved. Mother and son regarded each other without speaking. It was Maria who looked away first. She pointed to a chair, and Edward's eyes followed the pointing. Little Ralph's paint-box, black enamelled, lay there, and his pad of artists' paper. "You will bring me the paper," said Maria. Somewhat dazed, Edward rose wearily and lifted the pad in his hand. There was something painted on its top sheet, something stiffly painted in water colours in a full and lifeless brown, something that perched on a twig. Ralph had evidently attempted to paint—a hen.

"Betsy!" said Edward. "Is this, Mother, a painting of my Betsy?" He was touched, even though this creature did not express his pet, though it was drawn with painful exactness, every brown feather outlined with thick black paint. The wattles were an unnatural red, the legs and claws bright yellow, the brown eye dull. There was not a single smear on this neat parody of a living bird, this careful, unimaginative parody. For some mysterious reason he could not understand, himself, Edward felt a twinge of pity for the child who had drawn and painted this. He turned to his mother; she was smiling sternly, as if pleased at his reaction and recognition.

"It is a gift to you, from your brother, who will be a famous artist and greatly honoured in the world," she said.

"Well, thanks," said Edward, awkwardly. He looked away from her to the painting. He could not understand why his youngest brother, the lusty and excitable Ralph, for ever demanding, for ever having artistic tantrums, should go to all this effort for a despised brother. Edward was very moved. But that eye; it was lifeless. He looked longingly at the paints forbidden him. "It is very good of Ralph. It is a very good likeness of Betsy."

He heard, rather than saw, his mother shift in her chair. "It is a sacrifice to be an artist," she said. "And others must sacrifice for those who are gifted."

A sudden foreboding, a sudden horror, came to Edward. He came to the table, and put the pad on it. He wet his lips. "Betsy?" he murmured. Betsy had somehow gotten free of her pen early to-night. "Betsy?" he repeated.

"Ralph permitted her out of the crude cage you made, Edward," said Maria, with severity. "He is very young. And, as an artist, he constantly searches for objects to paint."

"I put her back in her pen before I left for the shop," said Edward.

"Yes, my son. And after you left Ralph wished to continue with his work. He released the hen. Unfortunately, she escaped from the yard."

Edward turned impulsively towards the outer door, with the wild thought that he must find Betsy alone in the night, Betsy who was just a pullet, who was tame and trustful.

"Edward!" said Maria sharply. "It is no use. You must be sensible. I know your attachment for that creature, which is ridiculous. It is no use at all. A cat caught her near the end of the street, and carried her away."

Edward sat down, his knees weak and trembling. He clutched them with his strong young hands. His breath came hard, and his grey eyes were stricken and terrible.

Maria, in spite of a tremendous effort, could not look away from those eyes. "It is only a hen," she said. "A mindless thing, a bird. It is true that you loved her, you, Edward, almost a man. One must have a sense of proportion in these matters. One must not be absurd. One can buy another hen for fifty cents, though it is a waste if one is not to think of eggs or the pot. If you are determined to be ridiculous again, and fondle a soulless creature when you have a sister and brothers to love and serve, you may keep fifty cents extra from this day's work and buy another chicken."

Edward had no words. He could see Betsy vividly, in the cat's bloody mouth, Betsy screaming for help when there was no help, Betsy whom he loved, and who had loved him. He closed his eyes convulsively, and when he did so Maria's harsh mouth quivered and she could look away at last.

"I am sorry," she said stiffly.

Edward, in his suffering, did not remark to himself that he had never heard his mother say such a thing to anyone before. Betsy was dead. There would be no joyous flutter to-morrow when he went to the pen. There would be no eager scramble into his hands, no frantic pecking of delight and effection. An awful loneliness, an awful grief, ran over him like a black and smothering wave, and he sobbed aloud without tears.

Edward swung his head aside, in his anguish, and dropped the pad on the table again. His eye fell on Ralph's paints, which he had bought. He stood up, slowly, like an old man and went to the chair. He opened the paints, gazed at them as if in a daze. Then he took up a brush, filled a glass with water and carried the paints to the table. With great care he placed water and paints near together, wet the brush, and, with amazing sureness, he swirled the brush on a bright yellow plaque, added a small amount of white. He drew Ralph's drawing to him. He bent his head over it. The dead eye, in a second or two, shone into life and fervour, brightened into intelligent love. Edward dipped the brush into the water again, swirled it into the brown plaque, then into the yellow, and softened the unbending outlines of the bird's body, so that it seemed to fluff into soft feathers and stand out from the paper. He muted the wattles, the yellow beak. He gentled the legs and claws. The painted bird arched its neck as if to call. The rigid twig curved, became a light-green branch, bursting into living leaf.

And all this time Maria said nothing, and only watched, and saw the rough strands of her son's shaggy hair as he bent over the pad. The cuckoo burst from its wooden nest and announced, with violent head-bobbings, that it was half-past ten. A polished copper tap dripped into the sink, with the faint sound of tears. The crickets shrilled violently, and there was a mutter of thunder in the sky.

At last Edward was finished. He had worked in a dream-like state. He pushed the painting aside, drew it to him again, studied it, and then once more rejected it. It was not Betsy, after all. It lived and breathed, but it was not Betsy.

Not looking at his mother, not speaking, he left the kitchen, shambling as if exhausted.

Maria's hands lay thickly in her lap. It was not for some time that she took up the painting. She looked at it long and thoughtfully. Her formidable eyes fogged and she was angry with herself. She was also frightened. She lifted her head indomitably and frowned. The strongest must be sacrificed for the best. She studied the painting again, and shook her head as if in denial. It was not to be considered. It is Ralph's painting, she silently and determinedly insisted.

She picked up the still wet and discarded brush. In the righthand corner she printed the letter R. Then the brush felt weighted in her hand, and something squeezed in her breast. She made the R into an E, and finished the name: E.L.E., 1904. She carried it into the tiny bedroom off the kitchen which she shared with her husband and covered the painting with sheets of tissue paper and hid it away.

When Heinrich fearfully and guiltily returned half an hour later he found the light burning in the empty kitchen. His wife, in their big white bed, was apparently asleep. She did not stir when he let himself cautiously down beside her. And he never knew that she had been weeping. It would have been incredible to him that a Von Brunner would weep at all.

It was after breakfast the next day that Edward Enger's re-education began remorselessly. He had not slept all night, grieving over his pet. He wrestled with a cold rage when he thought of little Ralph, a fury which continued to surge up in spite of his reasoning that Ralph was only a child, and careless, and had meant no harm. However, towards dawn the rage subsided into the exhaustion of common sense. There was that cat I accidentally hit with a baseball bat, and killed, he told himself. It was like that, with Ralph. The fool kid didn't know what could happen to a little hen when it got loose.

As usual Edward appeared in the kitchen before anyone else, except Maria, who was at the stove. She gave her son a sidelong glance of commiseration, but her voice was without emotion when she greeted him. What was done was done. Only the stupid bewailed what could no longer be helped. She placed a large plate of pancakes before Edward, and poured a cup of coffee for him. The house was quiet, the sunlight still on walls and floor, and the breeze cool and fresh as it gushed through the small windows.

Ralph came bounding into the kitchen, laughing his usual boisterous laugh, and capering. He began to shout at his mother, then saw Edward. He stopped at once, staring at his brother, and blinking, his red underlip moving in and out warily. Edward avoided looking at him, for the fury boiled in his throat and he felt nauseated. Ralph sidled towards his mother, and said, "Where's my picture, huh, Ma? My picture of that ole hen?"

"I put it away," said Maria severely, and tried to silence her youngest child with a twitching gesture of her white apron. "Never mind. Sit down and have your breakfast."

Edward neither turned his head nor spoke. He slowly drank his coffee, warning himself wearily that Ralph was "only a kid, and kids don't mean harm." His averted profile, the sternness of it, and his silence, aroused the excitable Ralph, for, like all young children, he could not bear to be ignored. There was that silly ole Ed, pretending not to see nobody, pretending to be real grown up! Stingy ole Ed, fooling around with that silly ole hen! Ralph's black eyes began to glow and flicker with malice. He capered to the table, seized a spoon and banged it down hard beside Edward's relaxed hand.

"Yah!" he screamed. "Your little old stoopid hen! Ran away, and got caught by the cat! Funniest thing you ever saw! I laughed and laughed——"

"Ralph!" exclaimed Maria, and her pallid face flushed. Ralph wheeled on her, with rising excitement.

"I laughed and laughed!" he shouted, and stamped his foot. "I saw that ole cat——"

"Ralph," said Maria again, and advanced towards him. He backed away, bursting into laughter and evading his mother's hand. Edward sat up in his chair, his pale lips falling apart.

"I saw that ole cat!" Ralph shrieked. "Licking her ole mouth for a Sunday chicken dinner. Real ole hungry cat. And I shooed that silly hen at her, and the cat grabbed it by the neck, and it squawked like crazy——!" He clapped his hands with delight, and jumped high once or twice as if in an ecstasy.

Edward stood up, very slowly. He said, and his voice was very quiet, "You let the cat get my hen? You meant to do it?"

"No, Edward, no!" said Maria. "It is not true. He is always making up the stories; he is only a child, and likes excitement."

"I did so mean to do it," said Ralph, and stamped his foot furiously. "He wouldn't give me a nickel Saturday, but he bought that ole hen some stuff from the feed store! Bet it cost more'n a nickel, too, and I said I'd fix him!" He glared at Edward, and his eyes were dancing with hatred, and Edward saw that hatred. And it stunned him like a blow over his heart.

Why should his brother hate him? What had he done to arouse hatred? It seemed terribly necessary for Edward to know that; in the intensity of his desire he even forgot his pet. "Wait, Ma," he said to Maria, who was reaching for Ralph again. His hand was lifted with new authority towards his mother, and Maria let her own hand drop. He regarded Ralph fixedly. "You're not lying," he said. "I know that. But I want to know why you'd hate me enough to hurt me. I'm not going to hit you, Ralph. I just want to know."

The little boy blinked at him, and with a curious smooth blandness moved over his face. He began to giggle. "Sure I hate you," he said, cheerfully. "Most everybody does. D'you have to have a reason to hate somebody, except they're that person?"

"You see, he speaks foolishly—like a child," said Maria, disturbed by Edward's expression. She moved between him and Ralph, not to protect the latter but with a vague thought of protecting Edward, himself, from some ugly knowledge.

Edward shook his head. "No, Ma. He isn't speaking foolishly. He isn't even speaking like a kid. He talks—why" —and Edward was stunned again—" —just like everybody in the world. And I never knew it before! I was too dumb to know what I'd been hearing all my life, everywhere; I just couldn't believe people would hate for no reason at all, no reason at all! But now I know. It's the way people are made."

Maria was silent, and Ralph was silent, and no longer grinning.

"I don't think I'll ever like people again," said Edward, in a low voice as if speaking to himself. "Why, they make me sick at the stomach." He thought, his head bent. "I can see it now. People hate, and then they've got to make up a reason for their hating. And all the time I thought it was the other way around. A reason first, and then hate; but it isn't. If there's—God—He must feel something like I feel now, about people."

"It's wrong to hate. You mustn't hate Ralph," said Maria.

Edward looked at her with wonder. "I don't hate him. I just understand," he said, with painful explanation. "I just know the facts now."

He turned and went out of the kitchen. Maria could see the top of his dark head passing below the windows. Then for the first time she raised her hand and brought it with cold and determined anger against Ralph's cheek, and the boy staggered and fell into a chair. He began to bawl loudly, and eyed his mother with fright as she stood over him.

"Just because of that ole hen, you hit me! Just because that ole hen got killed——!"

"It wasn't only the hen you killed," she said without emotion, and moved away, and sat down at the table.

Chapter Three

"What is this, that makes Eddie not speak, or explain to me why he is so quiet and stern?" Heinrich asked his wife. He was bewildered, for he thought he guessed or knew the reason for Edward's occasional "sulks," as Sylvia called them.

"It is nothing. Or it is only the hen he lost," said Maria. But she said to herself, my son has the *weltschmerz*, the pain of the world. No one knew that she also suffered this pain in silence, this strange and paralysing pain which afflicted the spirit and silenced its very voice so that it could not pray or have joy or contentment, but only a depthless anguish without sound. One did not speak of suffering, as she and Edward understood.

Heinrich thought that she spoke indifferently, and he felt some small indignation. He faltered, "It was no small thing to him, that hen." He had contradicted his wife, and he was amazed at his courage, and then he wilted. These aristocrats could never understand an earthly soul who had only love to offer, and who loved for love and duty, and so appeared gross to the patrician.

The family was impatiently accustomed to Edward's infrequent silences and withdrawals, which baffled all but Maria, though Heinrich invariably believed that he knew the causes. These withdrawals usually lasted only a week at the very most. But now it was early December and he was still remote. He worked harder than ever; he drove himself. He had even taken on jobs after the shop closed at night. He silently gave the money to his mother, who as silently accepted it. Once she thought, It is not possible for him to understand that I love him, and that I know what he truly is. It is good that he does not know. He is all the hope we have; in his withdrawals he gathers strength. If he knew he had love, also, he would weaken, and we should be lost.

"You have been despondent for many weeks, Eddie," said Heinrich one day when the shop was empty. "You must not brood. It is very unkind. The mother feels it. I have seen her watching you. There is a very strange look in her eyes, such as I have never seen before."

Edward wiped up some shreds of ham from the spotless counter. Under the brownness of his skin he had a sallowness, and he had lost weight. He did not answer his father. Heinrich saw his profile, sharpened now, fixed in suffering, "Do not sulk," Heinrich implored, in German. "It is not well for the young to sulk, to have grievances."

Edward looked at him, then, and tried to smile. "I do not have grievances," he said. He said in English, "Pa, stop worrying. We're almost out of ham. I'll have to go to the market myself, to-morrow, and pick up a few pieces."

Heinrich was cheered. "It comes Christmas soon," he said. He blinked imploringly at his son. "I am thinking of a dog for you, Eddie. You have always wanted a dog. A loving puppy, perhaps?"

"No," said Edward. He turned to his father, and saw the humble, blinking eyes, and he felt a squeezing of his heart. Poor Pa. He was an awful worry to his father. "You know that Ma wouldn't stand a dog. We've talked about that before. Never mind. I've just been in the dumps. We need more corned beef, and salami. How's the English tongue going?"

"We've sold it all," Heinrich said, enthusiastically. "All but four tins. Such a genius at selling are you, Eddie. I have ordered another case."

"We've got to get some Christmas specials soon," said Edward. He opened a catalogue. "Let's see. French artichokes in vinegar and oil. Um. A case, perhaps. Listen to this! *Pâté de foi gras*. Stuffed anchovies. Caviar, English chutney, Chinese teas. English marmalade, Seville oranges, smoked kippers, English biscuits, Dutch cheese, Roquefort, Camembert, Swiss chocolate. Look at the pictures, Pa! Never tasted them in my life; bet they're wonderful." His young face lighted up with pleasure. "They'll make you think of the countries they came from. Look; here's some Italian pepperone. You can order them all from that place in New York. Things no one here ever dreamed of."

"You are not serious," said Heinrich, appalled, and retreating. "That is all very well for New York, or even Albany, where the Senators are and the Governor. But not for this city, this Waterford. Who would buy such delicacies?"

"Everybody," said Edward, with a large gesture. The darkness left the smoky pupils of his eyes, and they were radiant again. "Who says people in Waterford, or anywhere else, can't appreciate good things to eat? Why do we have to have just staples all the time? We can educate people to luxuries. We'll be a success!"

"A success we are, already!" cried Heinrich, very frightened.

Edward leaned his elbows on a counter and contemplated his father soberly. Heinrich nervously smoothed down the little black rim of hair around his skull. He tried to avoid Edward's stare.

"Look, Pa," said Edward quietly. "What are we? A delicatessen. Some good Wisconsin cheeses. Some better ham. Some better corned beef. A service to the neighbourhood, yes. When the grocery stores are closed. How much did we net last year? Two thousand dollars. You were very pleased, weren't you? How much do we have in the bank? About six thousand dollars. And here the kids are growing up. How're you going to give them what they want, the advantages they want, and must have? Ma knows they're geniuses, but she isn't going to part with that six thousand dollars and I don't blame her. We have a separate account for the education of the kids. Two thousand dollars. That's going to send Dave to New York, isn't it, and Sylvia too, and take care of Gregory, who wants to study medieval literature in Europe, and Ralph, who has to study in Rome and London. Where's the money coming from?"

"I toss and toss on the bed at night," said Heinrich, almost in tears.

"I can't make enough with my Sunday jobs, and my work here, and the other jobs I have, to get the money for them," said Edward. "It's about time we faced facts. We need a lot of money." He pointed at the window. "Delicatessen. Why can't it just be Enger's?" Look, there's a store on each side of us, empty. Renting for almost nothing. We can break down the walls between us and them. Expand. Sell things people can't get in other places in town. ENGER'S! You've got to do more than toss and toss on the bed at night, Pa. You've got to do things."

"This America," groaned Heinrich, wringing his hands. "It gives the young people strange thoughts, unnatural, foolish thoughts. It gives dreams. They are wrong."

"It gives us opportunities," said Edward. He bent over the catalogue again. "Pa, we'd better have a talk with Ma. She understands things. She's very worried about the kids. They're growing up, fast."

"The mother will swoon," said Heinrich, with gloomy positiveness. "It will anger her, your dreams and foolishness. I will stand beside you, while you talk with her, and plead that it is only your youth and then we shall forget it all."

Edward smiled. "We'll talk to Ma to-night," he said. He pulled out a large glossy piece of cardboard from under the counter and began to letter on it, carefully, "ENGER'S WITH THE FIRST! EXOTIC IMPORTATIONS FOR CHRISTMAS, AS GIFTS OR FOR FAMILY ENJOYMENT! TASTE DELIGHTS BEYOND COMPARE! AFTER DECEMBER FIFTEENTH! WATERFORD DESERVES THE BEST FOR THE BEST PALATES!"

He set the card on a prominent place near the English tongue and stood back to admire it. Heinrich peered at it with horror. Edward, wetting a pencil between his lips, began to make out an incredible order on some blanks. "We'll get these in the mails to-morrow, and I'm marking the orders rush."

"The prices!" exclaimed Heinrich, wildly. "Who will pay those prices? Have you considered our neighbours? Working people, poor people!"

"I'm after the carriage trade," said Edward easily, printing his orders.

Heinrich sat down abruptly on his stool. His dark little eyes sparkled with real anger on his son. "And the carriage trade, the ladies and gentlemen, will come to this shop, this delicatessen?"

"Why not?" said Edward calmly. "We've just got to advertise." He pulled a small pad of paper towards him, wet his pencil again. "Here's the ad. for the two Waterford papers: Why send to New York or Albany for the imported delicacies you love? Enger's have them! Now I'll list what I've ordered. Um. Now, Pa, wait a minute. You confuse me, whimpering like that. 'Enger's Quaint Old-World Shop. Sussex and Bradford Streets. Both phones. Deliveries made, if desired.'"

"*Ach, Mein Gott!*" shrieked Heinrich, rolling his head in his hands. "You will ruin me, you will have us on the street, in the snow. Eddie, this you shall not do!"

"I'll make the deliveries myself, and when business gets better, we'll hire a couple of kids, too," said Edward, ignoring his father's frenzied hysterics. He had gone through this many times before, but not, he admitted to himself, over such a stupendous idea as this.

Without haste, he picked up one of the two telephones on the counter and called the owner of the shops on each side of the delicatessen while Heinrich, blinking with stupefaction and despair, could only sit in paralysis. "Mr. Enreich?" said Edward, in a deep voice. "This is Edward Enger, your tenant. My father and I have decided to rent those two stores next door to us. They've been empty for nearly a year. We're willing to meet a fair rent, better than you had before, if you can give us a promise that you'll break down the walls between and throw all three stores together, completely finished, before December fifteenth. We're expanding."

Mr. Enreich, a middle-aged and wealthy childless man who greatly admired Edward and who knew him well, and had often dreamed that Edward was his son, chuckled. "Up to the fine old tricks again, eh, Eddie? One of these days, Eddie, and I shall help you. Did I not tell you many times that it is you who have the Enger brains? Ach, but you would not listen. All those geniuses. *Ja.* But the genius is you, the American genius. Who is it that made the delicatessen? It was Eddie."

Edward smiled. "Thanks, Mr. Enreich. But about those stores."

"So, it is the expanding, *hein*? Good. It is what I suggested to the father six months ago." The old man relapsed into "low" German. "The father did not tell you? That is to be understood, yes. He was very frightened, he has the timid soul. Eddie, I will break down the walls for you. I will make you a good rent. I will have it ready for Christmas, two weeks before. That English tongue—it is very good. Save me two tins. You are expanding on the imported delicacies?" He chuckled again. "Good luck again, to you, my genius."

Edward replaced the receiver, thoughtfully. "He said no, is it not so?" asked Heinrich eagerly. "The Herr Manager of the coke mills and such said no? That is to be expected. Ach, you should not have trespassed on his office, at his desk!"

"The Herr Manager said yes," said Edward. "He's very pleased. He likes—us. He thinks everything's fine."

Heinrich moaned. "The Herr Manager is a burgher. He has no soul. He knows nothing of music. He is not impressed that the mother is a Von. He scoffs at geniuses. But he was born in Prussia, of no noble family, and we know those Prussians! He wishes to ruin us!"

He bowed his head dramatically. "It is enough. When the mother knows that the Herr Manager, the Prussian brute, the Prussian burgher, the man with no soul, approves of this nonsense, the mother will set her foot down firmly, and we shall have peace."

Edward did not reply. He was pacing the small floor now, frowning, planning. Heinrich watched him, more affrighted than ever. Edward said, "We'll have one side given over to the imported canned meats, and the bulk meats. Over here, we'll have the other delicacies, on a special round table draped with a lace cloth. Only a few tins and cans at a time. Then we must buy one of those new glass counter ice-boxes, for the tinned fish and caviar and the *pâte*. Blocks of ice; the tins tossed among them. They don't need ice, but it gives a clean fresh look, and people like that. A row of electric lights above them. We've got to get rid of this gaslight. Four big electric globes from the ceiling." His intense grey eyes were sparkling brilliantly between their thick black lashes. "No more sawdust on the floor. Blocked linoleum, black and white. Like in the catalogue of the big New York stores. A display."

"My son is mad, mad," whispered Heinrich, with genuine terror. "What is this that my son would do?"

"I think a thousand dollars would do it all," said Edward, meditatively.

Heinrich lifted his head, cheered. "The mother will refuse," he said. "The mother is wise. Ach, here are some customers."

At noon, Edward went home. He knew his mother would be alone, the children at school, including fifteen-year-old David who was in "second year high." Maria was polishing the already glistening floor of the tiny dark parlour, with its navy-blue velvet draperies, its shining hard tables, its poisonous green settees and repulsively carved red velvet chairs. Her wonderful hair was wrapped in a big handkerchief and a huge white apron covered her brown woollen dress. A white handkerchief, with a lace edge, peeped from her sleeve, as usual. She said coldly, "You have left the father in the shop? You did not have your meal there?"

"I have to talk to you, Mother," said Edward.

Maria formally removed her kerchief and her apron, put them out of sight, and sat down with her natural stately dignity. On these occasions, when she talked alone with Edward on business matters or matters concerning the family, a curious rapport and understanding rose immediately between them, during which they conversed as respectful and self-respecting equals, having esteem for each other's point of view.

Edward sat stiffly upright in a chair, facing his mother, while a December blizzard began to lash the little windows with their heavy blue velvet draperies. The room was cold; Maria conserved on fuel during the day. The panes of glass became moist, and crystals of ice crept along the lower edges. Edward was careful not to shudder. He told his mother of his plans, and his conversation with Mr. Enreich.

"There will be no money for the educations unless we expand, and very quickly," he concluded. "In two years David will be ready for his serious music studies. In three years Sylvia will need theatrical education. We have not come, of course, to Gregory, and Ralph, who are younger. Is this small shop to pour out gold easily? Or, shall it be shown the older children that they must work for their educations, if possible, as others do I have heard, waiting on the tables in the universities or working outside their classroom hours?"

"That is not to be considered," said Maria. "My children are not vagabonds."

"Then, we must have some courage," said Edward. "We must risk the one thousand dollars. We shall not fail."

Maria thoughtfully smoothed her handkerchief on one massive knee. She had known great poverty and humiliation in her life, as the daughter of a Herr Professor in a very small school in Munich. She had come to her more affluent relatives in Dorfinger almost penniless, even after three years of being a Fräulein to an English family. She knew the value of money, and understood only too well that if poverty is not a crime it is treated by the world as such. The thousand dollars Edward spoke about now was the harvest of two years of very hard work. She glanced up and saw his young eyes, and their inflexible surety.

"The father is afraid," she said, and smiled her cold and infrequent smile.

"The father," said Edward very gently, "is always afraid. He is very kind and very innocent. He is also worried."

Again, Maria gave that significant smile. "It does no good to worry. Worry is a waste, unless it is accompanied by a plan. Then, when one carries out a plan, there is no time to worry."

Edward sighed, and smiled. He had won. "You, Mother, will speak to him about it? He must not know that I have gone behind his back."

"Do I do that?" asked Maria, haughtily. "Such a thing is ill-bred. I shall speak to him to-night, as if it is my own suggestion." She paused. "You said that the Herr Manager Enreich hinted of assistance to you. Why did you not suggest that he assist the geniuses, as a patron?"

Edward stood up, trying not to scowl. "The Herr Manager is a business-man and not interested in geniuses. I do not think he would understand about being a patron."

Again, Maria was thoughtful, scrutinising her son. She said, "In America, it is a genius to be a good business-man. I think you are that genius, Edward."

She had never complimented him before, and Edward's eyes brightened. He took a step towards his mother, involuntarily, but was interrupted by the loud and furious banging of the kitchen door. A boy shouted, "Ma, where are you, Ma?"

"David," said Maria with consternation. "Why is he home? Is he ill?" She rose quickly, just as David charged vehemently into the parlour. He was taken aback at seeing Edward, then dismissed him and turned to his mother.

"The teacher's an idiot," he said in English. "I suggested Mozart for the Christmas theme and the play. Sylvia's directing the play, and she wants Mozart. And the teacher doesn't want Mozart! She wants the silly little American Christmas songs! I said, no. And she said that she'd choose somebody else for the piano. If that wouldn't make a fellow dippy and go out of his mind I'd like to know what would!"

Edward was interested. He said, "Look, Dave, the kids

like the songs they know for Christmas. What does it matter to you what you play for them?"

David swung on him passionately. "What would a fool, smelling of pickles and garlic, know of anything?" he demanded. "Shut up, will you?"

David was taller than Edward, who was, himself, unusually tall for his age. But David was as thin as a long stalk of grass and very dark and very elegant and temperamental. His cheap, neat clothing hung on his elongated body as if the suit he wore had cost over a hundred dollars rather than fifteen, and his shoes were polished to an almost impossible glitter.

"If your teacher won't have Mozart, are you going to bow out of the Christmas business?" asked Edward, undisturbed by his brother's jibe.

"No!" cried David. "I need audiences!"

"Then, why don't you do what she wants?" said Edward, reasonably. "She's got a right to choose and so do the kids."

"Quiet," said Maria with icy anger. "What do you know of these things, Edward? Is my son, the pianist, to be insulted this way?"

Edward shrugged. "I don't see what else he can do," he remarked. He picked up his cap and worn overcoat, which he had inherited from David, nodded to his mother and turned to go. But he was almost knocked down by the wild charge of a young girl who burst into the parlour in a mood almost as furious as David's.

"I won't, I won't!" she shrieked. "I will *not* direct a play about fuzzy lambs, and Christmas carols and silly babies bouncing around in hay! Where's David——?" She saw her oldest brother and threw herself dramatically into a chair. "I'm through with that school. I'm not going back, and if Dave's got a brain in his head, he won't either!"

"There's a matter of law," said Edward anxiously. "You're only thirteen, Sylvia."

"Shut up, boob!" howled Sylvia, and burst into excitable tears. She bent her head on her black cotton knees and wept noisily. David came to her, walking with carefully dignified steps and put a narrow hand on her bobbing head. Sylvia, at thirteen, was not particularly prepossessing, being all spindly arms and legs like a dark spider, her fine black hair pulled back from a white and bony face in two long pigtails, her tilted black eyes starting from their sockets in an aghast expression.

"What do you know about an artist's soul?" asked David. He gave Edward a devastating look, then turned to his mother. "You see how it is," he added.

"I see how it is," said Maria sternly. "But this is America. What can an artist do?"

He can stop being a damn' fool, thought Edward, irreverently. Then he crushed down the thought. Who was he to judge, who was not a genius? He was ashamed of himself. He walked slowly and despondently into the little dim dining-room with its big oval table which reflected back the stark and shifting light that drifted through the one window. Darkness was falling, as the snow fell. Edward could hear Sylvia's wailing and David's perorations and Maria's indignant voice behind him. He went into the kitchen. She frowned. "I thought you had returned to the shop," she said. The rapport and understanding between mother and son had gone, as it always went when others of the family were in the house.

"Ma," said Edward, hopelessly, "I'd send Dave and Sylvia back to school right now if I were you." He looked at the alarm clock on its little shelf near the sink. "If they hurry up they'll only be about five minutes late."

"Were you asked?" said Maria.

Again Edward shook his head. He pulled on his woollen mittens and went out into the increasing storm. He walked slowly, his head bent. About his feet the sand-like snow whirled in miniature cyclones, boiling almost to his knees and sloping from the sombre sky. He rubbed his ears as he walked, thinking. David had missed school too much since September. There was no law that compelled a young man of fifteen to attend school after his fourteenth birthday, but still he ought to take advantage of the opportunity, thought Edward. David "despised" school. It was filled with numbskulls of boys and girls, and idiots of teachers. Yet, Edward reflected with worry, David's report cards were very poor, though his deportment was listed as above average. Sylvia's cards were as bad, except for English, and the younger children's cards bore the lowest marks. Only he, Edward, had made an excellent record in school.

Edward spoke aloud, smiling grimly. "I suppose that proves something or other." The city was engulfed in silence, except for the storm. His hurrying feet made no sound on the rising snow. He blinked his lashes free from clusters of flakes, turned up the collar of his coat. He wondered if Margaret, in the P's, were walking in the storm as he was walking, and if she was warm, and if she had enough to eat, and if she went to school. She was living on a farm with the Baumers, near Albany. There was a law that would force the Baumers to send her to school, Edward consoled himself, aching with loneliness. But still, he was apprehensive. At fourteen, approaching fifteen, he had already seen enough of the world to know its cruelty and its deformed viciousness and its relentless hatred for the undefended.

Heinrich glanced with hurt significance at the clock when Edward entered the store after carefully stamping off the layer of snow on his shoes. "It has been forty-five minutes, Eddie," he said. "You take but half an hour for a walk after you have had your lunch."

"Sorry, Pa." Edward hung up his clothing.

Heinrich relented. "It is the worry that made you walk long," he said. "You must not worry." He brightened. "I, too, have been thinking of our problem with the gifted children. And," he paused meaningfully, "I have come to the conclusion. The children must have scholarships to the universities, to the theatrical and music schools!"

What, on their marks in school now? asked Edward of himself, incredulous. He turned to his father, amazed at this innocence which could constantly conjure up impossible dreams in the face of reality. He said, as kindly as possible, and knowing it was a lie, "But, Pa, you know very well that scholarships are given only to those who cannot afford higher education, or those who have no parents to support them."

Heinrich was crestfallen. He looked about the shop with mingled pride and mournfulness. "Ach, I can understand that, though in Europe it does not matter about parents or money. Scholarships are given without such consideration. But in America—ach, they do not care about these things. Eddie, what are we to do?"

"Some way will be found," said Edward. "Don't worry, Pa."

Ways had been found before, and Edward had found them. Heinrich was cheered. He shook an arch finger at his son. "I am not going to speak to the mother about the wild and strange ideas you suggested this morning, Eddie! That would make her very angry with you, and her anger is very cold and long, and it is your birthday on Christmas day. We must not spoil the birthday. Fifteen, my son! A man!"

"It's also Christ's birthday, Pa," said Edward, narrowing his eyes at his father. He paused, a wet cloth in his hand. Heinrich became a little pinker; he looked aside and rubbed an eyebrow. "Ach, yes," he murmured. "It is so. It is a folk festival as I have told you. All religions have celebrated that time, before the Christ was born."

"Yes?" said Edward, and he leaned his elbows on a counter.

"It is not that I am not a Christian," said Heinrich. "But what is a Christian? He is an altruist. He must be concerned with political ideas, the progressive, the welfare, the good working conditions."

Edward's smile became even darker. "Isn't that putting the cart before the horse? First, shouldn't a man be a good and practising Christian? And then wouldn't good ideas come of it as a result?"

Heinrich regarded him with tender pity. "Ach, you are almost a man, but you do not understand. Christianity is old, but still we have the wars, and the sweat shops and the oppression of labour, and the big profits for a few, and governments, like this America who do not understand that the means of production should belong to the State."

"Should they?" asked Edward. "Would you like the government to grab this shop and tell you what to buy and sell, and how much money you could make? Eh, Pa?"

"This is different," said Heinrich, stiffly. "I am only a small shopkeeper."

Edward chuckled. The little fragrant shop was warm; the windows dripped with moisture. He shovelled more coal into the red maw of the hot little iron stove in the rear. "We won't have many customers to-day," he said. "With this storm. How about shutting up early, at half-past five?"

"No," said Heinrich, reproachfully. "We have established that we are open until seven every day, but Wednesday and Saturday, and on those days we are open to eleven or later. We cannot break the rule."

The storm increased in its savage white intensity. The walls of snow shut off any view of the street, which was deserted. Edward, while his father was not watching, slipped his orders into an envelope, filched a stamp, and put the envelope in his pocket. Heinrich, humming absently to himself, was standing at the washbowl in the little closet, carefully scrubbing his celluloid collar under the running water. He did this, fastidiously, twice a day. He wiped off the collar, put it on again, secured it with a stud to his striped shirt, and neatly adjusted his black bow-tie. He combed his fringe of black hair. Then he modestly closed the toilet door. I feel like a dog, thought Edward. Going behind his back. But I've had to do that for a long time. Poor Pa.

Sometimes one or two of the children stopped at the shop on the way home from school to fill their mother's orders. It was half-past three when David, Sylvia and Gregory stamped in, groaning with cold. "Outside!" shouted Edward. "Shake off that snow and wipe your feet! I've just cleaned up the floor."

"Honest?" said Sylvia, scornfully, taking off her red tam-o'-shanter and shaking the snow from it.

"Old Garlic and Pickles," said Gregory, in his light, snickering voice. "What do you do, anyways, when you're not washing floors? He deliberately removed his snow-covered coat and swished it through the air. Hard pellets dropped on everything. Edward's face darkened. David merely stood and watched, smiling slightly. One of these days, Edward thought, I'll beat hell out of them. But Heinrich was coming out of the closet, beaming with love. He spoke to the children with delight, and in German. "Ach, it is the little ones, like sunlight! I have the new candy." He pushed his hand under a counter and fished out three suckers and extended them. "I don't like peppermint," said Sylvia, scowling. "You know that, Pa. And talk English. Haven't you got cherry?"

"We all like cherry," said Gregory. "Give me a ham sandwich," said David, leaning his elbow nonchalantly on the counter and staring at his brother. Edward saw this stare, and frowned again. This was something new David had acquired, this thoughtful and unreadable contemplation of Edward, this peculiar calculation.

Do they hate me, as Ralph hates me, and for the same reason? Edward asked himself. Or for the same no-reason? And why? What've I done to them except work for them? Could that be the reason after all? A hard thrill of vengefulness suddenly ran through his heart, and he was appalled at himself, and then, a moment later, he was not appalled at all. A fellow had the right to get mad when all that he did was just snatched and no thanks, and just expected! I'm flesh and blood, too, aren't I? What's that damn' Dave doing anyway, just staring at me like I was a specimen, or something?

Dave said to him, as Edward roughly thrust the sandwich towards David's elbow, "You know, this family has about as much mystery as this ham and bread. Except you, Ed."

"Me? Mystery?" Edward scowled at him.

David smiled his slight smile again, and thoughtfully bit into the sandwich. "I wonder what you think," he murmured. "What?" demanded Edward, not catching the words. But David only shook his head, and he did not smile.

Sylvia's and Gregory's eyes roved over the candies laid out in a glass case. "I want some of those liquorice shoestrings," Gregory said, with that chronic whine in his voice. "And I want two of those pink wax frying-pans with the goo in it."

"And I want three of those chocolate bottles," said Sylvia, arrogantly.

"You know Ma doesn't want you to eat candy before dinner," said Edward. But Heinrich was already eagerly obeying his children. They snatched the little striped bags as though starving. They filled their mouths and their eyes mocked their brother.

Gregory was a true Enger. At eleven, he had an extraordinary resemblance to Edward, and it was perhaps this resented fact which impelled him to imitate David. He was newly striving for that well-bred appearance, but he did not have David's patrician face. He had Edward's smoky-grey eyes, but without their steadfastness. His own were excitable and volatile and too acutely alert. Moreover, his expression was all-knowing, all smug, all wise, and this invariably irritated Edward. What did a kid of eleven know about the world anyway, that he should look at it so distrustfully?

Sure, he wrote wonderful stories, Edward supposed. At least so said his teachers, and his parents. He was intelligent, but beyond the subject of English and history his school marks were deplorable.

Gregory, sucking on his candy, began to inspect the pickles with a critical eye. " Why don't you get more sour ones?" he asked, discontentedly.

" Because we have more calls for dill and sweet," said Edward.

Sylvia slapped her mother's list before Edward. " Make it fast," she said. " We've got to skedaddle. Can't wait all day. The storm's getting bad. Hurry up."

" And what did my children do in their classes to-day?" asked Heinrich, with fatuous adoration. " Do?" asked Sylvia, in her sharp voice. " Why, what we always do in the dumb school. I want three white eggs, not those old browns," she said to Edward. She watched her brother, closely, as he silently filled the order. She began to tap her narrow foot and hum under her breath. Her black eyes became keener, and there was an uncomfortable line of colour under them. Then she tossed her head as if throwing off a disagreeable thought. Oh, what did it matter about old Ed, anyway? Why should a person feel funny this way, sometimes, about him? What was he made for, except to work? She wished she'd stop having these thoughts, which came often lately.

She said, crossly, " I want those Norwegian sardines, not the American."

" Dainty appetite, haven't you?" said Edward. " The Norwegian are too expensive. You'll take the American or nothing."

" If one has the dainty appetite it should be encouraged. It is discriminating," said Heinrich, reproachfully. He smiled tenderly at his daughter, who did not smile in return, and dropped a tin of the expensive sardines into the big brown bag for her.

" Never mind! I don't want them, if he doesn't want me to have them!" cried Sylvia, and was angrily amazed at herself. She snatched out the tin and almost threw it at Edward. " Eat them yourself, you greedy thing!"

" I'll do that," said Edward. " I haven't tasted them yet." But he put the tin back on its shelf.

"Greedy thing," repeated Gregory. "Hey, I need a dime. Give me a dime, Ed. Your pockets're always jingling. It won't kill you." He extended his slender palm imperiously.

Edward's first impulse was to slap down that hand. And then he saw his father's anxious and imploring expression. "All right, all right," he said, wearily, and put his hand in his trouser pocket. Fifty cents there. He'd be able to put only forty cents on his bicycle to-morrow. He gave Gregory a shining silver dime, and Gregory gloated over it, as if he had accomplished something triumphant. "And now, go on home, all of you," said Edward shortly, controlling his temper. He was rarely angry, as others were angry. His anger took the form of a dark and cold resentment, which built up steadily over days and weeks.

"How about a dime for me, too?" asked Sylvia. "I want to buy a new hair-ribbon."

"What is a dime?" murmured Heinrich, pleadingly.

"Yes," said Edward, with an inward thrust of that cold rage. "What is a dime? Give Sylvia a dime, Pa."

Never before had he embroiled his father in small arguments, but now there was a hard aching behind his eyes, and a pain under his breast-bone. Heinrich, in bewilderment, began to protest, his hand on the till. And then he saw his son's face, the wide cheek-bones shining whitely under the sallow skin, the grey eyes fixed on him steadily. And he shrank. No one saw David's watching face, or the delicate bunching of flesh between his eyes, as he regarded his brother.

Heinrich swallowed. "Dear children," he implored. "A dime is a large sum of money. It is a profit on four pounds of tea, on two pounds of butter. It is hard work. As Eddie says, you must go home. See how the storm is. It is not good for children to be walking in it. There is the pneumonia."

"Why should Greg get a dime and not me?" said Sylvia, and held out her own palm smartly. But this time it was directed at Heinrich, whose distress was growing.

David said, languidly, "Why should Ed give two dimes? It's up to you now, Pa."

Edward was startled at this sudden championing, and uneasy, and newly resentful. Dave was "up to something." He and Sylvia had no right to badger their father, and confuse him. A dime was a dime to Heinrich; it was a symbol of his work. So he raised his voice harshly, " Go on, now. Get out, all of you. If you don't I'll throw you out."

It was very seldom that he spoke with such mature authority, and his brothers and sister looked at him with amazement. Then David smiled to himself, and nodded imperceptibly. But Sylvia, in umbrage, saw Edward's clenched fists on the counter, and she suddenly decided that a dime was not worth the indignity of a blow.

" Let's go," said David.

" God be with you, my children," Heinrich called after them, but they did not turn their heads. Gregory slammed the door and the bell tinkled violently. Heinrich sat down on his stool and looked before him with melancholy. Without speaking, Edward cleared up the mess his brothers and sister had left behind them. He washed and wiped the counter. He took a broom and swept up the wet and dirty sawdust. Heinrich, after a while, began to watch him.

" Eddie," he said at last, and in a weak voice.

" Yes, Pa," replied Edward, bending to sweep the sawdust into a pan.

" I am not well, Eddie. I am hurt by discordant voices and quarrels."

Edward threw the fragments of bread and ham, and the dirty sawdust, into a galvanised pan and replaced the cover. There was a throbbing in his chest, a painful throbbing. When he had been twelve years old he had had what Heinrich had called " the growing pains." All his joints had been swollen and painful, for a short time. Since then Edward had suffered these occasional throbbings in his chest, especially when he was angered or overworked or tired. Sometimes he could not sleep. It was like a knife in his chest.

" It is my heart," said Heinrich, with a tentative and wounded reach for conciliation. There were times, these days, when Edward frightened him, with his strange new manner and the strange new look in his eyes. When had all this begun? It was some time in the past—some time in the summer . . . Was it still that foolish hen?

" Sure, Pa," said Edward. " Never mind. You mustn't pay too much attention to the kids. I'm not mad. Honestly."

Heinrich sighed with relief. " There are times when you are truly understanding, my son. One must be particularly understanding of the artistic temperament."

" Sure," repeated Edward. He was very tired.

The lousy, damn' world, he thought, with unusual bitterness. He was taken aback by the thought, which was so new to him. What was the world but an aggregation of self-seeking and murderous shark-mouths? It didn't deserve the prophets who had died for it in blood and torture; it didn't deserve the heroic ones who had fought for it.

The storm bellowed at the door. The windows dripped. The day darkened. The globes of gas hissed from the ceiling. A lamplighter darted past the store, an old man with no topcoat, his battered hat layered with snow. Edward could dimly see him, with his lighted stick, turning on the street lamps. " Look, Pa," he said. " It's after four. Almost half-past. And the storm is getting worse. Why don't you go home now? I'll manage until seven. We won't have many customers, anyway."

" Eddie, you are sometimes very thoughtful," Heinrich said, with gratitude. Something had depressed him, had disheartened him. He peered at his son, and moistened his lips. " I will go, Eddie, if it will please you." He spoke as if granting a favour to an importunate person, in a surrendering tone.

" It'll please me all right," said Edward. " I won't have to worry about you."

He helped his father on with his coat. He wrapped his father's woollen scarf about his short throat. He buttoned his father's coat, bending his knees to do so. He put his father's cap on the round bald head, and found his father's gloves and rubbers. He felt he was assisting a child. Impulsively then, he bent and kissed his father's cheek, which was still too pale. Tears came into Heinrich's eyes, easy tears.

Edward held the door open for him. The throbbing was really painful now, in his chest. " Good night, Pa," he said gently. " I'll be home around eight, after I've cleaned up a little. Tell Ma to leave something out for me. I can help myself."

He watched his father plunge into the storm, a small rotund figure. Poor Pa. Edward closed the door, looked about the warm and silent shop, so brightly lighted, so good-smelling. It was wonderful to be alone, sometimes. He began to sing softly to himself. Then, without his volition, his voice soared out, a rich baritone which shook the walls and the shelves, like a triumphant pæan.

Silent Night, Holy Night!
All is calm, all is bright!
Round yon Virgin——

The storm swirled around the shop. There was thunder at the windows. Edward's spirits rose exultantly, as he sang. The day of the Lord's birth was also the day of his, Edward's birth. His Germanic heart found some mysterious message in that. He wished he knew more about God, and His coming. There was the Bible at home, of course, but when he arrived at night the parlour was firmly closed, and icy.

Surprisingly, considering the storm, there were twelve customers in the next hour, and Edward waited on them briskly. He sold the rest of the tongue. All the customers were excited by his placard announcing the treats for Christmas. The till opened and shut with a heart-warming frequency, and the bills and silver mounted. The customers were fond of Edward. They told him their troubles and their difficulties, as if he had been a hoary man of much wisdom. He listened sympathetically. He knew them intimately, and was really concerned with them. He managed deftly, however, to increase their original orders. The slicer whirled, the bread diminished, the sardines dropped satisfactorily, the salami and baloney almost cut themselves to the butts. The pickles dwindled in the barrels. The women, grateful for the warmth after the cold outside, lingered, examined, recklessly bought more. The coffee mill ground on and on, and filled the hot little shop with the most entrancing odours. When a customer bought more than a dollar's worth her child was rewarded with a sucker. The customers left the shop reluctantly, the women wrapping their wet shawls over their heads, the children sucking joyously. Everybody left messages for Heinrich.

And then they were gone, and Edward restored neatness. His father would be pleased. He was alone again, and again began to sing. The door bell tinkled and a very squat, very stout man, in a black broadcloth coat with a fur collar, entered, his glasses immediately steaming. He took off his excellent derby hat and shook it, and stamped his feet, which were protected by elegant spats.

"Mr. Enreich!" said Edward. Mr. Enreich frequently

patronised his tenants, but always through his coachman. He rarely came himself. Then Edward saw the fine carriage outside, with the coachman on the high seat. Mr. Enreich smiled at Edward and showed a number of gold teeth between his pink lips. His tiny fat nose wrinkled and his shrewd greenish eyes looked on Edward with affection.

"I thought we'd better have a talk, between ourselves," he said. "Just you and me, Eddie. By the way, I saw your father stumbling through the snow and drove him home. That's why I knew he wouldn't be here."

"Let me make you a sandwich," said Edward, impulsively. "And I've got some root-beer on ice." He never saw Mr. Enreich without pleasure. He looked at the gentleman warmly. Mr. Enreich had a square head with a stiff crop of red hair standing up on it like a bristling fence. Edward wished there was a chair for such a customer, and he pushed out his father's stool to the other side of the counter. "Such ham," said Mr. Enreich. "Yes, a sandwich, but not the root-beer! *Mein Gott*, not the soft beer!" He heaved his fat haunches on the stool, and wiped his glasses. He looked at the close walls of the shop, and nodded.

"I can make you some coffee," said Edward.

He turned up the gas on the hot-plate, rinsed out the granite coffee-pot and brought out the best coffee. He'll probably buy at least five dollars' worth, he thought, contentedly. Pa might deprecate Mr. Enreich but he invariably bought large quantities of foods and was not to be underestimated. Besides, the Herr Manager was a rich man and should be cultivated. He did not patronise Edward and this was a wonder to the boy. He treats me like a man, Edward said to himself, setting down two cups and spoons and sugar and cream. The screaming white storm outside, the night, the lights and the clouded windows inside, filled the boy with contentment and peace. And now the shop was permeated with the fragrance of coffee. Edward made a sandwich for Mr. Enreich and one for himself. During all this neither spoke, nor found reason for speaking.

Mr. Enreich, waiting, lit a fine Havana, and puffed it. He had removed his fur-lined coat and had thrown it nonchalantly on a pile of cartons, and had crowned it with his derby and gloves. His black broadcloth suit was as rich as silk, and his stiff white collar gleamed about his huge red neck. A monster black pearl glimmered on his thin blue tie, and a heavy gold chain, swinging with seals and other impedimenta, shone on his paunch. He gave the impression of enormous strength and physical vitality, at which Edward marvelled, considering that Mr. Enreich must have been at least forty-eight, a precariously elderly age in Edward's youthful opinion.

Edward poured the coffee. Mr. Enreich set big gold teeth into a sandwich, nodded his head blissfully, drank deep of the liquid, which he had generously diluted with yellow cream and sweetened with four teaspoons of sugar. His glasses steamed again with delight. " Ach," he said, " I say it now, and will say it again, there is nothing like the simple food and good fresh coffee off the fire. Another sandwich, Eddie. This time the mustard I will try." His ruddy cheeks bulged.

Edward sat on the edge of the counter, and the two ate with contentment, and drank another cup of coffee. Then, replete, Mr. George Enreich wiped his hands fastidiously on a big square of fine linen faintly perfumed with lemon verbena. " We shall now get down to business, Eddie, and you will tell me all your plans."

He listened intently as Edward spoke with quiet enthusiasm, and occasionally he nodded, and turned to look when Edward pointed to the spots where the new counters would stand. He read the placard Edward had printed, and smiled. " It is the advertisement that pays," he said.

He took out a gold toothpick, and cleaned his teeth meditatively, his green eyes, like full marble agates, fixed on Eddie. He had a deep and purring voice, not in the least " refined " or " genteel." " Eddie, I have said I will break down the walls, and rent you the two stores. I will finish it twelve or fifteen days before Christmas. I have already called the workmen. They will begin to-morrow. How much are you going to invest in the expanding, *hein*?"

" I'm not investing, Pa is," said Edward, a little uncomfortable.

Again Mr. Enreich chuckled. " Does he know?" he asked. " Ach, I thought not. But invest he will. Eddie, I will make you the proposition. Ten per cent of your increased sales when the shops are thrown together. Ten per cent gross."

Edward frowned. He did not know whether it was a good

offer or not. He said, "Mr. Enreich, I think rent would be better."

"No." Mr. Enreich slapped his hand on the counter. "I take the gamble. Maybe more than the rent, maybe less. I am the business-man."

"For how many years?" asked Edward, cautiously.

"Why, for ever," Mr. Enreich replied genially. "Unless you close up the shop. No leases, we gamble together. Yes?"

Edward reflected. He forgot he was not yet fifteen; he forgot that this was his father's shop, not his. He folded his arms and stared into space. "All right," he said, "we'll make a contract, Mr. Enreich."

"I have it already," said Mr. Enreich, and drew out the papers from an inner pocket. "With the new fountain pen, the wonder, that holds all the ink so no one stands back and says, 'I will sign it to-night, or to-morrow, at home, at the office, where I have the pen and ink.' Eddie, when the customer is there is the time for the signature. To-morrow never comes."

"But, my father is the one to sign," said Edward, coming to himself. "I only work for him, for five dollars a week. And I won't be fifteen until Christmas Day."

"Sign, Eddie. Your signature is as good as gold to me. The father? Who writes and sends out the orders to New York, and keeps the books? You. Yet under law, you have no right to do so. But you do it."

"All right," said Edward, and neatly wrote his signature below the few lines of agreement. His writing was small and firm and compact. Mr. Enreich nodded to himself, as he watched. "I hope it stands up," said Eddie.

"It will," replied Mr. Enreich cheerfully. Eddie was holding the gold pen in his hand. It was engraved with the letters GE. It felt very good in Edward's big fingers. "You like it, *hein*? Well, Eddie, you will have a pen some day like this, for yourself. You will not stay with the delicatessen all your life. No, no, I know men. You will be a rich man."

"I hope so," said Edward, returning the pen reluctantly. "I mean, I've got to be. All the kids, and Pa's getting old. He'll soon be thirty-five." He coloured when Mr. Enreich roared with laughter. Then Mr. Enreich became serious. He rested his elbows on the counter and studied Edward intently.

"You must tell me, Eddie. I am curious. How is it that

you got into this, this belief in the geniuses, this belief you must serve them? You are not a fool; you have the intelligence. They call you the fool, but you know they are wrong. So. What is it?"

"I'm not gifted," Edward replied. "They are."

"So," said Mr. Enreich, sardonically. "That is a matter of opinion."

Again he studied Edward's square, dark face with the resolute grey eyes, the good chin and short, sturdy nose. It is the son I should have had, had not my wife died, he thought. We shall see. "So," he said, "you will give your life to your brothers and sister, your life that is not yours to give, but which God gave you. You have not told me why. You have said only words."

Edward considered, his colour brightening. He bit his lip. Then he spoke quickly and impulsively. "It's my father. He must not be—be—well, he must have his beliefs. It would just about kill him if they weren't so. You see, Mr. Enreich? And maybe he's right. I'll do all I can, just for him, I kind of—kind of——"

Mr. Enreich smiled at him gently.

Edward burst out, "They are geniuses! It's a dream, for me. I'll make the dreams come true."

Mr. Enreich no longer smiled. He sighed. He said, "I want a lot of delicacies, Eddie. Get out the big bag, and I'll call Ellis in to take it to the carriage."

He walked about the shop, puffing on his cigar, Edward following him alertly. Five dollars, six dollars, seven dollars! The bag bulged to the very top. Edward was elated. The coachman came in and carried the bag to the carriage, and Mr. Enreich put on his hat and coat and gloves, slowly and carefully. Then he went to the door. He turned and looked at Edward, his hand on the handle.

"It was Shakespeare who said something, in the Hamlet. The soliloquy. It is something for you to remember, Eddie. '. . . and all the spurns which patient merit of the unworthy takes——' "

He closed the door silently behind him. Edward stood still a long time, frowning, trying to understand. Then he shrugged. He would have to hurry, to close the shop by seven.

The snow was very deep now. Its drifts lay against the windows.

Chapter Four

Mr. George Enreich was one of the richest men in Waterford, and he might have been considered rich even in New York, as well as in a small city of some quarter of a million souls. Heinrich, who had read much of what he called, with mingled awe and envy (being a Socialist), " the robber barons," had decided that Mr. Enreich was not to be numbered in that esoteric company. He did not resent Mr. Enreich much, for after all, the most dedicated of Socialists excluded the rich men of their acquaintance from an onerous company of faceless men with silk hats, diamonds on their fingers and in their ties, and with big stables full of blooded horses and magnificent carriages. The " robber " barons had mysterious and evil associations with something called Wall Street, and, as Heinrich said, he had never heard that Mr. Enreich was committed to the inhabitants of the Street who " ground the faces of the poor."

Yet, Mr. Enreich was, and in his own genial and hard-handed way, a " robber baron " and entrepreneur. Over the years it had become his custom to enter a sound company in Waterford as a manager, and then, by manipulation, to become at least one of the directors of the board if not a vice-president. He not only was " interested " in the Walz Cope and Coal Company, but in Waterford's lumber mill, in a number of small and flourishing factories, in the Everingham Iron Works, in the one steel mill, and in a chemical plant.

He was outside a number of pales. Once, he had been seen in the one good restaurant in the town in the company of a woman who SMOKED! To add to all this, he was rough, even brutal at times, contemptuous of almost everybody, and lived as he wished. When he gave parties he rarely invited the " Society " of Waterford. He preferred politicians from Albany, New York and Washington, many of whom he regrettably influenced and bought. He thought it a very comfortable arrangement ; politicians were not easy to buy in proper England and in stern Germany, and this often inhibited men with ideas.

Edward's part in the " generosity " and the strange contract with Mr. Enreich passed notice. Maria it was who had "talked" with her husband about the expansion, and after a few such talks the whole family except Edward, agreed that the mother had formulated the exciting new plan. Heinrich would even say to Edward, with trembling enthusiasm, "Is not the mother herself a genius? Alone in the house, she conceived this magnificence!"

In the odd way of humanity, he had totally forgotten that it was Edward who had proposed the expansion, for he never knew of Edward's talk with Maria. There were times when Edward smarted, during his family's superior and patronising eulogies of Mr. Enreich. They just took my contract I signed and put it in the tin box with the other papers and never looked at my signature! How do they think the contract happened, anyways?

Nevertheless, he had long moments of inner excitement and happiness. The walls were already torn down between the three little shops and he and his father had to wear coats and mittens to wait on the customers, for the small iron stove could not heat the gaping holes on each side. After the work was finished there would be one big stove, adequate for heating the expanded shop. Then, to everyone's awe, Mr. Enreich grandly had radiators installed, and a marvellous central heating system in the dank basement. Heinrich had qualms about this. The monster furnace would devour coal. "Not much more than the big stove, Pa," Edward said. "Besides, Mr. Enreich wouldn't do this unless he knew we're going to be rich!" Heinrich moistening his lips and blinking thoughtfully, agreed that Edward was right. "Besides," he said largely, "it will give the prestige, the newness. It is not every shop which has a furnace."

The small windows were removed and suddenly there was one big plate window and children and men and women often gathered to stare at its blaze of overwhelming crystal. And then, across it, in giant silvery letters which sparkled, "ENGER'S." During lax moments both Edward and his father would step outside to look in speechless pride.

Big squares of black and white linoleum covered the old boards, gleaming like marble. The counters were beginning to arrive, and the dozens of exotic cartons of delicacies from New York. Edward inserted expensive advertisements in the local papers, designed to attract the carriage trade. There would be a "grand opening." In the meantime, the shop continued to serve staples and a few of the cheaper delicacies to the local customers. They no longer engaged Edward in accounts of unemployment, derelict husbands, "the drink," the ailments of babies and children, the worries about adolescent daughters who wanted to put up their hair too soon, and were showing signs of being flighty at seventeen, and their sons, who at fourteen, were obstinately pleading to be allowed to continue school for a year or two more, when they should be at jobs to help the family. Edward vaguely and anxiously worried about this. He did not as yet know that the new big shop was already overawing the humble and the neighbours, and especially the big plate-glass window. It was not his intention yet to frighten away the backbone of any business, the steady, small purchasers.

Mr. Enreich, though the Hero, did not pay a return visit to the shop, though he sent his coachman for the new and expensive goods. Once Ellis said patronisingly to Edward, as he disdainfully lifted big bags, "Mr. Enreich doesn't buy from New York or Albany any more. You should thank your lucky stars. Twelve dollars this time."

After the "grand opening" there was a constant parade of carriages on the street, which first intimidated the local customers. And then they were happy and preening to be allowed to brush elbows with ladies in sable coats and smelling of wonderful scents. The mothers no longer sent children who would not appreciate this splendour; they came, themselves, in their head shawls and in their dragging coats and skirts and with coarse hands, to stare, to pretend for a few moments, that they were one of the fine ladies, and that one of the carriages outside was their own.

The neighbourhood, conscious of its shabbiness in all this grandeur, decided to be worthy. Windows were washed frequently, and shone. Curtains suddenly became white and stiff with starch. Walks, usually left covered with beaten snow and ice until spring suns melted them in due course, were shovelled feverishly. The working men became particular about their dress and never entered the shop with dinner pails, as they had done in the past. Children were protestingly scrubbed within an inch of their lives, and holes disappeared in their stockings and clothing. There was much talk of house-painting when the summer came.

To crown it all, the plank walks were removed and concrete poured before the big new shop and for some distance beyond it. Concrete carriage steps appeared. New cartons from New York arrived daily. There was almost always a van before the door. Then Edward hired Billy Russell after school to help with the harder work in the back and in the basement and to assist with the cleaning. Heinrich no longer went to the market even for staples and hams and corned beef and pickles. Edward took over, with Billy. "But a Negro boy!" Heinrich had protested at first. "He is my friend," said Edward, and had looked at his father sternly. "Don't Socialists say all men are equal?"

"That is true," Heinrich admitted with some uneasiness. "However, one draws lines."

"What lines?" demanded Edward, with a new hard eye which disconcerted his father. To this, Heinrich had no reply. There was no use, sometimes, in arguing with Edward. He had the stubborn, blind soul that refused to be sensible on occasion. The selfish soul that did not understand, Heinrich would think, not the selfish soul that does not give of its heart, but the soul that did not consider other points of view but its own. And what was this "friend" matter? Edward had no friends but this Negro boy. Heinrich discussed this with Maria. Edward invariably chose acquaintances among the inferior, but that was because he had inherited the full impact of the Enger blood. "One has only to consider that priest," Heinrich would remark. "I understand Edward speaks with him often."

In the meantime, in his spirit, Edward talked to God, gratefully happily, as a child talks to its father in joy over gifts. God was not in His heaven alone. He was in a snowflake, in the bellow of the north wind, in a sudden glimpse of blue sky among ominous winter clouds, in an instantaneous smiting of the sun on a snow-bank, in the majesty of bread and butter and milk, and in the drowsy pleasure a weary body experiences in a warm bed after a day of bitter labour. Sometimes, at night, before falling to sleep, Edward said in his spirit, "Father?" And God always answered in a gentle and comforting voice, "My son." It was enough.

It was three nights to Christmas Eve, and during the last week

Enger's kept open till eleven at night. Heinrich, exhausted, would leave at eight, and it was Edward's business to conduct the store's business for the next three hours, with the help of Billy. Sometimes, however, the boys could not leave until much later, and they would walk part of the way home together, hardly speaking from weariness, but content. It had begun to snow again this last week and the white crispness would crunch under their plodding feet, and the air, in the light of the golden street lamps, would sparkle and stream and blow like bits of diamonds. The boys would catch the tiny flakes on their sleeves and study the miraculous beauty and mystic wonderfulness of them with a kind of awe. "Look," Edward would say, "they never have more than six points, any of them, and how do you suppose that happens?"

"Guess God told them not to make more than six, or something. Look at this one, Ed. Like lace or something. A design. Nobody could make anything like that." Then Billy, as if he had seen a miracle, would be inspired to pull out his harmonica and play reverently as he walked along, the small but rolling organ notes rising above the wind and the fall of the patient snow. Edward, after a while, would sing with the music.

Nobody knows the trouble I've seen,
Nobody knows, but Jesus!

Man, Billy would think with compassion, listening to the rich and youthful baritone, you ain't seen anything yet of trouble! I've got it in my bones that you'll see plenty, yes, sir.

It was three nights to Christmas Eve, and it was on that night that Edward had his first serious and violent quarrel with his father.

Billy, who took care of the furnace which supplied the fine new radiators with steam, always ate his evening sandwiches in the basement. At seven o'clock, as usual, he went downstairs with several sandwiches and a pint of milk. Edward was very tired. He was suffering from what his parents called "one of his black moods."

It was a slow time in the shop between six and seven, and Edward was cleaning up the broad new counters and polishing the wood of them. Heinrich, happily inspecting the till, and unaware that his son had been quiet too long, remarked, "Is it not marvellous, Eddie? We have taken in this day twice which we took in a month ago in a week of days! We shall be rich, as the mother prophesied!"

"I prophesied that," said Edward, in a loud, hard voice. Heinrich started apprehensively. "You've forgotten," Edward added. "Funny how people forget things." He suddenly threw down his damp cloth. "Pa, I've got to talk to you before you go home. Billy's been coming in here after school every day, at three o'clock, and working sometimes to midnight. Nine hours a day. And you pay him three dollars a week, and only charge him fifteen cents a day for a lunch at four o'clock and another sandwich or two at seven or eight! Now, isn't that wonderful? Ninety cents a week out of his three dollars! He can take home two dollars and ten cents. Wonderful!"

Heinrich blinked. He could not understand. He stared at Edward's wrathful face, at the fiercely glittering grey eyes. He stammered, "You think fifteen cents is not enough, Eddie, for the meals?"

Edward's large fist clenched on the counter. "Pa, I think it's too much. That's what I think. You shouldn't charge him anything. And you should pay him at least five dollars a week. You know what I'm going to do? I'm going to tell Billy to quit unless you give him his meals free and pay him five dollars."

"What is this?" cried Heinrich. "Have you become mad, Eddie? The boy eats what he wishes, and it is worth more than fifteen cents, and two dollars and ten cents a week is very good! It would be a fortune in Bavaria, for a boy, with the good ham and the corned beef and the milk, and the cakes——"

"This isn't Bavaria," said Edward. "This is America. Well, Pa? Does Billy quit or do you raise his pay and stop charging him for meals?"

"I do not understand you, Eddie," faltered Heinrich, retreating before the cold blaze of his son's eyes. "Do we not work and save, only for the children? You would rob the children of their future?"

"What of Billy's future, Pa?"

Heinrich, very frightened, stammered, "The boy—the Billy—he has no future."

Edward's big mouth became a whitened ridge in his face. "Who says that, Pa?"

Neither father nor son had seen Billy's bronze face and thick black curls rise above the floor at the rear of the store, where the stairs descended to the basement. Neither ever knew that Billy had been listening from the start, caught unexpectedly by the sound of his own name.

"Maybe you haven't heard, Pa," Edward continued, in a voice growing progressively more inflexible and bitter. "We aren't considered too much, either. We're foreigners, even if all of us except you and Ma were born in this country. The people in this town, most of them, don't think we've got any future to mention. We're just the delicatessen keepers. Even people with our ancestry look down their noses at us, because we're new here. I heard Ma laugh about it one time, but I don't laugh. And I'm not laughing now."

Heinrich's small plump stature seemed to dwindle. He shook his head feebly. "Well, it is to be expected of barbarians, my son. We do not think it of much importance."

"Billy might think it important. For him. And that brings me to another suggestion. You've been giving me five dollars a week since June, when I left school. We're making a fortune now. I'm not going to put four of my five dollars into the fund for educating the other kids any more, unless you raise my pay to ten dollars a week. Ten dollars, Pa. Maybe I've got a future, too. I've started to think about it."

Now Heinrich was truly appalled at this blasphemy against his family. He wet his round, pink mouth and his eyes became big black circles in his face. "Eddie!" he whispered. "What is wrong with my son, who has dedicated himself to the geniuses? He would exploit them, deprive them. . . . When was it that he began these thoughts?"

Edward, almost as amazed as his father at what he had said, could have answered with truth, "Right this minute and not a second before." He contemplated his own words, and then, before his inner eye the past few months rose up before him clearly, and he thought, It all began the day Ralph killed Betsy, and it went on to Billy, and all the insults I've been taking lately from the kids, and Ma's letting everyone think she thought up the idea of expanding. All of a sudden I've begun to think, and thinking of ten dollars for me, putting in all that work and never anything in sight just for me, sounds like a damn' good idea! I'm willing to work the way I do, not getting any education, not asking much, just as anxious as Pa is and maybe more, for his sake, that the kids develop themselves, but I want a little justice for myself!

He looked at his father without speaking for some very long moments, and in those moments he stepped for ever from boyhood into manhood. He could even say with gentleness, "Pa, maybe I've been thinking you ought to be just to me, too. I haven't seen a vaudeville show since I was twelve, maybe eleven years old, because I was always here after school. And what you gave me, mostly, went to the fund for the kids. I had that drummed into me all the time—for the kids. Ever since I can remember. Maybe I'm not a genius, but I'm a human being. I've got a right to something, after all my work. And I want a bicycle and some other things."

Heinrich sat down heavily on his stool and rested his elbows on the counter and held his face in his hands. He shook his head sombrely, rolling it in his hands, and sighing deeply.

"I'm going to make myself a couple of sandwiches and go down to eat with Billy," Edward said. "And I've got to know if you're going to be just to Billy, too, so I can give him the good news, or tell him to quit. I hired him; he won't stay just for you."

Heinrich groaned. He thought of Maria, and winced. "I do not know my son," he muttered pathetically. "Over and over, he has agreed with me that all must be for the geniuses and their education. He understood. And now, all at once, he does not understand, he refuses his burden, his destiny, his place in the world, his obedience. What is it, what is it!" he cried.

Edward straightened up and turned away and began to slice pink ham for his sandwiches. He said, almost as if to himself, "Who says it's my burden, my destiny, my place, my obedience? I took it on myself. Maybe I've been wrong all the time. Maybe I've been right. I don't know. Maybe I'll find it out too late. But I've got to have a little justice for Billy even more than for myself."

Heinrich, feeling that he was alone in the big shining shop with a stranger, and feeling a fear of that stranger, sat and shook his head over and over. None of Edward's plea for himself and Billy seemed comprehensible to him. A spark of indignation quivered in his misery. It was all so plain to him, the sacrifices for the geniuses. In a way, those sacrifices were noble, and should be accepted almost with gratitude. Was it not Luther who had said, "To be singled out by Almighty God to carry the burden of service, yes, even of martrydom, is an awesome sign of His favour?" He and Edward had been so singled out. Without them, the geniuses would languish in dark obscurity, and the world poorer for it.

Edward laid the sandwiches on a piece of butcher paper and turned to his father. He saw that Heinrich was very pale, almost grey, and for an instant his heart lurched weakly and he was remorseful. Then he thought of Billy. He said, "Well, Pa?"

Heinrich said faintly, "What of the mother? When it is a matter of money I always tell the mother."

Edward smiled grimly. "Well, just don't tell her this time. In fact, I absolutely insist you don't tell her. If you do, I'll tell Billy to go, and I won't work here any longer."

"Eddie!" wailed Heinrich. "What is this you are saying? But you are not serious!"

"About my quitting? Pa, I mean it. I'll be fifteen on Christmas, and I can get a job somewhere in town, or maybe I'll go to Albany. Anybody'd pay me twelve or fourteen dollars a week—anybody." Edward was smiling, and it was a cold white smile. "I can pass for older than I am." He leaned against the shelves and looked before him and not at his father. He wondered, a little, how he could feel this hollow emptiness, this peculiar lack of compassion, this imperviousness, in himself.

Heinrich was gazing at him as at something he found incredible. But his son's eyes, when they met his, made him almost leap from his stool.

"Yes, yes!" he stuttered, throwing out his arms despairingly. "I agree! But Eddie—Eddie——!"

"What?" asked Edward, his voice remote and gentle.

I have lost my son, thought Heinrich. In these minutes, I have lost my son, and never until now did I know what the loss would mean to me.

He dropped his face into his hands in a gesture of real anguish. Edward, watching him, frowned again, thoughtfully. He said, "Now, Pa, don't be dramatic, as Ma says." He waited, but Heinrich seemed to have forgotten him in his misery and Edward was ashamed. He took a step or two towards his father, and then he halted.

"You've only agreed to the right thing, Pa," said the boy. At that moment two women and three children entered through the wide doors of the shop, and Heinrich, still trembling and pale, automatically smiled his kind and naïve smile, got to his feet to wait upon them. Edward began to put down his sandwiches in order to help, then firmly took them up again. His father would be leaving very soon, and then he would have to work far past eleven o'clock. He went down the stairs, and his whole body was heavy and listless.

The basement was warm but dim, for only one or two jets of gas were burning. Billy was shovelling coal into the red mouth of the furnace, and he turned his head and greeted Edward with his ineffably sweet grin. "About giving up hope you'd be coming down, Ed," he remarked. "Man, this furnace sure eats up the coal! Can't hardly leave it for more than half an hour, or the steam goes down." He wiped his sweating forehead with the patched sleeve of his striped blue shirt, and rested, panting, on the shovel. He, too, was tired, tired to the point of shivering.

Edward laid his sandwiches beside Billy's on one of the wooden chairs. "Here, let me help you for a minute," he said. "I'm sorry I didn't have time to-day to come down and help you, but we could have used two more hands up there. I'd better start to think of that before long." He took the shovel from Billy, who was too weary to protest.

Edward tossed the coals into the furnace, shovelled up more. His knees were shaking a little from exhaustion. Then suddenly they were shaking heavily and uncontrollably and there was an awful feeling of emptiness in his bowels and a curious sensation of collapse. He let the shovel slide out of his hands and he raised his head, looking about him blankly. Then there was the pain in his chest and his side again, but this time the pain was like the blow of a hatchet over his heart. He could not breathe, for every attempt to take his breath brought the hatchet blows to a pitch of unbearable intensity. He staggered, and threw out his left arm to catch blindly at anything to prevent falling, and did not know that his body and arm sloped rapidly towards the very mouth of the big furnace. He was not conscious that Billy had caught him and had uttered a great, alarmed cry of terror, and he did not begin to recover from the reeling dizziness until Billy, half-carrying him, half-pushing him, had let him down on a chair.

His hands seized the sides of the seat, and Billy supported his upper body against his own. "Holy Jesus," said Billy, softly and reverently, and he gulped. "You almost went into that furnace, Ed. Jesus. What if I hadn't been here? You'd have died, burned up like a cinder."

The basement was still a whirling darkness before Edward, but it was slowly coming into focus, slowly subsiding from its mad spiralling. The pain too, began to recede like a red-crested sea. It was dull and threatening, but bearable, and now Edward could breathe. He did not know that his face was absolutely livid and that his lips were blue and that he was gasping weakly. He leaned his head against Billy and waited until the last throb of pain ebbed away.

Then he thought of death.

It was the first time that he had every thought of death in connection with his own vital young life. It was something that happened to the old and the ill, the faceless ones, the people a person did not know. It never came to youth, to strength, to hope and courage. But now, all at once, Edward understood that it had cast its breath on him in dark passage and that he, like all the strangers, was in jeopardy. Never did he think it was his heart which had almost failed. It was still a mystery to him, but a most terrible one, and, as the forces of his vitality surged in him again he was filled, not with fear, but with indignant wonder. He, too, could die mysteriously, and it was not fair that the young should die.

"Here," Billy was saying. "Drink the cold milk from the bottle. Jesus, you sure scared me almost to death, Ed. What's the matter?"

The cold milk in his dry mouth was revivifying, and he swallowed gratefully. "Guess it was all that rushing this week," he said. "And all the work. Ten times the customers we usually have, and maybe I've got a cold. That makes you weak."

"I don't know what it was," said Billy, still quivering with dread. "But you looked like you were dying for a couple of minutes. You got too tired to-day. Well, it'll soon be over, all this Christmas buying and things, and then you can settle down. But don't forget about hiring more help." He sucked in his own breath through a tight throat. "Maybe I'd better get your Pa, and he can call a doctor for you."

"A doctor!" exclaimed Edward, sitting up straight. "What for? Don't be dippy. Just for a cold or something!"

Billy cautiously stepped back from him, but with his hands ready. However, Edward was smiling. "I'm fine now," he said.

Billy sat near him on the coal and they ate together. The Negro boy's handsome face was very sober, and he kept glancing anxiously at his friend. He started when Edward suddenly laughed.

"Billy, I've got good news for you. Pa decided to-night that you're worth five dollars a week, and all the food you can eat, free. What do you think about that?"

Billy's eyes glowed. "Honest? You mean that, Ed! Gee, your Pa is a prince! I'll go up right away and thank him. Five dollars! No taking out for the meals, either!" He jumped joyously to his feet, forgetting his weariness. Edward stopped him.

"Don't bother Pa now. Can't you hear those feet coming in and out? Thank him some other time. Look, I brought a cheese-cake, half of one, anyway. Just for us."

They ate the cheese-cake happily. The furnace roared. It was warm and good to be here in the basement, resting and eating. It was better than anything Edward had ever known before. He looked about him and everything seemed more clear to him than at any other time, sharper, more exciting, more meaningful. He did not know how it was, but it was enough for him to know that it was.

Chapter Five

Billy thanked Heinrich the next day, and Heinrich received the thanks with a stateliness that Edward found amusing. He was unusually solicitous all that long and rushing day, and Heinrich, believing his son was repentant, became more dignified as the day went on. He was cheered that his appalling vision of the loss of his son had been only the result of a moment's weariness.

At five that night Heinrich decided he would use Edward's remorse as he had used the boy's remorse before, to bring him to "understanding." There was a lull in customers, and the two were alone, Edward whistling abstractly through his teeth as he worked briskly. "Eddie," said Heinrich in a wounded voice.

"Yes, Pa," the boy answered, the old brightness in his tone. Heinrich drew himself up to his diminutive height.

"Eddie, I have considered that you were just in asking that Billy receive the extra money, though I will reconsider again after the work of the holiday is over. But it cannot be you were serious about yourself—the ten dollars a week—which would deprive the children." He shook his head admonishingly at his son, and with reserve. He waited for Edward's sheepish smile. He, Heinrich, would not forgive immediately. Edward did not smile. To Heinrich's astonishment Edward was looking at him with that strange hardness again, and that glitter of grey eye.

"Five dollars extra a week won't 'deprive' the kids," said Edward. "Seven times that, or more, is being put into their fund every week. I know. I helped earn it. I don't intend to be deprived myself, Pa."

Heinrich shrank, not from what his son had said, but from the dismal terror of his knowing that the vision of loss had been true and not merely his imagination. Impulsively, to destroy that vision, he put up his small pink palms in a gesture of warding off, of denial, of supplication.

"Eddie!"

Edward, not understanding, was not moved. "That's right, Pa. I don't intend to be deprived, myself. Not too much, anyway."

"Eddie," said Heinrich, and put his hand over his heart in an appealing gesture, such as a child would make. Now Edward smiled. "Oh, come on, Pa. What's five dollars extra for me with all the money we're making these days? It's almost Christmas. Let's forget everything and let things be as they always were!"

Heinrich flushed with joy. "Then, it is not the five dollars you want?"

Edward still smiled. "Yes, Pa, it is the five dollars I want. The extra five dollars. Now, where do we put these new smoked sardines from Denmark? They deserve a special place."

Heinrich thought, I would give five times five if I could have my son again. I shall not speak of the money; it is a silence in my heart from this time on. Perhaps, then, he will be once more my son. I cannot endure that look in his eye, or that smile, as if he repudiated me, or removed himself from me. I confess it to myself now that of all my children I love this son more than all the others.

He said, in a meek and faintly tremulous voice, "Eddie, it is you who always choose the best places, and the red and the green paper, and the little artificial berries, to make the nice display. It is the imagination you truly have."

Edward was touched. He put his strong young arm about his father's shoulders, and squeezed them so vigorously that Heinrich gasped for breath, but it was a gasp that had the sound of weeping in it, and gratitude. He said, "You love your father, do you not, my son?"

Edward squeezed him again, but said cautiously, "Why, Pa, sure I do. You know that." That extra five dollars! How his father gripped on to it. Then he saw Heinrich's face below his and he was troubled. He did not understand that pleading expression, that expression of hope, of asking. He patted his father's shoulder.

"Eddie," said Heinrich. "I am sorry about your bicycle. I know you are saving the money in the bank for it. And for Christmas I shall have the present for you." He nodded like a child asking for love, and his eyes dimmed.

"Pa!" exclaimed Edward, incredulously. "I only need about nine dollars more."

Heinrich was full of mystery, and importance. "We shall see, we shall see," he answered, and moved away with a majestic tread while Edward followed him with his eyes and was troubled again.

It was not until he was almost fifty that he said to his wife, Margaret, "God, for His own reasons, which I don't think are just, has deprived us of understanding those closest to us, or understanding anyone at all. And that is the real tragedy of man, that he never knows the motives of his brother, and never knows that his brother is asking for love when his lips say something else, usually foolish, or stupid. But perhaps it's not God's doing. Perhaps it is man, himself, who never listens to his brother."

It was two nights before Christmas. The shop was gay with streamers and festoons of twisted green and red paper. A huge wreath of holly hung at the big window. Tinsel twined itself around the displays on the several tables and counters. Oversize crêpe-paper bells dangled everywhere. Edward had used extraordinary imagination. He had bought a very small fir tree and had prepared a mixture of flour and water, sprinkled with diamantés, and had carefully smeared it over the tree. He had then hung the tree with bright little globes of yellow, red, blue, silver and green, and strips of tinsel he had cut from the " tin " foil of old cigarette wrappers. He had then set the tree in the window, where passers-by gathered to admire and exclaim. Heinrich was proud. He strutted about his gleaming shop and received compliments graciously. Edward did not mind. It pleased him to see his father so happy, for there were uncomfortable interludes between them when Edward intuitively guessed that his father was begging him for something in a poignant silence. But what it was his father was asking him he did not know.

Billy, too, noticed that Mr. Enger treated him with unusual kindness, and that he pressed extra candies and cookies upon him. With the subconscious awareness of his race, Billy saw that when Mr. Enger gave him something unexpected Mr. Enger would glance at Edward, as if for approval. Edward, sometimes noticing, would smile at his father, and Heinrich would beam happily. The old man wants something, thought Billy, but Ed doesn't know what it is, and neither do I. Yet, Billy had his intuitions, stronger than Edward's, and he began to feel sorry for his employer.

Edward decided to send his father home a little earler than usual, for Heinrich was showing the effect of his enormously increased trade, which, though it sometimes stunned him, was very arduous. His son had not yet suggested more help, as he wished to see if the large holiday trade continued after the New Year. Heinrich was being assisted into his coat by Edward and the boy was just wrapping the mud-coloured wool scarf carefully about his father's throat when, to

Edward's pleasure, George Enreich entered the shop, stamping his feet and shaking his hat.

Heinrich, overwhelmed at this visit, ran forward, bowing agitatedly. But George held out his hand and Heinrich, after a startled moment, shyly accepted it. "I haven't been around lately," said George, without condescension. "Too busy. Ellis has been doing my shopping for me." He put his hands under his coat-tails and surveyed the big shop approvingly. "Looks as if we're all going to make a lot of money," he remarked. "Good boy, Ed. The imagination is here. I have been hearing of it, and so I came." He smiled broadly at Edward and continued: "I wonder what my percentage will be on January first?"

"Too much," responded Edward, laughing. His father gave him a horrified glance. One did not speak so casually, so almost impudently, to the powerful, to the benefactor, to the Hero, even if he were only, as Goethe had said, with some contempt, "the thatched-headed Prussian." George Enreich no longer seemed gross and brutal to Heinrich, the sensitive and more perceptive Bavarian. There could be good even in Prussians, thought Heinrich, palpitating with delight at this magnanimous visit of the great man. But he must talk to Edward about his casualness, about his raw youth, about his assumption of equality with Mr. Enreich.

To Heinrich's sense of values it seemed incredible that Mr. Enreich was laughing at Edward's remark. "To be certain, I shall demand that I examine the books myself," he was saying jokingly.

Heinrich relapsed into German, hastily. "It is the Herr Enreich's privilege and right, and we shall welcome his examination." He was agitated again. George regarded him with amused surprise. He said, in his rougher gutturals, "I was speaking, Herr Enger, only in jest. I trust your son as if he were myself."

"I hope that is a compliment, Herr Enreich," said Edward, laughing again. In confusion, Heinrich blinked and looked anxiously from his son to the Herr Manager, and he was even more confused when George roared appreciatively and slapped Edward on his back. George said, in English, "Eddie, you have the sharp head and the sharp tongue, and it is fortunate that I have the sense of humour."

Then he said, "I came to-night to give you a present, Eddie, as we are in a way, partners. And it is Christmas, is it not?"

Edward was no longer a man at this mention of a present. He was a boy again. "A present! That's wonderful! I love presents." He held out his hand eagerly. George fished in his pocket and pulled out a small thin parcel and shook it teasingly at the boy. "It is what you wanted," he said, then gave it to Edward. Heinrich, freshly overcome by this benevolence, almost danced with obsequious impatience as Edward took his delicious time to unwrap the shiny white paper. A box covered with grey velvet was revealed and Edward paused to rub his thumb over the silken fabric. Now his heart was beating rapidly. He opened the box slowly, and there, on white satin, lay a gold pen.

Edward's mouth opened but he could not speak. Heinrich bent over the pen in disbelief. A fountain pen! Of gold, gold! It was not to be believed that such magnificence should be given to only a boy! Heinrich involuntarily extended a trembling hand and Edward let his father lift the pen from its bed. Along its length there was an inscription in fine German script and Heinrich, in a hushed voice, read it aloud:

"To E.E. For the Stalwart."

Heinrich's eyes suddenly swam with tears. He looked mutely at Edward and gave him the pen. He was deeply shaken; he tried to speak but his tongue felt thick and useless. Edward read the inscription aloud, wonderingly. The pen was smooth and glittering in his palm. He glanced at George with gratitude. Then he said, "But I am not so stalwart." He thought of his mysterious attack last night when he had been aware of the dark passage of death near him.

George misunderstood. He wagged his head. "But you are," he said. "I have no use for those who are not stalwart. It is first necessary that a man have courage, for courage is the greatest of virtues. Without courage, even an angel is a weakling."

Heinrich's head had been swimming dazedly. He stared at the pen on Edward's palm, and moistened his lips. No boy should have such a gift; it was all a dream. The Herr Manager must be cruelly joking. Or, the pen was only plated. That would be much better. Almost praying that the pen was only gold-washed, and thus bringing it into the realm of reality and propriety, Heinrich took the pen from Edward and peered at it. He caught his breath when he read in tiny print: "18-K." There was no doubt of it. It was gold. It was worthy of a count, a duke, a prince, a kaiser! It was royal.

George watched Heinrich quizzically, his thick red eyebrows arched. At that moment three customers entered and Edward hurried to serve them. Glancing about him distractedly, Heinrich murmured to George, "The Herr Manager is more than generous. He intends to keep the pen until my son is old enough to have it?"

"No," said George, a little hardly. "He is old enough. He was never, I think, a child. He never had time to be a child."

Heinrich could not comprehend. "My son is a good boy," he stammered.

"He is a good man," said George. "Despite all he knows and understands, he is still a good man, and that is a miracle." He took the pen gently from Heinrich and replaced it in the box and nonchalantly set the box on a counter. He added, "I am not a good man, and so it is that I can appreciate a good man, if he is stalwart and courageous. You are lucky in your son, Herr Enger."

Heinrich was almost overcome again. "The Herr Manager is very kind. The Herr Manager has not seen my geniuses?"

George was silent a moment. Then he said, "I have seen Herr Enger's genius."

Edward, having disposed of the customers, returned, breezily. But he looked for his pen, and having found it on the counter, he put it into the pocket of his long white apron. "I shall keep it," he said, "all the days of my life."

George put his hand on the boy's arm. "All the days of your life, Eddie. Remember that. They are your days and the days of no one else." His voice was stern and Edward looked at him. His grey eyes narrowed, baffled, George leaned against the counter and there was a greenish flash from under his red lashes. "Eddie, I want you to do something for yourself. To-night, or to-morrow, look at your family. Look closely, Eddie. You may see something you never saw before. There was a time when I considered you the victim. I am not so sure now." He tapped his florid forehead. " On some occasions I can become quite mystic. I am not so certain now, among humanity who is the victim and who the exploited and the weak. It is not my thought alone. Nietszche has asked it."

Edward was silent. He was thinking. Then he looked at his father, and thought, he believes, he knows, they are geniuses! They had better be!

George said, almost bashfully, though his eyes remained stern, " I never ask more of a man than he is capable of doing."

It was not until he was almost fifty that Edward understood what had been said that night by George Enreich, just before Christmas, 1904. And then, in his agony, he thought, how was it I was so stupid?

But to-night he said to George, " I don't think I'm weak, or exploited."

George shrugged. He turned to Heinrich and said, as if in pity, " My sleigh is outside. Permit me, Herr Enger, to put it at your service, for there is a storm. It will return for me when I have made my purchases."

When Heinrich, still more overcome, had gone, George said to Edward, " You are a good man, Eddie. And that is sometimes a crime against others. Do not ask me what I mean. You will know some day; let us hope before it is too late. And now, I have my list thoughtfully written by Ellis."

Edward waited on him, following him about with a basket on his arm. A crime against others—kindness. That was foolishness. Sometimes it was very hard to be kind, especially when a customer became oppressive or arrogant, or the children at home hurt their father with contemptuous words or laughed at his ponderous English or neglected the things they should do. He almost forgot the marvel of the gold pen in his pocket in his vexation with George Enreich, who seemed to talk in puzzles to-night.

" What's wrong, Eddie?" asked Mr. Enreich, stopping suddenly. Edward started and coloured. " I just don't know what you meant, Mr. Enreich, when you said it was a crime to be kind."

" I didn't say that at all, Eddie. I said it was sometimes a crime against others to be a good man. Certainly a different thing." He motioned to the basket and took out a cigar. " Take care of your customers. I can wait. I think I shall have the sandwich with you as we did when we made our bargain."

Highly pleased, Edward waited on his customers. Not one bought less than two dollars' worth of delicacies. George nodded to himself, as if speaking inwardly and commenting on his thoughts. The boy is a natural merchant, he thought. We must have a talk about his plans for expansion, for he must have them. He has a great imagination, and boldness also, and courage, and these things are the raw material of an entrepreneur. I never made a mistake. He felt a deep affection for Edward, and he smiled to himself at the plans he had for the boy.

The shop was empty again, except for the boy and the man. Edward cut ham for the sandwiches, prepared the coffee in the rear. Then he hesitated, and glanced over his shoulder at Mr. Enreich. Finally he laid down his knife and firmly marched up to his friend. "Mr. Enreich, when I'm alone Billy, our helper, comes up from the basement to eat with me. He expects to come up to-night, and that's why he didn't take anything down to eat. I can't disappoint him. We—well, we have talks. And he's always afraid of being slighted. He's got a sore spot about that."

"Well," said George, impatiently, "why do you not call him up? We can all have our sandwiches and coffee together." He wondered why Edward appeared uncomfortable, and why the boy eyed him dubiously. Then Edward said, "Billy is my friend. My best friend. The only friend I have."

George detected something interesting here. "So? And why is it you have only one friend, Eddie? You have a genius for friendship. Have I not felt it myself?"

Edward looked at the long knife in his hand. "I don't know why I haven't more friends. I guess it's because I never had the time. I always had to hurry home from school, since I was ten or abouts, to help Pa, or help Ma. Never had time to play."

"Then, why is it you have made a friend of this Billy, you who never had time?"

"Billy's different. In a way, we're the same kind of people. Billy's worked just the way I've worked. We met in the third grade at school, and he still goes to school, though I don't, and he brings me his school books every afternoon and goes over the lessons with me. I'm right up to date on the work; I study when I have time, either here or home. Billy plays the harmonica, too. He's awfully bright; gets the best marks in school. You should hear him play! He'll be a famous musician one of these days. He's taught himself to read notes. He can play anything on the harmonica."

George spoke in German, and very kindly, "This Billy must be a genius. Why do you hide this genius, Eddie, this other genius?"

"I don't hide him," said Eddie. Then he, too, spoke in German, and defiantly, looking at George with challenging eyes. "There's something else about Billy. He is not a white boy. He is a Negro."

George puffed on his cigar a moment. Then he said, "So?" And raised his eyebrows.

"You do not . . ." Eddie began, much relieved. Then he saw that George was sincerely annoyed. Mr. Enreich said, "Eddie, do not take prejudices for granted. I am a gross man, it is said. I am a man without sensitivities. I am not polite, not cultured. That is why, perhaps, I do not have the discriminations of the delicate and the well bred." He smiled, "Do not look so puzzled. You are more intelligent than that. Call your Billy, your friend, the wonder, the genius. And always remember this. I am no intellectual, and so do not despise my humbler fellow-man if he is worthy of respect."

Edward laughed, and called to Billy who came up at once. When he saw George Enreich he went down two steps precipitately, so that only his head and shoulders appeared above the stairway. George waved his hand to him genially. "I have been hearing about you, Billy. Join us with the sandwiches."

"It's Mr. Enreich," said Eddie. Billy bobbed down another step, and Eddie called, "Come on, Billy. We're all going to eat together."

Billy came up diffidently, his soft brown eyes uncertain and disbelieving. The great Mr. Enreich! The rich and powerful Mr. Enreich! It must all be a mistake. He washed his hands in the closet and ran a comb through his black curls. He mistrusted "tolerance." He and his race suffered more from the hypocritical "tolerance" of the North than they had ever suffered in the "lynching" South. Acceptance, in the North, meant the lowest and dirtiest and hardest of work, and an ostracism and rejection never encountered in the South where there was a strict line of demarcation between the white men and the black.

So Billy slowly and mistrustfully came into the shop, warily regarding George. And then he saw at once that the geniality was not false, but casual and warm. He relaxed, in wonderment, and when George smiled at him he smiled back, and George was moved by the sweetness of his smile and the brilliant intelligence in his eyes.

Edward had always liked and admired George Enreich but now he loved him. He took special care with the sandwiches, assisted by Billy. The damp snow was clotting in big blobs on the windows; a dank wind blew in even under the tight doors. It was half-past eight.

Edward spread a white cloth on a counter. The shop, at Edward's suggestion, had been supplied with chairs, so ladies need not stand while they awaited attention. Sometimes the "carriage trade" ladies would sit and gossip with friends, lulled by the shining lavishness and the celestial fragrance of the shop. Edward drew up a chair to the counter for Mr. Enreich, and thought, with some cynicism, that the presence of Billy eating would be overlooked in the presence of a powerful man who, if he was not liked in Waterford, was respected and feared.

Edward and Mr. Enreich talked happily, but Billy was silent and awkward. He still could hardly believe in this. There was a lump of excitement in his throat, and, for the first time since he had been a very young child, he felt hope.

"Now," said Mr. Enreich, as he comfortably drank his coffee. "You must tell me of your plans to expand again, Eddie, for you have the plans. That I know."

Edward was surprised. "But I've only talked about them to Billy. How did you know?"

Billy said, "Mr. Enreich knows many things." Then he was embarrassed. But George nodded at him. "And Billy is a very wise boy, not like this *dumfkopf*."

Edward blazed with excitement. George became very familiar with that incandescent look in the years following, the sudden hot glaze of eye, the sudden flush, the sudden broadening of the wide mouth and the shine of big white teeth. "All right, sir!" Edward exclaimed. "I'll tell you! I haven't told Pa yet, or even suggested it to him. I want to open another shop, in the best part of town, where only the rich people shop, and where it'll be more convenient for most of them than this place. A bigger shop! More elegant. More expensive delicacies, more imports. Best shop outside of New York! People'll drive from miles away! Why, they'll come from Syracuse, maybe. We can advertise in the Albany papers, and customers can buy from us cheaper and quicker than they can buy the things from New York; we don't have New York overhead. And we can send big orders by canal, or by railroad. Five hours by rail for delivery on receipt of order! New York can't do that. And clerks in the store, not in white jackets. An elegant store! An out-of-town department where we can send rush. Think of it. Isn't it a grand idea?"

George studied that young and glistening face and smoked placidly. George said, "A grand idea. Of course, it is many years too early even to think of it, this delicatessen Great Atlantic and Pacific Tea Company! Four—five—years too early."

When Edward frowned George went on imperturbably. "You were thinking that you are not too young, you who are barely fifteen. But I do not eat green fruit. I prefer it to ripen on the tree. Otherwise"—and he spread his hands with an eloquent if brutal gesture—"one gets the bellyache. I will tell you, my Eddie. I will give you books to read, and I will speak with you twice a month in my house, and I will teach you to be the entrepreneur it is fated for you to be. I recognise men of fate, even though they have just been elevated to the long trousers out of the knickers. And why am I so interested in this so raw fruit? Because I expect to make the large profit. One does not do things for charity, *hein*?"

Edward's impatience vanished. He gazed at George Enreich with intense gratitude. This is the father I should have had, he thought. Affection replaced the hot glaze in his eyes. "You are very right, Herr Manager. I was just too enthusiastic."

"Enthusiasm," said George, "is very good. One admires it, but not if it is without substance. We do not expect, naturally, to stop with one shop. Shall we begin the tutoring on January the tenth?"

"You will do all this for me?" said Edward, marvelling.

"I have said, one does not do things for charity." But George smiled, and all his gold teeth glittered.

Edward suddenly remembered Billy. He said, "Herr Manager Enreich, we are being discourteous. We are speaking German before my friend."

Billy spoke with careful slow awkwardness but also with triumph, in German. "I have learned a little German from listening to you and your father and some of the other German people who come into the shop. And I have been learning it at school, and in study at night."

George turned to him, unsmiling, and gave him one of his long and penetrating regards. "It is a boy of intellect, this Billy. His syntax is perfect. His accent is admirable. We must discuss him later."

Astonished and proud, Edward stared at his friend, while Billy beamed with importance. He managed to give the impression of strutting though he did not move his feet or body.

The door opened and young Father Jahle came in, in his thin coat, his face blue and pinched and cold. Edward went to him at once and shook his hand, and George, strangely interested now, watched. He knew of this earnest and youthful priest, though he had never seen him before. He made it his business to be interested in all priests. His expression became stiff and solid, and all his Prussian nature expressed itself in his ruddy jowls, set and unyielding, and in the little green pinpoints under his lashes. This priest made a nuisance of himself. He had a friend in the two local newspapers, and the newspapers never failed to give Father Jahle's newest ideas of the Fatherhood of God and the brotherhood of man some prominence every Monday morning, much to the irritation of less shabby and more prosperous priests, and especially ministers with excellent parishes. Father Jahle's ideas, it was believed, were very dangerous and provocative, and George had heard the invidious words, "Socialism," on more than one occasion.

Edward was drawing Father Jahle affectionately to George, who merely grunted at the timid words of greeting. He saw that the priest had no warm gloves; his worn hands were purplish. He was trying to repress shudders of cold. George noticed that this poverty-stricken, this starveling, priest, was not intimidated at learning who he was. He stood on his dignity, as a man of God before whom the rich and the powerful were only as all men, to be enlightened and brought to the Lord.

The priest greeted Billy as a friend, and then turned to Edward and said, "I only want a quarter of a pound of butter, Simon, and a quarter of a pound of cheese. And, yes, a quarter of a pound of ham. My mother likes your ham so much."

His clerical collar was stiff but showed severe signs of wear as he loosened the black scarf which his mother had knitted for him. George said in a slow and brutal voice:

"You have called Eddie 'Simon'—and why is this?"

The priest blushed, bent his head and said in a low voice, "It was St. Simon who helped carry Our Lord's Cross."

Then George said to the priest, "I never make a mistake in things, and in ruthless men, and men who are equal with me. I know my humanity. I should not call Edward 'Simon.' I should call him one of the Atlantes. There are times when they hold up a useless arch. But am I to quarrel with humour?"

The priest regarded him with surprise. A gross and illiterate man, he had heard. The priest's kind young eyes, so brown, so serious, so ingenuous, became humble. He must remember again that one never judged another by rumour or malice.

"However," said George, "it may be you are wiser than I. It may be that in a distorted fashion Eddie is indeed 'Simon', but it is a papier-mâché cross he is carrying, by his own will, and perhaps by his innocent ruthlessness."

Edward came back to them, careful to lay the parcel on the counter.

"So," murmured George. He said to Edward, "Will you call in Ellis for me—Simon?"

Edward grinned. "One of these days Father Jahle is going to tell me why he calls me that." He missed Billy's look of incredulity at this statement, and then his following thoughtfulness. He ran to the door and called Ellis, who was gloomily stamping his cold feet up and down on the snow-covered sidewalk.

George fumbled in his breast pocket. There was a fifty-dollar bill there. Hastily, he pulled it out and pressed it into the priest's hand. The priest looked at it, stupefied. George said, "Say a prayer for me—a prayer for me—Father. God and I have a quarrel, a quarrel since I was an immigrant of twenty. I have not been to Mass since, nor have made my confession. Nor"—and he scowled ferociously at the priest, who was suddenly pale, and whose eyes were suddenly shining—"do I ever intend to do so. Let us say nothing about this."

The priest's lips trembled. "I shall pray that you return to the Church, Mr. Enreich." And he leaned across the counter to the returned Edward and shook his hand, and then Billy's hand. "Happy, holy Christmas to you both, boys," he said, hurriedly, and left with a flap of his long black coat. He paused at the door. "And to you, Mr. Enreich, a joyous journey home."

George smoked, as the boys, glancing at the clock, saw it was nearly ten. The cold air outside rang with the sweet sound of bells, as sleighs raced past the shop. A child's wan face pressed itself against the window to stare at the tree, and then was gone, like the face of a ghost.

"Slow night," said Edward. "It usually is, two nights before Christmas. Then everybody comes in on Christmas Eve. Rush, rush, rush."

George looked at Ellis, who had picked up the loaded bags of goods which his employer had bought. Ellis licked his lips. Let anybody talk about Mr. Enreich being greedy. The help in his house ate what he ate. There was no locking of cupboards, or any inspection of them. Ellis carried out the bags to the sleigh, and George lifted his bulky body from the chair.

He hesitated. It was at Billy he looked now. "I never make a promise I do not keep, my Billy. I shall remember you, and your future."

Chapter Six

But Christmas Eve was not busy, much to Edward's surprise. On this night the shop closed promptly at half-past eight, as there were only two customers from half-past seven on. However, the day had been exceptionally busy. Now the people were preparing either for midnight church services or Christmas parties.

All of Edward's family were in the parish house to see the Christmas play, the dialogue of which had been written by Gregory and the play itself produced by Sylvia. Sylvia, it was, too, who had designed the sets with the assistance of young Ralph, and David had composed the music. It was a proud occasion for the Engers. Edward had been left with the shop.

It was customary, over any holiday, for Edward to carry the day's receipts home, for Heinrich's frugality had not as yet extended to a safe for the shop. The money was kept in a strong-box at home, to be deposited in the bank after the holiday. As there had been some robberies in the neighbourhood Billy insisted on accompanying Edward home as a bodyguard.

It was a fine night. The boys locked up, banked the furnace, left one light burning in the shop. Then they went out on to the street. The marble silence of the winter night surrounded them. The streets were almost empty. The lamps glimmered brilliantly in the clarified purity of the air. The snow crunched under their feet and the black skeletons of the trees cracked with the frost. The boys felt exhilaration. There would be no work to-morrow, except that Edward would remain home to keep the furnace fired well, and to watch the goose in the oven. The rest of the family would be at church services up to noon.

"They never think I might want to go, too," Edward grumbled.

"You got the Bible I gave you," said Billy mildly. There was something in his voice that made Edward glance at him sharply. Billy continued: "You can read the whole thing yourself. Specially St. Luke. I like him best. He never saw the Lord, but he wrote best about Him. He saw His Mother. She told him all about it. You can read it to-night, or to-morrow."

Edward was silent.

"I like the Magnificat," Billy went on. Still Edward did not speak. Billy pulled out his harmonica and softly made it sing to the night, a song of reverence and beauty and young triumph and joy. Edward looked at Billy. There was no confusion, no doubt, no resentment, in his dreaming eyes. He sure lives a simple life, thought Edward, with some vexation. He doesn't have any problems or my worries.

He was not aware that Billy had stopped playing until the latter said gently, " Easy, boy."

" What?" said Edward, and shrugged his big shoulders. How long had Billy been annoying him with his sudden insights, his sudden understanding which embarrassed him, Edward? " All I'm doing," said Edward, " is just walking along, thinking."

" Sure," said Billy. " And what you're thinking isn't so good. Ed, you've changed since last summer. Not all at once, but just steady. I don't know what the change is, but I've got a feeling it's wrong for you."

" I've got my problems," said Edward, curtly, and moved his neck against a sense of smothering.

" Maybe you made them," said Billy, in that soft voice.

" Now look here!" exclaimed Edward angrily. But Billy began to play again, a Christmas carol, and Edward subsided. He listened with reluctant pleasure. Billy was a genius. He should have a violin, and he would be famous. Edward said, " One of these days, when I'm rich, I'll give you a violin, and you can take music lessons."

Billy said, " If God wants me to have a violin, He'll get one for me. Didn't He give me the harmonica? Sure, it was yours, but all at once He fixed it so I had it. You know something? God gives you what you ought to have, if you'll just believe He will."

Simple, repeated Edward inwardly. Very, very simple.

" Don't push me," said Billy, but he grinned at his friend affectionately, and pranced forward in a little dance which prevented any reply from Edward.

They reached the Enger house. To Edward's surprise the parlour was all lit up, though when the family was absent the whole house was frugally dark. Someone was playing the piano, and as the boys neared the icy wooden steps of the porch the music could be heard clearly in the quiet night.

" Listen to that!" said Edward, furiously. " It's Dave. He's supposed to be at the church party to-night. Does he call that music, that crazy, daffy noise, that ragtime? He always does that when he thinks nobody's around! It makes me sick, after all the——"

The music was loud, gay, clamouring, full of frolic and rhythm and pleasure. It gambolled and ran up and down the keys in a dance of release and merriment. It strutted and stamped and whirled, sometimes with a bass like drums, sometimes with the lilting tinkle of the high octaves. In spite of himself and his own anger and outrage, Edward found his feet moving and his knees swaying. He came to himself when he heard Billy's harmonica joining in the frenzied and abandoned melody that underlay the twinkles and the drummings. He caught Billy's arm and stopped him. Billy stared at him and his eyes were very bright and fixed in the light of the street lamp.

"Boy," said Billy, in a hushed voice. "He sure can make that piano roll!"

"You make me sick," said Edward with disgust, and he ran up the stairs and flung open the door. Billy looked after him, and hesitated. Then he forgot he was a Negro and that he had never been in this house before, and he followed his friend. Something had impelled him to do so, something instinctive and urgent. He stood in the doorway of the small hot parlour with its ugly, crowding furniture, and, with the piano between the two little windows. And he saw David. David's dark and narrow face was alight with a kind of ecstasy and abandon, his eyes sparkling, his body swaying, his slender hands racing up and down the keys in a blurr of dancing movement. "Boy, that's music," whispered Billy, and his hand went to his pocket and pulled out the harmonica. "Real, happy music."

"Shut up!" shouted Edward, and advanced into the room.

David's hands stopped on the keys with a loud, discordant sound. He swung about on the stool and looked at his brother, and his distinguished features tightened.

Edward still advanced upon him, as if to strike him. "After all the goddamn money I've spent on that piano!" he said. "After all the lessons I've paid for, working like a dog in that goddamn store, and never going anywhere, and putting money in the fund for you! After all your genius, when you can play like a real concert pianist! And you've got to fool away your time, and my money, playing that trash!"

David sat on the stool, long and slim and graceful, and his black eyes flashed on his brother like dark fire. There was a sudden violence in the air, a sudden enraged silence. In spite of his natural diffidence, Billy came into the room, and David's eye fell on him. He knew Billy slightly, and his mouth, open as if to snarl, closed.

"Look," said Billy, to the outraged Edward. He took Edward by the elbow. "There's all kinds of music. It don't mean that this isn't music, too. There's all kinds, and this is GOOD." He smiled at David gently. "Man, you sure can make that piano talk! Make a wooden Indian dance."

Edward tore his elbow out of Billy's grasp. He turned on the boy with an almost brutal gesture. But Billy was putting his harmonica to his lips, and to David's amazement, and to Edward's dazed fury, he began to play the melody which David had composed himself, and which he had been playing. The harmonica sang out lightly and rapidly, romping, fairy notes of youthful dancing, and Billy rolled with its excitement, stamping his foot on the red Brussels carpet to keep time, his shouders twitching.

David laughed out, swung on his stool, and his hands fell on the keys in perfect harmony. The two played together, the harmonica soaring like a tiny violin in accompaniment, the keys of the piano rising and falling in a movement almost too fast to be seen. To Edward it was repulsive, discordant and incredibly vulgar, for his rage was making a shrill humming in his ears. It was a repudiation of all his years of work, of all the loss of his youth. It was a disdainful rejection of his grief over Betsy, and the insults he had taken in silence, and of the denial of his own importance. Mixed with it all was a wild dismay, and a challenge to him, a challenge he would not acknowledge, or permit.

"Get out of here! Go on, get out of here!" he yelled at Billy, and struck him on the shoulder with his clenched fist.

The music stopped abruptly. David rose slowly from his stool and confronted his brother, and Billy stepped back, wincing with pain, his eyes sombrely staring at Edward. "I said, get out," repeated Edward, and his friend did not know his face.

"Now, see here," said David.

But Billy, still staring at Edward as at a stranger, walked backwards to the door. He opened it behind his back, stepped out, and closed the door. To the last Edward could see his eyes, questioning, mournful and compassionate, shining with still golden lights.

"That was a hell of a thing to do," said David, slowly, and there was no sneer in his voice. "Hitting him like that."

Edward turned from him and ran to the door and flung it

open. But Billy was gone. There was not even a shadow of him on the street. A great pain pierced Edward's chest. I'll make it up to him, he thought, confusedly. I shouldn't have done that, he's my friend. He's all the friend I have. He called out, "Billy! Billy!"

His shout came back to him, with emptiness and desolation.

He slammed the door and turned to his brother with a black face. "It was all your fault," he said in a low tone full of passionate anger.

David shrugged. He was eyeing Edward queerly. "Was it?" he asked.

Edward was almost blind with that anger. "Wasting your time," he said, quickly. "Wasting my time. Wasting—all the days of my life. That's what you're doing. Since I was ten. I was willing to work, because Pa says you're a genius. And I've heard you play lots of times, and I know he's right. But you can't go on wasting my life and my money and the work, all the goddamn work, I do! You hear me?"

David regarded him as if seeing him for the first time, and as if what he saw frightened him. He felt Edward's powerful strength, his iron determination, and it was as if the bars of a prison closed about him and there was the clang of a steel door. Edward, he saw, was no longer the despised and toiling numbskull of a brother, but someone to be feared, to be placated, to be restored to acceptance, for the things he could do, the nameless, implacable things he could do, the destroying things he could do. Edward's grey eyes were distended and inexorable, glittering almost with malignance.

"Hey," said David, quietly. "What's the matter with you, anyway? I know how you work. But you've got brains." He paused. "Yes, you've got brains. You work because that's what you want to do. You think it's because——"

"Shut up!" cried Edward. "I do it all because you're a genius, a concert pianist, a composer! I do it all for all of you! And you're not going to waste your time or I'll—I'll do—something! You hear me?"

David did not answer. Neither boy was aware that the back door to the parlour had opened and that the family was crowding on the threshold and listening with mute amazement and disbelief.

"You're all going to develop yourselves, like Pa says." Edward's voice was the voice of a ruthless man now, and not a youth. "I didn't choose what Pa calls your futures. You did, all of you. You aren't going to throw over his ambitions for you; I'll take care of that!"

"Yes," said David, thoughtfully, still gazing at his feet. "I guess you will." He raised his head and gave Edward another odd stare.

Maria Enger thought this the proper time to interfere. "What is this quarrel on Christmas Eve? What is this stupidity, this ugly conversation? Was it for this occasion, David, that you decided to remain home at the very last moment and practise, as you said?"

Edward swung to her, and Heinrich, blinking distressedly in the doorway, surrounded by his children, was struck again by the extraordinary resemblance between his second son and Maria, for all their physical differences. Edward said, wrathfully, "I returned home, Mother, with the day's receipts, and discovered David playing that ragtime, that clashing ragtime, on the piano again! You did not know that when he is alone he plays nothing but that?"

Maria paused. In any quarrel between Edward and her other children she invariably decided in favour of the "gifted ones," for they had "temperaments." But this was serious. She turned formidably to her oldest son. "Is it so, David, the thing your brother says?"

It was usual for David to answer angrily and impatiently when pressed, even by his mother. But now he only continued to gaze at Edward as he said without emotion, "Not always. There are some times when I must have relief from the classic music. It is unfortunate that Eddie has heard me then."

"Not too many brains," said Gregory, with his knowing wink. He wore a new suit to-night, and he had tried for David's elegance without success. His broad face, so like Edward's, wrinkled with amused spite, and intelligent malevolence. "He's always fighting with somebody around here. Why can't he sleep in the store, with the pickles? Jeepers, Christmas Eve, and he's got to raise a fuss around here!"

"Children, my children," murmured Heinrich, full of misery. He peered at Edward, and thought again, my son has changed, he has become like iron, he has lost his heart. Heinrich's woollen scarf, as if reflecting his despondency, uncoiled itself and fell over his belly. He could always appeal to Edward with one eloquent look of pleading, and Edward, however stirred or angered, would subside. But to-night Edward did not subside; his anger brightened at that meek and imploring glance. His throat felt thick, turgid with bitter emotion.

Sylvia followed her father into the room. She was not yet fourteen, and she was dark and thin and spindly and restless, and had no obvious beauty, but she possessed what Edward did not know was chic, a flair, a style.

She looked at Edward with cool contempt. "I don't know what's the matter with him, since last summer," she said. "He's been acting dippy, as if he owned everybody around here, and he gives orders, and glares, and thinks he can scare us."

Maria lifted one of her big and fleshy hands commandingly. "One forgets that Edward is making money for us all, though I should prefer that it not become his obsession. Wait," she said, severely, as Edward opened his mouth to speak. "I have not done. Edward has some justice on his side. David should not be wasting his time, for it is blasphemous to waste a gift."

"I told you, Ma," David said, replying to her in obstinate English. "I've got to have some relief, sometimes. Like stretching your muscles." But he coloured.

"That is to be expected," said Heinrich, timidly, peeping apologetically at his wife. "It was that way with my flute. I did not always play the classics. I, at times, played for the dancers, at the *gasthaus*, and it was relaxing and pleasant."

"Genius cannot relax, as you say, Heinrich," his wife remarked with haughty disdain. "You were not a genius. We were speaking of the gifted. David, I command you to play only what is right for you to play. One wonders where you hear this tawdriness."

"I can tell you," said Edward, bitterly. "He hears it in other houses, on the gramophone. He goes to the Witlocks and the McCarthys and the Bergers, down the street, with all the kids. He even composes the stuff himself!"

"Is it true?" asked Maria, of David.

The boy coloured again. "Well, yes. But I've got to have some recreation. It doesn't hurt—anything. And, though you'd never believe it of anybody raised in this house, I happen to like people. That's funny, isn't it, to like people?

I like to play for the kids I know, and I like to see them dance, and I like to dance, too." He said the last, defiantly, and everyone listened aghast, except Sylvia, whose thin lips smiled in sympathy.

"Do you call that jumping, dancing?" asked Maria.

"It is Christmas Eve," said Heinrich, piteously. "We must remember the occasion." But no one heard him.

"It is all vile and common," Maria continued. "It is not expected of a Von Brunner. It is expected only of the base and the stupid and the vulgar."

"That's not all," Edward interrupted. No one ever dared to interrupt Maria before, but Maria did not express any outrage now, much to the astonishment of her family. In fact, she turned majestically to Edward, and said, "Speak, my son."

Edward pointed at Sylvia. "She made those clothes she's wearing, wasting her time, when she should have been studying her drama. And we pay three dollars a week for her lessons with Madam Bilinski!"

Sylvia glared at him. "What's the difference if you design clothes as well as stage sets, and learn how to make your own hats as well as to direct plays?"

"I do not object to the thrift which leads one to make one's clothes," said Maria. "But I, too, have observed that too much time is spent on this, Sylvia. You are endlessly altering your frocks or changing the style of your hats, when you should be studying. I will allot you, hereafter, only three hours a week on the clothing."

A scarlet stain appeared on Sylvia's white cheek-bones, and she gave Edward a glance charged with hatred.

"She spends hours looking in store windows at dresses and hats, and I've seen her sketching them on her school paper, outside the windows," said Edward.

"This will cease," said Maria, with icy finality. "Sylvia will return from school by the clock."

Edward stood in the centre of the hot and crowded room, yet there seemed to be a space about him like the space given a dangerous chieftain. He dominated the room, and his grey eyes were like smoke filled with fire.

He looked at Gregory and Ralph, who shrank and tried to make themselves as inconspicuous as possible. "These other kids," said Edward, pointing to them mercilessly. "Greg writes what he thinks are funny stories, and you should hear them scream down in the basement, or in the parlour, when you and Pa aren't around. And he's supposed to be learning to do serious writing, novels and biographies!"

Gregory straightened up. It was significant, now, that he spoke to Edward and not his mother. "Gosh darn it anyways!" he cried. "You got to have some fun sometimes! I'm not an old man, like Pa, and not a dummy like you! You never hear anybody laugh around here; it's all work and study, and I'm only eleven years old, not even twelve, and if I play I'm murdered or something. I'm wasting my time! What if I do write funny stories for Dave and Sylvia and Ralph? They like to laugh too. It's like a funeral around here all the time, and you're the undertaker, you dummy!"

Ralph had begun to sniffle, knowing himself next. Edward, ignoring Gregory's outburst, fulfilled Ralph's apprehension. "And here we've got the artist, the one who's going to be the famous artist. Money put out every week for his special art lessons. Money given him for car fare to the museum. And what does he do, every chance he gets? He studies higher mathematics, things I never heard of, though I like maths and wanted to be . . ." Edward paused, and white ridges sprang out about his mouth. "And he draws geometry pictures, and he's got a slide-rule from somewheres. And he only paints real things when he's afraid someone will know what he's doing on the sly."

"Wait," said Maria. "Here I must intervene. Sylvia designed the sets for the Sunday school play, and very excellently, and Ralph was most original in the painting of them, and Gregory's work brought much appreciation. However . . ." And she paused formidably again. "This does not expiate the hours wasted on foolishness, about which I have now just learned. There will be no more of it. Gregory will confine himself to serious literature, Ralph will do mathematics only with his schoolwork. Life is too short for frivolities and uselessness."

"A funeral parlour," said Gregory, hopelessly.

Edward looked at them all with a darkling smile. "I had no time to play," he said, "I had no time to study, to dance. I never learned to play the piano or paint or read books. I didn't have the money to go to the nickelodean. Why, we had a ball team on this street, and I could run better, hit better and throw better than anybody else! But there wasn't time, after I was ten. There was the store. And all of you."

David gazed at him, and his slender face became moved and tremulous. "Edward has justice on his side," said Maria. "If he works so hard then it must be appreciated. But I do not like his tone. He will never join——"

"Merry Christmas," said Edward, ironically. And he went to the door and for the first time a passage was made for him. He could feel the disturbed eyes of his brothers and sister on his back, and he straightened his shoulders and he was no longer tired.

"Merry Christmas, my son," said Heinrich, imploringly, but Edward did not answer.

Maria watched him go. She thought, My son has removed himself from us. He removed himself a long time ago, though doubtless he believes we have rejected him. Is it possible that the rejected have, in reality, rejected others first? Who is, in reality the destroyer, Cain or Abel? Was Cain goaded beyond his strength by his brother? Were their mother and father truly the guilty ones? Who can tell, in this terrible and most confusing life? I know only one thing with surety: Edward is the reflection of myself, and I know my weaknesses, and he shall not suffer from his own, if I can prevent it. He is too strong to expire into nothing, as I expired.

She moved ponderously towards the kitchen, and her expression was remote and determined. Edward's lonely door, in the attic, banged behind him, and Maria winced. It is the eve of his birthday, she thought, as she removed her coat. He thinks we have forgotten. He does not know that each man must travel a lonely way to himself, and that the journey is frightful, but at the end is God. This, he will learn, and no one can help him but the Father. The road is more terrible, but more rewarding, at the last, for the strong, than the sheltered way of the weak.

Edward lit his one oil lamp, which was unshaded, but whose chimney was brightly polished by himself. It stood on an old round oak table, discarded from the parlour, and it was scarred by the years, having been second-hand in the first place. Neatly arranged about the lamp were a number of Edward's books on physics, and three copies of the *Retail Merchant*. After lighting the lamp, Edward lit his meagre second-hand oil-stove, a round small affair like a cylinder. It gave little heat; he stood over it and tried to warm hands which remained cold and stiff and trembling.

He looked about his attic room. He alone occupied it. He could have shared a room with David, but would not, and had given no explanation. "He is so obstinate," Maria would say, after she had urged her second son to move in with his brother in the larger, warmer and more comfortable room on the middle floor. "A recluse. If he were an artist, one would understand."

The room was very narrow but ran the full length of the house. Only the part occupied by Edward's old iron bed was walled and papered in a sleazy fashion. It had been so prepared four years ago when he had demanded the attic for himself. There was no ceiling, however, except the steep and slanting roof, all its rafters bare, all its nails revealed.

Once, three years ago, when Edward had had bronchitis and a doctor had had to be called after long family consultation, the doctor had glanced indignantly about the "room" and the rest of the attic. But young Edward had smiled and had said, "I could have a room downstairs with my brother, a nice room. But I like this. I made them give it to me."

Here he could be alone; here he could think; here no one could intrude. Here he could dream and read and study. Here was silence. Until a few months ago the attic had been filled with peace and tranquillity for him. Now there was no peace.

Well, Edward would say to himself, with some misery, I guess it's because I'm a man now, and not a kid, and I know what I want. I'm on my way. I suppose you have to pay something for that.

The attic seemed particularly cold and dingy and repellent to-night. It was the sleeping-place of a stranger whom he did not know, though once he had known very well. The coldness of his hands was in his body, too; even his bones felt cold and tremulous, and the pit of his stomach. His face was dark and as fixed as granite, and there was an Arctic grimness in his mind and a feeling of triumph which gave him no pleasure. He was too young, as yet, to know the source of all this. He only knew that where there had once been a softness and sweetness in him, in spite of all his work and strength and worry, a gentle yet powerfully urgent love for life, and bright excitement, there was this as yet nameless rigidity and glacial induration, this icy objectivity. He did not regret the loss of what once had been his. He did not regret it until he was nearly fifty. On this Christmas Eve he could almost rejoice that he had lost what now seemed his "babyishness and silly ideas." He did not know that what he was feeling was largely mixed with hatred, for hatred heretofore had been unknown to him, and only a perplexing word.

No sound came to him from downstairs; the family was still in the kitchen lingering over their coffee and cake. Edward lifted his head stiffly, and the frail lamplight fell on his clenched face. Mr. Enreich had told him to "take a long look" at his family. Well, he had taken that "look" to-night. Weaklings! David, Sylvia, Gregory, Ralph—all of them! Having been given gifts, they trifled with them. There was no dedication in their spirits, no determination, no drive. Well, thought Edward, I'm the boy who can drive them! They'll toe the mark and make all the days of my life count. They'd better! I'm not giving up my life for nothing.

The bells of the Catholic churches in Waterford began to ring at midnight. Edward heard them and they were voices behind him in exile, in an ecstasy he could no longer share, and he did not know why he could not share.

When the shop opened after Christmas, Billy was not there. But a letter for Edward lay on the counter. Billy had written:

"Maybe I should have told you, Eddie, that I can't come back. It's been on my mind for a long time and it's got nothing to do with you, or anything. My folks won't miss me. I'm going down to New Orleans. They've got little bands and things down there and maybe I'll get myself a job playing the harmonica."

There was a postcript. "P.S. Now, don't you go thinking that anything you did or said made me make up my mind. It didn't. Cross my heart and hope to die."

"An ungrateful boy," said Heinrich. "And it was you, my son, who insisted I raise his wages and give him meals without payment. Eddie, why do you weep? Billy was only a coloured boy, and he showed you no gratitude. Ah, that is the way of friends! Dry your eyes, my son. There are two customers entering. I do not know why you are so affected, and you must forget."

Chapter Seven

"It is well, now," said George Enreich. "I have taught you all I know these four years. We shall proceed to establish the fine shop of which you spoke."

"I have already chosen the place," said Edward. "A large store. It hasn't been doing well since the Panic last year, and the man and his wife are old, and their sons are indifferent. They won't work; they think nine hours a day is enough, and only half a day Saturday. When did a man ever succeed if he watched the clock? Clocks are for lazy people. I can buy the store at a bargain, and the stock, too. I've talked with the owners, and they haven't any choice but to sell to me or go into bankruptcy. Did you know what they asked me to do, Mr. Enreich? Lend them the money to get back on their feet, as they say! The banks won't lend them a cent."

"Ah," said George, thoughtfully, looking at his cigar. "That would not be the Goeltzes would it?"

"Yes," said Edward, his features hardening. "It would." He watched George warily.

"They did well until a year or so ago. I remember them. What did you offer for the shop and the stock, my Eddie?"

Edward hesitated. "They bought the shop, and the flat above, in 1895. They paid four thousand dollars for the whole thing. I offered them five thousand dollars for the building, and all the stock. They refused, of course. They said they had put three thousand dollars extra into the shop and the flat, plumbing, new floors, counters, store room, a heating plant, not including the stock."

"So," said George, his small green eyes still on his cigar.

"I should guess that they want at least nine thousand dollars, pleading that prices are going up, and that their location is centred in the best shopping streets."

"Ten thousand," replied Edward. He shifted his big and muscular body in his chair, and there was an edge to his voice. "I told them that they could take my five thousand dollars, or leave it. If they don't sell to me, and there aren't any other prospects, they'll lose it all, anyway. I knew that. And they know it, too."

"They owe the banks two thousand dollars," said George. "A mortgage. This they borrowed when the Panic began."

Edward had ceased to be surprised at the extent of George's vast knowledge of the city and its inhabitants and history. His uneasiness arose from another source. "Yes," he said, flatly. "That would leave them three thousand dollars. The old folks are in their late sixties or early seventies. Their sons can get jobs somewhere else. In fact, the younger one, Walter, could have a job with me, though he'd have to learn how to work, and he's in his early forties, I think." He rolled a cigarette for himself from a pack of Bull Durham and a sheaf of rice paper, and George watched his large hands do this with delicacy and neatness. George, himself, took out his gold match-case and struck a light for the young man who accepted the courtesy with a brief "thanks." His mind was still pursuing the Goeltzes.

"With that three thousand dollars, old Goeltze could open a smaller delicatessen somewhere else," suggested George. "Perhaps nearby. After all, they have friends in the neighbourhood."

Edward squinted through the smoke of his cigarette. "I took care of that, too. I said I wouldn't buy if they did not sign an ironclad agreement that neither they nor their sons would open a delicatessen within five miles of this one, and not even that, for two years."

"So," said George again. "No doubt you have visited the bank and discovered that the mortgage falls due in three months."

Edward's broad dark cheeks coloured slightly, then he smiled, and shrugged. "Yes, of course."

"And you have offered to buy the premises from the bank at a slightly smaller figure in the event it is seized by them for the mortgage?"

"Yes," said Edward, with no inflection in his voice. "That's business."

Once on a time, thought George, you would not have considered that "business," my Eddie. You have gone a long way and I am not certain as to where you have gone. In my direction? It is possible. But I did not tutor you in these things, these expedient things. Were they latent in you all the years of your youth, or has life corrupted you as it corrupted me? I look at your face and if it is harder and too old for your nineteen years, and if your eyes are cold, there is no hypocrisy there, no cruelty for the sake of cruelty, no meanness or ugliness. You are driven, and only the Great God can know what drives you.

George, who unconsciously relapsed into German whenever he was disturbed, said, "Father Jahle often speaks to me of your enormous generosity to him, Eddie. Ah, you are blushing like a girl. Do not blush for good acts, though I suspect you do not blush for exigent acts. You thought, of course, that I would lend you the five thousand dollars, and you have reason to expect that. You have no five thousand dollars of your own. Will you tell me what you have?"

"Five hundred," said Edward, curtly, and again that stain of colour appeared on his wide cheekbones. "After all, the kids are growing up and the fund has to grow accordingly. Will you lend me the money for the Goeltz property? If I have it in my hand, how can those old people resist, in spite of their sons?"

George meditated, his red eyebrows drawn together. Four years had increased his girth but had not lessened his thatch of coarse red hair or added more than a few lines to his ruddy face. Then he slapped his hand on the counter. "You have a partner, Eddie. I will lend, as a partner. Five thousand dollars is my investment."

"I don't want a partner, Mr. Enreich." Edward's voice was colder than before.

"A partner you have, or you have nothing." George's voice became rough with brutality. "And do not think, Eddie, that you can go to the bank for a loan. On your merits, yes, you could get a loan of five thousand dollars from any bank here, and on your statements. But, my Eddie, I would forestall that. That would be my business."

Edward was both amazed and aghast. "You can say that

to me, Herr Enreich, after all these years of your teaching?"

"My Eddie, you are still young and do not as yet know men. When George Enreich goes into any business George Enreich makes a profit and not a small one. Yes, I taught you, but that, too, was my investment." George suppressed a smile at Edward's expression.

The store was closed, for it was after ten, and the two clerks and Heinrich had gone home, and Edward and George were alone in the shining expanse of counters, polished nickel, gleaming linoleum and glass. ENGER'S had grown these past four years: one other shop had been added at the left. But beyond this expansion, and the necessary two clerks ENGER'S had remained what it was, a fine delicatessen, extremely prosperous even during the Panic of '07, the year before. It had, indeed, as Edward would say—"spruced up the whole neighbourhood," and property values had increased. There was no better delicatessen this side of New York, and it did a good business as far as Albany, to which many packages and cartons were sent as a consequence of Edward's skilful and luring advertisements in the Albany papers. It also did an excellent business with Syracuse and even Elmira, and there were special German delicacies imported by Edward in great demand in Buffalo, where Edward also advertised in the *Buffalo Evening News* and the *Express*, and in the local German language paper. He had just recently imported a most unusual item—Polish ham—and the growing Polish population of Buffalo, learning of it in their own newspaper, sent in very satisfactory orders.

The Engers, according to the standards of Waterford, were "rich." But greedy, envious competitors would say, sourly, "Look at them! They live in that old shack on School Street, and they don't even have a carriage, and Ed Enger rides all over town on a bicycle his dad gave him years ago. Save all their money; dress like working people; never go anywhere. That's the German! Save every penny, even if it comes out of their own hides!"

Edward, for some reason, was not popular except among customers, and even they now preferred the kindly and timid Heinrich who still had an eye for children and kept a large box filled with lollipops for them at Christmas. But few poor people came any longer to ENGER'S. The prices were too high, even for staples. Carriages lined the street all day long. Heinrich, walking home in his old coat, or in his shirt-sleeves in hot weather, could always spare the time for a gentle conversation with a long acquaintance who lived in the neighbourhood. But Edward had forgotten that art, or had decided that those who did not spend money in the shop were not worth the spending of his time in acknowledging them. The smiling and generous boy of over four years ago had been replaced by an alert, quick-eyed, stern-lipped young man, with a fast frown and an authoritative voice for delivery men and clerks and an occasional shabby stranger who wandered into the shop. It was not that he was " mean," as the neighbourhood said, and he was just to employees for all his demands on them, and he had forced his father to pay them unbelievably high wages, and no money was ever deducted from their wages when they were ill or late. He had also insisted upon granting them two weeks' vacation with pay every summer—and this had occasioned a furious battle with his parents who had been aghast at the very suggestion—and a small bonus at Christmas in accordance with their sales for the year. He was, at this very time in March, 1908, plotting to set aside a regular fund for the two clerks and the janitor in case of their deaths, in order that their families would have enough for a decent funeral and a little over. Edward thought these wild innovations secret from everyone except his father, but George Enreich, who knew everything that happened in Waterford, knew of this also, though he did not speak of it to his protégé.

It was unfortunate that the employees were firmly convinced that Heinrich, himself, was responsible for their high wages, their bonus, their vacations, and their steady income during illness. Heinrich never disillusioned them, not because he wished them to believe these things of him, but simply because it had not occurred to him that they believed them. He accepted their humble thanks in the name of ENGER'S, graciously and with kindness. He was not aware that his old acquaintances pitied him and had affection for him, and hated his son, Edward, for his brusque ways, his impatience, his silence as he rode home on his bicycle, his air of ignoring those who once supported the shop with their small purchases. No one, of course, was perceptive enough to understand that Edward had his hard material dreams and ambitions for his family and himself, and was preoccupied with them with a kind of unshaking ferocity.

It was only during especially crowded periods that Edward now waited upon customers. He left this to his father and the clerks. He had built an office in the rear of the fourth shop added to the other three, and here he made out his orders, kept his books, planned new imports. He was often in the shop to supervise, to watch, to greet a favourite, distinguished customer, to mutter a short and severe admonition to a lagging clerk, to let his rapid eyes run over the shelves, to inspect for absolute cleanliness, to encourage his father who was complaining more and more of his heart. He had a typewriter on his desk on which to compose enticing advertisements, write letters and do other needed work. He was the powerful spring that kept the clock of ENGER'S ticking constantly and prosperously, and his energy seemed limitless. But there was one place to which he never descended, and that was the basement.

George Enreich, on this unusually mild March night, thought of all these things as he sat and smoked his cigar and ate the sandwich and drank the coffee Edward had prepared for him. He continued, tranquilly, to enjoy all this, waiting for Edward to recover from his indignation.

"You didn't lose anything by your 'investment' Mr. Enreich," said Edward. He straightened up the full length of his six feet of height, and he squared his broad shoulders. "You get your percentage of our gross profits, and they're about ten times what you would have received in rents."

"Not to mention my free lunches," said George, placidly chewing. "This Polish ham, my Eddie. It is remarkable. What was I saying? Yes. I would prevail on the banks not to lend you the five thousand dollars to buy that shop. No. I am your partner, or you have nothing, *hein*?"

"What's your proposition, then?" asked Edward.

"Remarkable ham," George repeated. "Ah, yes, my proposition. But you have not told me what you will do with the Goeltz shop—if I am greatly persuaded into investing."

Edward was too vexed to see the twinkle in George's little eyes or the faint smile on his gross mouth. "All right," he said, "I'll go over it again with you. I told you about it years ago, and I've been telling you all along. A big shop, elegant, more expensive delicacies and imports, in the best shopping part of town. A shop that'll send orders all over New York State, and maybe into Pennsylvania and Connecticut, too. We can undersell New York City; we don't have the overhead they have there, and we're more central. But I've told you all that! There's one thing I haven't told you, though. I intend to open an office in New York and call it the Enger Importing Company. Imports, direct. Not through New York dealers. I can use the money myself."

George nodded, approvingly. "That, of course, is what I expected. We shall make the lot of money, is it not? *Ja.* The father, of course, is not to be part of the new shop. *Hein?*" He lifted his eyes and guilelessly fixed them on Edward's face.

Edward glanced aside. "*Nein,*" he said, bluntly. "A year ago I talked it over with Pa and Ma, and you'd have thought I'd proposed to blow this shop off its foundations. So, I knew I had to go it alone. There's fifteen thousand in the fund for the education of my brothers and sister, and though Dave and the others draw on it all the time, the money is always replaced fast. And my parents have twenty-five thousand dollars in their own name. I have five hundred." His lips curved in a hard line.

"I'm going to call the new shop The Fine Food Market. And then I plan branches of it, in Waterford and in other cities."

"What will happen to this shop?" asked Enger.

Edward looked about him and for a moment there was nostalgia in his eyes. "My father will have it, and he can manage it, with the aid of another clerk. I will retain my interest in it, of course. Supervision. Once or twice a week. Pa will pay me for it. I will do all the ordering myself in New York. Pa will get the goods from me for what I pay for them. He won't have any complaint there. And he'll still pay me my salary of twenty-two dollars a week, which I'll put in the fund as usual." He looked at George grimly. "I could pull out entirely, but Pa couldn't manage without me. And I've got to run it right, or he'll learn that without me he must fail, or go down to what he was before I made it what it is to-day. So, I'll keep my interest, and get my salary. But Pa won't be part of the new shop, though I'll be part of this. I have my obligations, and my brothers and sister will need all the money they can get. And I am the one who can get it for them."

"You have never considered letting them get it for themselves, my Eddie?" George's voice was deceptively mild. "You have never considered the character that would strengthen in them?"

Edward stared at him incredulously.

He blurted, "They have no character, they are weaklings!" And then his face was suffused with a dark wash of blood. He walked down the length of the counter as if escaping from the shrewd point of a rapier presented near his heart. He stood at the end of the counter, in profile. He drew a deep breath, and the colour left his face, leaving it very pale and harsh and quiet. "I shouldn't have said that. I don't think it. Dave's doing wonderfully in his music in New York; his teacher has confirmed that he is a genius. He takes three lessons a week and practises at least eight hours a day in that little apartment I rented for him. He's only twenty, but he'll be able to begin a tour in about three years, the teacher said. A limited tour at first, and then all over the country. And then he'll study in Europe. I'm thinking of sending him to Europe next year, and not letting him stay in New York."

The gas-gloves hissed warmly in the shining stillness of the shop. George did not speak.

Edward went on, "And Sylvia's doing fine in her drama and stage art school here, and she'll be ready for New York next year, and she's only seventeen now. And Greg's in that expensive boy's school in Pennsylvania, and he gets good marks, specially in literature and composition, and he's only fourteen. And Ralph will be going to Greg's school in two years; he's only twelve."

Edward came back along the counter and faced George. "Do you think they'd do better working in this shop for wages, or in factories, and then studying at night, and paying for their own educations?" His voice was very loud and furious, and there was a quality of breathlessness in it.

George spread out his hands. "I have known you were emotional, my Eddie, but not this emotional. *Nein*. It is as if I have attacked you." He narrowed his eyes. "Have I attacked you, my Eddie? It is not necessary to answer.

But I will say this: I have known great men who have worked for their ambition, and have studied in attics, and have struggled, and have succeeded. Because they had character, and character is not a commodity which you can buy. It is not a quality you can acquire in your best schools."

Edward, so careful these past few years, lost his temper. His anger rose from some enormous and secret wound in himself, which he sensed with an endless pain but which was consciously not known to him. "You have character, sir," he said, rudely. "And——"

"It is not the sort of character you prefer for your brothers and sister?" George smiled oddly. "That is what you would say, and it would not be the truth. You will not speak truth to yourself and that is the flaw I find in you. My Eddie, have you studied Bismarck?"

Edward frowned darkly. "I never always understand you, Mr. Enreich."

"You will, my Eddie, you will. One of these days. One of the very sombre days. Perhaps not until it is too late. For you, for your brothers and sister."

He wiped his fat hands, which were covered with rings, on the white napkin which Edward had given him. Edward said, "I'd rather not discuss my brothers and sister. I am doing my very best for them, and I intend to do a lot more. I can't do it here. That's why I want the Fine Food Markets. What is your proposition, Mr. Enreich?"

"Ah, it is a realist, this Eddie," said George. "Well, this is so: twenty-five per cent of the net profits, and I will assume the responsibility of all future financing in the expansion of the business. Am I not generous? Am I not reckless in this investing? But I was always so." He smiled with mock ruefulness. "Too, I have much trust in your ability, or I would not propose it."

Edward was appalled. "Twenty-five per cent!" he exclaimed. "You aren't really serious, Mr. Enreich? You can't be! I'd considered offering you six per cent interest until I could pay you back your money."

"I am no banker, Eddie. I do not need to lend you five thousand dollars and help you to expand, for six per cent. My investments pay me that now. I do not take risks for nothing. You are not yet twenty. You are not yet of age. I violate the law, I think, by negotiating a contract with you before you are twenty-one. But, you must understand, I am investing, if I invest, not just in the shops. I am investing in that quality which you have repudiated with such anger—character. Your character, my Eddie. And that is where I am generous. For, you have that flaw which some men would call strength but which I call weakness. A most terrible and devastating weakness, and it has caused all the world's greater agonies."

"What weakness?" Edward demanded, amazed and affronted.

George grunted as he shifted his weight from the stool to the floor. He changed the subject. "I am to expect you at my home to-morrow, Saturday night, for the usual discussions? The contract will be there. And now, good night to you, my Eddie. I suggest you sleep a little more. There are times when I am not pleased with your colour."

He began to walk weightily to the door, then wheeled like a behemoth. Edward was still standing at his counter, wrathful and fuming over the "proposition," and it was several moments before he realised that George had not left the shop. He started when he saw the older man, who was gazing at him formidably.

"No, I am not pleased with your colour. It could not be because of one or two of the trollops of the town, *hein*?"

Edward stiffened at this intrusion into his private affairs, and his pride was outraged. He said, in formal German, "Herr Manager Enreich, I am a man and not a child caught in some small and obscene act. Nor am I your son who needs chastisement. The Herr Manager has eyes in the back of his head, it is evident, and I request that his eyes do not remain on me constantly."

George perversely replied in English, "Your words are a man's words, my Eddie, but your annoyance is a child's annoyance." He grinned broadly. "You should have said, 'George, mind your own business,' and laughed. My Eddie, let me give you advice about women. Let them alone. That is not to say you must be a monk, no. But involve yourself in them not, with your heart and your emotions. I have heard you are attached to that particular trollop, one Annabelle, who has a very sensitive face and is a waitress to hide what she is."

Edward coloured. "I know what Annie is. Well, sir, mind

your own business. Quotes. Annie takes her—I mean, I give her half a ham or some delicacies once in a while, besides money."

For some reason utterly bewildering to Edward, George burst out laughing with such an uproar that all his jowls and his big belly shook as if with an ague. He was still roaring with mirth when he left the shop. Now Edward, his face still warm and flushed, was angrier than ever. He finished cleaning up George's cup and plate and emptying the coffee-pot. Then the door bell rang and a mildy chill and fragrant breath of the March night flowed in as the door opened. Edward said impatiently, "The shop is closed. I'm sorry."

He looked up and saw a very shabby but neat man of about thirty-five approaching him, a slight and wiry man wearing a workman's cap on a mass of curling sandy hair. Edward scowled. "I said . . ." he began. The man airily waved his hand with a gesture of peculiar flair and grace. "It is not the food I am after, young sir," he said, with a brogue unfamiliar to Edward. "It is a job."

Edward thought of the stout safe in his office, and the gun he was permitted to keep in a drawer in his desk. He eyed the man closely, concluded that even if he were an armed robber, he, Edward, had the advantage over him in size and youth.

"Funny time to come in asking for a job," he said. "It's after eleven. How about to-morrow?"

The stranger came easily to the counter and sat on George's stool and regarded Edward with dancing hazel eyes, so bright, so vivid, so full of laughter and intelligence, that they gave a shine to an otherwise nondescript face, yellowish and sprinkled lavishly with brown freckles. It was a pointed foxlike face, almost cunning, with a tilted nose and a mobile mouth, thick sandy eyelashes and brows, and a forehead so lined and dry that it was evident that he had spent the major part of his life under the sun. He took off his cap, smoothed his hands over his light curls, then laid the cap on the counter.

"What does it matter when a man looks for a job?" he asked, reasonably. "I just dropped into town only half an hour ago." He coughed. "Inadvertently, as it were. By no will of my own. However, it is an axiom that railroad men have no hearts."

In spite of his wariness and annoyance, Edward found himself smiling. A tramp. He was also intrigued by the stranger's manner and his evident air of culture, and his language. Here was no ordinary man. Among other things it was apparent that he found life amusing, and Edward was invariably attracted to those who found life amusing. They satisfied a lack in himself.

He studied the man a little closer. The body, for all its slightness, showed strength and agility even under the shabby brown suit. The hands were long and the fingers flexible and the nails well kept. The stranger shrugged his coat down into place with the instinctive movement of a gentleman, and showed a real linen collar and a striped pink and white shirt with a black knotted tie. The clothing was all very cheap and worn. Nevertheless, he gave polish to it.

In his turn the stranger studied Edward with those lilting eyes of his, and nodded to himself. "It is, indeed, an odd time to be looking for work," he said, and Edward was pleased at the deep inflections of the brogue. "I might add, if you please, that just at this moment I am also looking for a place to spend the night. I saw the lights in this shop"—and he glanced about the shop approvingly—"and you at the counter, and so tested my luck, which has been abominable lately. If the accommodations, young sir, are worthy, I will consider a position with you."

Edward laughed involuntarily. He was more and more fascinated by this peculiar stranger. He leaned his elbows on the counter. "It couldn't be that you'd consider a couple of ham sandwiches with Swiss cheese and English mustard, with a piece of cheese-cake on the side, and a big cup of coffee, too?"

The stranger made so comical a face of mock gravity that Edward laughed again. "Young sir, if you insist, I will join you in that slight repast. To tell you the truth I haven't eaten for three days, with the exception of a can of beans." He made a grimace. "Beans are, no question, redoubtable food, but I have a delicate digestion. That, too, was good luck, for the beans kept me from feeling hungry for the past two days."

He scrutinised the deep shelves behind Edward, and coughed again. "Ham, too, has its merits. But I see you have Madras curry, there, *pâté de foi gras*, English smoked chicken, and an excellent chutney. Not to mention some tins of savoury. English biscuits, too, and some delightful jasmine tea."

"I thought you were hungry," said Edward.

"That I am," said the stranger. "But a wise man respects his palate and never insults it. Even when he is hungry. Better starvation than plebeian food."

"Oh, rats," said Edward, with good humour. Nevertheless, he took down the tins the stranger had indicated, and found a can opener. "You would not have a sherry, a Bristol Cream, perchance?" asked the engaging intruder.

"I perchance would not," said Edward, laying out a plate. "We're not a saloon."

The stranger sighed. "A saloon," he said, meditatively. "What a perversion of language! Salon—saloon! A whole culture and world of difference, yet these two words have merged in a frightful miscegenation. Ah, well. The world decays, elegance is abandoned, life is dusty. *Après moi le déluge.*"

"The only deluge I can see coming after you is just plain working for a living," said Edward. "When did you last indulge in that awful thing?"

The stranger was delighted. "Now, then, I thought at first you were an unlettered churl," he said. "My apologies, my boy. Sometimes, to my chagrin, I am not always perceptive."

"Let's stop the fancy language," said Edward, laying out the contents of the can with careful appreciation. "Who are you, what do you do for a living, and what do you want?"

The stranger waited until Edward put a kettle on the hot-plate in the rear. "Enough water, please," he said, "so that the teapot can be heated by it. No American knows how to brew tea properly. You have a teapot?" he asked, apprehensively.

"Sure we have," said Edward. "We keep it for the swell customers who pretend they like tea better than coffee." He found the teapot under the counter, and wiped it off. "We aren't a restaurant, though. This is just one of those touches for customers we appreciate."

"I have," said the stranger, "exactly fifteen cents."

"You're still a customer," said Edward. He forgot time. He was enjoying himself for the first time in years. "By the way, what's your name? Mine's Ed Enger."

The stranger bowed profoundly from the waist. " I, young sir, am William Montgomery Percival Chauncey McFadden, of the McFaddens of London and Belfast, and, regrettably of County Cork. Perhaps not so regrettably after all. Those of my family in County Cork had a genius for living, sadly lacking in London and Belfast. There is something in the air of London and Belfast that inhibits joy. I have been thinking of writing a small book on the subject. Very provocative."

He pulled down his face in a risible expression, for he was an actor at heart. " However, just call me Bill," he said, woefully. " Just plain Bill."

" No," said Edward. " You aren't a Bill. You're a William. Are you a writer?"

" Very perspicacious," answered William, with an eloquent glance at his frayed cuffs and worn trousers. " The garb of those born with a pen in their hands. My last book sold exactly two hundred and twenty-one copies. The first two hundred and twenty were purchased by the loyal relatives. The extra one remains, to this day, a profound mystery."

" What is the name of the book?"

" The book? Ah, yes, the book. It was a treatise on that old fraud Plutarch. A snob. I flayed him from pillar to post. Somehow, no one particularly cared, least of all Plutarch."

Feeling lighthearted for the first time in many months, Edward carefully brewed the tea under the anxious and strained scrutiny of his guest. He was often to say in the future, " William told so many stories that you could never know whether or not he was ever telling the truth. At any rate, he was entertaining. And a good story is a good story."

Edward ceremoniously spread a fresh white napkin on the counter and elaborately polished the plain silver. William, his eyes clenched shut, daintily sampled the various delicacies on his plate. " Ah," he said of the Madras curry, " truly authentic. I ate it last in Delhi. Odd to say, the chef was an Englishman. That in itself was a miracle. Have you ever partaken of English cooking?" He gave an elaborate shudder, drew up his shoulders, winced, and rapidly blinked his eyes, giving the impression of a man presented with a frightful dish. Even his freckles gave the impression of flinching.

" What were you doing in Delhi?" asked Edward, folding his arms on the counter.

" I was a younger son, Edward. And younger sons have a

reputation to maintain, a reputation for debauchery and recklessness inflicted on them by lady novelists. Being gallant by nature, and never one to refute a lady, I was debauched, I was reckless. A bore, and very expensive. So, I became a remittance man."

"Are you Irish?" asked Edward, more and more enchanted.

"I am that strange manifestation known as a Scots-Irishman, my lad. Neither fish nor fowl nor good red herring. My sainted mother was of the Doyles of County Cork, and never without her rosary. My father, not so sainted, was the Scot, McFadden, and he was an Orangeman. To turn an Orangeman into a Catholic is only a little more difficult than to turn granite into flesh, but my mother prayed. Holy Saint Francis, how she prayed! And the Blessed Mother performed the miracle for her."

"You must meet a very good friend of mine, Father Jahle," said Edward. William immediately became Mephisto shrinking in terror from the Archangel Michael, cowering on his stool, protecting his head with his thin arms and freckled, clever hands, shivering violently, and knocking his knees together. Entranced by this realistic performance, Edward laughed aloud, throwing back his head.

"Priests affect me that way," said William, immediately becoming the connoisseur of excellent food again.

The telephone rang shrilly and abruptly, and both men jumped. Edward answered somewhat irritably. It was Heinrich. It was typical that Heinrich was worried over his son's long delay because of the large amount of cash in the safe. "What is it, Eddie?" he asked. "Why is the lateness? It is the safe that causes me anxiety. In these days there are many robbers."

"No robbers," said Edward, curtly. "But what if there was, and I'd just had my head shot off?"

Heinrich laughed feebly. "My Eddie can take care of himself. You have closed the safe?"

Edward glanced over his shoulder at his appreciative guest. "Yes," he answered. "Don't worry. Just some late customers, I'll be home after a while." He hung up the receiver and frowned at it, and William, the keen-eyed, watched him. Edward returned to the counter, and his youthful face was eager again for fresh stories. It is a hungry face, thought

William, compassionately. What little pleasure there must be in that young life!

"Well, if you had a remittance, why did you sneak a ride on a train?" asked Edward. "And why are you looking for a job?"

"It is a painful story," said William, discreetly. "I prefer not to speak of it. Suffice to say, there is no longer a remittance, no love and kisses in letters, for I receive no letters. I am a vagabond on the face of the earth. I have committed no crimes, though some would be boorish enough to disagree. There is a judge or two . . . That is irrelevant. I wandered to this remarkable country when I was twenty-five, ten years ago. The streets are paved with gold. I have not found gold. My occupation? Frankly, I am a jack of all trades. And I never stole but three quid in my life. Honest William."

He sipped the tea with the absorbed and critical air of a wine-taster. "Nectar," he said reverently. "The jasmine flowers are abloom in it. It takes a knowing hand to brew tea like this. I was born in Belfast. My father had a large stable of horses. He hunted with the hounds. A damned hullabaloo every autumn. Stupid animals, horses. The hounds are only a little better. The hunters are the most stupid of them all, in their pink coats, and their ruddy faces swelled and red and boorish. It is quite a spectacle; you must enjoy it some day. You will never be the same again. My sympathies were always with the fox."

He looked more fox-like than ever. Hypnotised, Edward could actually see pricked-up ears, the nose sharpening to a point, the bright hazel eyes startlingly wild and excited, the sandy hair gleaming like a pelt.

"Nevertheless, I like horses," said William. "They are malicious people, and not innocently so. I am malicious, myself. Consequently, they knew I was their master. I have attended horses all over the damn' world, racehorses. I firmly believe they decide among themselves, in the paddock, who shall win the day's race, and they have their small joke, which disconcerts their masters. We've had many a laugh together, the horses and I. What fool said that only man has the gift of laughter? I have seen the fox laugh, as well as other animals. And all animals are cynics. Yet they enjoy life. They understand that the green garden of the world was made for joy and frolic. Only man never learned that. So, he is serious. And being serious he is murderous. Frankly, I detest people."

This made Edward uneasy, with a nameless uneasiness. He drummed on the counter with the fingers of his right hand, and stared into space. "What else can you do besides joking with horses, William?"

"Anything," said William, with a dramatic spreading of his arms. "Name it. I'm your man."

Edward thought. Then he told William of the Fine Food Markets, and William listened to him with as much fascination as Edward had listened to his own stories, and his head was tilted courteously.

"I will need help in my first shop," Edward concluded. "Someone I can trust." He studied Honest William warily.

William nodded. "No sticky hand in the till. It so happens that I have managed a haberdashery, about four years ago. I increased the volume of customers, and I received ten dollars a week at the end of the first year. Unhappily, there was only that one year. There was the matter of the daughter of the owner of the shop. She insisted upon marrying me, and I recoil in horror at the idea of marriage. So I departed in a dust."

Edward scrutinised him openly. "You'll make a wonderful clerk," he said. "But it'll be some weeks before I have that first shop. In the meantime, you can help the janitor here. He's an old man, and overworked. He sleeps at home, mostly, but sometimes he sleeps here. We've got quite a comfortable room walled off in the basement, with a cot and clean blankets and a lavatory. Fritz is very neat. He's home to-night, and you can sleep down there. It's warm. And help yourself to breakfast early in the morning. We open at half-past seven." He paused. "I'll give you fifteen dollars a week as helper to our janitor, and twenty-five dollars a week to start when I open my new shop. And all you want to eat, free."

There is a lot here that I don't as yet know, thought William. He smiled, and his yellow teeth were the teeth of a pleased fox. "A fortune," he commented.

Chapter Eight

"Damn these old oil lamps, anyway!" Sylvia said aloud. "You can go blind trying to read under them. But Ma and Ed like them and the rest of us can get ourselves white canes in a few years." She took the chimney off the lamp and poked at the black wick disconsolately with a hairpin. It sputtered, and stank, and a blue smoke rose from it to circle about the room. Sylvia hastily replaced the chimney.

Her bedroom was small and ugly, with a crazed wallpaper of green lattices and bulging, bloody roses, with, here and there and incongruously, little bunches of strawberries growing as nature never permitted them to grow. Sylvia never looked at the walls without shuddering.

Everything's terrible around here, she thought, bitterly. Then her bony face, which had a white luminosity in the lamplight, became dreamily and intensely absorbed as she bent over the fashion magazine. Now, here was an elegant blue linen suit! Draped skirt, tapering down to nothing at the ankles. Peg-top. A flat tucking over the hips would be better than those little pleats. The jacket could be flared a little more, the bodice tightened, and crystal buttons instead of those pink ones. And that white lawn shirt-waist would be stunning without all that lace jabot and the fussy pin. Stunning!

I can make it up in blue cotton, cheap, Sylvia said to herself. But how I'd like to have linen, a fine handkerchief linen! And a hat like this, big yellow straw like a cartwheel, the brim overflowing with blue water-lilies and flat green leaves. And those real patent leather slippers! And the French heels and spats! We can afford it, too, just once. But, oh no! You mustn't waste money. It's sacred.

She lifted her eyes and fixed them on space. Then she turned her head aside, away from the lovely picture, and brooded. A clean-cut angle appeared sharply under her white chin, a tri-coloured angle as clear as if painted by a black brush. Her distinct and narrow profile had a look of desolation, and her hair fell away from it, bleakly. She let the magazine slip from her knee with a rustle. She listened to the disembodied voices and the house, her attenuated shadow high and bent on the wall and the ceiling. The lamp burned with a repulsive odour, and the room grew colder moment by moment as the banked furnace sent up no heat. The rug smelled of dust, though the strong and ardent spring wind flapped at the little window. Maria and Heinrich were already in bed, and little Ralph slept like a rosy cherub in his own room. The nickel alarm-clock on the chest moved its arms to midnight.

We'll never get out of here, never, Sylvia thought, her desolation increasing. But no one wants to, but me, and perhaps Dave. Nothing must be spent to make life nicer and more beautiful; it must all go into the bank. "For the future." What if there's no future for any of us? What if we get sick and die?

Her forehead was damp. But her dreary thoughts went on. We're all weak, all of us. But Ma. And Ed. She shivered, hugged her long thin arms about her flannel bathrobe. There's got to be a way out for me, Sylvia implored the unanswering sky. She no longer prayed to anything. Maria insisted on church, and her children obeyed, but none of them believed in the God spoken of by the minister. Nor did they believe in the God of their father—the heroic masses of which he spoke so fervently, and with such a glow in his eyes. Sylvia leaned on the window-sill and said aloud, "I wish there was really Someone you could pray to. Someone who could hear you, and promise you things, and give you hope. Pa's masses?"

She became aware that she was speaking aloud, and laughed again. "I think I'm going crazy," she remarked. "Don't crazy people talk out loud to themselves?"

Black despondency closed about her. There's a way out for me, she thought. I know it. Why don't I go? Who's to stop me, when I'm eighteen? I'll be my own mistress then. But I know I can't go. Not because of Ma and Pa, and Ed. No, not because of Ed. Just because of me.

This sudden confession terrified her. She put her hands to her cheeks and pressed fiercely. She mustn't think those thoughts! They weren't true! It was everything that imprisoned her. Mostly, it was Ed. Ed, the jailer, the monster, who pushed her remorselessly through the empty days.

Someone was coming down the street, footsteps echoing. If

was Edward. Sylvia looked down at him and now her face turned sharp with malevolence. She did not hesitate. She ran, her carpet slippers flopping, to the door, opened it swiftly and silently, and raced down the stairs, to meet Edward at the foot of them. He started back at this white-faced vision with the swinging lengths of black hair, and Sylvia pushed by him. The lower floors were unlighted except for a gas jet near the stairs.

"Hey," said Edward, in a low voice. "What's the matter?"

Sylvia turned and faced him. "You," she said.

"Me?" A dull flush passed over Edward's drawn face. "Are you dippy? What've I done?"

"Everything. But you're too stupid to understand." Then she stared at him narrowly and her mouth twitched. "No," she said, slowly, "you're not stupid. You never were. I just found that out, right this minute. You're brighter than anybody else in this house!"

She came closer to him. His grey eyes were gleaming oddly, and though he did not give the impression of smiling Sylvia knew that he was secretly amused. There was something terrible and yet defenceless in Sylvia's piercing regard of him. The gas jet sent eerie flickering shadows over the stark bones of her face and in the hollows of her eyes. She was peering at him now, her head thrust forward, and the intensity of her expression quelled his amusement.

"Is it just because of Pa?" she asked. "You've got to tell me."

Edward put his hand on the newel post. He turned his head and gazed at his sister in a silence she confusedly thought was threatening.

"No," she said, softly and thickly, "it isn't just Pa, is it?"

"I don't know what you're talking about, Sylvia. Why aren't you in bed?" The dull flush had deepened on his cheek-bones. "I've been working since seven this morning. I'm not going to stand here and talk to you. Good night."

But she put out her almost fleshless white hand and caught his big arm. She was trembling. "Why don't you let us go?" she demanded.

He shook her off. He stood there, large and powerful and dominant, like a young man carved from immutable rock.

"Who's keeping you?" he said. He no longer pretended to misunderstand her. "Are any of you prisoners?"

Her hand dropped from his arm and hung at her side, as if exhausted. " I could forgive you, if it was just for Pa. But it's for you, not Pa. When did it begin? Years ago. It was in a summer. That's the time you began to think, wasn't it, and began to hate us?"

" Hate you?" he repeated, meditatively. " Haven't I worked for all of you?"

Sylvia was too young to grasp the immensity of the instinctive thoughts she was thinking, the thoughts that rose from a kind of helpless terror out of the depths of her soul.

" You're not just working for us," she stammered, intimidated by her brother for the first time in her life. " What are you working for?"

Edward smiled, and it was not a youthful smile. " You can think what you want, Sylvia. You're a genius, aren't you? Can't geniuses think?"

She was stammering more than before. " I'll tell—I'll talk to Ma, to Pa—I'll talk to Dave——"

" Go ahead, Sylvia. Talk to them all. But just what'll you say?"

" That you—that you——"

" Yes?"

Sylvia was silent. Her brother was looking at her with adult indulgence, but his eyes were like granite struck by light.

Then he said, " You're not going to ruin what I started out to do, what I'm doing, what I'll be doing. For all of you."

Sylvia was trembling violently. " You think we are geniuses?"

He studied her. Then he said, with hard sincerity, " Yes. And you'd better be!" For an instant, an instant only, there was a sick quailing in him.

" The Chopin," said Professor Emilio Autori. " That is not the way we play the Chopin. Not so fast, not with the lilt. It is blasphemy. It is most the blasphemy with a young man with your gifts." He blew his pallid old nose on a soiled silk handkerchief on which a red and blue crest had been embroidered. Then he smiled. " But it is not the so bad. It is gay. There is no gaiety in this country. Tell me, my young friend, why is there no gaiety in a country which calls itself young?"

David smiled briefly and fleetingly at his teacher, and ran

a trill of light and flexible notes on the great piano. "Who says we're young?" he asked. "I've been thinking. We're barbarians. Millions of barbarians, born into America all these years. The Goths. The Visigoths. I've been thinking. Man isn't really created equal. The ancient savages are born in every generation, totally incapable of culture, just healthy, war-making, simple savages with a primitive inborn code of their own. Things-worshippers. Not idea-worshippers. A man who worships things can't ever be taught to worship abstractions. It's a waste of time to try. And barbarians aren't ever gay. Only a civilised man, born of civilised ancestors, can really laugh at—things. And even life. Barbarians can only get drunk, and fight, and they're serious as all hell, like all other animals."

"You have no high regard for humanity, David?" asked the old man, gently.

David shrugged, ran his beautiful hands tenderly over the keys. "I accept it," he said.

Signor Autori sat down very slowly on an old plush chair and contemplated his young pupil with amazement. "Ah, so it is!" he murmured. "It did not come to me before. We Italians, we are an old and cultured race; full of laughter and art and music and philosophy. We have given the world our civilisation. But among us, in every generation, are born some bear-eyed barbarians, who cannot comprehend music or the philosophic laughter or the noble tenets of Christianity. As among other nations, so are the barbarians born among the civilised Italians. I have often marvelled that in some of these fellow Italians of mine there is not the multi-coloured Italian soul."

David said, "Look, it's almost seven o'clock, Professor. Time to eat, isn't it?"

The old teacher laughed silently, his wrinkled mouth widening to show two rows of mottled teeth. He said, "It is good to be young, and long for the fragrance of excellent food, and the taste of it. But it is also good to be old, when digestion is more important."

A glimmering evening light, colourless and sad, filtered through the two tall thin windows near the piano. There was one tree on the miniature lawn outside. The three-story gaunt house had a spindly look between two wider houses, for it was only twenty feet wide and of dull grey brick.

But its ceilings were grotesquely tall and moulded of faded white plaster, and this room possessed a black fireplace in which a fire sullenly muttered to the voice of the wind in the chimney. An old, old room, with darkly polished parquetry floors covered by dimmed and ancient rugs whose pattern was almost obliterated by time, with high antique furniture of carved mahogany and crimson plush seats, with a Florentine mirror, octagon-shaped and blurred, over the mantelpiece, which held bronze candlesticks dripping with crystal prisms and a marble head of the Madonna. Between the two windows stood a high ebony stand bearing a cloisonné vase, all dark red and blue and black enamel and gilt traceries. Against one streaked white wall had been placed a Florentine chest of mahogany, its carvings flaking with gold, green and dying scarlet.

Yet it was an august room, and David loved it for all its majestic bleakness and age. He loved the whole house, this Italian house on West 4th Street, and he especially loved his tiny apartment on the third floor which enclosed rather than contained his own piano for practise after his lessons in the parlour below, and his severe white bed and the Italian chest of drawers and minute fire.

Only David lived in the house, for only David could afford the rent of the little apartment on the third floor. The other piano students lived in wretched tiny rooms in the neighbourhood, working as waiters or scrubbers or dish-washers in restaurants in the village to pay the very modest fees of Professor Autori.

"Why did you and Mrs. Autori come to America, Professor?" David had once asked. The old man had given him a peculiar and quizzical glance, and had coughed. "It was a slight affair of politics," he had murmured. "You are surprised, my David? In this America a man does not leave his home for politics, which are regarded with humour, and which are not too dangerous. And that is good, very good. There are many other excellent things in your country, even if it does laugh too easily and without true laughter. But that again may be good, for it is laughter without malice or cruel subtlety. It is all very paradoxical."

David remembered this remark this cold spring evening, as he looked at the one bare elm outside, its back running with sooty rain, its branches dripping. Paradoxical. He was learning of paradoxes for the first time in his twenty years. There were never any paradoxes at home, in Waterford. Only stringencies, severe and harsh, which rose from the nature of the Engers. For some reason, he thought of his brother, Edward. He put his hands on his narrow hips, and wondered why he was disturbed.

Professor Autori joined him at the window. He was so tall an old man that he was even taller than David, and he seemed all bone and string under his greenish broadcloth coat and slender trousers. Even his face, long, furrowed and pale, appeared fleshless beneath a rolling mass of silver hair like a mane. His sunken eyes glowed impetuously under enormous silvery brows, and his wise old mouth was etched into a pattern of sceptical drollery. The corners twitched meditatively as he, too, thought of Edward Enger, who had brought his brother to this house and who had bargained smartly with him about the rent of the miniature apartment, but not about the fees. "My friend, Mr. George Enreich, has told me about you," Edward had said, without unnecessary preamble, and with a straight gleaming of his grey eyes directed at the professor. "He recommended you highly. He says that you conducted in the La Scala Opera in Milan, and that you've forgotten what the ordinary conductor knows. And so, here is my brother, David, and he is a genius, and I want the best for him."

The professor coughed now, and said to David, "It has come to me that I am thinking of your brother. Eduardo? That is the name?"

David started, and smiled moodily. "Funny. I was just thinking of him, myself."

"I have been told that I have the perception," said the professor, gravely. He regarded David tentatively, and without apology. "It is not often that you speak of your family, though when you do speak of them you speak almost always of Eduardo."

For a moment David, who had been brought up in an atmosphere where one did not inquire into the affairs of a family, paused. But the professor was smiling at him with bland inquisitiveness. David shifted in his narrow and polished boots. "I suppose," he said with irritable candour, "that the whole family is really Ed. I've suspected that for a long time. Maybe Ed knows that, and maybe he doesn't, but he sure acts that way! I remember when he brought me here. I didn't bring him. I think that sums up Ed." He paused again. "Genius," he continued reflectively. "I don't know about myself, but Ed's a genius. Sometimes he scares the hell out of me, and I don't know why. He sacrifices himself all the time for all of us, but——"

He thought of the Christmas Eve when he had played Bach-Gounod's "Ave Maria" for his brother, and his heart, so volatile, so easily annoyed, so strangely distressed, softened. "You can live in the same house with a brother and not know him at all. I thought I knew Ed. We used to call him The Dummy."

"The Dummy," repeated the old man. "And what is The Dummy?"

David's fine-boned face coloured. He ran one of his extraordinarily elegant hands over his smooth black hair. "A fool," he said, ashamedly. "That's how stupid we are, my brothers and sister and me. And my father," he added. He thought again. "You know, Professor, though my mother always say that Ed doesn't have any genius, and that he's not gifted, I don't believe she thinks that. And now I don't either. There's something—well, something terrible about Ed. It's impossible to explain."

"But he sacrifices his life for the family," said the professor.

David was silent. Then he nodded, slowly. "Yes. He reminds us of that all the time." He laughed faintly. "And he reminds us we're geniuses; never lets us forget it for a single minute. It's gotten to the point where I'm—I'm frightened. And it's not Ed's fault. He's had it drummed in him all his life that we're gifted, and he believes it as much as we do, maybe more so."

The professor turned thoughtfully to the piano and touched the keys with love. "You do not believe you are a genius, David?"

David followed him with anxiety. "Do you, Professor? I've been with you since last September. You ought to know by now. I've been afraid to ask."

Or, perhaps, thought the professor with compassion, you have been hoping that I would reply no. He danced his fingers over the keys and the most fragile and delicate notes answered him, like a harp.

He said, in Italian, "We must speak in Italian, for it is

necessary for you to be proficient. A cultured man knows several languages; with only one he is like a man who knows but one song. Yes, David, you are a genius." He smiled at the young man with a deeper compassion. (But, not as you think, not as your brother thinks, he thought.)

He put his hand on David's tense shoulder. Ah, nerves. This is a youth of nerves. He is never at rest. The old man smiled. "So, I have told you, and I would not deceive you. We must pray for you, must we not? When I was young," he said, with a musing and dreaming expression, "I was the agnostic, the atheist. There are years of youth when it is in rebellion. It becomes daring, bold, to announce that God does not exist. It shocks the parents; it outrages the clergy, who are more simple. It is exhilarating. But the intelligent youth knows he lies, while he rejoices in his lies. He is the man now, the knowing man, the emancipated man, and he swaggers, with his books under his arm. He is the scientist, the youthful Darwin, the man of the Age of Enlightenment, free of superstition. He is also a child. With the years comes wisdom, and it is not the wisdom of fear but the wisdom of knowledge. So, we must pray."

It was Edward who had taken over the "management" of what he sometimes, and bitterly, stigmatised, to himself, as the Fund for Fools. It was he who decided how much should be spent for his brothers' and sister's clothing, and their tuition, except where there were fixed fees. Now that David was in New York, his music fees and board provided, it was necessary, according to Edward, that he "dress the part." Therefore, David had a good if limited wardrobe, Edward instinctively understanding that a poorly dressed man is severely handicapped. Too, Edward had a secret but powerful pride, daily growing more obsessive, and as David was an Enger, and a student of a famous teacher, Edward wished him to surpass the other students in dress, thus impressing upon teacher, acquaintances, possible "interests," and students, that here was an important personage. But pocket money, "for foolishness," was strictly doled out.

"What do you need a lot of money for?" Edward had demanded of David. "You have good clothing, better than I have or ever will have, an apartment, a piano, your fees paid, your music bought, concert tickets provided whenever you want them, opera tickets, money for books. Besides, you'll be studying and practising most of the time. So where, and when, could you spend a lot of money? I'm not working my head off so you can swagger around New York like a millionaire."

So David, affluent in every other way, was miserably circumscribed in any spending for pure pleasure, and this to a young man going on twenty-one, was intolerable.

His conversation with Professor Autori this afternoon had stirred him deeply. He was unusually quiet during that night and ate little. He was somewhat moody and restless. The soft and sooty rain had stopped, and there was a quickening movement in the spring night, a promise that danced over brick and concrete and brightened the yellow street lamps. David decided that the house was unbearable, and that he must walk endlessly. He had received his monthly cheque to-day from his brother, and recklessly he considered spending most of it, if the opportunity offered.

He put on his short but costly broadcloth overcoat with its narrow velvet collar over his well-cut black suit, and adjusted his glimmering derby hat. He put on pearl-grey spats over his polished boots, and drew on pearl-grey gloves, and took up a small and shining black cane with an ivory head. He looked at himself in the old Venetian mirror, and was pleased. Then he set off.

He glanced with covert eagerness at some of the girls who passed him in the mild March night. But he was disappointed to see that they were not the kind he had seen before. Most of them were dowdy and preoccupied, their skirts not lifted in a gloved hand, but dragging on damp pavements. Their faces were white and worried and plain, under wide felt hats of the poorest quality, and their coats and suits were frowsy. They looked furtively, and with admiration, at David, but he looked away. Working girls, seamstresses or office girls, on the way home from work.

Most of those who lived in the neighbourhood were at supper, and David soon found himself practically alone in the narrow and winding streets. He heard the distant rumbling of traffic, but here it was quiet. Now he was coming to the neighbourhood of the little restaurants and cabarets, and he walked with more intensification of his mysterious excitement. He imagined he felt hungry. He would find a restaurant, dark and small and lighted with candles, where he would treat himself to an exotic dish and a bottle of expensive French wine. He would sit among " people " and watch, and think of himself as a man of the world, a suave and polished stranger, condescending to visit the Village. A Frenchman, perhaps. Or a French-Italian. Better the Italian; he knew that langauage more fluently.

He found a restaurant he had never seen before, and he stopped on the sidewalk to study its exterior, thoughtfully twirling his cane. The curtains were drawn across the steamed windows. There was a poster on one of the windows, a noisy poster lettered in green and red: " Prince Emory! Two weeks' engagement! Just returned from the Mardi Gras in New Orleans! New music, new rhythms! Extraordinary Effects from Dixie! From Ten to Two!"

David glanced at his pocket watch. It was hardly nine. He hesitated. The restaurant would be empty. But he knew that it was open, for there were shadows on the curtains moving rapidly back and forth. Then he heard music, the sudden brilliant flare of a trumpet, like a joyful cry of delight, the sudden clamour of a piano, the sudden ripple of a drum, teasing and audacious. He had never heard such music before, and his flesh tingled ecstatically. The music stopped. They were practising, apparently. Then a violin sang alone, with a voice and with music which sounded like a dusky girl on some hot mountain with hibiscus in her hair, her skirts flashing and whirling. David was enchanted; he breathed lightly, so as not to miss that wild singing that cried of palm trees and shining Southern oceans and islands, green as jade, haloed in warm golden beaches, and people who lived to love and to laugh, far from concrete and gas-lights.

David pushed open the door. As he suspected, there were no customers in the restaurant, which was not very large, but was very intimate, with bare wooden tables and candles stuck in wine bottles, and with a bare floor. On a dais, against one wall in the middle of the restaurant, two young Negros were practising at a piano and at a drum, while two others stood near them, one with a violin, one with a silver trumpet. They turned their heads, startled, as David entered, and one of them said in a liquid and courteous voice, " Not open yet, mister. Not till ten." Their eyes were curious, roaming over his clothing and face, and their expressions took on constraint.

"That's all right," said David. He stood near the door. There was not a waiter in sight. He hesitated. "I think I'll sit down anyway, and wait, and listen to you practise." The young Negroes glanced at each other, shrugged, and turned back to their instruments. David seated himself at a table near them. He brought out a package of cigarettes, and lit one, and though he did not know it his every gesture was that of a grand seigneur, and antagonising.

Then one of the young Negroes, exceptionally handsome, and tall and slight, and possessing a smooth face the colour and texture of finely polished bronze, and with features of unusual clarity, suddenly swung about and stared intently at David. David was pretending to be absorbed in thought, and he studied the burning end of his cigarette with an aloof expression. He was deciding to be a Fifth Avenue gentleman waiting for a mysterious feminine companion. The companion would not come; he would sit alone. But he would be interesting.

The young Negro who was staring at him lifted a hand to silence the other musicians, and put his silver trumpet on the top of the piano. He stepped down from the dais, and his companions watched with curiosity, their hands on their instruments. He walked with a feline grace to David, who started when a shadow fell across his table.

"Excuse me," said the young Negro, and his beautiful voice trembled a little. "I kind of thought I knew you, from somewhere. I'm Prince Emory, and this is my band, a new kind of band, just come from N'Orleans."

David coloured with embarrassment, then he said, awkwardly, "Sit down, Mr.—Emory. Guess we can have some wine, if we can find a waiter. I don't seem to know you. Who did you think I was?"

Prince Emory sat down, after a brief hesitation. He studied David earnestly, moving his head to catch a different angle of David's warm face. Then, to David's astonishment those soft brown eyes filled with tears, and he smiled tremulously. "I know you!" he said, gently. "You're Dave Enger!" He, too, was astonished. "I'd know you anywhere! Dave Enger!" Now his eyes shone with happiness.

"Yes, I'm Dave Enger," David replied. "But I don't seem to——" Then he stared fixedly, and slowly he smiled, a young and touchingly inhibited smile. "Why, for God's sake, you're Billy Russell, from Waterford! Ed said you'd gone to New Orleans, years ago." He stretched out his hand enthusiastically to Billy and Billy, after another brief hesitation, took it and shook it with delight.

"What do you know?" marvelled David, suddenly at ease at finding someone who knew him in this enormous city where he was so lonely. "Prince Emory! What've you been doing all this time, Billy?"

"I've been in N'Orleans," said Billy, accepting one of David's cigarettes. "Learning. New music, wonderful music. I'm making money," he added, pridefully. "Lots of money. I guess you could call me rich, now. I get five hundred a week anywhere I go; can keep half of it for myself, the rest goes to the other fellows."

"Honestly?" said David, incredulous. He looked about the small and somewhat dank little restaurant. "Here, too? Five hundred dollars a week!"

"Sure," said Billy, with a contented smile. "Don't let this place fool you, Dave. All the rich folks from uptown come to this restaurant all the time; you can't get in, even on Monday nights. And it's been crowded every night I have been here. This is my second week. I got notices in the big newspapers in New York; theatrical fellows been here almost every night. One's a music publisher; he's going to publish some of my music. We're a sensation, first time they ever heard our kind of music in New York." He flourished the cigarette with an air of modest pride and assurance.

Then he said, "What're you doing in New York, Dave?" His astute eye had noticed the expensive clothing, the elegance, the watch-chain.

"I'm studying with Professor Autori. Piano. I've been here almost a year. Concert music. I live on West 4th Street, an apartment of my own. We're doing very well in Waterford, Billy." And his mouth, suddenly expressive, jerked a little.

A small silence fell between them. They were remembering the very young Edward of almost five years ago, who had struck Billy and who had upbraided and denounced his brother.

"Professor Autori," said Billy, in an awed voice. He had

never heard of Professor Autori, but he was too natively polite to reveal that fact. "A real genius. You're lucky." Then they both thought of how David had played the piano in the hot little parlour in the house on School Street, and of how Billy had spontaneously accompanied him. Billy's eyes flinched with pain. "You'll be a concert pianist, too, I guess. One of these days. Not my kind of music, though. Mine's special."

"I like it," said David, gloomily. He shifted on his wooden chair. He said, "I like it a damned lot better than I do mine! I understand it. I——" And he was silent.

An elderly waiter in a long white apron appeared from the rear shadows of the empty restaurant. He came to the table and looked at "Prince Emory" with an expression of mixed superiority and resentful respect. "Want something, Prince?" he asked.

"Yes." Billy regarded David's drooping face acutely. "No wine. Maybe two ryes and water. Not the water in the same glass with the whisky, Hugo." The waiter sniffed antagonistically and trundled away.

"If you don't watch them," said Billy, "they'll put a quarter inch of whisky in the bottom of the glass and fill it way up with water." He was concerned that David appeared to have sunken into brooding gloom. When he was like this he resembled Edward, and Billy sighed. He did not want to be the first to mention his old friend, for the memory of that last night was still like a wound in him.

"I suppose so," said David, absently.

Billy was silently praying that David would speak of Edward, so he adroitly led the conversation in that direction. "Why shouldn't you like my kind of music, Dave? What's wrong with it? I tell you, you've got to be just as much of a genius to play it as you have to be to play your kind." He paused. "Or, maybe it isn't your kind. Remember how you played—that night—and I came in with my harmonica and pitched right in with you? Man, we made it roll!"

David moved uneasily. He lit another cigarette. Billy put his hand in the rear pocket of his trousers—he was in shirt-sleeves, rolled to the elbow—and placed Edward's harmonica on the table between himself and David. The two young men gazed at it with sadness. It was worn, at the mouthpiece, down to the underlying piece. " I play it ; I can still make it sing like all get-out. Tried other harmonicas, costing up to a hundred dollars, but this here thing runs away from 'em." He paused again. " Ed gave it to me."

" I know," said David. He glanced up at Billy, and his eyes were vivid. " Poor Ed. He wanted Pa's flute, but Pa wouldn't let him have it, so he bought the harmonica for two dollars. Nobody ever heard him play it, except me. He wasn't allowed to practise in the house. You see, he wasn't a genius." David smiled wryly.

He went on, musingly, " It's funny, but I've remembered something. It was a long time ago, when Ed was about fourteen. Maybe thirteen. We'd all gone to the park on a Sunday, for a picnic, and Ed had to stay at home to open and run the store at six o'clock. My mother asked me to stop in on the way back and pick up some sliced boiled ham. The door of the shop was open, and Ed was all alone in it, sitting on the counter, with his back to the door. And he was playing the harmonica."

He snuffed out his cigarette with a strong and twisting movement. " Well, I stood there in the doorway and listened, and it was like a little organ, that harmonica. Ed was improvising on a theme he had heard me play on the piano. A phrase from Beethoven's Fifth. I couldn't believe it, Billy! It seemed impossible to believe it, myself. And would you believe this?" He looked at Billy with gleaming self-contempt and regret. " I was angry. I was the musical genius. I felt that Ed was insulting me! I didn't know at the time that he could make circles around me. He's the genius of the family. The rest of us are just fakes." He laughed shortly and bitterly. " Fakes! Farces! Oh, I'm not saying we don't have—something, but I've got the idea it's mediocre, and what we are really fitted for is the thing we are not learning. We're caught on something, like an insane carousel that never stops and which won't let us off, and it's not Ed's fault. It's ours."

Billy nodded soberly. " I guessed all that a long time ago. He'd talk about stage art, from looking at Sylvia's books on it, and about music like a professional, and he used to sneak in a couple of hours a month at the art gallery and describe the pictures to me like a painter, himself, and he'd get books from the public library on medicine and read them in the basement, and physics books, with all kinds of jargon and charts in them, and when he talked, it looked like he was on fire, just burning up. You couldn't stop listening to him; it was like listening to somebody hypnotising you. I guess you're right. He could have been anything he wanted to be. But he runs the store and he's sure making something out of it! Yes, sir! A real genius at selling, and plans. Maybe he decided, all by himself, that he was best at that."

To-night, to his astonishment, in that little restaurant in the Village, David was hearing fully about his brother, and he could not help it, in his youth and jealousy and resentment against Edward, that he discounted almost everything Billy was saying. The music, yes. But not all the rest! It was impossible. Billy was just enlarging his friend, in his affection, to the dimensions of a god. David smiled indulgently, and Billy stiffened.

"Ed's a first-class merchant," said David. "We're getting rich out of the delicatessen and getting what we want. Perhaps we'll never know what it is we really want, but that's our own fault."

The waiter brought the whisky. David had never drunk whisky before, and he watched covertly as Billy dealt with it like a man. Then he sipped. It nauseated him, but he controlled his affronted expression.

Billy subsided in thought. He watched the candlelight shining on the gold cuff-links. Then he asked, as if idly, "How's Ed? I mean, how's he feeling?"

"Ed? Why, Ed's an ox! He never gets tired; he can lift a hundred pounds as easily as I can lift ten. He's like a wrestler, all broad muscles and limber as a snake. Make two of me, though I'm a little taller. He lives in the shop, though we've got two clerks now. Pa has to stay home a great deal, with his heart."

Billy pursed his finely carved lips. "Maybe Ed's big, and ambitious, but I don't think he's very healthy. He almost fainted in the basement one time, and almost fell in the furnace. Caught him on the way in. He looked like he was dying."

"Ed?" repeated David, incredulously. "Why, Ed was never sick a day in his life! He must have just tired himself out. Fainted? Ed?"

Billy changed the subject. " Dave, in about twenty minutes people'll start coming in. I've got an idea! I've composed a couple of pieces, myself. A new one, I call it The Royal Street Blues. It's just been published in a place down in N'Orleans. I'm trying it out, to-night." He became very excited. " Wait! I'll get it off the piano and I want you to run your eyes over it."

He ran to the piano, where his musicians were straining to hear the conversation. He snatched a sheet of music from the piano, and ran back to David, who was suddenly feeling the whisky. There was a golden haze shifting before his eyes, yet everything appeared preternaturally acute and clear, and there was a rising lightness and pleasure in him. " There," said Billy, proudly. " You just read it! You can follow it while we run it off for you."

He returned to the dais and picked up his trumpet, and his musicians prepared to play. He put the trumpet to his mouth and made it sound as David had never heard a trumpet sound before. The other instruments joined in, and David, following the music with his eyes, was enchanted and dazzled. He listened intently, as he read. Why, this was something new, something never heard before, something so exciting that it made a man's heart jump!

Billy put down the trumpet, and began to sing in a rich baritone.

David, entranced though he was, had begun to furiously edit the sheet of music. His face was flushed with damp, and his pencil raced. He would lift his head, listen intently, his mouth parted and smiling, then he would bend his head again and scribble faster than ever. His heart pounded. He was uplifted, carried away. The trumpet blazed again, and it was voluptuous. This was music he could understand! This was his own kind, his own music! The other musicians now sang the song, dolefully, movingly, and the trumpet now followed them as if mourning, in notes David would have thought, before to-night, utterly impossible with that instrument.

It was the whisky, of course, and his own suddenly released youth, and his rapture, that made him seize the sheet of music, and Billy's harmonica, and run to the dais. The musicians grinned at him, and Billy laughed around the mouth of the trumpet. Then David threw the harmonica on the top of the piano, pushed the pianist fiercely aside, and took his place. The piano, to the amazement of everyone but Billy, took on new expression, new depth, new feeling. Billy softened the trumpet, the violinist let his notes sink, the drum murmured, and the piano "rolled" out, triumphantly. David was now scarlet; he looked drugged yet fervid and ebullient, lost in his music.

The waiters crowded at the back to listen, and their eyes glazed, and their feet tapped. They rolled in unison. One or two hummed the melody. When the music came to a wild end, they clapped without their own volition, and stamped their feet. The musicians rose and screamed a passionate hosannah, and beat David's shoulders in a frenzy.

David sat now, in silence, and grinned, all his white teeth glittering. He could feel the blood rushing in his body, the tingling of his flesh. He shook hands with all the four young Negroes, and accepted their accolades.

"You're for us!" cried Billy. He turned to his musicians. "I've known him since we were kids. I knew all the time what he could do, yes, sir! Yes, sir; yes, sir! Did you hear that piano? Man, that piano! It'll never be the same!"

"Oh, now," said David, and he was a little hoarse. He gave Billy the sheet of music. "I've made some corrections. Billy, you've got a wonderful voice."

Billy looked at David, and though his bronze face still glowed, he became sober. "Man, you got a job with us any time you want! Any time! Two pianos! That'll DO something to 'em. What're you wasting your time for?"

David was suddenly sobered, and a chill settled on him. He was full of yearning, and there was a reckless passion in his blood. But still, he began to grow cold. He looked at the piano wistfully, and all his soul longed for it.

"Tell you what, Dave," said the sensitive Billy. "You just keep my card. You think about it."

David whispered, and he was trembling: "I—I can't, Billy. Not yet, Billy." Then he lifted his head and his eyes sparkled. "But maybe sometime, Billy. Sometime, Billy!"

Chapter Nine

"You are certain, my Eddie, that you do not wish me to be present when you tell your parents of our new plans, and our partnership?" asked George Enreich on the telephone.

Edward smiled. "You mean, you think I might need moral support?" His smile became unpleasant. "I'm not that delicate. I can handle things myself. No, thanks, Mr. Enreich."

Over the past few years he had frequently called "conferences" between his parents and himself, and both Maria and Heinrich, upon being told by Edward to-night that he wanted to talk with them, were pleased. Edward's "talks" inevitably were the prelude to larger income. Sylvia and Ralph were banished to their rooms and Maria took up her endless knitting and Heinrich loosened the buttons of his vest, as they sat in the parlour with Edward. Too, in order to produce a proper and "cultured" atmosphere, the conversations were invariably conducted in German rather than in frivolous and "formless" English. "One must have precision, during important discussions," Maria would always say. "There must be no room for ambiguous meanings, which could cause trouble later." To Maria, German was like a legal document, embellished with red seals and firm signatures.

Edward did not sit down. Heinrich lit his pipe and looked anxious and meek as usual, waiting to take all his cues from Maria. His wife knitted with massive serenity and patience, not lifting her eyes from her work. It was always so, from the beginning, thought Heinrich, with uneasy surprise. Maria has respected Eddie, not despised him. Ach, they are alike, these ones!

Edward glanced about the tiny parlour. It was warm, this spring night, but the windows were not open, to conserve the heat for cooler hours. He looked at the gas globes. He was done with this place! It enclosed him like a constricting shell which was now too small for him.

"I do not speak," he began, "until I have made up my mind, until I have closed all contingencies, all retreats, and there is no turning back. I must have this understood from the beginning."

"Yes," said Maria, with a nod, indicating that all sensible and intelligent people proceed in this way, while only fools discuss plans before resolving them into action. Her needles clicked decisively. "Ach, yes," murmured Heinrich.

Edward put his hand in his pockets. "We have come a long way. We've taken several steps. Small steps. Now we must take the large step. And I must warn you, my parents, that nothing you can say can cause me to turn back. We go on together, or"—and he paused—"I go on alone."

Maria lifted her bulbous blue eyes and fixed them on her son. For an instant the large impassiveness of her face became intent. "You have threatened that before," she said. "I do not believe for a moment that you make idle threats. But, why is it necessary to threaten? Have I not always been reasonable?"

Edward smiled that unpleasant smile which more and more had a habit of dislodging his former agreeable expression. "You have been reasonable, Mother, when all my plans indicated that my brothers and sister, and yourselves, would be the ones mainly to profit from my ideas."

Maria knitted in silence for a few moments. Heinrich pulled himself up in his chair. He did not like this! Then Maria was saying calmly, "It is a strange thing about humanity. It considers its sacrifices solely for the benefit of others. But altruism, as a great philosopher has said, is deeply rooted in a desire, an egotistic desire, to benefit the altruist first of all, and himself enormously more than others. However, where is the man who is honest with himself? Edward, you have not reached understanding yet. No one can give you that understanding. Time alone can accomplish that."

Now she's talking like George Enreich, thought Edward, angrily. I'm a simple person, an American, and I don't like these oblique references. It's impossible for Germans to think or talk without mystique.

Maria continued, in that same calm and detached manner. "I, too, your mother, have an existence apart from my children, though perhaps it has never occurred to you."

Edward pondered on this, then shook his head irritably. It was so like his mother to get away from the subject. She was exhibiting no curiosity. She was never in a hurry, or eager. Her son had no doubt that she would be willing, now, to discuss philosophy for quite a while, and delay discussion of the momentous thing in his mind and will.

"All right!" he said shortly. "I have had a talk with Mr. Enreich this evening."

"Ach," said Heinrich, with mingled pleasure and apprehension. "One can always be certain that the Herr Manager never speaks lightly."

"Not when it comes to profits for himself," Edward agreed, sullenly. He drew a deep breath. Now he addressed his mother alone, and he talked for a full ten minutes without interruption. The gas hissed in its yellow globes; the spring wind felt along the edges of the windows. Maria knitted inexorably. Heinrich's face began to take on a look of shock and disbelief and terror. He kept moistening his full pink lips, and sometimes, frantically, he chewed on a hang-nail. But he never glanced away from his son; he gazed at him as one gazes at a fascinating and appalling spectacle.

There was a long silence when Edward had finished, broken only by the click of Maria's needles, the hiss of the gas, the restless rising of the night wind, and the creakings of the little old house. Heinrich suddenly leaned back in his chair and closed his eyes in faintness. It was not possible that his son, Edward, was proposing this, in such a hard and implacable voice. It was a dream; one had only to keep quiet and one would awake.

Then Maria was speaking, without raising her tone, and almost dispassionately. "You have considered your father's health, no doubt."

"I've told you," said Edward. "He keeps his clerks; I will supervise. In an emergency, I will be there. After all, I'm not going to the moon."

Maria put down her knitting, and folded her hands in her lap. She regarded Edward with cool and detached curiosity. Inwardly, she smiled, recognising her own irresitible force of character in Edward. "You will say that this new—venture—will increase the fund for the others. Yes, I admit that. If Herr Enreich believes in it, then it cannot fail. In reality, however, you are separating yourself from us. You are like the eagle, who, though preserving its nest and what lies in it, is unrestrained in the unreachable air, a flying shadow on a mountain top, always hovering, always alert, but free in itself." Ah, yes, she thought, and that was I, too, but I did not know until it was too late.

Heinrich came to himself. He was aghast at his wife, appalled at his son. The old awful loneliness came to him again: I have lost my Eddie. He was more shaken at this than at Edward's proposals, or decisions.

"What are you saying, Maria?" he cried. "You are not agreeing to this?"

His wife slowly turned her head to him and considered him. "Agree?" she asked. "I believe we have no other alternative but to agree. As that man, Goeltz, has no other alternative."

"I can't see the comparison between us and Goeltz," said Edward, and he flushed.

"Can you not?" said Maria, with cold surprise. "But then, perhaps it is fortunate that we are your family, unlike Herr Goeltz. We shall not suffer; we shall profit. That, I know. But still, Herr Goeltz and your father and I have much in common."

Edward was deeply angered.

"There was a time," Maria continued, "when I considered you, Edward, incapable of hatred. That was unwise and stupid of me. It was latent in you, from the beginning. I have nothing against hatred, when it is righteous and directed against evil. But it is a dangerous thing when one hates humanity and not evils."

"Eddie was always so loving," said Heinrich, feebly. "I do not understand . . ." He wiped his face, as if perspiring, but in reality it was only a cover to dry his stinging tears.

Maria nodded. "True. But he has not found love yet."

She picked up her knitting again. "You have not told us all, Edward."

"No," said her son. "I have not. And when I do, you will not be so sure that I hate my family."

Maria smiled faintly. She again lifted her eyes and scrutinised the young man. "Did I say you hated your family? No. It is you who have suggested it."

Edward furiously thought of all that he had done, not only in benefits to his family, but to many others. However, there was no use arguing with his mother. Let a fellow think of himself, occasionally, and she immediately accused him of "hating" his family! But it was like her to be unjust and narrow. He was tired of being accused, of being put on the defensive, of having motives ascribed to him which had never entered his mind!

"Coming back to your allegory about the eagle and the nest," Edward said, contemptuously. "Very good. And now I want to tell you that this nest, right here, this house, doesn't suit me any longer. We live like beggars, when we are rich. I've been thinking of building a house. Herr Enreich has offered me eighteen acres three miles outside of this town, at only forty dollars an acre. A manufacturing company, beer, I think, has offered him one hundred fifty dollars an acre for the land. I am going to buy that property."

Now Maria was disturbed for the first time, and Heinrich was speechless, looking at his son with his mouth dropping open idiotically.

"And," said Edward, inexorably, "we are going to think about building on it. Perhaps not this year or next, or even in the next five years. But we are going to have a decent home, an estate."

For an instant Maria thought of her family's *schloss*, and she was struck with nostalgia. Then she said, "On the profits of the shops, I assume."

"No. That would be impossible, then, for a long time. I am going to invest in some of the stocks and bonds Herr Enreich has suggested. I am going to put my own profits into them. A man cannot get rich merely by working. And I am going to be rich."

"Stocks? Bombs?" exclaimed Heinrich, with the despair of one confronting a madman. Horror distended his eyes. "Do you mean, Eddie, WALL STREET? That bloated organisation of wicked men?"

Edward looked at him in contempt. "Socialism, again. Accursed industry, again. Haven't you ever learned what the Industrial Revolution has done for what you call the masses, and what it will continue to do as it expands? The masses have only just begun to prosper in this country, and you can talk all you want about exploitation and long hours and low wages. They'll go, too. It's in the nature of things. And I am going to buy those stocks and bonds with every penny I have left for myself."

Maria listened with deep interest. She did not share her

husband's fetish about Socialism. Her eyes softened with a dreaming expression. She did not like, in particular, those whom her husband called " the masses." In fact, she did not believe in their actual existence. America was in a state of flux, the " classes " constantly changing. " Let us have no foolish discussion about what does not exist. Wall Street is merely a trading place, a market place. I have no doubt that shrewd men can profit there, though I know so little about it. However, if Herr Enreich is committed there, then it cannot be a stupid thing to do."

Though he had been steadily losing to Edward over the past few years, Heinrich stubbornly tried again to exert his authority over this granite-eyed young man. " I cannot permit the gambling, the Wall Street gambling, over the lives and souls of oppressed humanity," he said, raising his voice futilely, as a wave lifts against a cliff. His throat trembled; he clenched his small fists on the arms of his chair. " And I shall give long consideration, my Eddie, to your other proposals. I cannot guarantee," he added, shaking his head, " that I will accede."

" Certainly, you will," said Maria. " You have no other choice, my husband. Let us not be absurd. As for the stocks and bonds, Edward is to be the judge about his own money."

Edward was not grateful to his mother for her practicality. He thought, with cynicism, She always knows where her own advantage lies. As for Pa, I don't have to consider him. All I need to do is to show him the bank-books, and stop him from trying to reduce the clerks' wages and get more than a decent amount of work out of them.

Edward, with more than a youth's arrogance, and more than a youth's ardent and uncompromising simplicity, did not understand that men are often more, or less, than they seemed, and that they had a secret and powerful existence of their own, locked in the yellowish cell of their skulls, and in the dark corridors of their hearts. He was not even sure of these things in himself. He thought of himself only as a driving force, single-minded and uncomplex.

He was getting ready for bed when his mother, puffing from her ascent up the attic stairs, knocked on his door. He admitted her grudgingly, and she sat down, without invitation, and fanned herself with her handkerchief. Edward snapped off his tie, ignoring her, though he wondered why she had come. He could feel her eyes on his back, and finally, as he unbuttoned his shirt, he was irritated and uneasy. "Well?" he demanded. "What more is there to say?"

Maria fanned herself. "Much. But I am wondering how to say it. No." And she lifted her hand. "Do not frown, my son. I am not here to discuss the conversation of this evening. I should like to talk with you about your brothers and sister."

"Don't you think I can get tired of the subject?" he suddenly shouted, in English. "What more do you want of me, than what I'm doing?"

Maria folded her damp handkerchief neatly and put it into her sleeve before replying. Then she fixed her pale blue eyes on her son's. She saw that Edward's eyes seemed full of sparkling steel fragments. She began to speak, slowly. "I have had some experience in the world: I have not lived a cloistered life. When I say my children are—talented—it is not vanity which makes me say so. It is a fact. I am only wondering if we could possibly have misunderstood something. It is very possible that they are talented in another direction."

"What!" exclaimed Edward wrathfully. He clenched his fists at his side. "What are you talking about? Isn't Dave a musician? Isn't Sylvia gifted in the theatre arts? Isn't Gregory a writer? Isn't Ralph an artist?"

Then, even Maria was amazed, for she saw stark terror on Edward's face, and a powerful rage. What is my son afraid of? she asked herself. What does he fear to lose? For, surely, he is frightened that he is about to lose something. She shook her head, dismayed. It would be impossible to explain to a frantic man so he could understand and be reasonable. How could she say, "My children are showing a puny mastery of what they are doing. They are desperately unhappy; I see this, now. Out of mercy, let us discover what it is they are really fitted for, so they will not hate you, and in their hatred try to destroy you. It is you, my Edward, who occupy my thoughts. Your life is dedicated to the less strong, yes; but still, there is your life. Even the strong should live, and not only for the weak. I must beg your forgiveness; in your childhood I did not lift a voice to prevent your exploitation, for adjustment's sake; there is the coward's way, the bloodless way, the way of the feeble. But there are inevitabilities, few but inexorable, which we must accept. Let us explore, now, for your sake, what your brothers and sister need, and where their greater talents lie. After all, art goes through phases, until it finally is crystallised into its final form."

But that, she considered, would make Edward's past life meaningless to him, and one does not destroy a man's past without destroying a vital part of him, perhaps for ever, perhaps even crippling his future.

But, then the others must be sacrificed to some extent. Maria sighed with despair. This was an inevitability which she herself, must face. Her face became stern. She prayed inwardly that her other children would find their own way, at least, out of the iron mould of Edward's conviction—and grim determination. There were so many things which one could not say.

She stood up. "You are right, Edward," she said. "I had only thought that perhaps your brothers and sister might develop talents—in addition—in addition to what they have."

"You can't scatter yourself," said Edward, angrily, but the terror subsided on his face, leaving it with an ebbed and relieved expression. "No," said Maria, turning to the door. "You can't scatter yourself, my son."

"And they are geniuses," Edward called after her, and there was power in his voice. "They had better be!"

Edward and William Montgomery Percival Chauncey McFadden were alone in the glistening and glittering shop. Heinrich had felt "unwell" to-day, he had piteously pleaded that morning. He had stayed home, to recover from the "shock." The clerks scuttled home to their suppers; they would not be needed to-night, for the shop now closed on Wednesdays at six.

The spring evening was still light, a study in luminous greys. Even the houses opposite were washed with that mute warmth. Through alleys the western sky could be seen—quiet as thought. Few people passed the lighted shop, and these few walked as if musing. Far in the distance a trolley clanged and rang its bell, but it only increased the evening silence. For some reason this air of expectant contemplation, this gentle call for creative communion, only depressed Edward.

He looked at William irritably. "Don't polish that nickel too much," he said. "You'll rub off the plate."

William, clad in a striped pink shirt which was pushed up to the elbows, and with the neckband unfastened about his lean, fox-like throat, rubbed his hands on his long white apron. He turned with a smile, and an inclination of his head. "Always did like things neat, laddie," he murmured. "By the way, did you tell your Dadda I'm on the employed list?"

"Yes," said Edward, and his depression lifted a little as he grinned. "He nearly had a seizure. I had to promise to pay your wages out of my own pocket, until we move into my own store. I gave him that concession. After all . . ." And he paused.

William nodded, as if all was explained, and in fact it had been explained to him by intuition. "You can sleep downstairs until you get your first pay, or you can get an advance from me and find a room of your own at once," said Edward.

"I'd prefer to save my first few wages," said William, loftily. "I have reached the age of discretion. I will provide for my elderly years. I will become a solid citizen. I will consider concerts again. You have concerts in this benighted town, don't you?" He looked at Edward with the eager expectancy of the animal he so resembled.

Edward laughed. "We have band concerts in the park on Sundays, in the summer. Fine banging, smashing, thundering Wagner, mostly, and Sousa. The Star Spangled Banner. And waltzes. Of course, no one can dance on Sunday."

William shuddered. "Victoria!" he exclaimed. "You should visit the Continent very soon and learn how the civilised half lives. Or, perhaps, Catholic Canada. 'The Sabbath was made for man, not man for the Sabbath,'" he piously quoted. He leaned against a counter dreamily, and crossed his neat ankles. "How well I remember Paris Sunday evenings, in the spring! I've frolicked there, boyo. Even Berlin is gay then. And Vienna! A man hasn't lived until he has spent a spring in Vienna. But London! If there is a hell, surely it is London on Sunday. I was once a Sunday school teacher. I can quote Scripture with the facility of the Devil, though why he should, when there is much more engaging literature, I don't know."

"The Bible has some pretty spicy stuff in it," said Edward. "At least, I remember some of it when I was a kid."

"But no finesse! A sinewy, masculine, brutal sort of 'spicy stuff,' as you say. No subtlety. No titillation. No awakening of ardour, of curiosity. Here is the bed, here is the whore, here is the pit, says the Bible. No details, if you gather what I mean. It would deter a man, and not arouse him, and I fancy that's the whole idea, though I imagine the old boys licked their lips when writing all about it."

"Sin isn't supposed to be gay," said Edward, smiling. He jingled his keys. William was a whole new source of education to him, and though he attempted to be incredulous he was not. The store felt suddenly cold.

"I'm tired. I'm an hour late."

"No doubt for the spare ribs and *sauerkraut*."

"My mother's cooking is the best of German cooking, and she also, sometimes, uses French recipes," said Edward, irritated. "She was a Von Brunner. What about the shops?"

"The new shop, where I'll be manager later, I assume," said William, calmly. "'Fine Food Shops.' What a brilliant name. You need elegance. A flair. A polish. Some name with sophistication. I have a suggestion. Shall we call it—let me see—something with initials, too. C. C. Chauncey's. That's the ticket! You will gather I am offering, modestly, the use of my name. Have you heard of S. S. Pierce's in Boston? A name that sticks. Unusual. Simple, yet not so simple. C. C. Chauncey's. What could be better?"

"People will laugh. They'll know who it is all the time." But Edward was intrigued.

"People never laugh at pretentiousness. They adore it. They only laugh at humility and simplicity, and why not? That is all they deserve, for they are a sort of affection in themselves. C. C. Chauncey's." He rolled the name deliciously on his tongue. "And, you must import the best wines, and put your own labels on it."

He scratched his chin, and his lean tongue rubbed the corner of his mouth. His expression grew brighter and brighter. "Aha," he said, triumphantly. "There's this new slogan: 'It pays to advertise.' Excellent. Do we remain snobbish delicatessens for a few, or do we reach for the sky. I have another man for you."

Edward forgot his dinner again. He picked up a fragment of ham and chewed it. "Go on," he said. "Who's the man? One of your fellow tramps?"

William looked hurt. "What is a tramp? A man who refuses to obey the mores of marrying, dancing off to a shack, and breeding a brood of brats. On three quid a week, if he's lucky. An individualist, the tramp. A free man. A man choicy about what he will do. The chap I am speaking of is Padraig Devoe. Not Paddy, mind. Padraig. There's not a man living who would dare to call him Paddy. He is not a man who can be bought, like any churl. I must send the word along the bally railroad chaps, and when I can reach him I will try to persuade him."

"I hope he'll condescend," said Edward, "after he's eaten his mulligan."

"It doesn't pay to be patronising, laddie. Curious chap, Padraig. He and I were on a commercial fishing boat, out of Jamaica—a hot, hellish place in the summer. We were down to our last few bob, and a man must earn a living sometime."

William swung himself up lightly to sit on a counter. He lit another cigarette, and his face was intent with remembrance. "It was very fine, to fish, to throw the nets, in spite of the blasted, everlasting sun that seared the hide. It was not sport; it was serious business. Man must eat. Still, a man's heart must misgive him to watch the poor creatures struggling, the big fish glittering like gold and silver as they throw themselves in the air and try to live and escape. It is not too bad, if one doesn't look into their eyes. It was very bad for Padraig, for like all philosophers he detests mankind and has the tenderest heart for the innocent ones. 'Don't look at their eyes, Padraig,' I would say. 'We have three bob left.' You see, boyo, I knew Padraig."

"How did you get all the way to Jamaica?" asked Edward.

"That is a long story, in more ways than one, and I will not bore you with it. That Montego Bay! Beautiful, but evil.

"Well, and now. Up come the diver chappies with the conchies, big shells with the sand and the water running off them. 'And what would they be, and what is it you would be doing?' asks Padraig. 'He sells 'em to the lady trippers and to the market,' says a Sassenach. A Sassenach always sells anything. These were no darkie divers. The darkies have more intelligence than gallivanting around sharks.

"So they get out their buckets and their scrubbing brushes and kneel on the deck, dripping the water off them and shaking it out of their hair. And they take a spike and hammer it through the turrets of the conchies, to kill them, or loosen them. Stubborn, poor creatures, trying to hide in their turrets, dark, liver-coloured creatures, shrinking from the death and no one to pray for them or ask their pardon.

"Padraig, now, is a still man, and that is enough to make a man a stranger in a shouting world. But never have I seen him so still. There were ten shells. A diver hammers away, and then he reaches in the turret, and he drags out the conchie, a big poor soul about sixteen inches long, all liver-spots and white patches and helpless head. It was then that Padraig gives a start, like a convulsion. He turns away his eyes as the conchie is plopped into the bucket to die. One of the divers said sometimes it takes a full twenty-four hours for them to die, in agony, and who is there to care?

"Then Padraig drops on his knees and stares at the waiting shells, and leans over them. The divers begin to laugh, for it is that Padraig is protecting them with his long body, and his clothing patched like the bodies of the conchies, themselves, whitish and black. I can see it as clear as if it is happening now. Padraig had thick black hair, all bristles, on that narrow head of his, and that sinister copper light from the sun lit up the ends like fire. He has a suffering face, by nature, but now it was all anguish.

"And then a conchie looks out from his turret, and the heart in me flopped like a fish, itself. A grey, leatherish head, with big, wrinkled, leatherish eyes, in grey folds. And it looks straight at Padraig, and damn it! You could feel they were talking to each other, and you could feel the fear of the conchie, and the pleading. He had come to the right man," added William ruefully.

Edward, listening, could see the dark and flowing ocean, the broken path of the dropping sun, the depths of the burning sky, the distant glimpse of palms rising above the waters. He could hear the hot silence, the murmur of waves against the boat. But most of all he could see the tragic figure of Padraig, thin almost to death, and his tragic face, and the baffled crew and divers.

William sighed. "He looks at the conchie and the conchie looks at him, and it was like big brother and little brother, and he says, 'How much for the whole damned lot?' And the divers laugh and stamp their wet legs, and Padraig repeats himself in that muted voice of his, like a harp murmuring to itself. 'A pound will do it, Irish,' one of them says. 'Setting up business?'

"And there kneels Padraig on his hands and knees over the conchies and their shells, and I know there isn't a pound between us. Is Padraig going to fight for the conchies? Never a man was born who could best Padraig in a fair fight, though he looks like a lath. But Padraig is a just man. The conch shells are the divers' way of making a living, and it is a Sassenach's ill fortune that he has no heart. Then Padraig heaves a huge breath, and without looking up he pulls a ring from his finger, all that he has in the world, a big gold ring with a ruby set in it, and never did he tell me who gave it to him.

"'This is worth a hundred pounds or more,' he says. 'Take it for the poor creatures.'

"They pounce on the ring, slavering. And while they're shouting how much they can sell it for Padraig picks up the conchies, one by one, and drops them back into the sea. He's got just three left when the divers come to themselves, and they screech. But Padraig throws the conchies into their waters, and wipes off his hands and stands up, and by the Blessed Mother, if he isn't smiling, and full of peace, like a man who's just taken Holy Communion.

"You should have seen the gaping divers, Eddie. Big eyes and falling mouths. It's a madman they've been dealing with, they are thinking. And they run off and tell the captain. And the captain gives us both the sack, on the spot. And we with three bob in Jamaica."

William looked at Edward, who was trying to smile. Edward said, "I think I can understand why he did it. But still, he's impractical. How did you get away from Jamaica?"

"We worked in the sugar-canes for over three accursed months, and then we shipped out." William slipped off the counter and the telephone rang angrily. "It's only Pa," said Edward, in bemusement, and answered the telephone impatiently. He said, over his shoulder, "I suppose Padraig never thought that the divers would probably pick up the same conchies the next day."

"What was that to him, then? They had another lease on their lives. And he's spaced them, in deeper waters. If they crawled home, it would take them some time. And, if there is a God, it is possible that He would remember Padraig's ring, which even when we were starving he would not sell, but cherished it with love, and He would protect the conchies for Padraig's sake. A man does not give his heart, and God not knowing."

Edward picked up his coat, and his face was dark and brooding. William watched him keenly. Then Edward was staring at the clean and empty counters. "What makes you think he'd make a good man, William?"

"There are very few things, or people, in which Padraig believes. I think, Eddie, that he will believe in you. And when Padraig believes, God or man cannot stop him. He has a way with him, and an eloquence, when he wills, that can move stones."

Edward glanced up quickly, and he could not understand William's shrewd but compassionate smile.

"Aye, laddie, he will believe in you." He will, it is possible, be your conscience, William added to himself.

PART TWO

"It is difficult for power to avoid despotism."
GASPARIN

Chapter One

Mrs. William McNulty, the internationally famous American actress, "never moved," as she put it, unless she "first consulted the stars." To sceptics, she would recall Montaigne's aphorism that a leaf on this planet cannot move without disturbing the most distant galaxies in their august courses.

The stars were unpropitious about her new tour, but ambiguously so. She had been a widow for five years, and the astrologer had hinted that she would meet "a dark and taciturn stranger of great tragedy, male." Almost puritanical in her private life, she had not comforted herself since Mr. McNulty's death in the conventional stage fashion, and as love to her meant marriage—with one at least as wealthy as herself, she would think, prudently—she was stirred by the astrologer's mysterious message. Men of tragedy, she had discovered, were usually men who could afford to be tragic. Gentlemen who worked hard for a living were necessarily cheerful, or, at least, they had no time to indulge themselves.

The tour, this early March of 1914, did not appeal to her particularly. She had just closed her latest play, *A Woman of Morality*, in New York. They play was a bad one, but had been saved triumphantly by her superb and majestically emotional acting. She had managed to keep the play alive, and prosperous, for four months. When diminishing returns had set in, she had immediately closed it, for she was a partner.

She had been invited to appear, solo, in Buffalo, Detroit and Chicago, for she had her own repertoire apart from large plays. As a woman who never spurned a dollar, and as she was not to appear in London until June, and as she hated idleness, she had accepted the offer, after doubling the amount of the original offers.

Mrs. William McNulty was thirty-eight years old. She was

advertised as thirty-two. She was a "fine figure of a woman," buxom, tall, commanding, theatrical in appearance and manner, and was thoroughly "black Irish," with a mass of hair as black as Satan, blue eyes as intense as an autumn sky, and a skin as white as foam. Her friend, Mary Garrity, alias Mme. DelaFontaine, had increased the drama of Maggie's appearance by designing for her dresses and gowns and coats of the utmost grace, and in a classic manner. Mary detested lavishness, in a very lavish age. "I'm not austere," she would say, coldly. "I'm just against vulgarity. The present styles are really vulgar, you know. It is not a matter of being puritanical. It is a matter of the woman setting off the clothes. I never design a dress for an average personality. What is there to display? If a woman has character and distinction, classic clothing will enhance them. If a woman has nothing, then she is nothing but a hanger, and I refuse to design clothes for her and have my efforts made into dowdy caricatures or dummies."

Mary Garrity, alias Mme. Honora DelaFontaine, was petite, vivid, acrimonious, and full of humour. She had finished with her spring showing in New York. On invitation, she had decided to accompany Mrs. McNulty on this dubious tour. "One never knows where one will get ideas," she had said. Moreover, Mrs. McNulty had offered to pay all expenses. Moreover, Mme. DelaFontaine would be conspicuously mentioned on the programmes as New York's "foremost Designer and Modiste." It never hurt to consider future markets, even among "the barbarians" across the Hudson. The fact that Mary Garrity had just invested in a pioneering firm which promised mass production on "original models" had nothing to do with the case, of course, even though the "original models" had been designed by Mary Garrity.

There were no secrets between these two devoted friends. Their conversation together was secretive, hilarious, and sometimes lewd. They had no other confidantes. They were also fond of whisky, though each pretended, to others, that sherry was a "ladies' drink." In short, they were women full of the lust for life, vital and eager, and ever ready for new experiences.

So, on an early March day in 1914, these robust two set out on the tour, leaving New York on a dank morning adrift with fog and wind. They were accompanied only by Mrs.

McNulty's maid and manager, two meek people who shared a Pullman seat in the coach that carried the actress's drawing-room. Maggie and Mary, after a brief shudder at the weather, opened a golden bottle and prepared to exchange confidences, scandal and laughter. " I don't know why I'm going with you, Maggie," said Mary, as she dashed the pungent liquor into a glass and disdained offered water.

" Except you want a little publicity, yourself," said Maggie McNulty, with a glass at her own lips. " My God! Look, it's snowing. And do I remember the snows! Listen to that wind."

" Pull your sables over your shoulders," said Mary. " I always said there's nothing better than Irish whisky. I hope our trunks got aboard safely."

Maggie rubbed the steamed window with a froth of real lace, and peered through the glass, at which the wind and the snow pounded furiously. " We've stopped at some station, I think," she said. " But I can't see any sign." She rang the bell for the porter, who came in almost immediately. " Where are we?" she demanded, imperiously. " What are we stopping for? I thought our next stop was Buffalo."

But the conductor pushed the porter aside, and looked at the two ladies with worried anxiety. " I'm sorry, but the train is stalled, ma'am," he said to Maggie, who appeared to him to be the most imposing woman in the drawing-room, and therefore in command. " At Waterford. We can't go on until to-morrow, if then. We are going on a side-track, and I'm afraid you ladies will have to spend a day or two in Waterford."

" In WHERE?" boomed Mary, incredulously.

" The man says Waterford," said Maggie. " I've heard of it."

The conductor saw the nearly empty bottle of whisky and his Yankee face became remote. No wonder that little woman there had such a voice, like a man's. Whisky voice ; her cords must all be cobbled. She was glaring at him in outrage. " Two good hotels in Waterford," he said, stiffly, and replaced his cap. Women who drank were no ladies and it wasn't necessary for a man to remove his hat for them. " The Whitney House's the best. We're in the station now, and you can get a hack. See them standing out there now, waiting."

Maggie sighed with resignation. " Nothing for it but to gather ourselves up, call Eloise and the jackass who calls himself my manager, or something," she said. Her voice, the conductor heard approvingly, was both sonorous and velvety. A lady's voice. The little woman was probably her maid.

" I'm not going to leave this damned train," said Mary, positively, pulling her own sables over her neat little shoulders. " Why it's death out there. Waterford! Where in hell is *that*?"

" You'll stay couple of days in here then," said the conductor, with happy gloom. " Better hurry, ladies, or the hacks'll all be gone, and then you'll have to walk three miles." His lanky face glowed at the prospect.

" Let's go. Don't be a fool, Mary," said Maggie, rising, and in so doing inadvertently upsetting the bottle of whisky on the floor. The compartment was immediately flooded with the fumes of alcohol. Maggie went to the door and shouted, " Eloise! Harry! Come on in here!" The conductor retreated.

" But your engagements!" said Mary.

" It stands to reason I can't walk to them," replied her friend. " We'll send telegrams. People in Buffalo understand about snows, and there won't be any hysteria if I'm a day or two late. Not like New York."

" Maggie McNulty and DelaFontaine holed up at the end of the world," protested Mary. She stood up, chic in her black broadcloth suit and white lace shirt-waist and small black sailor hat of the finest beaver. Beside her, in crimson velvet and lace, with a wide crimson velvet hat, Maggie towered like a rather lush goddess. She swung her sable cape expertly over her round and well-nourished shoulders as her maid and manager came rushing in, aghast at what they had just heard from the porter. " Don't look like carp," said Maggie, annoyed. " Perhaps you'd both like to take shovels and clear off the tracks in front of the train. Gather things up, Eloise. Where're my gloves?"

The two ladies emerged into the coach, and Maggie, looking for her gloves up her sleeve, where she usually kept them, dropped her purse. It was immediately picked up by a man even taller than herself, who returned the article to her with a slight and formal bow. " Thank you," she said, and then looked at him again.

"A dark and taciturn stranger of great tragedy, male."

He had not spoken, he had not even smiled at her, and he certainly had a tragic face, all sombre lean angles and muted handsomeness and still grave eyes, black as faintly gleaming coal. He was narrow and almost fleshless under his excellently tailored clothing, Maggie saw at a glance. His thick black hair was cut shorter than the fashion, and he had fine ears, seemingly without blood, so pale they were. Even his mouth, wide and stern, had no colour. A wave of excitement ran over Maggie.

"Thank you," she repeated. (He could not be over forty.) "I am Mrs. William McNulty——"

"I know, Mrs. McNulty," he replied, and his voice was so gentle and yet so resonant that Maggie was thrilled to the heart. "My name is Padraig Devoe."

Little Mary was peering at them inquisitively, and then when they did not appear to know that she was present, she discreetly pinched her friend on a vulnerable and highly improper spot. "Ouch," said Maggie, absentmindedly. "Oh, Mary. Mary, this is Mr. Padraig Devoe. Mr. Devoe, my friend, the famous modiste, Mme. DelaFontaine."

Padraig bowed again, but he looked at Maggie. "I've had the pleasure of seeing you several times on the stage, Mrs. McNulty," he said, and Maggie felt as young as a girl. Her fair cheeks coloured entrancingly, and her blue eyes deepened in colour. "How kind," she said, and her voice trembled. She caught her breath, as Padraig half-turned away to leave her. "Oh, Mr. Devoe. Isn't this terrible to be stalled here in Waterford?"

"It isn't so bad for me," he said. "I am stopping at Waterford for a few days or a week."

A drummer? Maggie's heart sank, then rose resolutely. What did it matter if he only sold soap? She forgot all her discretion.

"One of your businesses?" she asked, eagerly. Surely, he must be someone important, noticing his clothing again, his hand-made boots, his English gloves, his broadcloth coat with the French velvet collar.

"I am the advertising manager of C. C. Chauncey's," he replied, and seemed reluctantly pleased at being detained.

Maggie's eyes became big with delight. "C. C. Chauncey's!" she cried, ecstatically. "Who doesn't know them in

New York and Boston and Chicago and Philadelphia! Mary! C. C. Chauncey's!" she almost sang, turning to Mary, who displayed great interest and pleasure. "Why, the original shop is right here in Waterford, isn't it, Mr. Devoe?"

He smiled faintly, and inclined his head. "I should have remembered," Maggie breathed. "I've heard that dozens of times."

"Yes," said Padraig. He had forgotten that a woman could be so beautiful. He had never really looked at a woman, since Norah had been killed by his horse, and she only seventeen. Little Norah Bellamy, with the dark blue eyes and golden hair and a smile like the sun, itself.

"Aren't you Irish?" blurted Maggie, desperate to keep him. The coach was emptying rapidly of its disgruntled passengers. "I am, too. And so is Mary—Mary Garrity." She looked down at Mary, and was annoyed, unreasonably, by her friend's trim and immaculate appearance. Her own crimson velvet was sprinkled with cigarette ash, as usual, and she was conscious of her size and the wrinkles in her clothing, as she had never been conscious before. If only she had had the sense to leave Mary in New York, as her astrologer had hinted darkly. What had the astrologer said? "The journey you are about to take will have its unpleasant aspects." Mme. DelaFontaine, at this moment, seemed to Maggie to appear to be a most unpleasant aspect, and definitely a nuisance and a drag.

"Yes, I am," said Padraig. He hesitated. He never involved himself with people, but another look into Maggie's intensely blue eyes undid him, and the sensation brought back a pang of anguished memory. "May I help you ladies to a hack? They seem to be disappearing very fast out there."

"We'll need two," said Maggie, suddenly remembering Eloise and Harry. She turned to Mary, who shook her head in silent negation. Maggie's hope that Mary could be induced to ride to the hotel with the maid and the manager, leaving her, Maggie, to ride alone with Mr. Devoe, disappeared dismally. The unpleasant aspect of Mary was becoming clearer every moment. Then Mary relented at the speechless plea on her friend's face, and, remembering her role, she gave a Latin shrug. "We're going to a place called the Whitney House," she said to Padraig. "I'll go along with

Eloise and Harry, Maggie. If Mr. Devoe can get us two hacks." Good heavens, was Maggie, the distant and virtuous, going to get herself entangled with a perfect stranger, who wore such a shadowy air of impenetrable sadness? He probably had a wife who was a perfect horror, blowsy, and without an ounce of taste, and a dozen brats besides.

"I hope we won't be taking you out of your way—home," said Mary, the loyal and loving, with immense tact. "Perhaps Mrs. Devoe will wonder what's delaying you."

Maggie's mouth opened soundlessly. She had never considered a wife. Her heart beat with sudden rapidity, as she waited for Padraig to speak. He said, quietly, "It happens that I am staying at the Whitney House, myself." He paused. He did not know what made him add, "And there's no Mrs. Devoe." He rarely made gratuitous remarks except when doing business.

Maggie shut her eyes quickly and passionately, and when she opened them again they were the colour of Irish skies in the spring, moist and with a violet overcast on the blueness. She put her fingers, long, white, plump, on Padraig's thin arm, and said, gaily, "Oh, let us go, let us go!" And her lovely voice was a song.

"I wouldn't go out even if St. Michael called me, in person, not in this damned snow and wind," said Mary, later. "What a night, what a town! And you accepting an invitation to see some amateur two-cent show put on by yokels! You, Mrs. William McNulty! Are you out of your mind, Maggie? Why can't you stay in this drummer's dream of a hotel, where it's at least warm?" She looked about her at the tiny "suite" which was the best the hotel afforded. It had a brown rug, brown velvet draperies at the tall and slit-like windows, brown plush furniture, and two depressing marble-topped tables. The brown and yellow walls boasted gas-lights, which offended Mary more than anything else. "Not even electricity. And going out with a man you practically picked up on the train. He didn't even have the manners to invite you to dinner first."

"He's the reserved kind," said Maggie. She glowed. She appeared even more incandescent than in her best roles. She shines all over, thought Mary, with disquiet. "Besides," said

Maggie, "he's having dinner with his employer and his family. And his employer's sister, Padraig says, is putting on the show. Why, it's one of my old ones, and I get a royalty on it! What he hell is the name of it? Yes, *Lady in Waiting*."

"It stank. Highly," said Mary. "Not one of your best inspirations, Maggie, darling."

Maggie shrugged. "Oh, that was eighteen years ago. Don't belittle, Mary. What's the man's name? Yes. Enger. Where did he get the Chauncey? It doesn't matter. They're rich as dirt. I understand Mr. Enger subsidises his sister's shows. You know," Maggie added, happily, "the girl may have talent."

"Don't get involved, dearie," said the discouraging Mary.

"I believe in encouraging young talent," said Maggie, with a superb gesture.

"That's not what I mean," answered Mary, darkly.

She suddenly resolved to go with Maggie. After all, the man had thrown the invitation casually to the both of them, not Maggie alone. And Maggie, in this dithering state, so very apparent, and so unique, could not be trusted with this man. He was such a strange person, and Mary, who had a very compelling imagination, could see her friend lying strangled, somewhere, in the snow, probably not to be found until summer, if it ever got to be summer here.

Mary stood up. "If you insist upon going, and making a fine high fool of yourself, Mary Regan McNulty, then I'm going, too," she said. "As your guardian."

Chapter Two

"I just can't believe that Mrs. William McNulty—the Mrs. William McNulty, is actually coming to our Little Theatre to-night," said twenty-three-year-old Sylvia Enger. Her spare white face, so angular, and so distinguished, almost softened with pleasure. It softened even more, it almost gleamed, when she turned it to Padraig Devoe across the rich damask of the tablecloth. Her intensely black eyes dimmed moistly in the candlelight. A pulse beat in her long white throat, and her pale lips trembled. He was smiling at her, that infrequent smile which could so charm, and her heart leapt.

"These stage people will do anything for publicity," said Edward, twenty-five years old. "Didn't her manager, or agent, or something, call up the newspapers to-night? There'll be headlines to-morrow, and that's what she wants. I never heard of her before." This was not true. He had seen her three times, in New York, and had admired her immensely. He had always sat in the first row and when he had caught the brilliant blue flash of her eyes in the lights something had stirred in him, like a quick current under ice, disturbing and moving. Somewhere, he had seen eyes like hers, large and radiant, but he could not remember. The blueness was so all-pervading that it seemed to tint the very whites, themselves, and fill the eye-sockets with enchanting colour.

"Don't be disagreeable, as usual," said Sylvia, bitterly. "What kind of publicity can she get in Waterford? This horrible city. What would it mean to an actress as famous as she is? You have no sense of proportion, Ed."

"You could be in New York, if you wanted to," said Edward, and his grey eyes were like stone. "But no. You preferred to stay in this 'horrible city,' though you never exactly explained why."

"I did. New York's full of stage producers. I'm no dilettante," said Sylvia, her voice growing more bitter. She could never tell him, though now she knew beyond self-deception, that she had no inspiration, no feeling for the stage at all. She could not even admit it, freely, to herself. She had attended many plays in New York, and had understood her own inadequacy. Too, there had been those two years she had spent in New York, studying, and her teachers' verdict, given privately to her, out of pity, and not to her brother.

"I was willing to—what do they call it?—angle a play for you," said Edward.

Sylvia drew a deep breath. She was terrified that he would guess. She threw up her small head, crowned with its Grecian coronet of glassy black braids. She was terrified that she might be forced, one awful day, to confess what she had not thoroughly confessed to herself. That would be the end of her pride. She needed to hate her brother in order to survive, herself. She had nothing else now but her deception, nothing in the world.

"You've never thought," she said, in a patient voice, "that the theatre isn't confined to New York. We do good plays here. People come for miles around. I think it's my duty to stay here, considering that not even third-rate stock from New York ever patronises this place. Our Little Theatre is the only centre of culture in Waterford."

Padraig watched her, from under his short thick lashes. He was full of pity for Sylvia. It was his compassion for all that lived that kept him apart from people, a compassion that was partly composed of a silent anger. Mankind was stupid, and there was no excuse for stupidity, for mankind possessed reason, and its stupidity was an obstinate determination to be blind. The "lesser animals" were different. They had innocence, because they had no reason, and only their instincts.

"And Ralph, when he's home, does an excellent job painting the sets," Sylvia added.

Edward frowned at the mention of his brother's name. Ralph was in Paris now, studying under the best masters in the art of portraiture. But he was costing a devil of a lot of money, far beyond his tuition, far more than a young man of nineteen should spend even in Paris. One of these days I'll go over there and see for myself, Edward thought. But he knew he would not. He did not often leave Waterford, and then only on business, and he did not know why he felt this reluctance. Waterford had become his cocoon, which he had spun about himself as if in protection.

There were only these three at dinner to-night, Sylvia, Edward and Padraig. Heinrich, who disapproved of "the late dinners," had his meal with Maria in his own suite in this fine new mansion, just completed eight weeks ago. He was also "unwell." More and more, as time passed, his periods of indisposition increased. There seemed to be some unknowable spiritual sickness in him, and during the past few years an unconfessed but total estrangement had developed between him and Edward. On many occasions poor Heinrich, in anxious despair, had tried to cross that abysmal crevice to his son, but Edward retreated more and more. He was the considerate son, kind and thoughtful. But he was a stranger. He stood alone. Once Maria had said to her husband,

" Edward always stood alone. It was your illusion, Heinrich, though never mine, that he was ever close to you or to anybody."

" You are wrong, Maria! When he was a child, he was as close as my own flesh. He was my only companion."

Maria had studied him thoughtfully. And then in a tone of unusual gentleness she had said, " He was a child. Now he is a man."

The years had gone like months, to Maria, who accepted everything calmly and with Teutonic fatality. David was " on tour," for the past eighteen months, after his studies in Paris under a famous maestro. No one but Edward knew that the agent who " handled " him did not receive large fees for David's appearances in the smaller cities and towns. It was Edward who, through the agent, had added an equal amount to the mediocre fees. The agent was happy. He collected his ten per cent on the bolstered fees, and it remained a secret between him and Edward. He had told Edward, in the very beginning, with careful tact, that it would be some years before David would actually be in what he called " the big time," such as Carnegie Hall and appearances before " important " audiences in Chicago and Philadelphia and Boston and San Francisco. Edward, during this private interview, had said nothing, but had kept his eyes fixed in a most disturbing way on the agent's bland face. " An artist must creep before he walks, and walk before he can run," the agent had said. " David must build up a reputation in the smaller places. But one of these days——! "

But Edward had thought, with hatred and anger like metal in his mouth: David has wasted himself, both in New York and Paris. He had not been dedicated; his chronic attitude was one of sullenness. He played brilliantly but without passion. There had been times when Edward, hearing him in some small dank hall in a distant city, had felt a surge of furious pain in himself, and had cried out to his brother in his heart, " Emphasise it there! Lift it there! Soften it there, slow it, increase it! God, don't you have any feeling for it, damn you?"

He was like a man whose whole being urges him to sing, but who is mute. He knew what was missing in David's musicianship. He believed that David knew it also and was too indifferent to try, to care, or, in malice, was deliberately restraining himself. "How are you ever going to be a pianist of importance and fame?" he had asked David once, in a rage. "Don't you care?"

Ask God, David had thought. He was always so tired. His life was a weariness. The only time when he came to life was when he played the music he really loved, in secret, apart from his expensive coach, apart from everybody but himself. When in New York, where he had never been asked to play, he visited the cabarets in which he could listen to the music that delighted him and filled him with fervour and a sense of youth. A few times he had come upon Prince Emory and his Dukes, and had spent many evenings, far in a shadowy background, listening and rejoicing, full of the excitement and passion and emotion so absent in his classical performances.

"You could do a lot with your stupid ragtime," Edward had said. "You could make it 'roll,' somebody said, once. The piano almost jumped off its legs. Deafening. If you could do that with worthless music, if you want to call that music, why can't you do it with something worthwhile?"

David had not answered. His only relief was to be away from Waterford, in the small and insignificant places of meagre audiences, and later he could console himself with his own kind of music. The place of his birth had become intolerable to him. The card Billy Russell had given him had grown yellow and brittle over the years, and he kept it in his wallet, carefully.

Edward was deeply in debt, in spite of his incredibly flourishing shops. On George Enreich's suggestion, over the past few years, he had invested all his spare cash, and what he could borrow, in munitions, steel, mines, woollen mills and sugar. "Why munitions?" he had asked, obscurely afraid and irritated. But George had only laughed at him silently, all his gold teeth shining. The stock had been picked up very cheaply, just after the depression of 1913, but the amount of stock was enormous. It carried a huge margin, also. Then the mansion, built on the eighteen acres of land Edward had bought from his old friend, had cost more than originally expected, though Mr. Enreich had managed to get most of the materials at cost for Edward. There was a large mortgage on the house, and Edward, the prudent, felt that the house would never truly be his unless he owned it free and clear. In the meantime, at George's insistence, he became more and more involved in the stock market.

Edward's brothers and sister were a gigantic drain on his resources. And were they grateful for all his work, all his guidance? They were not. On holidays, at home, here in the resplendent mansion he had built for them, for their enjoyment and pride, they were sullen, irritable, secretive and uncommunicative. His questions about their progress were met with monosyllables, and when he pressed them their eyes would become congested and they would leave him without further words. "If they'd had to work for their education, it might have been better for them," he had once said explosively to William, now the head of his purchasing department.

"Aye, and that it would," William had replied, with a sidewise glance at his employer, an unreadable glance. Edward had paused; he was disturbed with what he believed to be an elliptical intonation in William's voice.

"There is not one thing they are doing that I wouldn't have given half my life to have had the opportunity to do," Edward had said, with deep resentment. "Music, painting, the stage, writing. I felt them all, inside me. But there wasn't time for my own development. I had to work."

He could not understand then, why the almost always merry William had suddenly looked grave, and why his foxy hazel eyes had sparkled so mysteriously on his friend. But William, at last, had only shaken his head and had murmured something about "it's a pity."

"I had no genius. They have. They clamoured to develop their genius, and so I worked, and sacrificed myself. And all they can do is to glower at me when they're home. Contempt for me, and I paying their damned bills!"

The grounds about the mansion had not yet been developed, though many mighty trees were scattered over the eighteen acres. This spring a score of gardeners would place flower beds and gravel walks, plant fruit trees, create arbors. The house stood in the midst of heaps of snow-covered earth; it had been built of greyish-white stone, in the English manner, all chimneys, severe porticoes, small latticed windows, stone steps and white doors. There were twelve bedrooms, each with its big marble bath, and three with private sitting-rooms. The servants' quarters, five rooms, were on the third floor. On the first floor there was what the architect had called

" an informal morning-room," a grand library full of leather furniture and mahogany tables, a dining-room of impressive proportions, a drawing-room of even more impressive proportions, two large kitchens and pantries, and a reception room. There was also a small music room for David.

" There is a saying, an English saying," George Enreich had said, contentedly, " to the effect, my boy wonder, that one should not bite off more than he can chew. It has been my experience that one should bite off more than he can chew, and chew it."

" I've certainly got a mouthful," Edward had replied, apprehensively. " I just hope those damned stocks you recommended to me will pay off. Otherwise, I'll go bankrupt."

" They will pay off," said George. " Be patient. Rome was not, I have heard, built in a day."

" Tell the banks that," Edward had retorted. There were times when he felt that he was walking on a very thin crust over a flood that might break through at any time. Sometimes he thought that he had come too far too fast. His personal life was ascetic. He spent little or nothing on himself. He had but four suits and six pairs of shoes, and only one overcoat, three years old. The income from the shops, though almost unbelievable, was not sufficient to pay all the expenses. Often his nights were sleepless. He was living beyond his immediate income, and this violated all his inborn instincts. It was fine to take chances ; he had taken many chances, audaciously, in his life, but they had been chances backed up by solid probabilities and his own sense of immediate control. Now he was dissipated over numerous enterprises in the stock market. He spent much time going over reports, and scowling at the sluggish stocks he had bought. Up a point, down a point. He could not control the stock market, and what he could not control he distrusted.

Munitions, for God's sake! Who wanted munitions in this peaceful world? Sometimes he hated George Enreich for this stupidity. And George, of course, collected his twenty-five per cent of the profits, with serene regularity. Nothing disturbed George, who was a multi-millionaire. Edward owed him, on personal notes, over seventy thousand dollars. For this infernal house, which no one appreciated but himself, and which no one loved but himself. In believing this, Edward was wrong. His family gloated over the house, but they would not give him the satisfaction of betraying their pride and their arrogant elation.

Edward did not reply to Sylvia's remark, to-night, on the subject of her Little Theatre being the "sole centre of culture in Waterford." His silence was contemptuous. But he was thinking. This Mrs. McNulty, the famous actress—it would not hurt for her to see *Lady in Waiting*. Perhaps she would be able to inspire Sylvia to take the woodenness out of the play. Like David's music, Sylvia's stage direction, choice of amateur talent, and timing, were flawless. It was a silly play, a tragi-comedy, but the exasperating thing about it was that it was never quite tragic and never quite funny. Once Edward had seen the leading lady, a charming girl of nineteen, in tears, and he had asked her the trouble. She had burst out, sobbing, "Oh, Miss Enger insists on restraint, where there shouldn't be any. The second act—why, Mr. Enger, an actress should let herself GO! I've tried it, and almost got thrown out. Miss Enger said it was cheap."

Edward said to his sister, "Padraig's invited her. She might be able to give you some tips——"

"She's too emphatic," protested Sylvia, "even if famous." Her pride smarted. "Too exaggerated, though I suppose that sort of thing goes in New York." She looked at the gold watch pinned to her very chic, very severe, black silk dress. "Heavens! It's almost eight, half an hour to curtain time. I must go, if the sleigh can get through the drifts." She smiled, and her smile was like sudden moonlight on her face as she glanced at Padraig. "It'll be warm under the rugs, though."

Padraig hesitated. "I promised to call for Mrs. McNulty and possibly her friend."

"I intend to go with you," said Edward. "So we'll get out the new Pierce-Arrow which seats seven, with the chauffeur. Ring for him, Sylvia. We'll pick up the ladies."

This was not pleasing to Sylvia, who had pictured herself being alone with Padraig under the fur rugs, as she had never been alone with him before. Her white face tensed, and seeing this, Edward smiled to himself. He, too, had his hopes. He could conceive of nothing more gratifying than a marriage between Sylvia and Padraig, for Padraig was not only a gentleman but his advertising manager, with an impressive salary, and worth every penny of it, too. Padraig was also his, Edward's friend. In this house Padraig appeared less melancholy. Sometimes he breached his withdrawn silences enough to enter into a conversation that was both wise and entertaining, spoken in a very pleasant brogue that, in its lilt, was expressive and musical. He was a man who could be trusted, and if he spoke in a friendly manner, it was with sincerity. Edward knew of no one of his acquaintance like this, not even William or George Enreich. Padraig never "spoke in riddles," as they did, nor was he frequently oblique or mystifying.

Why had Edward decided to come to-night, Sylvia wondered, instead of sitting in his library surrounded by books? He spoiled everything, as usual. He was spiteful and malicious. Angrily, as she pulled her gloves over her slender hands, Sylvia paced the room. She could see her reflection in the many narrow glasses of her dressing-table, and dresser, and pier mirror. She stopped suddenly, and stared at herself again. She never "painted" her face, not only because it was coarse and suspect to do so, but because beyond her clothing she gave little heed to her appearance. Now, her full attention was on her extreme pallor, which, though luminous, suddenly seemed unpleasant to her. She rubbed her wide thin mouth with a handkerchief, and bit her lips. There was no rush of warm blood to them. She thought. She remembered a red silk handkerchief she sometimes used with a black suit, and darted for it in a drawer. She wet a corner, and rubbed it briskly over her mouth. A little delicate colour was immediately imparted to it, and she smiled, showing her perfect teeth. It looked very natural, and she threw up her head in its customary proud arching.

She ran down the broad white staircase with a sense of excitement, her feet hardly touching the dark-red carpet that covered the steps. The baronial hall below was warm and a fire burned in the black marble fireplace. Large black walnut and mahogany chairs, upholstered in crimson and deep-blue velvet, stood near the fire. An immense crystal chandelier, imported from France, swung down from the second story, ablaze with electric candles. Old Pierre, once a teacher at the Waterford School for Girls, was now Edward's butler, receiving twice the customary wages, and he stood in the hall expectantly.

"Where are the gentlemen?" she asked Pierre peremptorily. He was anxiously watching her lips. He bowed gracefully, in spite of his age. "They will be here almost at once, Mademoiselle," he said in his soft voice.

She hated to have her mouth gazed at so intently. Then she was ashamed. She knew her own temperamental rigidity in which she took pride as a rule; it ought not to extend, however, to those afflicted in any sense, or crippled in body. I just can't help it, though, she would think. I demand perfection. She began to pace restlessly up and down the deep-coloured Oriental rug which covered the floor, shifting her hands with impatience in her ermine muff. Surely, Padraig, after all these years, knew that she loved him! And surely, she was not wrong in believing that he was less remote and quiet when he visited this house. Her heart felt hot and choking in her unfashionable small breast, and the palms of her hands sweated with love and longing.

Pierre was watching her discreetly near the cloakroom. In her restlessness, she paced even faster, her frail silk skirts rustling against the slim ankles in their black silk stockings. She kept glancing, in her impatience, at the large and opulent and excellent paintings on the walnut walls. Everything was opulent in this house, huge and dim and muted in an Old World splendour, except for her own room. But she did not really dislike the furnishings; there was something solid and rooted in them, something which gave her a sense of safety, though she affected, in Edward's hearing, to deprecate his taste. Oh, when she and Padraig were married, they would have one of the suites upstairs and they would be so happy! The tautness in her would dissolve away; she would do as she wished. She would go with him on his travels to all those shops, and while he also visited the many stores in the many cities which carried C. C. Chauncey's fine wines and delicacies (all with their distinctive gold, blue and scarlet label) she would visit the fashionable places to see the new styles, she would attend concerts, she would buy. Then, there would be the evenings alone, in expensive hotels and in this house, she and Padraig together, and it would be enough for her, more than all the world enough, just to sit beside him and smile at him as he read.

She wanted to give him all she had, her austerely virginal

soul and body, the sweetness he could arouse in her, the yearning tenderness that often seemed to ignite her cool heart to a conflagration. She had loved him from the moment she had seen him, six years ago; she had not, then seventeen, ever dreamed of being married one day. She had dreamed, since, of being married to Padraig, and he was never out of her mind, even when she slept.

Edward and Padraig entered the hall, Edward smoking one of George Enreich's cigars, Padraig attentive as he listened to his employer's new ideas. They both seemed startled at seeing Sylvia. Can't he dress, even for one evening?" thought Sylvia, scornfully, as she looked at her brother. He was so big and uncouth and bulky, to her, in his worn clothing, his stiff collar, his undistinguished tie. Beside him, Padraig was a British gentleman, moving with grace and ease. Edward's dark hair, which needed barbering, his big shoulders, his heavy legs and arms, his looming height, his broad features and granite-coloured eyes, and even the way he walked, setting his feet down hard, antagonised his sister more than ordinarily. The famous Mrs. McNulty would have nothing but disdain for him, and Sylvia was mortified.

"Oh, there you are," said Edward, without apology for his delay. "Well, Pierre, is the automobile waiting?"

The snow had stopped; the air rang with clarity; the alabaster drifts glimmered and sparkled under a fresh moon. "I don't suppose the theatre will be half-full, after that storm," said Edward.

"Why not?" demanded Sylvia, but her voice was not as acid as usual, for she was sitting between the two men and her arm leaned on Padraig's. The contact made her feel exquisitely happy and content. "We've had worse, and people came. Besides, I shouldn't wonder if the whole town knows that Mrs. McNulty is here——"

"Were they the newspapers you were calling to-night?" asked Edward, in a disagreeably amused voice. "I thought I caught a few words through the door of the library. It's too late for the newspapers, until to-morrow."

Sylvia's face was hot; her eyelids felt touched with flame. Padraig said with unusual quickness, "Mrs. McNulty, as an actress, would be grateful for any publicity. After all, we have news services. Besides, she said she would have to telegraph, and the hotel would pick up the information. I wonder if her friend is coming, too?"

"Her friend?" Sylvia swallowed over the burning lump of rage in her throat.

"Yes. You may have forgotten that I mentioned her," said Padraig. But Sylvia had spoken only in her desperation to change the subject. "I don't think I told you her name, though. It's Mme. DelaFontaine, of New York. At least, Mrs. McNulty explained that's her professional name."

Sylvia forgot her rage in this new wonder. "Mme. DelaFontaine! Why, I read she designs all Mrs. McNulty's clothes! Everything! She's the most famous designer in the whole country, and people who can afford to go to Paris for their gowns and coats and hats go to her!" The limousine was passing a street lamp, and Slyvia's face was lustrous with joy and excitement. Padraig smiled down at her with kind understanding, and then he sighed.

"A dressmaker," said Edward, in an uninflected voice.

"A modiste, a *couturière*!" cried Sylvia. "You've been taking French lessons for years, Ed, and I supposed you'd had a little French culture rubbed off on you or had acquired it through osmosis. I see I was mistaken." She turned her head to Padraig. "Her professional name? Isn't she French?"

Padraig hesitated. If Mary Garrity wanted to reveal her real identity that was her affair. "I'm not sure," he said, quietly. "She's a very interesting woman, though."

Sylvia jealously mulled over his last words. Had they been admiring? But then, Mme. DelaFontaine must be old, very old. She'd been famous for years. When the limousine, which had lumbered majestically through the snow, drew up before the dimly lit entrance to the Whitney House, Sylvia leaned forward avidly. Padraig and Edward left the limousine and went into the lobby. In a few moments they emerged with two ladies, one tall and swathed in sables, with a glittering scarf over her head, and one very small and vivacious. Sylvia recognised Mrs. McNulty, and dismissed her after a brief glance. Handsome, but florid, and entirely too big, bigger than she appeared on the stage. The small woman—and how stylish she seemed even in that brown suit she was wearing and that short sealskin jacket!—had a little impudent face which Sylvia happily designated as monkey-ish. Sylvia was not a girl to like people on sight, or even to like people, but suddenly, without warning, she liked Mary Garrity, and smiled at the flash of striking and animated eyes as Mary said something amusing to Edward. So engrossed with Mary was Sylvia that she missed Maggie's intimate hand on Padraig's arm, and the smile he gave her as he bent his head a trifle.

The two ladies were tucked in beside Sylvia, after the introduction, and the two gentlemen sat on the unfolded seats in front of them. Sylvia had hoped to sit by her secret idol, Mme. DelaFontaine, but Maggie sat in the middle. Her perfume was rich and subtle, and her profile, Sylvia thought disinterestedly and with reluctance, was the profile of a Roman goddess. Her only desire was to discover what gown Maggie was wearing. She had lost interest in her as an actress. Her answers to Maggie's warm and generous questions were brief almost to the point of curtness. What a fascinating face, thought the kind-hearted Maggie. Not beautiful, but distinguished, really extraordinary. And so young, too. But as Sylvia seemed not to wish to talk, Maggie gave her attention to the back of Padraig's head and shoulders. She was truly in love, and, if she knew men at all, he was attracted to her.

Mary, who had no aversion for money, had been duly pleased by the big limousine, the fur rugs and the chauffeur. She had expected to sleep to-night in Buffalo, and here she was in some out-of-the-way little city which could boast of a man with enough money for one of the finest automobiles she had ever seen. She had been much impressed by Edward, a fact which would have astounded Sylvia. A man, she had thought, really a man! The forceful kind, not exactly homespun, and certainly not the yokel she had expected. There was a power in him, steadfast and exigent. Of course, he's at least ten years younger than I am, she thought, wistfully. And to-morrow, she and Maggie would be leaving. Ah, well, ships that pass in the night. . . . She had glanced only briefly at Sylvia. She did not like these intense people, and the girl was not old enough for that intensity. Mary hoped that Sylvia was not going to be tiresome and cling to Maggie, in the hope of acquiring her influence on the stage.

The world was full of these hopeful young people, yearning to leave the hinterland.

" I'm not an actress," said Sylvia, shortly, to Maggie, after another polite question. " I put on plays."

" Oh," said Maggie, absently, wondering what she had asked the girl in an effort to make conversation.

Mary gave Sylvia another glance, and waited for a street lamp. Then she was caught by the hat Sylvia was wearing. Was it possible the girl sometimes went to Paris? A beautiful, a marvellous, a unique hat. She leaned across Maggie's heroic bosom and said, " I've been admiring your hat, Miss Enger. Did you buy it in New York? I've never seen anything like it."

Her voice, to Edward, was " tough " and inelegant, with its masculine huskiness. But to Sylvia, it was alluring and delightful, because of the questions. She said, with shy eagerness, " I made it myself. I design and make all my clothes, when I have time." She paused, with a furtive glance at the back of Edward's head. " And I design all the women's clothes, in my plays."

" That's what makes them so infernally stark," said Edward, ruthlessly.

" I don't think this luscious hat is stark," said Mary, suddenly disliking him. " I'd like to look at it close at hand." Then she was astonished. How was it possible for a backwoods girl to have this genius? She could scarcely wait to see the dress and the coat Sylvia wore, and the dresses of the amateur actresses. She sometimes had these intuitions that something exciting was about to happen. Now her sixth sense was quivering. Only once or twice before had she had this anticipatory awareness. There had been that little blonde girl from Minnesota, who had come to the DelaFontaine establishment six years ago, shyly begging a job as a seamstress. Mary had looked at her, and had been excited, though the girl was not in any visible way remarkable. Within six weeks she had revealed, even to her own amazement, if not to Mary's, a flair for exquisite draping of sleeves and uncommon buttons. Mademoiselle Louise, neé Signe Arundsen, was one of the more important employees of DelaFontaine now.

Sylvia said, almost without volition, " Madame, if you'd like this hat—as a—as a—model, I'd be glad to—give—it to you." Her voice trembled a little, humbly.

"I'll take it," said Mary, promptly. "To-night. And if I can make it go among my clientèle, I'll send you a royalty." She did not see Sylvia clasping her gloved hands convulsively, but she felt it, and she smiled with sympathy.

Both Maggie and Mary were struck by the good taste and impressiveness of the Little Theatre, into which Edward had poured thousands of dollars. Small, yes, but perfect, thought Maggie, surprised. A crowd had already gathered in front, among them a number of newspaper photographers. Maggie lifted her head; she became the famous White Way actress again. She accepted Padraig's hand, when alighting, like a queen condescending to a courtier, but the smile she gave him resembled noonday. The photographers lifted their sticks, filled with powder, and there was a flare of light while the cameras clicked. A small cheer went up from the spectators, who had hurriedly bought tickets. Edward marvelled at the subtle and unseen power of publicity, which had brought out these people, without previous newspaper columns, despite the snow-filled streets and the tiger-toothed cold. The theatre would be filled, no matter that the damned silly play had been thoroughly assassinated by the two local newspaper critics.

Moving grandly, on Padraig's arm, Maggie sailed into the theatre, bowing and beaming at her admirers, who gazed at her with awe. The others in the party followed unnoticed. Maggie was surrounded in the lobby by reporters. "Yes, yes, indeed," she was saying, all charm. "*Lady in Waiting* was one of my earlier plays. Delightful. I simply had to stop off to-night to see it, in this delicious theatre. It brings back lovely memories. Charming. Charming. Yes, indeed." She stood there, with her sables thrown back, and revealing her noble white shoulders and bosom, to the entrancement of the reporters. Mary, in the meantime, was not wasting time in cynicism. She was examining Sylvia's coat and dress, and again she was quivering with excitement. "My dear," she murmured to the bemused Sylvia, "you and I must have a little talk." She lifted part of the velvet coat, and sighed with deep pleasure. "Between the first and second acts? At intermission?"

The Enger box was in a royal position, and filled with plush chairs. The play began, but the eyes of the audience were fixed stolidly, and almost without blinking, on Maggie.

In spite of her preoccupation with Padraig, Maggie was not insensible to this adoration. While she talked with him, she preened, turned her head so that the fullness of her white throat was revealed, drew back breaths which enhanced her bosom, and smiled radiantly. The black silk lace on her breasts fluttered. She fanned herself occasionally so that her large white arm was displayed in all its famous perfection. She inclined her face, and let the dim light play on her glossy curls and waves. The audience sighed at each fresh revelation. And Padraig gazed at her and thought, This is a dear child, as Norah was dear, and she is innocent and kind and warm as a fire, and her smile is Norah's smile. In all these years since Norah's death he had never reached for a woman's hand, but now he did.

The play, thought Edward with anger and shame, was appalling. Or, rather, the actors and actresses were abominable. They moved perfectly, spoke perfectly, timed themselves perfectly, but they were wooden figures without accentuation or life. It was, though a slim play, filled with possibilities. But one wouldn't know that from these people on the stage. Where was the vitality, the lightness, the sudden change of mood, the originality, the fire, the colour, the sentiment? They had been washed from the words, the actions, so that all hues and nuances had faded into dull blacks and whites and uninspired lethargy. Come on! he silently shouted to the actors. Move faster there, speak louder! You aren't talking to yourself!

No one in the box but himself was studying the play. That New York actress was "showing off." Padraig looked fatuous, almost foolish; Edward, in his rage, did not deduce anything from this then. Sylvia, of course, was down in the wings. And that little woman with the disgustingly masculine voice was looking at—what? She did not smile at the arch lines, did not show any gravity at the dramatic ones. She sat absolutely still. Edward did not know that she was scrutinising the miraculously beautiful and original gowns the actresses were wearing, the subtle lines, the perfect sophistication of the neck designs and the chic draping of the sleeves. To Edward, the clothing was without lure or attractiveness. But Mary was thinking, What subdued worldliness, what ingenious under-statement, what refinement, what aristocracy! The girl's an absolute genius, and I must have her at once.

Edward was so bitterly engrossed with his fury and humiliation that he was not aware, for a few moments, that the curtain had fallen on the first act. When he turned about, to confront eyes he was sure would be derisive, he found that he was alone in the box. He was too mortified, for some time, to move. Then he went looking for his companions. He did not find them, to his relief. He did not even wonder where they were.

Padraig and Maggie had discovered a little dim corridor off one of the exits, and they paced there together, undisturbed, Maggie's arm closely entwined with Padraig's. She was smoking one of her little gold-tipped cigarettes. There was no need for her to speak, she knew. It was enough to exchange serious glances and faint smiles.

Then Maggie said, softly, "I'll be in Buffalo, to-morrow."

"I'll be there," replied Padraig.

"And then Detroit, and Chicago."

"I'll be there."

Maggie squeezed her eyelids together, then looked at him with all the blueness of her eyes so vivid that, hypnotised, he could not glance away. "I know," she whispered.

They walked up and down slowly, the warmth of their bodies mingling.

"I must go back to Ireland some day," said Padraig. He paused. "I can never be an American citizen."

Maggie did not care. She was not even curious. The circumstances connected with Padraig were of no importance to her. If he had suddenly confessed to the darkest of dark pasts she would have smiled at him serenely.

"But you are an American citizen—Maggie," he said. "You may lose that citizenship."

Maggie, the proudest American patriot of them all, pressed her cheek to his tenderly. They had known each other only a few hours; marriage had not been mentioned. Yet it was understood that they had always known each other, that marriage was as inevitable as to-morrow. Padraig put his thin hands on her shoulders and regarded her gravely. "I know who you are, Maggie, my darling, but you don't know who I am."

"You are my heart's treasure," murmured Maggie. "That's enough for me."

He tried to smile. His angular face sank into melancholy.

"You didn't really hear me," he said. "I must go back to Ireland some day. To County Mayo. You didn't ask why. I have a duty, Mavourneen." And now his voice strengthened, and his brogue slowed his words.

"Yes," said Maggie, dazed with happiness, and she nodded. "You'll always have a duty, Padraig."

He sighed, released her. "A duty I'll not be wanting, Maggie. You must listen; you mustn't look at me while I tell you. My father—he is Sean Lord Devoe. I'm his only son, his only heir."

The buzzer, announcing the rise of the second act curtain, was unheard by them. Maggie tried to understand; her winged eyebrows drew together in an obedient attempt. She said, brightly, "Sean. That was my father's name, may his soul rest in peace near the Blessed Mother. Sean Lord Devoe. I like it, Padraig."

He had to laugh his short and reluctant laugh. "Maggie. My father is a peer. A lord. An Irish lord. One of the few with money. He could sit in the British House of Lords, if he wished, which he does not and never will, himself hating the English more than the devils in hell. He's almost seventy now. One day I will be Padraig Lord Devoe. And you, my darling, will be Lady Maggie."

Maggie's black eyelashes trembled, and her fine colour faded. "You . . ." she began, then swallowed. "And I . . ."

He put his arms about her and pulled her to him. "You'll not be saying it, Maggie, now or ever." He put his mouth against the top of her head and closed his eyes on a spasm of pain. "I was tried for murder, Maggie." He waited, but she did not stir in his arms. "It was my horse, and it was I riding the fiend, that killed the child I was to marry, Norah Bellamy. A cruel beast, a stallion, and himself had told me not to ride the animal, but I was wilful, and I rode him, and Norah came running out of the paddock, hearing the commotion, and he wheeled and struck her down with his forelegs. It was her head, Maggie, her golden head, which he crushed, and the hair like sunlight, and the blood—I was twenty years old, Maggie."

She put her arms around his waist tightly, and moaned.

"Murder, the judge called it, though the jury would not convict me. And it was so, Maggie, because I had always been an arrogant lad, the only son, the spoiled and selfish son, who cared only for his pleasure. But I loved Norah, and for twenty years I've wandered the world trying to forget, not taking money from my father, and doing penance. Maggie, do you think I have repented enough?"

She leaned back in his arms to look at him, and her eyes were crystalline with tears. "Oh, Padraig, and you could not go home, and that poor lonely man, your father, and all the pain——"

"Surely God has forgiven me," he said. "If He had not, I should never have known you."

"But, my dear child, you haven't a bit of feeling for the stage!" Mary Garrity repeated again and again in despair to Sylvia, as they sat together in Sylvia's private room near the dressing-rooms. "You are a genius, though, in something just as important, or even more so. And you've been telling me what it is that you've always wanted. Don't cry. Just give me a reason why you refuse. Just one sensible reason that I can understand, why you won't come with me in New York."

"I can't, I can't!" cried Sylvia, full of nameless terror and shrinking. "No, you can't understand, Madame. My mother is a Von Brunner. It was always this way—it isn't something I can explain."

"Is there a man?" asked Mary, with cold flatness.

"Yes, yes. But that isn't the reason. Believe me. He—he wouldn't mind my doing what you want me to do. He'd even like it, I think." Sylvia sobbed dryly. "No, no, you can't understand. You've seen my brother, Ed?"

"Not a very agreeable character, though attractive," conceded Mary. "What's he got to do with all this?"

Sylvia crouched on her chair in the raw electric light, and she wrung her slender fingers together. "I—I am afraid," she stammered.

"Of Ed?"

"He has all the money. He has the house, our new house. . . . Oh, I can't explain!" She jumped to her feet distractedly.

"You're afraid of your brother, and you a woman?" said Mary, incredulous.

Sylvia stared before her emptily. "I hate him," she said.

"Well, good," responded Mary with vigour. "Then, pull

away from him, from this awful town, from your family, and assert yourself, be free, independent."

Sylvia swung to her, and her white face expressed such utter horror that Mary rose involuntarily. "You can't run away and leave your whole life. . . ." Sylvia groaned. "It isn't that easy."

"Why not? I did," said Mary, and now her eyes narrowed with a wondering contempt. "And I was only seventeen. Seven years younger than you. My girl, could it be you haven't any guts?"

She was sorry for Sylvia, who seemed to her much younger than her years. But all that genius, that wonderful, artistic genius, that find of a century!

The vulgar last word brought a stain to Sylvia's wide cheek-bones. "You don't understand! I can't possibly make you understand."

Mary picked up her gloves and purse. "I'm afraid," she said, "that you don't understand, yourself, or are afraid to let yourself understand. Well." She paused. Then she opened her purse, took out a card-case, and removed a card. She put it on the table before the stark mirror. "There's my address, my telephone number. One of these days, I hope to God, you'll stiffen your backbone and you'll come to New York and you'll call me. I'm eleven years older than you, and the world isn't as frightful—not *quite* as frightful, as I suspect you think it is."

She waited. Sylvia's hard breathing filled the little room. Then Mary shrugged, and walked out, muttering profanely. Sylvia watched her leave, heard the hard banging of the door.

"Oh!" she cried aloud, in anguish. "I—I'll make him pay for this! I'll make him pay!"

Edward sat alone in his box for a full ten minutes before he was joined by Padraig, Maggie and Mary. He stood up slowly, while the ladies seated themselves. The actors jabbered listlessly on the stage. The audience yawned, gave up the struggle, and stared at Maggie again. Then even Edward, angered and humiliated though he was at this fiasco, saw that both ladies appeared disturbed. Maggie was pale, though she smiled constantly. Mary was scowling. "Is there something wrong?" asked Edward.

Maggie took up the cue at once. "I'm so sorry," she murmured. "I have a terrible headache. And we must catch the early train to Buffalo to-morrow. Six o'clock—in the morning! Perhaps—perhaps Mr. Devoe . . ."

Padraig rose at once, with an eagerness Edward found more humiliating than ever. "I'll be glad to take Mrs. McNulty and Madame DelaFontaine back to their hotel," he said.

Maggie put her hand coaxingly on Edward's stiff arm, and managed to summon up a wan expression. "You will forgive us, won't you, Mr. Enger? It's been charming—charming—really exciting. One of my own plays, you know. I've always loved it. Do tell your sister—the theatre is a gem. It's been such an unexpected pleasure——"

Edward wanted to pull away rudely, but he restrained himself. "After all, they're only amateurs," he said. "I thought, though, that my sister has done pretty well, considering."

Maggie was distressed. Even in that dim light from the stage she could see the cold inflexibility of his eyes. She hated to hurt anyone; he was offended. But Mary said in a loud and positive voice, "I'm really dying for some sleep." She hesitated. "Your sister is a genius, Mr. Enger."

He smiled at her for the first time. "I know," he said. "It's just that stupid play."

Maggie's mouth opened soundlessly with affront. But Mary said, "I don't mean about the stage." She stared at him. "I mean her creations. She could make a fortune, with me."

"You mean, as a DRESSMAKER?" Edward demanded, insulted. "My sister?"

Mary rose abruptly. "My head is aching worse than yours, Maggie," she said, and the hoarse boom of her voice attracted interested stares from the orchestra.

"I didn't mean to offend you," Edward began.

Maggie smiled at him sweetly, and again touched his arm. "Why, of course you didn't, Mr. Enger. But you will excuse us, won't you? And give your sister our congratulations? She's really . . ." Maggie glanced at Padraig with helplessness, and he helped her rise and put on her sable cloak. Maggie, her warm heart still feeling for Edward, continued, "She's really a genius, and I should know, Mr. Enger. Thank you, thank you for thinking of us. If your sister ever comes to New York . . ."

Edward, not standing now though the ladies were standing, looked at Padraig over his solid shoulder. "Call for the limousine," he said, and his voice was pent. "Then send it back, please, for us, Padraig."

"I've never seen such a brute," said Mary, when they were rolling and heaving over the snow on the way to the hotel. "He's got that gifted sister of his frightened out of her wits." She had explained, briefly, her preoccupation with Sylvia.

"No," said Padraig, sadly, "he isn't a brute. It isn't his fault at all. That is, not entirely. I've known the family for at least six years now. No, it isn't his fault. It's hard to explain."

"Don't begin that, too," said Mary, laughing.

"There are intangibles," Padraig offered. He was so at ease. He could not remember ever having been at ease before in all those long and twenty years.

"Intangibles, hell," said Mary, with fervour. "How can you stand him?"

"You don't know Ed," said Padraig.

"And I don't want to. I just want that stupid girl."

When they reached the hotel, Mary, who knew that Maggie was now committed beyond recall, and that Padraig, though "mysterious"—and she disliked mysteries—was a man to win your heart if you weren't careful, and was all respectability, discreetly retired into the bedroom leaving the lovers alone. She had her own melancholy. She was frustrated and hot with anger against Edward and "that stupid girl."

She had left her card with Sylvia. One of these days, she was certain, Sylvia would appear suddenly at her salon, and life would become sensible again.

"And now," said Maggie, in the brown little "parlour," and coming at once into Padraig's arms, "you must tell me how much you love me. You haven't said a word about love at all, and we engaged to be married!"

"When will you marry me, my darling?" asked Padraig.

Chapter Three

Whistling cheerfully, though his sandy brows were knotted in thought, William McFadden, purchasing manager for the C. C. Chauncey's Shops, climbed the steps to Ralph Enger's pleasant little apartment and studio in a pension in the Latin Quarter of Paris.

Number five. William knocked on the door; he heard, with sly approval, a slight scuffling inside, a girl's muffled giggle, something upsetting, and then the scrape of a chair. Ah, what it was to be nineteen, in Paris in the spring, and all the money to spend, and an excellent dinner cooking, and flowers, and a nice piece of twist on the side. The door opened, and Ralph Enger, somewhat flushed, his handsome auburn hair dishevelled, and carrying a paint brush ostentatiously in his hand, stood on the threshold. "What?" he said. Then recognising William, he smiled a little sullenly, and said, "Oh, it's you again. I thought you weren't coming until to-morrow evening."

He was tall and plump and he exuded an immense and earthy vitality. His dark eyes were exceptionally quick and restless, his colour ruddy, his features a little too fleshy. He was naked to the waist, and his body had a strong pinkish tone, and was warmly damp. His body scent, young and lustful, was not unpleasant.

"I have other plans for to-morrow, I found," said William. Ralph stood aside and William entered the large studio with its north window, its views of roofs and chimney-pots and pigeons fluttering, and balconies, and wisps of smoke curling along a chaos of eaves and tiled roofs. Ralph's studio consisted not only of this room where he painted, but an agreeable living-room, a bedroom and a kitchen, all in precise order—the order, William thought, of a mathematician who detested confusion. There was nothing "artistic" in the studio but the window, the neat stacks of canvases against the walls, the easel, and the young naked girl sitting demurely on a small platform, and trying to control a curiously rapid breathing. Trust him not to have a model who's blowsy or too highly coloured, thought William, smiling to himself.

This is a neat little piece, compact and clear cut and well laid out. The girl, small, dark and exquisitely formed, gazed at him from under long black lashes, and drew in generous rosy lips to quiet her impulse to giggle again. Her nose was carved to a pure tilt, her eyes were oval and full of mischief, and her dark chestnut hair was coiled on her nape without a curl to distract its smoothness and order. Even her breasts were trim and distinct, and her legs and arms, though not long, were firmly moulded. A sum, well added up and complete, thought William, approvingly.

"Mademoiselle Violette Carré," said Ralph, with some sheepishness. He added, "My model."

"I didn't think she was here just for a cup of tea," said William, artlessly, with a pointed glance at the damsel's nakedness.

Ralph laughed loudly, and the girl tittered. She was utterly at ease. She crossed one leg over the other, and William, with more approval, saw that her knees were dimpled. "All right, honey," said Ralph, to Violette. "Throw something on. And you'd better see how that ragout is doing, Vi. Go easy on the wine," he called after her, "and the garlic. Never could stand garlic much, after the shop," Ralph explained to his visitor. "Old Garlic and Pickles, you know."

He, too, lit a cigarette. "Finished with your buying in Paris?" he asked.

"Yes," said William, thoughtfully, "and for a long time, I'm thinking."

"What? Business bad?" For a moment Ralph frowned.

William pretended not to notice the sudden concern. "Not our business," he replied. "The world's business. Where are your bally ears? It's not been using them, you have. Don't your professors talk, or are they up to their ears in their dusty books all the time? The students? Drinking too much wine and coffee in the cafés, I'll wager."

Ralph scratched his pink cheek, and frowned again. "Oh. You mean the rumours of war? Nonsense."

"My advice to you, boyo, is to clear out as fast as you can," said William, and he was not smiling. "First boat, bag and baggage."

"You and your plots and counter-plots," said Ralph.

William shrugged. "I've given you my advice, laddie. Ease my conscience a bit, and at least buy a ticket."

Ralph sat down abruptly, and rested his bare elbows on his knees, and stared at William through the cigarette smoke. "Enger," said William, musingly. "It's not a name that'll be popular in France. But you're an American, too, my lad. Clear out. There'll be a rush for boats, and you mark my words."

Ralph yawned. "I don't believe any of it," he said. "Let's change the subject. You're giving me the willies."

William leaned back on the sofa. Then he stood up and went to the easel and gazed at it contemplatively for a long time. He cocked his head, mused, hummed to himself, stepped back, stepped forward, screwed up his eyes.

"Well, what do you think of it?" asked Ralph, aggressively.

"What do you think of it?" countered William. "Honestly."

Ralph bent forward from the hips and regarded his own work. "Everything's there," he said, trying for lightness.

"So it is. Just like a calculation in logarithms. But where's the soul, man?"

"All right," said Ralph, impatiently, and his ruddy colour deepened. "I've trusted you; I've told you everything. I've been studying at the Sorbonne and paying for it with the measly pocket-money old Garlic and Pickles has been squeezing out to me. I'm a qualified engineer; I can design bridges. I can stop this damned painting." His voice rose. "Don't you think I know I'm no real artist?"

"At least you're honest, and that's more than the others are," muttered William. "Poor old Ed."

"What?"

"I was talking to myself, a bad habit of the elderly," said William, and his soft brogue deepened.

"I hate it," said Ralph, with passion. "But Ed insisted I was an artist. What could I do, with him and his ambitions?"

"It's not the truth you are speaking," said William. "It is not the engineering you want, not at the expense of a breach with your brother and his money." He shook his head. "It is the easy safe life you want. You know that in your heart. Two years more of lolling, of not being a man—that is what you want, laddie. And then perhaps two more, pretending to be the artist. But time has run out; the world is exploding. Crash. Boom. And never the same thereafter. The end of life as we know it. You must take your chance like a man;

you must do as you were created by Our Lord to do. Or be damned to you for ever!"

Ralph stopped his pacing. "Why the hell don't you mind your own business?" he shouted. He pushed his auburn hair into a tangled mane over his head. His life, as he had made it, so gay, so irresponsible, so pleasant, was being threatened.

Ralph looked at his big hands, the sensitive finger-tips: the hands of an engineer who could throw glittering steel arches across rivers. Who was stopping him? The single pronoun stood in ruthless fire before his inner eye, but he shut his vision against it. It was all Ed's fault, he said in a desperate litany to himself. All his fault, the smug black bastard, the slave-driver, the dreamer of silly dreams. All his fault, all his fault!

Chapter Four

The City, New York's newest and smartest and most sophisticatedly ribald magazine, had been a success since its birth two years ago. It had protested from the beginning that it was a "New York magazine for New Yorkers," but to the surprise, or perhaps not to the surprise, of its owner and editors, it had become immensely popular with the despised hinterland. Its smoothly urbane articles, its short but clever stories, its "news of the world," and other features, were an innovation in a world of facile magazines with their wordy and flowery and diffuse offerings. The subtle cartoons held up a mirror to mankind, and mankind, professing to be shocked, laughed at the gently lewd reflections of itself. The people were beginning to tire of drawings of Gibson and Dana girls, and crude humour and sentimental stories. *The City*, etched, as someone said, in pure gall and acrid urine, and conceived in mannerly contempt, was entirely mature, entirely impertinent, and had convinced New Yorkers that they were as suave, worldly and knowing as itself.

Harry Suffolk, as editor-in-chief, passed the lightest paragraph, the smallest cartoon, the most minute "squib," as well as the major features. He was a fat, gross man, untidy and ink-stained, and had a voice like a minotaur. He boasted that he never combed his hair, shaved his black beard only twice a week, and took only one bath a month. Nobody questioned these statements, for obvious reasons. *The City* was his darling; the small offices, rarely swept out, and in a constant state of disorder, hummed like a nest of hornets. The staff, indeed, resembled hornets themselves, lean, slight young men with sallow complexions, fast-moving but precise, sharp of speech and sharper of pen, and their stings were not without toxic results. Harry had only two words to express approval or disapproval of any manuscript or cartoon: "O.K." Or "stinks."

Harry's office was so small that he seemed to fill it to the very corners, as he sprawled in his battered chair, or slumped over his splintery desk which was heaped, always, with masses of material. "You have to edge around his bulges," his editors would say. One of them edged around the bulges on this warm day in March. Harry snarled as usual, and wiped his inky hands on his hair. The editor said, "That young writer, Gil Enderson—you know, the one we bought three stories from, and that article on Wilson's 'New Freedoms,' is here with your letter."

"Send the yokel in," said Harry, irritably.

He thrust a cigarette in his thick mouth, and it appeared as small as a match in the mound of his face. His coarse black eyebrows twitched. Gil Enderson. Harry did not believe in encouraging anyone, even his best writers. He prepared to demolish the artful young man.

Gil Enderson, even in those three stories which *The City* had bought, had become a Name for his risible lampooning of tycoons and robber barons, not with the heavy hand of the current "muck-rakers" who used indignation and polysyllable words and thunderings to denounce those they envied, but with a deft and sprightly touch that was much more devastating than all the moral screams of the deadly serious. He had created a character called Mr. Thor, and the subscribers had demanded more, and subscriptions had gone up gratifyingly. Harry suspected that "Mr. Thor" was an actual person, though caricatured, and that Enderson secretly admired him while he hated him. There was a distinct impression of a feline licking-of-wounds in the debonair tales.

The creaking door opened and a shaft of sunlight tried to penetrate the dusty windows. A young man entered, and, to

Harry's secret surprise, he seemed hardly more than twenty-one, though he was tall and with a largish frame. The frame, Harry noticed, was clad in excellent tweeds, and just managed to miss elegance imperceptibly, though considerable endeavour had been made to achieve that effect. There was an impression of deliberate struggle to attain ease and grace of movement and assurance and even hauteur.

But Gil Enderson had an engaging air, and his broad face, dark and alert, had an expression of lively pugnacity and vivid intelligence. His nervous eyebrows were quirked over small grey eyes, and they gave a look of animation to the rest of his features, which inclined to weak bluntness. There was something familiar about him, and Harry frowned, trying to remember. "Wher'd I see you before?" Harry grunted. He waved his soiled hand. "Never mind. You're Gil Enderson. Sit down, unless you don't want to dirty the seat of those Irish tweeds."

Gil laughed, and it was a laugh of pure humour. He sat down. "I brought your letter, Mr. Suffolk. I want to talk to you about it."

Harry took the letter, grunted again, turned it over in his hands, staring at Gil with his round brown eyes. "New Haven, eh?" he said, almost with loathing. "What're you doing there?"

"Yale," said Gil.

"A student?" said Harry, aghast.

"Senior," replied Gil. His voice was quick as his eyes. He coloured a little. "My last semester."

"I'll be damned," said Harry, more and more aghast. "I thought you'd be older and . . ." He paused. "How old are you, anyway?"

"Twenty-one."

Harry combed his hair with his fingers again. He reread his letter. "I am offering you a job as editor for *The City*—one hundred seventy-five dollars a week—you'll have to live in New York, of course. You can write your stories about 'Mr. Thor' in your spare time—they've attracted some slight notice——"

Harry studied the young man again, more narrowly this time. Just his meat. This kid could be trained into fine editorial work; he had the touch, the lightness, the awareness. There was no use, of course, in praising his stories too much; that led to egotism and egotism led to dullness. The editor, whom Harry wished Gil to replace, had just had what Harry called "a rush of respectability to the head." And there was nothing like respectability to ruin a writer or an editor.

"What made you think you could fit in here?" demanded Harry.

Gil raised his eyebrows. "I didn't. You did, Mr. Suffolk. That's why I came."

Harry tossed his letter aside with taurine contempt. "Some damn' clerk must have written it, and I signed it without reading it."

Scepticism gleamed in Gil's eyes. He laid an envelope on the cluttered desk. "I brought you two more stories about 'Mr. Thor'," he said. Now his face took on gloom and sullenness. "I can't take the job, sir. Not even when I am graduated."

"You can't, eh? Maybe I'm not offering you one. This is just a discussion. Never thought I'd be discussing anything with a damned schoolboy, at my age! But just suppose I was offering you that job, why wouldn't you take it?"

"I can't." The words were flat and vicious. "It'd be a risk——"

"Well, what in hell isn't? From the look of you, though, I wouldn't say that you'd ever suffered any privation. And you're young. And I've a faint idea I've read one of your scrawls, or a few paragraphs, anyway. School assignment?" he added tauntingly, though he knew better.

"No," said Gil, almost angrily.

Harry leaned back in his chair. "Um. Somebody you know. Now," he went on, observing Gil's flush, "you could write maybe ten or twelve or fourteen more stories about 'Mr. Thor.' I'm not saying you haven't some small talent, you know. Then maybe you could get the stories together and publish them. Maybe. I've seen, though, the best stories we've published shoved together in a book and they've made just about as much sound as a pancake falling on a carpet. Books are different. And there'll come a time when our readers will get tired of 'Mr. Thor.' They'll want something different. You're callow. You've got yourself a character you know, somebody you hate, somebody you've caricatured. You can write the way you do about him because you despise his guts, and admire him, and are scared to death of him. . . ."

Gil's colour had so increased that he looked inflamed. Harry shook a rocklike finger at him. "I know," he said. "And I repeat, you've got a talent. But you're going to run out of characters because you haven't lived long enough or experienced enough, and you're just writing biography, now. If you come here—and I haven't offered you the job yet—you'll learn, you'll meet people in New York, you'll listen, you'll get experience—and your gift for satire will develop naturally in a natural environment. Some people have the genius for invention; you haven't. You write as you see a man, and that's both good and bad. And I'm not saying that 'Mr. Thor' does Mr. Thor justice. There's just too much malice in your things. People are sons of bitches, sure. And 'Mr. Thor' is a prize one. But I don't think he's as mean or as stupid or impervious a son of a bitch as you write. He wouldn't have made all his money if he were. Some people are so superbly stupid that they can't help succeeding in anything they do, but Mr. Thor isn't that stupid. It leaks out here and there, in your work, that he's got a mind, though you probably wrote that subconsciously. When you get tired of Mr. Thor, or bored with him, or you've written him out, what're you going to do?"

Gil said, and his voice almost trembled, "My family believe—want—me to be a famous, serious writer."

Harry slowly straightened up. He stared at Gil with bullish antagonism. "And you don't believe a word of what they say. You know better. You know what you are and what you can do. It isn't enough, eh? You're not scared of your family; you're scared of yourself. You haven't any belly."

He creaked in his chair. "You're not a solid, really serious writer. You're no Tolstoy. When you learn that, and if it isn't too late, write me a letter. In the meantime, we'll look over these new stories."

His eyes were points of fury. "Good-bye," he said.

Gil stood up. He felt an answering fury, and a deathly shame. He started out of the room just as an editor, with a green eye-shade, entered. The editor blinked at him uncertainly. "Oh, hallo," he said. But Gil pushed by him and was gone.

"D'you know that young bastard?" asked Harry, lighting a cigarette with fingers that enraged him by trembling a little.

"I've seen his picture, somewhere," said the editor, puzzled. He pushed up his eye-shade. "Yes, I'm sure of it!" He snapped his fingers, frowned. "Why, that's Edward Enger, the delicacy prince! C. C. Chauncey's! What do you know about that? There's an article about him this month in *Harper's*! What's he doing here? Trying to buy the magazine?" And he laughed.

"You're crazy," said Harry. "He's only twenty-one; he's at Yale. Student. Get me a copy of *Harper's*!"

The magazine was brought, and the two bent over it with excitement. The article was admiring but acute. They studied the photograph, the older face, the harder, more powerful face, the more intellectual face, the sterner and bitterer face. But the strong resemblance was there, though the resolution and force were not. "Portrait in iron," said Harry, "copied in wax."

They rapidly skimmed the article. The names of brothers and sister—"David Enger, famous pianist. Sylvia, promising director and producer of plays. Ralph, studying in Paris. And Gregory Enger, at Yale, majoring in English, editor of the university paper——"

"Gregory Enger! Gil Enderson!" said Harry, and swore with mingled amusement, regret and disgust.

Chapter Five

When men were proud of what they had created it was rare to find jealousy among them. Their delight in what they had created made them eager for approval and even for emulation. The "original" finds both flattery and pride in mimickers. Creators are often anxious that those who copy them shall do so with such care and nicety that they enhance the prestige of the creators.

So Edward Enger had found with S. S. Pierce's of Boston. Years ago, when he had bought the Goeltz property he had visited S. S. Pierce's almost humbly. He was received with the utmost courtesy and was compelled to take many notes, so profuse and generous were the suggestions, so patient and kind were the executives, buyers, advertising men, managers, and the clerks themselves. Young, he had been despairing that he could ever approach this perfection, this influence, this pride, and the absolute faith lavished on S. S. Pierce's by their customers. " We buy and sell nothing but the excellent," said one of the gentlemen Edward interviewed. " Anything else wouldn't be worthy of us, and it would be an offence to our friends. Quality. That's the keynote. Customers must trust you absolutely."

Caveat emptor, Edward discovered, had no place at S. S. Pierce's. He also found that these busy gentlemen could spare the time to sit down with him and discuss his problems and his ambitions with the most attentive sympathy. If they thought he was wrong, they said so; if he had an original idea, they applauded. He returned to Waterford with his bundle of notes and spent months studying them, to his great advantage. His pride was not hurt when customers in various big cities told him enthusiastically, " C. C. Chauncey's reminds me so much of S. S. Pierce's." Rather, he was highly pleased.

He did not want to start as modestly as his mentors had started, and therefore, after long study of the Pierce methods of merchandising, he approached George Enreich for much more than had been originally agreed upon. George had said nothing; he had gone, unknown to Edward, for his own scrutiny of the establishment in Boston. Then he had advanced the money. " You are in competition with them, my Eddie, but I have the conviction that this will not alarm or annoy them."

The Goeltz property had been bought. Then, to the astonishment of the people of Waterford, and their ominous predictions, Edward had rebuilt the property entirely. There were six floors now, in this April of 1914, and the shop and its departments covered an area of half a block. Small old houses adjacent had been purchased, removed, and the shop extended.

In an era of small shops and small windows Edward introduced, in Waterford, huge expanses of plate glass. He invented his distinctive labels for his shops in other cities, and for the outlets in other stores who would carry some of his products. The Waterford shop, however, was what William called The Home.

The vast store in Waterford was the wonder and pride of the city. Glass, beautiful lighting, clerks in white jackets, managers in frock-coats and striped trousers, carpeting and scattered chairs for weary customers, and rest rooms " like palaces," all mingled together to make a trip to C. C. Chauncey's an event. There was no dark wood anywhere or dark counters or dim spots. The areas, " acres," some people said in awe, of counters glowed with glass and light. Islands stood in inviting places, heaped with esoteric imports. There was a special " wine cellar " downstairs in a cool basement, where customers could linger over cobwebbed bottles and champagnes and liqueurs and whiskies, with a deferential and knowing clerk in attendance to advise or discreetly suggest. Big wagons stood in line at the rear, loading and unloading, and motor vans busied themselves at the many doors. There was a special candy shop carrying only the best imported of " Chauncey brand " sweets, glacés, and brittles, a honey shop, a special meats shops, a coffee shop, a tea shop, all small and beautifully decorated off the main shop, and reached through arches.

The executive offices were on the third floor. Here business was done not only for local purchasing but for business abroad. Here letters flowed in a steady river to the C. C. Chauncey warehouse in New York, and to outlets and to out-of-town Chauncey shops. Here conferences were held between Padraig Devoe and his assistants and advertisers, and William McFadden and his own circle. Here was the board-room where Edward met with his officers once a month. Here, in offices, typewriters clacked and files slammed and clerks and stenographers bustled. Here was the heart of the enterprise. On the fourth floor was the experimental kitchen, to which visitors were invited. The other top floors were store-rooms.

Edward's office was larger than that of his officers, and was furnished in the style of his home: rich Oriental carpets, heavy velvet and leather furniture, two chandeliers, brocaded draperies. He often worked to midnight, his big windows lighted brilliantly, while the only sounds were that of men unloading the wagons and the vans. Sometimes he would go downstairs to the silent shops, light them here and there, and simply wander, looking at everything, occasionally making reproving notes, investigating, studying. He lived only two lives, that of his family and that of his enterprise. He liked to pick up a porcelain pot of honey, with his impressive label upon it, and open it and taste it, and put it on a plain

English biscuit. Sometimes he went into the kitchens and brewed himself a cup of coffee, and ate a sandwich made of his best imported English or Polish ham. He would sit, then, on a table and eat contentedly. During the day he would only descend to the shops when his buzzer sounded to indicate that a valued customer needed special attention or pampering. Otherwise, his peaceful and agreeable moments were spent alone.

He was alone, this warm late April night, in his office. It was nearly ten o'clock. The broad windows stood open, and the air was like balm, sweet and languishing.

Edward never could recall at what precise instant he thought suddenly of suicide.

The instant before he had been preoccupied with an important decision. He had made the decision and he had known it was good. He had also known that he was hungry, even after the plenteous dinner at home. He had decided to visit the experimental kitchens and treat himself to his best brand of coffee and some spiced imported meat in a sandwich. He had contemplated the idea with pleasure.

And then, without warning, he had thought of suicide, and had leaned back in his chair and had considered it simply. Why? he asked himself, curiously. The impulse became more demanding. It was like a command which must be obeyed. Objectively, he examined the idea, coldly and analytically. Debts? Of course, they were mountainous, but they could be overcome in time. Health? It was superb. Disappointment? No. David's agent had just jubilantly written him that the Carnegie engagement was assured, and that David had just received an offer from Albany, where he would play on 23rd April, to-morrow. The rest of the family? With the exception of Sylvia, all was well. Business? It had never been better, even in these days when there was an uneasy feeling abroad, everywhere, a kind of formless premonition of disaster. Within a month, he would open two new shops in other cities. He came back, in his thoughts, to his family.

Sylvia, whom he disliked more than he disliked the other members of the family, could not be the cause of this command to die, a command not accompanied by any despondency or despair or hopelessness. He considered Sylvia for a moment. Only he knew the real cause of her sudden illness and collapse, and he would not speak of it even to her. Padraig Devoe had married Mrs. Maggie McNulty in Buffalo over a month ago. Damn it, he *had* been disappointed, but it was Padraig's business and not his. He was positive, too, that Padraig had never once suspected that Sylvia loved him. There was no guile in Padraig. After the marriage, upon which Padraig had sent him a quiet telegram, Padraig had completed his business and had returned to his apartment in New York, and his offices in the importing branch of C. C. Chauncey's. Edward had wired his congratulations and had ordered an expensive gift for the couple. But Sylvia had suddenly collapsed and had been forced to go to bed.

It was not Sylvia, or anyone else, or anything else, which had commanded Edward to die. It had surged inexorably up in him like an imperious mandate, without sound or pain or desolation. It was simply there, a fact. He liked his life. But in comparison it was nothing to this darkly secret urge to die.

Now, he could be entertained by the idea. He played with a pencil, and examined it from every angle, looked at every facet. Once, when he had been young—and he could not remember just when—he had been afraid he was dying, and had been appalled by the thought. There was no fear in him now, no aversion. There was, suddenly, no longer any appetite in him for living. It was gone, and he did not know why, or how.

It's a good thing I don't have a gun at hand! thought Edward, and then he laughed. The impulse for death blew away on his laughter, and life rushed in on him. Shaking his head, and laughing again, he began to rise from his desk. It was then that an awful trembling seized him, an intense sickness of the spirit, a passionate recoil, as if he had just confronted a most terrible danger. Sweat broke out on his body; his hands were nerveless. Tremors ran over him. His affrighted body, aware of the escaped destruction, clamoured in all its cells. Quiet, he said sternly in himself. Quiet, quiet. A knife seemed to flash through his heart, and then it was gone. The carved clock on the wall struck a melodious eleven. He started. Somehow, he had lost an hour, and had not been aware of it. I must have been insane for an hour, he thought. Well, I'll never have such an idea again. Damn' fool.

Edward ate his breakfast alone in his lofty dining-room, for

Heinrich and Maria did not rise so early. Since Heinrich, or, rather, Edward, had engaged an excellent manager for ENGER'S, Heinrich preferred to arrive at his own shop about ten in the morning. There was a silent *malaise* about him lately, a slackening of energy, though he was only past his mid-forties. When he complained that he was an old man, in a very piteous voice, no one contradicted him, for Heinrich was indeed old. He felt abandoned, lost and ill, and would look about him, when spoken to, with a seeking expression, like a blind child. Maria would sit with him in their rooms and read to him in sonorous German, all the sentimental poems and stories which he remembered from his youth, and which would fill his eyes with tears.

On this particular morning, after Edward's inexplicable urge to death, Maria came downstairs alone for breakfast. Edward glanced up in surprise, then rose. "Early, aren't you, Ma?" he asked. He liked to be alone. The hunger for solitude was growing in him, like a lonely but heavily rooted tree.

Maria sat down, as formidable and massive as ever, and as dominant. There was some grey in her hair, but it blended so perfectly with the lengths of silver-gilt that it was perceptible only as a silver shine in certain lights. She was dressed as formally as if she were about to leave the house, in a brown satin dress which enhanced the size of her great body. She spoke in German to Edward, gazing at him with an odd penetration, as she shook out the big square of white linen beside her plate.

"It may appear strange to you, my son, but a mother has her intuitions. I felt, this morning, that all was not well with you."

"Nonsense," said Edward. Embarrassed, he looked at the windows. They were mullioned rectangles of grey mist and shallow green, as the damp morning slanted through the new trees. "I was just thinking about those two adjoining acres. I'd like to get them."

Maria's protruding and glassy eyes fixed themselves intently on him with new searching. "There is an old saying: 'How much land does a man need?'"

Edward laughed. His broad face had a slight ashen overcast. He had eaten very little this morning. It was that confounded stomach trouble again, he thought. The sharp but fleeting spasms of pain irritated him. He swallowed another soda-mint, and Maria watched him gravely. "I need those two acres," he said. "I don't want a farm, but those two acres are on the highway and there's no real zoning laws in Waterford, and it's possible that someone will build a blacksmith shop or a meat market on the land. Another road borders it, and that will end any threat to my property."

Maria nodded. "That is understandable, your apprehension," she said. "But I was not speaking literally. I was speaking in a symbol."

Edward frowned. "I don't understand," he said. "Enlighten me."

"It does not matter. Allusions are for scholars, and not always in good taste. You must forgive me."

Old Pierre brought in fresh coffee. He glanced at Maria, and bent his head to listen to her order. When he had gone Edward said, "How much land does a man need? Meaning what?"

But Maria shook her head and ate her dish of fine imported figs, a speciality of C. C. Chauncey's. It was baffling, but Edward thought of his impulse last night. Then he suddenly understood. How much land does a man need? Only enough to make him a grave, and a grave, finally, was all he had. He pushed back his chair abruptly.

"Yes?" said Maria. "The acres again?" Her gaze was inscrutable.

"That's right, Ma." Edward's hands were on the table, and they had closed into fists. Maria saw them, and put down her coffee cup. She saw that he had flushed. He was speaking rapidly, as if to drive away a terrible thought. "I've been hounding the bank to get in touch with the person who owns that land, without any result at all. She lives in Albany; her name is Baumer. That's all they can tell me, they say. Probably some old hag who's waiting for me to raise my price."

By the time his limousine had taken him to the shop his mind was busy, as it was always busy, planning, thinking, weighing. There was to be a board meeting this afternoon.

There was, among all the messages waiting for him, one that was interesting. The bank manager had called. Edward's secretary made a call to the bank, and the manager said respectfully, " Mr. Enger? The lady, Miss Baumer, who owns those two acres, will be in my office at ten o'clock. I think she is willing to sell that land now——"

" For how much?"

The manager approved of rich men's caution. Only bankrupts never asked the price. " At what you offered. To tell you the truth, Mr. Enger, she hasn't been in the country for nearly a year. She found my letter with your offer a few days ago, when she returned home to Albany. She wrote me, and I honestly think she didn't even remember she had those two acres here!"

" She must be very wealthy," said Edward, with wryness.

" Not extremely so, Mr. Enger. I should say—comfortable." The banker coughed. " Her parents owned a farm near Albany, and when the city expanded they sold a large section of it to a manufacturer for a factory. Then the rest was divided into lots for houses for working men. The land you want was bought by her parents at least twenty years ago when they lived in Waterford. They're dead now, I understand. About five years ago."

Some old spinster who had finally inherited, thought Edward. " I'll be in your office at ten," he said. " I hope the old—lady really wants to sell."

He was pleased. The small piece of land had been a real threat to his estate. At ten o'clock he called for his limousine and was driven to the bank. He did not deal here. It was neither impressive nor very prosperous. The manager greeted him effusively and led him into his dingy office. Edward was oppressed because of the meagre size, and there was a constriction in his chest. He sat down, refused one of Mr. Erhlich's eagerly proffered cigar. Mr. Erhlich noted Edward's worn clothing, and he approved. Only bankrupts dressed to the hilt, he thought. A rich man could afford to be shabby. He studied Edward out of the corner of his eyes; he had caught glimpses of Edward occasionally, but he had not remembered that he was so tall, so broad, and so harsh and obdurate of expression. It was said that he was still in his twenties; he looked much older. But then, all that responsibility, all that money! Mr. Erhlich wistfully wondered if Edward would ever do any business with his bank. He doubted it.

He did not know what to say to Edward. The young man sat there, his long right leg impatiently swinging over the other. He glanced at his watch. " Miss Baumer should be here," he said, apologetically. " But ladies, you know, aren't very punctual."

The door opened and a clerk said with obsequiousness, " Miss Baumer, Mr. Erhlich." The banker rose and Edward rose, reluctantly as always, for he had no great reverence for women and only impatience or contempt. He especially disliked elderly women who, he had discovered long ago, objected to parting with cash and liked to haggle for the sheer sense of importance it gave them with browbeating clerks or asserting their faded personalities, or pretending to be very shrewd indeed.

The clerk stood aside and a young woman entered, a pretty girl not more than twenty-one or two. " Miss Baumer!" exclaimed Mr. Erhlich with delight. " And how was Europe?" He took her hand, which was covered with a white kid glove.

" Oh, I came back from Europe some weeks ago. I've been touring America since then." She had a sweet voice, not thin, not particularly clear, but gently strong and firm. She let Mr. Erhlich lead her to a chair, and then looked up at Edward, who was standing near the desk and staring at her with what she considered brutal forwardness. What an unpleasant-looking young man! she thought. And so, this is David's brother. Poor David. Now I'm beginning to understand a little.

Edward was thinking, I've seen her before! But where, where? Why, she's as familiar to me as my own hands. I couldn't have forgotten her!

He had seen she was tall, but very slight, and that her figure, though not as buxom as fashion preferred, was perfect. The blue silk suit, with the long tight skirt reaching to her ankles, had not been bought " off the hook." Even Edward could see that. The hat, broad velvet the colour of her suit, was loaded with coral velvet roses, the exact hue of her smooth coral cheeks and full coral lips. The froth of white lace at her neckline was no whiter than her throat and temples and brow and chin and hands. Edward remembered it all, but could not remember where and when. He thought this girl the most beautiful woman he had ever seen.

He said bluntly, "I think we've met before, haven't we, Miss Baumer?"

She shook her head slightly. "No, I don't think so. Unless you were at one of David's concerts, in a little town in Illinois a month ago."

"David? You know my brother, David?" He did not know that his voice had risen. The girl sat back in her chair. What a rough voice he had, strained and thrusting out at a person. David had been reticent about his brother, but she had caught undertones in his conversation.

"Yes, Mr. Enger. I know David." The coral in her cheeks deepened, and Edward's powers of observation, always acute, became preternaturally sharp. "I think he is a wonderful artist."

No, no, said Edward in himself, and again there was that searing in his chest, and he felt suddenly ill and full of compressed fury. Not David; not this girl. Outrage constricted his throat.

"It's a small world," said Mr. Erhlich, feebly, and attempted to chuckle.

"Too small," said Edward. His eyes had become bits of steel under his thick black lashes.

Miss Baumer stared at him, affronted, and she paled. She finally turned her shoulder to him and said quietly, "Mr. Erhlich, I have an appointment almost immediately. Can we conclude this business at once?" Her slender shoulder, her sweetly rounded breast, visibly trembled. "Too small," he had said, implying that she had no right to know any member of his precious family! Her hands clenched over her purse.

"Why, certainly, certainly!" said Mr. Erhlich, relieved. There was something very singular in this atmosphere. Young Mr. Enger was still fixedly glowering at this nice, pretty young woman, as if he wanted to hit her, or shout, or overturn things, and Miss Baumer appeared to be about to dissolve into tears. The necessary papers were all on Mr. Erhlich's desk, but it perhaps would be best if he pretended they were not and left the room for a few moments. Then, probably, when he returned, the bursting tension in the air would be gone. He excused himself with haste, and went out.

"You—you can't possibly——" Edward began, in a pent and almost stifled voice.

"I can't what, Mr. Enger?" asked the girl, still half-turned from him.

"You can't—I mean," said Edward, and his congested throat made him cough. "Dave. My brother——"

She blushed angrily. "David is a friend of mine," she said. She swung to him suddenly, and the blueness of her eyes flashed in a blaze of offence. "Have you any objections, Mr. Enger? What do you know about me, anyway?"

To her amazement his voice dropped, became very slow and quiet. "I've known you all my life. I've never forgotten you. I've . . ." He stopped.

Her blush brightened. She lifted her head proudly. "I don't remember you. As far as I know, I've never seen you in my life. I lived in Waterford until I was about ten, with—with—my parents, and then we moved to Albany. That was a long time ago."

Why, the man must be insane! His eyes were absolutely mad! He was leaning over the desk at her, and his brows were one slash of black. Miss Baumer was frightened. She grasped her gloves and purse and moved to the edge of her chair, as if gathering herself for flight.

"Where did you live, in Waterford?" Edward asked. All his faculties were concentrated on the girl; he forgot even where he was.

"I think it was Sherwood Street. I only lived there a little while." The colour suddenly went from the girl's cheeks and mouth and she was absolutely white. "Oh, I see. You've found out something about me. David must have written, and so you investigated." Her voice curved out loud and clear with scorn. "Don't worry, Mr. Enger. I'm not serious about David—yet. But when I am, you won't matter at all!"

"You can't—want—Dave," said Edward, and he stood up, and his air of wrath terrified her. His big body, his massive shoulders, bulked over her like a rock.

But she spoke as clearly as before. "Because I was brought up in the orphan asylum here? Because I don't know who my parents were? Mr. Enger, the Baumers adopted me when I was fifteen. They left me everything they had; they educated me. I'm a decent person." She caught her breath. "And I'm going to write David, to-night, that I'll marry him, just as soon as he wants!"

She looked at him with cold blue defiance, though her lips trembled. Then she was again astonished. He was approaching her. Now he was standing beside her. He was a very queer ashen colour, but he was smiling.

" Margaret—in the P's," he said, and his voice was low and shaken and marvelling.

Her mouth opened on a little gasp. He was bending over her. His stiff arm was supported by the hand he had placed on the desk, and she saw the tight fist. " I just remembered," he was saying. " I remember where and when we saw each other. Just one time. Try and remember." His voice had fallen even lower, and it was desperately pleading, and even the startled girl recognised there was no threat in it. " We had a small delicatessen store. My father and I. It was a hot day. I can see and feel and smell it right now, just as if it was yesterday. You came in ; you were just a little girl. The Baumers weren't good people ; they'd taken you from the asylum to work for them. You hadn't had any dinner. I made a ham sandwich for you, and gave you a glass of milk——"

" I don't remember," the girl faltered.

Edward did not seem to hear her. He gently took one of her hands, though she shrank again. " I remember your hands that day. They were all cut and bruised. You said you weren't afraid of work ; you used to wash all the floors in the orphanage. You said you didn't want charity, as you chewed the sandwich. You were hungry. I never forgot you, though I thought I did. I didn't know who I was looking for, since then. I was looking for you, all these years."

She was afraid to pull away her hand. Her fingers were rigid in his. She blinked her gilt eyelashes and moistened her lips. She was more frightened than ever. She repeated, " I don't remember."

" You were only ten," he said. " Margaret, in the P's!"

The rigidity went out of her fingers. She looked at him as if hypnotised. Something was forming before her: a small shop, the glitter of glass counters, a little rotund man, a tall and lanky boy giving her something to eat, the sputter of gaslight. Faint, far-off, distant, almost a dream. That was just before the Baumers had taken her to Albany, because she had satisfied them that she could work. There was the sweet taste of bread and ham and milk in her mouth, and the pungent odour of garlic and vinegar in her nostrils, and the dingy, dismal past was all about her, including the clamour of the orphan asylum, the endless floors to be scoured, the harsh smell of soap-suds and dirty water in pails, the ugly feel of a scrub-brush against her fingers.

Tears ran around the edges of her eyelids. She smiled unsteadily. "Why, yes," she said. "I do remember now. You were awfully good to a little girl." Her eyes widened. "And you had a tree! And there was the tree they cut down at the orphanage! Eddie!"

They did not see Mr. Erhlich in the doorway, gaping at them, stupefied. Mr. Erhlich was in confusion. He had left this room in haste, because of the huge hostility in it, the baffling hostility, and here they were now, smiling at each other and holding hands and the girl had just cried, "Eddie!"

"You said I was an 'Eddie,'" Edward was saying.

"It was a long time ago," said the girl. "I never thought of it after we left here. I didn't want to remember anything about Waterford." Her voice was stammering. "When we lived in Albany, near Albany on a farm, the Baumers were nicer to me. I worked awfully hard. Mr. Baumer was nicer than . . . Anyway, they adopted me years later. They left me a lot of money. . . ." Her hand clung to Edward's involuntarily, and she was looking up into his eyes like a child. "I must have remembered a little, though. When I met David, I—I liked him. He seemed to remind me of somebody—somebody who—I know, now, it was you. You were the first person who had ever been kind to me. . . ."

A pool of pure light shone under her chin, the reflection of the sun. But, to Edward, it seemed like a thing belonging to her alone, an emanation of her, just as the full blueness of her eyes were hers, shining on him behind a mist of tears. He could not look away from her. He stroked her hand and she leaned a little towards him.

"I never forgot, I never forgot," he said, and he was young again, and buoyant and full of joy. "I've looked for you in every woman I've seen." Quite simply, he raised his free hand and touched her cheek, and it was the hand of a loving husband whose wife had returned from a long journey.

Well, thought Mr. Erhlich. Well, this is very curious, very.

He was quite dumbfounded when Edward put his hand under Margaret's elbow and she rose with implicit obedience and sweetness and walked out with him. They passed Mr. Erhlich as if he were not there. They were looking only at each other.

Chapter Six

"But, what shall I do about David?" asked Margaret, troubled. "How can we keep from hurting him?"

She laid David's last letter to her on the stiffly white and glimmering tablecloth in the dining-room of the Whitney House. Edward and she had been sitting there having lunch for over two hours, Edward completely forgetting, for the first time, that he had a board meeting which had already been in session for half an hour without his presence. Most of the midday diners had gone, and with them their long and inquisitive stares at the engrossed man and young woman who occupied this table in a far corner. The spring sun filled the big dining-room, melted brownly on its panelled walls, sifted on its thick crimson rug, sparkled on its silver and chandeliers, and enamelled the edges of chairs and plates.

It had been understood from the moment that Edward and Margaret had left the bank together that they were not only in love but loved each other, had always loved each other, and that they would be married very soon. It had been understood without declarations, questions or doubts. It was love at its most tranquil yet most sensual; it was embedded in them like their own hearts; it was a fact that neither questioned nor hesitated over; it was not a marvel or a miracle. It had existed from all time.

Never before in all his life had Edward spoken to another in absolute faith that he would be understood, that he had no need for explanations or wariness, that he need not withdraw before some imminent incomprehension. Margaret knew exactly what he meant when he spoke, and he knew exactly what she meant by a glance, a smile, or a word. He was released from a confinement of spirit which had always been with him from his first consciousness of his self. He now possessed a freedom he had not known existed. His mother, Maria, had made only one comment when she had learned of Padraig's marriage: "And so, he is free." He had thought it a ridiculous remark; marriage was bondage, not liberty. Now he saw that to love was to have freedom in its most mystic sense, and that a man who did not love was a prisoner.

They had talked with each other for two hours, and they did not remember of what they talked. The communication had been perfect, serene and content. Edward felt an enormous sense of well-being, buoyancy and health. He had not known that he was lonely. Now he understood that he had always been lonely, and waiting, and deprived, until to-day. Sometimes he would touch Margaret's hand across the table, and she would smile at him with simple delight, and he would think, I knew all the time that she was somewhere. Why, I prayed for her a long time.

It was when Margaret had extended David's letter to Edward that the first discord appeared. But it was not a discord between him and Margaret. It was an intrusion and a problem that both must settle. Edward frowned at the letter, and hesitated. "You're sure you want me to read this, Margaret?"

"That is why I'm giving it to you," she answered, surprised. "You have to know everything. I met him in New York before I left for Europe; it was at a party given me by a friend, the lawyer who manages my—parents'—estate. David had been invited to play. There were a lot of people there. He played beautifully."

She sighed. "I thought, and still think, that David is one of the most interesting and handsome men I've ever met." She looked up and twinkled at Edward. "Outside of you, of course, you shaggy brute. Stop glowering. And I think David is extremely sensitive. And unhappy."

Edward settled back in his chair. His face had hardened. "Unhappy? Why should he be unhappy? I've worked for him all the days of my life; he's never been denied anything. He's had the best money can buy in the way of teachers and clothing. He has what he wants."

Margaret's gilt brows drew together in anxious sympathy. "I don't know if that's what he wants, Ed. I think he wants something else."

Edward, for the first time in over two hours, felt the old hot constriction in his throat and chest. " Then why didn't he say so, for God's sake? I would have worked just as hard to give him what he wanted—if he had wanted something else."

You believe that, my darling, thought Margaret, sadly, with the wisdom of love. But it is not true. I can see it in your face.

" He was the musical genius of the family," Edward went on, in a tight voice. " I bought his first piano. I gave up all my youth for him, and the others. I suppose he never mentioned that to you?"

" Yes," said Margaret, with deepening sadness. " He told me all about it. Ed, David has a strong—affection for you—and pity."

" Pity?" exclaimed Edward, with strong violence and humiliation. " For what?" He had darkly flushed. " Because I'm a success, and have made his success possible?"

" It's hard to explain," said Margaret, in a low tone. " David didn't quite explain it himself. Perhaps he couldn't. Please don't be angry at him, Ed. Perhaps I was wrong; he wasn't pitying himself, and he wasn't insulting you with his compassion for you. I got the idea, somehow, that he felt that you had been deprived in some way. And he was sorry."

Edward said, " What do you think he wanted, if he wanted something else besides the thing he said he always wanted, as long as I remember?" His light eyes jumped with inner rage.

" He didn't say," replied Margaret. " Perhaps I just imagined it. I only know that he seemed unhappy, and that he didn't mingle much with the people. We began to talk together; he looked familiar to me in a way, and as I said before, it was because of my memory of you."

Edward said nothing. He did not look at Margaret; he stared at the silver knife in his hand. He did not know that he was holding it by the handle and that he was making small stabbing motions with it. But Margaret saw and understood, and she was alarmed. Her new and total peace ripped apart.

The taste of hatred was like a corrosion in Edward's mouth. Again, watching him, Margaret was afraid, and again she shrank. Then Edward pushed away David's letter with the point of his knife, and it was so quick and so violent a movement that it was like a deadly attack. " I don't want to read it," he said.

" Have I said something to offend you?" she asked, in consternation.

Edward looked at her and saw her distress. " Never mind," he said, trying to smile. How to explain to this girl that he felt like a husband whose wife had been grossly insulted? " I just think that reading Dave's letter to you would be an invasion of his privacy."

She was relieved. His smile was not reassuring, but his words were. " You're probably right," she said. " It was bad taste on my part to give you the letter. I just thought that we shouldn't have any secrets between us. You see, David knew I was coming to Waterford to sell the last property here of my parents. He asked me to get in touch with his family; he wanted me to know them all. Including you." And she smiled gently. " Particularly you. He sends you all his regards." She watched Edward and hesitated. The unhealthy flush on his broad and heavy face alarmed her. " He mentions he's going to play in Carnegie Hall in a week. He's arriving here to-morrow for a visit. He wanted me to tell you that. I had already told him that you wanted my two acres next to your house, and he said, ' Then you'll see old Ed right away, by himself. And that's very good. He's different when he's with the family.' You see, dear, he wanted me to like you."

Edward threw the knife from him. " He didn't tell you, of course, that it's costing me a fortune to have him play at Carnegie Hall, at a benefit performance for a charity, to which I'm contributing? And that it costs me a fortune in supplementary fees wherever he appears—because his agent can't give him important engagements? And that he and his agent couldn't survive on what he really makes?"

Margaret was stunned. " No, he didn't tell me," she stammered. What was wrong with Edward? What had she said to him to give him that murderous expression, and to light up his pale eyes with such fury? Then the mysterious intuition of love explained it all to her. She leaned towards him and said with quiet sternness, " Ed, does he know, himself?"

He did not answer. But she understood.

" I'm so sorry," she said, mournfully. " So terribly sorry."

"For Dave?" His voice was loaded with affront.

"For both of you. But, perhaps, a little more for David. I think he knows his—limitations."

"He hasn't any! I've talked with his teachers. It's his own deliberate doing that he's a perfect mechanic. It's his way of frustrating me. Just as the others do. Weaklings! That's the only way, they think, of revenging themselves on me."

"Revenge for what?" Her words were gentle but insistent, and her blue eyes fixed themselves on him.

"For giving them what they've always wanted, for them having been dependent on me."

Then, she, too, was angered, but not at Edward. He had given all his life to his brothers and sister. She had learned that from David, himself. And in return they had given him ingratitude and frustration and contempt. Her compassion for David vanished in the fierce loyalty of love.

"Never mind, dear," she said. "Never mind. You have me, now. And we'll never be lonely again, will we?"

It had been agreed between them that Margaret would tell David the next night that she could not marry him, but that she would not speak to him of Edward. Margaret had had doubts about this; it seemed like an unnecessary falseness to her.

"It's not falseness, or deception," Edward had said, before they had parted. He spoke reasonably, and with an air of fairness, though there was something about his smile which disturbed Margaret. "Just think about it a minute, darling. He comes to you for a definite answer, and you blurt out that you're going to marry his brother. When did you meet his brother? Oh, just yesterday. Dave's not a complete fool. You wouldn't be able to blame him for not understanding. So we'll wait a month or so, and then be quietly married. Perhaps in Albany, perhaps in New York."

"Without your family being present at all?"

"Why should they be?"

Margaret had a few answers to this, but she was now so bemused and enthralled and joyous that the answers immediately seemed foolish.

She was occupying the very same suite that Maggie McNulty and Mary Garrity had occupied, and it was in the little brown parlour that she received David when he came to get his answer the next night. He entered the room, and again she was struck with admiration for his elegance, poise and grace. Yet, at the same time, he appeared too tenuous to her, in comparison with Edward, too polished, too without virility. And she resented his fine clothing. This Edward denied for himself, in order that his family might have luxuries she thought, bitterly.

David, the extremely sensitive, felt this elusiveness, this withdrawal. He was bewildered, and his spirits sank and his whole impressionable nature was disturbed. He took Margaret's hand, and felt its unresponsiveness. She had never seemed so beautiful and so desirable to him, and he had come to her for the warmth and gentleness and sympathy he remembered and which had alleviated the awful loneliness which he suffered always. Yet, now her eyes were half averted, her coral lips set, her manner distant. She's decided not to marry me, thought David, and he was overwhelmed with sorrow and despair.

"Do sit down, David," she said. "I've ordered tea."

David sat down. He said to himself, Why, I've never loved anyone before. He wanted to stop the words he dreaded to hear from her, and so in pathetic haste he said, "I've been thinking of you every minute, Margaret, and counting the time until I could see you again."

She was touched, and vexed with herself that she was touched. She began, "David." He broke in. "I've told my parents about you. I have a note here, from my mother, asking you to have dinner with us to-morrow night. Margaret, will you come?"

She suddenly blushed. The pink tide rose from her throat and covered her face. She stammered, "What did you tell your family about me?"

"That I loved you, and wanted to marry you," he replied, and moved to the edge of his chair as if to get up. She looked fully at him now, in distress. "Do you mind? Was I too hasty?"

But Margaret was preoccupied with her rapid thoughts. "You say your 'family,' David. You mean, just your parents know?"

"No. I told them all at dinner last night. My sister Sylvia, my brother, Ed, and my parents."

Margaret looked down at the hands she had clenched

together in her lap. She wore a dress of light-blue silk lace and it moved agitatedly over her breast. She had never seemed so beautiful and so precious to the lonely David. "Your—sister—and your—brother—what did they say?" she asked faintly.

She hadn't protested, she hadn't said no! Hope lifted again in David. "Well," he said, with his reluctant half-laugh, "Sylvia's been ill, as I told you, and it's made her bitter and cynical. It must have been a nervous breakdown. She made some flippant remark, and then apologised. You see, Sylvia and I have always had a lot in common, and have understood each other. My father looked happy but uncertain. He was never very certain about anything, as long as I remember. He's always been overawed by Mother and her—pretensions. And then Ed has bullied him all his life. Mother? I've never understood my mother, except that she's ambitious and has pride of family. She was interested; she asked me a number of questions about you. She——"

The blushes had intensified on Margaret's face. She interrupted, "And your brother, Ed. What did he say?"

David frowned, trying to remember. His black eyes narrowed. "I don't think he said anything, and that's odd, for he always has an opinion and it's usually dogmatic. He just looked at me as if he was very interested. Yes. And he smiled. Ed rarely smiles pleasantly. And this wasn't one of the exceptions."

"And he didn't say anything?"

"No. Does it matter?"

Margaret was silent. She swallowed against a lump of dry anger, and this anger was directed against Edward for the first time. He had had his opportunity, then, to speak for himself, but he had not spoken. She tried to control her emotions. After all, Edward probably had some consideration for his brother, she told herself, struggling against her indignation. Yes, yes, that was it. She sighed in relief.

"Does he know about your mother's invitation to me, David?"

"Yes. In fact, he did say something after I had finished telling the family about you, dear. It was the first and last remark he made." David was, all at once, agreeably surprised. "To be perfectly truthful, it was Ed who suggested to Mother that she invite you to-morrow night."

"No!" cried Margaret, and she stood up in her agitation at this enormity and implied cruelty. She was struck with pain and confusion. How was it possible for a man to do this to his brother? Her eyes shimmered with tears. But of one thing she was sure: she would not meet Edward's family the next night. No, not so soon!

David rose, bewildered. "'No,' what, Margaret? Won't you come?" He was full of dread and sorrow again. "I'd hoped you would. Ed said nothing about meeting you to-day, but he's always so busy."

I never want to see Ed again! the girl thought, passionately, gazing through her tears at David, and feeling the hurt of compassion at her heart. But she knew she was lying to herself. She pressed her lips together, and again looked for an excuse for Edward, as she would look for excuses the rest of her life. He was a direct man. He wanted her to meet his parents. In some way, he was planning to clear the situation between herself and David, once and for all. Yes, that must be it, there could be no other explanation! Yet, how blunt he was, how impatient! She found herself smiling a little. He hoped, apparently, that she would play her part, too. But she did not know what her part was to be.

"I'll come, David," she said.

He smiled happily and his tired face shone. He took her hand and did not feel the slight resistance. Before he could speak she continued rapidly, "I'm sorry, though, that you made any—announcement—about—about us. I don't know you well enough, David. You were awfully premature. I haven't given you much encouragement, have I? You should have asked me first."

But David was certain, now. Margaret was only showing a woman's natural modesty and reticence. He waited until she sat down again, and he saw the soft silk mould itself around her body in exquisite lines. The lamplight glittered on her curling, light-brown hair, and lay along the curve of her chin and cheek radiantly. Then he said, "Perhaps I did speak too fast, dear. But, you see, I can't imagine living without you."

She turned her head quickly towards him. "David! You mustn't say that!"

Her colour left her face, and the blueness of her eyes became intense with a return of her distress. "I never told you I'd marry you. We've been very good friends. I listened when you suggested marriage——"

He was shaken again. "You didn't refuse me, Margaret." He looked into her eyes, bending over her to hold her attention. "You know you didn't. You asked for time. Perhaps I haven't given you enough time." He wanted to touch her, to hold her, to kiss her, and the desire was almost more than he could endure. "It's just that I haven't given you enough time, isn't it? That's all it is, isn't it, Margaret? You do like me, don't you?" His voice broke.

She was sick with her compassion, and her guilt. She put out her hand impulsively and rested it on the black broadcloth of his sleeve. She could feel the thinness of his bones and flesh under the material, and she bit her lip to keep from bursting into crying. "Yes, David, I do like you. I'll always like you. But"—and she began to stammer—"I don't think I love you, David. I don't think I ever will."

He moved away from her slowly, and she saw his misery and anguish. He stood in profile to her, his head bent, his mouth drawn and pale and sunken. She wanted to console him, and cried out, "Don't look like that, David! I'll go and meet your parents to-morrow. I want to meet them. Oh, sit down, David. Let's talk, at least, as we always did, as friends."

He turned quickly, and saw the tears on her lashes, and he hoped again. "I've frightened you, dear, haven't I? But I loved you from the very first time we met, in New York. I've been pretty wretched most of my life, and then, there you were, and I had a friend. I felt I'd known you for ever. No, please let me finish, and then we'll talk about other things. I'm willing to give you as much time as you want, Margaret, if you'll just give me a little encouragement."

"I can't," she whispered, and twisted her hands together in her lap. "I honestly can't, David."

"I'll wait," he pleaded. "Years, if necessary." Then he paused, ill with a powerful premonition. "Margaret, there isn't anyone else, is there? You told me, weeks ago, that there wasn't."

"There is," she said, despairingly. "I'm terribly sorry, David, but there is. I met him—recently."

He sat down, abruptly. "I can't believe it, Margaret! I

got your last letter only a week ago. You didn't mention it then. You couldn't just have met another man in the last few days——"

"I did."

"But you've accepted my mother's invitation!"

What did Ed want her to do? He knew his brother was visiting her to-night. He knew that David would speak urgently. She put her hand to her forehead and rubbed it in a stronger agitation than before. David was staring at her, disbelieving, and waiting.

"We've been good friends," she faltered. "And I thought —I thought perhaps I'd like to meet your family. I think I've made a mistake in accepting."

"Do I know the man?" he asked, and his face was full of suffering.

Margaret was quiet. If she lied to him now that would be unpardonable. "Yes, you know him. But do we have to talk about this now, please?"

"I think so," he said. He still could not believe it. "I don't know many people, in spite of my touring," he went on pleadingly. "I can't remember any man we've met together who might interest you, Margaret."

"I told you I met him recently!" Margaret cried. "David, do let me alone."

But his love and grief made him relentless. "Someone I know. Do I know him well? You owe that much to me, to tell me, Margaret."

Yes, she owed him that, she acknowledged, dejectedly. Her meetings with him, the long hours she had spent with him, in pleasant affection, her implied acceptance of him, though hesitant, in all her letters, the hope she had given him, the comfort she had offered him when he was most dispirited, were debts of the utmost urgency.

"Yes, David, you know him well. No, I can't tell you his name, not yet."

"Why not?"

She was silent. She did not know that tears were running over her pale cheeks. She looked at his hand, the long sensitive fingers, the whitened knuckles, and she could feel his love for her, and his desire to console and protect her from her own pain.

He could hardly hear her when she spoke. "David, I've

not just met him. I've known him almost all my life, since I was ten years old. I must tell you that. He was the first person who was ever kind to me. You know I lived in Waterford until the Baumers took me to that farm near Albany. I never forgot—him. I thought I did, but now I know I've been looking for him for over ten years. I did forget his name, except the first one, and when I saw him, I didn't know him at first. But he remembered me."

"A boy from the orphanage, Margaret?" His voice was very kind and steady.

"No, David. Not from the orphanage."

"But, if he remembered you, and you didn't remember him, he must be too old for you. He must have been a man, even when you were a child."

Her throat felt thick and stiff, and she was crying again. But honesty was one of her strongest characteristics. "He is about four or five years older than I am, David." She closed her wet eyes. "And he told me that though he'd forgotten my name, too, he hadn't forgotten me, and had been looking for me everywhere. You musn't hate him, David. It's terribly necessary for you not to hate him."

"Why, Margaret?" he asked, quietly.

She did not answer him. Her hand lay in his like the hand of a desolate child. He began to think. Margaret had arrived in Waterford this morning. She had told him that she had never returned to this city before. The man lived in Waterford. Who had Margaret seen to-day? She had written him that she was to be here to settle her affairs and sell her two acres of land—the land his brother, Edward, had wanted.

A sudden and intolerable blow struck at David's heart. A sudden and intolerable knowledge which made him open his mouth in an expression of agony. He dropped her hand, and both his hands fell slackly between his knees. Not Ed! Oh, God, not Ed, his brother! Anyone else but Ed, please God, anyone else but Ed!

Margaret opened her eyes and she knew at once what he suspected, and she was overcome. He stood up slowly. He stretched out his hands and took her shoulders in them. She was trembling, and the trembling passed from his hands to his arms and then to his whole body, and he trembled in reply.

"Where did you meet Ed for the first time, Margaret?"

She tried to pull away from him, but he tightened his hands, and she had no strength to resist or struggle. He was looking at her with a most terrible intensity, and his eyes were stark and bright.

"In your father's shop," she whispered. "When I was ten years old. He gave me something to eat. I was hungry."

She had betrayed Ed after all, and he would never forgive her.

"I didn't want to hurt you, David, believe me, I didn't want to hurt you!" she cried. "Please believe me."

"And he knew all the time, all the time, while I was talking to-night," said David in a sick and wondering tone. "And he never said a word. And he suggested that you come to dinner. Why? Why did he do that to me? Why didn't he say something about you, and him? That you'd met to-day?"

So, in spite of all that she had done, David hated her, and his brother. The hatred would last for ever. David would forget what he owed Edward; David would forget a lifetime of sacrifice in his behalf. To spite Edward, he might repudiate him and go his own way, and destroy all Edward's work. Margaret's frantic thoughts were like a scattering of terrorised birds.

"You're unfair, you're cruel!" Margaret exclaimed, in frenzy. "Do you think he wanted to do this to you? We talked it over for hours to-day! I gave him your letter, but he wouldn't read it. He asked me not to tell you about us; he just wanted me to discourage you, and then after a while we would be married quietly, after you had forgotten all about me. That's why he didn't speak to-night. It was you he was thinking about!"

David stared down at his feet. He was sick to the point of violent nausea. "I suppose you believe that, Margaret. Yes, I suppose you believe that. I'm sorry, but I don't. You see, I know all about Ed now. I think I always knew, and that's why I am sorry for him."

"You never knew anything about him, none of you!" Margaret was scarlet with anger and resentment. "You never even tried to know! He gave all of you his whole life, and you repaid him with contempt, and took all he had to give!"

David raised his eyes and looked at her with a strange, long look. "I suppose you believe that, Margaret," he repeated. "For, you see, he believes that, himself. We weren't angels; we were worse than he was. I'm not condoning anything. But now we're his prisoners, and we can't get away, because we haven't any courage. None of us. He took our courage away from us."

Her face was high and coloured with indignation and scorn. He shook his head. "You don't understand yet, Margaret. Perhaps you'll never understand. I hope you won't, anyway."

Chapter Seven

Edward was driving in his limousine through the cobbled streets of Waterford in the late May sunset. Children were playing under the new green trees. Hopscotch. Ball. Jumping rope. Jacks. Marbles. The braids and ribbons of the little girls plopped behind them. The little boys ran and shrilled. Wistaria was climbing in purple plumes over old porches. The thick white candles of chestnuts blew in a gentle wind. Men were coming home in work clothes, carrying pails, and they moved quicker in spite of their weariness, and smiled or shouted at the children, or stopped to study their small patches of lawn. Women talked on stoops, aprons tucked over their plump arms. Beyond the trees the western sky burned in scarlet and gold and magenta, and above the conflagration a silver star pulsed alone.

It was on such a street that he had known his early childhood and youth. For the first time in all the years since, he felt nostalgia instead of his usual anger. He forgot, for a moment or two, the crowded years of his young life, the bitterness, the weary days, the suppressed rage and depressions, the silent revolts. He could even imagine that his boyhood had been rich and carefree, filled with promise, and that he had played as these children now played, blithe and joyous and content.

The streets were peaceful. It was impossible to believe that anything menaced this peace, this freedom. Nothing sinister lay in the long red beams of the sun as it illuminated the boughs and coppered the leaves of the trees. The little lawns seemed to quiver with green vitality. Kitchen windows lit up, one by one. There was an odour of corned beef and cabbages, of roasting pork, of good soup, drifting out of open doors. Someone was playing a gramophone, and the metallic music and lilting voice clamoured on the warm air. A train wailed in the distance, and a street-car rattled and rang. Peace had a power greater than war. America lay in peace as a happy man lay in summer waters, dreaming.

He suddenly rapped on the glass, and it slid aside. "Henry, stop at that next corner for a few minutes. In front of the church and parsonage."

The car slowly wheeled to a halt and Edward got out. He gazed at the church critically, and was pleased. His gifts to Father Jahle had made an enormous improvement in the building, a small church but fine and secure in its little lawns.

Edward fumed, thinking of all this, and then he climbed the scabrous steps of the little parsonage and pulled the bell-rope. Mrs. Jahle, the priest's mother, as tall, thin and starved as himself, and with the very emaciated but shining face of her son, and his own large and tender eyes, smiled joyously as she saw Edward. Her grey gingham dress was the colour of her thin hair, and hung on her slat-like body in folds. Her white apron was stiff and spotless. She shyly gave Edward her hand. The Father was in the garden, tending his precious roses, which he cultivated for the altars. She would call him. Edward sat down in the dark and narrow little parlour, with its horse-hair furniture, its cold and tiny fireplace, its dimmed windows over which patched white curtains had been drawn. The old house had a dank and chilly atmosphere, and gave off an odour of dust and age. The worn red carpet had been neatly darned, but it was as thin as paper. Edward was depressed; he had forgotten how wretched the parsonage was.

Father Jahle, whose clothing had been covered with a workman's blue denim apron, came in, drying his thin hands on a towel. He was happily surprised to see Edward, who stood up and shook hands with him. "Eddie!" he exclaimed. "I haven't seen you for almost a year!" He held off the younger man and studied him, and still smiled, though he sighed. "You look well, thank God."

He sat down and began to fill a very charred pipe with cheap tobacco. His eyes fixed themselves affectionately on his visitor, who was frowning.

"I wrote you about seeing a doctor, about six months ago," said Edward. "Well?"

The priest blushed like a boy. "That was Christmas," he said. "I couldn't go then. And before I knew it, it was Easter. There's nothing wrong with me, Eddie."

"Nothing except starvation and overwork and worry," replied Edward. "Now, you listen to me. I don't like that cough of yours. You'll go to my doctor to-morrow or we won't be friends any more. Is that understood?"

"To-morrow, there are confessions," protested the priest.

"Then, you'll go to-night. Here's my card. He has office hours between seven and nine. Give him my card. He'll take care of you."

The priest turned the card about in his fingers and looked troubled. He hesitated. Then he lifted his eyes and they were filmed with tears. He said, simply, "Eddie, I can't leave my church. If your doctor should find—if he should say I need a rest—it would be impossible. I am feeling much stronger."

"Seven to nine, to-night," replied Edward, inexorably. "Is that a promise?"

The priest was silent. He looked about the little parlour, where he had heard so much grief, so much despair, so much seeking, so much anguish. He could hear the faint and broken voices of those he had comforted, exhorted and brought into the light. He could not endure the thought of leaving this place even for his health, even for a little while.

"You might have something contagious, and that isn't fair to your people," said Edward. "It isn't fair to your church. What if what you have kills you? Then you won't be coming back at all. Be sensible."

"All right," the priest said. His people came first, and then there were the children whom he might be endangering. Too, his bishop, a few months ago, had sternly asked him about his health. He had evaded his bishop. He had only a bad winter cough. He closed his eyes convulsively. What if it were tuberculosis? That would mean months in bed, endless treatment. Would his replacement understand his "children"? Would he be kind and forbearing and everlastingly patient?

Now that he had the priest's promise, Edward stood up

and restlessly prowled up and down the room. "Father," he said, stopping in front of the priest. "I'm going to be married four weeks from to-day. To a girl I've known since I was fourteen."

The priest brightened with pleasure. He seized Edward's hand and pressed it. "God bless you both!" he said, fervently. But Edward's brooding expression did not change and Father Jahle comprehended that Edward was only abstractedly thinking of his marriage and that he had come here to-day for some other reason than this announcement. "Do I know the young lady?" he asked.

Edward shook his head impatiently. "No. But you will, when I bring her home from Albany. That isn't why I came here to-day, though. Father Jahle, you know George Enreich and William McFadden well. They've been telling me there is going to be a war soon, and that it will involve America. What do you think?"

Father Jahle dropped his eyes and poked at the bowl of his pipe with a match. He seemed distressed. "There is little in the papers," he answered. "There is always some mention of the Balkans. But the Balkans are always seething." He paused. Then he said, "I think there will be a war. I've been reading many books. There are the Secret Masters. But why should there be a war that will involve America?" he cried. "We're too far away from Europe!" There was no conviction in his desperate cry.

Edward nodded gloomily. "I did hope that you'd laugh at the idea," he said. He took up his hat and cane. "Father Jahle, the Church must know something. The Pope must know something. Why aren't they doing what they can about this?"

"They are, Eddie. But if men overwhelmingly choose evil, what can the clergy do? Besides, there are always the liars, and the liars speak louder than God, and men prefer lies to truth. Eddie, if and when the grand assault comes, the Church will be the target of the sinister men, for so long as the Church endures the spirit of men will endure, and a measure of virtue and faith and justice and a will to resist tyrants. That is why, in the conviction of the murderers, the Church must be destroyed." He stood up, and his gaunt face glowed. "But the Church will never be destroyed! The destruction has been attempted before, and it never succeeded.

Out of the ruins and the darkness the faithful men emerged with candles of everlasting love and confidence and civilisation rose again and the murderers were silenced. For a little while."

"This time may be the end," said Edward.

The priest shook his head. "No, it will never be the end. For God lives."

He seemed invigorated and trembling with life and exaltation. Edward regarded him with dull amazement. He could not understand that unshaken confidence, that light of supernatural glory that was leaping in the priest's eyes. He, himself, preferred facts. The thought of America engaging in planned wars was horrifying and unacceptable to him. He said, "I'm thinking about my country, not about—God. I happen to love my country. I want to see her remain free."

"All countries belong to God," said the priest. "Not only America. Not only the white men but the brown and the black and the yellow. It's selfish to think only of America."

Edward said, with hard simplicity, "The hell with the rest of the world."

The priest sighed. He put his hands on Edward's shoulders. "It was Lincoln who said a country cannot endure half-slave, half-free. Neither can the world. All men must be free or all men will be slaves. It is of the freedom of the world that we must think, and it is the enemies of the world that all of us must fight. With every spiritual and just weapon at our command."

"So," said Edward, pulling away, "we must get into wars to 'free' others, whoever they are?"

He went out of the parsonage quickly, and he was boiling with anger. The clear scarlet of the western skies had dimmed to a foreboding crimson, a lake of blood motionless in the heavens. The streets lay in dusky shadow, as if crouching before some imminent terror. And there was a profound silence in the air, like a caught breath. Edward said to himself, It's funny how a man projects his own emotions on the rest of creation. These are just shabby, quiet little streets, and the houses are full of tired but contented people eating their dinners! The premonition is in me, not in them. I'm catching at nightmares.

The streets became progressively more expensive and formal, set back on cultured lawns and among pruned bushes and evergreens. Then the limousine was moving over the winding gravel drive to George's house, a monstrous affair of purplish grey wood with many false towers, false balconies, false thin turrets and "candle-snuffers" and battlements, and wide verandas. Here the evergreens had been shaped into cones, squares and balls, but there were no flowers. A green gloom hung over the house and darkened the brown roofs. It was, thought Edward, the ugliest mansion in Waterford, which was not distinguished for lovely architecture. He saw a distant light through one of the long thin windows and he knew that George was in his library, indulging himself in his usual brandy and soda before his dinner.

But the library was breezy and cheerful, if ponderous with old-fashioned furniture. Rows of books mounted to the ceiling on all four walls, books which George had read through the years, and a small fire crackled cosily on the black marble hearth. George greeted Edward with his usual shrewd and expansive affection, invited him to a drink, which Edward accepted. The older man saw at once that Edward was in a bad mood, and he wrinkled his reddish brows thoughtfully. The years had planted grey tufts in his bristling red hair, had fattened his bulky body and given him a paunch, but had not taken the keen light from his green eyes. When Edward had settled himself in a brown leather chair George said, "It is a fine evening, *hein*? One to give pleasure to the soul after the long winter."

Edward replied in German, "I never noticed. I don't have time to notice these things lately. I have been talking with William recently."

"So," said George, and lit a fat cigar and leaned back in his chair. "What is it that William wails of to-day?"

So Edward told him of William's view about the coming catastrophe in brief harsh sentences, and George listened without a change of expression. Then when Edward had finished he puffed contemplatively and stared at a wall. He said, finally, "So? It will surprise you to learn that I am also convinced, and that I know? But I have told you before, a little."

"Who would we fight?" asked Edward angrily.

George shrugged with eloquence. "Who? *Ja*, who? Perhaps England, perhaps Russia, perhaps Germany. It does not matter. We will fight. That was decided long ago."

"What can we do to stop it, in America?" Edward demanded, full of a solid if uncomprehending wrath.

"Nothing, my Eddie. We have already lost the fight, in the darkness, in the silence, bloodlessly."

"Then we can only cut our throats? Is that what you are implying?" asked Edward irascibly.

George shook his head. "*Nein.* That is a foolish question. We can make much money, and inevitably the men of evil compromise with the men of wealth, and men of wealth inevitably compromise with evil. That is entitled expediency or common sense, in the name of what the French call *le fait accompli.*"

Edward was silent, smoking. He stared at the book on the arm of his chair. His face slowly swelled and became suffused with dark colour. He turned the glare of his light grey eyes on George, and it was inimical. "I came to tell you to-night that I want to sell you my munitions stocks, at the market price. I do not want any part of murder, if there is going to be murder."

"So," murmured George. He carefully deposited the ash of his cigar in a silver ash tray, and, as he turned his body he exuded compact potency. He said, "I did not think you a fool, my Eddie. What will it profit you to sell those stocks? Will it save the world, your selling? You are going to speak to me of principle? Who can afford principle, in the days to come, which are already reddening the eastern skies? If I buy your stocks, or you throw them on the market, you can wash your hands as did Pontius Pilate, who, I have heard, died a miserable and agonised death. He did not prevent the Crucifixion of God, and you will not prevent the crucifixion of man. It is a quixotic gesture, this you contemplate."

"I am going to fight against war, and I need money," said Edward.

George laughed softly. "Then you will need the munitions stock, which will bring you the great, the very great, profit." He smiled at Edward with irony. "More money than what you will amass with what, perhaps, you would call innocent investments."

Edward fumed to himself. Then George became grave. "It is a dangerous task you set yourself."

Edward stood up. "I intend to take it on, nevertheless," he said, "if what you have said is true."

George shrugged, and spread out his hands. "If a man is determined to destroy himself, how is it possible to interfere? And the wedding?" he added. "You have said in four weeks? You have told the family?"

"Not yet. But to-night," said Edward, shortly. "Margaret now insists that she will not marry me until I have told them first."

"Ah, the young lady has steel, and honour. It is good."

Edward looked at him with directness and cold fixity. He was thinking, I've got to get you out. I need that twenty-five per cent you're getting out of the shops. I have steel, too. George smiled, cocked his head as though he had heard Edward's thoughts, and was amused.

Back at home, Edward spoke without ceremony to his mother and Sylvia. "I sent a cable to Dave and Ralph to-day. I've ordered them to come home at once."

"What for?" demanded Sylvia, in her edged and bodiless voice.

But Edward said only to his mother, "I've been hearing rumours that there's going to be a war in Europe. It'll be no place for Americans."

Sylvia laughed scornfully. Heinrich pulled himself up in his chair. He said, feebly, "Is it not what I have said for years, my Eddie? And so it comes."

Maria said, as she knitted, "I have respect for your judgment. If you think it necessary, then it is necessary. It is unfortunate for my sons, however."

"Just when they're doing so well!" exclaimed Sylvia, malevolently. "Could that be your real reason, Ed?" She twitched her shawl closer about her, and her thin hands trembled.

"Why should it be?" asked Edward, with contempt.

"I know! You want them under your thumb again!" cried Sylvia. "They're free in Europe, free of you!"

Edward sat down slowly and smoked a cigarette. Mr. Faure came in with his tray of soda and whisky. Everyone fell into silence, but the old man glanced with anxiety at Edward, whom he loved dearly and devotedly. There was something very wrong with Edward, he thought; he recognised that pentness, that grim stillness, on his face. But Edward merely thanked him and waited until Faure had left the room. Then he sipped at his drink and looked at his sister with quiet loathing.

"Free?" he repeated. "Free of me? What is holding any of you here? Have you any idea of what you are all costing me, and what my debts are? Even my house isn't my own. What is to prevent you, for instance, leaving this house and going where you want to go? This is Greg's last year at Yale. He chatters now of writing 'his book,' right here, of course, at my expense, living in my house. Dave can manage to get engagements on his own, and pay his own agent, and as for Ralph, he can go to New York and make his own way as a portrait painter."

He sipped his drink again; his big hand shook with suppressed wrath. His grey eyes became points of fire under his thick black brows. "Well, why don't all of you do what you want to do? You've been costing me a fortune, in time and money, all the days of my life. And you speak of freedom for yourselves!"

"Edward," said Maria.

But Edward looked at his sister, and did not hear his father's faint and desperate murmur. "But the geniuses! It is expected that they have a patron . . ."

Sylvia had turned whiter than before, and she shrank in her chair. She moistened her pale lips. Edward must never know of the hats she designed for Mme. DelaFontaine. If he did he would evict his sister from this house, insist on her going to New York "on her own." She would have to live in some cramped apartment in the city; she would lose her security, the luxurious, effortless luxury of her home. She shivered, feeling the coldness of freedom, the uncertain and shifting footing of freedom, and she was swept with terror.

"We have a right——!" she cried, in her fear.

"A right to what? And who are you to talk of rights?" asked Edward, and a thrill of caustic triumph shook him. "You don't have any rights except those I give you and have given you. I've noticed that those who take finally believe they have a right to take—at someone else's expense. For weeks, now, you've sat here in your shawl, and have had your meals carried up to you, and a doctor dancing attendance on you. Are those your 'rights'? What've you done to earn them? You haven't even taken an interest in the theatre I bought for you, for months now."

Sylvia's terror disappeared in hatred and helplessness. She saw Edward's eyes and shrank again.

Maria broke in, calmly, "A slave is not a slave until the moment he accepts his slavery. And the master commits the crime when he offers slavery to kill the responsibility of free men to provide for themselves. Who are so strong as to prefer liberty and the hardships of living, when an easy thralldom is offered which demands neither thinking nor manhood?"

A glimmer of understanding came to Edward, and he flushed duskily. "I'm offering freedom," he said.

Maria shook her head. "To those already in chains?"

Edward surged with rage. He stood up. "You didn't sing that song years ago, Ma. You sang the songs of the 'geniuses.' Everything for the geniuses, remember? You've changed your tune. When did the change begin?"

Maria put her knitting in her lap and gazed at her son contemplatively. "There is a great difference between assistance and enslavement. When the one who assists becomes suddenly obsessed with power, then he has committed a great crime against those to whom he first extended help. I am convinced," she went on, "that a man and a law become evil when they begin to oppress those who have offered themselves for oppression. You see"—she smiled inscrutably—"as I grow older I become wiser. But then, I was never a Socialist, and I never hated my fellow-men enough to believe that I knew what was best for them."

"You're too subtle for me, Ma," said Edward, with new contempt.

Maria nodded. She picked up her knitting again. "But some day it will be clear to you. That will be a sad day. Edward, I have noticed that you have studied much about Bismarck through these years. And you have begun to love liberty more than anything else. Yet, you have denied liberty to others. Is that paradoxical? No. Not in good men, and you are a good man. And as a good man, you feel guilty in your heart."

"I feel guilty because I've let myself be exploited!" said Edward. "And not because I wanted power. Power over whom? A pack of weaklings and spenders?"

Maria said nothing. She continued to knit impassively.

Edward made a furious gesture. " Why don't they get the hell out and make their own way, and leave my house?"

Maria said quietly, " Do you think they can, now?"

" That doesn't even deserve an answer, Ma."

Edward turned to his sister. " You've heard," he said, to her taut white face. " This has been a very interesting discussion. Perhaps you've got enough intelligence to understand it. So, you tell Ma why you don't stand on your own legs and amount to something. You tell her what's keeping you here, you who are going on twenty-four years of age."

But Maria said, " How can she answer you, when she doesn't dare answer?"

Sylvia drew her shawl more tightly about her and her very lips were icy. Edward said, " What I've done for myself, they can do for themselves. They're old enough."

" But no longer free enough, in their spirits," said Maria. She turned her profile to her family and it was heavy with sadness. " Why have I not interfered before? That is what I ask myself all through the nights. And now I know there's a terrible inevitability in the affairs of men. Not even God can interfere, for it is by their own wills that men become despots or slaves. And, who is the victim? The despot, or the slave? One can only have compassion."

" I'm a fine despot!" said Edward, with irony. " I've worked ever since I can remember. I've sacrificed everything I could have had. I work sixteen hours a day. I take nothing for myself. I only give."

Maria nodded. " There was never a tyrant who did not say the same thing, never, in the history of the world. Before they died, either naturally or by violence, they cried out that they sacrificed themselves endlessly, and worked endlessly. And so they did. Most of them lived austerely, wanting nothing of pleasure. They worked to their deaths for their people, and one cannot doubt their sincerity. But still, they were despots and murderers. For they took away liberty and gave slavery. They destroyed souls, and there is no greater sin than that."

A great darkness and sickness swelled up in Edward. Then, with renewed fury, he turned on Sylvia. " Have I destroyed your soul?" he asked.

Yes, thought the terrified girl, simply. But I helped. I didn't have any real courage.

But she shut off the bleak horror of her silent confession, for she could not bear it. She looked about her quickly, like a threatened animal seeking escape from death. She clasped her hands together in a convulsive movement. "I don't know what you're talking about, either of you," she said hoarsely. She could not stop herself from glancing at Edward, and she hated him.

Edward laughed, and his laugh was ugly. "You see, Ma," he said.

Heinrich, as was common those days, had fallen into a sickish dose. But he started when he heard Edward's laugh, and woke. "Is it dinner?" he said, hopefully, for he found comfort in his meals. His belly would warm from the wine, and he could believe once more that he was a man and a father and the master of the home, and was loved and needed.

"Not yet," said Edward, noticing him for the first time. He did not know why he rarely, in these past years, ever looked directly at his father or why he never talked with him alone, or easily, in the presence of others.

"I've got something to tell all of you," he went on, for Heinrich's eyes, so childlike, so mournful, so seeking, unnerved him. He was dimly aware that his father wanted something, and was even more dimly aware that the giving could only come from him. But what it was his father begged, and what he, himself, could give, he never knew.

"I'm going to be married soon," he said shortly.

"Married?" said Maria, putting down her knitting again. "Is this not sudden, Edward?" Now even Sylvia and Heinrich sat erect, in astonishment.

"No," said Edward. "I've known the girl since I was fourteen." He spoke carefully and slowly, and avoided looking at them. "She was about ten then. Pa, you knew her, too."

Heinrich, overjoyed that his son had spoken to him and had seen him at last, exclaimed: "I? It is I of whom you are speaking, my Eddie?"

"Yes." Edward snuffed out his cigarette. This was going to be very bad, but it had to be faced. "She came into the old delicatessen when she was a little girl. It was a Sunday night. She was hungry. The—the people she lived with didn't believe in feeding children too much. And you—we—fed her. You gave her a lollipop, and some ice-cream, too."

"Oh, the poor little one," said Heinrich, and his eyes filled with easy tears. "But I fed many of the poor children, and it is hard to remember."

"She left Waterford with her—parents," said Edward. "And I didn't see her again until some time ago. I recognised her, and she recognised me."

"And you both fell in love!" said Sylvia, scornful and sure again. "How romantic. Naturally, she didn't mind recognising you again, since you're a rich man! What is she doing now? Working in a shop, perhaps? Or somebody's kitchen?" It was like her brother to be attracted to the coarse and the vulgar and the cheap! "And we're supposed to receive some pauper or shop girl and make her welcome! Don't rely on me, Ed, to be the loving sister-in-law. After all, I have my standards."

"Which I made it possible for you to have," said Edward, in a deadly voice.

"It does not matter what the young lady does to earn a living that is honest," said Maria, the aristocrat. But Heinrich cried out feebly, "My Eddie, one must think, one must ponder. We have few friends, but their opinions must be considered. One must think of the Bullocks and the Fosters and the Freudhoffs. . . . One must think of the position of the family, and the brothers and sister."

"But this is a democracy," said Sylvia with sober derision.

"What is the young lady's name?" asked Maria, ignoring her daughter.

"I don't know, and neither does she," said Edward, and now he was coldly beginning to enjoy himself. "She was an orphan, in the asylum here."

"An orphan?" Sylvia gasped. "She doesn't know who she is? Why she might even be—be . . ." She paused, and her pallor was relieved by a flush.

"Illegitimate?" said Edward, with fine carelessness. "Perhaps. Probably. She was left in the orphanage when she was a baby."

"Oh, you can't, you can't!" Sylvia cried, in real and horrified despair. "Not a woman without a background or family or money or anything! You can't do this to us!"

"I'm going to do it," said Edward. (It wasn't going to be so bad after all. In fact, it was going to be pleasant.)

"Tell us," said Maria, not disturbed at all. She did not look at her daughter, who had begun to cry.

"I told you. We recognised each other. And I asked her to marry me about two hours later. I never forgot her. The people who adopted her had taken her to a farm near Albany. She didn't return to Waterford until this year, when she came to dispose of some property her adopted parents had left her."

"Property?" repeated Heinrich, with some hope.

"Property." Edward nodded. "You see, her parents became almost rich, when they sold off parts of their farm to real estate men for new houses. She inherited their money when they died."

Heinrich beamed. Maria gave her whole attention to her son, and even Sylvia abruptly stopped crying. "Ah, it is property," murmured Heinrich. "It is not so bad, with property."

"What is her adopted name?" asked Maria, quietly.

"Pa's heard it; he heard it years ago. He knew the people." Edward paused. "Her name is Margaret Baumer."

Maria's hands stopped knitting; Sylvia's mouth opened soundlessly; Heinrich stared at his son, and blinked. The dinner gong rang through the house but no one heard it.

"Baumer?" said Heinrich, faintly. "That Baumer. I have heard it before. Yes, yes, I have heard it before, and not in the long ago."

Maria's large pouched face became rigid and stiff. "Baumer," she said, slowly. "I have heard it in this house. Margaret Baumer."

Then her pale-blue eyes shone with a hard light. "Yes. I have heard it. I have written it down." Her hands closed tightly over her knitting, and she drew a deep breath, and bent her head.

It was then that Sylvia jumped to her feet with a muffled scream. Her black hair, though neatly braided in her Tudor style, gave the impression of dishevelment. She pointed a trembling hand at Edward.

"Margaret Baumer! But she was the girl Dave was going to marry! He told us so, when Ma invited her. . . . Margaret

Baumer! Oh, God, it can't be the same woman, it can't, it can't!"

She was overwhelmed with agony. She thought of David, whom she loved. She wrung her hands together. Now her agony centred on herself. So she had suffered, when the man she wanted had suddenly married another woman, a stranger. She could not endure her pain. She pressed her hands against her small breasts. Edward had been responsible for that marriage, she knew! Edward had done that awful thing to her! David's pain was her pain; she even forgot her brother. She was freshly wounded, freshly mortally injured. She cried out again, and bent over, as if struck in the heart.

"Why all the damned dramatics?" said Edward, in a loud voice, but he had coloured. "Yes, she's the girl Dave thought he was going to marry. But she didn't want him; she never gave him any encouragement. She was only a friend of his, as far as she was concerned. If he had any stupid ideas, they weren't hers."

Sylvia groped for her chair, fell into it, and covered her face with her hands. She sobbed raggedly, her thin shoulders heaving, for grief unutterable.

"Don't be a goddamn fool," said Edward. "What's it to you?" But he knew, and the pang of pleasure the knowledge gave him was involuntary. He was immediately ashamed, in spite of his detestation for his sister.

Maria gazed at her daughter, and understood suddenly. Sylvia was weeping for herself, not for David. How had she, Maria, forgotten the dark stars in Sylvia's eyes when she had looked at Padraig Devoe, and the trembling voice, and the sweetness of her face? But, she had forgotten, and had not remembered until now. Maria paled. So, this was the explanation of Sylvia's illness, and the long weeks of her invalidism. Maria stretched out her hand and took one of Sylvia's gaunt wrists in her fingers, in an unusual gesture of maternal gentleness. "Hush," she said, softly. "Hush, my daughter. Let us be calm."

Heinrich was gaping at his son. "It is the girl David loved?" he stammered. "The girl who was invited to this house, and who did not come? My Eddie, this is not possible."

"I suppose you think I should be miserable, or feel guilty,

or something," said Edward. "But I'm not. These things happen. I'm sorry for Dave, but he's probably forgotten Margaret by now. She told him about us."

"And that is why he suddenly went to Europe," said Maria, and looked at her son straightly.

"Ma, be reasonable," said Edward. "It isn't my fault, and it isn't Margaret's. Do you think I like it this way."

Maria continued to gaze at him. Then she shook her head. "I do not know, I do not know," she said, slowly. "I do not think you planned it; no, Edward, I do not think so. But I also do not think you regret it."

"It doesn't make me happy!" said Edward, angrily. And believed it.

Sylvia raised her deathly face with its running tears. "It does, it does!" she exclaimed. "You'd rather have it this way than any other! I know!" She gulped desperately. "How can you do this to Dave, your brother?"

"Don't be an idiot," said Edward. "Do you think that if I didn't marry her she'd want Dave?"

"What a dreadful person she must be!" said Sylvia, brokenly. "What a dreadful, conscienceless, hateful person! Dave wouldn't have told us he was going to marry her unless he was sure. And then, and then"—her voice failed for a moment—"she meets you, understands that you have the money, and throws Dave over for you!" (As Padraig, with Ed's encouragement, had married a rich woman in preference to Sylvia Enger who had to rely upon her brother for her support!)

Edward's hands clenched into fists. "She didn't throw Dave over, you fool. She never accepted him. Get that into your stupid head."

He was suddenly sick of them all, sick of his mother's gleaming stare, his father's tear-filled eyes, his sister's hysterics. This was his house; they were his dependents. The food they ate, the roof that sheltered them, the clothing they wore, the money they spent, were the things he had given them freely. They could sit there, looking stricken and wounded or accusing, because, for the first time in his life, he wished something for himself, and had taken it!

He spoke to them all, very quietly but with malignance burning the edges of his words, "If it's so terrible to you,

Ma, Pa, Sylvia, and you can't stand it, you don't have to stay here when I marry Margaret in a few weeks. You'll have time. You can get ready to leave. You don't have to receive her. I'll look for a house for you." He smiled sombrely. "I hear our old house on School Street is for sale again. I'll buy it for you."

"This is all unnecessary," said Maria with hard coldness. "It is no occasion for threats."

"I'm not threatening," said Edward. "I'm just not going to have my wife embarrassed. This is going to be Margaret's home; she is going to be mistress here. I want decent behaviour towards her. If any of you think you can't give it to her, then you can leave."

Maria ignored this. But Sylvia stopped crying. She was looking affrightedly at her brother, and blinking her wet lashes. Maria said, "You have considered what David will think, how he will feel?"

"Yes, I have," said Edward, flatly. "And that's why I wanted to marry Margaret before telling you. Do you think I enjoy all this? But Dave will have to get over it, if he hasn't already gotten over it by now." Then his anger flared again, and he said with new violence, "But if he hasn't, and no matter how he feels, I can't help it. It's happened. It's got to be accepted. If any of you feel you can't accept it, I've offered you an alternative. It's the best I can do."

"I just can't receive her!" Sylvia sobbed.

"You don't have to," said Edward. All at once he was exhausted.

Maria said, "Naturally, we will accept her. Naturally, she will be my daughter. We must be sensible." She smiled, wryly. "Have we any other choice?"

She rose and went to Edward, for she was deeply concerned for him because of the dark colour of his cheek-bones and the sudden hollowness of his eyes. She put her hand on his arm. She could feel the throbbing of some large artery under the shabby cloth of his coat, and was alarmed. She tried to smile.

"But if I am to be the welcoming mother, I must make a request, Edward. I must request that you see a physician. It is only just that you find if your health is good. It is only just for—Margaret."

He wanted to shake off her hand, then was caught by her expression, which was almost tender. He had never seen it before. And he was grateful.

"All right, Ma," he said, smiling. But he had no intention of complying.

The dinner gong rang again, with impatience.

"It is dinner," said Maria. "We must descend."

"I don't want dinner, I won't go down, I can't bear it!" Sylvia groaned. "I'm going to my room. I'm going to bed."

Maria said, "You will be sensible, you will join us at dinner. I am still mistress in this house, and this is my command."

Chapter Eight

Maria sat down at her big mahogany desk in her sitting-room and wrote to Margaret Baumer.

"My son, Edward, and I have had a quiet discussion of your coming marriage, my dear Margaret, though we have not as yet met you. It was his first intention, and so he told me, for you to be married in Albany, with only strange witnesses present, and a brief appearance before public officials. I have now convinced him that this would be an injustice to you, and would leave you with no memories. A young lady, on her wedding day, is entitled to her memories of that most important occasion in her life, and to pleasant and happy recollections of which she will tell her children.

"The young lady is also entitled to know and become intimate with the members of her husband's family, and to acquire a familiarity with her new home where she will pass her life. I have also convinced Edward of this, and he has suggested that I write you. However, had he not made this suggestion I should have written in any event. To do otherwise would be an injustice to you.

"It is fortunate that you will be married on 28th June, in your new home, and under the auspices of our minister, the Reverend Mr. Yaeger. For, by that time my other children will be in residence, Gregory from Yale, and Ralph from Paris, where he has been studying art. My daughter, Sylvia, who is much gifted in the theatre arts, has not left home and her health is delicate. My son, David, whom you knew slightly, I believe, will not be present, though he has just returned from Berlin. He has many piano recital engagements to which he agreed some months ago, and is compelled by the terms of his contract to fulfil these engagements."

Maria paused, and her stern, light-blue eyes bulged with tears. She gazed through the windows at the sun-struck lawns and flower-beds beyond. A gardener was mowing the grass, and she could smell the sweetness of the cut blades and the scent of roses from the rose gardens. A small cloud of white butterflies blew up against the screen of the opened casement, and a warm wind whispered in the trees. Then Maria resolutely wrote again:

" My son, Ralph, is at present spending a few days in New York, consulting with the establishment where he will study again, beginning in September. He has paid us a short visit, bringing with him his bride, the former Violette Carré, a young French lady of distinguished family. . . ."

Maria took her lace handkerchief from her sleeve and pressed it against her lips. How silly, and stupid, it was of Ralph to tell his mother that fiction! She had known at once that Violette was a cocotte, and that she had probably been Ralph's mistress as well as model. Still, it had been a concession to his mother, and a tribute to her sensibilities, and her aristocracy, when he had lied.

I trust, thought Maria, that Margaret's knowledge of French is too limited to detect the grossness of Violette's patois, her paucity of education. Maria was too intelligent, too subtle a woman, to believe that because Margaret Baumer's birth was clouded, that she had been an inmate of a public orphan asylum, that she had been adopted by mean people, she would be a young woman of Violette's type. For Maria knew her son, Edward, too well to fear that he would be drawn to vulgarity or cheapness or mediocrity. Moreover, Edward had given his mother a small photograph of Margaret, and Maria had immediately, if silently, approved of that fine young face, those candid and beautiful eyes, the circumspect dress, and the lovely sensitive mouth. Whoever Margaret's parents had been there was the signature of patrician birth upon her features.

The blow of Ralph's marriage had been one of the worst calamities of Maria's life. But, as she was an indomitable woman she had neither cried out nor protested nor rejected Violette. There were matters one must accept. This catastrophe was one of them. Ralph was married, and appeared to be much enchanted by his young wife, and Violette seemed to have an amused and sardonic affection for him, and a humorous tolerance. She had, in addition, the intuitive Frenchwoman's training in the art of pleasing men and making their lives agreeable. It could be much worse, thought Maria, sighing again as she picked up her pen to continue her letter to Margaret.

"Ralph," Maria wrote, "will be home for the wedding with Violette." Maria turned the pen in her big fat fingers. "I wish at this time to extend to you, my dear Margaret, not only my affection but the affection of the family. Though we have not as yet had the pleasure of becoming acquainted with you, we know that we shall love you. You have brought to my son, Edward, an air of lightness and contentment, which I have never discerned in him before, and I know that your gift to him at your wedding will be a lifetime of happiness and fulfilment. He is inclined to be too serious, too much devoted to his work and his family. It is well that he is marrying.

"Permit me, as your future mother, and the mother of your bridegroom, to urge that you come as soon as possible to our home, before the wedding. This will not be improper or indiscreet or without propriety! My daughter and I will act as your perfect chaperones. I am already preparing quarters for you, and will wish to consult you as to the decorating of the suite which you and Edward will occupy."

But what should she, Maria, tell this young and inexperienced girl about Edward, her tragic son, absorbed in his desperate and secret misery, his unconscious insistence that his brothers and his sister give him a meaning in life? And what should she tell her about the exploitation of his youth, because he was strong, and must be the hand that lifted the weak, and supported them?

Chapter Nine

Margaret Baumer, though still very young, was well acquainted with the brief, unlit agony of life, and for this short time before she married Edward Enger she was still possessed of a lucid eye.

And so she was troubled and thoughtful this golden 23rd June, five days before she was to be married. Like Edward, she was of a solitary disposition. While his solitariness was invaded by cold and speechless resentments and colder anger, hers was contemplative, sometimes sad, and often an interlude which she used for summing up. Her childhood had been drab and full of pain and hopelessness, until comparatively recently, and it was still too close to her not to be part of her life and to affect her thoughts. It had not left her bitter, only frequently depressed and mournful, and quite often compassionate. Though she loved Edward as she had never loved before, and would never love again, she understood that the years of his life had hardened and congealed him. He had given her his first full confidence, and she had listened for hours in mute consternation and pity, not for what he had endured and not for his struggles, but for what his life had done to him and what he had permitted life to do to him, even with his own abetting. Later, she was to forget, in the very unfocusing of her devotion, the clarity with which she had first seen and understood.

She had been in his house for almost a week now, and at sunset, while the rest of the family gathered in Maria's and Heinrich's suite to talk and to drink coffee, she would quietly leave the house and wander in the gardens. She had found a favourite and hidden spot a long distance away, which Edward had preserved in a state of semi-wilderness of crowding great trees, thick grass and wild flowers. Here, on a weathered wooden bench, out of sight of the house, she would sit, her hands folded in her lap.

The bees hummed about her, catching little beams of light on their wings; the grass bent and changed colour in the warm wind; the trees towered over her in heavy shade and their tops glittered and moved. Margaret was sad and uneasy.

She was making up her mind how best to approach Edward on the subject of his family, not for the sake of the family but for his own salvation. Once or twice before she had attempted this tactfully, but he had looked at her with umbrage as if she had become a stranger who did not speak his language, and she had hurried to assure him that she understood, but . . . Once she had commented to herself, dryly, that if love overcame all things it also blinded all things.

Margaret was still not quite sure that Edward's explanation to her was correct—that his brothers and sister detested him because they were ungrateful. She was still able to suspect that their insulting way with him, and their fear, not open but to be easily discerned, rose from a secret detestation of themselves. She remembered David's last words to her on that night in March. "He doesn't despise me half as much as I despise myself."

Margaret folded a tuck in her green skirt, and shook her head despondently.

Gregory. Quick, mercurial, intelligent. There was an alert brain there, and a ruthless one. But he was without potency. He was like a sharp thin stick that could be easily broken in strong hands.

Now, there was Ralph, tall, plump, ruddy and handsome, with his curling auburn hair and big, bold black eyes, his cunning eyes so without illusion, so full of greed and so often morose and angry. Margaret felt an aversion for him. But somehow he reminded her of a big boastful young boy who was deeply frightened and who used a bullying manner to conceal his fright. For this, she pitied him.

At that moment Margaret came closer to the understanding of the whole *malaise* of the family than she was ever to come again.

She still could not think of David without a sharp pain. She was glad he was not here. But inevitably he would return some day. She prayed that he would, by then, have forgotten he ever loved her.

It had become alarmingly clear to her that not even the probable marriages of Sylvia, Gregory, and David would relieve her of their presence. Edward had said, "This is their home. Even when they're married I'll expect them to be here often, or always. They understand this."

Margaret had been incredulous. Why should Edward insist

that his brothers and sister, who hated and feared him, and whom he despised, should be under his roof? It was beyond her comprehension. She wanted to know why. So far, Edward had not enlightened her. Or, perhaps, he was incapable of enlightening her. She had thought it was a sort of clannishness in Edward, or even that he loved his family in spite of all this discord, this resentment, this hardly hidden malignance.

There was only one hope. Gregory had demanded post-graduate study. Ralph, brought home from Europe, wanted to study further. David had engagements all over the country. Sylvia, however, was a permanent fixture here, even if she married. But it would not be too bad! Things changed; not even Edward could stop the changing.

She turned her head and saw Edward approaching her across the tall thick grass, and, as always, her heart rose on a high crest of joy. He, alone, knew of this hiding place of hers. "The think-place," he had teased her. "It's mine, too."

She stood up and held out her hands to him with a low happy cry. He took them. It was then that she saw that his dark broad face looked sick and tense, and that his eyes were sunken and that his whole big body expressed despair.

Chapter Ten

"Tell me, darling," said Margaret, as she and Edward sat side by side on the bench, their hands together. She was frightened. He seemed ill and shattered, and yet full of rage. "You went to see Hans Bohn to-day and Congressman Sheftel. And Senator Bonwit."

And so he told her.

He had gone to see his friend, the prosperous newspaperman and publisher of the Waterford *Evening News*, who also published a newspaper in Albany and one in Rochester. Hans Bohn was known for his somewhat austere integrity, his publishing ethics, and his taciturn nature which rebuked too enthusiastic attempts at friendship from others. His deep cold passion was freedom of the press, truth and fair play; he had a hatred for sensationalism. He was a friend, a close friend of Edward Enger's, though Edward would have laughted at the idea. A middle-aged man, he was as lean as a fleshless stick, and gave a uniform impression of greyness, from his hair, his eyes and the colour of his skin, to his controlled cool manner. He never indulged in conversation for conversation's sake, and so was rarely seen in gayer society.

Edward had made an appointment with him a few days ago, and Hans received him in a large office as chill, grey and featureless as himself. He waited courteously until Edward had seated himself. On his smooth desk there was a pile of neat papers, and Edward saw that these were his own, which he had sent to the publisher. Hans put his long colourless hand on him as he saw Edward's glance. " Smoke, if you wish, Ed," he said in his toneless voice, and Edward lit a cigarette nervously. " Well, Hans?" he demanded, and his strong voice sounded too loud in the quiet office.

Hans went to a file and brought out a small old newspaper, so old that its edges were rusty and crackling. " I have here," he said, without expression, " a copy of the Buffalo *Courier and Republic*, published on 4th May, 1869. A good, sound newspaper. I sent for it, for I remember my father speaking particularly of this newspaper item, which was also published in other newspapers."

He paused. He found an immaculate tray for Edward's cigarette. All his movements were controlled and quiet. " I will read it to you, Ed.

> " Commercially, as well as from a military point of view, Russia is soon to be our chief rival. We are both advancing towards the coveted regions of Asia, and the influence of our settlements along the Pacific coast will soon be powerfully felt on the opposite—to us the western—side of the ocean."

He looked at Edward with his reserved eyes. " You see, now, that what you have given me I have known for some time. Socialism has already been adopted by Sweden. Bismarck brought much of it to Germany. It remains for Russia to give it—ah, eh—bloody impetus. There is something else you do not know. The bankers of Europe, the bankers of America, have long been dissatisfied with the Tsarist régime, in Russia. It has repulsed the Amsterdam-Frankfurt-Paris-London-Vienna cartel of those interlocked bankers. No foreign banks, said the Tsars, could carry on their business in Russia, if managed outside of Russia. In 1893, the Russian Minister of Finance advised all bankers in Russia that if they assisted speculative operations in the Russian rouble, it would be 'considered as incompatible with their privileges.' Because of this policy, the Russian banks are not as volatile, for instance, as the German banks, which are involved with politics."

Edward sat and listened to this usually monosyllabic man give him information which stunned him. It was much worse, much more involved, much more terrible and sinister than what he had thought! The papers he had given Hans now seemed puerile and superficial. Hans turned his swivel chair with slow dignity and stared through his polished window. His profile was stern and quiet.

"But evil, Ed, has a thousand eyes and a thousand brains and a thousand hands. Evil men are the most loyal in the world—to other evil men. The foreign bankers have already made an opening in Russia. The Rothschilds have an agent, the Bleichroeder Company of Berlin. One Carl Fuerstenberg, of the Berliner Handels-Gesellschaft, has already managed relations with the private Russian banking house, the Petersburger Dissonto Bank. The director of that bank was a partner in the Berliner Handels-Gesellschaft. So, now there is a bank of this in Russia."

A pattern, huge and malignant, though still vague, began to loom in Edward's mind, like a gigantic weaving machine. The threads darted in and out, red and gold and black, manipulated by unseen hands.

Ed stood up. He thrust his shaking hands into his trousers' pockets. His breath was shallow, because of the constricting heat and agony in his chest. He turned to him and said in a passionate voice:

"You know! How many men like you know, Hans?"

Hans sighed. "Thousands of us, Ed, tens of thouands of us, in every country in the world. But, who would listen? Should I publish an editorial about this, who would listen? I would be laughed out of circulation. The only ones who would believe are those who know. I am a publisher of three newspapers, but I am vulnerable. I could be stopped. You stare. Yes, I could be stopped in America. It would be simple. I happen to love my newspapers."

"America!" said Ed, with anguish. "Surely not America!"

"Surely, America," said Hans. "Surely America, too. It has already begun."

"Then, we can do nothing, Hans."

The publisher smiled dryly. "We can try, Ed. We can have it for our spiritual salvation, that we tried."

Edward sat down, crushed and overwhelmed.

Hans took up one of Edward's pages and scanned it. "You wish to form a Save America Committee. People will ask: 'Save America from what?' You speak of wars. There is no war on the horizon—yet. I recommend that you begin to form that Committee after a war breaks out. It will not be long, I assure you. Who will we fight? people will ask. Perhaps England or Germany or Russia. It doesn't matter. War is the thing, and continuing wars."

Congressman Henry Sheftel was a small and active man, young, ambitious, and absolutely innocent. He had not been in politics very long. He still believed that it was the duty of Congressmen to obey the wishes of the electorate, and to represent them with honour, integrity and devotion. His thick yellow curls crowned a slim and open face, like a boy's, and he had small and sparkling blue eyes. He did not belong to Edward's Party, but the two young men had known each other from school days, and both had had a background of hard work and responsibility. He had wondered why Edward had asked him to go to the office of the Honourable Senator Thorne Bonwit, who was of the opposite Party, very wealthy (he owned an apartment house in New York), and a man of devious mind, expedient and too suave. In Washington, they called him Gentleman Bonwit, and he was much liked except by the few of Henry Sheftel's calibre.

Henry was uneasy in the senator's rich law offices on Mandrell Street. His own little law office was shabby and usually filled with poor and desperate people. Henry had seen the well-dressed men in the senator's office, men with gold watch-chains, spats and polished boots. He had not envied the senator his clientele. He had not been in politics very long.

The senator had been condescending, but agreeable. A big

and florid-faced middle-aged man, full of jokes and ever tactful and amiable, he had large features which gave a meretricious impression of candour. His large fingers were manicured, and glittered pinkly. Seeing them, Henry hid his bitten finger-nails in his pockets. He accepted one of the senator's excellent cigars, and put it in his pocket for his father, who had a small shoe store and could only afford a cigar on Sundays.

"One of Eddie's little mysteries," said the senator, affably.

Henry frowned, politely trying to understand. Ed was never mysterious. He was hard and blunt and thrusting, and he meant what he said when he said it.

"We've been friends all our lives, in a way," murmured Henry. "And he did contribute something to my campaign two years ago, even though we don't belong to the same Party."

"Friendship," said the senator genially, and nodding comprehendingly. He thought of the large contribution Edward had made to his own campaign. Yet, Edward was no personal friend of his, and he did not believe that Edward particularly liked him. The senator, who called himself very democratic, had an aversion for people not of his own social stratum and who had made their own fortunes. But Edward was wealthy and he was a friend of George Enreich's, and George Enreich called the tune in State politics. "Ah, here they are now, Ed and Hans," said the senator, as his secretary entered. "Now we'll soon have the solution of this little mystery! Come in, come in, gentlemen! How are you, dear Ed, and Hans? Hans, are you here in the capacity of a reporter? Hah! Fine day, isn't it, fine day! Always happy to be home among my own friends. Sit down, sit down! Cigars? Why didn't you ask me to be your best man, Ed? No, no, I was only joking; don't take me seriously."

Something's wrong, he thought cunningly, under his unctuous and bounding chatter. What's Hans doing here? Bill 1792? I'll have to be careful and watch it. Never liked Hans, the cold grey fish; he gave me some bad days after that editorial of his last October. Never liked Ed, for that matter; you can't trust men who have no subtlety and who never ask you for favours. They save up for the day when they have a definite and serious demand, and it's hell trying to satisfy and deceive them at one and the same time.

Yes, it was serious. Hans was regarding him with his chilly eyes and Edward, the senator thought distastefully, looked like a driver of a brewer's big wagon. Why did he have to look so shabby and so bulking? "Yes, yes," said the senator, happily. "Henry and I have been wondering why you asked him to meet both of you here. Not the same Party, hah, hah! But friends, yes, friends!"

"Stop babbling, Thorne," said Hans, indifferently. "You never keep your big red mouth shut, and you don't have to advertise the fact that you visit your dentist at least twice a year. I'm not here as a newspaper man; I'd have sent a reporter instead of coming myself, if I wanted an interview with you. I'm here as an American, and a private citizen, and so is Ed." He held up his hand, and the senator's loud gay laugher stopped abruptly. "For once, Thorne, listen and don't talk. You're wasting our time. All right, Ed, begin."

Edward talked in short and precise sentences, with a kind of cold vehemence. He talked, without interruption, for over ten minutes, and his voice was the only sound in the room. And, as he spoke, Hans acutely watched the faces of the two politicians. Henry's face expressed in turn, confusion, alarm, incomprehension, incredulity and then greater alarm. He leaned forward in his chair, his fingers laced tensely together, and kept his eyes on Edward's face, as in a kind of appalled trance.

But Senator Bonwit's face slowly took on the aspect of smooth pink marble, his handsome brown eyes expressionless and watchful. He smoked steadily, and with an air of ease. He knows, thought Hans. Yes, he knows. But not poor little Henry. This is all news to him.

Edward had finished. Then Hans took up the story in his remote and unaccented voice, judicious and without passion. Henry gazed at him with mounting horror; the senator was very still and curiously impassive, though wearing an air of polite interest.

"Well," said Hans, finally, "you've heard us, both of you. We're not hysterics; we're businessmen, and we're well informed. We not only believe what we've told you; we know it to be the truth. The question is, what are you going to do about it?"

Henry looked at the senator; his small features were squeezed together as if he were about to cry. The senator took his cigar from his mouth and studied the glowing end contemplatively. Then he smiled, and sighed. He raised his eyes and looked at Edward and Hans ruefully, and shook his head.

"I don't believe a word of it," he said, as if with wonder. "Oh, I'm not doubting that you believe what you've both told me. Now, I'm in Washington. There isn't even a rumour, and I give you my word of honour as your senator! Everything's calm and placid. It's true that the President is an unworldly scholar, and has strange ideas, but we have a sensible Congress. I assure you, boys, that if there was the slightest rumour—the very slightest, please understand—I'd be almost the first to know. Colonel House is a personal friend of mine. We dine frequently together."

"We never said that President Wilson is part of the plot," interrupted Hans, contemptuously. "He'll probably be the last to know, if he ever knows." He gazed at the senator, who became ruddier than ever. "But you know, don't you, Thorne? I know a lot about you; I understand you have about a million dollars' worth of munitions stocks. Besides, you'd like to be President, wouldn't you? I've heard rumours."

He turned to Henry, kindly, while the senator sat in speechlessness. "Well, Henry?"

The young man's sensitive mouth trembled visibly. "Hans, if you are really convinced—I can't believe these terrible things, but you know more than I do—Hans, you can count on me to vote against getting America into any war. . . ."

The senator suddenly turned his head to the youthful Congressman, and for an instant there was a malign flash in his eye. Then he gave his attention to Hans and laughed gently.

"Hans, I'm going to overlook your remarks about my munitions stocks, and what you allege are my ambitions. I am going to ask you a hypothetical question, purely hypothetical. What if the British or German Fleet should ever stand in New York harbour with guns trained on the city?"

Hans smiled slightly. "You know that'll never happen, Thorne. And you also know that can be used as a lying threat to get America into some long-plotted war."

The senator assumed an expression of sadness and open dismay. "Hans! I honestly don't understand you. You and

Ed, here, have been talking about plots and counter-plots and wars, and, frankly, it sounds like Alice in Wonderland. I've not been contradicting anything either of you has said, for, to me, it has no meaning whatsoever. No basis, no reality. But, I've been interested, as one would be interested in a new game. That's why I asked you that hypothetical question, without real seriousness.

"But"—and now his face stiffened and he watched them—"would you not defend America, in the very improbable circumstance that we should be attacked? Would you be—pacifists?"

Pacifists. Hans pondered the word. It was new. And it was terribly dangerous. "Pacifists?" said Edward, in a loud and brutal voice. "Explain that."

The senator waved his hand largely. "I meant, isn't America worth fighting for or even dying for? I think so."

"Yes," said Edward. "She is. I love my country. I want to keep her out of fighting and dying—permanently."

Hans stood up, and stretched his lean body. He seemed casual and relaxed, but the senator watched him with sudden alertness. "I'm thinking of something the fourth President of the United States once said, James Madison: 'Of all the evils to public liberty war is perhaps the most to be dreaded.—War is the parent of armies; from these proceed debts and taxes. And armies, and debts, and taxes, are the known instruments for bringing the many under the dominion of the few. In war, too, the discretionary power of the executive is extended—and all the means of seducing the minds are added to those of subduing the force of the people! No nation could preserve its freedom in the midst of continual warfare.'

"That, Thorne, was said by President Madison generations on generations ago. And I suggest that you understand it all too well, too well for American peace. 'Armies, and debts, and taxes, are the known instruments for bringing the many under the dominion of the few.' You expect to be one of the few, don't you, Thorne?"

The high colour left the senator's face, and Edward, watching him, wondered if that hard white pallor meant guilt or anger or fear. It could be all of them. He was convinced this was true when the senator lost his jocund manner, his affability, his genial air of tolerant appeasement, and replaced it with menace and quiet fury and threat. The time had come, the senator had apparently decided, when the politician's amiability was of no further use.

"Hans," he said, "don't use those remarks of yours in your newspapers. We still have libel laws. And in Washington——"

"Yes, I know," said Hans, with bitter coldness. A word in Washington, from you. My newspapers are mortgaged. Somehow, through your banker friends, and your friends in Washington, my loans could be suddenly called in. But, I have friends, too. My newspapers almost defeated you last November. The next time, I can really defeat you, even if I lose my newspapers. But, do you know something, Thorne? I don't believe you'll move against me. Not yet, anyway. You wouldn't dare."

He turned to the Congressman, Henry Sheftel, who was much shaken after this exchange. "Henry," said Hans, "let's get out of here. There's a stench in this place."

"So, you see," said Edward to Margaret, in the blowing green light of the early evening, as they sat side by side on the wooden bench, "Hans wasn't sure about Bonwit. He wanted to be sure; he wanted to learn something. And he did. He learned about Sheftel, too. We talked about Sheftel, later. We're going to support him against Bonwit, at the next senatorial elections, though he isn't of our Party."

Margaret looked at his worn and haggard face, and her heart squeezed together, and she put her head on his shoulder. She was deeply frightened and stricken. The warm wind blew stronger, and lifted the scent of the earth into the air, like an overpowering perfume. The sky dreamed in a soft blue, and a few radiant clouds stood motionless in it. There was such peace here, such coolness. It was almost impossible to believe in hot if quiet plottings, and terrors, and unnamed wars, and the furious calculations of evil men. But Margaret believed Edward. However, she wanted to soothe and comfort him. Before she could speak, he went on drearily:

"Bonwit knows about my plans for expansion into large markets in most of the big cities. General grocery, meat and and vegetable stores, like the Atlantic and Pacific. Just before we left him—and he'd lost all that ruddy pleasantness of his by then—he said to me, 'Ed, there's some rumour in

Washington of bringing an anti-trust suit against the Atlantic and Pacific. It would be unpleasant, wouldn't it, if a similar suit were brought against you? Or an order of restraint?'"

"Oh, Ed, you're not afraid of him!"

"No," said Edward, grimly. "But there was another thing. At the door, he said, 'You're a German, aren't you?' And he looked at Hans from me. So Hans is now convinced that the war will be against Germany."

"Impossible," said Margaret, quietly. "At least a third of the American people are of German stock. And America and Germany have always been good friends, and the American people don't like England."

"It doesn't matter," said Edward. "Nations 'like' or dislike, other countries whenever their rulers tell them to do so, with lies and libels."

Margaret was silent for a few minutues. Then she said, "But, Ed, if there is an inevitability about all this, what can you do? What makes you so intense about it?"

"I don't know," he answered, slowly. "So help me God, I don't know. But when I think of it I almost lose my mind."

He held her hand so tightly that it hurt her. "You make me, even now, love life, and have hope," he said, in a voice that none of his family ever heard. "As long as I have you I won't be completely desperate, Margaret." He kissed the gilded lashes, and then her lips.

After a while Margaret said, "Your family is giving us a party to-night, inviting most of their friends. We must hurry."

Edward was quite aware of his family's reactions to Margaret. He stopped, but Margaret coaxingly locked her arm in his and laughed. "Your mother is really a most remarkable lady," she said. "A grand lady. Your brothers and sister are spoiled, I admit, but they have possibilities. And your father is sweet. He told me this morning that he was coming down for the party."

"There's nothing wrong with him!" said Edward, with a violence that startled her. "Nothing! He's just indulging himself. He can afford it. I made that possible for him. He has what he wanted, a mansion, money, servants, and people fawning on him and visiting him."

But, no one notices the poor thing, thought Margaret sadly. And what he wants isn't what you've said, my darling.

Now they were out in the last long sunlight, and approaching the formal gardens with their flower-beds, their grottoes, their dusky paths and little glades. A fountain sang before them, a bowl of water in mossy stone. A marble child stood in the centre, naked and laughing, with a big fish in his arms, and from the fish's mouth poured a sparkling stream. The child had a gay and mocking face, in spite of the chubby cheeks and the stony curls and the dimpled chin. Edward stood with Margaret to look at him.

"Somehow, I don't like it," said Edward. "William picked it up in Italy. The face's too wise, too knowing. Too—decadent."

Margaret thought so too, but she said, "I think it's charming."

She hugged his arm briefly, and they went on. They came in sight of the house at an angle; it loomed against a dark-red sunset, all its windows cold. Edward said restlessly, "It'll never be my own until I lift the mortgage. And lifting the mortgage is the first thing I'll do when I can stop pouring money into the business and open my markets. I'm going to call them the Green and White markets, and I've got ideas better than the Atlantic and Pacific Tea Company. I'll give them some good competition."

He seemed more vigorous. He lifted Margaret's hand from his arm and kissed it. All at once he was buoyant. "Perhaps the things I know won't happen in our lifetime. With you, darling, surely I'll have some peace now, all the days of my life."

"'Surely goodness and mercy shall follow me all the days of my life, and I shall dwell in the house of the Lord for ever'," she quoted softly.

"What?" he said annoyed.

"It's the twenty-third psalm," she said, with surprise. "Didn't you know what you've been quoting?"

"No," he said, shortly. "And I'm sorry I know now. And I'm going to forget it. I like it the way I thought it was."

She knew his moods as well as she knew her own. She walked with him in silence. The air seemed to darken as they approached the mighty and solid house. There was a sudden flash of lightning in the east, and then a low rolling of thunder. A willow's long hair suddenly lashed in the strengthening wind, and blew against the red sky in green dishevelment. Margaret, oppressed all at once, hoped it wasn't a bad omen. She looked at the eastern sky, and saw new and looming clouds, as dark as Edward's face, and as unquiet. "Let us run!" cried Margaret, and there was an urgency in her voice which was not connected with the gathering storm at all.

Chapter Eleven

The wedding day was dim and oppressively green, so that the gardens, where the marriage took place, lost colour, and, in spite of the smothering heat of the weather, held a kind of remote desolation and colourlessness. It was Sylvia who had designed the altar, near the fountain, and Margaret thought it perfection. Sylvia received this compliment haughtily, and turned away in disdain. Did this shop girl, this cheap creature, think she could please her, Sylvia Enger, with this superficial gratitude? It was actually an insult. Sylvia said ungraciously, "I'm glad you like it. It was the garden altar I designed last summer for our play, *The Golden Lady*."

The altar was in an arch painted soft green and covered with yellow roses, each one perfect, and seeming to shine vividly in the spectral light of the ominous afternoon. The arch itself was banked with Chinese jade-coloured pots filled with towering ferns, and in its centre was a low altar covered with a green and silver cloth, which glimmered dully. The sound of the fountain seemed unduly loud, almost crashing, in the hushed quiet, and drops of quicksilver water floated on the ferns closest to it. A green grass carpet stretched all the way from the house to the altar, which stood in wide isolation. At a considerable distance tables covered with white damask and bowls of flowers and glimmering silver were prepared for the bridal party.

There had been considerable scornful and derisive conversation between Edward's brothers and sister because he had chosen William McFadden to be his best man, and Margaret had chosen as her matron of honour Maggie McNulty Devoe. Sylvia and Violette were the bridesmaids, and Gregory and Ralph the ushers. Sylvia, who had spitefully hoped that rain would spoil the wedding, now was anxious that it would not, for she had designed not only Margaret's wedding-gown, but the gowns for herself and Violette. Pride in her secret profession had prevented her from her first impulse to make Margaret seem dowdy and unattractive, and when she heard the sincere exclamations of delight from her sister-in-law, Maggie and Margaret, she almost liked the bride.

But when Padraig had arrived two nights ago with his imposing and beautiful wife, Sylvia had been freshly devastated. She could not beg her mother to let these guests stay at the hotel in Waterford; that would be betraying herself. She hated Maggie; the very sight of her made Sylvia physically ill. She avoided Padraig, and did not see him until the day of the wedding. She detested William; his bright hazel eyes saw too much, and he had a sharper repartee than her own. Moreover, he was attached to Edward and that, in Sylvia's estimation, branded him as a person of low taste. Her whole being, body and spirit, was in a state of tense and aching turmoil these days. She supervised the dressmakers, and her cutting voice could frequently be heard in the sewing rooms. But she would not come downstairs for her meals and lay for hours, sometimes, on her bed, staring blankly at the ceiling.

Violette was malicious; she had guessed that Sylvia loved Padraig. But she admired Maggie to Sylvia with such an air of absolute innocence that Sylvia was deceived. "I think Mrs. Devoe's too lush," said Sylvia. "But, after all, she is quite old. Did you see the gown she is wearing to the wedding, Violette? I didn't." She paused. "Tell me."

Violette described the blue silk lace with enthusiasm, and the wide garden hat to match and the blue lace parasol. "The magnificent eyes: they will be—increased," said Violette, in her uncertain but descriptive English. "I suggested a touch, an accent, one pink rose, on the bosom, embossed on the lace. Ah! She kissed me. Like a mother," added the clever Violette, seeing the sick darkness on Sylvia's face.

Sylvia had designed a daring gown for Violette, her artistic eye guiding her to enhance the girl's trim and impudent prettiness. The gown was of fresh golden silk, sophisticated in its lines, which brought out the firm young bosom, the short narrow waist, the swelling hips. It clung to the trim thighs, then flared from the knees to the floor. To Sylvia, Violette was the perfect model, though her figure certainly was not American. Sylvia also designed the golden silk little sailor hat, which Violette was to perch on her chestnut curls and chignon. All this brought out the amber lights of Violette's skin, and the vivid oval eyes, and naturally red mouth, with its naughtily pouting lower lip.

For herself Sylvia had designed a dress of mauve faille, demure yet unusual. Violette suggested padding for the bosom of Sylvia's dress. "It is too thin, the figure," said Violette. "It is—it is the virginal. One may be a virgin, *non*? But one does not display it to the gentlemen. It is like fruit, the green fruit, hard like the stone, biting to the tongue."

"I'm sure you never had to worry about that," Sylvia had said, colouring angrily. But Violette had laughed with high merriment, and had not been insulted in the least. She liked Sylvia very much, but she thought her naïve and provincial.

Sylvia did not attend the family dinner the night before the wedding. She was not only anguished and bereft; she was also exhausted from her work. She could not endure the thought of seeing Padraig in candlelight, at the very table where she had often gazed at him with secret and devouring love.

Margaret did not speak at all. She sat at Edward's right hand but rarely saw his face, which was turned to his friends. For some reason she felt despondent and alone. It was only when the beautiful Maggie Devoe smiled at her across the table, with such affection and encouragement, that her spirits rose a little. After dinner, Margaret went upstairs, in accordance with custom. She would not see Edward until to-morrow.

No one was on the second floor, not even a servant. Margaret went silently to the newly decorated suite which she and Edward would occupy. She had timidly asked for ivory walls, with touches of gilt, a pale Aubusson rug in tints of blue and rose and yellow, for the sitting-room. This had been done. She had suggested the decorations, for this was one of the few rooms filled with Parisian furniture: small gilt chairs in blue and rose brocade, small marble tables and crystal lamps, and love-seats in light gold silk. She had chosen the draperies of blue and gold and rose brocade, with their silken fringes. Her bedroom was similarly furnished. Even Sylvia had grudgingly conceded that it was all very beautiful and perfect. The casement windows overlooked the gardens, and a small white marble fireplace was filled with white roses.

Edward's bedroom was large and somewhat ponderously furnished, and all in heavy mahogany and dark rugs and draperies. A single lamp was lit, on a big table near the bed with its high and intricately carved mahogany headboard. Margaret entered the room and approached the bed. She touched the crimson velvet spread lovingly. She wandered to the chests of drawers, with their oval, wood-framed mirrors. Here were Edward's leather cuff-link boxes, his silver brushes. She touched them shyly, and her heart trembled. No man had ever been born who could compare with dear Ed, she thought. Dear Ed, with his beset face, his tired grey eyes, his deep and gentle smile. She clasped her hands suddenly to her breast. She had almost nothing to give him, but her love and all her life and her devotion. So little to give!

The lamplight shimmered on her hair, on the pure curve of her cheek and chin, and on her white shoulders which rose from her pearl-coloured gown. She caught a glimpse of a shadow, and turned swiftly and fearfully. It was only Pierre, who was entering to turn down Edward's bed. She smiled at the aged and bent old man, and he returned her smile. His ancient eyes had watched her for a full minute before she had seen him. It is a lovely lady, he had thought, a very tender and innocent child, who has suffered. It is a lady worthy of my Edward, for she has known pain and loneliness and it has not made her harsh.

"Good evening, Pierre," said Margaret, blushing because he had found her here. "It's lonely to be a bride, on the night before the wedding."

"Yes, Miss Baumer," the old man replied. He turned down the velvet bedspread with deft hands, mottled and tendoned. "You will permit me to bring you a glass of wine? It is good for the sleep, on a troubled night."

Margaret accepted gratefully, and went into the sitting-room. The house was so hot, and so very quiet. The clouded sky was streaked with dark veins, like vaulted marble. Margaret could hardly breathe. She sat in a chair near the casement, and waited for the wine. It was brought to her soon, and she thanked Pierre. He hesitated.

"Miss Baumer will permit me to speak? She will not think me presumptuous?"

Margaret took the crystal glass from her lips. Her blue eyes widened kindly on the old man, but with some surprise. "I'd never think you presumptuous, Pierre," she said. "Do say whatever you wish."

"It is about my Edward," he said, in the low voice of one who is seriously deafened. He looked at her anxiously. "He is my friend. He is not only my employer. I was lost and abandoned, and he took me into his heart and into his house. I regard him as my son, my dear, beloved son. Miss Baumer understands?"

"Yes," she said, very moved. "I know how you love Ed, Pierre."

He sighed, and clasped his hands listlessly before him. "It is not easy to speak, for all is elusive. For my Edward's sake, I ask Miss Baumer not to look with unseeing eyes. All is not what it seems, and I say this, who loves him. The loyalty of love can deceive, when one is young. The old can be loyal, but they are not blind. For Edward's sake, it is necessary for Miss Baumer to see clearly. Most necessary, for his sake."

Margaret tried to understand. The old man was urgently trying to convey something very subtle but very important to her, and she was baffled. She said at last, while he waited, "I think I know what you mean, Pierre. He's been exploited all his life. He's given all his life to his family." Her voice rose on a little crest of anger. "You want me to help stop the exploitation? That's it, isn't it?"

Pierre sighed again, as if his last hope had gone, and he half-turned away. "He is destroying himself," he murmured. "Because he is destroying others."

Margaret caught the murmur, but not the words. She watched the old man go to the door. He paused there, and looked at her desolately. "Perhaps," he said, "it is enough to love. Perhaps love will finally see, and save."

How had he deceived himself that so young a woman, so innocent and unworldly a woman, so passionately loving a woman, could understand? "Good night, Miss Baumer," he said, mournfully, and went away.

Margaret spent a restless night. Occasionally, waking from a dose, she heard the growl of thunder, the sudden lashing of trees. Her nightgown was damp and clammy, and she turned her pillows frequently. Occasionally she thought, I should have been married as Edward wanted to be married, alone in Albany. This family is so unfriendly to me; they'll never like me. And I'll never like them! How cruel they are, how absolutely cruel and unfeeling. Oh, if we could only live alone, and never see them again. Never, never. Her braided hair felt too heavy on her neck and shoulders. Her whole body, mind and spirit felt heavy and foreboding.

Edward waited at the altar for his bride. Damn all this ceremony. He felt ridiculous. "Quiet, quiet, boyo," William murmured at his side. "It's committed you are, and did I not warn you?" "Shut up," muttered Edward, out of the side of his mouth. "Don't lose that ring." William chuckled under his breath.

A portable organ had been set up nearby. It looked absurd to Edward, and so did the wife of the Sunday school superintendent, in her bunchy, apricot-coloured dress. She sat on the bench, with a prim and reverent expression, and blinked her eyes behind her spectacles. Edward thought that the waiting minister, in his expensive black clerical garb, was too pompous, too grave, too important. It was enough to make a man laugh, Edward said to himself, to see him under that silly arch with all those roses. There was a strong scent in the air, like the scent of a coming storm, though the misty trees were absolutely still. The fountain, to Edward, positively clattered.

The wedding guests were waiting also, seated on little chairs in a semi-circle facing the altar. Yes, Senator Bonwit was there, though Edward had hardly expected him, and Henry Sheftel and Hans Bohn, and all "the friends of the family." His brothers hovered in the background, conducting late arrivals to seats. There sat his mother, regal and massive, in dark blue silk, and beside her was his father, round and plump and pale, and next to him, George Enreich with his square, cynical countenance and stiff red hair. There, too, was Padraig, kingly in his striped trousers and Prince Albert, his tragic face softened by the months of his marriage. When he caught Edward's eye he smiled slightly, the smile of an affectionate friend. The mayor of Waterford was there, with his wife. The waiting and expectant faces appalled Edward, whose body felt hot and uncomfortable, and " foolish " (in his opinion), in his formal clothing. There was no sound but the flutter of the ladies' fans and the gush of the fountain. He visibly started when, at some unseen signal, the organ crashed into the wedding march and started brooding birds out of the shadowy trees.

Maggie appeared on the grass cloth carpet, carrying not wearing, a pink rose. Edward saw a tall blue blur, which excited admiring murmurs from the ladies, but Padraig saw his heart's darling, his Maggie, the mother of his child, who would be born in six months. Then, walking slowly came the bridesmaids. Everyone stared at Violette, shining like a figure of fluid gold against the background of the motionless trees, her pert face falsely demure. That was the French girl, of a hinted noble family. Too much bosom, thought some of the ladies with disapproval, and too accentuated. Sylvia, pacing her, was tall, and thin almost to emaciation, her feverish eyes and white face fixed and sightless; she moved as if all her muscles were rigid. Nevertheless, she was admired. The girl certainly had taste and style; if the mauve gown was not quite her colour, she so dark and without vividness, it was exquisite. She walked with her head slightly bent under her yellow hat. The two girls carried yellow roses floating in lavender tulle.

All held their breath for the bride. And then she was there, a radiance in white lace, her lovely face half-hidden by a veil. Maria still felt affronted. It was most improper for no one to give the bride away, but for some peculiar and unexplained reason, Margaret had gently insisted that this must be so. She had refused Padraig's kind offer, relayed through Edward. She had said to her groom, " I don't know who were my parents or if I have relatives. I lived alone, all my life, and I want to come to you, Ed, all alone. Maybe it isn't just right. I can't say what I mean. I want to walk to you, all by myself, giving what I am to you."

The minister had disapproved at the rehearsal. " A lady doesn't give herself away," he had politely pointed out. " This lady does," Margaret had said.

The virginal veil showed only the colour of her lips, the faint hint of her blue eyes. But the wedding-gown was absolute artistry, and Sylvia, awakening from her trance of grief, felt a thrill of pride at the way the fabric outlined the tall and slender figure, the long slender waist, the girlish hips, the soft bosom.

Edward had hardly seen the bridal attendants. He remembered what Margaret had said. " I want to walk to you, all by myself, giving what I am to you." Neither he nor Margaret heard the swell of hushed admiration, nor saw handkerchiefs touched to sentimental mouths and eyes. She came to him in her dignity and her girlhood and all her beauty, her hands, with their Bible, already lifted towards him. In spite of a restraining gesture from William he advanced a few steps to meet her. Then he drew her before the altar and the ceremony began, against a background of murmurous music. And the two gazed at each other, and not at the minister.

He had had to dispense with the " Who gives this woman . . ." Pompously he asked the usual queries. He was startled at Margaret's clearly heard " Yes ! " and at Edward's emphatic reply. They appeared not to be answering Mr. Yaeger's questions ; they were answering each other, in some secret dedication of their own, some secret vows, something fervently promised for ever.

Their kiss was less a clinging than a profound consecration.

Bemused, shaken, they were assailed by family and guests. But it was strange that no one demanded to kiss the bride. The guests had seen what had transpired between Margaret and Edward, and any boisterousness, they vaguely felt, would have been a violation. Those who had intimately questioned Margaret's origins forgot their reservations against her. George Enreich and Padraig kissed her hand only, bowing over it as if in reverence. Even the ladies were content to touch her fingers. Not even Maria kissed her new daughter ; she just approached her and gave her one of her inscrutable smiles and pressed her hand against the girl's arm.

But Margaret gave one kiss only, other than that to Edward. She kissed Heinrich, who cried silently and mopped his eyes.

There was a gigantic cake at the bride's table. The next few hours passed in a dream for Margaret and Edward. All the guests were only mouthing shadows. Their hands touched each other constantly. The veil thrown back, Margaret's eyes were as blue and radiant as an effulgent sky. Edward's face, usually so dark and blunt and cold, became the face of a young man, caught up in pulsing delight and rapture.

They never forgot that day. It lived in their memories as fresh and as deep-felt as at the first moment, in spite of the spectral tragedies that were almost upon them, even in those hours. " We were man and wife from the very beginning, perhaps from the instant we met," Margaret would say. " The wedding was only the culmination." To Edward it was the one day when he was young again, hopeful again, and full of gentleness, as he had been as a child.

After the bridal lunch they still clung together. The meal was excellent; they could not eat. They drank the champagne, and the sprightly liquid enhanced their enchantment and almost unbearable ecstasy. Hand in hand, they walked over the grass, speaking, smiling, accepting good wishes and congratulations which they hardly heard. There was no dancing; it was Sunday, 28th July and Mr. Yaeger had had to secure special permission from his bishop to perform the ceremony then. " I will assent, if it is decorous," the bishop had said. " And no dancing, no hilarity, and, if possible, no spiritous refreshments."

Hours went by in a dream. There was no hurry. There would be no honeymoon until next week, when Edward had to go to New York. More food was brought out by servants, who glanced apprehensively at the crepuscular sky, and listened to the wind which was beginning to torment the trees. Candles appeared, though it was now only six o'clock. Thunder boomed like a drum in the background; no one heard it. Everyone was caught up in the spirit of the lovely marriage, and its mysterious meaning. Glimpses of Margaret had the quality of hypnotism. Her face had regained its usual charming colour; she appeared to sparkle; there was an iridescence about her. Even Sylvia, who had been almost overcome at the sight of Padraig, reluctantly conceded that Margaret was beautiful. " But a common beauty," she had murmured to Violette who had squinted her eyes humorously.

It was about seven o'clock when Hans Bohn was called to the telephone. The guests were still enjoying themselves at the table. He came back to Edward and said in a low voice, " Something has happened. I must go to the office. I know you'll excuse me, Ed."

Edward began to say something pleasant; his face was alive with his happiness. Then he saw the eyes of the publisher, and the hard cloven lines about his face, and the bitter significance of his manner. He stood up, dropping Margaret's hand.

"What is it, Hans?" he asked quietly, and moved away from the table. "You look like a corpse. It's not your family; they're here. Some—catastrophe?"

Hans hesitated. He was resolved not to spoil this wedding day. And then he remembered that Edward was his friend, that Edward had a powerful right to know the news. He said, "Don't say anything about this to anyone. Not that they'd care," he added sombrely. "Ed, it's broken loose, at last. I didn't expect it to come, not for a while, but it has." He dropped his voice even lower.

"There's been a cable just a few minutes ago. The Archduke Francis Ferdinand, heir to the Austrian throne, and his wife, the Duchess of Hohenberg, were murdered by an assassin in Slavic Bosnia. To-day, at noon, in Europe. About dawn in America."

Edward stared at him uncomprehending for a few seconds. Then his face thickened and reddened, and then suddenly paled. He glanced about for Senator Bonwit at one of the tables. The senator had left. Edward then remembered the senator passing his table a few moments ago, murmuring how delightful the wedding had been, but that he had been summoned urgently to his office.

"So, it's begun," said Edward, and his heart was a lump of hot iron.

Chapter Twelve

Austria-Hungary was at war with Serbia. That was 28th July. On 1st August, the Kaiser declared that Germany was at war with Russia. On 3rd August, France was at war with Germany, and Germany was at war with Belgium, Great Britain with Germany on 4th August, Austria-Hungary with Russia, and Serbia with Germany, on 6th August. France went to war with Austria-Hungary, and Great Britain with Austria-Hungary, on 12th August.

"The guns sounding in Europe are the guns aimed at the heart of all mankind," William wrote to Edward. "But this is only the beginning. I'm not a religious chap, but this is

Armageddon. . . . The nations aren't fighting each other, though they think they are. They're fighting the bloody fight for Socialism ; nobody's told them that yet."

On a hot day in middle August Margaret called on Father Jahle. She had never met the priest before, and when she saw his face, so exalted, so suffering, and so kind, she felt she had not made a mistake in coming to him for help.

She looked about the little dank parlour. Milk bottles and cheap glass vases and bowls overflowed with zinnias, yellow daisies, late roses and summer lilies. They possessed a coloured light of their own in every corner, on every table, and masked, by their effulgence, the dull shabbiness and mildewed walls on which they seemed to cast a living radiance. Their scent flowed over odours of decay and poverty. Margaret sat on a small horse-hair chair, beautiful in her white linen suit and big blue hat, but her eyes were full of pain and set in dark circles. She had taken off her gloves, and unconsciously twisted them in her hands as she spoke.

" Father Jahle, I'm afraid you'll think me presumptuous, or silly, in coming to talk with you," she said in a low voice.

The priest smiled at her with tender encouragement. How many times he had heard those exact words in this room! " Presumptuous, silly," the anguished souls called themselves, as they cried out for succour in their despair. " Why should I, Mrs. Enger?" he asked, gently. " What else is a priest for, except to help, if he can?"

" Yes," she said, faintly. " That's what I've come for. Help." She paused, and her eyes implored him. " Ed talks about you so much ; you see each other so often, he's so devoted——"

The priest said, with some sadness, " It's true that I've known Eddie since he was a child, and that he has done so much for me, so much! I think I know Eddie almost more than anyone else does, except, of course, his wife." (The pretty, loving young girl, the poor child!) He went on, looking at her earnestly. " But I don't see Eddie very often, not in these past years. In fact, I haven't seen him this time for several months, or many weeks, at least. I was just going to write him a letter. You see, the last time I saw him he insisted on me going to a doctor ; he thought it was something very serious. But it wasn't, thank God. I just have asthma ;

I've had it all my life. Perhaps you can reassure Eddie for me."

"Oh, no," said Margaret, dropping her head. "I don't want him to know that I've been here."

The priest waited, and Margaret, her face hidden, felt his large humanity, his compassion, and his profound innocence that was also wisdom. It was never good to urge confession or confidence, thought the priest. The seeking soul had its own tempo.

"It's about Ed," Margaret murmured at last.

"Yes. Of course," said the priest.

Margaret lifted her eyes and the pure blueness of them was magnified with tears.

"Since the war broke out, in Europe, he—he hasn't been well," she said, her voice breaking. "I mean, there's a kind of dustiness, a dusty shadow, over his face. He told me, even before we were married, that there was a war coming, against the world, by men who had arranged it a long time ago. He seemed to be one of the few who knew . . ." She paused. "He seems ill. He doesn't talk about it much any longer, even to me, but I know he is busy about something.

"But that isn't just why I came. It's—I'm afraid for him. He's my husband. I love him. He's tearing himself to pieces inside; you'd almost think the war meant something to him, personally, that it had a personal meaning for him. That's what I can't understand! When terrible things occur, it's only right that a man should fight them, if he cares anything about other men at all." She stopped, and gazed at the priest despairingly. "But I don't think that he——"

Father Jahle nodded, sorrowfully. "Yes, I know. What you wish to say, and don't wish to say as a loyal wife, is that Eddie dislikes people intensely, and cares nothing about them. Mrs. Enger, it's been my experience that when men begin to dislike people violently, and to give an impression that the fate of other men is not only not their concern, but that they derive pleasure from seeing calamity visited on others, it's because they once loved their fellow-men and cherished them and worried about them. And then they were terribly hurt. It isn't possible for men like Eddie to become indifferent to their fellows, for they've been involved with the world too long. The dislike and the derision and the malice is the reverse side of the coin of their original love and hope and dedication."

"Yes, yes!" said Margaret. "His family has disappointed him so much! They're detestable."

But that's not what I meant, or it's only part of it, thought the priest. Yet, how much, really, do I know of such a protean man as Eddie?

He was disturbed by the anger and indignation on Margaret's face.

"I think," faltered Margaret, "that in some way the war is tied up in his mind, though he doesn't realise it, with his family. It's just a guess on my part, a sort of intuition. I think it's beginning to kill him, day by day. On the few times that he's mentioned the war, he never fails to speak of his brothers and sister right afterwards, as if it was a continuing theme in his thought, without his conscious knowledge. I know that sounds stupid, but——"

The priest was disturbed and greatly startled. He pondered over what Margaret had said, one thin finger pressed against his lips. He coughed, over and over, apparently having some difficulty with his breath. He thought, while trying to overcome his paroxysms, The child hasn't spoken stupidly. There's truth in what she's said, but I never saw it before. I am the stupid one.

He said, "Only Our Lord understands the tortuous and devious ways of the human soul and mind." His voice was weak from his spasm. "Eddie, is by nature, a man of deep feeling and emotion. I don't know his family well. At one time," he said, musingly, "I called him Simon." He looked at Margaret questioningly, wondering if she were as little versed in religion as Edward. But Margaret nodded.

"He still is," she said, with some bitterness and vehemence.

Father Jahle sighed and shook his head. This girl wanted to help her husband; she could not help him if she believed what she had said. Her love and fierce loyalty would blind her. As gently as possible, the priest went on, "Mrs. Enger, I don't call Eddie Simon any longer."

She was puzzled. "I don't understand," she said.

He wondered if he could reach her, for Edward's sake. He sat on the edge of his chair, his clasped hands between his thin black knees. He did not want to hurt her. He said, "Words are very inadequate; I find that out all the time. It's a clumsy way to try to convey what you mean. At one time, Mrs. Enger, I believed Eddie was terribly exploited by his family, that he, the strong one, was being oppressed by the weak, and that he couldn't escape. I don't think that now. Oh, from what I've heard over the years, his brothers and sister are weak. And Eddie is very strong."

He regarded her hopefully. But she was frowning a little. "You mean, they're weak because they and their parents think they're geniuses? But they do have gifts?"

"Yes," said the priest. "They have. But I think that's beside the point. I've said that Eddie is strong; he is. And he's been exploited. Why? Because he believes in his family's genius? Perhaps that's part of it. But there's an enormous resentment in him, even a kind of hatred for them."

Margaret nodded. "How can he be blamed? They've disappointed him; they don't use their capacities to the limit, in spite of all his work and his money. I—I know one of the brothers very well." She coloured, and the priest wondered why, anxiously. "It's David. A wonderful pianist. He could do better; his technique is perfect, but it hasn't any true colour or brilliance. It's mechanical. Ed knows; Ed could have been a pianist, himself. He has the spirit for it, the feeling, the intensity. I think he could have been a painter, too; he knows all about painting. He's haunted all the bigger galleries in this country, and he can talk about art like an artist, himself. He speaks, and writes, eloquently; he knows literature. And he's built that theatre for Sylvia, and she's no more interested in it than I am. Don't you see why Ed should feel as he does about them?"

Again the priest shook his head. "I can see. On the surface. But I don't think that's the real reason, somehow."

"But he was deprived, so they could have the chance!" cried Margaret.

The priest stood up, slowly, and leaned his arm on the little mantelpiece near him. He dropped his face into his hand. Yes, he thought. That is a part of it, but only a part. But why did he let himself be exploited? That's the dark and hidden answer to it all. He's strong; he could have gone his own way. Why didn't he? Was it because, in a kind of revenge——? I don't know! And Eddie probably knows the least of all.

He often had these moments of absolute bafflement and

pain. Even a priest could see only the surface, much of the time. A man's soul lay hidden, like a creature in a shell, far below the bright roof of the ocean, dwelling to itself, known only to God.

Margaret's shoulders drooped with weariness. The priest did not understand at all. She said, lifelessly, "I know I'm right in thinking that the war is somehow tied up in Ed's mind with his family. I sense it. But I haven't a way of bringing it to his consciousness! What could I say? He would look at me as if I was insane." She laughed drearily. "Perhaps I am, after all. What could that awful war have in common with Ed's feeling about his family?"

"I don't know. But I think you're right, Mrs. Enger."

She looked at him in astonishment. "You think so? Then, what can we do to help him?"

"God will have to reveal it to him. You see, Mrs. Enger, God, like the sea, has His own tides, and nothing can hurry them. A man has first to understand himself, and feel contrition, and confess, and then ask for forgiveness, before he is free."

Margaret was outraged. "You're speaking of Ed? What has he to feel contrite about? What has he to confess? He's given his life to his family!"

"So he has," said Father Jahle, mournfully. "Or, has he? I don't know. There's something here neither of us can understand. Men aren't mathematical equations; they can't be measured by scientific instruments. No man has the identical aims, emotions, passions, loves, and desires, as another man has. Every man is unique, because he is an immortal soul. He shares in God's infinite variety, which is never duplicated. He is beyond science; only his body is the field of the biologist. The new psychology you read about, here and there, can never be a science, for science is exactness. Its experiments can be repeated over and over, with always the same results. But man's soul is beyond science, for no man's spirit can be analysed by other men, because they have not experienced exactly the same thing he's experienced, nor thought the same thoughts, nor loved nor hated nor suffered as he has."

He half-turned from Margaret. "There were the two thieves on their crosses, on each side of Our Lord. One of them reviled Him; the other recognised Him and loved Him. Yet, they were both thieves, both miserable wretches, both abandoned creatures, in the sight of the crowd, both criminals caught in the same crime. But modern psychology would declare them to be the same, objects which could be measured scientifically, reacting identically. Part of Mass Man. Yet, one repented, the other did not. Was the repentance a sudden Grace from God? Or was it a bursting into light of what had been cramped and chained and oppressed, and was now suddenly released?"

Margaret twisted her gloves in her hands and regarded him steadily. Then she began to shake her head over and over, as if denying something in herself.

"Please, my child," said the priest. "Try to help Eddie. You can do that by helping his brothers and sister, perhaps to—to free themselves. . . ."

Margaret exclaimed indignantly, "Ed constantly urges them to stand on their own feet! He's not imprisoning them! They haven't any courage!"

"And you can't help them to have courage?" asked the priest. "A new sister, a gentle sister, a sister with pity?"

"Pity them?" cried Margaret, jumping to her feet. "For exploiting Ed, for worrying him to death, for disappointing him? For frustrating him, for muttering ridicule of him behind his back? I've heard them, when they thought I wasn't there. Oh, they don't dare to say anything to his face, except Sylvia, and then even she realises she's gone too far, and tries to appease him. Pity them! Grown people! Only Ralph's younger than I am, only a year younger. How long should they be children?"

"Until God makes them adults," said the priest, hopelessly.

Margaret went towards the door, then stopped and turned a mutinous face on Father Jahle. "And so, you won't help Ed?"

"What would you suggest, Mrs. Enger?"

"You could tell him not to get so emotional about that war. You could tell him to do what he can, objectively, even if it won't help now. At least, he'll know he's trying. But he can't be objective, and that's the awful part of it. Unless he's helped."

"And you can't help him?"

"I've tried," said Margaret, listless again. "But he gets too excited. Even violent. I've even asked him to talk it over with the family's minister, Mr. Yaeger. But Ed doesn't like religion. . . ." She blushed awkwardly.

"I think," said the priest, "that he believes that God's estranged Himself from him. But Eddie has estranged himself from God. I don't know when, or how. I tried to get him to explain, but he couldn't, or wouldn't. By nature, he is deeply religious. Please believe that, Mrs. Enger. I knew him when he was a boy. And, why would he do as much for me, as he's done, and for Mr. Yaeger, too, if he were irreligious?

"The only hope Ed has for understanding himself is to come again into the presence of God. There, you can help. He won't be on guard, as he is with me, and his minister. Your love for him can lead him to God." He paused, then continued urgently, "Mrs. Enger, you must help him. You must ask God to give you the wisdom and the strength and the fortitude. You must forget his family in relation to him, and think only of him, as an individual soul, needing enlightenment, the enlightenment that only God can give him."

"Forget his family?" Margaret was freshly outraged. "They're the cause of his misery! Why should he need to be enlightened about his family? He knows too much about them as it is!"

The priest went to the door with her. He had hoped so much from Margaret. He had thought, for a moment or two, that he had reached her with subtle knowledge that could spring only from a loving soul. But Eddie was almost lost now, through love.

I had hoped so much from him, thought Margaret, with despair. But he's like everyone else. He thinks the strong can take care of themselves; he never thinks for a minute that they are vulnerable, too. I can't talk it over with Mr. Yaeger, either. He doesn't know much about Ed, and he's afraid of him, and he's under the family's influence. I did think that priest would be more understanding, for he's known Ed for so many years. But he understands the least of everybody!

When she was settled in the gleaming black Victoria, she looked back at Father Jahle. He was going into his church and he walked slowly, his head bent, as if in prayer. Pray! she cried wildly, in herself. It won't do any good at all!

"Is it *enceinte*?" asked Violette, with twinkling sympathy.

Margaret was annoyed. She felt that her sanctuary under the trees, so far from the English mansion, had been violated.

"I think that's my own business, Violette," said Margaret, shortly. Then she relented, though Violette did not appear in the least crushed. In fact, the smart little French girl sat down on the bench beside her and regarded her humorously. "It is a mistake," she said, with frankness. "This, having a child at once—is it? A lady does not know her husband very well, so soon, and there, *voila*! is a stranger, a stranger who is uncouth, a nasty stranger. But Americans are children, yes. They must cover themselves with children, or they are the lonesome. American ladies are dull, dull. It is the children."

"Thank you," said Margaret, but she smiled. She liked Violette; she preferred villainy to be charming and adroit and gay. The villainy of Edward's family was repulsive, in its sullen and selfish insistence on gratifying itself, its lightlessness, its childish petulance and greed.

Violette spread out her hands expressively. "The Americans—they have no *élan, non*. They are busy, busy, busy. Like the ant, like the bee. They confuse motion with the intellect." And she tapped her golden-tinted forehead significantly.

"But you married Ralph," said Margaret, with human curiosity.

"Ah, Ralph! The child! It is the life he has, and a measure of *élan*. When," added Violette thoughtfully, "he forgets to pretend he is the artist."

Margaret stirred; the green leaves overshadowing the girl made a pattern of quick light and shade on her face. "You don't think he is an artist, after all?"

Violette shrugged. "*Certainement, non*. Not the great artist. The artisan. It is something else he wishes. But he must discover that himself; he must have the *esprit*. No man can say it to the other: 'This shall you do and not this.' A man must discover his own way."

She sounds like Father Jahle, thought Margaret with some resentment.

"I think it is the wife's business to help her husband discover, as you say, Violette."

Violette shook her head so strongly that her mound of rolls and coils of hair vibrated. "No, no, no! It is the wife's business—business?—to amuse, comfort and be the coquette. (What is this 'business?' Always, it the business with Americans!) Then if the gentleman fails, he is not mortified, for it is his secret. If he succeeds, then he shall say, 'It is my wife, or my *petite amie*, who inspired me.' And it is the truth."

Margaret considered this thoughtfully. Violette watched her lovely face with inner compassion and some amusement. It is a child's face, she thought, trusting, confiding, valorous but without understanding. She smoothed her very extreme but very chic frock over her tidy thighs, and regarded her tiny feet, in their stilted shoes, with gratification. Her moods were like bubbles, but under them her nature was iron.

Margaret sighed. "It's hard to know what to do," she murmured.

"Then, it is best to do nothing," said Violette. Her pert face, her impudent eyes, smiled. She studied Margaret. "The trousseau, designed by Sylvia, is the delight. But reserved. It is the American style, with importance."

Margaret was youthfully pleased. Her simple rosy dress, a long sheath reaching to her ankles, was devoid of all ornament, except for tucks under the breast. It cast a rosy reflection below her chin and on her throat. "It is all that soap," said Violette. "All the American soap. *Eh bien*. Why is all the soap and the water?"

"What? Oh, you mean our baths. We like to keep clean." And Margaret smiled with a little malice.

Violette made a wise moue. "Then, it is not clean in the soul? All this washing of hands and so?"

"I don't know what you're talking about," said Margaret. She was not feeling well, and she was troubled. She had visited a doctor that morning, and he had given her some disquieting news. In her childhood, he had told her, she must have had rickets because of malnutrition. It had not affected her limbs, not her long slender body's outline. But it had affected her pelvis, narrowing it dangerously. She must tell her husband, he had warned her. She was over three months pregnant, in this warm and winey October; the doctor anticipated a great deal of difficulty at the birth, if, in fact, she ever carried her child to term. Then a Caesarian section should be considered, and the mortality in such an operation was high.

Margaret resolutely pulled her thoughts away from this subject. She was certainly not going to worry Edward until the time came. She turned again to the weary thought of the war.

" Aren't you glad, Violette, that you and Ralph came home just in time?" she asked. She was surprised when Violette's small and lively face hardened, became older.

"*La guerre*, the war? The vile Boche! Again and again and again! It is always the vile Boche! Ah, if I were a man! It is unfortunate that I have no brothers to inspire me, no brothers in France."

Margaret was offended. She said, " But the Enger family is German, and they're certainly not vile! Mother and Father Enger were born in Germany; they're not even American citizens, Ed tells me. And your own husband, though an American, is of German stock. You don't know what's behind this war, or you wouldn't talk like that. And coming down to it," Margaret continued with heat, " I'm probably of German stock, too."

She was astonished to see that Violette was twinkling again.

" One's husband, and his family, though Germans, are never the Boche," she said. But the hardness lay about her large dark eyes and red, pouting mouth. " One must be realistic. If one is not, he is the poet or the fool."

She stretched out her dark little hand, with the quick, prehensile fingers, and took Margaret's chin firmly in it. She studied the blue eyes, which seemed to fill their sockets with light, the delicate coral colour, the long cleft chin, the gilded lashes and brows and the bright brown hair. "*Non*," she said, thoughtfully. " It is not German. It is Swedish, perhaps, or English. *Non, non!* Not English, not Swedish! There is too much—what is it?—the vividness. The shine. There are Normans like this." She nodded her head decisively. " It is definitely the Norman. And so, we are sisters."

Margaret laughed. " What does it matter? All people are the same."

" All the same," agreed Violette, with a laugh. She stood up, and Margaret admired again the compact trimness and prettiness of her figure. Violette yawned, her small mouth opening to show a large expanse of very white and flaring teeth.

"I find you charming, my Margaret," Violette added. She waved her hand lightly, and moved away through the tall thick grass, off which came the autumnal odour of ripeness and harvest. Margaret watched the provocative swaying of her small and dainty figure. She reflected on Violette. Here was a girl not even her own age, a girl only nineteen or twenty. And yet, she was old and wise and knowing, and yes, thought Margaret uneasily, decadent—decadent as Americans could not imagine decadence. It was a matter of soul, and not even of morals or the lack of them, or virtue, or the lack of it. Though Violette did not resemble the marble child in the fountain in the last, there was a certain affinity between the girl and the statue.

Margaret sat alone, and looked, troubled, about her. She was afraid of Violette, as she was not afraid of the other members of the household, not even Maria. Edward's brothers and sister could be disliked, but could be dealt with on their own ground, or so Margaret thought. They were rude, bad-tempered, grasping and exploiting, and full of selfishness and petulance. They were children in the bodies of men and women, and she could still almost pity them for their mystifying retardation of character. She had come to the conclusion that she must help them, for Edward's sake. Gregory was taking post-graduate work in English at Yale, for his Master's degree. Ralph would certainly go to New York for further study, if he did not succeed in nagging Edward into sending him to Mexico, or Central America, "for the colour." David had not yet returned home, and his promises to do so were still vague. That would leave only Sylvia.

Margaret decided to help Ralph persuade Edward to finance him far away from home. That would remove Violette also. I can stand open enemies, thought Margaret, but not smiling enemies who like me.

The great trees murmured in the autumn wind, ruffling their high mantles of russet, scarlet, green and gold. A few leaves drifted down, crackling faintly, at Margaret's feet, and for a moment or two she was diverted by her endless wonder over the world. She saw the dry veins which only recently had swum with life; she studied the intricacies of form and pattern and colour, and involuntarily she clasped her hands. How marvellous, how exact, how awe-inspiring, was God! No detail escaped His notice; His laws were fulfilled as much in the shape of a leaf, the curve of a blade of grass, the contour of a flower, the movement of an insect, as they were fulfilled in the thunderous blaze of constellations and in the beat of a man's heart. She looked at the high bright sky with its mounting and radiant clouds, and she thought, Surely, goodness and mercy shall follow me all the days of my life. . . .

She was suddenly no longer afraid or doubtful or anxious. Of what had man to be afraid? Only himself, his own passions, his own angers, his own vices, his own rejections, his own blindness.

She looked at the leaves again, as they floated down about her. Sighing, she stood up and left the small hollow for the higher terraces that led to the gardens and the house.

She stopped at the fountain, and musingly dipped her forefinger in the sparkling and living water, and looked up at the marble child who stood in the midst of it. The child was beautiful, in its depraved way; the marble face and shoulders and legs and arms ran with brilliant drops of water, like liquid diamonds. The laughing face looked down with human eloquence and mischief. The fountain splashed, as if speaking to the statue in an unhuman language which they both understood; the scales of the marble fish in the arms of the child flashed through the water prismatically. The nakedness of the child was not innocent, Margaret thought, with part of her mind. It is even a little evil. The cool wetness flowed over her finger, but could not cool her disquiet.

She turned her head and saw that Violette had paused beside Sylvia, who sat under the shade of a small clump of trees. Sylvia had a book on her thin knee; she was all delicate blackness and white shawl. Neither of the young women glanced at Margaret, poised at the fountain, but somehow she guessed that they were speaking of her, and not with kindness. She could hear the murmurous sound of their voices, but not the words. She wandered off through another section of the gardens, reluctant to return to the house, reluctant to remain outside, reluctant to speak to anyone.

"He'll leave the major part of his money to that woman,"

said Sylvia, bitingly. "Especially if they have a child, as you say they are going to have. Then we'll get practically nothing but the leavings from Ma and Pa."

"Then," said Violette, in a gay voice, "we must busy ourselves, *non*? I shall have the child, too. And you must marry, and have children."

Sylvia elaborately shuddered. "I shall never marry," she answered, her white cheekbones colouring a little. "Don't smile, Violette. This is serious. I never did like that woman! She's cheap and—anonymous. She doesn't even have a name she can rightly call her own, except what Ed's given her." She bit her lip and frowned intently. "He should begin to settle money on us right away. After all! Ma should make him see his duty towards us——"

"After all!" Violette echoed, with a twinkle.

Sylvia gave her a sharp glance, and was annoyed. "You really don't understand, Violette. Everything is a joke to you."

"It is so," said Violette. "One must laugh, or weep. It is a matter of temperament."

"But this is very serious!" said Sylvia, more and more annoyed. "If he refuses to settle money in all of us then we should try to get as much as we can, whenever we can, and put it quietly away. He does give us big allowances, after all those years of parsimony when we were younger. He likes to play the grand seigneur now, just to humiliate us." She thought of the five thousand dollars already paid to her by Mary Garrity, and smiled her chill smile. No one knew of that account, no one ever would. She was awaiting another cheque for her autumn designs for three hats. There were ways of investing cash. Sylvia, unknown to anyone but Maria, who pretended not to see, sedulously read Edward's discarded financial journals and magazines. The market was rising, even in these days of temporary depression, since Wilson had been elected two years ago. Steel. Copper. A dozen things. She would write to Mary Garrity about it.

"He provides the home, *voila!* he is indeed the grand seigneur," said Violette, refusing to be sober. "He provides the meat and the fish and the bread; he provides the servants. He provides the money. I am willing to be pleasant to the grand seigneur for these kindnesses." But her merry eyes were thoughtful.

"Maybe he'll stop being kind very soon!" said Sylvia.

"She's probably whining at him all the time to throw us out. But she won't get her way. Ma is with us." She laughed grimly. "Did you ever see such an unintelligent face? All eyes and chin and hair. Like a milkmaid. She resents us."

"*Certainement*," said the other girl. "And why not? Do we love her? Do we regard her as a sister? Yet, I do not believe she is urging our Eddie to evict us. It is 'evict,' is it not? It would be the part of discretion to be pleasant to her, though she is not malicious." She smiled down mischievously at the bright and febrile stare directed up at her from Sylvia's tilted eyes. Ah, it was a naïve one, in spite of the cleverness with the clothes and the hats, and the reading of many books!

"I will not play up to her!" said Sylvia, vehemently. "I have my pride. I was born an Enger, and my mother was a Von Brunner. I would rather starve than pretend to like her!"

Ah, you will never starve, my little one, thought Violette. You are naïve, but you also know when you must stop. She waved her hand affectionately at Sylvia and went into the house, leaving the other girl wretched with uneasiness and apprehension.

Margaret, in the meantime, was continuing her slow wandering about the vast grounds, and with increasing unhappiness. She walked over the grass, feeling the cool and fragrant wind against her face. She paused to study, in assumed nonchalance, a bed of mauve, yellow, pink and white mums, then a bed of crimson callas. She then approached the long Italian terrace which stretched from the house under a symmetrical line of trees. Two of the chauffeur's children were playing there slyly, knowing that this was forbidden territory and enjoying their trespassing. They stopped abruptly when they saw Margaret, eyeing her alertly, their eyes as bright and wild as an animal's. With the prescience of children they well knew that Margaret was unwelcome in this grand house, and in this family, for they had often seen her disturbed face, the snubs visited upon her, and her loneliness. They were very young, the boy about six, the girl but five, but they had heard their parents' smothering comments and snickerings about Margaret, and they had understood.

Margaret hardly knew them, but she was aware that they should not be here. Nevertheless, she remembered her own deprived childhood and humiliations. She approached the children, smiling at them, thinking of the child she was carrying. She was ready to be tender to all young things. "Hallo," she said, gently.

But the children's eyes, bold and disingenuous as only children's eyes can be, fixed themselves upon her with sparkling malice. They were not afraid of her, as they were afraid of Sylvia and the others. She was nothing! Daddy and Mummy said so. They watched her approach, then backed away a little. The girl tittered evilly, and the boy made a face. Margaret stopped. Then the children, shrieking with meaningless mirth, ran off, looking back at the young woman over their shoulders.

How could I have forgotten how children really are? Margaret asked herself, miserably. They have no real innocence or kindness. They have no gentleness or consideration or understanding. These are the things they must learn, or pretend to learn. I suppose my own child will be as bad. . . . She was freshly depressed.

She entered the house at its side and less formal door, and passed the music room. Ralph was sitting at the pianola piano, gaily manipulating the mechanism, which mechanically rattled out the newest ragtime. Violette stood beside him, rapidly inclining her head from side to side in time with the blatant music, and humming and snapping her fingers. Margaret slipped by the door rapidly, hoping that neither had noticed her. But Violette had. She closed the door, and Ralph stopped beating the pedals with his big feet. His wife ruffled his auburn hair, kissed his lips seductively and said, "We must have an infant, *mon petit*. That Eddie is about to become a father. We must compete." She made a distasteful moue.

"You mean that tin lizzie of a woman is going to be a mama, so that she can grab off our money better?" said Ralph, his ruddy face swelling with affront. He stared at his hands, and pursed up his thick red lips. His drawings of a proposed bridge over a tributary of the Mississippi had been accepted. "A beautiful, engineering marvel," the constructor had called it in a letter which contained a substantial cheque. The bridge would be small, of course, but it was Ralph's first concrete effort. He had not told even his wife.

Margaret went silently down the wide and dusky hall, with its lofty furniture and vaulted ceiling and fine paintings on the panelled walls. She was just passing the door of the library when it opened quickly. Gregory was on the threshold, and he started when he saw her. Behind him the sun poured through the library windows, showering its autumn gold on red and blue and black leather, on mahogany tables and lines of books. He had been typewriting; the instrument was uncovered, and an ash tray smoked with rejected cigarettes. He was holding a sheaf of papers in his hands, and he half-folded them guiltily.

"Ah, the lass with the delicate air," he said, with light mockery. Damn it, did she have to look both stupid and beautiful at the same time? She had, he commented, eyes like aquamarines as the slanting sunlight struck them, eyes like jewels. Why were most lovely women confounded idiots?

"Hallo, Greg," said Margaret. He was insufferable, but he had a certain gaiety and quickness, and he resembled Edward. "Have you started the Great American Novel, yet?" She glanced at the sheaf of manuscript in his hands. Her tone was not taunting, but interested, yet he coloured with annoyance.

"Briefing it," he said. "Writing's the most hellish work in the world."

Why did she linger? He couldn't push by her rudely, though he wanted to, and he couldn't slam the door in her face. She was looking at him wistfully, and all at once he was embarrassed. "I'm sure it is," she was saying. Her colour, he thought, was like a tea rose. Under other circumstances, he might have fallen in love with her, or, at least, greatly admired her. The thought startled him, and a page slipped from his hand to the long Oriental rug that ran the length of the hall. He bent down precipitously for it, but not before Margaret's eye had caught the title: *Mr. Thor Takes a Wife*, by Gil Enderson.

Margaret was dumbfounded. She read *The City* regularly. She knew the "Thor" series, and had thought them amusingly and vividly done, but cruel and filled with malignance. Oh, it wasn't possible that Gregory Enger was Gil Enderson! Her mind swam in rapids of confused and revolted thought. Yet, the evidence had lain before her for an illuminated moment. She began to tremble, and ripples of cold ran over her flesh. I must get away at once, and think, she said to herself. She made herself smile at Gregory, but her suddenly acute eye saw the guilty hand clenching the sheets of paper. " Everybody expects so much of you," she murmured, and went down the hall, her knees trembling.

She didn't see anything, and if she did, it wouldn't matter, thought Gregory, watching the rose-coloured retreating figure. She's practically illiterate ; I bet she never read a book in her life, not to mention *The City*. Pollyanna in person! Sweetness and light, enveloped in an orma of Cashmere Bouquet!

Margaret ran up the stairs to her own suite. Her head was aching wildly. She sat down near a window, shivering, her clasped hands tight between her knees. " Mr. Thor! " Now she saw it clearly. Edward was " Mr. Thor." He had been depicted as a brutish but animal-shrewd tycoon, without sensitivity, except where money was concerned, a laughable buffoon and boor, a gross and lumbering creature, the butt of the clubs into which he had stormed his battering-ram way, a provincial whose pleasure it was to insult gracious gentlemen, and manipulate them so expertly that he ruined them out of revenge. She did not like *The City*. She read it for its cartoons, its comments on the theatre and the opera, its foreign news, only. She found its stories pointless, its " moods " trivial, its sophistication shallow, its air that of a *poseur* who is very blasé and who has never been in contact with reality. Clever, yes, like a precocious adolescent, but never adult. It was like Gregory!

In this, Margaret was somewhat in error. If *The City* affronted her it was because it was frequently malicious, and malice, to Margaret, was an evil thing, and not to be excused by cleverness or wit or fine writing.

Her first impulse was to tell Edward when he came home. Then she shook her head. No. It would only infuriate him. He was so beset these days. Let Gregory write the libellous stories about his brother, if he wishes. It was nothing to her. *Mr. Thor Takes a Wife*. Me, she thought, dryly. It'll be interesting, at any rate. All at once, she hated Gregory, the great American novelist, who exploited his brother and then derided that brother malignly, and kept his counsel, and, naturally, the cheques that he received for his stories. She had never hated in all her life before, and the power of this new emotion shook her and sickened her. She was appalled at the burning taste of it in her mouth, the clenching of her heart, the heat in her face, the surge in her mind.

I hate them all, she thought. All of them. And to think that I pitied them and wanted to help them! What a buttery imbecile I am! Well, they have a real enemy, now, and I'll stand between them and Ed—all the days of my own life. Nobody understands but me, not even his friends, if they are friends, not even that priest who's known him since he was a child. She began to cry, with mingled hatred, anger and despair.

The door opened and Edward entered, a grey and thinner Edward, with lines cleft about his heavy mouth, and with darker lines about his sunken eyes. Margaret jumped to her feet and ran to him, and put her arms about him, mutely, her head on his shoulder. There was a fierceness in her embrace, a protecting, a tumultuous protest against all the world which so badgered and oppressed him.

"Well, now!" said Edward, lifting her wet face from his shoulder. He was suddenly anxious. "What is it, darling?" Has anybody been annoying you?" His eyes narrowed and pointed, and his mouth tightened.

"Oh, no, no," she said, and tried to smile. "I was just lonely for you. . . ."

"But you didn't meet me downstairs, as usual, when I came home."

"I forgot the time," she faltered. She tugged at his hand. "Sit down, dear. You look so tired." Her hand was feverish in his, and he restrained her tugging motion. "Margaret, there is something wrong. You've got to tell me."

She thought, distractedly. He must never guess how much she now hated his family, those "geniuses!" He must never know what she knew. It would break a heart already too burdened. She laughed shakily. "I've got something to tell you. And, I hope it'll make you happy. Sit down, dearest, do sit down. No, you're not going to look at the newspaper, not to-night! We're just going to be Mr. and Mrs. Ed Enger, to-night, in a nice peaceful world, after a nice humdrum day, at sunset in a little house of our own." She stopped, and her fingers touched her betraying lips.

Edward still stood and held her hand more tightly. "Margaret, don't you like my house?"

"I love it!" she cried. "It's beautiful. It's your home, and mine! Ed, I was just trying to amuse you, just trying to get you into an ordinary mood, so I could tell you."

"Has anyone said anything to you to-day, to make you look so wretched?" he demanded inexorably, his light eyes fixing themselves on her face. "That's something I want to know."

"No, no! In fact, Violette and I had a very interesting talk to-day. And everybody was so—pleasant. Please, Ed, sit down. Right near the window. And I'll ring Pierre for a drink for you, and I think I'll take sherry, myself!" Her voice and manner were almost distraught in her false gaiety. She tugged at him more strongly. Her bright hair curled in moist tendrils about her face, and her imploring eyes were a blue largeness.

"If anyone ever says anything to you, or annoys you," he began, in a threatening and ugly tone.

"They wouldn't," she pleaded. "There, that's right. Throw that newspaper aside. Now, sit down." She ran to the bell-rope and jerked it, then ran to Edward and sat on his knee. She held his face in her hands and kissed his mouth ardently, over and over. She forced back her tears and swallowed them; the taste of them in her mouth was like salty blood. His big hand fondled her neck, her soft and vulnerable neck, which throbbed under his touch. His thumb rubbed the delicate flesh with rising passion and love.

"You're all I have, Margaret," he said, with unconscious desolation. He pressed his lips in the hollow of her throat.

Yes, all you have, my darling, she thought with hard ferocity, and for the first time. No real friends, no real family.

Pierre came in with a silver tray. He looked at Edward and Margaret, and he saw the silvery wetness on Margaret's cheek. But she smiled at him brightly. He put the tray on the table, bowed, and left.

"Poor tragic old man," said Margaret, but no longer with any feeling. No one mattered but Ed. She got up and mixed whisky and soda for her husband.

"That reminds me," said Edward. "About Padraig. He came in to-day."

Margaret shook her head so violently that curls dashed against her cheeks. "No, no! Nobody but us to-night, nobody. I don't want to hear. And I want dinner upstairs to-night, here, just the two of us. I've got such news for you!"

"Not dinner," said Edward, but he smiled. "After all, most of them will be leaving soon, and I like having the family around me at dinner-time."

"Then, I'll be here alone," said Margaret, mutinously, pouring a small glass of sherry for herself. "In fact," she added, with a mysterious glance, "I think I'll go to bed early."

"What in hell's the matter with you, pet?" he asked, with tenderness. "All right; sit on my knee again." He hugged her to him. "Now, tell me the wonderful news. I suppose it's news? You're all excited."

She drank a sip of sherry, and smiled at him over the crystal rim of the glass. "Guess," she said.

He thought. It couldn't be bad news, though her eyes were moist and her colour too high, her manner too artificially vivacious. She was pretending, she was hiding something. "All right," he said. "I give up. I can't imagine anything happening in this house that would make you so bouncy."

She flung out a hand dramatically, and rolled up her eyes. "Mr. and Mrs. Edward Enger, of Waterford, New York, announce the birth of a son—or a daughter—on—on—perhaps 31st March or 1st April, 1915!"

He caught her hand quickly, and held it. "Margaret! Are you sure?" His face was suddenly young and ebullient and alive. "Who told you, and when?"

She laughed with real delight now. "I'm sure." And she told him.

He cradled her in his arms as if she were a child, herself. They sat together, her chin on his shoulder, her forehead pressed against his cheek. The autumn sunset, swift and golden and red, stood at the windows. They were silent for some time.

Then Edward said, "He, or she, will be a genius, of course."

Margaret sat up, and her face was suddenly stern. She looked at Edward with direct fervour and simplicity. "Oh, God, no. Dear God, no. Anything but that. Anything but that!" And she clasped her hands together as if praying, and her face, turned to the sunset, was white and set.

"Do you want it to be a fool?" asked Edward, a little vexed.

"Ed, dear, there's a middle way between being a genius

and a fool. A person can be good and sound and gentle and intelligent and kind, without being gifted. In fact, goodness itself is genius, and there's precious little of that sort in the world."

She was frightened. She fervently prayed that her child would not be a " genius." For Ed's sake, for Ed's dear sake. And for the sake of the child, itself. If I see any sign of a " gift " I'll nip it right in the bud, I will, I will! she promised herself resolutely. And then she laughed.

" Ed, I want the baby to be exactly like you, for you are an authentic genius, though no one knows it but me! "

PART THREE

"Surely goodness and mercy will follow me all the days of my life, and I shall dwell in the House of the Lord for ever."

TWENTY-THIRD PSALM

Chapter One

David Enger sat, wrapped in his long, fur-lined broadcloth cape, in the little dressing-room. It was very cold, this January night, and the room was not heated adequately, and even the blaze of lights around the mirror seemed glacial. He smoked and read the evening newspapers, his fine dark forehead puckered with gloomy anxiety, his aquiline profile sharp in the mirror, his sensitive mouth drawn in. Finally, he threw the paper aside, and lighted another cigarette from the one he had smoked down. He tapped his narrow foot on the gritty wooden floor, and shook his head as if throwing off some tormenting thoughts. His eye touched a large photograph on the dressing-table; it was a sepia portrait of a young and very beautiful mulatto girl with a smile that appeared to illuminate her face with its own light. David involuntarily smiled. He knew Melinda Russell very well, and her two small children. She had introduced his last song on the programme of her husband, Prince Emory, on Christmas Eve, and the sheet music had already sold over half a million copies. It was a "popular" song, but very melodious, and everyone was singing it, in its minor key and smooth rhythm: "Song for a Sad Day." Melinda had a voice like velvet, deep and rich, and vibrating with some natural melancholy which did not appear in her ordinary mood of cheerfulness.

David could faintly hear the insistent and rapturous applause from the stage of the theatre. No one had expected that a band, even Prince Emory's band, could fill a theatre dedicated to "serious" plays and ballets, or an occasional and "stupendous" five-reel picture from Hollywood or New York. Yet, Prince Emory's band had not only filled every seat in orchestra and balcony, but every inch of standing room also, to the immense disgust of austere critics and those who professed to believe that Prince was a "desecration." David reflected that here, in New York, he, himself, had drawn only one hundred men and women this week, but he was not inclined to cynicism, nor, indeed, inclined to any thought but satisfaction, considering the tremendous popularity of his six songs which his friend had introduced over the past three years. He had over forty thousand dollars in the bank now, and, as an Enger, he was not averse to money. He was considering investments.

The door blew open, and a gale of applause rushed in, even at this distance from the stage. Prince Emory, né Billy Russell, bounded into the dressing-room, his handsome face ashine with excitement and gratification. More than ever, David thought, he resembled animated bronze, even with his crown of thick black curls.

"Ho!" he cried to David, and he grasped David's hand and slapped him on the shoulder. "How did it come along?"

"Fine. As usual," said David. "I came away just as you started 'Song for a Sad Day.' As I hear it at least three times every twenty-four hours I thought I'd miss it this time. Well? Do you think you can hold this theatre for the next three days?" He smiled at his friend artlessly.

Billy lit a cigarette, and began to pace up and down the room as if his excitement were a fire in him. He waved his arms. "Three days? The manager's already asking me to stay at least another week. Do you know who was in the audience to-night? Irene Castle! She sent a note to me; she wants to see me to-morrow night!" He laughed joyously. "She and her husband probably want to adapt your song for their dances. More royalties, friend, more royalties, for both of us." He looked over his shoulder at David with pure delight.

He sat astride a chair; his vitality crackled about him. "I'm going to send Melinda a wire to-night." He glowed at David, then his face changed. "I wanted to tell you I went to the Town Hall yesterday, to hear you. Dave——"

"Now, don't tell me I'm a genius. I'm just an excellent mechanic. We've gone over that before." David flung his arm over the back of his chair and his expression was serene. "Anyway, it keeps me in practice, and what if I steal a theme or so from one of the Masters? Bringing the classics to the Masses."

"Don't put on that cynical pose," said Billy, laughing. "Davey Jones is doing very well in the financial department, or am I mistaken?"

David looked solemn. "Davey Jones, popular song writer, couldn't be doing better. Thanks for the last cheque. By the way, how long can we keep the press from poking around and discovering who Davey Jones is?"

"That's a thought that keeps nagging at me," said Billy. "So far, I've ducked out with a mysterious expression and a sly wink. That makes them dance tiptoe on hot coals, and slaver."

David nodded. "I'm getting a little disturbed," he said. "There's my Negro opera, *Samson Smith*."

Billy jumped to his feet again. "Man! That's going to set the country to pounding and shouting and singing and whistling! The boys have been practising it, just for their own enjoyment, and then they get up and sing and stamp, and whirl around like tops. That aria for Delilah Brown in the second act: 'One Wonderful Kiss.' When Melinda hears that I'm going to keep her down on the farm; she'll insist on being the prima donna."

"Of course," said David. He rocked one elegant leg over the other. "I had Melinda in mind all the time. Who else but Melinda?"

Billy chewed one finger-nail thoughtfully and stared at David. "And now we come back to the Press boys. Who's going to play Davey Jones? Don't you think it's time you stopped impersonating a classical concert pianist, and be David Enger, composer of *Samson Smith*?" He sat down again and regarded his friend with eager demand.

"No," said David, shortly. "No." His face darkened. Now Billy, for the first time, saw that David was even thinner than usual, and that some heavy misery was shadowing his glittering and restless eyes. David turned his head aside from the penetrating study of his friend. "After all, I can't do this to my parents, and my brother, this late in the day. The money, and even the fame, wouldn't matter to them, if I stepped out of this damned cloak and let them see what I really am."

"Hum," said Billy. He had discerned fear in David's

voice. Why should he fear? Forty thousand or more dollars already received for only six songs, and records, and a fortune to follow *Samson Smith*! The hectic ballet in the third act would become a classic in itself. Why should any man be afraid?

David stood up, long and poised and graceful. "Let's go to Delmonico's for a late supper, Billy," he said, and took up his cane and gloves. Billy hesitated. "Well, now," he murmured, and rested his chin on the arms he had folded on the back of his chair. "The last time I was there, there was some murmuring from the clientele." He smiled ruefully. "Oh, I'm not insulted or anything. But I hate to hurt people by exploding one of their precious myths. In the North, I'm an abused young Uncle Tom from the Deep Lynching South. In the South, I'm a coloured gentleman, and my white friends shows me off proudly. After all, they helped me get started, you know. My friend in Raleigh was the first to suggest a theatre for me, and he rounded up all his friends and spread the word, and it was a great success. That's what made me try this theatre in New York."

He puffed at his cigarette and squinted thoughtfully, and with a smile, through the smoke. "I'm sure that my audience to-night, and my Northern audiences in the cabarets, think that after I and my men leave their lily white presences we slink away meekly into some slum, where we sit and wail darkie plantation songs and wipe away our tears. Even though they must know we get paid a fortune up here, I haven't the slightest doubt that they believe that when we take off our striped trousers and Prince Alberts we put on rags. Who am I to destroy such a pathetic dream?"

He chuckled. "When they swarm around, after a session, avoiding shaking my hand, of course, I have to talk what they think is darkie talk. In a thick Southern accent. They feel very happy with themselves, congratulating me. Why should I take that pleasure away from them? So, why don't you come to my hotel and have a late supper in my suite, with some of the boys?"

"People are damn' fools," said David.

"Not very original. But, who isn't?" And Billy fixed his eyes meaningly on his friend.

"You couldn't be referring to me, could you?" said David,

smiling painfully. "See here, Billy, I struggled for three months, after writing my first song, before sending it to you." He paused. "I suppose that makes me a fool."

"Am I to judge any man?" asked Billy, with a pious expression. "Come on, Dave. The boys get hungry after all that playing." He put on his fur-collared black overcoat and a shimmering top hat, pearly gloves and silk scarf. Dave thought, There's some aristocratic ancestor in that woodpile, and he's probably got some very patrician relatives in North Carolina. Billy inspected himself happily in the mirror. He arranged his scarf meticulously, and gave his hat a debonair tilt. Still studying his reflection, he asked with transparent carelessness:

"How's Ed?"

"All right, from my mother's letters." David's voice was stifled. Billy looked at him furtively in the mirror. David's fine-drawn features had become thin, almost wizened, with some secret pain, which Billy suspected did not arise from the thought of Edward. David drew a deep breath. "He's opened ten new stores, the Green and White Markets, in the big cities." His voice was more easy. "My mother says he'll have at least eight more by the summer. There isn't any end to his energy."

"You wrote me he got married last June," said Billy, fastening the buttons on his kid gloves. "But I read an item about it in a Chicago paper. Ed's famous in his own right. I always thought he would be." He had trouble with the last button, and blinked.

"Billy, when you're in Albany in February, why don't you go to Waterford to see him?" David spoke impulsively, as he watched the suddenly clumsy manipulation of the refractory button.

"I don't think so," said Billy, quietly. "No, sir, I don't think so. He probably knows who Prince Emory is. If he wanted to see me, or know about me, he could write."

"Sometimes you're an idiot," said David, impatiently. "Ed thinks popular music is as degrading as opium smoking, and just as much to be avoided. He probably never even looked at a sheet of modern music, so how would he see your photograph on it? I may be wrong, but I think he never forgot you. I think the memory of you plagues him sometimes. My mother wrote me that he is one of the big supporters of that private settlement house for Negroes in New York."

Billy's head jerked up, and his smile was radiant. "You mean the Russell Home House? Was that for me, do you honestly think?"

"Who else? I'm sorry I never mentioned it before; I thought you knew. There's no other 'Russell' there."

Tears sparkled in Billy's beautiful black eyes. "I never knew," he said, his voice trembling. "Honest to God, I never knew." He paused. "And I have an idea he doesn't know, either, that Russell is for me. Not consciously, anyway. He probably picked it out of the air."

David considered this, then nodded. "Possibly. Ed's the most complex person I ever knew. Protean. One moment he's as dull as tarnished brass, and the next he's mercurial. Volatile. I'm the only one in the family who knows that, except my mother. And now, after all these years, I'm beginning to suspect he was always her favourite child, and that she knows he resembles her in character a good deal and that's why she was hard on him. She was punishing herself, in Ed. And determined that he'd make none of her own past mistakes." He looked at the gold head of his cane. "Even now, I'm sorry for Ed, though I haven't seen him since last March, almost a year ago." His mouth changed, became intensely mournful and sad. "At first—well, I thought I'd throw the whole thing up, my pretence of believing I was a pianist. And then, I couldn't hurt him."

"What's wrong, Dave?" asked Billy softly. Dave glanced up, startled, then saw his friend's compassionate eyes. His face became rigid. He had never confided in anyone fully in all his life, not even his old teacher in New York, not even Billy. But there was such an agony in his heart now, such a desire for surcease. He put his gloved hands over the top of his cane, and leaned on it, and stared at the floor.

"Billy," he began, then stopped. His head drooped. In a lower voice, he said, "Ed married the girl I thought loved me, the girl I thought was going to marry me. I never told you. Or anybody. It was impossible."

"I see," said Billy. He paused. "Did Ed know? Did you ever tell him?"

"He knew," said David. "Yes, he knew. Don't think he

married her to thwart or injure me. He didn't. He met her, the first time, when she was a child, and apparently never forgot her, and then one day he met her again. That was all. I suppose it was as much a shock to him, knowing about me——"

"I see," said Billy again. He took David's arm. "Let's go," he added.

His touch, his sympathy, almost unnerved David. They left the theatre together. The air was full of dark cold and snow. "I have to take a cab," said Billy. "I don't dare use my limousine openly. Uncle Tom, you know." He was silent a moment. "I'm sorry, Dave. And that's why you haven't been home since last March."

"That's right," said Dave. "But now I must. My father is very ill. I can't avoid Ed—and Margaret—for ever. By the way, I'm going to be an uncle soon."

The newsboys were crying in the streets, holding up papers with black headlines:

"U.S. Protests English Interference with American Mail!"

"Berlin accuses France of fresh atrocities!"

"Britain Seizes American Seamen on Neutral Ships!"

Billy bought a newspaper. The two young men scanned the various shouting headlines. Then Billy took a coin out of his pocket and tossed it in the air.

"Who do we fight, boys, who do we fight? Heads, England. Tails, Germany." He threw the coin higher; it fell into the snow and its message was lost.

"And for what?" asked David, angrily. "And for what?"

"But my son should know," objected Maria, calmly. "Why should anyone be spared the stresses of life, man or woman or child? Life is stress and fury and grief and pain, and there is little joy but much suffering. Why it should be I do not know." She put down her knitting and looked thoughtfully at space. "It is an old question: who is the creator of man's misery and uncertainty and sorrow, man, himself, or God?" (She thought acutely of Edward.)

The purplish-white February twilight stood at the windows of Margaret's sitting-room. The grounds below and beyond lay in ghostly mauve shadow as they swelled under the snow in waves like a small sea. A fire fluttered on the hearth in the ivory and gold room, threw its lance-like reflections on the ceiling. Margaret sat in a comfortable chair near the fire, her listless hands clasped in her lap, her swollen body heavy with life.

She had no affection for Maria, but only a profound respect, and an absolute belief in her integrity. So she had confided her fears about the birth to Edward's mother. She knew, now, that she would bear twins, and the doctor, sworn to silence, had been dubious about the children's, or her own, survival.

"I don't believe in worrying anyone until the time comes," said Margaret. She looked down at the snow and the silence and the massed, empty trees, and she thought it all resembled a cemetery. She shivered. "He has enough to worry him," she added, with a touch of resentment.

Maria said nothing. She knew that Margaret was referring to Edward's family. She, Maria, had hoped much from this marriage. Part of her hope had been fulfilled—Margaret had brought Edward the first real happiness he had ever known in his life. But it had been a narrow happiness; his understanding of his wife had not broadened to an understanding of others. His concern for her, his merging with her, his tender consideration and new subtlety about the thoughts of others, ended with his wife. In fact, in connection with other people, his perceptions had hardened and darkened, had even, at times, become ruthless. Love, thought Maria, while sometimes it can wear the wings of an angel, can also become a short chain in a hidden cell.

Maria said, in a tone of remote indifference. "Who does not have worry? Why do we have a tendency to look upon our neighbours' smiling faces and say to ourselves: There are the blessed of both the world and God, who are never tearful or oppressed or despairing. Why do we say, He has never spent an anxious night, or sighed in his sleep or contemplated death? We hide from each other, in a regard for manners or in pride or conceit."

They were speaking in German. Maria had been pleased that Margaret spoke the language so well, with such careful diction and without idioms, which were vulgar.

What have you to worry about, and your children? Margaret asked her in her mind, with indignation. Ed's given you all his life and all his work, and none of you have returned those gifts with affection or gratitude, but only with an air that all this is your right! You live a life of luxury and protection and safety; you never think of Ed who's so terribly worried constantly and who works so hard.

"I am not going to tell Ed," said Margaret. "And it will probably be all right. I am in good health, and I have heard my doctor is too conservative. Why should I add to Ed's burdens?" she asked, meaningly.

But Maria could not be goaded when she knew silence was the best.

"He thinks about the war all the time," Margaret said.

"So do I," replied Maria, very quickly. "I have cousins and nephews in Germany. I have not heard from them. I write, but receive no replies. That is because England is censoring and suppressing letters to and from Germany. She also cut the cable between America and Germany almost immediately."

"I know, Mother Enger. That is why, among other things, we almost declared war on England last December. Only our Ambassador to London, and the President, prevented the indignation of the American people from culminating in a war with the English."

"Naturally," said Maria, resuming her knitting. "It is not in the plan for America to fight the British. So the anger of the American people must be guided against Germany. So it is that the brave editor of Berlin's greatest newspaper, who has been denouncing the war, has been imprisoned by that stupid German Government, which does not understand. The Kaiser does not understand that he is only a puppet of those who have planned this monstrous thing over the years. He, too, is stupid. But where are the wise men? The Bible says that the children of darkness are wiser in their generation than the children of light. However, it is not necessary for good men to be stupid as well as virtuous."

Margaret sat up, surprised. "Then, you know also, Mother Enger?"

Maria smiled a little. "Did you think wisdom, or knowledge, begins and ends with Edward? When I was a girl, and young in my family's *schloss*, one of my cousins, who was a colonel in the Imperial Army, disclosed to us, with much anxiety, what he knew even in those days. For his presumption, in bringing this to the attention of his superiors, he was retired. Did they know all too well, or did they think him mad? That, we shall never know."

"Then," said Margaret, hopelessly, "there is nothing we can do now."

"I do not think so—not just now," replied Maria, knitting faster. "Those who tried to warn us, from every country in the world, have been silenced, or are heard no more. But is it necessary to discuss this? Edward is doing what he can, with his 'Save America Committee,' and I suppose it is expensive and too much for him. However, a man must act in accordance with his principles, so I say nothing."

Margaret lifted her weighted body with difficulty and went to a window. The evening light deepened more and more; now the snow dunes were carved in marble and dark purple and the cobalt sky pulsed with one quicksilver star. It was one of the last days of February, and Margaret wondered how she could endure another month of this semi-helplessness and discomfort and apprehension. But the thought ran over her mind lightly, as a ripple runs over a lake. She must tell Ed when he came home that his mother knew what was troubling him, and that she not only believed but was fully aware of the truth. She rubbed a finger on the leaded glass, and a little auro of warm moisture spread out from her flesh.

"It is not hard, having children," said Maria from her seat near the fire. "Birth is the very least. It is the life of your children about you which is hard. Always, we conceive and bear strangers, and as the years pass those strangers rarely become friends of their parents. It is not unusual for hatred to grow between them. Shall the parents be blamed, or the children? That is impossible to know. If this were my wedding day I would vow to myself that I would not bear children."

Margaret's eyes widened and she turned as swiftly as she could. She looked at Maria's calm and placid face which showed no vehemence, no bitterness.

"It is not that my children are different in an important way from the children of other mothers," said Maria. "They have not disappointed me more than the children of other women have disappointed them. But children inevitably bring sorrow and regret and sadness and fear, as they become men and women. She who denies this does not speak the truth."

"What are you trying to tell me?" demanded Margaret in a rising voice.

Maria lifted her big head and smiled at the girl. "I am not a Catholic, but often I think of Mary, the mother of Jesus, that young girl. Hers was a mortal's pain and a mortal's fear and a mortal's love. Her Son's were God's. He suffered as God suffers, but still it was a Divine suffering, not to be understood by us, not even by His Mother. I think of her standing at the foot of the Cross and gazing up at her Son, and seeing the blood on His brow and in His side, and to her, I am certain, it was only her Son hanging there, the flesh of her flesh and the blood of her blood. Her knowledge of Who He was was submerged, in those supreme moments, in the agony of a mother."

"You are telling me not to forget Ed, in my children," said Margaret, in a soft and trembling tone, and for a moment she almost loved Maria. "Do not be disturbed. Ed will always be first and last with his wife, for she loved him from the moment she met him as a child."

Maria nodded vastly. "It is so. I am also warning you that when you are a mother you will never forget that you are a mother. Bút your children will forget that they are your children. You must prepare for that day. It has been said in the Bible that a man and his wife are one flesh, but it has not been said that their children are their flesh."

Margaret stared at her in humble wonder, as if seeing for the first time. What did she know of Maria, after all? The huge woman knitting so placidly and so surely by the fire was an enigma, and no questions Margaret might ask would be enlightening. Moreover, they could not be asked. All at once, Margaret was afraid of the answers.

She felt a short and savage twinge in her side and put her hand hastily over the spot. The children moved in her, and it came to her that though she had conceived them and would bear them, and had given her blood and her life and the beating of her heart to them, they were mysteries. She could not imagine their faces. Even their sex was hidden from her. They knew themselves, in the vortex of her womb, but she did not know them. She was dazed by the thought, and vaguely frightened.

The telephone rang by her bedside and she lumbered to it. It was Edward, and his first question, rich with love, was about her health to-day. Her voice shook in answering. "When will you be home?" she asked. "I've been expecting you every minute."

There was a slight pause, and his voice changed and seemed to fade a little. "I won't be home until the day after to-morrow, darling. I am leaving for Cleveland in an hour."

He usually kept a packed suitcase in his office, for in those days he was quite often away overnight in behalf of the "Save America Committee," or on sudden business concerned with his burgeoning new stores.

"Oh," said Margaret, disappointed. She wondered if it were the fault of the line that he sounded so pent and yet so guarded. "When you go away, Ed, it seems that you're away for ever. Is it necessary——"

"Very necessary, Margaret." He paused. "How're Castor and Pollux getting along?"

"Lively. Your mother has been keeping me company this afternoon."

There was a pause. Then he said a strange thing, as if involuntarily, "That's good. My mother is a wise woman." Apparently he was surprised at his own words, for he went on in a different tone, "That is, she isn't as stupid as the rest of the family."

Margaret smiled. "He who calls his brother a fool is in danger of hell fire." He was tired; she could hear it in his voice. She wanted to cheer him. But he said with grimness, "I'm in it already. Never mind, dear. Don't worry." He gave her the name of the hotel in which he usually stayed in Cleveland. "I'm within reach," he added.

"I don't expect you to be away for a month," she said. "Is it one of the shops?"

"Two of them," he said.

At four o'clock that afternoon he had called George Enreich. That was an hour ago. He had received a telegram from his local manager in Cleveland. Then he had called George Enreich.

"Two shops this time," he had said, trying to keep his voice level though his heart was a sickening pain in his chest. "Cleveland. You can't explain it away this time as you did the Pittsburgh shops, the Albany shops, and the Chicago shops. Jealous and frightened independent grocers and butchers, or hooligans, or thieves. No, no, not this time."

George said coldly, "I never believed it myself, my Eddie. The first, yes, but not the others. However, I hoped it would not spread. It is your Committee, naturally."

"I know it, but I can't believe it, George. The Green and White Shops aren't identified with me. My name doesn't appear on the letter-heads, I'm not known personally in Cleveland or the other cities, to anybody. No one knows we own those shops——"

"No?" said George, in that same cold voice. "Do not be naïve, Eddie. It is true that only we know the facts, and not even the newspapers. But, my Eddie, the enemy has a thousand eyes and a thousand ears. You are dangerous to them, in their time-plan of involving America in that war. How much have you spent so far of your own money in newspaper advertisement, in the name of the 'Save America Committee'? At least twenty-five thousand dollars, is it not? Yes. You have written the advertisements, yes, and they are eloquent. Many times they have been quoted in editorials, in anger or approval. Do you not think the sleepless enemy would make it their affair to discover who was the power behind the 'Save America Committee'?"

"But I sent in those advertisements in that name, not mine!"

"So," said George.

"Then, I have spies somewhere."

"No," said George. "You underestimate our foes. Who could tell them? I know and William knows, and that tragic Irishman, Padraig. Are you accusing one of us?" He chuckled sourly. "Your advertisements have been paid for in cash, by the banks, who are notoriously discreet, and who do not know you are the donor, themselves. Yet, eight shops, in different cities, have had their fine plate windows smashed, their products fouled, their tables overturned. You cannot stop them. Your insurance company has been unpleasant; you have been reimbursed only a fraction of your loss. Eddie, I did not approve of your Committee, though I gave you money. As a matter of friendship. Principle, have you said? But there are few men of principle; the enemy is ubiquitous. Are you to take my advice, and desist?"

" No," said Edward, wrathfully. " I can stand this. I am going to Cleveland to-night."

Now George was alarmed. " It must not be so! You will finally lose concealment. It is true that the foe knows who you are, but do the populace? You will have boycotts, to add to your loss."

" The American people don't want war, and you know it, George. Most of the letters in the correspondence columns of the newspapers approve my advertisements. So do most of the editorials. It won't matter if they know, at last."

" It will," said George. " For surely we will go to war with Germany. To-morrow, next month, next year. But surely we will go. And, in the meantime, the Press is being harassed by men in Washington. Has your Hans not told you? Yes. The Press, in the main, is resisting. Newspapers are very jealous of their freedom. But in the end they will succumb, especially if there is a terrible incident. Be certain the incident is being prepared. I have seen signs of it. The German Embassy is pleading with Americans not to go to Europe on British boats, for it accuses the British of carrying contraband in the holds, for our so-neutral country, our so-peace-loving country, has men who manufacture that contraband for a profit, and other more powerful men who want war with Germany, for their own ancient and sinister purposes. But, do the Americans not sail? Ach, yes. It is 'fun, it is exciting, it is bold and daring,' say these fools. They love to be convoyed by British destroyers; they love shrieking that they have sighted a submarine, a U-boat, in the distance; they use binoculars; they prance in exuberance and pass the binoculars to their wives. And the British captains smile darkly. Tell me, my dear American Eddie, why are your countrymen so stupid?"

" They aren't," said Edward, doggedly. " Very few of them."

" There is another thing," said George, ignoring his remark. " When the incident comes, then you will not be an American at all. I have read a few hints in the more vociferous newspapers. There is a name they are calling: the hyphenated American, the German-American. That, you will be called, and your Committee remembered, and treachery attributed to you. Have you not been reading the national newspapers? Have you not seen some of the cartoons? The Kaiser is being depicted as a cannibal; Germans are being depicted as swine-headed monsters. Only here and there, tentatively. But there. It is called the new name-propaganda. But the thing is old, old as the ostrakismos of Greece. My Eddie, I am not a young man; I dislike the shell being placed against me."

Now Edward could not contain his fury. "Perhaps," shouted, "you'd like not only to stop donating to the Committee, in the name of America, but would like to pull out of all the shops, too?"

He was sorry an instant later, for losing his wild temper. And then, incredibly, he heard George say, "It is possible. Have you my quarter of a mililon dollars available at this time?"

Edward jerked the receiver from his ear, and stared at it blankly. Then, with a suddenly wet hand, he put it back to his ear. He could only mouth stammering words incoherently. George went on, "It is more than a quarter of a million. There is my next quarter of profits, twenty-five per cent. Yet, I am willing to lose future profits. You have only to return the money I have advanced."

Edward was silent. He had been planning for a long time to get George out of the business. But the plans had been for the future. Not just now, when he was more heavily in debt than ever, because of the Green and White stores. He had thought of ten years, fifteen years. Then, he would manipulate cleverly. There was a thick congestion in his throat as if his heart had risen there, and was bleeding. More than anything else that affected him was George's ruthless repudiation of their friendship, his casting off of Edward as one would cast off something that had become perilous and noxious. A worthless acquaintance who was now unstable and held in contempt. (Edward forgot in his extremity the fact that he had been planning to relieve himself of the twenty-five per cent paid out to his old friend —in the possible future.) Worst of all, in repudiating Edward, he was repudiating America.

He said in a dwindled voice, "And you don't care about helping my country, at all?"

"No," said George emphatically. "No, I do not. And why, you will ask, when this country has been 'good' to me, as you might sentimentally say? I have worked; in my own fashion I have returned the benefits, if they were benefits. But America will be willingly, and joyfully, through propaganda, prepared to destroy me—as a hyphenated American. When the time comes. So, I cannot any longer be connected with the Committee." He paused. "And with you, Eddie: My quarter of a million dollars . . ."

Edward closed his eyes on a spasm. Then he said, "One time, long ago, you gave me a gold pen, engraved with the words: 'For the stalwart'——"

"Yes. But I am not ready to be destroyed with the stalwart. I have told you. I am not young. I love my life, and what it gives me." He laughed, a short harsh laugh. "For that, I will be the American patriot; I will hate the German, when I am bidden to hate him. I am a man. I have worked hard. For the years that remain for me I will enjoy myself. Shall I destroy all this, fruitlessly, when America goes mad also? I am not a man to carry banners in a cause already dead."

Enormously ill, and trembling, Edward said, weakly, "You believe the cause is dead. How can you believe that of America?"

"Because it is true. If not to-day, then to-morrow. You will see. Are Americans less vulnerable than other nations? No. They are even more vulnerable, because they lack cynicism. They never doubt the invincibility of truth; they are simple. And what they will believe, to them will be the truth. It is the mark of an innocent man. Yet innocent men can be destroyers—in the name of the truth which will be manufactured cunningly for them."

Edward, out of his numb shock, could only say, "I love my country."

"Love her, my Eddie. She will destroy you—in the name of truth. I have warned you. And so I ask, when may I have my money?"

Edward did not speak for a few moments. Then he said, quietly, "When I am prepared to return it to you, and not a minute before. I am the one to decide that. There's no clause in our contract that binds me to any specific date."

George said, almost sadly, "But there is a clause which states that I, if I am not satisfied, may give you six months' notice. I am giving you that notice now. I will withdraw it—if you halt your Committee."

Edward clenched the receiver. His cold dry lips formed the words: " I will not halt the Committee. You may sue me, if you want to, but remember, if you do, I shall give the whole story to the Press."

" If I sue," said George, " it will be at an appropriate moment. When the American people have absorbed enough lies, as they surely will. When did ever a people not prefer lies to truth?"

Edward's head was shattering in a splintering thunder. " I can't betray my country. You are asking too much. I have to live with myself."

" A man can always live with himself, when he has convinced himself that he has acted sensibly. It is a matter of delusion, and such a delusion is not hard. It is really very easy, my Eddie, as is all self-interest."

Edward's grief was almost too much for him, but he said, steadily, almost imploringly—and the money did not matter now—" You have always been my friend, and for years you were the only friend I had, George. You have been like a father to me."

George said, kindly, and his own voice changed, " I am still that, Eddie. My sole wish is that you do not destroy yourself, that you think of yourself. Do you think this is a matter of no moment to me?"

Edward's eyes roved desperately, and blindly, about his office. Finally he said, " I shall, some way, find that money for you. And never again will I speak to you, or think of you. I'll wipe you out of my mind, George."

He took the receiver from his ear, and ignored George's urgent voice that cried in it. He replaced the receiver, put his elbows on his desk and his hands over his eyes. He was so undone that his whole body felt paralysed. He had broken with George Enreich, finally, irrevocably. He had done that for America, but still it was a thing too terrible to bear. Then he was full of terror. George would not have said what he had said if he had not been convinced of the truth. He would not have cut Edward off—if he had not tried to save him, and had failed. No, God, said Edward, in the first prayer he had offered in many years. No, God. Preserve my country; save her. Give her peace; don't take her hope and her belief in the moral law from her. She is good and generous and vast, and her simplicity is noble. Don't abandon her to international plotters, who want to destroy her and overthrow her, and enslave and corrupt her. I love my country; I would give my life for her, to preserve her. I would give my life to uphold her principles. I would give my life . . .

There was something from Shakespeare; he could not, just now, in his awful confusion and devastation, recall the source. It was something about an English general, pleading with his king that all was lost, and that their armies must retreat. But the king had remained on the battlefield and had won a great victory. The general returned in joy to congratulate him. The king had said with powerful loathing, "Hang yourself, brave Crillon. We fought at Arques. And *you* were not there."

Edward said to himself, in a fainting, childish promise, I must look up the quotation. I must find it. It seemed of the most tremendous importance to him.

George, in his own office, wiped slow and unfamiliar tears from his cheeks, and then cursed himself. After some moments of thought he called New York. There was a long and exasperating delay until he was connected with William McFadden. George said, in a voice that was hoarse and halting, "William. Eddie must be stopped from going to the Press." He gave William a quick outline of what had been said between him and Edward, and William said, "The bucko is daft."

George said, "He will call in the Press and reveal himself and appeal to what he believes is the American conscience and American indignation—for he loves his country. I must ask you to go to Cleveland at once, in the name of our affection for him. You sound cheerful. I assure you, my friend, that this is no occasion for cheerfulness. Ah, you have news? Good. But take it to Cleveland; I have made inquiries. There is a train at eleven o'clock; it will bring you from New York to Cleveland in time. He does not know that whatever he does now will be no good. In the end, if he destroys himself, it will do no good."

Maria showed no signs of leaving Margaret alone, as usual, for her late afternoon coffee and little cakes. The house was very silent. Only Sylvia remained of the children. Ralph and Violette were in Mexico, a long way, Margaret would reflect complacently. Sylvia, at this moment, was brooding in her own room; she preferred tea, and her own company. Since almost a year ago she had shown only the slightest interest in her theatre, which Edward had bought for her at such expense. She had delegated her duties, in the name of invalidism, to a young and vigorous woman who was bringing successful plays to Waterford. But Margaret was puzzled by the fact that Sylvia was almost always engaged with mysterious large pads of paper, paint and pencils. Was it possible that Sylvia was trying to attract the attention of prominent producers in New York? If so, Margaret would think, I hope she suceeds, and will leave this house permanently.

Pierre brought in the silver tray which held a steaming coffee-pot, cups and saucers, and a plate of dainty cakes. Margaret noticed the two cups. She had not requested the extra cup. But Maria was tranquilly pouring, a little to Margaret's vexation. She liked this twilight hour alone. Then she was ashamed of her annoyance. It had been very good of Maria, and most unusual, for her to devote all this afternoon to her daughter-in-law, leaving even her husband, and not visiting Sylvia. Is it possible she really likes me? Margaret asked herself, with discomfort. Is it possible that she likes anybody, coming down to it?

"The coffee is strong and hot," Maria said approvingly. "Is it cream and sugar for you, Margaret?" Then she looked fully at the girl and said, "I have told nobody. But my mother's name was Marguerita. It is a name I love. If the children are girls, perhaps you would consider naming one of them Marguerita Gertrude, my mother's full name?"

Margaret was touched. "No one likes her own name," she said, frankly. "So, I would not want to call a girl by mine. But Gertrude shall be the name of one, if both are girls."

I'm sure they know their sex, and who they are, thought Margaret, dreamily. But I, their mother, don't know a thing about them. Oh, I'm getting mystical! The stab of pain in her side came again, and she winced and cowered a little, under Maria's alert eyes. But the children were not expected for another month; this must just be another of the discomforts a mother must suffer. When a great pain seemed to crush her back for a moment or two she trembled. It was a while before she could straighten up. Then her forehead was moist, and a trickle of water ran between her shoulder blades. The fire on the hearth seemed, suddenly, too hot, and the air in the room too oppressive.

Pierre entered the room silently, and the women started. "I am sorry, Madame," he said to Maria. "I ought to have knocked. But Mr. David has returned. I have just conducted him to his room. He wishes to join the ladies, if they have no objection."

"David!" exclaimed Maria, and her puffy face coloured with pleasure. "He said nothing! He did not send a telegram!" She rose, and her black dress rustled. "Send him in at once, Pierre."

David! Margaret was all sick confusion, and embarrassment. But she thought, For all our sakes I must be casual and friendly. Besides, David has probably forgotten me entirely by this time. She set her face in an appearance of pleased and sisterly expectation, though her colour rose, and her inner embarrassment moistened the palms of her hands. She was hardly aware of another wave of pain in her back.

David, smiling, came into the room and his mother went to him and put her hands on his shoulders and looked into his face. "My son," she said, gently. She rarely, if ever, had kissed her children, even when they had been very young, and they did not expect it. But her eyes caught the slightest nuances of their expressions, the slightest involuntary gesture. David, in turn, put his hands on his mother's arms, lightly. She was almost as tall as he and they exchanged an eloquent glance in which everything was asked and everything answered, as much as David permitted himself to answer in that poignant silence.

Margaret's first thought was that David seemed excessively thin and very haggard, and that his once arrogant profile with the aquiline nose had softened and matured. The girl felt a rush of sadness for him, remembering his kindness and devotion and his love, which had asked nothing of her but had only wanted to give. She was no longer much perturbed; she wished she knew what to do for this young man. Part of her feeling was based on his very faint resemblance to Edward, and part on her real affection for him. She did not resent, very much, his air of dignity and elegance, his quick but harmonious movements which came from some inner assurance.

"And now, our Margaret," said Maria, calmly, turning to her daughter-in-law. Her early training had taught her that difficult situations could best be managed by ignoring the difficulty. "Edward has left her for a day or two under my care." And she smiled briefly at Margaret.

David crossed the floor and held out his hand to Margaret and she took it. He pressed her hand. It was kind and comforting. He smiled down at her, and said, "It's been a long time since we saw each other, Margaret. I'm glad I'm here now."

His dark eyes were still restless, but not as restless as she remembered. Nor were they embarrassed. They expressed his love for her, but it was a gentled love, and an accepting one.

"I will ring for some more coffee and cakes," said Maria. David sat down near Margaret and asked, "And how are you, Margaret?"

"Very well, David," she answered. It was so natural for him to be here, and she felt an immense relief. She was grateful for his tact, and his casualness. But then, everything David did had the touch of the *soignée* about it; it was impossible for him to be either awkward or crude. She settled her tightened body back in her chair, and returned his smile. He was studying her with a penetrating look, open and friendly, and she did not know that he was suffering.

"I thought I'd surprise everybody," he said. "I can only stay two days, because I've an engagement in Philadelphia. You say Ed is out of town?"

"Yes, in Cleveland," said Margaret. "He'll be back day after to-morrow. You'll see him, won't you?" She could, because of David's infinite tact, speak naturally of her husband.

He said, with real or assumed regret, "No, I'm afraid not. I'm leaving to-morrow night. Why, I haven't seen old Ed for almost a year! But I'll be back by the end of March for a week." His face did not change as he spoke of his brother. It remained intent and kind. If his eyes retreated behind his eyelids it was so quickly that Margaret did not catch the flicker.

He turned to his mother and gave her an amusing résumé of his concerts. Yes, he had received some very good reviews. Of course, concert pianists were a specialised breed, and did not, as a rule, draw anyone except those with a real interest in classical music or an assumed one. "I think," he said, "that the pretenders are in the majority." He spoke without cynicism or bitterness. "Usually they're the *nouveaux riches* who want to impress their new friends. They have all the jargon, down very pat. I've learned not to ask searching questions, when I'm invited to dinner at some mansion, obviously new, after a recital."

"Then, what do you speak of?" asked Maria, interested.

"I take the embarrassement out of the situation by immediately beginning to admire some *objet d'art* on the premises. That takes their uncomfortable minds off me. I've found that the best way to be a good conversationalist, and popular, is just to ask questions. You don't even have to listen to the answers."

Again there was no cynicism in his voice, but only indulgence. The once intolerant David, through his own grief and despair, had learned to look at others with a large measure of compassion, even fools and rascals. He's good, he's kind, he's a gentleman, thought Margaret, and began to enjoy his company as she could not remember having enjoyed it before. Ed was wrong about him, she said to herself, not in the least shocked by this treachery. I must tell him about David. He's the only one in the family who has real character and depth. Still, she caught herself quickly, he also exploits Ed. She frowned a little, uneasily, unable to reconcile her two emotions.

David talked almost exclusively to his mother, contenting himself by smiling at Margaret frequently, as he made a point. His thin arm, in its black sleeve, was very near her. She could see the prominent veins on his narrow hand, the long and sensitive fingers, the ring, set with an emerald, on the third finger. Though in good taste, it was an expensive ring, she saw. If David could afford such an article, then he had no right to take money from his brother, with or without David's knowledge that he was being subsidised. I really must speak to Ed, thought Margaret, annoyed, and this time her thought was not touched with kindness for David.

Then her musings vanished as a pain, like a pounding wave, struck her back once more, and circled her body. She gasped, then compressed her mouth and lowered her head. David and his mother, talking animatedly, did not see her wince and shudder. Her forehead started with drops of water.

Pierre came in again to light the lamps and replenish the fire with large lumps of cannal coal. The fire spluttered and turned a brighter red. Night stood at the windows. Margaret clutched the arms of her chair and cried in terror in herself, Ed! Ed! But Edward was on a train, nearing Cleveland now. I'm afraid, she thought. I'm awfully afraid; something is going to happen. I suppose we could reach him at a station, with a telegram. But perhaps it's too late for that. Or at his hotel, when he arrives. No, no, I mustn't worry him. I need him, but I mustn't worry him! His voice—it was so strained and stifled this afternoon. Something is wrong, very wrong. And, after all, it won't be for a month or six weeks; the doctor said. This is just part of the whole thing; I can't start to scream and be foolish.

The door flew open, violently, and Sylvia, with her everlasting lacy white shawl over her crimson wool frock, stood upon the threshold. She looked wild and breathless, and her black eyes were gleaming with rage and affront. She cried out in a furious voice, "You came home, Dave, but you never thought of seeing me, or asking about me! Oh, no! I'm not important enough to my brother! I had to find out you were here through that damned old Pierre, who mentioned it casually when he brought my tea!"

"Sylvia," said Maria, coldly. But David rose slowly and went to his sister. She stopped him half-way with a gesture which resembled the savage wielding of a steel whip. "Never mind, Dave. Just forget me, that's all. Poor old Sylvia, the old maid, shut up in her room." She laughed with sudden shrill scorn. "There are other people here more important to you." Her eyes flicked on Margaret, cowering in bemused pain in her chair.

"Sylvia," said Maria again, and this time her daughter heard and was silent, only gazing at Margaret with steady loathing and repudiation. Her emaciated body shook with passion. Even David had never seen her so aroused, so wild. He said, "I'm sorry, Sylvia. I did ask about you, immediately. But Pierre said you weren't well, and were resting, and I thought I'd wait until later." He was greatly alarmed. He had guessed that his family was not cordial to Margaret, for his sake, and because she was Edward's wife, but he had not expected such hatred, such rageful rejection, even from his favourite sister. He was extremely concerned for Margaret.

Sylvia drew an audible breath; it was almost a hiss. She dared not attack her mother, nor Margaret now. So she attacked David, and acid tears spurted into her eyes.

"Always so tactful, aren't you, Dave?" Her voice was taut and thin. "Always ready with the smooth explanation and excuse." But even in her passion she saw how worn and haggard he was and she was struck with grief and fresh rage against Margaret. Her voice changed and shook when she had swallowed with difficulty and she could speak again. "But some people aren't worth your kindness, Dave, believe me. Some people are low and detestable and coarse and cheap. You shouldn't waste yourself on them, Dave!"

"I meet all kinds of people in my profession, and travels," said David, quietly, still hoping to save the situation which even his mother did not seem able to control. "Would you want me to insult them or treat them with contempt?"

"Yes, yes!" cried Sylvia. "Yes, yes! That's all they deserve!"

Her voice broke in a sob, and she stood with her hands clenched at her sides, and looked only at Margaret, whose face was very pale and remote, and whose head had fallen forward.

"Then," said David, with a painful smile, "I'd soon have no engagements, Sylvia. Suppose we go to your room and have a little talk, alone together?"

She started back from him, and her white and angular face gleamed like bone in the lamplight. "Oh, no, Dave! I wouldn't deprive you of your wonderful company——"

Maria stood up massively. "I think we should leave Margaret alone to rest until dinner," she said. "Come on, Sylvia, I believe it is time for your tonic."

"Rest, rest!" exclaimed Sylvia, hysterically. "There's nothing but damned rest in this accursed house! Pa rests; Sylvia rests; Ma rests. And she . . ." Her eyes were a fierce blaze on Margaret, an annihilating blaze. Her face became contorted, and the delicate lavender veins at her temples stood out.

Why, thought David, his consternation increasing, she acts as if she's out of her mind. She's lost all sense of decency.

It isn't all just because of me, either. It's something deeper than that. He had known grief and despair as old acquaintances this past year, and he saw that they were also haunters of his sister. But why this was so he could not imagine. Sylvia had never mentioned, in her letters to him, any man she had met or known, except Padraig Devoe, and then only in passing. She had stopped mentioning him when he had married that actress.

" It is time for your tonic," said Maria, inexorably, and took her daughter's bony elbow firmly in her hand. " Also, there is something I wish to discuss with you, Sylvia. You are certainly not well."

Sylvia snatched her arm from her mother's grasp, tried to speak, then burst into a storm of weeping. She covered her face with her hands. David stood by helplessly, profoundly shocked and grieved and bewildered.

Shameful, shameful, thought Maria, with no pity at all. It is a plebeian's outbreak, without reticence or pride. I cannot imagine any of my cousins or nieces losing self-control like this, and forgetting themselves. She was full of umbrage and disdain for Sylvia. " You are a fool," she said, in a hard, low tone. " You are not a lady." But Sylvia did not hear; she was lost in her agony and her sorrow and hatred, the tears splashing through her fingers.

David gave his mother a quelling glance, an appealing glance, and put his arm about his sister. His one desire was to remove her from this room, and the sight of Margaret, and the knowledge of Margaret. " All right, dear," he said gently. " Come into your room with me, and we'll talk it over. Dear Sylvie," he added, using his childhood nickname for her in a last appeal.

Sylvia heard, dropped her hands from her ravished face, and leaned against her brother. " Oh, Dave," she said, brokenly. " You don't know, you don't know. Dave, I can't stand it. Dave, I'll lose my mind."

Maria understood, but still a lady, an aristocrat, did not break under any sorrow or stress, except when alone. " I am afraid you do not have any mind," she said, with controlled harshness. " Or any manners. Go with your brother, Sylvia."

She ventured a look at Margaret's chair near the fire. But it was empty. Maria nodded her head with approval. A lady always removed herself from a shameless situation, which she could not accept. Margaret had retired to her bedroom, and that was correct.

Then, even above Sylvia's incoherent weeping Maria heard a faint and agonised wailing, which dwindled almost immediately into silence as though a hand had been put forcefully over a tortured mouth. Forgetting even her daughter, Maria lumbered quickly to Margaret's bedroom. Margaret was crouching on her bed like an animal, on her hands and knees, her head fallen between her stiffened arms. She did not look up as Maria closed the door. Drops of water dripped from her face, and her lower lip was caught between her teeth. A sudden spasm seized her, and her whole body shook as if a wave had struck it with powerful force. But she did not utter a sound now.

"So," said Maria, softly, "it has come. Do not be afraid. We must send for the doctor at once."

The wave of torment receded, and Margaret dropped on her side like a felled deer. Her face was glazed and blank, her eyes sightless. Maria rang for a maid.

"We must be calm," said Maria, who was terribly concerned. The children would be premature; it was possible they would die. "We must find Edward, and bring him home."

Margaret said, and her voice was almost normal, "No. I must go through this alone. It would worry him——"

"It is his duty, to be worried," said Maria. But Margaret suddenly took her hand in a wet grip, and her eyes became alive once more. "No. He's almost in Cleveland now. And there's no train back here to-night. I know. So he'd be in misery all night, until to-morrow, at noon, when there is a train." Her voice was weak, and yet firm. "Don't send him a telegram—until it's all over. I can't worry him; it wouldn't do any good, you see."

She was in enormous and relentless pain, even though the onslaught of the excruciating wave had receded. She tried to smile up into Maria's sober face. "After all," she said, "other women have children, when their husbands are away. So, I'll have these."

A maid came in and Maria briefly told her to call Margaret's doctor. After the girl had left on swift feet, Maria said, "We must get her undressed and comfortable in bed." She approved of Margaret more and more; there was character here, and fortitude, and consideration for others. She could see the anguish in those strained blue eyes, yet Margaret was not crying or screaming. She even assisted Maria in her own undressing. Once, when her petticoat tangled about her knees she could even laugh.

The maid, frightened and inquisitive, returned to say that the doctor could not be reached for at least four hours, and that a message had been left for him. Maria in her alarm: "It will not be for some time," she said to Margaret, who now lay on her pillows spent and quiet. "The first is always long delayed."

"Yes," said Margaret, as if from experience. She was bracing herself against a new onslaught of the wave. She thought she could actually see the distant wave against a black horizon, and it was crested with threatening agony as red as blood. In a moment it would strike her, and she cringed in expectation. She turned her head into her pillow and caught the white slip beneath her teeth. Then the wave struck, and she writhed in silent and inhuman suffering. She watched the wave recede, behind her closed eyes; it went back, thundering, and she lay on some beach in the darkness, wounded and broken.

Hands were touching expertly, but she did not feel them. Even when she opened her eyes she could hardly see. The room had tilted drunkenly; everything was too bright, but too out of focus, like a nightmare. There was the taste of salt in her mouth; she did not know that her lip was bleeding. There was a tremendous bloated face bent over her, and she did not recognise Maria. A bubbling sound rose in her throat, and she did not know.

She was not conscious that David had just come into her bedroom. "I heard, from the maid," David said in a low voice to his mother. "Is it very bad?"

"Very bad," replied Maria, straightening the silken quilt over Margaret's collapsed body. "She is practically unconscious, the poor child." With a tenderness she had never shown her own children she smoothed Margaret's disordered hair, and touched the wet cheek. She could hardly endure the glazed stare fixed on the ceiling. "I do not like this," said Maria. "A few moments ago she was aware, and talking with me. And now she is not aware of anything except her pain. Her doctor has told her that she would be in great danger, that she might lose not only her children but her own life."

Dave uttered an exclamation. "Oh, no," he said, feebly. He sat down beside Margaret and took the soft, flaccid hand. "Does Ed know?"

"No. She would not tell him. She is a lady of much character," said Maria. "Where is Sylvia?"

Dave gave a short, miserable laugh. "Crying on her bed. But what are we going to do about Margaret?"

He did not hear his mother answer. Margaret was gripping his hand fiercely, and her body was slowly arching. Her stark face became livid; her staring eyes darkened. She uttered a long deep moaning, which, to David, was unendurable. Margaret's whitening finger-nails sank into his fingers, and he did not feel their piercing. He forgot that his mother was present. He said, clearly, "Margaret. Margaret, my darling. I'm here. Margaret."

He bent his head over her and kissed her forehead, and then pressed his cheek against hers. Her moaning faded away; she was still, as if listening. But her body quivered under the quilt. After a moment or two, she whispered, "Yes. Yes, dear."

She spoke like an exhausted child, out of her half-delirium. Her bright hair was a fan about her face, which was so suddenly small and dwindled, and of such a frightening colour. The blueness of her eyes gleamed from between her half-closed gilt eyelashes.

"We must have another doctor. We cannot wait," said Maria and she rang the bell again. Her heart was hurting intolerably; she could not remember when she had last felt this sting of tears along her eyelids. She looked at the sleek narrowness of her son's bent head, at his absorbed and passionate grip. "Ed, Ed," whispered Margaret, and David replied with confident love, "Yes. I'm here. I won't go away."

Maria averted her head, and her big chin quivered beyond her control. She started when she saw that Sylvia stood in the doorway. "What are you doing here?" she demanded, and without kindness. She noticed, with abstraction, that Sylvia was no longer wearing her shawl. The girl was looking as if with fascination, at Margaret and David. She said dully,

"The maid just told me. I . . ." She stopped, and drew nearer the bed, wrapping her thin arms about her breast and shoulders. "Oh, my God," she murmured. "She looks very ill. Dying." Her own face, in the lamplight, had changed subtly.

"Do not be so sure," said Maria, with coldness. Sylvia turned her head to her mother, and the tilted eyes widened in astonishment.

"Do you think I'm that base?" she asked, with deep shame and humility.

Maria shrugged her enormous shoulders, but her face softened. She said, "We have sent for another doctor. In the meantime we must do what we can. She is in a state of sudden shock."

In an illimitable darkness Margaret thought, quite objectively, pain isn't hot. It's cold—cold as death. Who is so cold? Who is crying? She floated above her agony, as if it were the agony of someone else. Yet, she could not escape it. She tried to rush into the darkness, like one pursued, but it overtook her, a mangling beast that rolled her over and over, her body in its jaws. Then again she would be apart, half-detached and wondering. Was that lightning in the sky, or in herself, or in someone she did not know, but whose screams were banners blowing in some unseen wind, banners the colour of blood? It was very strange. But she was not afraid; Ed was holding her hand, and talking to her softly. She could not see him, but he was there. When the beast overtook her again and again, and she sank down in a whirling blackness, his hand became tighter and he drew her up from the abyss. I am having a nightmare, she thought. In a minute I'll wake up, in just a minute. I'm very tired. If Ed should take his hand away, I'd just lie down, or let go, and die.

The anguish diminished, and then her coldness was warmed; she could feel the warmth against her flesh, and she sighed with pleasure. She felt hands moving her, and was relieved. But this, too, was strange. It was not Ed who had lifted her from her spasmodic position, for he was still holding her hand strongly. She could even hear his voice, comforting and soothing. Far off, in some space not to be known, she could hear other voices now, retreating, advancing, like the fringes of the sea. One of the voices was weeping, and she wanted to console the weeper. But she was voiceless. Suddenly, high above her, she saw a vast glittering. Stars. But that was impossible, she saw. The glittering shifted, formed a thousand dizzying patterns, flew together in a single ball so bright that her eyes ached—yet she could not close them—and then exploded into fragments which began to form their endless patterns of torture again.

Young Dr. Streit came into the pretty, lighted bedroom, carrying his bag. He had been practising only a year and though he knew of the Engers they did not know of him. The distracted maid had called him, because he was nearer the mansion than any other physician. He was afraid of the wealthy Engers, but his fear disappeared at the remarkable sight before him. Maria, a very mountain of a woman, had rolled up her sleeves competently, and she was bending over the half-hidden girl on the bed, her hands expertly manipulating the prostrate body, her fingers wet with blood. A dark, very thin girl was assisting her, in silence, and with cleverness, her crimson dress spotted. Beside the bed sat a young man—the husband probably—holding a white and writhing hand with all his strength, and murmuring steadily, his head bent.

Maria gave the doctor one of her formidable glances over her shoulder. "It is an hour since we called," she said, abruptly.

"I came as fast as possible," said the young doctor, with apology. Was this some midwife, this great shapeless woman, and the girl her assistant? In these modern days—a midwife—and for the Engers? He advanced to the bed. David did not look up. The doctor stood at the foot of the bed and looked at the tortured and struggling girl upon it, the quilts and sheets thrown aside and red and wet and splashed with hæmorrhage. After that one quick and competent glance, the doctor was horrified. This poor girl, this pretty thing, was *in extremis*. That overly swollen body indicated twins, which could not be delivered. He dropped his bag and ruthlessly shouldered Sylvia aside. "A minute," he said, tersely. Yes, a poor pretty thing, in spite of the sprawled white legs so purely formed and streaked with blood, in spite of the leaden face, the rolled-up blue eyes, in spite of the open mouth that panted and gasped and groaned.

He lifted the twisted other hand and felt the pulse, looking at his watch. The pulse bounded, faded, was tremulous, almost stopped, then tripped on too rapidly. The groaning was the only constant sound in the room, a groaning that became weaker and weaker every moment. "I'm Mrs. Enger, and this is my son's wife," said Maria. "You must do what you can; her own physican cannot be reached. The children are not expected for a month."

"She must go to the hospital at once," said Dr. Streit, who was a slender young man. "I'll call the ambulance."

Maria, not stopping her ministrations for a moment, said, "Nonsense. Can you not see that she will die if she is not helped almost immediately? Too, I do not believe in hospitals."

The doctor was discomfited because he had mistaken Maria for some gross midwife, possibly called because the other doctor was unavailable. But he forgot this in a moment. He knelt beside Margaret, listened to her heart, which raced and ponded like a terrified animal, then sank away, to be almost inaudible, then to start again. Old Mrs. Enger was right. The girl would not survive long enough to take her to the hospital. What could be done must be done now. Maria, in a few words, explained what she had already done, and the young physician spared her a glance of admiration. "I have had many children," she said, quietly. "My first was born alone. There was no one else in the house but me."

The doctor continued his examinations. The girl in the crimson dress and Maria assisted him. Tears ran down the girl's face, but she, too, was competent, her hands deft and light. "The head of the first child is in presentation," he said, as to colleagues. The groaning went on with every labouring breath, and the quality of it dwindled and hoarsened. Yet, Margaret's hand clutched the hand of David. Her husband certainly is a help now, thought the doctor; composed sort of fellow, able to talk to the girl like that, and hold her. Edward Enger; that was his name. Dr. Streit had heard rumours from his fellow physicians that young Mrs. Enger was "expecting." He had imagined Edward as a more bulky and dominant man; he was, in fact, thin and elegant, never removing his attention from his wife, and murmuring lovingly to her, and tightening his hand when an arch of agony raised Margaret's body from the bed.

"Dr. Conover had said there must be an operation," Maria

remarked. She stripped back the tangled sheets and quilts and blankets, and threw them over the foot of the bed. Birth did not embarrass or dismay her, the doctor commented to himself. One of those earthly women, one of those dogged German peasants.

"An operation?" repeated Dr. Streit, with a pleased smile. He thought of himself relating this to his friends, who would laugh behind their hands at the prominent Dr. Conover and his infallible prognoses. "I don't think so. This won't be easy, but I think we'll make it, if we're fast. Take away those hot-water bags, please. And now, if you'll help me turn Mrs. Enger across the bed; I have the high forceps here. I won't promise that I can save either or both the children, but I think we can save the mother."

Maria watched him, and approved. He might be young, but he knew what to do. She liked his quick movements, the sureness of his hands. "Certainly, you will save the children also," she said. "They are a month premature, but you will save them."

I'm glad you think so, thought the doctor, ruefully. He glanced up sharply at the girl in the crimson dress. "I will need the forceps sterilised," he said, tersely. She seized the instrument at once, without a word, and ran from the room. Not a girl to be overwhelmed or hysterical, said the doctor to himself. Who was she? A friend, a nurse? "The young lady is a nurse?" he asked, fixing Margaret's knees.

"My daughter," said Maria, and there was pride in her voice. "My daughter, Sylvia. She has been of much help."

The doctor gave Margaret a stimulant for her heart, plunging the needle deeply into her thigh. He began to sweat. The pelvis was narrow, dangerously narrow. The presented head was wedged. "Hold her still," said the doctor, to Maria. "Her struggles are complicating things, though she's unconscious. Don't let go her hand," he said to David. The husband's face was sunken with strain and fear, but he was calm. "I'll never let go her hand," he said. Never, never, he repeated to himself.

The bed was a bath of blood; Margaret wallowed in it, restrained only by Maria's hands, which were so strong. Her chin pointed at the ceiling, her neck cords straining in her stretched throat. But her colour was better now, her groaning stronger. If her heart holds out we can make it, thought the doctor exultantly. And, if we hurry. He pushed the filmy nightgown, with all that lace, under Margaret's armpits, so that her body was fully exposed. Her breast rose and fell and heaved. Her mouth was badly bitten. Margaret's head, near the side of the bed, dropped its weight of shining hair over the edge, in a cataract of light and colour. She was so helpless, so tortured, so lovely. I will save her if it's the last thing I do, the doctor promised himself. Over the hoarse groaning he could hear the flutter and crackle of a fire in the other room. "Yes, yes," said David, in a strong voice. "I'm here, darling. Be patient, darling. It'll soon be over."

I wish I believed that, too, thought the doctor. I'm afraid I'll have to crush the child's head. And from the looks of her pelvis, she'll never be able to have another child, Caesarian section or not. He regretted this; so lovely a poor creature, and so devoted and steadfast her husband. He was amazed that she had brought the children even to eight months.

Sylvia returned, the forceps not wrapped ignorantly in a towel, but dripping and hot from their immersion in boiling water. "Now," said Dr. Streit. "This is going to be very bad." He inserted the forceps. He was amazed that they had room to grip the baby's head. Suddenly, he was elated. He might, after all, save at least one of the children. Sweat rolled down his back, wet his shirt, for he had thrown aside his coat. Intent, his eyes screwed together, he gently drew the baby's head from its imprisoning cage. Slowly, slowly. Thank God, it wasn't a breech presentation. That would have been hopeless.

Margaret's child, a boy, was delivered eventually, a boy who immediately howled. "A blanket," said the doctor, but Sylvia was ready with one of the warm small blankets she had found in a drawer in Margaret's room. She took the child without fumbling, and wrapped it closely and with tender hands. What an awful, red, contorted little face! But a big one, and with a crown of pale silvery hair. "Take the child into another room," said the doctor, his face streaming and exultant. "Don't leave it. I haven't time to do anything about it just now. If it begins to choke, call me. We can do other things when I'm ready."

Margaret was suddenly still, not moving at all. The doctor

watched her, then gave her another stimulant. She lay like one dead, one who had given up, had surrendered to death, her head fallen aside. The doctor examined her. "The next child," he said, "probably won't be born for an hour. I'll attend to the first baby now. Don't let Mrs. Enger struggle and waste her strength." He looked up at Sylvia. "I think we'd better have nurses at once. Three of them. Will you call, Miss Enger? The Lutheran hospital; I'm on the staff. Tell them I'm here." The hospital would be thrown into a flurry! By to-morrow, all his friends would know that he'd saved the wealthy young Mrs. Enger's life, and at least one of the children.

He left Margaret in Maria's and David's care and went into Edward's ponderous bedroom, where Sylvia was holding the baby and crooning over him. The baby was howling satisfactorily, throwing his tiny hands belligerently in the air over his blanket. "Now," said Dr. Streit, after a kind smile at Sylvia. "Let's look at this scoundrel. No obstruction in the throat; listen to him yell. Now I'll examine the cord; tied it hastily, you know. Good. Big boy, considering he's premature."

He bent over the baby. Fortunate kid, fortunate to be alive, fortunate to be an Enger. "I don't believe in washing babies right away," he told Sylvia, confidentially. "That's heresy, in the maternity wards. He'd better be oiled. Think you could find some vaseline, somewhere, Miss Enger?"

Margaret, in her own bedroom, had begun to thresh again in her gory bed. Now she cried out for Edward, but was immediately soothed and quieted when her dull mind caught David's urgent strong voice. Once, she actually smiled, in her unconsciousness. She could even whisper, "Yes, dear, yes, Ed." Then she writhed powerfully and groaned.

At ten o'clock, her daughter was born with less difficulty than the boy. "Girls are always easier," said Maria, cryptically. Her arms were reddened to the elbows. The girl howled as reassuringly as her brother, though she was smaller. Sylvia, at hand again, was ready with another blanket.

At eleven o'clock Margaret, without regaining consciousness, fell into a deep and exhausted sleep, the coral already faintly in her cheeks, in spite of the blood she had lost. Her hand still clutched David's. He did not leave her until midnight, when the first nurse arrived. He did not want to leave her. Her blood was on his hand also.

No one had given the slightest thought to dinner. Maria, Sylvia, David and Dr. Streit, utterly spent, gathered together in the big drawing-room over coffee and cold roast beef and bread. They did not speak, while they sluggishly ate and drank. The men had had a considerable glass of whisky first.

"Mr. Enger," said the doctor at last. "Your wife will live, of course, and the children. I didn't think so, in the beginning. And we owe a lot of it to you."

Maria hesitated. But there was no help for it. "He is not her husband," she said, keeping her voice neutral. "This is my eldest son, David. Margaret and he are friends, of a long time."

The young doctor coloured, and he said, helplessly, "Of course." He had seen too much. He diffidently glanced at David, and thought, "There's something very funny here." Brothers-in-law did not usually show such solicitude for their brothers' wives. The man looked absolutely undone, leaning back in his chair, very limp, very pale under his dark skin, his hands hanging over the sides. He did not appear to have heard. His face was remote and blank, his thin body long and almost sprawled.

Sylvia ate and drank very little. Tears ran over her cheeks; they were abstracted tears, and she did not know of them.

Dr. Conover, announced by Pierre, bustled importantly into the room, a tall and florid man with dignified silver hair and a genial manner. Then he stood in surprise, staring at the group around the blazing fireplace. Maria said, merely glancing at him, "It is too late, Dr. Conover. The children are born, and the mother is asleep."

But Dr. Streit stood up, thinking to himself, Hell, he's an old man and all he has besides his money is his reputation. So the younger man said respectfully, "I delivered the children, Doctor, as I've often watched you do, in the hospital. I used exactly your own methods."

Chapter Two

Edward could not sleep in his hotel in Cleveland. A blizzard shrieked outside, and he felt that he was entirely alone in the world with his desperate thoughts. Foreboding chilled him, though the large room was warm and comfortable. He lay in bed, smoking rapidly, the evening papers scattered about him. When he attempted to bring his thoughts to Margaret she retreated from him like a dream. At three in the morning he was still formulating what he would say to the Press. First of all, he would talk to his managers and their assistants. Nothing mattered any longer, not even George Enreich, but that the American people should know of the doom that had been prepared for them decades ago.

Finally he got up and went to the desk and wrote out a statement to be given to the Press, after he had explained—but on what evidence? never mind—that his Green and White Stores had been wrecked because he was the founder and chief supporter of the " Save America Committee." The Euporean war was the first gigantic move of the despots against humanity. It was necessary for America not to be enticed or forced into it, no matter the " provocation."

Edward wrote on and on, while the blizzard increased in fury, and the first dull light of dawn stood in the east. He had just finished his statement, written in his small but cogent hand, when, without warning he was struck again by an irresistible urge to die. He clenched his hands on the desk, and resisted the relentless cold passion of the urge, and his body stiffened with the effort. Again and again a disembodied voice spoke to him in his mind. Why should a man live? For what am I living? To what end must I live? " To-morrow, and to-morrow, and to-morrow. . . ." The to-morrows stretched before him without a horizon, level and monotonous and infinitely weary and without profit or joy. A dark weight seemed to settle on the top of his head, like the lid of a coffin, and his heart pounded in terrified protest against the voice. An icy loneliness closed about him, like a shell, like a casing of stone, and he thought, It is better for a man to die than to live.

There was no reality for him, in those awful minutes while he automatically resisted the urge. There was no sense of obligation, only a sense of surrender, a brittleness of perception, a sick void in his heart. He could not even summon up a clear memory of Margaret: his children, about to be born, had no substance to him. He leaned his elbows on the desk and dropped his head into his hands. His temples throbbed against his palms, and he was conscious of nausea both physical and spiritual, and a sinking desolation. Finally, he got to his feet, swaying, and went to the window. The snow-shrouded streets, with their yellow paling lights and white emptiness and starkness, lay twelve stories below him. Without his will, his hands began to lift the window, and it was not until the freezing air blew on to his face that he came to himself. He discovered, then, that he was drenched with sweat and that he was gasping, and that the old crushing pain was constricting his chest.

"Well, now," he muttered, aloud, in a daze. He closed the window, and it took all his strength, and he went to the bed and fell on it, face down. He began to tremble violently, and to retch. What is the matter with me he asked himself, savagely. It's true that life doesn't seem to have any purpose, or any goal, or any aim, or any satisfaction—at least none that I can see. Just now. But neither does death.

He remembered nothing else until he heard a loud knocking on his door. He pushed himself up on the bed, and blinked. I must have slept, he thought. A lonely winter sun poured through the windows. The knocking increased in tempo. His mouth and throat were so dry and tight that it was a moment or two before he could demand who was knocking.

"Why, and it's your old friend, William Montgomery Percival Chauncey McFadden!" cried a cheery voice. "And a very good morning to you, sir. Open up!" The door knob rattled.

Edward was stupefied. He stared at the door and rubbed his eyes. Then he got up and opened the door. "Now what the hell brings you here?" he demanded, fastening his dressing-gown around him. He still could not believe it was William there, jaunty as always, the hazel eyes dancing, the foxy face quivering in greeting. "How did you know I was here?"

William bounced lightly into the room. "Aha," he said, tapping his brow. "It's a little pixie I have up here, who whispers to me." He threw his bag on the bed and rubbed his freckled hands. "It's starving I am, boyo. Shall we order a light refreshment, say several poached eggs and some good ham?"

He pushed his black derby hat to an acute angle on his sandy hair, and laughed at Edward's face and expression of disbelief. "The telephone, the blessed room service," he said. "It's nine o'clock, and I just disembarked from the Pullman. Blessed Pullman. Well, I remember the days I rode under it and not in it, and you may take my word for it, laddie, there's a bit of difference, and a different point of view."

He radiated zest and innocence, as he pulled off his smart topcoat and gloves, and hurled them after his bag.

"How did you know I was here?" demanded Edward again, wondering vaguely at the sudden rise of his spirits. He peered at William suspiciously.

William looked at him pleadingly. He clasped his hands in an attitude of prayer. "Let me have my delusions."

Edward went to the telephone and ordered a large breakfast for two, and he wondered why he was hungry after that night. "I don't believe you," he said.

William sighed. "How did I know? There is the newfangled thing called the telephone, and I had occasion to put in a call for you from New York, and it was gone you were, on the wings of the wind, to Cleveland. So, I am here."

"Why? What's so important to bring you down here?"

"That, my dear young friend, is a gruesome story. It is a personal matter."

He pretended to be unaware of the greyness of Edward's face, and the strained and sunken pits about his eyes, and the purplish shadow on his lips. He pretended not to see the pile of paper neatly stacked on the desk. "Close in here," he said. "Let's have a breath of fresh air." He opened the window and took deep and audible breaths. Then he swung about alertly, sniffing. "I smell the breakfast, and hear the musical clangour of dishes and a table."

They ate breakfast in warm contentment, and Edward was surprised at how spiritually satisfying good coffee was, and how food could lift the heart after agony. He leaned back in his chair, and smoked a cigarette, and said, "Now, come on. What brought you here, and no lies, understand?"

Then he saw that William was not smiling, and that he was staring at the bottom of the cup. "It's Padraig," he said. "I'm to bring you a message. He is leaving soon, with Maggie, and the brat, Sean, for Ireland."

"What?" cried Edward. "What the devil for? Is he going to get himself in that war, after all he's said about it?"

William shook his head. "No, it's not off to the wars for Padraig. It's to save Ireland, he says. Did I not tell you? His Dadda just served two months in the prison, for 'insurrection,' says they, and he's an old man but full of ginger. 'My country needs me, and this is the time for freedom,' says Padraig, and it's off he will be, with the lovely Maggie and the heir."

Edward considered this. "Good God!" he exclaimed.

William studied him shrewdly, his sallow face wrinkling and thoughtful. He said, after a moment, "Life is short and principles are long, and I'm a man who doesn't believe the mob is worth principles. It's comfort I want, as long as I can get it. Principles! Do they put money in the bank or bring a man a comfortable old age, surrounded by the wet-nosed grandchildren and a garden? They do not."

Edward was angry. "Yet, you've been telling me for years what we are going to face! You're the one who's given me a lot of my information. Didn't you warn me about the Federal income tax?"

"So I did. It was conversation, not warning."

"You were the one who suggested that I do something, and you contributed to the 'Save America Committee'." Edward's anger was rising.

"Ah, there's the touch of the Don Quixote in me, I must confess. You must permit me my sentimentalities."

"You call it sentimental to try to save your country from disaster and bankruptcy and slavery?"

William shrugged. Then he shook a lean and sallow finger under Edward's nose. "Hearken to words of wisdom. When a people are bent obstinately on enslaving themselves—and never was a people enslaved without its willing—then Our Lord, Himself, cannot stop them."

He leaned back in his chair and pushed his hands into his trouser pockets and stared at the ceiling, and now his face, that lively and expressive face, was sombre. "You're a priest at heart," said Edward, uncomfortably. "Let's not talk foolishness. You wanted to know why I was here. I'll tell you."

William listened, as if this was news to him. He clouded his face with the smoke of Turkish cigarettes, to conceal any expression which might betray him.

When Edward had finished, William smoked out his last cigarette. Then he said, "Permit me a discourtesy. You are an idiot, my benighted young friend. You will call in the Press and give your life away. Let me remind you. Millions of the American people are of German stock, as you have said. Yet, I must tell you, out of my observations. When Washington gives the word to the American people that they must hate Germany, then they will hate Germany. They will chant the slogans of murder the government will give them."

He shook a finger in Edward's frowning face. "And it is the government you would defy, who has already chosen the 'enemy.' It is the government you will try to control. You? You, and a few other men? It will set the blessed people against you; it will look at your income tax returns and declare that you have cheated! And then will come boycotts, and ruin. And where will you be? Economically excommunicated, you with your family, and your wife, and the children who will be born. Will that make you happy? Will you look at the wreck of your life, and say to yourself, 'I tried. But it was no good.' Yes, that you will say, in your exile, and when you are eating your crumbs."

"What do you think I should do?" shouted Edward, furiously. "Just sit and collect profits, and work, and do nothing?"

"I just ask you not to tell the Press who you are, and what you are doing. Then you can keep on with your 'Save America Committee,' until the day war is declared against Germany. You can hide behind your mask. Prudence. Sense. A few will remember, later. And on that few, weak though you are, you may bank. They may grow into a chorus, that'll defeat the murderers through the ballots, not to-morrow, not next year or next decade. But surely, sometime. Not that I believe in the virtue of the people. No. But self-preservation's a mighty thing, and God has hinted over and over that liberty is His gift. They'll remember; they always do, when the chains grow too heavy. And when that day comes, you'll have your money as your sword, to fight, to publish, to help."

"Maybe I won't be alive then. Maybe it'll be too late for my country. You want me to be a coward!" But Edward was desperately thinking, and as desperately despairing. "And, in the meantime, my shops will be sabotaged. I've heard from my managers in the other cities. The men who did that weren't hooligans or thieves. It was a design, because our enemies know who I am."

William chewed the toast with enjoyment, and then in his soft brogue he quoted:

Now hand you there, y're out of sight,
Below the fatt'rils, snug and tight;
Na, faith he yet! ye'll no be right
Till ye've got on it,
The very tapmost, towering height
O' Miss's bonnet.

"What are you talking about?" roared Edward irately.

"I consult with the pixies in the dark of the moon, while I'm grousing around on my knees. 'Now what,' I ask them, 'do we do about the big laddie, the Senator Bonwit? For, gentlemen, I've smelled mice.' When you have enemies, my boy, you look into their closets. Everybody has a closet. So I found the skeleton in Bonwit's."

Edward, glaring and bewildered, sat down abruptly in his chair, and threw his big arm over the back. "Bonwit?" he exclaimed. "Of course, Bonwit!"

"Ah, now you see. So, after the other shops are smashed to bits, I go to Washington, two days ago, smelling the mice. And with a top of the morning he greets me, and slaps me on the back, the beefy bastard. 'And how's my good young friend, Ed Enger?' he asks, beaming like the blinking sun. And I look him in the eye and say, 'Bad, very bad.'"

"That swine," said Edward, not seeing, and his impatience growing.

William inclined his head in agreement. "But a swine with a closet that holds a big stout skeleton. That I found out. Twenty years ago he was a Socialist, one of Debs's friends, a contributor; he furnished counsel for Debs, of dour reputation. And I know our Senator has ambitions; Vice-President, or President, he wants, or perhaps the Supreme Court, or a Cabinet little job.

"So I says to him, says I, 'and I've been an admirer of yours, dear boy. Your campaign manager in New York is closer to my heart than breathing,' and that's the God's truth, Siegfried. 'Always cuddle up to a political fella,' my old Dadda told me. 'Never know when it comes in handy.'

"So our senator beams once more, though he blinks a little. And I says, 'Your campaign manager whispers in my ear, and I nod, Senator.'"

William pursed up his lips and assumed an expression of great distress and trouble and doubt. "'And what would be the matter, dear William?' asks the senator, seeing my near tears. 'Oh,' says I, 'and it's delighted I'd be to support you. With cash. With a word here and there. But there is something. Debs.'

"And he looks at me and clutches his chest, and almost strangles. Then he says, 'I haven't seen Debs—if I saw him at all—for years.' And I shakes my head dolefully, and says, 'But if the word got around you'd be back on your ass, if you'll pardon me, Senator, in your office in Albany, with nothing on but counting your dividends and attending pink teas. Now, Senator, what're we to do?' And me knowing, of course, and he knowing, that he's still one of Them, though undercover, like the British Foreign Service, or is it Scotland Yard, or whatever? You can't make a Christian gentleman out of a traitor or a blackguard."

"I still don't see what it's all about," said Edward, glancing at his watch, which showed eleven o'clock. "You weren't thinking of a spot of blackmail, were you, as you'd say? What for?"

"Now what would I be doing blackmailing that ham that walks like a man?" asked William, virtuously. "Not I. Let a man have a dozen skeletons in his closet, and I'd respect them. A man's skeletons are a private affair. No, my boy, not blackmail. Just a discussion, between friends.

"And now the senator is eager for my advice. So I change the subject. I talk about you, my mutton-headed friend. I tell the senator about your shops. And he squints up his eyes. But never does he ask questions. He knows. And I say, 'Bad it is that a fine young lad like that has hooligans destroying his property, his sacred property, for which he worked so hard. Sad it is that no one can help him.' And I look him straight in the eye and he shakes his head sadly, and after we smoke a cigar together, we shake hands, and we part with mutual felicitations. And when I open the door a bit, there he is at the telephone, as red as a tomato."

Edward glowered at him. William smiled gently. "And there's a feeling in me that from this day on there'll be no more clouting of your shops. All will be serene. Like a Sunday seen from Richmond Hill. Placid. Like aspic."

Edward jumped up, excitedly. "Why can't we expose him? Now? Call in the Press, and tell them what you know!"

William lifted a mild hand. "And we'll have the senator on his buttocks in forty-eight hours; recalled. Sure, and that would help us. But what about the shops, eh? You wouldn't have a sou left in a month. Perhaps not even a house. And that would suit you splendid, wouldn't it?"

"But he's a menace, it's our duty——!"

"Never did I crave to be a martyr, lad. ''Twas a famous victory.' And if we throw out the senator, there're twenty more or more, rising up right in Washington, and it's your blood they'd have, very soon, one way or another. Duty? Now, I'm a chap that loves duty, if you can do something with it. But not now. Too late. You should have started fifty years ago."

Edward considered, biting his lips, fuming. Then he burst out, "So we're to let Bonwit go on doing his dirty work! I'm to stop fighting! What has a man when he stops fighting something? What purpose does he have in living?"

William sighed patiently. "As for Bonwit, it's too late, but you don't listen. Washington's full of him. Sure, and you can fight. You've got your Committee. That is your purpose. And you've got a bigger one. You can train up your children to respect America, and all her institutions. Then, after the war, support the newspapers and magazines that call for peace. Shore up the ramparts; take an interest in politics. There'll be plenty of time, boyo, plenty of time, and plenty of work cut out for you. Did you think this fight was the beginning and the end?"

Someone knocked at the door and Edward cursed, and ordered the knocker to come in. It was a boy with a telegram, and Edward took it, and said, grimly, " You and your blackmail. This is probably to tell me I've lost another shop or two." He began to read aloud:

" You have a son and daughter born last night, and Margaret is well and waiting for you." It was signed by Maria.

" We must talk," said Maria, firmly, to Edward, grasping his arm and preventing him from rushing upstairs to Margaret. " There is much to say."

She sat in the morning-room but Edward stood and listened. " And so," said Maria, " it is to your brother and your sister that we owe the lives of your wife and children, in great part. David has gone." She paused. " But Sylvia is here."

Edward, whose face had darkened gloomily while his mother had been speaking, said in a cold, hard voice, and with a disagreeable smile, " I will give them extra money."

Maria looked down at her hands. " And you think money will repay them for their devotion?"

" Why not? Isn't that all they ever wanted?"

" No," said Maria.

" Let's not be sentimental," said Edward. " I know them better than you do."

Maria raised her large light eyes and studied him. " There, I do not agree. I must ask you: do not insult David and Sylvia with money. Hatred, expressed through money, can never be forgiven."

She stood up. " Let us not forget. Margaret is still under sedatives; she is not yet completely awake and aware. She believes you returned last night, and that you were with her. The doctor is certain she struggled for life, because of that belief, and because your brother, whom you would insult, never left her."

They stared at each other fixedly. " It would be best," said Maria, " for Margaret never to know it was David."

Edward looked aside, and his face was sombre and inscrutable.

" Sylvia will never tell her," Maria added. " Nor will David. It will be our secret for ever."

Chapter Three

" I know, I know, all about principles!" Edward exclaimed to Padraig a few weeks later. "I talk about principles with William——"

"Then," said Padraig, with a gentle smile, "why do you object to my having them also?"

I don't want to lose you; I don't want to lose a friend because I have so few, thought Edward. And you've been my conscience, in your grave and stately way. He said, "I can't explain it." He looked at Padraig with dark restlessness. "I just have a feeling I'll never see you again, if you go back to Ireland. You and Maggie."

They were sitting in Edward's office, and Padraig gazed thoughtfully through the window at the cloud of snow blowing against the glass. "There's the submarines, too," said Edward. "What right do you have to expose Maggie and the child to the dangers of them?" His face changed.

"I'll never forget the day you first worked for me," he said, "and when you put on the long white apron. Aprons always looked funny on William, like a clown's get-up. Hanging to his ankles; it always made me laugh. But when you put on one it—well, it acquired dignity. It became part of you. Everything," said Edward, trying to smile, "becomes part of you and you dignify it, Padraig. You dignified even the dirtiest, hardest work."

"Thank you," said Padraig. "But I think you exaggerate."

"Without words, you made me understand that work, in itself, is prideful, outside of the money," Edward went on. "All my life, you see, I was regarded as the drudge of the family, and though I had my ambitions and liked the shops and the money they brought, still I thought of it as—drudgery, and not as important—as genius."

"All work is important," said Padraig, and he looked at Edward with compassion. "It is as important to men to lay bricks and mortar as it is to listen to a symphony, or to read a book. To labour is to pray, no matter the labour."

"You gave me a feeling of importance, the first I'd ever

had," said Edward. " In my own right. And because of that I've been able to stand—a lot of things."

Padraig stood up with finality. Then he paused, " Eddie, there is another thing. Your quarrel with your good friend, George Enreich. He has been like a father to you. Wait, please. I know the circumstances ; William has told me. But George was thinking of you. Just," he added, with his sad smile, " as you have been thinking of me, and all the danger."

" I tell you, he threw me off! And demanded his money! Don't be a sentimental fool, Padraig! Oh, you're going, are you? All right, go." Edward stood up, tight and shaken. " The hell with everything. I was alone for a long time. I can be alone again."

Chapter Four

" You don't look on top of the world," said William. " It's fifty Green and White Markets you have now. Are the Washington blighters after you again for restraint of trade or monopoly or whatever?"

" No," said Edward. " Not again. Not when they found we could kick out Bonwit and make Henry Sheftel senator in his place. Just to show there's no discrimination or pressure in it, they've turned their attention—again—to the Atlantic and Pacific. Just a small flurry, to clear themselves after Hans gave them a little exposure in his papers." He laughed, grimly. " Sometimes when I'm low in my mind I remember how they tried to get me by calling me in for the draft in late 1917, even though I had a wife and two children and other dependents. I still don't know how I got out of that. A perfunctory examination by the doctors, and I was out on the street. Another attempt to scare me, of course."

" Hum," said William, eyeing him with concern. " Seems there was more to it than that. Didn't they tell you to see your own doctor?"

" Probably. But they knew damn' well I was in the best of health. My own doctor? What for? I haven't had a doctor since I had pneumonia when I was a child, and those swollen joints that made me limp for a few weeks, and kept me awake a few nights. Look at me. Ever see anyone in better condition? I play eighteen holes of golf without an effort, since Margaret made me join the Waterford Country Club. Waste of time, but she insists. But to please her I waddle around in the pool, too."

William studied. Edward was thirty-four, yet he looked older; there were patches of random grey in his thick dark hair, and his broad face had a chronic expression of pent harassment and was lined with constant anger. It was only when with his wife and children that his face softened and became youthful, and the purplish tint in his wide mouth faded to a more healthy colour. His big body still moved with fast vitality, but there was a nervousness in him that betrayed itself in the trembling of his fingers when he struck a match or began to write.

"I'd go to one of those bally medicine chaps just the same," said William. Edward shrugged, lifted and studied some papers on his desk. He was never without a cigarette. One hung in the corner of his mouth now.

"I haven't time; don't bother me," said Edward, and then, as if without his volition, he struck his desk with a clenched fist. He threw aside his papers, and rested his chin in his palms. "I still can't get over their killing Padraig, in 1918. And hanging him with a silk rope because he was a peer! The only good thing about it was his father dying suddenly six months before that. A silk rope! What a concession!" He put his hands over his eyes. "And Maggie with two boys, then, one just a baby. And it was all our Ambassador could do to keep them from confiscating Padraig's property, because he was a 'traitor'! Well, we gave them some publicity in the New York newspapers, and got the Irish stirred up, and I suppose that's the only reason Maggie still has the ancestral property, or whatever they call it."

"It was a good thing, that you did," said William, and his merry face was grave with sorrow. "Do not think that Padraig was murdered uselessly. No good man dies violently without Our Lord taking note of it."

Edward uttered an obscene word in contempt. "And there weren't good men dying in Europe for years, were there? Young men. And what was the result of it? The Bolshevik Revolution, and the active rise of Socialism all over Europe. How d'ye explain that, eh?"

"I told you once. Satan's in it."

Edward was profane again. " Don't let's talk imbecility, please. I'm tired."

" I've been reading my Bible again, a book I've ignored a number of years. It says the last battle will be between God and Satan, for men's souls. There's all the signs of it. Not an actual bloody battle on battlefields, perhaps, but a battle in the minds and hearts and spirits of men—between Good and Evil. The Bolshevik Revolution in 1917 was the opening engagement—the Communists are the bloody legions of hell."

" At least, since 1920, we've stopped the advance of Socialism in the United States!" said Edward. " You've got to admit that."

" I admit nothing," said William, soberly. " The devils are just gathering forces. Let there be a remittance in this wild prosperity we're having now, and there they'll be, waving their red flag with the hammer and sickle on it, and calling to the proletariat to throw off their chains. The devils never sleep; they never did. They're a special breed of men, descended right from Cain, I'm thinking. Why, look at Cato, with his shrieks that Carthage must be destroyed. Look at 'em, all right down through history, legions of them. Now they're ready to take over the world, five years, twenty years, forty years. If we let them."

" And how do we stop them?" asked Edward, derisively. " Shoot them down in the streets?"

William nodded slowly. " It may come to that, laddie, it may come to that. I do hope. But before that, they'll have the world, I'll be thinking. Socialism, and the club and the bayonets and the prisons and the all-powerful government of murderous bureaucrats."

He rubbed his lip with one freckled finger. He coughed. " And in your household . . . A man like you can start in his own house; every man can."

Edward stared at him, frowning. He thought of his brother, Gregory, who, after a very brief, and very safe, billet in France, during his short army service, had become one of the young men now grandiloquently called " The Lost Generation." He had had one lurid novel published, *The Sun Rises West*. A very bad novel, purporting to be a story of the " oppressed " in America, the " submerged," and their awakening since " the dawn " of Communism in Russia. It had sold two thousand copies in the United States, and the critics had jeered at in, in the main, with the exception of a few of the " progressives " in New York. These had been ecstatic. The novel had been published in 1922. Edward had written his brother: " Another such piece of trash, and you're on your own." And Gregory had thought, " I've got to be more subtle. That bastard doesn't threaten emptily." Unknown to anyone in his family, Gregory was contributing, under a pseudonym, to various inflammatory pulp-paper journals in Europe and in the United States, and was writing another novel of America which was more discreet, but hardly less dangerous than his first. It was not in Gregory, as yet, to understand that in attacking orderly government and time-proved traditions, and in supporting chaos and ruin and death, he was actually assaulting his brother and all he stood for.

Edward wrote to Gregory again. " I notice that in your foolish novel you speak reverently of Lincoln and his 'humble' beginnings and his love for the oppressed, as you call them. Well, let me quote something else to you that Lincoln said: 'You cannot bring about prosperity by discouraging thrift. You cannot strengthen the weak by weakening the strong. You cannot help the wage earner by pulling down the wage payer. You cannot further the brotherhood of man by encouraging class hatred. You cannot help the poor by destroying the rich. You cannot establish sound security on borrowed money. You cannot keep out of trouble by spending more than you earn. You cannot build character and courage by taking away man's initiative and independence. You cannot help men permanently by doing for them what they could and should do for themselves.' "

Gregory, on reading that, was much startled. Why, Lincoln sounded like the modern reactionary sons of bitches!

Sylvia was listlessly running her theatre again, in Edward's belief. But her assistants, enthusiastic young women, were in reality the true managers, the true producers, the true set designers. They listened to Sylvia respectfully, then did as they wished, and she was too indifferent to notice or to care. The theatre was paying its way, but no more. In the meantime, Sylvia designed hats and frocks and gowns for Mary Garrity, and her private bank account, in Albany, was fast approaching respectable dimensions. Her large allowance from Edward joined that account regularly, while Edward paid her bills for clothing and other necessities and luxuries and trips to New York, and to Paris.

Edward said to William, still frowning, "I don't know what you mean by starting in my own house. My family's settled down. Greg's not writing his fool stuff any more. And he did show real genius even in that one stinking book; even his adverse critics said so. And whenever Ralph makes a sale he tells me about it and suggests I cut down his allowance for the next quarter. So, he isn't robbing me, though I do send him money. Yes, they're settling down."

William said nothing. Though Edward was considered, and rated, an enormously rich man, he had not thrown off his debts, though he had cleared away the mortgage on his house. In fact, his debts were rising steadily. "His family eats him like cannibals," William would comment to himself. Whenever Edward was in sight of complete solvency, he opened new stores. He poured into them his huge dividends from stocks and bonds. He was deeply entangled in the speculative market. He was a driven man. He never stopped expanding. To him, the status quo was repugnant. He spent little on himself, nor did money, in itself, gratify him. He was like a top, William would think. Set spinning and then keeping on spinning, in its own inertia. But, who knows what makes a man do the things that are killing him?

Edward was saying, "And I don't have to subsidise Dave any longer. Funny, he's the only one who won't take money from me any more." He did not like the thought, and his deep hostility for his brother grew in consequence. "I don't know how he manages to support that apartment of his in New York and his elegant clothes and his car and that valet. But I don't care."

"Thrifty, no doubt," murmured William, with hidden irony. But he, too, wondered. David had numerous engagements, all over the country; William doubted that they brought him much money. The chap probably had invested some of the money Edward had previously given him. Still, you had to give him credit. He was no longer a leech on his brother. He was unique in that damned family.

"It isn't the fault of my brothers and sister that their genius isn't widely acknowledged," said Edward, gloomily.

He picked up the papers on his desk again, and a tide of

grey exhaustion washed over his face. "The three stores in Kansas City aren't paying their way. I think you'd better run out there, William. Something's wrong. I'm paying my managers top salaries, and the other employees, too, yet——"

That's part of your damned trouble, thought William, compassionately. There's not a chain or any other shop in the whole country which pays the wages you do. And pensions, too, by God, and sick benefits, and big holidays, and no pay taken out for anything. And yet, you do have strikes! Rum that your competitors don't. God, people are the scaliest lot of dogs the Almighty ever created. Give them marmalade on their bread and butter and they'll howl for caviar. And the farmers you buy your meats and vegetables from—you pay them over the market price. Are they grateful? They are not! If you can pay that much, they tell their black hearts, it's because you're the rich man you are, and they want to dig deeper into your pockets. But they don't ask the same prices, or get them, from your competitors.

It had been a relief, William thought, when George Enreich had been paid off, at a tremendous sacrifice, by Edward. But George Enreich, in his fashion, had acted as a brake. Now that brake was gone. Nor had the friendship been resumed. George had made overtures, many times, had actually humbled himself. But for some perverse reason Edward repeatedly repudiated his old friend. Edward explained it: "He pulled out when I most needed him, when I was working almost alone for my country. He has contempt for the American people——"

"He has contempt for all people," William would say. But Edward would only shrug and change the subject.

"All right, go out to Kansas City," Edward said. He rubbed his hands over his face, and the pressure put red streaks over the greyness. "One of these days," he continued, "I'm going to take a vacation, myself. A long rest."

Margaret was chairwoman of the Ladies' Lutheran League of the Enger Clinic, which Edward subsidised, and also a member of the Ladies' Medical Auxiliary of the Enger Wing of the Waterford General Hospital, which was devoted to children ill of cancer. In these capacities she organised entertainments for the occupants of the fifty beds of the Enger Clinic, helped manage their disorganised domestic affairs during their hospitalisation, and assisted in the procurement of nurses and other specialised technicians. She had, in these nine years of marriage to Edward Enger, become exceedingly popular with the leading ladies of the city, because of her beauty, delicacy, tact and modesty, and willingness to give of herself to any good charity. She was not often at home during the day; she had a little office of her own, and an assistant, in the Enger Clinic, where she conducted her humanitarian work.

This worried her. She was a passionately devoted mother to her two children, Robert and Gertrude. She wished she could spend more time with them. To her dismay, they hardly seemed to miss her, though they loved her with charming devotion. And, to her greater consternation, they seemed extremely attached to their aunt, Sylvia. Often, Margaret admitted her jealousy to Edward, half-laughing. The love and tenderness and pampering Sylvia heaped upon the children was incredible to the parents, who did not know that Sylvia cherished the little ones because she was partly responsible for saving their lives. "She's trying to usurp us, out of malice," Edward would say, angrily. "Turning our children against us." But Margaret did not believe this in the least. She saw that Sylvia not only loved her son and daughter but that she was quite a disciplinarian, and taught them to respect and honour Margaret and Edward, a fact that puzzled Margaret more than ever. When Margaret was with the children Sylvia never interfered to any great extent.

Her former open hatred and contempt for Margaret had been strangely, to Margaret, replaced by a wary civility and curt politeness. There were even times when she talked to Margaret in her short, taut phrases, almost in a friendly manner. This, too, was because she had helped save Margaret's life. Unobtrusively, she had taken over the management of Margaret's wardrobe; she designed Margaret's clothing, to the younger woman's confused gratitude, or she shopped for it in New York. Margaret did not know that her more fetching costumes, bought in the best shop in New York, Mme. DelaFontaine's, had been designed by Sylvia and made to her meticulous requirements in that establishment, in which she now owned a share. Sylvia could not resist beauty in hats and garments, and Margaret was a perfect model for her.

"She's sometimes almost kind to me," Margaret would confess to her husband. "But I do wish she'd get married!"

The family was becoming a weary obsession to her. They all lived, of course, in Edward's mansion, including the little quick son of Ralph and Violette, André, a sly, intelligent and ingratiating child of seven, a year younger than Robert and Gertrude. He appeared much younger, being at least half a head shorter than the tall twins, and he was very lively and gay and lied atrociously and winningly, and was very slight and active. He had a round hard head covered with a thin black fur, sharp and diminutive features, except for his eyes, which were extraordinarily large and dark and shining, and fringed heavily, all around, with the thickest but shortest jet eyelashes his family had ever seen. This gave him, according to Sylvia, a "Hindu" look. He was as foreign in that household as a gipsy. In addition to the odd appearance of his eyes, themselves, his eyelids had a brownish stain, enhancing the shine and the peculiar expression. "He whirls," Sylvia often said, with cold disapproval, for she did not like the little boy, and at times actually hated him. She thought him a bad influence on her darlings, Robert and Gertrude, whom she sometimes considered her own.

Margaret pitied the child, because he had last seen his parents nearly two years ago. She thought him pathetic. In truth, he was not pathetic at all. He was a compact person in his own right, sure of himself, careful of himself, subtle and wheedling, and caring for no one but André. He enjoyed life with an intense and cunning zest, and had a high sense of humour, and considered himself, even in his few years, as a most remarkable person. He did not miss his parents at all. He hardly spoke of them. His existence was too interesting, and he had an alien handsomeness of his own which Margaret appreciated. His exploitation of everybody, which amounted to actual genius, kept him delightfully employed. His pretty eagerness about "presents," a mention of which made him clap his dark and little prehensile hands so like his mother's, induced even the sombre Edward to gratify him. Edward was not without his own sentimentality in connection with this disingenuous child. Only Sylvia, and Margaret and Maria were not deceived. And David, the few times he was at home.

Margaret, always hungry to be alone with her children and Edward, nevertheless did not urge him either to establish another home for his family, or for himself. She did not understand his insistence that his brothers and sister be his dependents, in his own house, for was he not always vehemently telling them they should stand on their own? He can't, of course, force out his father and mother, at their age, I suppose, Margaret would think, nor Sylvia, either, seeing she's unmarried, nor André, as his parents are always leaving him on everybody's hands.

But they stick like flies in honey, Margaret would think, sighing. She had hopes that Gregory would marry someone in France, as Ralph had done, and never come back, except perhaps, for a visit every year or so. She did not resent Dave much, for whom she had a cool regard, which was a mystery to her, except that he was so kind and thoughtful on his rare appearances, and seemed to love the children. Besides, he had an apartment in New York, and travelled all the time. Sylvia was a fixture; she showed no indication of marrying at all. Besides, Margaret told herself dolefully, even when they married they remained an incredible drain on their brother, Edward. They were like bloodsuckers, Margaret would think, with not much originality, but with truth.

For some reason, on this August 3, 1923, Margaret was more troubled than usual about Edward's friendlessness. It was four o'clock in the afternoon, warm and golden, strident with cicadas, alive with hurrying bees, shining of hot sky and burning of wind. She had just returned from a meeting on behalf of the Clinic, and felt despondent and listless. She sat under the shade of a clump of glittering trees, in sight of the house, her short blue dress revealing her beautiful legs, her bright hair clipped about her pretty face. There was some coolness here; from a distance she could hear the sound of children's voices, and their vehement laughter. This enhanced her loneliness, but she did not particularly desire the company of the children just now. She thought only of Edward, who was more to her than her children, more to her than life. If only he had a confidant besides herself! If only he could relinquish his brusque and faintly derisive manner when among others! Surely, among the hundreds of people he knew in Waterford and in New York and Albany and in other cities, there was at least one man, besides William, who could give him honest friendship. He maintained that in essence humanity was vile, weak, stupid and cruel. To a certain extent, yes, Margaret thought, but there is heroism and idealistic self-immolation and goodness in men, too.

She looked up, from her seat under the trees, and saw a nurse wheeling a wheel-chair towards her. Margaret sighed in pity. The chair was occupied by Heinrich, who had suffered a paralytic stroke two years before. He sat in the chair, lolling, shrunken and as passive as an infant, his sparse hair white, his face smooth and blank and apparently at peace. His attempts at speech were incoherent, and when he timidly smiled it was a grimace. He had utterly given up; there was no need, now, for him to struggle to be needed and important. His illness had settled, once and for all, his necessity to be the father of the family and a man of affairs, and Margaret suspected, in her compassion, that he was content with this, even happy, behind his helpless façade. He wore, constantly, silk pyjamas and a light dressing-robe and slippers, which enhanced his infantile appearance. He could lift his right hand and move his right leg slightly. Beyond that he could do nothing, not even feed himself. "But his mind and intellect have been little damaged," the doctor had assured the family. This, to Margaret, was more pathetic than anything else.

"Ah, there we are!" said the short and muscular nurse cheerily. "We thought we saw you from the sun room, and so we came out for a little airing."

"Hallo, Jane," said Margaret. She helped the nurse place the chair near her own. Heinrich grimaced at her, and uttered a few unintelligble words in a slow grunting voice. "The children?" said Margaret, who seemed the only one able to understand him. Heinrich nodded with painful eagerness. "I'll get the children," said the nurse. "They're playing around the conservatories. I do hope André hasn't broken another window. The gardeners complain so, and with wages so high these days you have to keep them in a good temper." She patted Heinrich's fallen shoulder maternally and went off for the children.

Margaret reached out lightly and touched Heinrich's cold and shrivelled left hand. He turned his head to her. His round dark eyes were faintly clouded, and filmed, but his soul implored her speechlessly. What is it he is always wanting? Margaret asked herself in distress. If I could only find out, the poor thing! She said, "Papa Enger, one of these days you must tell me what you want; I'll try to understand. And I'll get it for you." His eyes brightened, continued their heartbreaking plea. He grunted, but this time she could not understand.

The three children came racing across the hot and radiant grass, André in the lead, as always. He did not shout, as Robert did, but he had an unpleasant voice, shrill and ringing like hard little bells, which irritated the ear. This was more insistent than the twins' voices; Robert and Gertrude, when they spoke, spoke softly and seriously, though they could be noisy in play. It was André who reached Margaret first, and she patted that hard round head with its topping of thin black fur. She loved all children, even André.

Her favourite child was Gertrude, who resembled her father very closely. Tall and slender and usually quiet, she had fine, frank grey eyes, an olive complexion, a pretty smile and a wide-boned face. Her straight dark hair was braided, and the braids hung down her back, which was as broad and upright as Edward's. She was as incapable of guile as her father, but was as quick as he to anger when confronted by injustice. There was absolutely no compromise in her; a thing was wrong, or it was right, and she could comprehend, as little as Edward, a mercy which took many things into account.

Margaret thought this somewhat hard. It puzzled her in Gertrude as it invariably puzzled her in Edward. Edward's treatment of David years ago had not been guileful; it had been brutal and deliberate and open, and sometimes Margaret was afraid that Gertrude, if she were ever maliciously injured, would develop this attitude. As for Robert, he was a little taller than his sister, more outspoken than Gertrude, more vigorous, more sunny, and even gentler in spite of his strength. He resembled his mother; he had her bright and curling hair, her absolutely blue eyes framed in gilt lashes, her delicate features, her quick smile, her cleft chin, her lovely colouring. He was his father's favourite, yet he was not as intelligent as Gertrude.

"What've you been doing, dears?" asked Margaret tenderly. Robert threw himself down on the grass beside her; his fair skin was moist with sweat, his eyes shining. Gertrude kissed her grandfather on the forehead, then stood beside his chair. His poor head bent in her direction, and he smiled in content. André bounced about the group, shrilling. "It wasn't fair, it wasn't fair!" he cried. "We played ball and Gertrude always threw it to Robert, all the time! Never to me, and it wasn't fair!" His peculiar black eyes glittered on Gertrude with an odd expression.

"You aren't telling the truth," said Gertrude, disdainfully, leaning against her grandfather's chair. "You're a big liar, André."

"Gertrude," said Margaret, admonishingly. "Well, he is," said Gertrude, coldly. "I don't like liars. He always wants to be first. We've got rules, when we play ball, and he doesn't want rules. He just wants what he wants."

Margaret tried to smile. André could deceive adults, except herself and Sylvia and Maria, but he could not deceive his peers.

"Gertrude's right," said Robert, soberly. "We play triangles. But André always jumps to get the ball first; he won't wait his turn."

"You're so slow!" said André, still bouncing energetically. He was like a cricket. "Pokey." He suddenly stopped, and draped himself with a winning smile over the arm of Margaret's chair. "Aunt Margaret, will you take us to the movies on Saturday? It's a bang-bang Western, all full of guns and Indians." He cocked his little dark hand in the shape of a gun, and shrieked.

"All right," said Margaret. "Do stop making that noise, André."

"I don't like Westerns. I like Mary Pickford," said Robert, frowning.

"I don't like either," said Gertrude. "Why can't we see the new Pathé pictures at the Globe? *Les—Les Miseries?*"

"*Les Misérables*," said Margaret. She smoothed Gertrude's pink cotton frock, which Sylvia had designed and made. "Isn't that a little too grown-up for you, Gertrude?" Gertrude was mortified at her mispronunciation, an error she did not often commit.

"I've read the book twice," she said. It was quite true; though only eight, Gertrude's taste in reading was adult and comprehending. She preferred study to play; she led her class, at the Waterford School for Girls, while Robert, at his own private school, was quite content to be in the low middle. At eight, she could read and speak French competently. Until he had died, six months ago, old Pierre had taught her the language, beginning when she was hardly five. He had adored the little girl, who so resembled her father. " In French," Gertrude added, " and in English."

André's eyes sparkled on her maliciously. " My Mama's French. So I'm more French than you are—Gertie. I'm brighter, too. Mama said so. French people are brighter than Germans. Mama said so."

" If you're so bright, why does she leave you here?" asked Gertrude, cuttingly.

" Now," said Margaret, with sternness. But André was grinning, showing all his predatory white teeth, so like his mother's. " It's cheaper," he said. " Besides, you're so dumb, and Robert, too, that somebody has to stay here to teach you anything."

Robert, on the grass, raised his head. " You're part German, too," he remarked. André blithely thumbed his nose at him, and began bouncing again.

" Suppose I take you to the Globe, Gertrude," said Margaret. " And one of the maids can take you two boys to another movie."

" Western," said André.

" Oh, all right," said Robert, the amiable compromiser.

" Here comes Skinny," said André, dropping his voice. Sylvia was approaching across the grass, tall and thin and aloof, her black hair closely bobbed about her white, planed, and distinguished face. Even in summer she wore dark colours, " as every cosmopolitan woman does." Her navy-blue silk dress rustled about her knees and thin calves, for she considered the very short skirts then in fashion to be vulgar. Besides, as she usually pointed out, longer skirts were " coming in." Only provincials were slow in following the trend. Her sole ornament, in her severe costume, was a string of real pearls about her long and stem-like neck.

Robert and Gertrude ran to meet her, racing. Her cold face softened ; she bent from her height to put an arm about each of the twins. Margaret felt a pang of jealousy, then laughed at herself. " Skinny, Skinny," muttered André, again leaning against Margaret's chair. " Hush," said Margaret, and frowned at him. Sylvia approached the group under the trees, her arms still about the shoulders of the twins. " I've been listening to the crystal set," she told Margaret. "President Harding died to-day."

"Oh, no!" exclaimed Margaret, sitting up.

Sylvia smiled wryly. "And a good thing, too, with all that scandal."

"He was a good, kind man," protested Margaret. She and Edward had attended the President's inaugural. "You can't blame him for his friends."

"Why not?" said Sylvia. She looked at her father. She raised her voice, though he could hear well enough, and repeated the news. He gazed at her with blankness. "A man's friends are a good indication of his tastes and his character," Sylvia added. She sat down near Margaret, and frowned into the distance, her aquiline profile, so like David's, utterly set.

"Loyalty," murmured Margaret. Sylvia shrugged. "A person shouldn't have blind loyalty," she said. "It distorts his vision."

She seemed abstracted. Margaret said, "And so Mr. Coolidge is now the President. A very quiet man. We met him. I don't remember ever hearing him say a word."

"He has character," said Sylvia. Her abstraction grew. She glanced at André. "Why do you have to jump so?" she asked, coldly.

"I like it," said André, and jumped higher to displease her.

Sylvia ignored him. "Why don't you children run off, somewhere?" she asked. "I want to talk to an adult for a change." But she smiled at the twins and for a moment her bony face was beautiful with affection. The children, even André, went away instantly, Gertrude admonishing André for something or other. "I can't help it," said Sylvia, following the children with her eyes, "but I detest that little boy."

"It's just that he's so lively," said Margaret, uneasily. "And so alone."

Sylvia snorted. "Alone? He's never alone. He's got his own precious self, and that's enough for him."

Her almost fleshless fingers played with the string of pearls about her neck. Margaret detected that she was choosing words for what she wished to say. It must be important, thought Margaret. She's so rarely at a loss. But when Sylvia spoke it was on an old matter, about which they invariably disagreed. "I've been reading another story of Gertrude's," said Sylvia. "It's wonderful, almost good enough to be published. I do wish you'd encourage her, Margaret. But you hold her back; you don't take her seriously. And she's a genius."

Margaret winced, as usual. "I don't believe in puffing children up," she said, and laced her fingers together tightly. "Gertrude gets enough encouragement. Yes, I know, I don't let Ed praise her too much, and sometimes we quarrel about it. Genius! Gertrude's still only a child. When she is eighteen or so, then we'll see."

Sylvia shrugged. "Of course, I'm only her old maid aunt, and can't be expected to know anything about genius," she said, spitefully. "You may think it will hurt her to encourage her, but I think your attitude may stifle her."

Margaret said nothing. Sylvia went on, "And Robert plays beautifully on his flute. I do think he should have supplementary training, besides what he gets with the school band. He has a real genius for music."

"Lots of children have," said Margaret, keeping her voice level. "I noticed that, in the orphanage. Music comes naturally to most children. But later on, that faculty disappears. If Robert is really endowed, he will keep after it, with or without our encouragement. You can't stop a real—talent. Then later, we'll see, when he is more mature."

"The twins have more than 'talent,'" said Sylvia. "How you hate the word 'genius,' Margaret!"

I hate the damned word, thought Margaret, and felt released by her silent profanity. She smiled. "We'll see," she said.

"The Engers have always been endowed," Sylvia said. But Margaret refused to be goaded. She noticed again that Sylvia was playing with her beads. The nurse had returned, and was now sitting next to her patient, embroidering, her glasses blinking in the sunhine. Heinrich, speechless, seemed to drowse in his chair.

Sylvia said, abruptly, turning her stark face to Margaret, "I thought you ought to be first to know," she said. Margaret stared at her, puzzled. And why should I be the first to know—anything? she thought. Especially Sylvia!

Sylvia lowered her voice to escape the ears of the nurse. "You know Mr. Lang, the violinist with the theatre? He's been to dinner a few times."

Margaret, still upset from the brush over her children, and her regret at the death of the President, was momentarily confused. Sylvia frequently invited her artistic friends for dinner, and among them had been a series of very silent musicians from the theatre. "Ellis Lang," said Sylvia, impatiently. "He was here only two weeks ago." Then Margaret remembered. Ellis Lang was an even more silent musician than the others, a bachelor in his middle forties, extremely colourless and humble, a tall man with a long meek face and shy eyes and a nervous manner. He had sat all through dinner, murmuring faintly, laughing almost without sound, whenever addressed. "Oh, the violinist," said Margaret. "A very nice man." She wondered how Sylvia, the sharp and vibrant, had been able to tolerate such a pallid specimen of the human race. She looked at Sylvia, and was astonished at the flutter of slight colour in the other woman's face.

Sylvia was smoothing her hands, one over the other, and staring at them. "I am going to marry Ellis," she said. Then she looked up, and the colour deepened under her cheek-bones.

"Well," said Margaret, helplessly. Then she was elated, as well as amazed. Was it possible that one of the family would be leaving this house soon? She said, "Well, that's wonderful. I didn't know you were fond of him, Sylvia."

Sylvia said, in a still cold voice, "I'm not. Very. But we have a lot in common." Then her colour faded, leaving her face starker than before. "I never cared for any man in my life, except one, and he is dead." She made a short gesture. "Never mind; don't pity me. It was a long time ago, and it doesn't matter that I've never forgotten him, and never will. But Ellis needs me. Surely you've noticed Ellis at the theatre, Margaret! He stands out, a virtuoso. Absolutely brilliant. But he's always been poor and had to struggle. He never had a chance."

Margaret was so bewildered at this stream of confidences that she could say nothing.

"I've not told anyone else, yet," Sylvia went on. "I expect to marry Ellis in two weeks, without fanfare, or engagement parties or even an engagement ring. No publicity at all. A very quiet ceremony, in Mr. Yaeger's study, with only our family present. Ellis hasn't any living relatives."

"I'm—happy for you, Sylvia." Margaret was touched. Sylvia was sitting very upright and rigid in her chair and gazing at the distance. "I suppose he's really a fine person," Margaret added, softly, "or you wouldn't—I mean, you wouldn't like him so much."

"He hasn't any money," said Sylvia, flatly, as if Margaret had not spoken. "He barely makes a living at the theatre, and playing, sometimes, at the hotels, or at private parties. But he never cared for money, and doesn't care for it now." She repeated, "He needs me. And I hope to take him to New York for further study, at the Juillard School of Music. Ellis is a genius."

Margaret swallowed her rising elation. "We expect to leave for New York immediately after the ceremony," Sylvia continued, "and I do hope we'll never have to come back to this town! Except," she added, cautiously, "for visits."

"Of course!" said Margaret, controlling her joy. "I understand perfectly!"

Sylvia eyed her curiously. "I wonder," she said, in a meditative voice, "if you do, Margaret. You see, we'll need money. We'll need an apartment there, a good apartment, not one of those places in the village. Ellis is very sensitive, and he's known only miserable rooming houses all his life, and that's part of what has been inhibiting him. So, he must have pleasant surroundings, and security, so he will feel free to develop himself." She smiled, tightly. "It will probably take at least four years, at the school of music, and all this will be very expensive. As you know"—and she paused—"all I have is my allowance from Ed, and I've spent it on clothing and on the few luxuries I have."

Then Margaret understood; and her heart began a sudden indignant beating. Edward was to pay for all this; Edward was to have another parasite hung about his neck like an albatross. Four years at one of the most famous music schools in the world, for a miserable stranger no one hardly knew, except Sylvia! Four years in a luxurious apartment for Sylvia and her husband, four years of increased allowances for clothing not only for Sylvia but for Ellis Lang, and for their private spending in the most expensive city in the country; It was a matter, probably, of at least eight thousand dollars a year—out of Edward's pocket. No, at least ten thousand dollars, in these days of wild inflation.

Sylvia turned in her chair and studied Margaret, saw the angry sparkle of her eyes and her compressed mouth. "Well, what am I to do?" she demanded. "Unless Ed helps us? Did you expect him to come here, and live on us, like a parasite? He has his pride, Margaret, even if perhaps you don't believe that."

"I'm not thinking of his pride," said Margaret, her temper flaring. "I'm thinking of my husband."

"Who is also my brother," said Sylvia, lifting her chin. "Have you forgotten that? And, after all, he owes me a great deal, more than you'll ever know."

Margaret clenched her teeth to hold back the bitter and tumultuous words that surged in her throat. For the first time in her life she wanted, desperately, to hit someone very hard, flat in the face, preferably Sylvia. Her mind ran on like a turbulent river. Ed would never be free from his family, never. Sylvia was still a young woman, just thirty-three. There would probably be children. Then the "genius" would have to study abroad. It would go on, everlastingly. There would never be freedom for Ed, who was so beset, and who had never taken a holiday in his life, and had only worked.

"What does Ed owe any of you?" asked Margaret, holding her voice down with a tremendous effort. It shook, however, with her struggles. "You're all men and women, now. He educated you, provided a wonderful home for you, gave you large allowances, paid all your bills, indulged you in every fancy, built a theatre for you, supports Greg and Ralph and Violette in Europe, takes care of André and his parents, and spares nothing and refuses nothing. And what has he gotten for his work, all the work he has done all the days of his life? Not even gratitude!"

The nurse overheard, and discreetly bent her head, and listened avidly. Heinrich slept in his chair.

"I didn't expect you to understand," said Sylvia, stiffly.

"He owes none of you nothing, now," said Margaret, and furious tears rushed to her eyes. "Why, you're not even young any more! How long does this have to go on, before any of you are self-supporting—in your genius?"

Sylvia smiled viciously. "Naturally, you are thinking of yourself, and your children's inheritances."

Margaret restrained the hand that trembled to flash up and strike Sylvia. "I am thinking of my husband," she said. "When it comes to him, I don't mean anything. Nor do my children. Have you looked at Ed lately, any of you? Have you seen how exhausted he is? Does he indulge himself in anything? You have your own car, Sylvia, and your mother has hers, with the chauffeur. Why, Ed doesn't have a chauffeur any longer, and he's the mainstay of all his relatives! What has he ever gotten out of life? Tell me!"

Sylvia said, "He has power, and that's all he ever wanted."

Margaret was shocked. "Power? Why, you're out of your mind, Sylvia! Power!"

Sylvia stood up. Her face was without expression. "I'd hoped you would help me, by telling Ed, and asking his help for Ellis and me. Of course, if Ed won't help, then I'll just have to persuade Ellis to come here, to our home, to live, and I'll get a private teacher for him."

Margaret was aghast. There was just no escape, no escape at all. Sylvia was smiling down at her again in that ugly fashion. "After all," said Sylvia, "this was my home before it was yours, or have you forgotten?"

She swung about on her heel and left Margaret, who swallowed painfully against her tears and rage. She leaned back in her chair, her hands clenched on the arms, and tried to control herself. Ellis Lang in this house for ever, with Sylvia and their children! The idea was unbearable. The alternative was even more unbearable. If only Ed could be persuaded to inform Sylvia that when she married she would have to establish a home of her own—Margaret closed her eyes and considered. If only he would be sensible! But this time surely he would. The situation was outrageous.

"Do you have a headache, Mrs. Enger?" asked the nurse. She was bending over Margaret solicitously. "Shall I get you an aspirin?"

"No, thank you," said Margaret, opening her eyes. She glanced at her wrist-watch, crusted with diamonds, which Edward had given her for Christmas. "Oh, dear, it's after five, and Mr. Enger will be here any minute. I must go to meet him."

She stood up. She found that her knees were trembling.

She braced herself and walked to the far spot where Edward met her every evening.

"Yes," said Edward, as he sat beside his wife under the trees. "I know how you feel, dear. Lang! I just about remember him, but only just about. He's like a fixture you overlook. But, let's be sensible."

"That's exactly what I'm trying to get you to be!" cried Margaret, clutching his hand, her heart sinking, as it always did, at the sight of his weary face and haggard eyes. "This time, you just have to set your foot down, Ed."

"Let's look at it this way, then. I'm supporting Greg, Ralph and Violette in Europe. Greg and Ralph, of course, will be self-supporting, one of these days, I know. But look at it all from Sylvia's point of view. Is she to be the only one to be thrown bag and baggage out of her home, without any help from me?"

Margaret was distracted. "You shouldn't be supporting any of them, Ed! Not one of them, except your parents. And they have their own income from ENGER'S. Never mind your parents, though. Do you actually think that Lang will ever be able to take care of himself and Sylvia? Don't be foolish, please, please! You'll never get rid of any of them. They'll take care of that." She clutched Edward's arm and wept. "You've got to start somewhere, Ed. You might as well start with Sylvia, as a hint to the rest of them. Do you know what she said about you? She said you have what you've always wanted—power. You!"

Edward's face changed. "Power?" he said, in an odd voice. "I want power?" The ashen colour ran under his dark skin. "I want power, I who hate men who want it, and who've fought such men for years?"

Margaret was frightened. "I shouldn't have told you that, that cruel and stupid thing! Sylvia doesn't know what she's talking about, and I told her so. Ed, you look so ill. Oh, never mind your family, damn them! Nothing matters but you." Her fright increased. Edward was staring at her blindly, as if she was not there, and his lips had a purplish tinge. He put his hand suddenly to his left side.

"Oh, what is it, Ed?" Margaret exclaimed, with a terrible sense of foreboding. "What is it, Ed?"

"Nothing," he said, weakly. "Nothing at all. What's the

matter with you, darling?" He managed a smile. "I never saw you so hysterical. Suppose we forget the family. I think I'd like a Scotch and soda; my bootlegger delivered some very good stuff last week. And I think I'll mix you one, too. It'll do you good. And we'll drink to the new President, Mr. Coolidge." He stood up and pulled Margaret to her feet. "Stop worrying, dear. Why, I've made over ten thousand dollars the last two days in the stock market. What is ten thousand dollars? Why does it worry you? What if it does cost that much a year, to get Sylvia out of the house? Isn't that what you've always wanted, even if you didn't say so?"

And he kissed her, and led her away, his arm about her waist.

Chapter Five

All the family was at home at Christmas, which made Maria contented, for though her children usually forgot their father even in his presence, and rated him of no importance, she believed that they had some affection for him. Ralph and Violette and Gregory had returned from France a few days before, and David was between engagements. Ralph had had to return for a few weeks to discuss bridge designs with his clients, and Gregory had completed his book and was in search of a publisher. Ralph was the most practical member of the family, and this, with his earthiness, did not make him the most popular. However, he was the youngest, and he was amusing if vulgar, and Violette could bring deft gaiety in spite of the mistrust in which she was generally held.

With the exception of David, whom Sylvia declared she could no longer understand, there was an immediate and confiding solidarity against Edward, even more emphatic than usual. Now that none was very young any longer, their dislike and hostility were more mature, more directed, and, in their belief, more rationalised. However, perhaps because of some emanation from Sylvia, whom all respected, Edward's children were great pets with their aunts and uncles, even with Violette. The brothers and sister spent hours bitterly discussing Robert's and Gertrude's "frustrations." "Of course," said Sylvia, "what can you expect of a man who knows nothing of genius and its needs, and of a woman who is absolutely stupid and ignorant?"

Violette made a moue and shook her head. "There you are wrong, my dears," she said. "Ed is not a fool, and Margaret is very wise, though sometimes childish in the American manner." She looked mysterious. "It is very wrong to underestimate the enemy."

Everyone stared at her. The enemy. They had fear for Edward, and something close to hatred, and in spite of themselves they had a frightened respect for their puissant brother. But they had never, even during their angriest periods, ever actually considered him as an enemy. Now they gave thought to it, acknowledged it eagerly and excitedly, and their last vestige of conscience with regard to Edward vanished in a surge of relief. Violette's statement had exonerated them from feeling obligated to Edward; he was now the open foe for whom there was no quarter. They smiled at Violette as at a deliverer. Later, Sylvia, who seemed brighter than in years after this session, told David of the general conclusion. He had regarded her with that strange look which never failed to disconcert her.

"Enemy? Ed?" he had repeated, slowly. "It's an unusual enemy who works himself to death for us. Yes, yes, I know your claim is that he always wanted power over us, and power for himself. You know very well, Sylvia, that he's not one of the typical rapacious tycoons you're always talking about, who thinks and lives only for money. He's neither gaudy nor grasping; he might complain often about our expenses, but he gives us whatever we want, and not out of love. Definitely not out of love. Perhaps because of power, but only a little because of power. It's something more subtle, and probably something more terrible, hidden even from him, and that's why I pity him." This so outraged Sylvia that when she reported this conversation to her brothers she betrayed David for the first time. "He's not to be trusted," she warned them. "Don't discuss Ed with him. Why, he might even be reporting everything we say to Ed! Let's change the subject when David's around."

So David, a little to his dismay, found himself a stranger in his home. His brothers and sister showed a cordial interest in his career and in himself, but there were no confidences any longer. He found the others overlaid with a bright and casual brittleness when he appeared. His loneliness increased. He spent most of his days at home with Maria and the twins. He tried, a few times, to be friendly towards Edward; he even strained himself in that direction. But the abysmal cleavage, dark and formless and without a name, which existed between them could never be bridged by words. Once he said to Edward, "I wish you'd rest. You look sick to me. And too tired." His voice was honestly concerned and anxious, but Edward had given him a glance charged with what to David was inexplicable rejection, and affront.

"It's a little late in the day for any one of you to be interested in me, isn't it?" he replied. "Let's drop it."

David spoke to Margaret of his growing concern for his brother. "Why, he gets greyer and greyer all the time," he said. "Margaret, you're his wife. In the name of God, what is it, what's the matter with him?"

Margaret had become cold. "Why, you ought to know, David. So long as all of you exploit him, and are such a burden on him, and such dead-weights, then he'll never be free, he'll never have any rest."

"Don't cry," said David, with a tenderness he could not keep out of his voice. "I'm going to try to help him. I don't know how, but I'm going to try."

Two days before Christmas he went to see George Enreich in the latter's home. George's bristling hair was completely blanched now, his florid face paler, his body heavier and more clumsy. But the green eyes were as vital as ever. He had come to have respect and even affection for David over the years, though he saw him rarely. He listened to David's words thoughtfully, shifting his cigar from one corner of his mouth to the other.

Then he said, "I have ways of finding things out, David. As you know, my good young friend, Edward is like a son to me though we speak no longer. It is not my doing. He does not know how I have helped him, and I will give you my confidence. You will remember the 'Save America Committee', which I told you he headed, and only you of the family know this. When America decided that Germany must be the enemy, against all the desires of the people, then Edward's personal enemies in Washington prepared to ruin him. I was soon informed of the plot by means of several friends. Enough. I need not tell you of the months of efforts in his behalf on my part. I employed all and everything without restraint, and there was much money involved. Few politicians there are who can resist bribery. It is not something to deprecate or bewail, but only something to accept as in the nature of humanity, unfortunate though it is.

"Yes. I have my means of securing information. I am also not a stupid man. Nothing can make Eddie's arid existence blossom, only himself. His wife can do nothing for him, for she loves him too much and so cannot see him. And there has been a little estrangement growing between them this year, which I deplore, but which I understand. The love is not injured, but the closeness is somewhat marred. It is because of the children. You seem astonished that I know so much, but Eddie is my business because of my affection. You did not know it? Margaret is a very sensible and discreet woman, and is suspicious of what your family calls genius. She has reasons, as you know. She is not a deluded mother; she will never stand in her children's way, but she considers them too young as yet to know what they really want, and for what they are really fitted. Eddie is not so wise, so temperate, so tolerant. Some vague talents on the part of his children—and do not all children in early years show some talent which later withers naturally?—convinces him that his children are geniuses, and that their genius must be developed immediately. My informants?" George smiled. "I, too, have servants," he said. "Do not be so annoyed. The consuming interest of servants is their employers, and I do nothing to discourage that interest, and the reports, for I am concerned with Eddie.

"What is wrong with Eddie, you have asked. Many things, many dark and violent things, which are beyond him to comprehend. I do not believe in this Freud, who has insights, powerful insights, but only narrow insights. Perhaps he never truly loved anyone. However, I will bow towards Freud this time, in connection with Eddie. I know the very year in which Eddie changed, not slowly, but all at once. I know the time of the year. It was not long before Christmas, of 1904. Something happened in his life, something which may seem insignificant to others, but was of terrible importance to him. I do not know what it is, and who is there to say what is significant or insignificant? He was injured; he suffered what is now called a trauma. He has forgotten it, in his conscious mind. But it brought out a hardness and a ruthlessness, and no doubt even a vengefulness, in him, which possibly might have lain dormant—if that event had never happened. Or, it is possible that he began to think, and thinking often leads to hatred as well as to enlightenment."

"1904," repeated David, slowly. He shook his head. "We were only kids, then. I can't even remember that Christmas. Except one thing: I had a fight with Eddie over Billy Russell, that coloured boy who used to work for my father. Yes, it was Christmas Eve! Wait, wait. Something's stirring in my mind. Ed had begun to change long before that, though. I think the fight was only the culmination of something that was distorting him. He had always been very close to Pa; the closeness was gone, by Christmas. Even then, Ed was showing hostility towards him, and contempt for him. Do you think it all has something to do with Pa? I can't believe that. Pa has always been so simple and childlike and kind, and he'd be the last person in the world to hurt Ed, who was his favourite child."

George considered. Then he said, "I think it is your father. How, or why, it is impossible for me to know. But there is sureness in me about it." He paused, and looked at David, who was frowning in bafflement. "You have said, my David, that your sister has asserted that Eddie is the enemy of all of you. I believe that. I believe that he wants to retain power over you. I have always believed it. And, is that not paradoxical in a man who loves freedom absolutely, and who detests the power-seekers? When we discover the nature of the paradox, which probably is not paradoxical at all, we will know what is wrong with your brother. But that will not help him. He must know, himself."

David was silent a long time, his handsome narrow head bent, his hands clasped between his thin and elegant knees. Then he spoke, without looking up. "I respect Ed. I can even say I love him. I understand him even more than Margaret does, though perhaps not as much as my mother. I would give anything, anything, to help him, for his own sake. You believe that?"

"Certainly," said George, with kindness. He smiled mischievously. "And that is why you do not tell him who the famous composer of *Samson Smith* is, and who has been writing all those undeservedly popular songs? Ah, you are amazed, yet I have told you it is my business to know all about my Eddie, and those surrounding him. I am glad that you have given me the occasion to congratulate you. It was my admiration for you which prompted me to give you the various tips on the stock market, and so to help you become a rich man. You are very ingenious and very clever, and you have found your *métier*, though I confess I do not understand this modern music. Nevertheless, it is your *métier*. I wonder," he added, artlessly, "if your brothers and sister have found theirs also. It does not matter. I am not much interested."

He poured more wine into David's glass. "I have this advice: continue as you are doing. I am growing old, and perhaps my German mysticism is increasing. I feel that some day Eddie is going to need you."

David talked with Maria. She sat silently as he spoke, larger and more shapeless than ever, her pale hair now one drift of thick white, her pallid eyes inscrutable. "I've always thought you knew more about Ed than anyone," said David. "And though no one else would believe it, I've always believed he was your favourite child."

"I love all my children, but I have loved Edward the best," Maria said, in a voice without emotion. "And it is the tendency of love to oppress and demand. Though Edward is the only one who can help him, I am partly guilty of his spiritual sickness and his suffering. Wait." She lumbered to her feet, raising herself out of her chair with weighty effort, and went into her bedroom. She brought out a flat parcel tied with tissue paper covered with brown paper. She sat down and slowly unfastened it, while David watched. She then handed him a stiff sheet of drawing-paper, brown at the edges, and brittle. David looked at it in wonderment. Even though many years had obviously passed since this water-colour had been painted the colours were vehement and alive. It was a painting of a young hen, vigorously soft yet strong, lifted on her toes as if preparing to fly. "Why, this is the best thing Ralph has ever done!" said David, admiringly. "Even if he must have done it when he was a child." He suddenly frowned, trying to remember something. "Wasn't it Ed's chicken—Betsy? I seem to recall his having a chicken, a pet."

Maria smiled slightly. "Yes." The smile vanished. "Little

Ralph let her out of her cage to paint her, and she was caught by a cat. Edward was heartbroken. I don't think he ever forgave any of us; he began to change then. A small thing, a little hen, but a small door can imprison, or free, as well as a large door." She paused. "Ralph painted the hen. But Edward, when he saw the painting, which I wished to give him, took up the paints, himself, and brought life to wood. You are astonished. Perhaps you do not know that your brother is a great genius, a strong and very vital genius."

"I had a feeling about it," said David, looking more closely at the picture.

"Good. But you and I are the only ones who know. He has an instinct for art, for science, for writing. For many things. In any of them, he would have acquired an imposing reputation, and fame. None of you can match him, in anything."

David stared at her. Then suddenly his face kindled with a great black anger. "And you let him waste himself! You never helped him, as you helped us! We were the geniuses, we——"

"Were weak," said Maria, interrupting. Her eyes were cold and fixed. "And I was cruel. But realistic. We needed money for our children, which we did not have, and which we would never have had, had it not been for my son, Edward. What talents you possess, and they are feeble, but still they are talents, were nurtured by the money Edward made. I am a Von Brunner; I could not bear for my children to be mediocrities."

"But we are," said David, bluntly. He was still blazing with quiet but enormous anger. "And you let——"

"Wait," said Maria. She picked up her knitting and her needles clicked for some moments, the fire crackling in the background. "A mother knows her children. I know much about all of you."

David looked at her, stunned. She raised her eyes, and they were almost gentle.

"Without Edward's help and money, what would you be now, my child? Perhaps a worker in a small delicatessen."

David stood up and agitatedly began to pace the room, his tall and elegant body passing and repassing before the fire, while his mother placidly knitted. Then he swung to her and exclaimed, "Yes! We didn't deserve Ed. Why should he have been sacrificed for us? We're weak. Why should the strong be sacrificed for us?"

Maria said thoughtfully, not looking up from her knitting, "In the history of the world the strong have always been apparently victimised for the weak. It is the weak who protect themselves from the strong, with more and more punitive laws, and, at the last, by shrill violence. But the strong would never be violent; they pursue their way like the gods in Wagner's operas, knowing only themselves, unaware of anything but their intrinsic power. And so they inspire the envy and resentment and hatred of the weak, who revenge themselves on what they cannot understand, and which is too great and lofty for their understanding. The historians ignore this, or do not know it, or are weaklings taking their own revenge. The strong are often magnanimous. They often permit themselves, in the name of humanity, to be tied by Lilliputian bonds. But strength constrained and bereft does not increase the stature of the weak."

David said bitterly, "That's all very nice. We're Lilliputians and we've put ropes around Ed. I've known that since I was fifteen or sixteen. Do you think that's fair?"

Maria's hands rested on her knitting. "Edward is not magnanimous. You think you have tied him. But you are tied, my son. All of you. That is Edward's own revenge. He will never be free until you all go free, until you have escaped him. Why do you not escape him?"

David said, "I don't know about the others. But I don't exploit Ed now. And he's so sure I'm a gifted concert pianist, and he's satisfying himself vicariously in me, that I can't tell him the truth. I won't hurt him. I'll never hurt him." He spoke with quiet passion.

Maria nodded. "Not because of Margaret; he knows she did not love you. But because he would realise that you escaped him a long time ago. He dislikes you because his intuitive nature realises that he never held you, though he was exploited for you." She added, "There are the magnanimous strong, and there are the strong who are unforgiving. Edward is the last."

David felt that they were speaking of cobwebs that could be felt chillingly but not seen. His mother said, "I learned that Edward had a genius for business as well as other gifts. It was necessary that, for all your sakes, he develop the first.

He is deluding himself. He could be happy, if he could know himself."

"There's more to this damnable situation," said David, with wrath. "It isn't as simple as you say."

"You are quite right, David. Nothing is ever as simple as any of us say."

David picked up the old water-colour again, and the tints blurred before his eyes. "What a waste!" he said. "What a terrible waste!"

Maria looked at him. "Do you not know? Edward is doing what he wished to do, though he does not understand that. The strong are never really bound by the weak, even if they believe so. They always do what they want. Paternalism is always given, though the weak by their nature seem to demand it. They merely accept it after it is an accomplished fact."

"But Ed knows he's been exploited, and that's why he hates us."

"In part, yes. But he agreed to the exploitation, because it gave him power over you. His hatred is his private means of hiding the truth from himself. He is just; it would destroy him, perhaps, if he understood. He wanted what he has, and he also wanted more. Despite his ragings against all of you, he is satisfying the whole range of his genius. When you disappoint him, you are striking at his hunger for satisfaction."

"There's more to this," David repeated. "There's something else."

"Certainly," said Maria. "And it escapes me, though I have thought."

She wrapped up the picture again, and put it away.

On Christmas Eve the entire family, with the exception of Heinrich, gathered for a festive dinner before church. Edward sat at the head of the huge and gleaming table, the candlelight not softening his drawn and exhausted face and greying hair. He looked much older than his oldest brother, David, and his eyes were stained with the same purplish shadow that hovered over his broad lips. He seemed out of place in that ponderous but stately room, in his old clothing, creased shirt and rumpled tie. Margaret, in blue velvet, sat at the foot of the table. She and Edward were the only silent ones, Edward abstracted and brutally remote, and Margaret thinking of no one but her husband and almost unaware of anyone else. The blue velvet made her flesh seem whiter and more translucent than usual, but David saw that she was also thinner, and appeared sad. Her beautiful eyes fixed themselves frequently on Edward, almost imploringly.

Ralph ate heartily, and amused his family with anecdotes about Paris. His strong auburn hair was like filaments of living wire, rising in a crest above his flushed forehead, which was always slightly damp. He was definitely becoming quite fat; his full and lustful features were a brighter pink than his forehead, and his full mouth was red. Violette sat beside him, trim and merry, in chic black velvet and diamonds. (David eyed the jewellery with suspicion.) Her black curls were modishly short, gaily poised on the top of her head. She was always highly amused by this innocence, which seemed to her stupid and childish, and too redolent of soap, bath-brushes and rude health. Even little French children, she would think, are more sophisticated than American captains of industry. There is no subtlety in Americans, no true and polished ruthlessness. Ralph was very foolish; he said that it was just that Americans were not depraved.

The conversation, when not dominated by Ralph, was disjointed, as if everyone was speaking only to himself and not listening to anyone else. Violette was aware of the tensions in the room, which rose over the tinkle of silver on the best china, and the voices.

Margaret said to her, "Are you taking little André to Midnight Mass, Violette?"

Violette stared at her, her eyes dancing. "No, no, my dear." Her tongue flicked against her lips, as if with secret laughter. "I have never done so. It is strange you should ask me. Yes, I am *Catholique*. But I have a husband who is not dead. We are divorced. And then I married a Protestant, and that is against the Church, and most against because of the divorce and the living husband." She laughed, joyously. "I am not really married to this, my Ralph. It is only a civil marriage. I am living in naughtiness!"

Margaret smiled painfully. "But André was baptised by Father Jahle."

Violette looked very demure. " Yes, yes. Shall I deprive him of baptism ? No, no. But I shall not force him to church, to Mass, to the Sacraments. I am a heathen, yes?"

" Will you let us take him, then, to church with us to-night?"

Violette tossed her brisk curls in negation. " No, no. That would be a mortal sin. I must consider my son's soul." She smiled at Margaret's puzzled face with pure enjoyment. How naïve were these Americans!

" Stop teasing, Vi," said Ralph, annoyed not because of what his wife was saying but because Margaret's interruption had destroyed the point of a joke he had been telling. It had escaped him that no one had been listening; it was enough for him to talk.

A blizzard had begun half an hour ago. The gale pounded like a solid mass against the windows. Margaret worried about the children; Gertrude was recovering from a sore throat and Robert had been peevish to-night, unusual for the gentle and amiable boy. Margaret never permitted anyone to interfere with her about the children, except Maria, and that was only with regard to the attendance at church on Christmas Eve. It was a family occasion; only desperate illness conld intervene. That was the law of the household, which only Edward dared disobey or question, or occasionally, David, and, of course, Violette, who immediately became a " *Catholique* " whenever it served her purpose. During her absence the past two years little André had been taken to the Engers' church regularly, something of which Margaret disapproved highly, and over which she had quarrelled with Maria. " The boy should be instructed in his baptised religion, Mother Enger," she had said. " But he is never instructed," Maria had replied, coldly. " Catholique " or not, Violette tactfully refrained on commenting on the situation.

" I do not envy you, my dears," said Violette, to-night, as a particularly heavy wave of wind and snow assaulted the long dining-room windows. " I shall be snug and warm in my room; I shall read the good and inspiring book. And you will be in the cold. What a climate this is, in America." She shivered elaborately.

The family, with the exception of David, Edward, André and Violette, left for church soon after the dinner. Violette sat with her son in her warm little sitting-room, near a very agreeable fire. She spoke to him in French, grateful to Margaret that she had volunteered, with excellent results, to instruct the boy in his mother's language.

André told his mother, whom he thought delightful and fascinating, for all her neglect of him, about the affairs of the family over the past two years. He sat at her feet, like an elf, perched on a footstool, his big eyes shining with malice and pleasure. *Tante* Margaret had taken him for catechism instruction a number of times, secretly, to that very old, and very foolish, Abbé Jahle. No, no! No one knew at all. André and Violette laughed together, clapping their small hands with glee. The poor *Tante* Margaret, who was so solemn about matters. André had given her his promise that he would tell no others of the family, and she had appeared most uncomfortable at having to extract the promise. "Their religion is so without charm," said Violette, speaking to her son as to an equal in age. "No *élan*. No beauty. It is like the English suet pudding, heavy on the heart. I am pleased, my child, though one should never take religion seriously. It can interfere with a pleasant life.

"And now, about the Grandfather. It is well? You are certain, André?"

"Yes, Mama. Before he was stricken I was the very good, the very loving grandson. There was the first year, before I went to school with Robert. The old man is lonely, because he is so stupid. But I noticed him and followed him, and sometimes went with him to that very unfragrant shop, and I sat on the counters and watched the money come in, and was much petted by the clerks. Grandfather sat in his office and did nothing, or he came into the shop, and the customers like him, but he began to forget their names. Ah, yes, I was the good and loving grandson, and Grandfather patted my head. I was like Uncle Edward, he said. I had the heart and the feeling."

Violette rolled up her eyes in mock horror. "I trust not, my dear. There is a man without joy, though I confess he is very potent. Where would we be if there was no Uncle Edward? It is terrifying to contemplate." She looked at André intently. "You are just eight years old. How can one so young know if the Grandfather was generous?"

André's eyes took on a feral glow. "It is because the

Grandfather called me 'Eddie' very often, and said the shop would be mine, as he had promised. He was failing then."

"Poof," said Violette, frowning. "That is not enough, the slipping of an old man's memory."

André smiled. "He never called Robert 'Eddie' and never made him such promises and never invited him to the shop, though he loves Robert also, and, in particular, that silly Gertrude who considers she speaks French better than I. And when he gave them a dollar, he would give me two dollars, and an extra smile."

"That is encouraging," Violette conceded. "He is dying, of course. We shall soon see. You are a most satisfying son, my dear."

A maid brought them hot chocolate with whipped cream, which they drank together by the fire, listening to the storm. "You will take me to Paris this time, Mama?" suggested André. "It is very tiresome here."

Violette had already given this some thought. She had come to the conclusion that André, himself, might be "tiresome" in Paris, a hindrance to the gay life his mother lived. Ralph hardly spoke of the child, and was certainly never more than mildly interested in Maria's dutiful accounts of his schooling and his health. Since the war it was very hard to obtain responsible women to care for children. Nanette would surely leave if André was imposed upon her, and Nanette was not only extremely discreet but she was an excellent cook and a frugal housekeeper. Violette said, "Paris is not the same as when I was a girl. You would not find it interesting, my dear."

André shrugged, without disappointment. He said, in English, "Okay." He was shrewd far beyond his years, and he was fond of his pretty, smart little mother, and did not wish to interfere with her. She bent and kissed him, and he could smell the enticing and heady bouquet of her perfume. She said approvingly, "You are a most understanding son. If you were truly an American boy you would kick and scream and pout, not because you had been crossed but because I had given you an occasion to be disagreeable and intemperate. You will be a civilised man. When you are twelve, then you shall come to Paris."

In another part of the house David was playing a Brahms concerto, and he was playing as he had never played before, not only with technical brilliance and faultlessness, but with passion and grandeur and humanity. He was absorbed in the music; he was expressing, for the first time, in classical music, his grief and despair and loneliness, his hopeless love for Margaret, his love for his brother and his impotence to help that brother. Now, like one in a trance, he passed from the personal anguish of a single man to a universal anguish, with majesty and tragic undertones filled with a prayerful resignation. It was as if an enlightened Job acknowledged not only the calamitous and unknowable fate of man, but the mighty dignity and mystery of God to Whom all was known. The conversation between man and the Divine seemed not only to fill this room but the thundering world outside, and to penetrate to the farthest star. It faded, at last, into reconciliation, into acceptance, into slow tender notes of mutual and confident love, into promise given and promise received, for ever and for ever.

David's hands lay exhausted on the keys; drops of water stood on his dark forehead. His face was peaceful and calm.

"So, you can play when you want to," said a harsh voice from the doorway. David started and swung on the stool. Edward stood there, wrathful, his pale eyes violent. "You can play as you never play for an audience—if you want to."

He seemed very excited and stirred, under the wrath and violence. He came into the room, walking with a heavy tread on the parquet floor. His breath was audible. "I've never heard such music," he went on, in a low and savage voice. "And no one else ever has, either, from you. You can create as I knew you could. But you never wanted to, did you? It was too much to ask of you, too much for me to ask! I was only old Garlic and Pickles, never a man who knew music. Why . . ." He choked, and a terrible greyness washed over his face, and he caught the edge of the grand piano.

"Ed," said David, getting up in deep alarm. But Edward waved him off, with greater savagery. "Shut up," he said, and his voice was suddenly weak and gasping. His eyes remained violently on his brother. "God," he whispered, "I could kill you!"

He stood there, and his rasping breath filled all the room, while David stood in agony and listened. There was nothing he could do, under the glare of those raging and hating eyes, those condemning eyes. He could not explain, for there was no explanation for him. And Edward, seeing his brother so still, so pale, and so obdurate, as he thought, and so defiant, as he thought, really was possessed with the urge to murder. He might have moved upon David, then and there, but the tearing horror in his chest was like an animal.

David shut his eyes suddenly. He could hear Edward's ragged breath, the quick gasps. The storm rose in power and fury, and it seemed less to come from the chaotic world outside than in this room. What is wrong, what is wrong with him? David asked himself in terrified despair. He's sick; he sounds as if he's dying. If only I could reach him . . . David opened his eyes. Edward's colour was a little better, but his hand still clung to the piano. He was still staring fixedly at the older man as at an enemy both despised and repudiated.

David clenched his slender hands at his side. "Ed," he said, "you must listen to me. I don't know how to say this. We never could talk. None of us could ever really talk to each other. I want to try now. I want to help you."

Incredulity and affront leapt like a blaze across Edward's face in a frightening flow of red. "Help me! You!" His voice was stronger, charged with renewed wrath. "You parasite! You've taken all I could give you, and you've never returned anything, until now, and it wasn't for me! You, help me?"

"I think I can," said David, and his voice broke. "If you'll let me try. Do we have to be like this? Let's sit down and talk——"

He came closer to Edward, his concern growing for his brother. "You look sick," he said, pleadingly. "Let's sit down. I've a lot to say to you—help——"

Then Edward raised his hand and struck David furiously across the face, and David, overwhelmed both by the force of the blow and the dreadfulness of it, staggered back and fell against the piano. His hand reached for a hold and crashed on the keys and a discordant sound cried out. Then he stood there, his head bent, livid welts springing up on his assaulted cheek.

It was as if Edward had struck involuntarily, for he said with the same unchanged violence, and with no satisfaction, "All the days of my life—all the days of my life . . ." And he turned and walked out of the room, his step heavier than before, and slower, like a man who had come to the end of his endurance. He stopped in the doorway, to hold the side for a moment. It was as if he had forgotten David.

Then David was alone again. He sat down on the piano stool, his head drooping. It was no use. There was nothing he could do. His cheek throbbed and he was only vaguely aware of it. There was a more torturous throbbing in his heart.

When Margaret returned home, cold and strangely disheartened as she was so often these days, she went at once to Edward's room. But the room was dark. The shaded light in the sitting-room filtered into the bedroom, and she saw the long mound of Edward's body, very still. She sighed with relief. He too often remained up half the night reading. It was not yet midnight, yet he was asleep. Somewhat cheered, she prepared for bed, herself.

The bells of the churches sang faintly through the snow and the gale. And Edward lay in his bed and cried silently in himself, "Help. Help." And did not know to Whom he cried.

There was a big and glittering tree for the children in the large living-room. The storm had withdrawn in the night, and the world shone as if polished into marble, white on the earth, bluish-grey in the sky. The adults gathered with the children, to be pleased with their pleasure. The aunts and uncles, remembering early rigorous lives, lived vicariously in the excitement and delight of André, Robert and Gertrude. Margaret thought the gifts too lavish and expensive, and too numerous. It wasn't a wholesome thing for children to be satisfied this way, as satiated they would be, later. She had given Gertrude two dozen fine, but plain, linen handkerchiefs, and a silver wrist-watch to Robert, and a similar watch to André. Sylvia, when Margaret was momentarily distracted, pointed out these gifts to the others, with disdain.

But Gertrude, who was so understanding, and Robert, who was so good and amiable, gave their mother a sincere and loving kiss, and she was comforted. André, thanking his aunt with a politeness she thought excessive and a little mocking, put the watch aside, to rejoice in a gold watch from David, and other wonderful things. Edward had given each of the children a twenty-dollar gold piece. "All he can think of is money," Sylvia whispered to her sister and brothers.

She had bought Robert a silver flute and Gertrude a small typewriter. André did not fare so well from her, however. She had given him a book of fairy tales, which highly diverted him. He showed it to his mother, who smothered a laugh.

Maria, who thought much as Margaret thought, had knitted the children sweaters and gloves.

"What is wrong with him—again?" Sylvia muttered to Gregory, as they knelt in a welter of gold and silver paper near the tree. Gregory, smirking contemptuously, glanced over his shoulder at Edward, who sat at the far end of the vast room reading his newspaper. "We've probably got a contagious and loathsome disease," Gregory replied. "He looks like hell, though doesn't he? Ten years older than a year ago. Business bad, or something?"

"Not that I know of," said Sylvia, indifferently. "He's just opened four more stores. What does he think of, when he isn't thinking of money?"

Gregory reached up to pat André as the child wandered by, his eyes inquisitive and his ears always awake to catch a morsel to be repeated to his mother. But Sylvia said coldly as André wandered on, "I don't like that boy. He's sly, and I don't think he's too bright."

Gregory gave her a shrewd look. "Don't underestimate . . ." he said. "By the way, old Garlic and Pickles is reading my book in manuscript. Insists on it, since *The Sun Rises West.* Waves the old money club which is all he has, but it's potent, unfortunately. Don't underestimate him, Sylvia."

Sylvia shrugged. She smiled, however, when she saw her shy husband playing with Robert's toy railroad; Robert knelt beside him, laughing excitedly. Then Sylvia said, "And what's wrong with Dave? His cheek is bruised; he said he slipped on the polished floor in the music room and hit his cheek against the piano. But he looks distracted to-day, and sick."

"We're a very mysterious family," said Gregory, in a light and jeering voice. "Hallo, sweetheart," he said to Gertrude who was approaching them. "How's the typewriter? Thinking of putting your old uncle in the shade, eh?"

Ralph came up to them, frowning. "Just had a consultation with old Burns about Pa. He came in early on his daily call. He says Pa is definitely failing."

"Oh?" said Gregory, without interest.

"He ought to be in the Clinic," said Ralph. "But Ma insists he stay here."

"Masochists, that's what we are," said Gregory. "What's your opinion? Think the old man will last out the winter?"

It was one o'clock. Dinner was at three. The noise in the living-room became more febrile as the children became more confused over the proliferation of gifts. "I really think that Gertrude and Robert should go to their rooms and rest," said Margaret. "After all, they've just had an infection."

"Leave them alone," said Edward, abruptly. He was thinking of his desolate Christmases, when he had been young. But Margaret was hurt at his tone, and went away without speaking. She saw Maria beckoning her from the doorway, and hurried to the older woman. Maria said, with no emotion showing on her large face, "Father Enger is restless. I am disturbed. I have been sitting with him for the past hour. A moment ago he turned his head to me and said one word, 'Eddie.' Very clear. Will you ask Edward to come upstairs at once?"

Margaret looked searchingly into Maria's eyes and saw the withdrawn grief there in spite of Maria's composure. "Of course," she said, and went back to Edward. His face was still shadowed and he glanced at her with some impatience. "Darling," she said. "Please come. Your father is asking for you."

The pupils of his eyes distended until they seemed to blacken the iris. "Asking for me?" he said, incredulously. "Why, he hasn't been able to do anything but grunt since he had his stroke. Who says he wants to see me?" He rattled his newspaper.

"Your mother. She's just gone back upstairs."

"Ridiculous," said Edward. He dropped the newspaper. "Why don't they let the old man alone, to sleep?"

"You're not coming?" asked Margaret, disbelievingly.

"Of course not. It wears me out, just to look at him. He died when he had his stroke. He's just a vegetable now."

"No, no, Ed," said Margaret. "I can understand him, often. And you know his mind hasn't been much affected. Please, dear. Go to see him. Your mother isn't hysterical; she said your father distinctly asked for you, and named you."

He folded his big arms across his chest, and his eyes

narrowed. "Funny," he said, with an unpleasant smile. "I've never been away from her. I've seen Pa hundreds of times since he was taken sick. And he never seemed to recognise me even when I spoke to him. He never even grunted at me, as he does at the others. And now, suddenly, all at once, he not only thinks of me but asks for me by name! Burns said he must be quiet." The unpleasant smile broadened. "And quiet is what Pa is going to get. From me."

Oh, God, thought Margaret, distractedly. What is it, what is it? I know his father exploited him for the others, but surely he can forgive now. Or is it something deeper? "Please, please," she implored Edward. He took up his paper again. "Let him sleep," he said in a tone that frightened his wife.

Margaret almost ran from the room, and up the stairway, stumbling once or twice on her long robe. She went into the elder Engers' suite. Maria was sitting by her husband's bed, holding his shrivelled hand, and the nurse was taking the pulse in the other hand. Margaret approached the bed, and winced with pity at the sight of the old ashen face on the pillows. Heinrich's eyes, so gentle and so childlike, fastened on her eagerly with full consciousness and knowledge. "Eddie?" he said, and his voice was clear and loud.

"Yes, yes, dear," said Margaret, and bent and kissed his forehead. She was horrified at its damp coldness. "He's coming. In just a minute."

Heinrich gave her his painful and twisted smile. He said again, "Eddie."

Margaret exchanged a desperate glance with Maria, whose face became expressionless. A question had been asked, an answer given. Maria sighed. The nurse said in a low voice, "His pulse is very weak. I think we should call Dr. Burns again." She went off to make the call, and the two women sat side by side at Heinrich's bed in hopeless silence. Margaret swallowed her tears. Her arm touched Maria's comfortingly, but Maria appeared not to know. She saw only her dying husband. A fire fluttered on the hearth, and the bright chintz at the windows and on the chairs gleamed vividly in the winter sunlight.

"Eddie," said Heinrich again. His face seemed to dwindle visibly.

"Yes, yes," said Margaret. "He—he was away a few

minutes. He will be here, dear Papa Enger." But Heinrich was looking at the doorway, and his whole simple soul was in his eyes, pleadingly. Margaret could not bear to see this, and so she stared dryly at the foot of the bed.

The nurse returned with an anxious report that Dr. Burns was away for Christmas dinner, and could not be reached for an hour. She felt Heinrich's pulse again. "Why," she said, in a more cheerful voice, "it's stronger. Now, isn't that nice?"

Margaret smoothed her short hair with her trembling hands. She prayed that Edward would come. She listened for footsteps in the corridor outside. It was unendurable to see that fixed bright stare of Heinrich's directed at the door. Maria said nothing; she had begun to rock massively in her chair in the ancient movement of sorrow. The quiet was so complete that the ticking of the old clock downstairs could be heard above the crackle of the fire. Once or twice Margaret caught the excited shout of a child in the distant living-room. A light wind lifted a veil of sunlit snow against the windows, and left diamonds of it on the glass.

"He's sleeping. That's good," said the nurse. The fixed eyes had closed, and Heinrich's breath came unevenly. After a few moments Margaret stood up. She said, in a shaken voice, "I'm going to my room. To lie down. And then I'll dress. Call me, Mother Enger—if there's any—change."

Maria nodded, without looking at Margaret, and continued to sway in her chair.

Margaret went to her room and lay down, and suddenly she was crying. How was it possible for Edward not to go to his dying father? It was incredible that even years of bitterness and resentment could induce him to refuse that last call. It isn't like Ed! thought Margaret. Oh, no, it isn't like Ed, who is so good and gentle and tender. It isn't like Ed, who gives everything and receives nothing. It's just that he didn't believe his father wanted or needed him or asked for him. After all, we've had a lot of alarms since Papa Enger took sick. Ed thinks it's just another one of them.

But she could not convince herself of this. There had been something final and bitter and inexorable on Edward's face, something cold and malign, as if he knew only too well. Margaret moved her head denyingly on the pillows. "No, no," she whispered. "Ed isn't like that."

She shrank from the thought of the family dinner; she was

tired, and her throat was sore. She fell asleep, with tears on her cheeks.

She dreamed that she and Edward were alone in the mansion, and there was no one else there at all, not even the children. She was sitting beside Edward, who was asleep. She was conscious of some agony in herself which devoured her like a beast. It was night; no, it was dawn. There was a greyness at the windows, and a magenta slash in the greyness, like a wound. She called to Edward, but he did not awaken; her voice was an echo. And then Edward turned in the bed and his eyes were glazed and without life, and as she watched him with increasing terror and agony he rose out of the bed slowly, not seeing her. She called to him, and he did not hear. Slowly, slowly, moving like one in a trance, he left the bed and flitted like a ghost across the floor. He reached the door, and went through it. Margaret tried to get up and follow, but she was paralysed. She called, and her voice was snatched away in a sudden wind. The agony became a death in her, and she thought, I am dying.

"Wake up, wake up, darling," said a strong voice, and she woke up, to find Edward standing beside her bed. "What on earth's wrong?" he said, and bent to kiss her. "You were moaning. Bad dream?"

She stared at him incredulously, the dream with her, and then a frantic joy engulfed her and she knelt up in bed and threw herself into Edward's arms and burst into wild sobbing. "I thought, I thought!" she cried.

He sat on the edge of the bed and held her. "What?" he asked, indulgently.

But she could only sob. She could not tell him, for the very words were too terrible. The sunlight strode into the room and it was only Christmas Day after all, and Edward was here, holding her, and her frenzied heart was slowing. She dropped her head on his shoulder and clutched the rough cloth of his coat in wet hands.

"It's time," Edward began, smoothing her pretty hair. But he did not finish his sentence. Maria had entered the room, and she stood near them like the figure of an ageing Viking goddess, very calm, very still. She looked only at her son.

"Your father is dead," she said, with no change in her voice.

"Oh, no," Margaret cried, dropping her arms from Edward, who stood up and faced his mother.

"He asked for you, Edward," said Maria, as if Margaret were not there at all. "You would not come."

Edward said nothing. His face was a face carved from grey stone.

"No," said Maria, beginning to turn away. "You would not come, though he asked for you, though it was the last thing he asked." She stopped in her turning and gazed at her son with majestic condemnation.

"There is much that you have endured," she said. "But there is even more that you do not understand. I wish only to say this: I shall never forgive you, no, not even to the day I die. Or you die."

Heinrich's will was very strange to all but Violette, and pleasing to none but herself and Ralph, and, though no one knew it, to Maria also. The old man had left his money, some four hundred thousand dollars, divided between his wife and André, his grandson.

"It is very good," said Violette to André. "And very sensible. We must now invest it carefully. It is in what they call the blue chips, and bonds. We must have consultations with very wise men who do not have the too eager spark in the eyes."

Chapter Six

When I was a child, thought Margaret, listlessly, there was not all this excitement about weather, as if it were a new calamity every year, to be shrilled about in little indignant voices, by little shrill people—who perhaps should never have been born in the first place. Everybody clamoured that "the government" should do *something* about everything, including the natural phenomena of nature. What a tiny little generation we are becoming!

Huddled in her fur coat, which could not keep her from shivering from some inner cold, she paced along the walks which circled the house. One blizzard had succeeded another since Heinrich's death, and final burial in the black and marble desolation of the cemetery. (She would never forget the stiff dark earth, the flailing snow and the bitter howl of the wind, the day of the funeral, and how, in some terrible way, the heaped flowers looked in their dying colour on the lifeless ground.) So high was the snow along the sides of the walks that it seemed to Margaret that she was walking through a white tunnel, a white hell of a tunnel. The grounds undulated away from her in their buried starkness, the spruces bearing on their branches broad white plumes of snow, which dissolved even while she looked at them into flying clouds of frozen spray. The house, at a little distance, appeared to have sunken into a vast mound of whiteness, a bog of whiteness, with chimneys futilely smoking, and the eaves drifting in mist, and the snow crushing down its great roof. Waterford had never known such snows, and it in what was called " the snow belt." The papers clamoured about the weather, the monstrous cold, the clogged roads, the zero temperatures, the isolation of the city. And in the clamour there was a mean petulance as though something or someone was responsible and should be punished.

She was sick with the sickness of living. She could not bear to turn her thoughts to the stricken and blank-faced family. With the exception of Maria, the family wore an air of outrage and bewilderment that one who had lived so long on the edge of the grave had finally toppled into it, with no sound, no voice, no protest, and no dramatics. What have we done that death should enter this house? they appeared to be saying. Even Edward. Even Ed, thought Margaret, with an acrid taste in her mouth. No one spoke of Heinrich. He had lived in that house for many, many years, and none had noticed him much except his wife. There was no room where any of them could say, " Here Pa stood, and this is what he said—and how he laughed. Or here he gave us this, or that. Or, I remember there was one day, and he was sitting there at the head of the table, and he said something. . . . Do you remember the time he trimmed the tree—or walked over there—it was the funniest remark . . ."

No, there was not a room, and not even his deserted bed now, that spoke of Heinrich. There was not an ornament which he had bought. There was not a picture anyone could remember that he had admired. There was not a footprint of his, or a fingerprint, which marked his former presence. He had left the world as unostentatiously as he had been born, and had lived. Yet, the muffled indignation remained in the family, the silly, voiceless indignation, that death had dared to walk into that house and had, for a moment, brushed them with his dark and noiseless wings. There was a hideous selfishness in their bewilderment. And a furtive uneasiness. Was each remembering, vaguely and reluctantly, or at least trying to remember, the sound of that meek voice, the murmur of that ineffectual laughter, or recalling, or trying to recall, the father of their youth? Were they indignant and dimly ashamed that they could remember so little of him who had given them life?

The children were worse, in their way, than the adults. They had been briefly awed at the thought of death and its presence. Margaret—and she was embarrassed now at her juvenility—had hastily removed the children to upper rooms, and had prevented them from seeing their grandfather in his coffin. "Children should be happy," she had said defensively to Violette, who had stared at her with open amusement. "Why?" Violette, the realist, had answered. "Who told you, *ma petite*, that anyone *should* be happy? Who informed you, *chérie*, that man was born for happiness? You do not want the children to have 'nightmares'? That is what you have said: 'nightmares.' It is absurd. Life is a nightmare which we disperse with laughter, when we can laugh. We must not"—and Violette shook her wise head—"protect our children from life, or give them the evil drug of happiness. They are not tender, these little ones. They are as hard as stone. It is, perhaps, because you have forgotten what children are, but I,—I have not forgotten children, who are monsters. Everything is an occasion for them, these barbarians, no matter if it is death or birth or weeping or quarrelling or hate. They revel—yes, it is revel—in drama and struggle. And you would deprive them of drama and their delight in tragedy!" She shook her head again. "You have deprived your Gertrude and your Robert of joy in terror and mystery."

Violette was quite right, of course, Margaret thought dolefully, as she paced her lonely way along the walks. Gertrude and Robert had protested, avidly, at her fluttering insistence that they not see their dead grandfather, that they not attend his funeral. Was that actually disappointment she had seen in their smooth young faces? Yes, it had been disappointment! Not grief, not subdued awareness—only disappointment and resentfulness that they had been robbed of excitement and the hungry satisfaction that all primitives feel at the calamity of others.

Young André had been conducted at once by his mother into the presence of his dead grandfather, and Violette had serenely answered his question. " He is dead. What is dead?" " *Mon petit*, you have seen a dead bird, or a dead flower, or a dead insect. So is *Grandpère* dead, and he is no more now than these." " And we all die, *Maman*?" " Surely, we all die, child, and this way shall we lie for a little time, and then the earth will cover us."

André had peered up at his mother, at her slightly smiling face, so amber-coloured, so pert, and from her calmness and casual manner he had derived considerable understanding. " But *Tante* Margaret has said we live again," he had remarked, with an academic thoughtfulness. Violette had shrugged. " So it is taught, and who shall answer, my child? It is enough that for this while we live, that we can laugh, that we can love, that we can know."

" Robert says *Grandpère* is in Heaven," André said. " Where do you think he is, *Maman*?"

Violette had replied, and her smile had disappeared, " That, *mon petit*, is a question for God to answer, and we are not God." She had then taken his hand and had led him to her own room where they had contentedly sipped hot chocolate and had eaten some éclairs, and had talked of life while Heinrich lay dead below them.

I am a fool, thought Margaret. Her children were discontented. They question André with that ugly avidity of children, and he had looked at them with the amused contempt which his mother reserved for the jejeune. He had teased Gertrude and had called her " a baby," and Gertrude, in return, had reproached her mother, who had no words to explain now. We protect our children when they only want to learn and live, she told herself miserably. Violette is quite right; we Americans are juveniles, not adults, and we treat our children as precious toys and not living creatures who must go about the business of life very soon.

She stopped and stood on tiptoe to look over the tunnels surrounding the walks. Then, as if in expurgation, she lifted her skirts and her coat, and deliberately plunged into the snow, and struggled against it as she had struggled as a child.

It was exhilarating; it was wonderful to defy and oppose the elements, to live as a human being and not as a protected fish in a warm bowl. The snow bore heavily against her legs and her flesh, and she exulted, with fresh pleasure and strength, as she ploughed against its resistance. Her heart felt strong and fearless; when she brushed against a spruce and it poured its shower of weighted snow on her head and shoulders she laughed a little, and was glad, as a child is glad. Now she was no longer cold, and she could forget that house, forget Edward's dark closed face, his silence, the withdrawal of Maria, the sullen indignation against death which showed in the eyes of Edward's brothers and sister.

When she emerged from the snow on to another cleared walk the colour glowed in her cheeks and lips and her eyes were washed clean of the wretchedness of the thoughts which had imprisoned her since Heinrich's death ten days ago. She shook the dry snow from her coat and legs. She stamped her feet. She was alive! A person had only to realise that he was alive, to live again. Except . . .

She looked up to see David standing near her, looming dark and thin and silent against the bitter azure of the winter sky. She blushed, and now the old sickness and animosity against all of Edward's family returned to her.

He smiled faintly. "I'd like to do that, too—walk in the snow," he said.

"Well, why don't you?" she asked, and half-turned away from him. Her expanded heart contracted again into chill and tiredness. She began to walk away, but he caught up with her. The sun, colourless as glass, and as bright, shone on the snow, and the skeletons of the trees etched themselves on the whiteness.

David said, "I know you don't like us, Margaret, and I don't blame you. You think we're childish, and we are. You think we're parasites, and we are. You think we're worthless, and we are. All of us. But we're also something else."

"What else?" she said, in a clear loud voice, stopping on the walk and looking at him with the merciless blue of her eyes.

"How can I tell you, Margaret?" His voice was gentle. "How can any man tell another what he really is? He doesn't know, himself." They paced along together, Margaret reluctantly, David absorbed in his thoughts. He began to speak again. "You think we don't care about Pa. We do. But we've thought so long about ourselves that it's a shock when we're called up to think of somebody else, and we can't escape thinking."

He paused for a moment to rub his foot against the side of the white tunnel. "I'm trying to remember Pa, and what he was really like, when we were children." Margaret paused involuntarily with him. "And there's only a loving little ghost of him. Yes, he loved us, and we didn't care whether he did or not. None of us attach enough importance to love, especially if the meek and undemanding offer it. Pa never refused us anything, except a little money, when he worked so hard to make it, and he was too anxious that we love him, too. A man should never be too anxious for love; he never gets it if he is. I've noticed that the least deserving of people receive the most affection. You see, they give others the idea that they're superior, and as superiors they're treated. Not a nice thing to think about, but it's true just the same."

The angry beat of Margaret's heart subsided. She said in a rush, "You don't like people any more than Ed does, do you, Dave?"

He looked at her with a curious expression. "I don't hate them," he replied, quietly.

She stood facing him, her colour high and vibrant, her eyes like the eyes of a vigorous child, her soft hair escaping in waves from under her fur hat. He saw the fine lines about her lips, the tremulousness of her mouth, the innocence of her look, and he closed his eyes for an instant on a pang of pain long familiar to him.

"You think Ed hates people?" she challenged him. "And if he does, why not?"

"Why not, indeed?" he murmured inaudibly.

Without any voluntary decision, they walked along together, until the house sank behind the snow dunes and only its chimneys fumed against the sky. Insensibly, they left the brick walls, so wet and red in the sunshine, and ploughed through more shallow snow, and were lost in a white wilderness broken by the stark black framework of frozen trees. As if by mutual consent they stopped and faced each other, and Margaret's lips began to tremble, and she bit them. She was terribly alone; she had no confidant; in many ways, now, she had no husband and she was filled with a deep sense of loss and mournfulness.

My darling, thought David, sadly. My beautiful, innocent darling. What can I do to help you? Dear God, let me help her.

He said, at last, and in the gentlest voice, "Margaret, what is it? No, don't answer; I think I know. You're terribly worried about Ed. You don't understand him. You only love him."

"Isn't that enough?" asked Margaret, trying to make her voice hard. Then, all at once, she was crying, as simply as a child, letting the tears run down her face without hiding them or wiping them away.

"Not always enough," said David. "I'm sorry, but there it is. I've watched you for years. You are kind and good, valorous and—this sounds sentimental—but you're pure-hearted. You've suffered; you told me about that years ago. But always you kept a single eye on the world, and you never really condemned anything with hatred, and you never pitied yourself. And," he added, more slowly, "you never thought of revenge."

"Oh, I'm not as good as that," she said, trying to smile. She wanted someone strong and loving to put arms about her and hold her, and the longing was suddenly so intense that it was a passionate hunger in her. Then she was no longer smiling and the lines of her mouth became rigid and carved. "Are you trying to say that Ed is looking for 'revenge?' On whom? All he wants . . ."

The tears were immobile drops of crystal on her face, and her eyes were large and strained and, to David, almost unbearably blue.

"Let us say that Ed isn't like other men, or, he's larger than other men," said David, pretending not to see the tears. "He isn't the average man, with average appetites or desires. Does that make him a monster? No. A giant cannot help his giantness. I know as well as you do that Ed is desperate, but I think I know a little more than you do why he is desperate. Because you don't know he's withdrawn from you to a great extent, not withdrawing his affection from you, but withdrawing because he's afraid that you'll find out how vulnerable he is. My mother even knows more than you. But I know the most. He won't let me help him."

"Have you tried?" asked Margaret, with hostility. She was deeply outraged that David could imply that she did not know her husband at all.

"Yes, I have tried," he said, simply. "That may surprise you, but I've tried. And he—pushed—me away more furiously than he would ever push you away. His weakness has become his armour. Yes, Margaret, I said his weakness, or perhaps I should say his illusion."

"Illusions! Because he thought you were all geniuses? Well, I never did, believe me!" Her voice rose. "I know exactly what all of you are, but I won't tell Ed. Yes, I know what you are——!"

"Do you?" he said, with great compassion. "Do you know what Sylvia is, and Gregory, and Ralph, and I? In another woman I'd think that was arrogance. But I know that in you it's only protectiveness, for Ed."

She pressed her gloved hands together in a convulsive movement. "Oh, I don't care about any of you! It's just that I can't stand Ed looking so terrible, so closed, so alone! I can't get near him any longer. It isn't just the children; he's using our quarrels to keep me off. Have you looked at him, really looked? It's like looking at someone dying." She moved closer to David, the longing for comfort stronger in her, and now her shoulder touched his arm. She cried out, "Help me, help me, David! I can't bear it!"

It was the simplest matter in the world, the most natural thing in the world, for David to take her into his arms and hold her to him lovingly, and it was all simplicity, all grief, and all loneliness, which made her put her head on his shoulder and cling to him like a lost child.

She was sobbing drearily, her lips near his chin. "When his father died he never said anything. He took care of all the funeral arrangements. I tried to talk to him—he wouldn't go to his father when he was dying. I saw him standing near the casket, and looking down—it was an awful thing to see. I couldn't tell what he was thinking. My husband, and I didn't know what he was thinking. I'm afraid—I can't stand it—I'm afraid——"

"Yes," said David, and held her more closely to him. Her wet cheek was against his now, and she cried so passionately that her whole body shook. Her hands clutched him in agony.

"And after the funeral, he went up to his room, and closed the door behind him. He never closed his bedroom door to me before! I—I tried to open it. It was locked, locked to me, his wife!"

"Yes," said David. My darling, he said in himself again. My dearest child, my love. He stroked the glossy curls that escaped her hat at her nape. I would give my life for you, he continued in his mournful inner conversation. You were all I ever had. And the only thing I can do now is to hold you and listen to you cry about my brother, who is your husband, and who is tormented, and whom you can't help. The bitterness of it was like a corrosion in his throat.

She was sobbing and gasping in her extremity. "If only something could be done! If only he and I were alone! Things are too much for him; there's too big a burden on him. He can't carry it any longer."

He can't carry himself any longer, said David sorrowfully. Leave him alone? That would deprive him of his perverted meaning in life.

Margaret pushed herself away from him. "I'm sorry," she stammered. She wiped her tears with the back of her glove. "I'm such a fool, about Ed. But if he isn't relieved, he'll die. I know he will."

David's arms felt empty and bereft, and fell numbly at his sides. He had thought he was reconciled. He had believed that he had sublimated his love for Margaret in the loveliest amorous songs in *Samson Smith*. There was one which the critics enthusiastically had declared was a classic: "Wherever you are." Wherever you are, Margaret, he had thought, while writing it. Living or dead, wherever you are, there I will be, too, though you'll never see me, or understand. For there was never anybody for me but you, from the very beginning, when you were a shy young girl timidly entering a room, and when you looked at me. And now he knew that he would never be reconciled. The old love was a devouring anguish in him.

She looked up into his eyes and she thought them obdurate and strange in their restless intensity. Nobody understands, she thought, hopelessly.

"Can't you all go away, all of you?" she said, stammering again in her extremity. "I suppose your mother will have to stay. But if you'd all leave us alone . . ."

He shook his head. "It isn't possible, dear. Not possible. For his sake. That is, for his sake at this time."

Now she was angered. "I don't know what you mean! 'For his sake'! To take everything he has and give nothing—for his sake! Dave, you're the best of them, yet you can talk like that. Dave, please go away!"

"I'm not here very much," he said. "Does it bother you to have me here, Margaret, the few times I come?" He spoke with the heaviness of grief.

She was ashamed, because of his wondering, sad tone. "Well, David, perhaps not you. Though Ed seems to get worse when you come. But the others. Won't you tell them to leave, Gregory, Sylvia, Ellis, André, Ralph, Violette? You could explain it to them."

He was silent. She thought he was considering. She put her hand pleadingly on his arm. "Please, Dave."

He was still silent, pitying her, loving her. She dropped her hand. She exclaimed, with incoherent despair, "No! You've got too much of a good thing here, at the cost of Ed's life and health! You won't go away. I hate you; I hate all of you!" Her eyes blazed at him.

She turned then and left him, running like a young girl, as if something were pursuing her.

All I ever had, thought David. But, for the first time, I held you, and you cried in my arms. That will have to do me for the rest of my life.

Chapter Seven

Prince Emory, né Billy Russell, stopped at the desk of the Waldorf-Astoria and gathered up a sheaf of mail. He glanced at it, happily, for among the letters was one from Hollywood. He put the mail on the desk and asked the clerk to keep it for him for later. He went to the door, and people in the lobby paused to stare at him, to whisper about him, or to hail him loudly. He responded to greetings with a handsome smile and a wave of his light-grey felt hat, and his step grew more buoyant so that he moved in one easy fluid motion like a bronze-coloured cat. The new talkies! he thought.

Now they'll have my band on the screen, with sound! Good thing I invested in them.

The October day marked over the turreted city like a banner of blue light, and the brisk wind carried a sparkle with it. There was nothing like New York, anywhere in the world! It was a southern city, grey, tan, white and cream, and its topmost towers reflected the sun vivaciously. Billy stopped on the sidewalk to inhale the strongly masculine odour of the city, and he could feel the sinews of Manhattan move about him. Paris, he thought, was for women ; London was for commerce and law. But New York was for men.

As he waited for his limousine he hummed the latest " hit " tune by Davey Jones. In a week, since he had introduced it last night, it would lead all other songs in the nation. Billy's vigorous eyes roved over the crowds approvingly ; he loved the quick movement of them. Then his eyes paused, hesitated, turned away, then turned again on a man who had followed him from the hotel, and who was now hailing a cab.

The man was tall and broad and had a look of power about him. He was inconspicuously dressed, in the age of flaring lapels, wide-pin-striped suits and jaunty hats. His thick grey hair was half-hidden by an old hat, and his shoes did not match his blue serge suit. Billy craned his head to look at his profile, which was strong and hard and impatient. Billy grinned. He strolled over to the man and said, " Ride, sir? My car'll be here in a minute, and I'll be glad to take you wherever you want to go!"

The man swung about ; he frowned at Billy. " What? A ride? I'm waiting for a cab."

Edward Enger stared blankly, and then as blankly at Billy's offer of his gloved hand. " Who are you?" he demanded, and his tone was an insult. His eyes roved significantly over Billy's lavish suit and London topcoat and polished English boots. A Negro gangster, no doubt, or a bootlegger.

Billy dropped his hand. It was hard to maintain his smile. " You don't remember me? Why, I'm Billy Russell. From the old days in Waterford, State of New York." His smile definitely ached, but he kept it. " In the delicatessen. Remember?"

Edward's face was still blank, and then it was suddenly amazed. " Billy Russell! I don't believe it!" And now he thrust out his hand and forcibly shook Billy's. He smiled, and his face, so like worn granite, became youthful. "Well, well, Billy Russell. How did you know me, Billy?"

"Your face in the paper, old pal. And on the cover of your Chauncey magazines."

Edward threw back his head and laughed. He retained Billy's hand, and people passed about them on the sidewalk, glancing at them curiously. Billy's limousine drew up, and Billy said, "How about having lunch with me, at my club? The Ivory Club, here in town, with my own band. Prince Emory."

"Who?" asked Edward, still laughing. "Who's Prince Emory?"

Billy caricatured high dignity. "I am Prince Emory, sir, at your service. King of Jazz."

"I don't believe it!" exclaimed Edward, to whom the name Prince Emory meant nothing at all except an unpleasant vagueness connected with popular music. "I mean, I'd never have recognised you. Or, maybe I would. You haven't changed."

"Neither have you, old Ed," replied Billy. "And we're nearly forty."

"Not nearly. Just forty," said Edward. His eye touched Billy's excellent garb again, and a little reserve crept over his face. Was Billy a bootlegger, or a gangster? "Live in town, Billy?" Probably in Harlem.

"When I'm in town. I'm staying right here at the Waldorf," and Billy grandly indicated the hotel. "Where you're staying. But, here's my limousine. Come on down to my club and have lunch with me. Unless"—and he paused—"you're in a hurry."

Edward was silent. He looked at the black and glossy limousine. He looked at Billy. Then he said, "Well, I was on my way to the warehouses and the offices. My wife and I are sailing for Europe, to-morrow. Ireland, particularly, to see the wife of an old friend." He hesitated. A club? One of those night-clubs? Was Billy a waiter there? Edward was confused. Then he thought, It's really Billy Russell, Billy with the harmonica, Billy whom he had struck and driven away, Billy for whom he had mourned for a long time! He said, "Never mind my own business. All right. Let's go somewhere together and talk."

The chauffeur had come around in a sharp, military fashion, and he bowed in the two men and clicked the door after them. The fittings inside the limousine were of heavy silver, and rich black leather. There was a fine fur rug over the bar. The limousine glided away, and the uniformed chauffeur swung through the traffic. Edward began to feel a slight unreality in all this. Waiters did not own such vehicles; waiters were never conveyed in them. His dazed conviction that Billy was a bootlegger returned to him. He said, "How's the Scotch and bourbon market these days?"

Billy heard this innocently insulting remark and did not change expression. He said, lightly, "Very good. My bootleggers are the best; no cut liquor, no fakes. My customers expect the best. In my club. The Ivory Club. I own it, you see."

Edward's sense of unreality increased. He considered what Billy had said. Then he asked, "In Harlem?"

Billy's mouth tightened for a moment, but he said, kindly, as one would say to an ignorant tourist, "No, Ed. In the East Fifties. Best and most exclusive club in town. Best floor show, too. Best band. Mine."

Edward was embarrassed. He wanted to apologise. But he was still suspicious. How did a jazz player get such a limousine? A club, he had said, in the East Fifties. One of those coloured clubs? Prince Emory . . . He said, "I'm sorry, Billy, but this is all news to me. Frankly, I still can't believe it's you. I'll wake up in a minute. Who in hell is Prince Emory? You, you said. But what is it?"

Billy relented. His bronze profile smiled. "I see you're an outlander, a foreigner. You've been wandering around the classical corridors, staring at busts of Beethoven and Brahms and Bach. Now, as the papers are nice enough to call me, I'm the king of Jazzland, the interpreter of blues, the joy of millions here and abroad. Last week I visited the White House, to which I had been invited by President Hoover, who doesn't particularly care about jazz, either, but is too much of a gentleman to say so. But it's the thing, as the English say, to invite me. I've been at Windsor Castle, too. So far, Mussolini's been the only boy who hasn't asked for my presence. My music is decadent, to the Fascists."

Edward pushed his hat back on his head, stared at Billy again, then burst into another fit of laughter. But he was overjoyed, as well as hilarious. "Damn it!" he shouted, "I'd never have believed it! Let me shake your hand again, Billy." His eyes were the eyes of the boy in the delicatessen in Waterford on a cold Christmas Eve, and frank and affectionate. He struck Billy again and again on the shoulder. Then he flung his arm about that shoulder and hugged his old friend like a child who was filled with delight. "Old Billy," he said, marvelling. "I want to hear all about it."

There was colour in his seamed cheeks, and light in his pale-grey eyes. Billy smiled at him, with an ache in his throat. Poor old Ed, poor old driven, bedevilled Ed. "And I want to hear all about your family, too," he said, a little huskily. "How's everybody?"

Edward's face changed. He looked away. "My father died six years ago, this Christmas. You remember him?"

"Why, sure," said Billy, slowly, as if he had never heard this before. "I'm sorry, Ed. He was a good man, a good simple man, and I think he loved you more than anything in the world, even his shop."

Edward looked through the window, and he was old and hard again. Billy lit a cigarette. "Yes," he said, "I want to know about everybody. I haven't been in Waterford since I left there, a couple of days after Christmas—1904, wasn't it? Twenty-five years ago. A long time."

They went through the club, which was closed during the day, and dim and shadowy. Edward noted the rich appointments, the long bar, the heavy doors with their chains, the excellent furniture, the bandstand with its silent instruments, the velvety carpet, the gaily painted walls, all bright green palms and purple mountains and dancing Negro girls and men in Latin costumes. "An open bar," he commented. Billy smiled. "And expensive, too, and I don't mean just the liquor." He rubbed one finger on the palm of the other hand, significantly. "I hope you don't obey the Prohibition laws. I hope you're a good sound scofflaw."

"Evil laws are meant to be broken, or they should be broken," said Edward, following Billy down a long carpeted hall at the back of the club, and looking with interest at the various shut doors of gleaming mahogany. "Resistance to tyrants is obedience to God. Isn't that what Jefferson said?"

Billy produced a very formidable key and unlocked one of

the doors. "The American people don't break laws," he said. "Except Prohibition. And that's what's wrong with the country. We've lost spirit. Put totalitarianism on us, with police like Mussolini's, and we'll all be salaaming meekly. Don't laugh. I mean it. You can feel the rottenness growing, all over the country, and I'm not referring to gangsterism, either, which is only a symptom. Talk about Mussolini! We're just waiting for a dictator, ourselves, and we'll get one eventually, for we're asking for him. A Mussolini, or a Trotski, or a Hitler, or a Stalin. Well, come in. This is my private dining-room, and I'll order lunch."

He carefully shut the door and locked it. "I've got competition," he said briefly, at Edward's look of surprise. "I live and work and make my money honestly, but that doesn't mean I haven't been shot at regularly. I won't play with the boys. Not any more than I have to, anyway. How do you like all this?"

"All this" was a magnificent office furnished with authentic antiques, Oriental rugs, and heavy brocaded curtains drawn over barred windows, whose faint outlines could be seen through the material. There were excellent paintings on the walls, and Louis Fifteenth chairs, and a leather-covered desk tooled in gold. Beyond this office waited a small but exquisitely appointed dining-room, with no windows at all; a self indirect lighting filled it with a golden glow. "I eat here, whenever I want to," said Billy, proud of Edward's admiration. 'I've two singers auditioning in a couple of hours, a pretty girl from Harlem, a college graduate with a voice like black velvet. Man, can that child sing! And a boy who's studying law at Columbia; working his way through. My fellows tell me they're finds, but I want to see how they'll sound in the club. Acoustics can be tricky."

They went into the dining-room, which had an Italian refectory table covered with handmade lace, and high, antique Italian chairs upholstered in old purple plush with tassels of gold, and the carpet was Aubusson. "A drink first," said Billy. Edward saw him make no move but a moment later a coloured waiter entered carrying a silver tray on which was a pleasing bottle of genuine Scotch whisky, soda, ice and two glasses.

"Our speciality to-night is squab with chestnut dressing,"

he told Edward. "I hope there're two already cooked. And there's a bottle of Sauterne in the kitchen. How does that suit you?"

He opened a golden box on a small nearby table and Edward took a cigarette and examined it curiously. It was long, and Turkish, and the thin white paper bore a bold embossed little crown, with the words, "Prince Emory," written in gold script below it. "You've done well for yourself, Billy," he said. "There must be more to this jazz than I knew."

Billy smoked carefully, blowing up the smoke to hide his eyes. "And that's for sure," he said. He paused. "Ever hear of Davey Jones, the composer of *Samson Smith*, the first American opera?"

"I think I did," said Edward, with some distaste. "At least, my children are everlastingly humming some song or other from it. Discordant. I'm sorry, Billy, but that's how I feel about modern music, if you want to call it music."

"I know how you feel," said Billy, and Edward looked up with some quickness. There had been a cryptic note in Billy's voice. Was he remembering that tragic night so long ago? But Billy was smiling at him affectionately. "Every man to his taste," he said.

The lunch was excellent. During it Edward told Billy about his family, while Billy, who knew the story only too well, listened politely, and smoked, and motioned, from time to time, to the silent coloured waiter to pour more wine in the crystal glasses. He listened with real intentness, however, to Edward's voice, and its intonations, rather than to the words. He waited for Edward to speak of David, but he did not.

"Well," he said at last, while they ate their *pêche bombe*, "you, too, have come a long way, and your family with you. But you haven't mentioned old Dave. I remember him a little, and it seems to me that we've played the same cities sometimes. At least," he added, hastily, "I thought I've seen his name mentioned in the newspapers. Or, am I wrong?"

"You're not wrong," said Edward. He put down his glass of wine. "He's—the worst disappointment I've had, and I suppose you've understood that they've all disappointed me. Greg with his damned idiot book, *The Forgotten!* All about the starving, noble, striving, voiceless working class. As if such a class exists in America! I read the book in manuscript, and I laughed as I hadn't laughed in years. Greg wouldn't know a working man if he saw one. He's seen thousands, of course, but he's never recognised them. The men he sees riding around in Fords or Buicks and such, and in silk shirts, aren't recognisable to him as working men. It would kill him, to know the truth. Well. His book was quite popular. I bet the working people who read it, if they hadn't sense enough to avoid it, didn't recognise themselves either, as those mighty heroes of his. But the critics here in New York loved the book. And none of them can afford dinners such as the American ' working class ' eats every night."

He drank another glass of wine, angrily. The unhealthy colour was deep, under his cheekbones, and Billy watched him with some apprehension. He remembered that David had told him that Edward had had a " breakdown " six months after his father's death. He had been in Chicago, then, and in the hospital for some time.

" I've told you about Sylvia. Her precious Ellis had a heart attack, just on the eve of a concert tour, which I don't believe in, not a damned word of it. They're home, of course, living on me. Oh, I suppose the man has some talent; I've heard him play. Anything would sound good on a Stradivarius, which I had to buy for him. Ralph's still with his wife, playing around all over the world, at my expense. Greg's now writing the Great American Novel, and I've given him up, after *The Forgotten*."

" I read *The Forgotten*," said Billy. " Not bad writing. What the critics call taut and sensitive, and full of social significance, though what the hell that is I don't know. They have a special jargon, especially in New York. Well, at least they're all busy, aren't they? But you haven't told me about your children. Two, did you say?"

Edward's dark face lightened. " Yes. Going on fifteen. They're geniuses, both of them, though their mother won't admit it. Gertrude writes; editor of her school paper. She's sold two poems to a woman's magazine, and wonderful ones, too. And Robert's in his school band, at the Englebert School for Boys. He composed a new school song. Nice kids. Robert's the handsomest, everybody says. Everybody says Gertrude looks like me, poor child. Robert resembles his mother; he grows more like her every day." Edward's voice softened with love.

"My two kids are in school, too," said Billy. "They're older than yours. They're in the South."

"Private school? In the South?" Edward was surprised.

"Sure. And the best, too." Billy looked smoothly at his friend. "But, go on. Anything else you can tell me about your family, and Waterford?"

"No. Except about Ralph's boy, André. I didn't tell you. He inherited two hundred thousand dollars from—my father. None of us ever understood it." Edward's expression became hard, and almost livid. "The least my father could have done was to have repaid me, just a little, for everything I did for him and his children. Well. The boy's in school, in Paris. At least I make his father pay for him, out of the allowance I send Ralph!"

Billy was disturbed. He had heard this before, from David, and he was distressed not at what David had told him but at Edward's look of pent rage and hatred. "Why, that was wrong," said Billy, sympathetically. "Is the boy that attractive, or something, so that your father could forget his own children, and your children, for his sake?"

"That's something we could never understand, not even my mother, not even the meat-heads, my brothers and sister. I didn't dislike André, the way the others did. I thought he was amusing, and lively. I like all kids, anyway, so perhaps I didn't look at him too closely. Perhaps my—my father—thought that my children would have enough, and didn't need his money, and André did. That's the only explanation we can arrive at."

He brooded on it. It had not yet occurred to him that he had been remiss in not showing as much interest in Billy's family, and how he had arrived at all this obvious wealth, as Billy had shown in him. But Billy was not hurt. There is something of Heinrich's simplicity in him, Billy thought. He accepts the obvious. Besides, he's floundering along under a heavy burden. Why? Why doesn't he kick all of them out? Poor old Ed.

Billy said, "You've never told me why you were so sick in Chicago. Was it pneumonia?" (David had thought it was, or a nervous breakdown.)

Edward looked at him, his eyes wrinkling under his frowning brows. "Who told you I was sick, in Chicago?" he asked.

Billy cursed himself for this slip. He lit another cigarette with a light air. "Who told me? Why, there was an item in the newspapers. That's where I must have read it. After all, you're famous for your stores. Why wouldn't you be newsworthy? That was three years ago, wasn't it? Seems to me it was three years."

"Five." Edward was still frowning. He tapped his fingers on the lacy cloth. "I never told anyone in the family. No one would have been interested, except my wife, Margaret. And I especially kept it from her. Besides, the doctors were fools. I'd been working too hard. It could have happened to anyone." He paused, and grunted. "They said I'd had a heart attack. No, not coronary thrombosis. They said it was an old ailment; I must have had rheumatic fever at one time. Something to do with the valves. Well, I never had rheumatic fever. If I'd had compensation, they said, it'd broken down. I'll never believe doctors after that. I'd been driving myself; I'd run into trouble with a new Congressional committee investigating monopolies. That's the third time. Well, I'd had a cold, and it developed into bronchitis, and I couldn't spare the time to take care of it. So, one day, in my Chicago office, I collapsed. That was all there was to it. The doctors wanted to send for Margaret, but I put my foot down. Then, after I'd made them promise not to tell her their imbecile diagnosis, I had to let her come. I was in the hospital for two months, and that was fine for her!"

Billy was silent. He was remembering the night in the basement of the Enger delicatessen, so many years ago. Old Ed had almost fallen into the furnace, and would have done so if Billy had not caught him. Then he had sat on the chair, shuddering and trembling and gasping for a long time. He had looked like death. He looked like death now.

"Look," said Billy. "You're probably right about the Chicago doctors. But, we're forty. Now, I have an electrocardiogram every six months. Good insurance. We have the best doctors in the world, right here in New York. I know a wonderful heart specialist. Let's have you checked, just to reassure yourself."

Edward laughed shortly. "No, thanks. I wouldn't believe any doctor, after Chicago."

Billy was sick with his own anxiety. "You don't look

well," he said. Edward waved that aside. " I feel fine," he said. " We're leaving to-morrow for Europe, Ireland first. We'd have left in September, but there was that flurry about the Stock Market. Stocks are still down and unsteady, but we're pulling out of it now. I'm the executor of the will of an old friend, who used to work for me, Padraig Devoe." He thought of Padraig, and his face squeezed into momentary anguish. " His American estate. He was an Irishman. We haven't seen his wife, Maggie, and their boy, Sean, since they left for Ireland, shortly after the war started. He—died, there." He drummed his fingers again. " I've invested Padraig's money here, and it has quadrupled, or more. Maggie doesn't need it, but we like her, and I want to report to her, and that's our excuse for going."

He smiled at Billy. " Here I've been unloading on you, and I haven't asked you about this mysterious prosperity of yours. Now, tell me. Billy "—and his voice dropped—" I never forgot you. It almost floored me when you left so suddenly."

The waiter came in again, carrying a telephone. He plugged it into a socket, and said respectfully, " It's Mr. Rodgers, sir. Your stockbroker. He sounds sort of crazy. He said he's got to talk to you."

" I'll call him back," said Billy, impatiently.

" But Mr. Emory. He says everything's crashed."

Simultaneously, Billy and Edward jumped to their feet, and Billy seized the telephone. Slowly, as he listened, the bronze glisten of his face dimmed, and it became as rigid and lifeless as dimmed metal. He listened; he did not speak. Then he hung up the telephone and fell into his chair and looked at Edward with blind eyes.

It was that Black Friday, of October, 1929. It was the end for many people, literally. It was the end of an era. Though no one heard it, the bloody curtain of revolution and death was rising all over the world. It rose on that Friday.

Billy said in a dwindled voice, " It's ruin. I've just lost about every cent I have." And in that same abstracted and distant voice, he told Edward.

Edward sat down, his own face dull and blank and shocked into an awful pallor. Sweat broke out on his forehead, on his temples. His lower jaw began to tremble uncontrollably. He swallowed over and over, and choked.

At last, he said, in a far and wondering tone, as if in a dream, "I'm ruined. This is the end. I've lost two million dollars or more, all my reserves."

Suddenly he dropped his head on the table, and fainted.

Chapter Eight

Gregory could feel the big living-room of the pent-house filling up behind him with cocktail hour guests. But he stood before the huge dark window gloomily, his hands in his pockets. Then he saw his reflection in the black glass, lighted by the lamps in the large warm room, and the firelight that twinkled far behind him. He was abominably startled. It was as if Edward were looking at him grimly from the other side of the glass. He knew that he resembled his brother in an extraordinary way, but, as he believed, in a more refined and delicately clear-cut way. Something had betrayed him, momentarily, some deep and secret thing in himself which he had never suspected, to give his reflection the very embodiment of Edward's strength, his crude outlines, his look of still violence and power. Gregory was revolted and outraged—he told himself. Yet, when he turned his head quickly, in half-profile, and saw himself as he was, he was strangely bereft, as if part of him had become cloudy and unstable and pallid, no longer puissant, no longer certain.

His agent, who called himself LeCroix—no Christian name, just LeCroix—came scuttling up to him where he stood before the great window looking out at the mountain-blue façade of New York in the growing twilight. "Still brooding, Greg?" he asked, in his intolerably amused voice, so thin and light. "How many times do I have to tell you that the reviews are raving? Why can't you be happy about them? Look here, I have more of them—just came in this morning."

"The book's been out a month—no, six weeks," said Gregory, sullenly. "How many copies have been sold? One thousand, and just dribbles of re-orders. Reviews? It looks as if the people never read reviews."

Gregory looked at LeCroix. But he did not see him. I'm a failure, he thought. I was never really a writer, in spite of the money I've made on the Thor series. No, I'm wrong. I *am* a writer. But, what's wrong with me? Why don't I make a success, the sort of solid success I want? I do my best; I'm up to my neck in this thing, this social significance and Communism and nothing happens. God damn the stupid masses!

The austere shadow whispered, But, you have no courage. You really have no integrity. And, you lie.

No, said Gregory in desperate answer, I do believe in what I write. Who could be worse than Ed?

He looked at his reflection in the window again, and once more he was bereft. Only Gregory Enger was reflected there, the pseudo-elegant, the shadow of a stronger man, and Gregory thought sharply of his brother, and hated him with increasing hatred. He took my strength from me, he told himself. He chewed me until all my juices were gone.

Gregory turned, with a feeling of profound exhaustion, to the masses of people in the room. There was Thornton Greene over there. A tall and distinguished man, as elegant as David was elegant. A wealthy man. And who had been his father? A sturdy bricklayer who had become a building contractor. The bricklayer may have been physically gritty from his honest mortar. But his son, in spite of the air of sophistication and quiet assurance, had a dusty look.

There were no labour leaders present. They were too gross for this delicate company, who plotted their subjugation as well as the subjugation of their unions to the Universal State, as the *cognoscenti* liked to call it, euphemistically. Gregory thought, Why, any labour leader would gag at them! He hurriedly quelled the heretical thought. What was the matter with him to-night, for God's sake?

You could really write—if you were an honest man, the rebuking shadow whispered to him. What are you doing here?

The bejewelled women, with their fierce, fanatical and cruel eyes, moving about the room in their individual haloes of perfume. The alert men, always watching, watching, and whispering and whispering. The discreet jokes; no robust and human laughter here! "I talked with Senator So-and-So this morning . . . in the palm of my hand—there's this bill coming up. . . . Serge Ovlov . . . wonderful, eloquent! Higher taxes, that's the thing. . . . Lenin . . . he told me about Stalin. . . .

Masses . . . re-education of the people—will not be easy, but it can be done. . . . Did you read what Molotov said yesterday? . . . The professor was thrown out; reactionary . . . a matter of indoctrination of the teachers; resistive. . . . Government ownership of the means of production . . . now Lenin said . . . it was in 1895 . . . the workers, the workers. . . . Machiavelli, of course, was the first. . . . Did you read——?" The conversation was always the same.

Gregory's eye lighted on a young woman who was standing uneasily on the periphery of the massed guests—who drank so little and so cautiously, and endlessly watched each other. A young woman, perhaps in the late twenties or early thirties. She stood out in this exotic and glittering company like an honest sunflower set among rich and poisonous blooms. She had a bold, full face, with bold blue eyes, and a very large red mouth, which she licked uncertainly as she grinned. Her very blonde hair was pulled back from her broad temples and wide cheekbones into a severe chignon, which looked like a gleaming ball of yellow light. She was very tall; there was an open sensuality about her, in spite of the discreet tailored suit of dark blue. But it was the sensuality of a female animal in heat, innocent and avid and unashamed. Her full figure appeared to be about to burst out of the rigid suit; her white silk blouse could hardly restrain the unaffected press of her breasts. Gregory saw her hands, big and rather coarse, and her big feet in the high-heeled slippers. She exuded vitality, earthy and demanding, in spite of her apparent attempts to be inconspicuous. It was evident that she was not one of this company; she was listening, and her impudent eyes had a bewildered cast over them. She was trying to understand, and sometimes her smooth white forehead, a little cowlike, wrinkled conscientiously. She was sipping at her glass with obvious enjoyment. Now, it was empty. She glanced about her for another. The butler passed, and she eagerly seized on another glass, and drank it down in one gulp.

LeCroix, bustling nearby with a lizard's rapid movements, saw Gregory's signal. He came at once. "Not drinking?" he asked. "What's the matter, Greg? You usually——"

"Who's that girl over there, the big, bad-eyed blonde?" asked Gregory. "One of us?"

"Who? Margo? That's Margo Montgomery." LeCroix grinned. "Née Mamie Elkins. From Ohio. A farm girl, now a model, and a good one, too. Earns her keep."

"Her keep?"

"Oh, not that way. A frigid piece of meat. You wouldn't think it, would you? I know—personally, brother! All that . . ." And he continued his description, obscenely. For some reason Gregory winced and felt outraged. "She came with Greene," the agent concluded. "Not that he'll get anywhere with her. And she's not a Lesbian, either. Likes the boys, in a hands-off way. I don't know why Greene brought her; she's as dull as milk. Not a Party member. He's wasting his time, both ways."

"I'd like to meet her," said Gregory.

LeCroix shook his head with coy rebuke. "Not in your present funk. She's the gay type. Likes to laugh a lot. You know, the typical stupid female. Tell her you'll buy her a dinner, and dance with her in some hot night-club, and that there'll be no fumbling in a taxi, and you'll kiss her chastely on the brow at her door, and that's all, and she'll roar off with you. Heard her voice? Big and husky, like herself; it grates on a chap's ears. You wouldn't like it. She wouldn't appreciate your wit—when you're witty, and you're not witty to-night. Look for something more your type."

Gregory studied the girl, and he became aware of a tremendous animal strength in her. He was always mysteriously drawn to strength; it had a fascination for him beyond his understanding. He was aware of this; he thought that it was because he was strong, himself. He was drawn to these people in this room because they were strong, and so he was attracted to them. But LeCroix was thinking, candidly, You want her because you're weak, and you're here, not even knowing what it's all about, because it gives you a feeling of power and fortitude that isn't in you. But what would we do without the weak, anyway, even if you aren't reliable? Darling boy, you'll be the first to be liquidated! After we let you have your personal revenge, of course.

"I like her," said Gregory, stubbornly. "Trot her over."

LeCroix shrugged. "It's your party," he said. "First thing, she'll tell you your tie is all wrong. The model-complex, you know."

He scampered off, and touched Margo on the arm. She

glanced over at Gregory, and what she saw evidently pleased her, after LeCroix's whispered comments. She arched golden brows, and simpered, and smoothed down the coat of her suit, and lifted her head in a model's attitude, and arranged her legs in a model's "stance," as she listened to what was apparently a thumb-sketch of Gregory. Her blue eyes never left him during the recital, and now Gregory could see the shrewdness and calculation in them. He did not like this; he concentrated on the dimples, strong and deep, that waxed and waned in her pink cheeks. Strong, strong, he said to himself. Strong as earth. A sound wench. LeCroix, standing near her, was like a black and lifeless twig stuck beside a flourishing tree.

They came to Gregory together, and LeCroix introduced them. "I've been telling Mamie—I mean, Margo—that you're a famous author, Greg. She's read all your books. She says." He winked at Gregory, with malice.

Gregory and Margo stared at each other, smiling. Then Gregory thought, She really isn't stupid. She's as bright as new tin-foil. Cheap, yes. But aware, too. You could never really fool her. And she'd be loyal to anyone she trusted; you could tell her the damnedest lies, and she'd believe them, and follow you.

"Why do they serve cocktails that taste like witch-hazel?" Margo was asking him, with humour. "Everywhere Thornton takes me it's like this. And they just sip at the drinks, so they wouldn't know they're terrible. Me, I like good bootleg bourbon."

"They're intellectuals," said Gregory. "Intellectuals sometimes go brawny, and drink needled beer to be one of the proletariat boys, but they hate it. And bourbon's too bourgeois." After this witticism he glanced about him uneasily, but they were still cloistered in the draperies.

"I guess my Dad is bourgeois," she said, wondering if she knew just what that was. "He really likes beer, and he swills bourbon, when he can get it. Do you like bourbon, Mr. Enger?"

"I certainly do—Margo," he said. Margo was pleased. Now, she could be intellectual, herself. "Thorn takes me around, and it's always martinis, with seven-eighths bad vermouth and one-eighth smuggled gin. What's your first name? Oh, Gregory. Greg. Thanks. If they don't like to drink, why do they drink anything? They could have Cokes."

"They usually do. At home," said Gregory. Then he was uneasy again. Why had he said "they"? After all, he was one of them.

"I don't get it," said Margo. "I've listened and listened. After all, a girl has to be sophisticated, doesn't she? Dad's a farmer; he makes hardly anything, these days. He thinks I'm living a life of sin. He lives with Mom in Ohio. He won't even write to me. But he sure cashes the cheques I send them."

Gregory thought of the cheques his brother sent him, and he frowned. Margo said hastily, seeing that frown, "Oh, I don't mind! After all——"

"The poor deserve to be supported; the weak must be nurtured by the strong," said Gregory. "That's what they—we—are determined to bring about in this capitalistic country."

"Sure, all these poor people in this Depression," said Margo, heartily. She pondered. "I came here without a cent, and I know what it's like to be hungry. But I got a job as a model almost right off. It's very interesting. And you get clothes at half-price, too. You just have to take care of yourself, and have some—some courage—and you get somewhere. You can't expect other people, who've got their own troubles, to take care of you, if you don't want to work, or think the world owes you a living."

For an instant, Gregory, namelessly smarting, disliked her. Margo, believing that she had made an "intellectual" impression on this famous writer, went on cheerfully. "I just went to ninth grade. That doesn't matter, though, if you've got sense."

She continued, frankly, "I don't get it, do you?" She glanced over her broad shoulder at the others. "All these rich people. They talk and talk of the Common Man and the little fellow. Who do they mean, anyway? You know something, Greg? I bet anything they never give a cent to charity; they're just the kind. And what's this dialect materialism?"

Gregory smiled, wrapped in billows of strength and heartiness. "You mean dialectical materialism."

"Well, it's foreigners who speak that, isn't it?"

Gregory shook his head, amused. "Well, in a way. Most people think it came from Russia, through Karl Marx. But it didn't. It started in western Europe. What're you doing here with Thorn Greene?"

Her eyes, not too large, almost disappeared in a small twinkle between thick eyelashes. Her big red tongue licked at the corners of her mouth. "Oh, he thinks he's making time with me. He isn't, though; he's got a wife. You can't blame him for hoping, anyway, can you? Besides, he thinks I should be educated; get into the 'movement'."

Gregory said, "What movement?"

"Well, all this. He told me the intellectuals can't carry it all; it has to be a Common Man movement, too. I'm common, you see." Again the eyes twinkled shrewdly. "I'm not ritzy like these other dames here; just a farmer's daughter. Dy'ever see Thorn's wife? She's in the movement. A real bitch. Oh, not because she's in the movement. But I've started to wonder if bitches aren't drawn to it—and I mean men-bitches, too—because they're the kind of folks they are. I don't know what it's all about; sometimes it sounds crazy, but then, as I said, I only went to ninth grade."

"And you're not a bitch," said Gregory, gravely.

She laughed with much boisterousness, and she caught the annoyed attention of some of the ladies nearby, who gave her what she would call "a look." "Yes, I am," she said. "But in another kind of way. I take care of myself. You've got to do that in this man's world. There was something our teacher told us in ninth grade: 'The race to the swift, and the battle to the strong.' Now, that's for me. You know how it is." And Margo had a "feeling" that Gregory indeed knew how it was, and understood. "In every litter there's a couple of runts. No good. And there's scrub cattle. You just get rid of them. That is, if you want to raise good stock, without disease. You build up a fine herd that way."

"People aren't litters and scrubs," said Gregory, and he flushed.

Margo shrugged. "Aren't they?" she murmured, archly. The shrug had pulled on the gauzy softness of her blouse, and Gregory could see the smooth roundness of her full breast, which needed no artificial aids of support and enhancement. Suddenly, he wanted to lay his tired cheek against that breast and close his eyes and be at peace. Peace, he thought, forgetting his annoyance. A place to rest, to take stock, to regain or gain courage and strength.

"Look, Margo, let's get out of here," he said suddenly. "Forget Thorn. We'll go somewhere and drink bourbon together. I have an apartment——"

Margo smiled broadly. "No, sir. I don't go to apartments without a crowd. You'll talk real intellectual to me, for maybe a couple of drinks, and then you'll try to take my clothes off." Her eyes sparkled, but her big mouth was severe. "The only fellow who'll ever take my clothes off will be the fellow who's put a wedding ring on my finger, and when I've put the wedding certificate in my bureau drawer. You see, I've been around. My minks, when I get them, are going to be legal." Her face shone with wistful avarice. "Not even for a ten-thousand-dollar mink, and God, how I'd love one of them! It's not that I'm frigid"—and the lascivious bloom was on her lips again—"it's just that Margo's going to take care of Margo, because nobody else will."

Gregory began to warm with pleasure and affection. "All right, Margo, we'll go to a speak-easy I know of. And we'll talk. There are things I'd like to tell you."

She regarded him with responsive pleasure. He was really awfully good looking, in a big, rugged sort of way, though when she saw his profile she was not certain of the ruggedness. And, he was rich, too. Everybody here was rich, except Margo.

The great room hummed with voices. The butler circulated busily with his pale, weak martinis, followed by the maid with her tasteless hors d'œuvres. More and more people were arriving, obviously not "rich." Quiet, tense-faced men in cheap clothing, vehement-eyed women in rough wool dresses and "sensible" shoes, their faces dark and watchful. Gregory knew them. They were the "leaders." They pressed against the ermine, sable and mink scarves, against the fine flannels, of the other people, incongruously. They had brought with them a sense of power, of inexorable hatred and purpose.

"We can get out, now," said Gregory. "We won't be missed."

"Sure," said Margo. "Look, Thorn's talking to those

three women. Besides," she added, practically, "he'll never get a divorce from his wife."

Within fifteen minutes they were cosily harboured in a dimly-lit bar, where there was no nonsense about food or "a band," or other entertainment. After the first copious drink of straight bourbon Margo and Gregory smiled at each other with confidence. The girl's strength embraced Gregory like warm arms, protectively. He ordered another drink, and then another. It was a relief to be with someone who knew nothing of books or music or "the dance," or The State, and to whom intellectual jargon was incomprehensible. The bar became roseate. "Say," said Margo, humorously, "are you ordering a fourth round? Not for me, brother. And you look a little high, yourself. No, not for me. Go ahead for yourself, if you want to." She had been amusing Gregory for nearly an hour now with tales of her adventures as a model, and surprisingly he had enjoyed the anecdotes. His busy writer's mind, fired rather than dulled by alcohol, was already evolving a series of sprightly stories for *The City* about a model's experiences.

Margo went on, "Last week there was this guy from out West, buyer for girdles. I don't do girdles, usually. Evening and cocktail dresses, usually. But this was a big account, biggest in the country. So, there I was . . ." The story was outrageously indecent and full of humour. Gregory, released, roared with joy.

"You're not having another?" asked Margo, suddenly, her eyes still bright with laughter. She tapped Gregory's hand with a big finger. Abruptly, he was horribly sober, and the imperative to corrupt was on him again. He began to talk of Edward. When he reached this state, he invariably talked of his brother, with hatred.

Margo, who had started to yawn with unaffected sleepiness, was suddenly interested. Why, those Green and White supermarkets! Why, Greg was not only a big writer, with millions; he was a brother to the owner of those big stores. And he was darling, too. All at once, Margo loved him, quite sincerely. She had loved before, but the gentlemen sadly, and inevitably, were not rich, and she had parted from them with regret, but with determination. Her mother had once told her, "It's just as easy to love a rich man as a poor one; easier." Her mother was nobody's fool.

Margo had a mind, and now that she loved Gregory, she was all sympathy and attention. A picture of Edward Enger was forming her own opinions, she was carried away on the wave of Gregory's thinning voice as he described his brother. She never doubted his word for an instant, for she loved him. What a bastard that Ed must be! A real bastard. Keeping everybody on his or her knees in front of him; taking the guts out of them. Everybody, of course, except Gregory. Greg was one of those knights, or something, riding against a dragon. A real dragon. He was right in taking Ed's money, all of it he could get. And saving it, too. Margo's eyes gleamed with mingled greed and powerful affection. She nodded her golden head over and over, emphatically.

"So, you see, Margo, it's his kind we're fighting against," said Gregory. "We're going to take their wealth, their fat profits, away from them, and share it. And, why not?"

"Why not?" echoed Margo, bursting with her indignation.

The corruption was off to a fine start. Gregory could not help himself. He must corrupt to blind the terrifying vision of himself.

Four weeks later, on April 10, 1933, Gregory made one of the few independent decisions he had made since he was fifteen. He married Margo in New York. As part of his wedding offerings were several modern books on Marxism, written simply "for the masses." Margo was enthusiastic. (After all, a girl had to keep up with her husband, didn't she?) She never quite related what she was reading to the world of reality. The objective was Edward Enger, the oppressor, the grinder of the faces of the poor, the profiteer. He was, in particular, the grinder of the face of Gregory Enger, whom she loved.

Gregory, with great fear, had had to notify Edward. He wrote, "I'd like you to meet my wife, Margo, who was a model, before anyone else in the family knows. You'll like her. She's strong and decent, though she hasn't much education."

So Edward, gloomy and enraged at this new calamity—a model, for God's sake!—had come to New York at once, and to Gregory's apartment. He had sent a telegram and the newly married pair were waiting for him. But when he entered the apartment he had looked at once, not at his brother, but at Margo, and he thought to himself, with pleased surprise, " Why, she's not bad at all! She's got health and strength, and there's something clean-looking about her. It could be—it just could be—that she'll be good for him."

Margo, herself, was surprised. She had expected, in a vague way, to be confronted by something monstrous in human form, something beetling and fierce and terrible. " Why," she thought, " he looks just like Greg, except he's bigger and stronger looking and older."

They shook hands gravely. It was an uneventful meeting after all. Edward asked the girl blunt questions, which she answered as bluntly, while Gregory winced. It was all right! Edward told himself. A farm girl, a hearty girl, a girl who looked honestly greedy, and not sly.

Gregory had warned his wife. " Don't tell him about—the movement. Keep it all very casual. You don't know what he is!"

So, during the hours Edward spent with Gregory and Margo nothing was said that might annoy Edward, or arouse his suspicions. He went away the next morning considerably satisfied.

It took Gregory almost two weeks to convince his wife that Edward was a menace, and a destroyer. It took him several months to make her hate Edward again.

Chapter Nine

The day after Gertrude Enger's graduation from the Waterford School for Girls she sat alone in the hot June sunlight where her parents used to meet, and talk, and where they never met, or talked, any longer. She rubbed the toe of her slipper in the coarse warm grass, and watched the glitter of the strong green trees, the intent coming and going of honey bees, the light and shadow which ran over the earth as the huge and brilliant white clouds passed and repassed across the face of the golden sun. She heard, without really hearing, the distant splash of the fountain in the molten quiet, the conversation and quarrels of birds, the monotonous clatter of lawnmowers. She thought, There's so many gardeners around here now, more than we ever had. More than we need. The servants' quarters are just jammed with people. That's Daddy's contribution to fighting the Depression. And he won't close a single store; he says that the men need the work, even though we'll probably all end up in the poorhouse if this goes on. Poor Daddy. What did Miss Thomson, who's so sly and mean, anyway, say last winter? "This Depression is the end of the capitalist system in this democracy!" I always thought this country was a Republic; when did it get to be a democracy? Did President Wilson do that? Or, was it really what Daddy says it was, that the words were put into Mr. Wilson's mouth? Daddy says Mr. Wilson was always so suspicious of idealists, though he was sort of an idealist himself.

Gertrude sighed restlessly, feeling strangely oppressed and threatened. She was greatly worried about her father. She had no one to talk over her anxiety with except her mother, who was so apprehensive herself. Robert, her twin, was not one to worry overmuch, for his nature was sweet and amiable, and full of trust in the goodness of man and the power of God. "Oh, Dad will be all right; he's just worried about this Depression," he would say to Gertrude. It was odd that Robert, who had no conception of his father's agonies and torments, and who preferred sports to studies, and who had an absolutely obtuse—according to Gertrude—attitude towards the ominous events occurring all over the world—should be the only effective consoler of his father. He had only to come into the room, smiling and serene, tall and masculine, and Edward would immediately brighten, turn from sombre meditation and solitary misery, and greet his son with a lightening of his voice and a quick eagerness of expression. Was it because, the astute Gertrude asked herself, Robert brought to his father a sense of security, of reassurance, of unshakable health and hope, in a world that was monstrously sick and in a state of savage and hopeless upheaval? Robert did not play particularly well on that fine violin his father had bought for him on his sixteenth birthday, but Edward would sit and listen to him with smiling pleasure, and would compliment him enthusiastically. And Daddy, thought Gertrude, with a rueful smile, really knows music, too!

Gertrude thought of the discussion she had had with Robert only a few days ago, when he had been graduated from the Englebert school. Robert showed no anxiety, but only confidence. "I want to study at a School of Business Administration," he had told his sister. "Oh, I'll go in for a dash of the liberal arts, too, but business is my meat. Besides, Dad can use me a little later. What? My music? Who cares for that? I've outgrown it. I've just been going along with Dad, because he likes to hear me play. But I'll have a talk with him, and get everything settled."

Gertrude said, "But he's settled it all that you'll have four years of liberal arts, and intensive music training right along, and then a concert career after that!"

Robert smiled indulgently. "Don't squint up your face as if I'm about to give the old man a body blow, Gertie. I'll tell him what I really want, and that's all there'll be to it, with no fuss or screams, and he won't mind a bit."

The strange and confusing thing about it, thought Gertrude, is that Robert was probably right, with regard to himself, anyway. Gertrude was another matter. She was already entered at Wellesley, to major in literature. She had talked with her mother about Robert, and Margaret was of the same opinion. "Robert is the least devious person in the whole world," Margaret had said. "He doesn't know what hypocrisy is, or double-dealing, or manœuvring. He is just himself. He has only to ask your father for something, whether your father approves or not, and he gets it. Perhaps it's because he *is* just himself, and is simple and kind and expects others to be the same. You and I, darling, are a little more complex, and we expect trouble. And we usually get it, too!"

"I suppose Daddy will blow up when I tell him I want to enter the University of Syracuse's School of Nursing," Gertrude had said, anxiously. "He won't understand that I'm not really a writer, and don't want to be a writer, and that the very idea frightens and bores me to death. Just because of all those silly poems I used to write, and the stories to amuse myself, when I was a kid! He really took Aunt Sylvia seriously, didn't he?"

"That's because he wanted to take her seriously," Margaret had said, with some anger.

"I never took myself seriously," said Gertrude. "But Dad did." Her olive face and grey eyes, her broad cheekbones and thick dark hair, her straight tall body and resolute movements, made her a young and feminine replica of her father. But Gertrude, unlike Edward, had few illusions about herself or others, and preferred, unlike Edward, to let others pursue their own way. She was, by nature, solitary and reticent and proud, while her brother was gregarious, open in personality, and had a high sense of humour which prohibited too much pride. He was deeply concerned with others, and generous-hearted.

"I never," Gertrude had said to her mother, "deceived myself that I was a writer, but it pleased Daddy to think I was. I thought it would all pass later on. But he's fixed on it. I don't care! I'm going to be a nurse. I want to get into Dad's Clinic."

"You're not exactly the tender and solicitous kind, dear," Margaret had said, with one of the smiles which were becoming rarer and rarer with her. "So, why the nursing fever?"

"Oh, I don't expect to spend my life bending lovingly over beds and emptying bed pans," Gertrude replied. "I'm interested in the scientific side. I want to do research. And nothing, and nobody, not even Daddy, is going to stop me. I want to get off Dad's neck. I'm not a parasite." Her face shone with sudden strong indignation. "Why doesn't Dad throw them all out, all the uncles and aunts? Why, they're eating him alive, and in these days, too!"

Margaret did not reply, and Gertrude had continued, "I love Daddy, I love him dearly. But he's not going to manage my life."

Margaret said, "You and Robert are good children. You are the only good things in this house. You are the only good things that ever happened to your father. He'll realise that, one of these days. He doesn't know, yet, that to give anybody everything that person thinks he wants, is to do him the worst injury in the world."

Gertrude burst out, "I hate my aunts and uncles, yes, I hate them! For what they are doing to Daddy."

"And I do, too," said Margaret, quietly. "Yes, and I do, too."

"I love Daddy too much to give him power over me," Gertrude said.

Margaret was stunned and outraged. "What do you mean by 'power'? Your father never wanted power over anybody! What a terrible thing to say, Gertrude! He has never wanted to do anything but help——"

"They're the same thing, mostly," said Gertrude. "But,

it's very hard to explain. You help people, when they should be helping themselves, and so you acquire power over them because they are weaker, and so they hate you. For their own weakness in putting themselves under your domination. And, in turn, you despise them for their weakness, and you're uncomfortable, if you're a decent person like Daddy, because you have that power over them. I think all help, all charity, should be absolutely anonymous. Then the weak could develop pride, and the strong wouldn't be humiliated by having to exert power they don't want—if they're decent people."

" I simply don't know what you're talking about, Gertrude! All this talk of power."

You can't see, Mother, because you can't take an objective view of Daddy and all the aunts and uncles, thought Gertrude, hopelessly.

As she sat under the trees now her sense of foreboding and distress increased. She knew the source of them clearly. Unlike her father, she had a stern sense of reality in personal and emotional matters, and understood that though he derided mysticism he was thoroughly saturated with it. But Daddy is really an artist, with an artist's temperament, she thought, in spite of his marvellous business instinct. I just see things levelly, and I don't know whether or not that is so wonderful either. Grandma's like me ; that's why we have so much in common. And all she's gotten out of life is a philosophy of endurance, but for what purpose I don't know. Life is surely something more than an endurance test ; if it isn't, then it's a barren and fruitless thing. Yet, Grandma doesn't seem crushed, as Daddy does, Daddy who's always looking for a meaning to things, even if he doesn't know he's looking.

And yet, and yet, she thought, if you stop looking for a mystical or religious meaning to life, then you live in a world of blacks and greys and whites, without colour. You live in a world of despair and violence ; a cold hell without values or escape or significance. I think Daddy has one foot in the world of meaning, and one foot in hell. I wish I could help him, as Robert does ; Robert who cheerfully believes everything is very simple and kind and exciting.

" Aha," said someone, and Gertrude started. " We sit and dream about the graduation party Saturday night, before we go off to get educated."

"Oh, it's you," said Gertrude, coldly, looking up to see her cousin, André. "Go away, child. I'm busy."

André, with an indulgent and debonair wave of his hand, sat down beside her. She drew to the edge of the bench. Then slipped forward, as if about to rise. André said, "You're only a couple of months or so older than I am, and you're terribly young—child. Chronologically a little older; mentally a lot my junior. You're always worrying about people, and trying to solve things about them, in your own mind. I just accept them as amusing spectacles. They have a right to be idiotic, if they want to, and it's impudent of you to try to change them."

Gertrude's smooth olive face flushed, and André smiled at her approvingly. "You're really a very handsome girl, Gertrude. Not pretty. Handsome. You'll always be handsome, when only pretty girls have become dumpy and frowsy."

Gertrude tried to retain her annoyance, but she could not help smiling. She had no aversion for André, though she was sometimes afraid of his worldliness, and what her father referred to as "spiritual depravity." She disliked his detached objectivity; mankind was involved in itself, and its own fate and its obscure reason for being. She did not believe that anyone was justified in standing apart, as at a theatre, and watching the "antics" of others with pleasure and mercilessness and cynicism, as André and his mother did. Such an attitude implied inhumanity and heartlessness and a kind of outlook which was frightening. Yes, it was truly depraved.

She studied André with cold sternness, which hid her fear, not of him, but of his kind of soul and philosophy. He had, at almost eighteen, grown to quite an impressive stature, leaving his little mother far behind and taking on the height of his father. But his look of "foreignness" had increased. His black eyes still had that peculiar shine of his childhood, the lids stained with "gipsy" brown; his features were delicate, yet strong, and full of mature mischief. His movements, to Gertrude, were too quick, too alien in gesture and controlled vehemence. In spite of this, however, he was not emotional in the sense that Gertrude understood emotion. There was a knowingness about him, a disturbing sense of the absurd, and Gertrude found very few things absurd about the predicament of humanity. Her humour was the abstract kind; his was personal, and without pity. Yet, she enjoyed his company much of the time. He could frighten her, but he could sometimes give her inner vision clarity, and he could frequently inspire her and make her laugh.

She said, her hands still on the bench in the attitude of rising, "Why can't you dress for the country, the way everybody else does? Blazer, or something? You always look as if you're going to a funeral or about to attend a formal soirée." But she thought, with charity, that he had something of Uncle David's slim elegance about him, something of David's impeccable air of poise and patrician surety. André was also ingratiating, and had considerable charm. It's the French in him, Gertrude thought. They're calculating in even the smallest things. But then, he's been away in European schools ever since he was twelve, and it's hard to think of him as an American, with American ways. She tried to dislike him, very strongly, and never succeeded. Robert would sometimes say to her, affectionately, "Oh, let him alone. He has as much a right to be what he is as you have, Sis. Besides, he isn't complicated at all, though you think he is." But then, nothing was ever complicated for Robert.

"Why should I dress in the uniform of suburbia?" asked André. "I'm a gentleman, not a fake countryman, and I don't play golf, stupid game, and I like wine better than bootleg whisky, and I prefer conversation to batting a tennis ball around, and I like music more than dirty stories which don't have any subtlety. Why do Americans lack subtlety?"

"You're an American, yourself," said Gertrude. "And you're not even eighteen yet, and you're giving yourself airs."

"Have a cigarette," said André, as an adult would offer a child a lollipop.

He opened a gold case, and Gertrude took a cigarette with reluctance. He lit it for her gracefully, and put one in his own mouth. He stared before him for a moment or two, the lighter in his hand, and Gertrude was uncomfortable again at the maturity of his profile and the unyouthful quirk of his lips. "I was never a child," he said, as if speaking to himself humorously. "And, to a great extent, neither were you, Grandmother. That's why I'm in love with you; of course, we'll get married in a few years, after you've completed that nursing course, and I'm finished at the Sorbonne."

Gertrude was mortified, as always, that she frequently and impulsively confided in André, as she never confided in anyone else, even her mother or Robert. She did not know why she gave André her deepest confidences, except that in some confused way she understood he would never betray her, in spite of his artfulness, his lack of conscience, and his perverted view of men and women, and his amused derision of the world.

She said, with some heat, " Don't be stupid. When I marry, if ever, it'll be to someone as unlike you as possible—child. And someone a lot older. I don't intend to be a nursemaid to a brat. Or to raise a husband for myself. Seventeen!"

" How you Americans use age as a yardstick," said André, smiling now. " A man can have twice as much verve and zest for living at fifty as he had at twenty, but he's old, in the American opinion. He can be healthier, more alive, even gayer. But he's old. And at twenty, a man can be dull and spiritless and sluggish and colourless, but he's young, by God! The calendar is the measure of all things. Why, I know American girls in their teens who are actually middle-aged and lightless and without imagination and appetites, and about as sensual as a bowl of oatmeal, and just about as exhilarating. And I know European women, and some American ones, too, who are vivid and charming and diverting at forty, fifty, sixty. Even older." He shook his head at Gertrude. " Oh, come on. You know better, even if you pretend not to. And I like the nursing idea. It'll be helpful, when we have our children, though of course we'll have nursemaids for the little horrors."

" On whose money?" asked Gertrude, trying for light contempt and adulthood.

André waved his hand, and a wisp of his cigarette smoke brightened in the sunlight. " Partly on yours, my dear. After all, as we French say, a girl must have a *dot*. And partly on mine ; my father isn't exactly poor."

Gertrude's face turned harsh and dark. " He hasn't anything but what my father—my father!—gives him! And you——"

André gazed at her with a secret expression. He shrugged. He knew all about Ralph, his father, not that Ralph had ever confided in him. He had simply and cynically investigated his father two years ago, as he had investigated the others, too. It was his opinion that everyone could be a fruitful source of investigation ; people always hid things, he had observed. What had been mere investigation, for the sole purpose of investigating, had become an adventure that had been most fruitful and enlightening. André could now name almost every bridge in America and in Europe which his father had designed, and for which he had been richly paid. Any clever person, he had discovered, could acquire the the knack of opening a drawer or locked bureau or desk, and could search without leaving evidence of the search behind.

"You forget I'm really a writer, unlike Uncle Greg," he said now. "I expect to make a lot of money at it. I know what people like to read, and I can write well in three languages, and I understand men and women."

"Oh, and so you, at seventeen, have found out how to write infallible best-sellers?" said Gertrude, with hard ridicule.

"I wish you wouldn't keep repeating that I'm seventeen," said André, distastefully. "What a *non sequitur*. I'm not a child prodigy, but I'm also not a child, either, and, as I've said to you often, I never was. Yes, I think I know how to write best-sellers. Dickens and Thackeray and Tolstoy—unlikely company though they are together—had the secret, even if they didn't know they had it. It's a matter of writing about the world as it is, and people as they are. Reality, in other words, not some private notion of reality, or the world as some writers think it ought to be. For instance, did you read that imbecile latest from the pen of Uncle Greg? *Morning Before the Wind?* All about a 'sensitive' child born in the slums. Uncle Greg never saw a slum in his life; I did; all over Europe, and in New York and other American cities, too. And children are about as sensitive as concrete; murderous little realists, red in tooth and claw. How many copies did he sell? About five thousand, I think."

Gertrude was slightly appeased. She remembered her father's irate comments on the book. She had also read it, and she had wondered where her uncle had gotten his odd ideas, and where he had found such a child about whom he had written. Uncle Greg could write, but it was a sterile and twisted writing, with no base of actuality.

"Besides, he's a Communist," said André, casually.

"Uncle Greg a Communist!" cried Gertrude, aghast, thinking of her father. "I don't believe it!"

"Oh, I don't mean he goes around brandishing a card, or anything like that," said André. "I only mean he's taken on the fashionable gloss of it. Or the fashionable bloodstains, synthetic ones. Everything about him is synthetic, like his books. The only thing he has in common with the real Communists, the Russian ones, is an urge to violence and hatred, and even then it's synthetic."

Gertrude forgot that André was a "child." She listened to him intensely, her grey eyes welling with distressed thoughts, just as the sunlight ebbed and flowed as the clouds crossed the bright sky. When André put one of his hands easily over hers she was vaguely conscious of a strange deep thrill in her body, but only vaguely. She was too engrossed in what he was saying.

"I'm not an ardent anti-Communist," André said. "I just prefer things as they are, and commonsense, and reality, and I hate people who delude themselves. I don't bleed for the plight of the Russian people, under Communism. People generally deserve their government, though that isn't very original." He opened his cigarette case. "Have a cigarette."

"You smoke too much," said Gertrude, abstractedly. For some reason there was a sense of relief in her. André's realism touched her own, strongly.

"And now," said André lightly, squeezing her fingers, "tell me what you were brooding about when I found you here."

"I was thinking about my father," said Gertrude, involuntarily.

André gave her a glance of sympathy, and he was suddenly grave. He smoked a moment without speaking, and Gertrude, watching him and seeing the thoughtful glint of his narrowed eyes, wondered how she had missed, before, the resemblance between the youth and her Uncle David. "Yes," said André. "Poor Uncle Ed. I often wonder why he doesn't kick all of us out, and then I don't wonder."

"What do you mean?" asked Gertrude, uneasily. André glanced at her again, and her colour rose. So, he was the only one who understood or wanted to understand. Tears smarted along her eyelids and she blinked and averted her head. For the first time she thought, "If he wasn't so young!"

"There isn't one, and I'm including my father, too, who's worth a cent of his money, or one of his thoughts," said André. "Except, perhaps, Uncle Dave. I'm not excluding myself, either, from the blood-sucking gang of us. There's a lot I know; but I'm not a tale-bearer. . . . Look at us!

Uncles, aunts, children, and Grandma. But no one can rid Uncle Ed of us, except Uncle Ed——"

"I know," said Gertrude, in a low and faltering voice.

André took her hand again. "At least, dear," he said, kindly, "I won't be a drag on him much longer, through my father. And you've forgotten something: I have two hundred thousand dollars in my own name, nicely gathering dividends from good sound investments, thanks to Mama. So, we'll have money, besides your *dot*."

Gertrude tried to pull her hand away from his, but he laughed at her and held it more tightly. "You're such a fool, just a precocious kid," she said, and was angered at him, unreasonably, for his youth. A lump swelled in her throat and she wanted to cry. All at once he released her hand, and stared at the distant glittering grass as if he had forgotten her.

I don't know why I sit here and listen to his nonsense! thought Gertrude, wildly. I never liked him; he was a terrible child. He was a tease, and sly—we always fought. . . . He never liked me, no, he never liked me! He said I was stupid, and Robert, too. He's only teasing me now, with his ridiculous talk of marrying me.

A bee, all iridescence and twinkling life, lighted on André's hand. He lifted that hand slowly and gently, and said, "'Fearfully and wonderfully made.'"

Gertrude was astonished at the tenderness in his voice, the sincere love and admiration, which were without his customary raillery and derision. She watched as André turned and twisted his head, the better to see the little creature which contentedly stroked its wings and stretched its minute legs as though it were sitting on a leaf and were utterly at ease.

"Look at it," said André. "How innocent it is. How good it is. And how beautiful."

The bee flickered its wings, lifted them and blew away like a living jewel. André watched it go in bemusement.

"You mean," said Gertrude, uncertainly, "that it isn't like people, don't you?"

"Yes, of course," he said, absently.

The lump was in Gertrude's throat again. He turned to her and smiled. "You're like that bee, dear. Even when you were a gawky and prickly little girl. Innocent and good, but not as people think of innocence and goodness. And you had a sting, too."

He leaned towards her and kissed her mouth without touching her otherwise, and she sat there, shocked by her own confused passion of sweetness mingled with revolt. This was a man's kiss, not the awkward kiss of a boy. She could see the closeness of his eyes now, wide and shining and unfathomable, and her heart jumped. The thick black lashes were so near her own that they almost touched.

Then she was pushing him from her violently, and in that same movement she rose from the bench and ran away. He watched her go, laughing a little to himself. Her black, rather long hair, as straight as an Indian's, but glimmering, floated behind her, drifted over her wide shoulders, touched her thin broad back which was covered with the light-grey silk of her dress. She ran as swiftly and as compactly as a boy, not throwing out her legs in a womanish way, and her waist was strongly slender. "Dear child," said André, aloud, and he spoke in the voice he had used to the bee.

Gertrude rushed into the house, high colour staining her dark cheeks, her grey eyes wide and dilated. Compared with the brightness outside, the interior was cold and dim, like a prison, and Gertrude halted.

It was all spoiled; it was all ruined. The wild sweetness was gone, and the breathless fear, and the queer, surging delight, and the revulsion, which was itself a delight. Gertrude felt flat and drained and lonely. Why had she wanted to think, and to be alone? A boy of seventeen had kissed her; her own cousin, the wicked André, had kissed her, she who had been kissed by young men at dances! He had only been mocking her, this schoolboy home from Paris for the summer. That child! She wanted to cry in her humiliation and the loss and pain.

Upstairs, everything was still and untenanted. It was evident that no one was at home, except Maria, sitting quietly in her room and endlessly knitting. On an impulse, Gertrude went to her grandmother's door and knocked, then entered. Yes, there sat Maria in the widow's black she wore summer and winter, majestic as always, her hair a thick drift of snow around the old face. But the eyes were wise, remote and patient. She smiled at Gertrude with no question in the smile, for Maria no longer questioned anything, though she understood at once that her favourite grandchild was in some trouble. Maria knew many things, though she did not often descend from her room these days, as her heart was labouring and burdened with her mighty flesh. She continued to knit now, rocking slowly in her chair near the window. In all these years she had refused to let her suite be redecorated; the once bright chintz had faded, the once burnished rug had dimmed.

Gertrude closed the door behind her, then leaned against it, looking at her grandmother silently. And Maria waited, her needles clicking. Gertrude knew that it was a sweater for her, a lustrous white sweater to be used at college. For some reason she was touched at the thought, and she thought how terrible it must be to be old and to have nothing left in life but one's thoughts and a busyness of the hands. She was suddenly rebellious. There must be something more to life than this, this meaninglessness, this inevitable dull end. And she was frightened.

"I—I do wish you wouldn't work so hard. For me," said Gertrude, still pressed against the door as if repelling something that threatened her. "It's so nice outside; Grandma, you should be sitting on the terrace."

Maria knitted, counted a few stitches, and a small smile hovered over the pouches around her lips. "Is that what you came to tell me, my child?" she asked.

But, I never really tell anyone anything, not even Mother, not even Robert, or Daddy, thought Gertrude. Just André. And her eyes smarted again, and she was again bereft and angry. She said, "I didn't want to tell you anything, really, Grandma."

"No?" said Maria. But everyone had something to tell, if nothing to say. She glanced up at Gertrude, and saw the girl's dark pallor, the grey suffering of her eyes, the stern young lips that quivered at the corners. It was, certainly, something of importance; at that age, it was, certainly, love or infatuation or the pure misery of discovering that the world was neither happy nor peaceful, neither safe nor sure. Maria said, "You are so like your father, *liebchen*."

Gertrude stood against the door, the whiteness of which outlined her feminine strength and slenderness and height, the width of her shoulders, the young leanness of her body. Her black hair was an almost Egyptian fall about her broad cheekbones, her stern forehead, her vulnerable temples.

"Yes, so like him," said Maria, in a strange and weary

voice. She said, in German, "There is a fatefulness about life, an inevitability. One is fixed in a mould even before birth. But circumstance can modify that mould, or the mercy of God. I pray that it will be so for you, little one."

"No one will ever hurt me," said Gertrude, and her voice shook. "I'm not like Daddy, in that, Grandma. I won't let myself be hurt."

Maria sighed. "And who has hurt you, Gertrude? To-day, perhaps?"

Gertrude caught her lower lip between her teeth. Grandma saw too much; that was the penalty, or the reward, for becoming old, a terrible and barren penalty, or reward. It was coin which bought nothing; it was coin given for memory.

"You do not want to tell me?" asked Maria, and counted another row of stitches.

"There's nothing to tell," said Gertrude, coldly.

"Ah," said Maria, and let her knitting drop. She fixed her eyes penetratingly on Gertrude. "You are very like your father. If he had a personal crest it would not be inscribed 'Mollissima fandi tempora.' It would also not be your crest, my child. He never found a favourable time for speaking."

"No one ever listened to him, except Mother!" Gertrude burst out, furiously.

Maria shook her head, but did not speak. Gertrude opened the door. She looked at her grandmother, but Maria seemed intent on her knitting again. "I'm sorry I bothered you," said Gertrude, formally.

She went out and closed the door with firmness, though her eyes were filled with wretched tears. "The most favourable time for speaking!" But she never really spoke, with all her heart, to anyone except to André, whom she hated! Life was no longer sane and clear to her. He had ruined it all.

"My boy, you're unrealistic, to use the new jargon," said William, earnestly. "The bleeding heart and the quivering soul are all very well—when a chap can afford it, though some of the rainbow-eyes in Washington just now say that some of us must afford it whether we can or not. But you're paying your hundreds of fellows in the shops everywhere what you paid them in the late twenties. Rot. Food's down, every blasted thing is down, rents, clothes, boots. It's like giving them a forty per cent raise in the wages. A dollar's worth more than one hundred cents, this day; it was worth fifty-two cents before the Crash. It buys more than twice as much. So, down must go the wages, or out we go, ourselves.

"Now, listen to me. Sure, and men must eat and food must be bought, either on the dole or wages. But the lass with the market basket is buying less, and she's buying inferior, and staples. Not two chickens in the pot every day; a chicken once a month. Not tinned, wined peaches from Argentine, but potatoes. Not a rib roast, but minced meat. Not Norwegian sardines in olive oil, but tinned salmon. Prohibition knocked our wine cellars into lumber and wee stones; that was a blow. We survived it. We closed two of the Chauncey shops only last week. The clerks in the cutaways stand idle and polish their finger-nails. The lads and lassies in the Green and White Stores yawn over the canned soup and the flour bins. But each and every week they carry home their quid, and it's merry they are. At your expense. And our outlets have cut down on our stock, and some have eliminated it entirely.

"I'm not a man to call another a fool. But the wages must come down to the national base; at least a third of the employees must go. Or we go into bankruptcy, and thank the Saints there's no debtors' prisons any longer."

Edward, in his office, answered him with rage, "And, if we let a third go, what'll they do, in this Depression?"

William shrugged, "I swear, and you should be in Washington, helping the President with his dreamer-lads! And did I not tell you, old boy, they are swarming there, with their little hands red with revolution and their little black hearts full of Communism? And their little evil souls full of hate? No matter. We'll face them in the future, and may the good God give us ropes and guns in time.

"And what'll our employees do when we give them the sack? You've got a plan that gives them two months' pay; they've tucked away the cash well in all these years, not having to fork out for the doctors and hospital and insurance, which was at your expense. Out of your own pocket. The thrifty souls have the quid in the banks; let them live on it, or find another job. Not easy. But, by all that's holy, what is? And are you the anointed who must roll yourself into a stroke over them? Did they bleed for you, in their blessed strikes, when you were paying them far above what their brothers and sisters were getting in other shops? They did not. You're not an Atlas." And William bent his shoulders ruggedly, panted, and lifted shaking arms over his head.

He pointed at Edward. "Look at you! Old before your time, white hair and you only forty-four. Lines in your face like erosions. Why, damn it, you can't even drink to keep yourself from going mad! Look at your colour; lead with a grey shine on it. Did you bring on this Depression? Did you drag America into that accursed war in chains? Did you smash Europe from end to end? No. But you would wear the hair-shirt, or give it away to a chap who wore silk shirts when you wore cotton shirts, and you the master.

"A mortgage on the house, and the poor wife with the white face and the loving heart, signing away with you what you worked for. What is that phrase of yours? All the days of your life. I've said enough. America blew a big wind into Europe; now the whirlwind's on her. Listened to the liars and the murderers, that she did. Jumped in with both big feet. If she hadn't done that England and Germany would have signed a cosy negotiated peace, and little bits of real estate would have changed hands, and there'd have been a drop or two between friends, and back to work racing each other for profits, and everything forgotten, and love and kisses. But America must be the referee, only a referee with boxing gloves loaded with nuggets of iron, and slugging away at the enemy that'd been chosen for her back in 1905. And knocking friends out too, in the wild way. Now the beggars are on their backs, thanks to America, and America's plopped down beside them. It'll not please you, lad with the shattered face, but your country's been a blunderbuss to the world, and it's not the end that's in sight yet. If she'd kept her bally nose out of Europe, listening to George Washington instead of her bleeding Socialist traitors, there'd be no Hitler and Stalin now, and God knows where they'll lead us to. War, no doubt. It's making a grimace you are. But I've warned you."

Hiss small stature had diminished even more. His foxlike face was still alert and vigorous, the hazel eyes still brilliant and quick, but his sandy hair had blanched and his freckles stood out on parched skin like old paper. " I'm not a frolicsome lad any longer; I'm approaching sixty. Am I to stand by and see you die of your folly? Like an undertaker waiting for the corpse, and it's a corpse you'll be before long, I'm thinking."

" I've paid back most of the one hundred thousand dollars you lent me, damn you," said Edward, savagely, but the old power of his voice had weakened.

" And, am I asking for the rest of the twenty thousand? I am not. I took no interest. I wanted to give you the blasted money. 'Take it,' I said, 'and forget you ever took it.' It's there for you still. Pay off your mortgage with it; count it as a gift.

" And now that we're at it, boot your family out of your house, all the leeches battening on you. Ah, no, and you'd not be doing that, like a sensible man instead of a Hamlet. That would lower your self-esteem; it's a castle you have, and serfs—fat serfs who live better than the joyless baron."

Edward's ghastly face swelled with turgid colour. " I'm not asking your advice," he said, and he struck the desk with the flat of his hand.

William sighed. " No, but I've given it. The advice of a friend. I'll not be leaving until you tell me you're to be sensible. And if it's not sensible, I'll be leaving you for ever. That's my ultimatum."

He stood up. He leaned his hands and arms, stiff and straight on Edward's desk. " And will you be taking my advice, or seeing the last dust of me?"

Edward tried to smile, and the attempt was agonising. " Where will you go?"

" I'll be off to a small cosy island, somewhere, with my cash, and I'll buy palm trees and live on the fat of the land, with only the sea to watch and the lassies dancing, and a thatch roof over my head. Mark my words. There'll be thousands like me, wishing they'd done it, in the years to come."

" You can't withdraw from the world—don't be an idiot."

" That I can. A man's a right to a little peace in his old age, and there's still enough life in me to cavort and eat the breadfruit that falls into my hand. Do I want to live in a world that's spewed up a Hitler and a Stalin—with the fine braw help of America—when I can pull up my braces and run for it? I do not. Only one thing will keep me: you being sensible."

Edward lighted a cigarette; his hand trembled violently.

William said, " And there's another thing, though I'm not a man that asks for gratitude. The traitors were out for your blood, with your Committee, and your German name, and your support of the newspapers against war—though what else could you have done, and been a man and an American? It should be a consolation to you, that you fought for your country in your own way. And it was only the mercy of God that kept you alive. Look what they did to poor Hans Bohn, and others like him. Broke his office windows; called out his men, who left him with the sound of trumpets. Shut up his papers; crashed him down with boycotts. And he died of it, and others died of it with him. But you had better friends. You had George Enreich; you had me; you had a dozen others. We kept the wolves from your throat."

Edward stared at him blankly. The cigarette dropped limply from his fingers. William nodded dolorously. " Did you lose money? Were you hung in effigy? No. Was that a miracle? Only the miracle of having friends."

" George Enreich?" Edward's voice was hoarse and muffled; he coughed to get his breath.

" Sure, and it's a little Boy Blue you are. It cost him half a million dollars to drag you out of the teeth of the dragons. But a dragon likes cash. They all like cash. They'd even become solid citizens, if they got their price, and would forget about the brave new world of Communism and Russia. Excepting the rich laddies rolling in it, who want power. You'll not be telling Georgie. It's his secret, among others."

Edward leaned back in his chair, and a dark film covered his eyes. He clasped his hands tightly together on his desk, and he looked old and sick and broken. William looked at him compassionately. " Buck up," he said. " Issue the orders. One third of the yawners out of the shops, poor devils. Give me your word."

" All right," said Edward, and he coughed again, rackingly, and the old familiar anguish squeezed his heart.

William put his hand on Edward's shoulder, strongly. " And you'll boot out the parasites in your house?"

" No," said Edward. " It's their home, as well as mine. I

built it for them. I'll—manage to keep up the Clinic; it's needed now more than ever, with decent people unable to pay regular medical fees. I can't throw my family out. What would they do?"

George Enreich, sitting in his grey-green and gloomy garden, with his two canes beside him, watched Edward crossing the dank and mossy grass towards him. They had seen each other, and only casually, once or twice during the past years, and then at the homes of mutual friends. George thought now, as he sat almost immobilised in the painful cage of his arthritic prison, My Eddie is a sick, old and tormented man, and no man can deliver him except God—in Whom I do not believe, naturally—and himself.

Edward was near him now, and he laboriously held out his swollen left hand, which was the least affected, and said, "My Eddie. I am glad you are visiting me. I have been waiting a long time." Edward was shocked, in spite of his fixed smile, at the change in his old friend. George had shrunken; his once red hair was white and thin, though still bristling; his bulk had melted under the onslaught of his devouring disease. Only his greenish eyes, strenuous and alert, remained in their original power and strength.

Edward said, and was surprised and almost stunned at his own words, "But I've never been away." He sat down near George on a rattan chair. He could smell the damp mustiness of the crowding trees and shrubs, the jungle-like effluvia of too much vegetation. Not even insects clamoured here; birds made no passage through the darkened air; there was no fragrance of flowers or the lightness of blossoms. The intensely blue sky shone in fragments through branches of enveloping trees, like light seen at the bottom of a huge green cave.

The two old friends had nothing to say to each other, few questions to ask. Everything was known to them, or too little, or too much. George said, and his voice was dulled by long pain, and as if they had met only yesterday, "You will have a drink with me." His butler came across the green and pallid shadows of the garden with a tray, and prepared the whisky and soda. "It is forbidden me," said George. "And also my cigars. The doctors would take from me the last consolations I have, and what is life without consolations?"

They drank together in silence, not peering inquisitively at each other, but each thinking his own wretched or depressed thoughts. In this way they communicated, asking and answering questions. Do you remember when I was young, and had hope? Edward asked George in his mind. And do you see, now, what it has come to? But I was young once, and had hope, too, George replied silently. And this is the end to which we are all destined. Unless—and I do not know what it is that makes the end less terrible, but surely there is an answer. In which, of course, I do not believe.

Their eyes met in a quick encounter of mutual commiseration. Edward said, " It's a hot day, but it's very cool here. Do you think the dampness is good for you?"

" Nothing is good for me, any longer," said George, and smiled. " But, should I complain? I have had an interesting life, my Eddie. I have money and I have power, and these I have had for a long time. I have eaten and drunk and made love, and there is not a pleasure I have not sampled. There is no spot on earth which I have not visited. I have worn the best, and I have seen the best. Where there has been the most glorious music, there I have been. Where there has been the highest laughter, there I have been. There is no luxury that I have not known. And yet, it comes to this, in this chair, as if I had known nothing and experienced nothing. And do not tell me that memories are consolations. They are not. They are destroyers."

He put a cigar in his mouth and Edward stood up and lit it for him. The younger man did not immediately sit down again. He stood near his old friend and regarded him with sorrowful sympathy. George smoked, however, in long, serene enjoyment, looking across the garden. He said, " I have seen the photographs in the newspapers of your daughter's début. I regret that I could not be present." He puffed again, as Edward remained near him. " It is a woman, rather than a maiden."

Edward's worn face brightened with pleasure. " Gertrude isn't my favourite child, but I love her very much. Everybody says she's very much like me, not only in looks but in character. I hope not! I've messed up my life a lit——"

" And who has not?" asked George, as if in surprise at Edward's words. " And shall your children escape?"

Edward's sick heart skipped a beat in anxiety. " I'm doing

my best. You've seen my son, Robert. He has a sunny disposition; nothing bothers him; he accepts everything, and likes everything."

George nodded slowly. And so, he thought, the boy will go through all his life and see nothing. Is that good or evil? Would I have preferred to live in a blind brightness, or to have seen? I am sorry for that boy. He said, "But Gertrude is not like that. And so, she will suffer much. She will also know more."

Edward again felt that sharp skip of anxiety. "Is it necessary to suffer to know? Robert's no fool; he isn't a smiling idiot. He accepts life."

And so does a tree or a bird, thought George. But that does not make them men. Acceptance is a passive thing. To struggle is to be vital. Never to accept without a question; never to conform; never to adjust, when adjustment would smother. A man is a man, and acceptance is the death of a man.

Edward sat down again. And again, there was a long silence between the two, a long exchange. Finally, in a far voice, without an accent, as if speaking only to himself, Edward said, "What have I accomplished? What is the meaning of my life?"

George looked at him quickly, and with vividness. So, he thought.

"What is the meaning of anyone's life?" he asked. "When I was a child the priest in Prussia told me. I cannot remember. Or it was a foolish telling, which I rejected."

"There should be a meaning," said Edward. And suddenly the old black terror was on him again, a terror without a name. Here were memories hovering liks clouds on the antipodes of his soul, but he could not see them. His throat tightened and his chest constricted, and he moved in his chair as if preparing for flight. "If I could just remember—something," he said, almost inaudibly.

"Man will never find any meaning in himself," said George. He closed his eyes in weariness. "But where else he will find it I do not know, though once I seemed to know. Does a tree or a flower or a dog ask for a meaning to its life? I am not certain that it does not. We are too anthropocentric. But let us talk of less weighty things. How is our friend, Billy Russell, with the bands and the cavorting?"

Edward frowned. " It's a funny thing. Even right after the beginning of the Depression his bands, and himself, were always in constant demand. He never had to worry about engagements. He was the most popular band leader in the country. And then he attended the Republican Convention in 1932, and spoke for Mr. Hoover. Since then, and it's probably only a coincidence, his engagements get suddenly cancelled, or he doesn't get them at all."

" It is not a coincidence," said George, slowly and emphatically. " You will see, my Eddie. You have had no trouble, yourself?"

Edward frowned more darkly. " Yes. But probably only a coincidence, too. The Bureau of Internal Revenue is suddenly and almost exclusively interested in my business. They hound my offices in New York for weeks at a time, and send out assessments which are frivolous. We always beat them, but it stops work, and my lawyers are busy, expensively busy. Good God, George! I'm a Democrat, myself; I support the Democratic Party. I supposed Roosevelt——"

" It is not a matter of politics, Eddie. Your work to preserve America and her Constitution has not escaped the notice of our enemies. The evil days are on us, and when I contemplate them I am glad that I am old and have only a little longer to live."

" I believe in the American people," protested Edward.

George laughed faintly. " I believe in nothing. When the masters call the tune the American people will dance to it, in revolution and blood, or in war and blood. The Pied Piper of Hamelin never played a more seductive tune leading to oblivion and death."

" We can play another tune——"

" Ah, but it will not be so attractive. It will not promise hatred and revenge and war and the satisfaction of greed, and power, and murder. Do you think men are civilised? No, it was only yesterday when they descended from the trees. The way to civilisation is long and bloody and full of pain, and the journey has just begun."

The fragments of a shining sky above the topmost trees was suddenly darkened by a passing cloud, and the garden plunged into ghostly dimness. Edward stood up. " I'm going to hope for the best, and still work for it," he said, glancing at his watch. George smiled again and said nothing. Edward looked at him, and their eyes held.

"I'll come again. Soon," he said, and took George's hand.

George watched him go, then closed his eyes. He said to himself, I do not believe in You, naturally. But You are everywhere, and there is nothing that escapes You. And so, I must ask You now: Give my young friend peace, even if he must die to attain it. Deliver him from evil. I do not believe in You, but I believe in Lucifer.

At sunset, the warm June day suddenly darkened, the west swam in dulled gold, and shadow-based clouds strode into the sky. All at once thin veins of brilliant fire divided the heavens and the sound of thunder rolled over the earth. Edward Enger barely reached the great doors of his mansion when the storm crashed about him. There was an oppressive pressure in the air, and his labouring heart was further constricted. He passed through the hall, which seemed hollow and empty to him, and went upstairs to his suite. Margaret had shut the windows; the house was pervaded with heat and dimness; the rain rushed against the glass, and glared as lightning struck it.

When Edward entered Margaret got up and went to him and kissed him, after her usual long and searching look of anxiety and appraisal. She said, in the careful voice of a worrying wife, "How are you, darling?"

And, in the voice of a husband automatically answering the question of love, he replied, "Well enough. What've you been doing with yourself?"

"I was at the Clinic," she said. "I came home about an hour ago."

They stood and looked at each other, and Margaret thought with pain, "When did we start to move apart? We love each other with all our power. Yet, it was the children who finally stood between us, the children who will not let their father direct their lives, as he directed the lives of his brothers and sister. I'm glad I was able to help them stand against him, for his own dear sake, more than for theirs! But still, there is that reserve between us, which he erected."

"I have your drink ready," said Margaret, moving away to a table. Her figure was still tall and girlish, her face hardly touched by her forty years, her hair only a little less bright. Her eyes were always anxious, but the blueness as always seemed to fill the entire socket with intense colour. Edward sat down and waited. Oh, surely it's only my imagination that he seems more tired than usual, more grey! thought Margaret, and the thought was a desperate prayer. Dear God, don't let him mind so much about the mortgage and dwindling business and all the other material things! Let him remember that love is more important than anything else, and cannot be bought and isn't based on materialism, and is the very breath of life.

She gave Edward a very large drink of whisky, for this his physician had ordered. "Too much," said Edward, but he put the glass to his lips and drank. Surely it was her imagination that the purplish colour of his mouth was deeper to-day. "Why do you stand in front of me like that, with your hands clasped together as if you had a spasm or something?" asked Edward, with mingled affection and annoyance.

"You never tell me anything any more, dear," she said, in a low voice.

He shrugged. "What is there to tell? Business is getting worse. My debts are bigger. I'm struggling along." He stared at the windows, which alternately flared and dimmed in the lightning. He's thinking about that damned mortgage again! thought Margaret, despairingly. She pulled a chair close to him and said, "Please listen to me. Ed, you're all my life. There's nothing else. The children are nice children, but I'd give them up in an instant to save you. You've said I don't sound like a mother. Ed, I was a wife before I was a mother, and I'm still a wife, first, last and always. Children start to leave you the minute they've finished preparatory school; when they go off to college they never come home again, except for visits. They're on their way to their own lives, and they're only visitors after that."

"So you've told me a hundred times," said Edward, and frowned at her. "But, this is their home. Even when they marry, this'll be their home."

Margaret looked at her hands. "Dear, I know you have terrible worries. I don't want to add to them. When Gertrude and Robert marry it's very likely they won't live in Waterford. They may marry people from distant cities. You can't keep them for ever. You can't keep them for ever!"

"What're you talking about?" asked Edward, roughly.

"Of course nobody can keep anybody! Who said he could?" She looked up with some sharpness and saw a sudden feverish terror in his eyes. "I see," she thought, sadly. "You've always been afraid, my darling, but sometimes fear can save as well as destroy."

"All I ask of my children is that they fulfil themselves," Edward went on, in an accusing voice, as if Margaret were the enemy of his children, or desired to frustrate them out of stupid selfishness. "And be happy."

"Happy?" said Margaret, outraged at such puerility. "Are you serious? How can you guarantee happiness for anyone, Ed? You speak as if happiness were a commodity that can be dispensed by someone else, and not come from yourself alone, with the help of God. You can't give anyone happiness! You can't legislate it; you can't will it for yourself or anyone. You've always loved Dr. Samuel Johnson; you read and quote him by the hour. Don't you remember what he said? 'Human life is everywhere a state in which much is to be endured—and little to be enjoyed.' Yet, you talk of making the children 'happy,' as if it is in your power to make them so!"

"Are you going to be hysterical—again?" asked Edward, with some cruelty, for whenever Margaret talked with him about the children now her voice, to him, appeared to become too loud and raucous, too vehement, though in reality it was always quiet though often indignant these days. "You can't talk calmly any more, Margaret. We can't discuss the children rationally. You fly up, as if I'm threatening them——"

Margaret lost her temper. "And so you are, in a way! Why do you expect so much of everybody, as much as you expect from yourself? Sometimes, when I'm not emotional about you I think of your whole family, and sometimes I feel a vague pity for them, while I despise them. You hold on to everyone! Ed, you're not going to hold on to the children, as you've held on to your brothers and sister. Your grasp on the children may be love, but your grasp on the others—my God, Ed, it's probably hate!"

He looked at her with intense and vengeful silence, and she thought, despairingly, Do you think for a moment, my darling, that I care about anyone but you; in fighting to set the children free I am trying to set you free. Force your family to be free—of them.

"Yes," said Edward, in a low and bitter voice, "you're hysterical. There isn't a sensible thought in what you've just said. I have a sense of responsibility. You haven't."

"Responsibility for your brothers and sister—now?" demanded Margaret, with a sense of growing sickness at the futility of this argument, which had been going on for the past few years intermittently. "In these days? Are they children? They're men and women. . . ."

But when, she asked herself, does a man so involved in others possess reason or understanding? Edward's face became violent, and duskiness spread over it. She tried to reach him again, though hopelessly.

"Haven't you any responsibility for me?" she cried. "Don't you think I know how deep in debt you are, and how too hard you work? Don't you think you owe me some peace of mind? Why can't your brothers and sister get out and stay out? Greg and that Margo of his, here at least five or six months a year, and André, and Sylvia, and Ralph and Violette who 'visit' for months, and Dave who came 'between engagements,' he as calls them, while staying for weeks and weeks. . . . They have money. You've given them fortunes over the years, and are still giving them more than you can afford—they never spend anything; you pay for Greg's apartment in New York, and there's Sylvia, who must have a big bank account, and Ralph who *does* sell pictures, and who never lets go a cent you give him . . ." Tears dashed down her cheeks, and she sobbed.

"You've always hated my family, haven't you?" said Edward, with slow ruthlessness. "Perhaps you'd like me to throw my mother out, too. And close the doors in Ralph's, Violette's and David's faces, when they come home—to their home. Perhaps you'd like our children to stay in a hotel when they'll be on their vacations from college?" He stood up and slammed his glass on the table. "I know what you're thinking. You're remembering that you lent me your ninety thousand dollars two years ago. You want me to economise, so you can get it back. Well, don't worry about it. I'll get it for you within a month. Just give me a little time."

Margaret gazed at him blankly, utterly appalled. Her heart squeezed in her breast. She faltered, "How can you talk like that? I didn't 'lend' you that money. A man doesn't have his own money, or a woman hers, not when they're married.

It's all one thing; what belongs to one belongs to the other. The money I had was yours; I never gave it another thought. And you know it!"

He was ashamed, and angered at her because of his shame. "I'll still get it for you," he said, sullenly. Then he shook his finger almost in her face. "I've told you a thousand times. I built this house for my family; this is theirs as well as mine. I have a provision in my will, leaving the house to you, on condition that my family have the use of it as long as they want to, and putting aside, in their names, the allowances I've always given them. But just the allowances. You'd like me to stop them, wouldn't you, after I'm dead? It isn't enough for you that I've left you the bulk of my estate, and insurance, in trust for you. You'd like everything."

Margaret face became absolutely white. "I never asked you about your will. I never talked it over with you. How dare you speak to me like that! I've always prayed that I'd die before you, Ed. I don't want to live without you, and I don't think I will! And I don't want this house, even if I decide to live, if your family is to live in it. I wouldn't dream of living here with them." She uttered a great dry sob of terror at the thought of Edward dying, and pressed her hands to her breast. A blaze of lightning struck her face and he could see the agony on it, the wideness of her eyes. "Leave it to them! I don't want it, I never wanted it."

Edward felt a passionate urge to take her in his arms, and to hold her tightly, and to hide her agonised face and eyes against his shoulder. He wanted to say, "Forgive me. I've been hurting you because I'm so damned beset and afraid and worried. Everything I've said to you has been cruel and vicious and unpardonable, my darling, my wife. Forgive me. Because I don't know, God help me, what to do!"

Margaret saw his change of expression, and held her breath and even began to smile piteously. And then Gertrude came in. Later, Margaret would think, Children always intrude; at the most supreme moments between a man and his wife they always intrude and ruin and destroy, and change things beyond repair and beyond hope.

"Oh, go away, Gertrude!" Margaret almost screamed at her daughter in her anguish and frustration. "Your father and I are having a talk. . . ."

But the moment of reconciliation and passionate coming

together had gone. As Gertrude hovered uncertainly on the threshold, her whole sensitive nature understanding, Edward said, "Why should she go away, Margaret? She wants to tell us something. Come in, sweetheart."

But Gertrude said, "It doesn't matter. I'm awfully sorry. I should have knocked, Daddy. What I came to say can wait." She glanced at her mother's stiffly white and tear-stained face, and she wanted to beg for forgiveness. She had seen her father slowly begin to raise hs arms, and she hated herself. "I—I'm not important," she said to her mother, imploringly.

"You're not important?" exclaimed Edward, angrily, giving his wife a look of affront. "Who told you that?" he added, accusingly, still looking at Margaret.

"Please," murmured Gertrude, and prepared to retreat. But Edward was on her, he seized her shoulders in his big hands and pulled her into the room. Margaret sat down, abruptly. She had almost hated her daughter, who was her darling, and she was sick at the thought, and most terribly sick at what her daughter had destroyed.

Edward, smiling fondly, pushed the resisting Gertrude into a chair. He sat down beside her and took her hand. "All right, sweetheart," he said. "Tell me. Have you run over your allowance again?"

Gertrude sat up straight, and her pale grey eyes, so like her father's, fixed themselves on him. "Daddy, do you think all I ever want is money? Don't you ever think"—and her voice broke—"that I might love you, sometimes? And I'm not the one who runs over allowances. That's Robert."

Edward's face tightened a little. "You're always criticising your brother, sweetheart. Boys usually spend more than girls; besides, he has to take his girls out, and that costs money. Did you come here to complain about your brother?"

This was so absurd to Gertrude, who never complained about anything, that she smiled in a tired way. Well, there was no help for it now; she had ruined something between her parents, so she had best go on with it. She waited until a particularly splintering crash of thunder had rumbled away before speaking, and then she said, "It really wasn't important, honestly. I've just been thinking, Daddy. I don't want to go to Wellesley, after all. I want to take up a nursing career; I've wanted that for years."

Edward dropped her hand, almost in a gesture of throwing it away. "What're you talking about? What's this nonsense? Of course, you're going to Wellesley. What about your writing?"

He stared at her, incredulously. "What did you say? Nursing?"

Gertrude looked at her mother, who had lifted her head, and who was regarding her with a strangely strong smile of encouragement. The girl was grateful, and so moved that she could not speak for a moment. Then her voice was steady. "Daddy, I'm not really a writer. Dozens of girls in my classes could write, too, and a few of them better than I. I haven't taken the thought of writing seriously for years. But I've known what I really wanted. I want a nursing course; that's all I can think of. I can get a bachelor of science degree in it; it's a marvellous profession. Then I'll go on to specialise in laboratory work; I want to be a technician." She paused, while Edward stared at her with complete disbelief. "I want to work in your Clinic."

Edward jumped up, and stood over her as if he would strike her. "Why, you young fool," he said, slowly. "With all your talent! With that gift of yours! Nursing! You're out of your mind. It's degrading even to speak of it. A drudge—my daughter!"

"Daddy." Gertrude's voice was still steadfast, and her eyes glowed. "Nursing's a profession. Things have changed. You have to pay to learn to be a nurse, these days. And only the best qualified girls are admitted for study. If I have any gift at all, it's a scientific gift. I'm not going to fritter away my life, like Uncle Gregory, pretending to be a writer, when I'm not."

"Shut up!" Edward shouted, knotting his fists. "Your uncle is a famous writer now, even if the illiterate public doesn't realise it, and even if I don't approve of his subject matter! He's made a name for himself; he'll make a bigger name. And he didn't have as much talent to begin with as you have! Why, you stupid little wretch! I never heard such arrogance, such imbecility! Did you know he just sold his last book to Hollywood for fifty thousand dollars?"

Gertrude stood up and faced him. "Daddy, I don't know what's the matter with you. Not entirely." She flung up her head with a proud and fearless gesture. "I don't know, and perhaps you don't know, either, but it's killing you. Daddy," she went on, and the lightning seemed to encompass her, "I know what I want and I'm willing to sacrifice for it. I'm not going to Wellesley. I'm not going to waste all the days of my life. If you won't help me—and it wouldn't cost much, not near as much as Wellesley, I'll manage some way, myself. . . ."

It was that phrase, "All the days of my life," which shattered and maddened Edward more than anything else. Such a chaos and a roaring opened up in him that he was not aware that he had slapped Gertrude full in the face, and with all his strength, until he saw her stagger backwards, catch at a chair, and then fall sideways on the floor. He stared at her, astounded, his hand still in the air. She lay there, sobbing, her black hair tumbled over her face and shoulders, and it seemed like an awful dream to him.

"Ed!" cried Margaret, running to him and seizing his arm. "Ed, what have you done?"

He thrust her from him violently, desperately ill with his crushed amazement and the horror of his blow, for he had never struck either of his children before. A huge nausea swelled up in him. "It's your fault!" he shouted at his wife. "It's all your fault! You've done this behind my back, treacherously! I'll—I'll . . ." He actually lifted his hand as if to hit Margaret, herself. And Margaret stood and did not retreat, and the sound of thunder was all about them, like a magnification of their own passions.

Gertrude got to her feet. The impression of her father's blow was red against the pallor of her cheek. But she did not put her hand to it. She moved backwards towards the door, and the steady light of her eyes was directed at Edward. Her parents stood there and watched her, Edward in an attitude of violence, her mother straight and tall.

Then Gertrude turned and fled, not only down the echoing stairway and not only into the hall. She wrenched open the big doors of the house and ran into the rain and the storm and the shrieking cries of the trees, and the tearing power of the winds.

André knocked lightly at Maria's door, opened it, and entered her sitting-room. The storm flashed and roared against the window, near which she sat, knitting. "You wished to see me, Grandma?" he asked in his perfect French. She replied calmly. "Yes, my dear. Will you sit beside me?" But André, made even more electric by the storm, preferred to stand near her chair where he had a view of the rain and the tumultuous trees in the furious green gloom and fiery light.

"I see much from this window," said Maria, as if there was no booming of thunder and glare of lightning.

"So I would believe," said André, politely. A red and brilliant vein snaked down the heavens, and it was followed by a deafening crash. "That was very close," André added. "I think we have lost a tree."

"Much is lost during any storm," said Maria. "I have lived long enough to know that. And much is cleared away and illuminated."

André smiled. He was accustomed to Maria's enigmatic speech, and enjoyed it. He knew that it was not some mere desire for his company which had made Maria send for him. While Maria distrusted him, she was also amused by him. Once, a few years ago, she had said, "André, you are a rascal, and we both know it without illusion, but your rascality is open. However, you are extremely intelligent, and I prize intelligence above all other things." They had, in this way, reached a *modus vivendi*, and they often had what Maria called "serious conversations." She was the only one in the family who had not resented Heinrich's will, which she understood was not inspired by a subtlety she would have appreciated, but only by his simple willingness to be deceived by artfulness if it came in the guise of affection. She had thought, It is very good, and though plotted, it will serve an excellent purpose in the years to come.

"You will be returning to France in September," she said now, counting her stitches. "May I suggest you remain in this country and attend some university here?"

André slid a quick and shining glance down at her, but she was absorbed in her work. "Why?" he asked, teasingly. "Because I'm an American and should complete my education in America?"

"Shall we call it that?" said Maria. "It is as sensible an idea as anything else." She paused, and it was extraordinary how her large and puffy features could flatten under an emotion she could control and keep out of her voice and manner. "You are not one of those whom my son, Gregory, calls the Lost Generation. You will be a truly great writer. I particularly admired your essay on man's infinite capacity to delude himself. When will you have enough essays to publish them in a book?"

"In, perhaps, another three years," said André. "You believe I cannot complete them in Europe?"

"A writer can write anywhere," said Maria, reprovingly. "And that you know. Still, may I suggest that you remain in America?"

André lit a cigarette, and studied the storm with increasing interest. "You have a reason, Grandmother," he said.

"Naturally," she replied. "And it is not concerned with you, of course."

"That I understand," he said, and turned his admiration from the storm to Maria. "There is little that escapes you." He put his hand on her massive shoulder in a gesture of genuine affection. "When I was a child—if I ever was a child—I believed that you were the only member of this family who was truly civilised. But now I know it. May I ask you what, in particular, inspired your suggestion that I remain here?"

Maria knitted busily, then she looked at the window. "When a young girl, who is all pride and innocence and integrity, who is all control usually, suddenly darts from a hidden distance with tears on her face, which is also flushed yet smiling timidly, and who is breathing with excitement and fear, and then runs into her home as if for a refuge she does not really want, it is obvious that something has occurred of considerable importance. And then when a young man studiously strolls, smoking as you are smoking now, from the very same spot from which the girl burst a moment or two ago, only a blind woman would fail to come to the proper conclusion."

André patted her shoulder. "And what would you say of a girl who cries about age constantly, and insists upon age, Grandmother?"

"I would say that that girl is a child, and not a woman as yet. She is still without sight. Nevertheless, that, too, was only a protest against the strength of the heart, which has awakened and has destroyed the level order of her world—a world that did not really exist except in her determined and juvenile illusion that existence must be governed by reason always."

"I admire reason," said André. "But not what is generally called reason. I am a very logical person. However, there is still the matter of years, though not of age. My education is not complete; the young lady's education is not complete. This would not interfere, so far as I am concerned. In a truly civilised world marriage would not interfere with education, which is a continuous thing. However, there are parents to consider, and the small affair of law."

"Absence from one loved frequently gives parents an opportunity to distort a girl's life," said Maria, nodding approvingly over what André had said. "A father in particular. The father we are now considering is as obdurate and as innocent as his daughter." She sighed. "He has plans for her. She is resisting them, being possessed of some common sense. But she also loves him. He may succeed in ruining her life, with the very best intentions, and out of some terror which possesses him. It is strange that a man can be a genius and a fool at the very same time. It is also tragic."

"The father is indeed a genius," said André.

"And geniuses frequently annihilate. They are elemental forces, like the storm outside. I have made my suggestion. Do you agree with it?"

André smoked intently. Then he said, "Grandmother, you are the wisest woman in the world. I would be stupid indeed not to listen to you. And I am happy that you approve, in the light of what you have called my rascality, and in the light of the fact that the young lady is your favourite grandchild."

He bent to kiss her smiling cheek. "Do you think I will make her the good bourgeois husband?"

She shook her head vigorously. "No. And that is why I approve. The girl is very profound; her profundity is still folded in her heart like a bud. It must be persuaded to flower into true wisdom. She must be rescued and taught and loved. Everything else is of no significance. And I——"

"Excuse me, please," said André, in a quick, changed voice. "I have seen something through this famous and enlightening window of yours."

He turned swiftly and ran from the room. He ran down

the dark stairway and hardly touched the stairs. A servant was beginning to turn on the lights in the hall, and she exclaimed as André fled by her, and almost screamed when he pulled open the doors and bolted outside. "What in the world!" she cried, as wind and rain and lightning gushed into the hall. It was very difficult to close the door after André. She shook her head. This was sure a very funny family. That boy, running out into the storm, bare-headed, not noticing anything, not even the rain. Well, he was French, and he was the funniest one in the whole house! Except for the old German lady who had a nasty cold eye and just sat knitting or embroidering all the time.

André was momentarily caught and whirled by the wild gale and rain. They were like solid blows on his face and body, and he was blinded both by water and lightning. He put his hands over his mouth and drew in a breath protectingly. Then he bent his head and ploughed into the storm. The soaked earth yielded under his running feet; sometimes the wind struck him aside and made him stagger; sometimes the lightning dazed him as it lit up and distorted the furious lashing world about him. Sometimes the ground rumbled under him, echoing the thunder. Once, his eyes streaming with rain, he collided with a tree.

Now he was running freely, and faster, over the sodden grass, towards the place where he and Gertrude had sat that afternoon. He was angry, alarmed and frightened. It was dangerous under those huge trees now, with the leaping lightning hovering closely, waiting for a place to strike. But he did not call out. It was all he could do to breathe in this world of smothering water, which was illuminated by constant glares of fierce and unearthly light. He passed the fountain, which gushed over its bowl in silvery cataracts. The small naked statue of the boy which dominated it glistened with pale life, the laughing and depraved face flowing with bright water. André, even in those concerned moments, could give the statue a glance of appreciation.

Now it was behind him, and he was running down the long slow slope towards the trees. Once he slipped on the wet grass, and sprawled upon it. He was up again in a moment, cursing quietly. The soft black hair of his head, cropped like fur, had picked up blades of grass as well as much rain. He was like a fleeing faun, tall and slender, his drenched clothing hanging on his body.

A particularly fiery and vicious blaze of lightning showed him Gertrude at last, crouching on the bench under the maddened trees, her face in her hands, her slight body bent and crushed in unseeing and unfeeling grief and despair, her grey dress blackened and flooded with water.

Someone called her name, and she started violently and dropped her hands. André was before her, holding out his arms and trying to make her understand. She stared at him with blank amazement. And then she uttered a deep and broken sob and sprang up and threw herself, like an abandoned and terrified child, into his arms and clung to him, and cried.

"There, there," he said, and held her tightly, and drew her away from the perilous trees to a safe spot where they had only wind and rain to battle. His arms became stronger about her. Her loose hair whipped about her contorted face, and the wet strands of it blew against his cheek. Her hands clutched his arms, his shoulders; even above the sound of the storm he could hear her incoherent cries, her piteous stammering.

"There, there," he said, again, understanding that something had driven the usually controlled Gertrude out into this primordial fury. But what did that matter? Her cold and trembling mouth, tasting of rain and the saltiness of her tears, her innocent mouth, was pressing against his, and her arms were about his neck, in an utter abandon of sorrow and love.

Now her lips were at his ear, and she was crying, "Don't go away, André! Don't leave me!"

"Of course not, darling," he said. "I'll never go away. What made you think I would?"

Chapter Ten

The grey autumnal rain drizzled against the wide windows of Edward's offices. The whole world was grey and still, a melancholy twilight though it was only three in the afternoon. Edward sat and looked at his papers, and the hushed blank stillness of the day ran like drowning water over his desperate thoughts. He struggled against this dolorous anæthesia, for, he told himself numbly, he must think! Think how to keep what he had; think how to fight against his huge debts; think how to prevent being ploughed under the glacier of the increasing depression, which grew worse instead of better in this November of 1936. All the President had done, and was doing, could not overcome this leaden horror that flowed like lava over the country.

His secretary came in. "Mr. Standard is here," she said, listlessly, for the weather and her employer's chronic mood of wretchedness disheartened her. She held the door aside and Mr. Edgar Standard, of the huge Standard Supermarkets, entered, smiling. Edward got up to meet him with reserve, and they shook hands.

When they sat down again Edward said abruptly, "I wrote you you were wasting your time, Mr. Standard. I'm not going to sell out to your chain. I can't. I built my own smaller chain up, myself, and it's been my whole life."

Mr. Standard nodded understandingly. He was a slender, quiet man with a shrewd and perspicacious face, a man about ten years Edward's senior. "Yes, we had quite a discussion at the home office about your letter, Mr. Enger. And then I thought I ought to come and talk it over, personally. We've gone over the whole thing in our letters, haven't we?" His small brown eyes appeared to shine with sympathy on Edward. "But a personal interview can be more rewarding, and points gone over. . . ."

He wore a perpetual air of benevolence, and there were humorous lines graven about his mouth. Though older than Edward his hair was smooth and brown. He went on, "You've accused us of being buccaneers. We aren't really, you know, Mr. Enger. We're not even entrepreneurs, though, as you've written, we *have* absorbed independent businesses wherever we've opened new markets. The day of independent business is over—we can't stop that ending. We're a big country now. . . ."

Edward leaned back in his chair with overwhelming tiredness. "I shouldn't have said you were buccaneers. That was childish. You aren't entrepreneurs, and that's the sickening part of the whole thing. There's no real vitality these days in most big business-men, no power or force. Everything's just the Organisation, as if any organisation has a life of its own, outside of the people who run it! You're so benevolent, that it's sort of—suspect. You're just as materialistic as the old robber barons—but you call this new materialism the 'adjusted life.' You've gone in for Freud, and you've taken away all adventure from your employees, and all meaning out of their life, in the name of 'security.'"

"Well," said Mr. Standard, with a faint smile, "what are the mass of men, anyway? Clods. We treat them, in these days, as kindly as possible, and don't exploit them as the old boys did. At least we've made them happy, and being happy is all they want, in their cretin way—beer, a two-bedroom house, a little adultery when they get tired of the old girl, and three kids in every kitchen, a used car that runs, and bowling every Wednesday. What more do clods want? In fact, they don't want anything more." He lit a cigarette. "Besides, isn't our Government trying to make people happy, too, especially the clods? And isn't its spokesman always talking of the 'more abundant life,' and 'security'?"

"Who made them clods?" asked Edward, flushing deeply. "A man isn't born a clod, or, at least, he has some capacity to become more than a clod. Who sold them on security and the other nonsense? Government? Probably. But you helped too, you know."

"'The more abundant life,' quoted Mr. Standard, his smile widening. He had thick brown brows that were very mobile. He seemed to be enjoying himself. Here, he thought, is a very desperate and beset man, with old-fashioned ideas that the Government will knock out of him if reality doesn't.

"And what the hell does that mean?" exclaimed Edward, his passion rising. "Cocktails instead of beer, four bedrooms instead of two, a more expensive prostitute, a higher-priced car, a country-club membership instead of the Wednesday night bowling, and one child in the dining-room instead of three in the kitchen! It's still passive materialism, and it's still meaningless, and without purpose. It's still a drug. A man can't be just a belly in a pair of overalls, or in a tailor-made suit. Industry and business can't go on for ever by taking conflict and victory and meaning out of men's lives. You won't always be able to take defeat from them; defeat's the price men pay for being men, and for their successes. One of these days your millions of 'clods' will suddenly wake up to the fact that they're living in a benign desert, a blank monotony, and they'll react! And somehow, when people react they don't do it peacefully; they do it with violence. You won't succeed——"

"We've already succeeded," said Mr. Standard, gently. "Our people in our chain are happy and contented."

"So are the dead," said Edward. To his own brief and savage amusement, he thought of Mr. Standard as an undertaker. "I know how you use psychiatrists in your personnel departments: smoothing out of people all that makes them men, ambition, hope, competition, struggle against environment, periods of exultation. Making them good adjusted organisation men. Why, this is worse than the old gruelling system of the old buccaneers. At least, even a 'clod' had his dreams then, and dreams for his children. But there's no place for real dreams in the Organisation. And no place for life, either. Life's so damned untidy, isn't it? So gross, too. Bursting out of all the tidy little strait-jackets you modern employers force it into—you think the jacket will crush out all emotion, make life creamy and predictable, and so goddamned nice——!"

Mr. Standard shrugged. "You may be right. But you're putting the cart before the horse, Mr. Enger. You seem to think we big organisations are some sort of Machiavellian villains, with a 'plot' against our thousands of employees. You think we thought up this benevolence and security all by ourselves. We didn't. The people forced it on us. If there's guilt in this—then the working man is the guilty one, not the officers of a company. The working man doesn't want to struggle against his environment any longer; he doesn't want to risk anything; he wants shelter and food and a new radio and car, and lots of sex excitement. Mr. Enger, to give our employees that has cut deeply into our profits, but we did it. It's the New Order, the sociologists call it." He no longer smiled. He glanced quickly about the office as if fearing an eavesdropper. "Don't you think we'd prefer to advance men on their merits, or fire those who haven't the brains to hold a job? But we can't—any longer. 'Everybody has a *right* to be taken care of.' That's what they say, Mr. Enger."

"Why don't you have the guts to fight this—this deadliness—then?" shouted Edward. "Haven't you any sense of responsibility—to men's minds?"

"We can't fight it," replied Mr. Standard, gravely. "It's

the present trend. We've become a mediocre people, a spiritless people. All we want is safety. The clods never think of working for themselves, in small businesses, any longer. They don't want risk, or the chance of failure. Everything guaranteed, so they can live their maggot lives in peace. Do you think these are the days of the Founding Fathers, when a man would bet his life and everything he had on just being free in his manhood? No."

"Then we're a sick country," said Edward, in a stifled voice. "A very sick country."

He seemed personally stricken. The graven lines in his face deepened. He rubbed his cheek with the knuckles of his right hand, and his weary eyes blinked in despondent thought. "But one of these days the maggots, as you call them, might want to grow wings again. . . ."

Mr. Standard shook his head. "No. That's not what history tells us. You've only to remember Rome, and her housing developments, her bread and circuses, her lotteries, her steady alms to those who wouldn't or couldn't work because they were too unfitted for life, her free entertainments for the mobs, her securities for the mobs—well, you know the end of Rome. The healthy barbarians came in. Sometimes"—and he leaned closer to Edward and dropped his voice—"I'm frightened, myself. I think of the Russian barbarians—and I think of the Visigoths. Governments, at the last, don't make people weak. They were born that way, and they have to pay the penalty eventually. Governments, at the last, give them what they want, because there're so many millions of them!"

He sighed. He looked at Edward, waiting for his comments, but Edward was silent, furiously thinking, furiously despairing. He was no longer antagonistic towards Mr. Standard. Before them both lay a situation that was terrible for humanity, because humanity had created that terror out of its own cowardice and lack of courage—a deep flush of blood ran through Edward's body, as if his very flesh was trying to call his attention to something in his own precarious life.

At last Edward said, "Well, I'm not going to pimp for the weakness in my own employees. I'm not going to cater to their lack of courage." He suddenly brightened, and brought his fist down on his desk. "Look! I don't pay them what your chain pays its employees! I do give them a certain amount of sick leave, and I do give them a chance to invest in my chain, but I do insist that they put some of their own money into our private pension fund! I'm not an Organisation, and my people stay with me. They aren't clods, and there goes your argument!"

"But you do have strikes—and we don't," said Mr. Standard. He was a kind and realistic man at heart, and he was sorry for Edward. "And you do have debts and God knows what else, while we're solvent. And so we're prepared to make you a good price for your Green and White Markets, to clear up your debts and mortgages, to get rid of your outstanding commitments. If you agree to sell to us, you won't have to worry about the future, yourself, Mr. Enger. Isn't that a consideration?"

Edward was aghast. "What, then, shall I do with my life?" He swallowed in humiliation at this involuntary outburst, and he shook his head to conceal his humiliation. "No. No! I'll struggle along some way. I don't know how, but I will. I feel I owe it to my country to remain independent; I owe it to my employees to force them to be men, not secure 'maggots.' I don't move them from city to city, as you do. I employ managers for my markets right from their own community, after we're satisfied they want to stay there. And our employees are local people, too. The clerks often quit to go into one of your Markets. But the managers stay, in spite of what you can offer them! And that's a gain—for America. It helps my managers to be independent, to make their own choices."

Mr. Standard reluctantly knew this was the time to be ruthless. "We know what you owe, Mr. Enger. We know you are getting deeper into the hole ever day. And perhaps next year, or the year after, or the year after that, you won't be able to go on. You can't compete in prices with us; the Government won't let you redeem its food stamps. Why? How long can you go on bucking the Government, who wants to give people what it demands?"

He stood up. He looked down at Edward, but Edward seemed to have forgotten him. "Think it over, Mr. Enger," he urged. "We're always ready."

A little later Edward looked about him with a start. He was alone. He had not even been aware that Mr. Standard had left him. The rain filtered against the windows, and there was no sound but the muffled clatter of distant typewriters. "Oh, God," he muttered. He was surprised to see that it was nearly half-past four. How long ago had his visitor left him? He could not remember. He looked at the piles of papers on his desk, and shivered. He would go home —but, to what? To the absence of his children, away at school, to the immured silence of his mother, to the scorns and barbs of his sister, Sylvia, to the anxious love of Margaret, from which he tried to run away? With the exception of Sylvia, Maria and Margaret, there was no one in that big mansion to-day, and all its rooms rang with dull quiet as if life had permanently withdrawn from it.

His club? His club bored and wearied him. He could not drink as other men drank; his life had been too much of a gamble to be satisfied with little cards. His Lutheran life had been too austere for him now to take pleasure in foolish and ribald stories. The pursuits of his contemporaries disgusted him. Their talk of their mistresses revolted all his instincts of stern morality. It was all very well for a boy to caper in his youth, but a man with a wife did not caper. Besides, thought Edward, with a dreary smile, there was never anyone for me but Margaret, in spite of her probing eyes and the fear in her face for me. What would I do with a mistress? She'd bore me to death, and give me a bad taste. Friends? He had no friends, for he did not share the interests of other businessmen, who thought him strait-laced and dull. There was just no meaning in his life—a pang of terror so strong that it translated itself to a physical anguish made him start up from his chair.

His secretary came in with a look of inquisitive surprise on her angular face. "I'm sorry to disturb you, Mr. Enger, but there's a—a priest—out here who wants to talk with you. It's probably charity, though he says it isn't. He says he's an old friend——"

"Father Jahle!" Edward blurted, with amazement. "Why. Why, send him in, of course." He sat down in his chair, and all his nerves twitched. He had not seen Father Jahle for years, and he was suddenly awkward and embarrassed.

Father Jahle, smiling gently and almost with supplication, came in, emaciated, old and worn, as always, but with that indomitable large brilliance of eye. Edward went to him, and in silence they shook hands, while the priest's merciful and understanding eyes studied the younger man sorrowfully Yes, yes, all that George Enreich had been telling him all these years was true. Edward was beset; he was distracted; he was lost. He needed the comfort of God; he needed to know that God was always with him, that he was not alone.

"Sit down, sit down, Father," Edward urged, his awkwardness making him stammer. "It's good to see you—it's been a long time—terrible day, isn't it?—I've been very busy—should have gone to see you before this. . . ."

"You never forgot me, Eddie," said the priest, and clung for a moment to Edward's hand. "I get your cheque every Christmas. It's done so much——"

"It wasn't anything," said Edward. He removed his hand and hurried behind his desk, as behind a battlement. He tried to smile broadly. "Well, you seem all right. I was sorry about your mother, of course. . . ."

"It was kind of you to endow a hospital room in the Clinic, in her name," said the priest. "She was old, and died in her sleep. In the Grace and mercy of God."

Edward said nothing. All at once his mind was blank and empty, and there was nothing in it but the sound of the whispering rain. The priest had suddenly lost reality for him, and his uneasiness increased. The priest's eyes, so searching, so tender, unnerved him. What was there to speak about? After all these years of silence and absence! A dull old priest with a child's unclouded eyes: what did he know about life of men and the world? All at once, while hot with a sudden resentment, there was envy in Edward. Not to be beset, not to lie sleepless, not to quarrel or argue, not to be despairing, never to be worried—a child's life, but a peaceful one. While looking at the priest with that false, fixed smile, Edward was besieged again with that awful desire to die, and not to know, and not to be aware. Little drops of moisture appeared on his forehead and on his upper lip.

The priest waited. He understood that his appearance had done something violent to Edward, and that the younger man was suffering. Then he said, "I've come to say good-bye, Eddie. You see, I'm a monsignor now; I've been assigned to Detroit."

"Good-bye?" Edward echoed, stupidly. He stared at the

priest, and he was bereft. He had not seen him for years—yet he was bereft.

Father Jahle nodded. "I'm very sad at leaving Waterford, but when it is God's will a priest must obey."

The rain quickened; now it was pelting, insistent like small stones against the glass. Edward did not turn on the office lamps. The big room lay steeped in deep greyness, like a cave.

"Well," said Edward, lamely, "when you receive orders, you must go. . . ."

Please help me to reach him, the priest prayed. He leaned towards Edward urgently. "I want you to know that you're always in my prayers, Eddie," he said. "You see, our old friend, George Enreich, tells me all about you, and I know what your struggles are, and all about your family. I haven't left you alone, Eddie. There isn't a day that I don't remember you, and pray for you. Eddie, what can I do to help you?"

What can you do to help me? thought Edward, incredulously. You, a priest? What do you know of my work, my business, my family, you who never had a business or a family, and who lived life at second-hand through your parishioners? He smiled with indulgence. "Why, there's nothing, Father. I should be asking you that question, not you asking me."

"Eddie." The priest looked down at his thin clasped hands. "When you were a boy you understood all about God. Don't you remember how we used to talk together, when I came into the old delicatessen? And the discussions we had? I would think then, Here is a soul that knows God deeply, and understands, and will never be overlaid with the heavy stones of the outer world."

"That was a long time ago," said Edward. "I was almost a child then. Now I have responsibilities."

"The great responsibility is to God," said the priest. "Eddie, have you forgotten that there is no reality but God?"

A foolish conversation, a silly, clerical conversation. Edward was really indulgent now, though there was a shocked sensation of loss in him.

"Of course," he said, smoothly. It was almost five. He wanted to go home, to get away, not to listen any longer to these medieval precepts. "We all understand that. But tell me about Detroit. . . ."

I've failed, thought the priest with humility. There is something I should have said, but I don't know what it is! His ears are closed, and perhaps it is all my fault. I shouldn't have let him drift out of my sight so long. He said, aloud, "Forgive me, Eddie. When you stayed away from me I should have come to you. I might have been able to help."

"I've done very well," said Edward.

The priest sighed. "That isn't what I meant, Eddie."

Edward was impatient; he wanted to rise, take the priest by the hand, and let him out of the room. He could see the office without the priest: there would be the empty chair, but he would be alone with his frightful problems. Father Jahle was gazing at him with that compassionate and piercing regard which was intolerable.

Then Edward heard himself say simply, and with astonishment at his own words, "No one can help me, Father. No one at all. You know that. No, no. Don't speak to me of God. I don't believe—my father was right. God is only an Abstract. In the light of that Abstract, I've done all I could. You see, for a layman, life isn't as simple as it is for you clergy. We have to deal with it, with our bare hands."

"Your hands are not the only hands which have bled in the world," said the priest. "Remember that, Eddie. God lived as a Man. He knows what it is to be a man. Won't you give that some thought?"

It was imperative to Edward that the priest leave. He couldn't endure his presence any longer. While the priest was here there was such an agonised stirring in him, such a stretching—as as if one were being crucified. Edward wiped the moisture from his upper lip with his handkerchief.

"Yes, yes," he said, "I'll give it some thought." Go away! he shouted in himself. Don't you know I want to die, and that every minute you're here the impulse gets stronger?

The priest stood up, and thankfully Edward stood up also. The priest stood with bowed head, his hat in his hands. Then he said, "Eddie, I will be in Detroit, but I'll be with you in my prayers and my thoughts. Some day, Eddie, you will know and understand."

"I hope you'll be happy with your larger responsibilities in Detroit," said Eddie, and took the old thin hand. "Keep in touch with me, won't you? Let me know if you need anything."

The priest was gone, and the room steadily darkened. Then Edward said aloud, "Don't go away. Let me talk to you. Let me tell you . . ."

He suddenly fell asleep in his chair. The clerks left, and the secretary. When he awoke the office was in utter blackness, and the blackness and emptiness were in himself.

Chapter Eleven

The view from the small upper bedroom in the sorority house showed only a quiet, snow-filled street, with students trudging under the twilight lamps. Sometimes they stopped in little groups to laugh and talk and brush the falling snow from their faces. It was very still; the snow fell patiently and inexorably, as if from eternity itself. In the corridor outside the dormitory room there was only an occasional footstep, only the occasional soft voice of a girl. The radiator hissed.

Gertrude returned her attention to the letter she was writing to André, and a sweet and gentle smile stood on her lips, for all the seriousness of her eyes.

"How can I thank you, dear, for the beautiful silver dresser set you sent me? It arrived to-day, right on time for my birthday. I feel terribly old, at twenty-one. But I remember that you'll be just as old in June, though twenty-one isn't as bad for a boy as it is for a girl. Now, don't smile. See: I'm wearing the ring you gave me secretly for Christmas. I only dare wear it when I'm alone like this. I'm turning it now to catch the light of my lamp. I ask you again, how did you know that I loved dark blue sapphires more than anything else? The diamonds around it twinkle like white fire. I want to show it to everybody! Well, I will, in June, when I'm graduated from the nursing school."

She lifted her left hand to her lips and kissed the large gleaming stone in its wreath of pure light. Then she held the ring against her cheek and her eyes dreamed in a mist of joy and contentment. It was several moments before she began to write again.

"I can't wait until your book is published in September. And dedicated to me, too! I like to know it's still only our secret. And the Yale University Press! I'm terribly, foolishly, proud. I can hear you laugh at me, but I don't care about that any longer. I'm not nearly as unsophisticated as you think I am. I'm really a very practical person. I've been thinking of that small neat apartment over the Clinic where Dr. Blenlow lives. He is retiring in July, and I'm determined to have it for you and me, when we are married in August. I think of August all the time. Of course, Daddy will want us to live in the house, but I simply can't consider it. . . ."

I hate the house, the house where I was born, she thought with a sudden surge of revulsion. It's filled with Daddy's enemies, except for Grandma, and Uncle David, when he's there. You can feel the menace and discord in every room, and the savage rage under the controlled voices. It's as if they're deliberately punishing him for something, and, in turn, that he is punishing them. Why can't human relationships be clear and defined, kind and honest? Why must we complicate not only our lives, but the lives of others, until we all wallow in the mud of our own confusion? I detest undercurrents. Are we the only creatures who must distort living, and the meaning of living, so that all significance is lost in a welter of complex emotions?

I would love my home, if only Daddy and Mother and Robert and André and I and Grandma could live there, free of that crowding and suffocating atmosphere of unspoken hates and resentments and contempt. It all seems to be concentrated around my father; he's like the centre of a hurricane which never blows itself out, never becomes violent enough to disperse itself. And yet, how little he speaks these days. How little he speaks to me, in particular. He was sorry he struck me, three years ago, and he tried to atone for it—as if Daddy would ever have to atone for anything he did to me!—by agreeing to let me come here to the School of Nursing. But still, something's been broken between us; I've disappointed him. It's better, though, that I disappointed him by insisting on my own life than to disillusion him later and make him even more desperate than he is now.

And how desperate he is, her sad thoughts ran on. Of course, there is twice as much unemployment to-day as there was in 1933, in spite of what the President tries to do. Three years, and it is worse than ever. It almost kills my father when he has to dismiss more of his employees, but there's nothing he can do. I can't stand looking at him when I go home, thinking of his mountainous worries and his debts and his struggles. He's only forty-seven, but he seems an old man too exhausted to speak much, too besieged to laugh or to have some recreation. Why, he's almost never taken a vacation, in all his life! But the aunts and uncles have a fine time, indeed they do—at his expense. Never once has any of them asked him how his affairs are, nor have they ever cared. Once I thought I understood, a little, but now I don't know at all. And there's Robert, who looks at me blankly when I ask questions about this, and then pats my cheek kindly and reassures me that I'm just using my imagination. Dear, good, sweet Robert, who looks at life serenely and contentedly, with good will towards everything and everybody, quite unaware that something very frightful is brewing in our house, and must, some day, break out into destruction. What will Robert think then? I'm sure he'll just believe that somebody lost his or her temper, and it will all blow over, and let's all be nice again—as if anyone was ever really nice in that house!—and he'll pull his neat shiny blinders over his eyes and smile at everybody happily. Is he stupid, or just one of those incurable optimists who are so infuriating? But I did notice, thought Gertrude wryly, that he had no battle with Daddy at all when he beamingly announced he was going to the School of Business Administration. Daddy looked shocked for a few minutes, and Robert kept on beaming innocently and affectionately, just exuding confidence and assurance that Daddy would be pleased. Could it be that Robert is wiser than I, and never forces an issue, and absolutely refuses to attack deep seriousness to anything, and is perfectly sure that everyone is innately reasonable and benevolent? The strange thing is that he projects that pretty opinion on to people, so that it never occurs to them to disillusion him of the lovely idea he has about them! At any rate, Daddy just stared at Robert and blinked, as if hypnotised, and then he said he deeply appreciated it that Robert wanted to study business administration in order to help him. And that was all there was to it. The violin was completely forgotten. Robert gives Daddy some comfort no one else can.

Gertrude thought of André's parents, who were still in Paris, and were still travelling on the Continent, at Edward's expense. Ralph had become a very close friend of Picasso's and was imitating the famous artist shamefully, and was selling a surprising number of his canvasses, though at a cheap price. Poor André, thought Gertrude, naïvely, with his foolish parents. At least my own parents didn't abandon me when I was a child, as André was abandoned. For a moment or two André seemed very piteous to her, and then she laughed out loud to herself.

Gertrude thought of Gregory's wife, with her bold, coarsely beautiful face, expertly enhanced with cosmetics, and her laughing, lustful mouth, handsome nose and sensually smiling blue eyes. Margo had a fine figure, tall and marvellously curved, and though Sylvia spitefully and openly doubted it, the colour of her heavy blonde hair was natural. Gertrude, in spite of herself, liked Margo, for the latter had a tremendous animal magnetism, a high if lewd wit, and was extremely entertaining, and laughed always. She deceived no one, and never tried to deceive anyone, that she was not greedy and ambitious, and held mankind in very low esteem. Perhaps I like her, thought Gertrude, annoyed with herself, because she is absolutely honest about possessing no moral values, and is honestly convinced that no one else has them, either.

" Did you know that Uncle Ellis had another slight heart attack last week? Just bad enough so he could lie cosily in bed surrounded by three nurses and Aunt Sylvia, who devotes all her time to him since Daddy had to sell ' her ' theatre because she had lost all interest in it. Why are you so indifferent to the family, darling, and why are you refusing to go there for your spring vacation? After all, I'll be home, but it would seem I'm not much of an attraction after all."

She put the ring to her lips and kissed it again. She re-read the section of André's letter in which he had suggested that she meet him in New York rather than return to Waterford for the two weeks' holiday. She believed she had refused very tactfully in the letter she was writing. After all, it was a somewhat shocking and unconventional thing he had suggested, even though it would be very innocent. She yearned, however, to see him again, and very soon; sometimes her whole body ached with that artless yearning. She shook her head with smiling negation at his letter.

Then she was no longer smiling. She thought of the letter her mother had written her, and which she had received to-day with a substantial cheque for her birthday. Poor Mother, thought Gertrude, so pretty, so sweet, so tender, so loving, and so brave. Her young heart warmed with love as she thought of Margaret, who would never escape the miasma of that house which might have been a place of joy and contentment instead of a place of peril and misery.

The corridor outside the small snug room was alive with the laughter and voices of girls preparing for dinner and exchanging confidences. Gertrude felt a pang of loneliness. She was too proud and reticent to make friends easily, and though she was respected and admired and envied she was rarely included in the warmth of room parties and other gatherings. True, she had been elected to the most desirable sorority, because of her brilliance and scholarship. But the girls made nothing more than the most casual advances to her. She had no words to express her longing to be incluuded as one of them.

Someone knocked smartly on her door, and she started. A girl called out gaily that she was " wanted " on the telephone downstairs. Gertrude, with a twist of misgiving, ran down and snatched up the receiver, while happy girls milled about her talking excitedly to each other, and shrilling with youthful mirth.

It was André, and at the sound of his voice her heart rose on a crest of joy and delight and trembling relief.

" Did you think I'd forget it was your birthday, dear little child?" he asked, and her eyes filled with tears. " Your twenty-first birthday! And now you are a woman. I hope."

" Oh, André," she murmured. " Oh, André! "

" I suppose your phone has been ringing all day, with charming messages from home," he said.

But no one ever called her from " home." Even her twin had not called, though it was his birthday also. " Of course they called," she said. " A girl isn't twenty-one every day. André——"

" Yes, sweetness?"

But she could only say, out of her loneliness, and again, " Oh, André."

Never had a winter seemed so dogged, so enternal, to Margaret Enger, nor the house so sombre, nor herself so lonely, nor her life so hopeless and without meaning. She had believed, three years ago, that she would not miss her children too much, nor would she have missed them with this deep longing had Edward remained the grimly optimistic and vital man of their first period of marriage. She was annoyed with herself that she had to depend on letters from Gertrude and Robert for any comfort and brightening. A woman should find all she needs in her husband, she would say to herself with depression. It is a sad day for a woman when she must revert to her children, no matter how beloved, for engrossment with children is not too far akin from engrossment with strangers who must inevitably go when they come. In an effort not to become too involved with these strangers and travellers of her flesh, she did not write them more than once a week, nor, in spite of a desperate inner urging, did she call them on the telephone, not even on their birthdays. " I should be a more loving mother, and more demonstrative," she said to Maria on a colourless March day, " and without fear of attaching myself to them like an old woman of the sea, if I knew what to do with and about Ed."

" But I have told you," said Maria, gently, " that no one can do anything about my son except God and himself. It is presumptuous of any of us to believe we truly and permanently can influence others. Each soul has its way and its cross, and only its own feet can carry it, and only its own shoudlers can bear that load."

" Then, it's a lonely road we travel," said Margaret, despondently. " With no one at all."

Maria shook her head. " No, we are never alone. But how often do we look up to see Who travels with us, and Whose Hand is ready to ease the weight of the cross? Few of us speak to Him, Who can tell us of joy and the glory at the end of the journey, and few of us say to Him, 'My burden is too heavy. Lift it from me for a moment.' "

Tears smarted Margaret's eyes. She said, humbly, " I always keep forgetting. Or, I'm so afraid for Ed these days that I can't look at God or speak to Him." She put her hand out impulsively and laid it on the large, knotted hand of her mother-in-law. " What a fool and a wastrel I've been! I could have had you all these years!"

Maria wanted to say, But we have no one but God, and I had to learn that myself, and it was not an easy thing to learn. However, she could not speak this truth to Margaret, whose anxiety was daily lining her pretty face more deeply, and who was so baffled and alone. She said, instead, and very quietly, " You have always had me. My daughter."

" Yes, I know," said Margaret, in a low voice. " I was just stupid. I thought you were in the conspiracy to rob and ruin and exploit Ed."

And so I was, long ago, and may God forgive me, thought Maria. I overestimated my son's strength, until it was too late.

Robert's letters, sunny and enthusiastic, if not very imaginative, never failed to make Edward smile, and never failed to arouse the old buoyont note in his voice when he discussed the letters with Margaret. My son isn't stupid, Margaret would think. He's what they call an extrovert, these days, one who expects life to be kind and pleasant and objective, and so he finds it. But it still puzzled her that the intellectual Edward could be pleased and made a little happy by her son's letters. Robert was everything Edward was not. Gertrude's letters, introspective, serious and thoughtful, had a dismaying way of arriving on the days when her brother's letters arrived, and their tone subtly annoyed and disturbed Edward. Had he expected more of his daughter than of his son? Or, did she echo himself? Sometimes he would say gloomily, " What a waste! And she had an authentic genius, too." Then he would add in all naïveté, " I knew from the start that Robert was really a business-man at heart, and so I'm not disappointed."

Between Margaret and the rest of the family at home there was now only bitterness and hatred and coldness. At least three nights a week she would have a dinner tray alone in her room, to Edward's anger and accusations of associal tendencies. But his own relations with his family had deteriorated to the point where the dining-room silence was rarely broken by an amiable voice, or laughter. Sometimes, from upstairs, Margaret could hear Edward's quick and violent words of disgust or disagreement or contempt. Afterwards, he would go into the library and slam the door behind him, there to read far into the morning. Often he had but two or three hours of sleep. And more and more he went to New York and other cities on business.

To such a pass was Margaret arriving that she looked

forward to Violette's return from France to-morrow, Violette who was wickedly wise and humorous, and who liked her. And there were even times when Margaret desperately longed for David, and his gentle sympathy and his understanding and affection. It did not matter to her now that even a mention of David's name could make Edward become almost savage in look and speech. Of course, David's concert engagements were few, and his notices brief, and his appearances only in the smaller towns and cities. He had disappointed Edward; but, who had not? There was just no explanation.

One day in March Edward said to his wife, "I don't know what's the matter with you. Once you were gracious and friendly to everybody. Once you used to talk to me, and laugh, and wanted to spend time with me, when I had it. Now you shut yourself away from everyone in the family, and especially from me."

Margaret did not reply, but she thought, It's true I can't stand your family any longer, and every time I see them I get sick. For what they've done to you, and what they're still doing. But it isn't true that I've shut myself away from you, my darling. You have turned from me, yourself, though I know how much you really love me. I just can't stand seeing you getting more broke, more grey, more desperate, every day. It tears the heart out of me. Oh, my God, what can I do to help you?

She knew that business was extremely bad. Edward could have helped himself a little there, but he would not do it. His Green and White Stores were not permitted to undercut and undersell independent dealers in their vicinity. If an independent dealer had a sale in these dark and terrible days of depression, Edward would not allow a competing sale in that particular item. His Stores would feature a different sale entirely. "This is not realistic," William had protested. But Edward remembered the Goeltz family, and would only become irritable. "I offer what the independents can't offer, poor devils," he would say. "Bigger, brighter stores, the better local help, and quicker access to goods. That's fair competition. Murderous undercutting isn't in my line. And don't talk to me about bankruptcy!"

But he was close to it now, in March, 1936. He did not often think of this, however. He had a more frightful problem. It was clear to him, as it was to a few other thinking men, that Hitler was becoming an ominous power in Europe, and that evil and plotting men in America were not halting him with threats of economic boycotts and moral quarantine, and were not heartening the German people with calls for resistance and freedom. He realised, as did a few men and some honourable Senators, that a war was developing in Europe. And now Edward had a more personal terror to haunt his days and nights. Robert was twenty-one. He might have to fight, not to "save the world for democracy," if there had ever been such a war, but to save the world for approaching totalitarianism. He might have to die to consolidate the growing power of ancient despotism and the true reactionaries. America might have to die in order that her people could become slaves.

So Edward drew on his dwindling resources to finance men of wisdom and freedom to bring their views to the public means of communication. He financed two radio speakers, helped to support a number of newspapers and magazines who were fighting the losing battle of liberty in America. He backed Senators and Congressmen who endlessly warned the people against entangling themselves in any war in Europe, and it did not matter to Edward to what political party they belonged. It was enough for him to fight with them to save America from her enemies.

All this was profoundly exhausting to this beset and almost dying man. It seemed to him that life had degenerated into a most awful nightmare, where he struggled against unseen terrors with leaden arms and paralysed legs. He could not talk of these things to Margaret. Once George Enreich had said to him, "There is an old couplet: 'Things unspoken —spirit unbroken.'" Despite the claims of psychiatrists that a man was relieved of much of his pain when he talked of his troubles and fears, Edward instinctively knew that such discussions could plunge the soul into unrelieved and hopeless despair. The throwing open of a closet that contained a skeleton did not meliorate instinctive dread, but increased it by displaying the terror in all its inexorable threat to life, all its inexorable promise that the living would one day be reduced to this. Silence frequently permitted the spirit to delude itself that all was not lost. The face of a confidant too often mirrored one's own hopelessness.

There were times when his exhaustion numbed him, prevented him from thinking, and he lived for a while in a black and stony quietude where his own voice, in speaking, seemed to echo hollowly in his ears like the voice of someone else. And there were more times when he was assaulted by that passionate urge to die; there was scarcely a week when he did not suffer these agonising urges.

When Margaret looked back to March 18, 1937, she wondered why no guardian angel, no hovering spirit, gave her any warning on awakening of what she was about to suffer and endure on that day. It had begun as bleakly as any of the other winter days, motionless, half-thawing, half-snowing, with a sky the colour of parchment. No sign of spring made tender the stiff, stark trees; the snow lay in heaps on the grounds like the swell of new graves. She felt especially dull and had a weary headache. It was one of her days to serve at the Clinic, but she decided that she would shop in order to lift her heavy spirits. Surely, spring would come. Surely, with the spring, some hope would return to this hopeless world. A new hat, perhaps, or a new coat, would act as an inspiration, she told her disbelieving heart.

She was about to go out when a maid informed her that "an old priest" wished to see her, and was waiting downstairs at that very moment. Margaret frowned. She knew no priests, old or young. Father Jahle had been transferred to Detroit, and was now a monsignor there. "Are you sure he isn't Mr. Hellar, our new minister?" she asked the maid. (Mr. Yaeger had died three years ago.) The maid was positive that the caller was a priest. So Margaret, sighing, picked up her cheque-book, certain that this was a charity affair.

A tall old man with very white hair rose from his seat in the hall as she came downstairs, a man with a serene and gentle face and large and brilliant brown eyes. He was very thin in his clerical black, but his smile was radiant. "Is it Father Jahle?" she asked in surprise and uncertainty, hardly recognising him. "I mean, Monsignor Jahle?" She gave him her hand and he shook it, and something warm and comforting enveloped her heart.

"Yes, Mrs. Enger. I'm glad you haven't forgotten me," he said.

"I never forgot you—Father," she said, and without knowing why she was glad, almost happy, to see him. He glanced keenly, but with tenderness, at her pretty, anxious face. He thought how young she still appeared, in her light brown suit, her yellow blouse, and with her hair still bright and curling. He thought he had never seen such a pure blue in anyone's eyes before, the purity of the blue in the Blessed Mother's robe. "Do come into the living-room," said Margaret. It was ridiculous that she should feel suddenly safe, in the presence of a friend, suddenly delivered from her pervading misery. "I can't tell you how glad I am to see you!" she exclaimed, and was astonished at the ring in her own voice.

She led him into the dim drawing-room; the sky was darkening; there would be a heavy snow. She turned on a light. "Have you had lunch?" she asked.

Yes, he had had lunch only an hour ago, at the home of the priest who had taken his place. "But, you must have some coffee," she said, and rang for a maid.

He had been in this house only once or twice, and that, many years before. He saw that Margaret's influence was responsible for some of the lighter and less ponderous pieces; they were like her, delicate and graceful. There was a twinkle of crystal here and there; the curving line of a fine piece of silver; a glow of ruby or amber glass. Margaret, strangely lighthearted, knelt on the hearth and touched a match to a waiting fire.

They sat and drank coffee together, and ate a little cake, while a rising wind began to thud at the windows. "I'm so sorry that Ed won't be back from New York until after dinner," said Margaret. "Are you staying in town long?"

He hesitated. "Only until to-morrow morning." He smiled at her, and all at once, and it was so absurd! she wanted to sit closer to him and cry. "But I won't go until I see Eddie." He hesitated again. His hands, she saw, were so frail that they were almost translucent. "Eddie hasn't written me for some time."

Margaret looked at her cup. "I know," she said. "Things haven't been easy for Ed. You know how business is, Father. And then—well, there are . . ." She stopped. She could not tell him; there was too much to say; it would take days even to begin. She glanced up, and saw that he was regarding her gravely, and that in some way he understood. He said, "But I often hear from my old friend, George Enreich."

Then, he did know. "Mr. Enreich and Ed," she began. "I mean, they see each other—now. And I call on him a couple of times a month. It's so sad that he's bedridden, so strong and vital a man."

"And not very patient," said the priest, and smiled a little. "He's been writing to me that he won't return to the Church, and won't have the Last Sacrament, and won't leave a penny to the Church or any of her charities, unless I hear his confession—which he hasn't made for over fifty years."

They laughed together, thinking affectionately of George Enreich, still virile in mind if not in body.

"So, that is why you are here, to minister to him," said Margaret.

Monsignor Jahle did not answer, and Margaret looked at him and saw that he was grave again, and that his pale face had coloured slightly. "I'll see him, of course," he said. "But what really brought me, right now, is Eddie."

Margaret was very surprised, then touched. "Perhaps," she said, "Mr. Enreich has been worrying you too much. About Ed."

He put down his empty cup and clasped his hands between his knees, and his eyes, suddenly fixed on her, were the eyes of a shy child. "Mrs. Enger, I hope you won't think me foolish or superstitious. Superstition is forbidden us, you know. But I had to come to-day, about Eddie. You see, I had a dream two nights ago about him, and it was so vivid and compelling that I was—I was . . ."

Panic tightened Margaret's throat, and she put her hand to it. "What do you mean?" she faltered. "A dream? Everybody has dreams. . . ." Her colour left her face, and even her lips. "What do you mean?" she cried. "What dream?"

"Please. I didn't mean to frighten you," he replied, concerned. "It was, after all, only a dream. Perhaps I shouldn't have mentioned it. But I really wanted to know that Eddie was all right, that he wasn't ill. Human and foolish of me, wasn't it, to think that he might not be well?"

Margaret stood up, the panic quickening in her. "Of course, he's well!" she exclaimed. "That is, I don't think he is any worse than usual. Tired. Worn out. Worried. But who isn't these days?"

He got to his feet, his head bent. "Yes. Yes, of course, Mrs. Enger." His voice was still hesitating, and expressed his contrition. "You see, Eddie is someone special to me. I've known him since he was a little boy."

"And I have, too," said Margaret, trying to smile over the pain in her constricted throat. "And, I love him, too. I love him with all my heart. I couldn't, wouldn't, live, if anything happened to him."

He glanced at her with gentle sternness. "You mustn't say that, my child. Who is any of us to challenge, to defy, God, to say 'I will not' to anything He demands of us?"

Now Margaret was distracted. She clenched her hands together and leaned towards him. "That's clerical talk!" she cried. "What do you know of human love? I've never had anyone in my life, but Ed! Don't talk to me about my children! Do you think for a moment I wouldn't sacrifice their lives to save their father's life? That I wouldn't agree to their life-long unhappiness if it would give him happiness?"

She was breathing very fast, for terror had struck her. "What is God to me, without my husband? What is anything to me, but him?" (What had he dreamt, this unworldly priest with a saint's serene face? What had he dreamt about Ed? She wanted to know, but dared not know.)

He put his hand on her arm to quiet her. "Mrs. Enger, it was God who gave you your husband. Eddie is as dear to God as any other soul. Do you think He would injure Eddie? Or you? Please listen to me. I've known from the beginning that you and Eddie had a true marriage, that you were indeed of one flesh. God has greatly blessed you, in your husband, and Eddie, in his wife. As for what I've said, and I see now I have greatly offended you, and perhaps have greatly offended God, it was because of George Enreich. He wrote me last week that Eddie was—well, he seemed very tired and distraught. I brooded on it, while I prayed for Eddie. And so my anxiety induced my dream. I should have just inquired about him, or have waited to see him. You see, I called his office this morning, and they said he was away and did not know when he would be back. And so, I thought I'd come to see you, for personal reassurance. My selfishness has caused you much concern. Please forgive me."

Margaret sat down abruptly and put her hands over her face. Then she began to speak, in short phrases, her breath catching. " Dear God, I don't know what to do! I'm almost out of my mind. I can't even pray to God, for Ed. I'm too frightened." Her voice came muffled through her fingers, and sounded like a long and muted groaning. " And now, I don't believe any longer. Ed's suffered so much ; there'll never be any relief for him. No one can deliver him from his . . . It'll go on for ever, until he dies of it, and I die with him. It isn't just his business. It's everything else. It's his whole life! It's something terrible I don't know about, and perhaps he doesn't know, either. What can I do, what can I do?"

She dropped her hands and huddled in her chair, her head fallen, her face and eyes as dry as dust with her anguish.

Monsignor Jahle regarded her with deep sorrow and pain. Many years ago, he had asked this pretty and frenzied woman to help her husband, but she had not understood. She still did not understand. But God was merciful. Perhaps He would give her understanding in time to save Edward from himself and his secret and fathomless agonies.

The priest wanted to say these things to Margaret, but he saw that if he spoke it would only increase her distraction and confusion. She was not ready. So he said, " You can pray, Mrs. Enger. You can, at the very least, try to pray. God hears every word. Believe me, I know it. Dark and furious though the world is, caught in its own darkness, and baffled though all men are, and terrified, even evil, and lost, they have only to lift up their voices and call, and God will know, and God will help."

Margaret shook her head over and over, without sound. He put his hand gently on her arm. " Dear child," he murmured, " don't despair. Pray, out of your love. And my prayers will go up to God with yours."

She did not look at him. And so he went alone out of the room and out of the house, torn with sympathy, his lips moving in supplication.

It was a long time before Margaret became aware that he had gone, and that she was alone. The fire was bounding in red leaps on the hearth, and she was as cold as death.

Edward had not gone to New York but to Washington. He

had stayed there a full day, and then the next morning he had left.

His train was approaching Waterford. He lay back in his chair, his eyes closed, and he looked like a man already dead, his face livid and sunken, his eyelids stony and smooth and purple. The porter passed and repassed him, glancing at him dubiously. That there gentlemen sure was sick-looking. Hardly breathing. Once he paused by Edward's chair and said, "You all right, mister?" And Edward without stirring or opening his eyes, had replied very quietly, "Yes, I'm all right. Just resting."

I won't think of it, until I get home, he said to himself. It won't do any good, thinking. I can't hurry the train; I can't do anything but sit here. And try to breathe. God, this pain!

Chapter Twelve

Margo sat with her husband, Gregory Enger, in their secluded suite at the far eastern side of the house. She was not smiling; her bold face had something harsh about it, for all its smooth coarseness. She sat at her dressing-table and pulled a brush angrily through her straight blonde hair, and watched Gregory in her glass. Her large white arms flashed in and out of her blue velvet dressing-gown.

"We can always get that friend of yours, that psychiatrist, what's his name? Lorensen. Damn it, Greg, stop running up and down the room and listen to me!" She swung her big round thighs on her chair and twisted around the better to see Gregory.

"You know what they're always saying in Washington, that people who disagree with progressive policies are mentally ill, that anyone who thinks the Constitution means anything in these days is insane, and that men like your brother, who hate the progressives, should be confined and treated in mental hospitals. Why, almost all the psychiatrists say that, and you know it! What more do you need?" She slapped her brush down on the glass top of the dressing-table. "Damn! I've cracked it. Who cares? Well? You've talked to Lorensen about Ed, haven't you? And didn't he say that Ed must be out of his mind, always talking about this country getting in some war in Europe? Didn't he say that Ed was crazy and mixed up, about Socialism? He should know Ed personally, and the booby wagon would be at the door before you could blink your eyes.

"God damn it, Greg! I want money, a lot of money. You can get a dozen psychiatrists to swear that Ed is out of his mind; why, you can buy them! Lawyers do, when they're defending criminals. You can get them to swear that it's their opinion that a murderer is what he is because he came from a broken home, or something, or his dad spanked him for wetting his pants when he was five years old. Or he had a complex because his mother had red or green or bright blue-pink hair. It's done every day. Get Ed certified, and put where he belongs. Then we'll all have money; we can sell out those damned stores, and divide it up, and we'll be rich. Rich! My God, rich! A couple of the best cars. Clothes! Diamonds! Stop staring at me like that, just because I have some common sense."

Gregory stopped near her, his eyes screwed up tightly, his mouth puffing erratically at his cigarette. Margo went on: "Didn't you say that the psychiatrists are getting up a symposium, or something, to say that reactionaries be given what they call 'loving and tender care' until they're cured and get on the progressive band wagon? Didn't Lorensen say that George Washington was mentally ill, and must have hated his father, and that's why he disliked the authority of England? Well! If he can publish that stuff, he can do something about Ed."

Gregory, in a stifled voice, "Ed's not crazy, and you know it. He's just on to people like us, and he knows as well as we do what we want."

"All the more reason he should be put in the booby hatch where he won't be so dangerous. It won't be long before there'll be a showdown—remember that Martin Dies, and his Committee! How'd you like to have to testify before that —— Texan, anyway? The White House couldn't even scare him; he's got the F.B.I. behind him. Maybe they'll get their own psychiatrists to say *you* are crazy. Don't laugh." Her loud hoarse voice rose to a brawling tone, and Gregory winced.

"Do you have to yell like a train caller? Let me think."

"All right. Think! I'm not too sure about your brothers,

either. You couldn't pull Ralph in, or Dave. And Ralph and Violette will be here to-morrow. You'll have to talk to them —Ralph and Violette. Cook up some story. Ed's emotionally disturbed, and all that stuff. As for me, I'll swear to anything, and you can, too. I'll swear he pranced around naked every morning, at dawn, and doused himself regularly in that lousy fountain, even in the winter. Cut up paper dolls, too. Anything, for a diamond necklace and a fourteen carat emerald-cut ring, and a big car of our own."

Gregory glared at his wife in the mirror. There were patches of grey at his temples, and streaks of grey through his thick black hair. Margo glared back at him. Then, all at once, he was sick. She was a fool, of course, with that talk about certifying Ed. A big, coarse fool of a woman. He had looked for strength in her, for comfort. He remembered the night they had first met, she had been like a sunflower at the edge of a poisonous jungle. . . . He shook his head dazedly. But I was the one who corrupted her, he thought with sudden starkness. I put that jargon into her mouth, and she believed it, and it was all truth to her. Because she loved me, I suppose. Ed liked her ; he always did like her. I don't suppose that he ever thought she was like me. What am I like? What am I, with all those articles for the Party's papers and periodicals? Did I ever really believe it? Do I believe it now? What am I? What was I ever looking for?

It was too late now to ask himself these questions. He was committed. He had committed his wife, who had never really known what it was all about, not once in her simple, avaricious, trusting and—yes—her loving life. He had been able to corrupt her because she loved him. Did he love her now that she was corrupt?

" Look," he said, through his teeth and his sickness, " I'm not a real Communist, Margo. Did you think I was? I just joined a number of fronts, and wrote for them, and for—other magazines and papers. I was on the committees, *sub rosa*." He paused, for she was staring at him in amazement, her eyes big and unbelieving.

" What're you trying to tell me?" she cried.

That I didn't, and don't, believe a damned word I've been writing and saying all these years, he answered her in his wretched mind. That I'm scared to death now. That I was a coward, and hated Ed. That there wasn't a stinking place in the world to which I belonged, and I had no moral values or morality, because my father had taken them from me with his 'abstracts.' Because I'm weak, and I needed to have an archorage, and a sense of belonging. Because I knew, deep down, that I was really nothing, only a trifling, vengeful fool. And Ed was handy for hating, for he always could make me despise myself, and because I had him fooled for a long time. Because I didn't have the fortitude to stand on my own feet. A thousand "becauses.' And now I can look at myself, for I'm frightened to my very bones; they're coming closer; they may even have my name by now, and know everything I've done. Does a man have to be frightened to see himself for the first time?

"Margo," he said through his sickness. He wanted her strong arms about him, he wanted a renewal of her simplicity, he wanted to be cleansed. . . . But he had corrupted her; he had given her hatred and lies. It had taken him months to make her believe what she now believed about his brother. Even then, during these years, she had doubted at times. She had laughed with Ed occasionally, and he, Gregory, had seen the wrinkle of doubt between her bold blue eyes. She had come to her husband to be reassured, to be convinced of the rightness of the "crusade." Each time it had been easier. All that was intrinsically kind and honest in her had been silenced with the clamour of jargon and propaganda. Why had he, Gregory, wanted to corrupt her? What had been the imperative? He had forgotten. He hated himself; he hated those he knew in Washington and New York, the smirking, or the fanatical, or the cruel and zealous, or the benighted fools like himself. The hating, cowardly, snickering fools like himself! He hadn't even sold himself for the legendary thirty pieces of silver, he thought, drearily. He had sold himself only for hatred, when he could have been a man.

It was never Ed, he said to himself. It was only ourselves, my brothers and my sister—and I. Why do I have to know it now for the first time, without lies? All these years—and for the first time! When I feel I'm cornered, and there's no one I can go to for help—not even my wife.

Margo, watching him, jumped to her feet affrightedly. "Greg! What's the matter? Honey, what's the matter?" She ran to him and put her arms about him and her warm breast was against him. "You're scared, honey. Don't you be scared! Why should you be afraid of him, when we're right, when he's our enemy? You're tired; all that writing you've been doing; all those friends of yours called up before the sub-Committee. But now it's going to stop. You don't have to be afraid any longer. Honey, don't shake like that!"

Her arms were warm and strong; her lips were against his cheek; he could smell her robust perfume and feel the sturdiness of her body. Yes, he loved her, even if he had corrupted her. He wanted to say to her, "Margo, I'm a liar. I've been a liar all my life." But Margo was not a liar; she would not understand. She would stand back from him and see him, and that would be the end.

She was standing back from him now, her hands still on his shoulders, and staring at him in puzzlement and concern and affection. Then the telephone rang, and she muttered an obscene word and reached for the instrument, her eyes still questioningly on her husband. She said sharply into the telephone, "All right, Fran." She waited, and her face changed, the sockets of her eyes widening. "I have it," she said at last. "Yes, yes. Yes, Arnold. Washington?" Her voice rose shrilly. "He was in Washington?" She listened again, and her pink cheeks whitened and her eyes stared at Gregory with hard terror and consternation. Then she put the telephone down.

"What's wrong?" cried Gregory. But he knew with all surety.

Margo looked down at the telephone without moving. "He—he's been to Washington. To see some—friends. They asked him to come. That's what Arnold told me. It's that Senator, that old man, Sheftel. He told Ed—Arnold got it through someone in Sheftel's office—that if you didn't stop right away you'd be called before the sub-Committee. Sheftel wanted Ed to do something, for Ed's and the family's sake." She shivered, and sucked at her lips. "Well," she went on. "Well. Jesus Christ."

Gregory's lips turned as dry as stone. Margo looked at him now, and she saw his demoralisation, his great terror. She sat down suddenly. "Well," she said, again. She leaned her cheek on her hand, putting her elbow on the dressing-table. She tapped her foot. "Anyway," she murmured, "they're not going to do anything yet—not call you, or anything. It's just Ed we have to handle."

The sleet and wintry wind pounded at the windows. Margo gnawed a hang-nail. She was not afraid for herself. All the powers of her healthy body and her simple mind were gathering forces to protect her husband who stood there and could not move and who could only stand and look at her desperately. She wanted to run to him again, and to hide his face against her shoulder. But she had to think. For him. She swung her leg, and pulled absently at a thread in her robe, dangled it, then let it fall to the floor.

Then she got up and forced a big smile on to her face, and went to Gregory and put her arms about him again. " Hell, honey. He's your brother, though he's a real bastard, and for his own sake, and the family's, he won't let you be hurt. And what can he do to you? Anything he'd do he'd have to explain. And it'd be the worse for him, too. Him, and his precious goddamn stores. He'd be more afraid of the newspapers than anything else. He'll keep it quiet. He'll even pay—somebody—to keep it quiet. You can buy almost anybody for money. Besides, didn't that old flea-bag of a Senator tell him? Would he have told him if they—they—had it all planned to call you? It was just a warning."

" A warning," repeated Gregory in a dull and fainting voice. He was very cold; he leaned against the warmth of Margo's arms.

" Sure, sure, honey." She kissed him smackingly. " I'm here, aren't I? I won't let him—well, do anything to you. We'll go away, if that's what he wants. But we won't go away without money! We've got him there, by the short hairs!"

The sickness was on Gregory again. The necessity for cleansing was on him like a wild fury and the necessity for confession. Margo would heal him; she loved him. It was possible, if he explained in simple words, that she would understand. But even while he tried to form the words there was a knock on the door, and a maid said, " Mrs Enger? Mr. Enger just got home. He wants to see Mr. Gregory in the library, right away."

Margo spoke over her shoulder at the door. " All right," she said, impatiently. " He'll be down in a minute." She smiled deeply at Gregory. " Now, honey, you just be sure of yourself. You'll have to talk to him. Here, help me off with this damned robe." She showed herself in her glistening silk slip. Her breasts thrust against the soft fabric. "I'm going down with you, darling. He's not going to bully you. He's not very bright; you said that yourself. You can explain it all away. Laugh. We'll both laugh. And we can tell him that some of the trouble he's been having lately with the Government is because you've got friends in Washington. You can promise him more, if he won't listen to reason. There, now; just pull that over my right shoulder." She patted his face lovingly, and gave him another big smile.

What can I say to him? thought the grey-faced Gregory, as he and Margo went out into the hall together. There's nothing I can say now, nothing he can forgive, or want to understand. "Look," whispered Margo, pulling him back a little. "There's Margaret going down the stairs. That's good. She knows he's home, too. She'll help us calm him down. I think we're just scaring ourselves to death."

They let Margaret go far ahead of them. They did not move until she had run down the stairs. She had not seen Gregory and Margo, and she was smiling almost happily. Edward had not called to her to come, but she had been waiting, and she had heard the car return. It was not surprising to her that he had gone directly to the library. He often stopped there first to put papers into the safe and glance at his mail, before going upstairs. He was safe! He was at home. That priest, with his superstitious dreams! She clutched Gertrude's and Robert's new letters in her hand; they had arrived this morning. She would mix Ed a drink; she would sit near him while he read the letters, and, for a while, for just a little while, they would laugh together as they used to, and discuss the children.

She opened the library door. The room was full of lamplight. She still smiled. "Ed, darling," she said. "I was waiting for you. I'm so glad you're home! Here are . . ."

And then she stopped. Edward was standing behind a table and his face was terrible and fixed and his colour was ghastly. He looked at her and said in a very quiet voice, "Go away, Margaret. I'm going to be busy for a few minutes. Go upstairs. Stay there until I can come up."

She had never seen him like this, not even when business was at its worst, not even when he was most beset and distracted. She had never seen that expression on his face before, that frightful expression, that steady flare of the eyes. Her heart thumped; she was sick with fear. He was too still, too motionless.

"Oh, what is it?" she cried, overcome with her fear. "What is it, Ed? Tell me. I have a right to know. I'm your wife." She held out her hands pleadingly. She prayed inwardly, Dear God, what is the matter? What is wrong?

"I said, go away, Margaret." His voice did not change, did not become excitable or annoyed. "I don't want you here."

She stood in the middle of the room, transfixed with her awful dread. He is dying, she said in herself. Ed is dying. Absolute horror and panic shook her heart. She advanced a little into the room, and he held up his hand. She could see him more clearly now in the lamplight, and his eyes were brilliant and immobile. Yet his voice was still quiet when he repeated, "Go away. I don't want you here just now."

She swallowed dryly. Before she could move or speak again the door opened and Gregory and Margo stood on the threshold. Margaret regarded them with wild confusion, but even in that confusion, and her fear, she saw with curious clarity that Gregory had a deathly look, that Margo, though smiling, was colourless, and that about them both was a disordered air of trepidation and shocked alarm and utter fright. They seemed to falter on the threshold, rather than to stand on it. Margo's arm was twined tightly through Gregory's; she appeared to be holding him upright, and then she gave Edward a glance of fearful challenge, defiance and fortitude.

"Well?" she said, and her bold voice was almost shrill. "You wanted to see Greg?"

Margaret moistened her lips; her eyes darted from the faces of Gregory and Margo to Edward, and her confusion made her head swim. She put her hand to her temple, and frowned vaguely.

But Edward looked only at his wife. "Do you want me to put you out?" he asked.

Margo shouted, "Why? Why shouldn't she stay? What do you mean, asking Greg to come down here, like he was a servant or something? Why shouldn't Margaret hear what you want to say? Are you afraid she wouldn't love you any more?"

Her big mouth, stained with scarlet that only pointed up her pallor, sneered. In a wheedling and lowered voice she said to Margaret, "Don't go, darling. He—he came back—from somewhere—and then like a slave driver or something he told a maid to send Greg down here. . . . Don't go," she pleaded.

"Why, why?" muttered Margaret. "What is it?"

Margo held out her hand to Margaret, and Margaret involuntarily recoiled. A sensation of unreality fell over her; objects in the room, and those three faces, began to blur.

Margo, gathering passion again in her panic, and her anger against Edward, and her concern for Gregory, exclaimed, "What's it all about? Greg, ask him. Don't just stand here. He—he can't kill you!" Still holding her husband by one arm, she reached across his chest and shook his shoulders with her left hand. "Oh, Jesus!" she exclaimed, "be a man, honey, be a man!"

Margaret, dazed and with increasing confusion, faltered, "What is it? What have you done to Ed?"

Gregory came feebly to life. His voice croaked impotently once or twice before he could say in a very weak tone, "I don't know. But just look at him! What is all this—a secret?" Something vital slipped inside of him, something that had never been very strong but which was completely demoralised now.

"Not any longer," Edward replied to him. "And I think you know."

Margaret said faintly, "I'm not going. There's something wrong with my husband!" She took a blundering step towards Gregory. "What have you done to him? It's something you've done! I can see it in your faces." Her eyes shone on him, distraught.

"I don't know, I don't know," said Gregory, in that weak voice. It was too unbearable now to look at his brother. "We don't know," said Margo. "He—sent for Greg. And then we came in—and he's like this. Maybe he's lost his mind," she added, her tone rising almost hysterically.

Edward said to his wife, "I can't throw you out bodily. And what I have to say won't take a but a minute." He turned his baleful glance on his brother.

"I've been to Washington. A friend asked me to come—to save me and my family from disgrace." He spoke almost in an uninterested fashion. "I know all about you now, you vicious halfwit. I know what you've been doing; I know about the people you've been associating with; I know the kind of writing you've been doing for years. Don't speak. It won't do you any good."

He caught a sudden breath, harsh and loud in the quiet of the leathery library, and he quickly pressed a hand to his chest. Margaret, stunned, stared at Gregory and Margo. Edward looked at his watch. "It's almost half-past seven. I want you, and your wife—your wife I thought might put some sense and decency into that feeble brain of yours—out of this house before midnight. That's nearly five hours." He caught his breath again. He said, very simply, "And if you aren't out of this house by then, I think I'll kill you, not because you've been so important, but because of the thing you are, and what you always were."

Gregory straightened up rigidly as if shot and as if at any moment he would fall heavily to the floor.

"How dare you talk to Greg like that!" Margo was shouting again in frenzy. "You're all crazy, mixed up. You're out of your mind! We're not going out of this house like a pair of refugees, just because you've got a brainstorm. You're not Hitler." Her voice, in her panic, dropped to an incongruous note of threat, for she was shaking. "I think it'll be more safe for you for us to stay, Ed. You've been having trouble with Washington for some time, Ed. Do you want more? Do you really want trouble, trouble that'll put you out of business for ever? Greg can do that to you, you see."

There were blinding tears in her eyes. She had had to force Gregory against the door jamb to hold him upright. What was the matter with him? Why didn't he stand and talk and smile surely as he always did? He was always so brave—he could stand up to anybody—he could speak and make people just wilt—Greg, Greg, she implored him silently, in her distracted mind. You know what to say!

Then Edward smiled, a strange faint smile, almost of compassion, and Margo blinked as she saw it turned on her. "I ought to have known he'd get around to corrupting you, Margo. I shouldn't have been such a fool that I'd have overlooked that. I should have told you to go home, Margo, where you belong, among your own kind of people, and not among diseased brains. Don't you understand? He's my brother, who's lived on me all his life. He's never earned a really honourable cent all the years he's lived. Nothing will stop his kind except a rope or a gun. I ought to have known what he was, from the very beginning."

Again and again that torn and ragged breath sounded harshly in the room, even against the sound of the wind.

"Nothing but a rope or a gun," he repeated.

Margo's eyes rounded and glared. "Really crazy!" she exclaimed. "I always said you were, after what Greg told me about you. You're nothing but a Hitler! Trying to scare people to death, trying to drive people out. Sometimes I thought maybe Greg was wrong; my dad never talked like Greg; my dad met Greg once, and didn't like him. But Dad's an old reactionary fuddy-duddy. . . ." She swallowed visibly, and her tears overflowed her eyelids and fell over her firm round cheeks. "And now I see Greg's right, and your kind don't have the right to live, and I can say it to your face now!"

Margaret listened, and it was all clear to her. She pressed her clasped hands deeply into her breast. She looked at Gregory, and the blue of her eyes was like lightning.

Gregory, who gave the impression of grovelling, whispered, "I'm not a Communist, Ed, if that's what you mean. Margo, shut up, you and your idiotic bellowing. Don't listen to her, Ed; listen to me."

"What?" whimpered Margo, and her arms dropped from him.

"I'm a liberal, Ed," Gregory went on, and his whine was louder. "I'm a progressive. I know your ideas and you know mine. We've argued with each other, and have had some quarrels. But, as you've said, I'm your brother. Your brother, Ed. Do you think I would do anything to hurt you? What would that profit me?"

"Why, what d'you mean!" Margo shrieked. "All you've told me——!"

Edward closed his eyes for a moment. When he opened them they were more terrible than ever. "Don't lie any more, Greg," he said. "You've lied all your life. Look at Margo, and see what you've done. You parasite, you liar. And now you're finished. I could let my friends in Washington do what they want to do. One call from me and you'll wish you'd never been born. One call, and that's the end of you. I'm letting you go quietly. I don't care where you go or how you'll get there. But I warn you, if I hear anything more you've done—then I'll find you, wherever you are."

Now Margo was sure she knew! This was what they all did, these reactionaries! Scared people out of their minds! Browbeat them and murdered them and robbed them, and chased them away! Greg was right. He'd been right all the time, and she'd argued with him sometimes. Poor Greg, poor Greg. She clenched her fists and leaned towards Edward, and shouted hoarsely:

"Don't try to scare us, you fascist! We don't scare. Oh, we'll go. But we want ten thousand dollars, right this minute, and an allowance, or you'll be sorry all your life, and Greg's going on with his work and you can't stop him! Your friends? We got friends too, and you'll find out." And she shook her head so passionately and vehemently at Edward that her smooth chignon loosened as if in a wind. "Look what you've done to him! Frustrating him and making him a prisoner, doling out money to him as if he was a beggar, scaring the pants off him all the time! I know! But you're not going to do it any longer." She caught her breath and began to cry furiously. "I'll take care of Greg. He's got a delicate, peaceful kind of temperament, but I'm here, and you'll find out!"

Edward said to his brother, "Get out."

And then they knew this was the end, even poor, betrayed Margo. She fell silent, moistening her lips, wiping away her tears with the back of her hand, like a big child. She turned with sturdy and pitying tenderness to her husband. "Let's go, Greg, honey. We don't want to stay in a house where there's an insane fellow. You'd never know what he'd do. He's absolutely out of his mind." She took Gregory's arm again, then started violently. Margaret had uttered a great and wailing cry, a cry of the deepest despair. Margo jumped, and looked at Edward.

He was swaying behind his table. His eyes rolled up. He clutched blindly at papers, at wood, at a lamp, which tottered. His face became the colour of clay. He made a strangling sound, fell against the table. And then he crashed to the floor.

Margaret ran to him, knelt beside him, raised his head in her arms and held it tightly against her breast. Gregory, coming to life, flew to join her, but he stopped when he saw her eyes. "You've killed my husband," she whispered. "You've murdered my husband."

Wildly, Gregory looked about him. Margo uttered a high scream, and he ran at her and struck her across the mouth. "You did it!" he howled. "You killed my brother, you tramp!"

Chapter Thirteen

How long had he wallowed in that pain? Edward asked himself. A long time, a very long time, all the days of his life. But now it was over, and he was free and at peace, and he could breathe easily, and there was a lightness in him like the very essence of youth. He did not want to open his eyes; he lay in the soft darkness which seemed to strum with some gentle and triumphant music. If he opened his eyes he would be assaulted by that pain again. The pain of living, he said to himself, the immeasurable pain of living. The endless, lightless, hopeless pain of being a man. He rested on billows of warmth and comfort, and sighed with pleasure that he had been delivered.

A woman spoke, close to him, a soft and groaning voice. "You'll be kind, won't You, God?" she prayed. He turned his head in the darkness. Who was speaking?

"Not Ed, God, not Ed—just anyone else in the world," the voice prayed. "I, for instance. Take my eyes, my life, give me an awful disease, strike me down, do anything to me, kill me now, give my strength to Ed."

"I must go," he said. "You must let me go. Don't hold me." And then, "Margaret? You are dreaming, darling," he said. "Wake up. I'm here. I'm not in pain any longer. I only dreamt I had pain." And then he opened his eyes.

The pain did not return. There was a dim light about him. It was like a grey shadow rather than a light. Very slowly, then, the shadow retreated like a wave and he could see, but it was as if he saw at a great distance. He was in the very smallest of rooms, almost like a coffin, and there stood Margaret at a window, but a Margaret as tiny as a doll near a window that was only the most minute of blurs. She resembled one of those diminutive Dresden figures his mother had brought from Germany.

He thought, surprised, How little life is, how infinitesimal, how fragile, how unimportant. And how little it really has to do with us. He could hear that soft, prayerful groaning of the woman at the window, who stood with her back to him, and he said, " Margaret, my darling, it isn't worth praying about or crying about. Look at me. I am bigger than life, all of us are bigger than life. Here I am. I haven't gone away. Turn around and look at me."

But Margaret stood there, that most Lilliputian of figures, sharp and clear in colour, but still so very small. She could stand in the palm of his hand. Beyond her, he could see a faint slice of magenta in that minute blur of a window. He was in a doll's house, breathing and seeing in a doll's house. Or, he was standing at an immense distance, not on Margaret's level, not on any earthly level at all. He was profoundly interested in that fact. He was certain he was not dreaming; he could move and feel and know. Suddenly he was filled with tenderness for Margaret, his wife, the deepest of loves, moved by a love he had never felt before, so universal and yet so particular it was. And, he was joyful and free. He called to Margaret again, in a loud and sonorous voice, but she did not turn. Her litany of agony continued, in the frailest of voices. " Not Ed, God, please not Ed. My life. Everything I have. Take them. Kill me. Just spare Ed."

" But I have been spared," he said. " I'm alive, dearest. Don't suffer so. Look at me." And he rose off his pillows, got out of bed and stood up. He seemed to tower out of the doll's house, to look down at Margaret's tiny body. This confused him for a moment. Then he was impatient. Margaret had only to turn to see him, to see him strong and young and vital. To see him free. She would be happy then. He began to walk towards her. A voice called him, a man's voice, and he turned sharply.

But he could see no one. The door stood open. He hesitated. He had to go through that door; he wanted, first, for Margaret to see and know him before he went away. You see, he argued with her lovingly and reprovingly, I can't say here. Someone's calling me. You'd understand, if you'd just turn around and see. I'm not going far, not too far to hear your voice. I'll be waiting, just outside the door. Or, not too far.

"Ed," said the man's voice, urgently and with a note of command in it. He could not disobey. He walked across the floor; he was so light and so buoyant and he wanted to laugh with pleasure at his freedom of movement. At the door he paused, and for the last time he begged Margaret to look at him. But she would not. So he went through the door with the swiftness of a young child.

The hall swam in soft light, and was very silent. He could feel it like a friendly presence. He went down the stairs. There were lights in the hall, and a fire on the hearth, and lights beyond in the living-room. He could hear voices, far and muted voices, the voices of tiny creatures. He hesitated, then the man's voice called to him again, and he said, in surprise, "Yes, Padraig. Where are you?"

"Here," said Padraig. And there was Padraig, young and smiling, at the big hall doors. He had opened them. He stood in the aperture, and beyond him the world was all summer and moonlight, a world wide and illuminated and filled with the sweetest of perfumes. Padraig held out his hand and Edward went at once to him, and again he wanted to laugh with pleasure and delight. "I dreamt you were dead," he said to Padraig, and Padraig laughed. "I was never dead," he replied. "You were dreaming."

But when Edward reached out to take his hand Padraig said gently, "Not yet. Just follow me." And he stepped into the sweet and luminous world of summer and moonlight and Edward followed. Everything had a luminosity of its own, as if shining softly from within. The leaves on the summer trees were pale jewels; each blade of grass was burnished. The stars were great spheres, burning in sapphire and ruby and emerald; they were so close that it was possible to see their majestic turning and to observe the flash of their ordered passage. The moon stood in the dark sky, an immense moon, giving out her own light, and not the light of any sun. Edward saw flowers along his path that he could not remember. Roses and lilies so fair and so tall, and so fragrant, that he knew at once that they were not insensate plants but individuals who knew him and loved him, and stood proudly in their coloured radiance. He saw the animals of the field near them, not afraid, but clothed in their shy and simple innocence. Their eyes glowed and regarded him with kindness.

Then he remembered that it was winter. He turned his head and looked back, and the winter was there, cold and stark and dead, the moon diminished, the patches of snow eroded and leprous. An icy wind struck his face. He saw the house, and it was indeed a doll's house, shrunken, huddled close to the unliving earth.

" Do not look back," said Padraig. " It is always winter, when you look back."

Full of wonder, Edward followed him. Padraig was so close, yet when Edward quickened his step he could not shorten the gap between them. Padraig was leading the way across the garden, which blossomed before them in that pure silver light. The fountain splashed in drops of mercurial brilliance, and the boy who stood in the midst of the bowl nodded his head at Edward in greeting. " I thought you were stone," said Edward in surprise. The boy replied, " But nothing is stone. Everything lives." His face was no longer depraved ; it was the face of a blissful child.

Now Padraig was standing and waiting under the shadow of the grove of trees, and the trees were in full summer, their leaves plated with light and ever-turning in a soft wind. " Let us sit here and talk," said Padraig, in the deep and quiet voice Edward remembered. They sat on the bench together, but Padraig sat at a distance, and his face was smiling and peaceful. " They sent me for you," he said. " And then you must decide whether to go with me, or return."

" Return to winter?" asked Edward, and it seemed to him that he diminished and became cold and frozen.

" You have forgotten," said Padraig. " Love is there, in the winter."

" We must go back for Margaret," said Edward.

Padraig shook his head. " Not yet. It is not her time. It may not be yours."

They looked at each other, and Padraig smiled with affection and serenity. " I have only a little time," he said. " God has been good. He let me come to you. There is so much you do not know, Ed. I am permitted to show you." He lifted his and and pointed. " See, and then you must understand."

Edward turned his head. It was still night. But a small and unlovely night now. He was looking at a street, lonely, narrow, the houses dark and mean. A summer night, with hammocks creaking on silent little porches. People were alive in the dusty darkness and heat. A boy was walking down the concrete sidewalk, and it was himself. He could hear his own thoughts: "I wonder what people live for? What, for instance, am I living for?" There was an arc light spitting and sparkling on the corner, all starkness, all without merciful shadows. Clouds of blinded insects blew about the light, hurling themselves to a burning death, trying to extinguish themselves. "Why, they're like those people on the porches, and in the houses," the young Edward said, and he was filled with pity. "Why were they born? Why was I born?"

"See," said Padraig, and the street swirled, became mist, and was gone, and only the gemmed and moonlit summer darkness was there once more. "It was never real at all," said Edward with relief. But something else was forming, and it became a small and narrow room, and Edward recognised it as the parlour of the house on School Street. There was David's piano, and the oak settees with their poisonous green plush and the stiff lace curtains at the windows, and the smell of dust stifling in the hot close heat of the room. Kerosene lamps stood on a table near the wall, with its pattern of red roses crawling over green lattices. Edward's breath stifled in his throat. And there he sat, in the oak rocking-chair, and his father, young and anxious and very serious, was sitting near him. They were alone. "We sold over twenty dollars' worth of stuff to-day," Edward said, and his voice was like a memory, and it was tired.

"It is good," said Heinrich, absently. Edward was very sorry for him. He said, "I didn't believe you were dying. I thought you were just awake, and I was punishing you. Forgive me."

But Heinrich did not appear to have heard him. He was gazing at Edward with the utmost earnestness. "You must listen to me, my son, for you are fourteen years old and it is time that you knew many things, for you are no longer a child but almost a man." He spoke in German, and his voice, too, was an echo.

"Yes, Pa," said Edward, wanting to soothe and placate him, for Heinrich was very serious. In a few moments Ma would come downstairs to ask why they were sitting there, at ten o'clock at night, and market day to-morrow.

"You have been saying, my son, that you were asking yourself what meaning there is to life. There is no meaning at all; the best philosophers have said so, and though we go to church it is to listen politely. Certainly, there is a God, but who shall ever know Him? It is not our concern. Our concern is men, and what all of us must do to change the world, to make it easier and more pleasant, to make days of work shorter, to make more luxuries available for the people, to give to the people their rights, which is the control of the means of production. There must be no profits, no rewards, no millionaires."

Edward became uneasy. He wanted to say with bluntness, "What about me? I do nothing but work, for the kids." But his father looked so earnest, like an enthusiastic child.

He said to his father, "But I do think there's some meaning to living. There's got to be. What've people to look forward to, if there's no meaning? They have kids and the kids grow up and get married, and then they have kids, too, and it's all repeated, like a nightmare, and there's nothing, no meaning. Just breeding, just working, just dying."

He told his father, then, about the moths blowing themselves to a witless and unlamented death against the spluttering arc light, and Heinrich listened, looking somewhat confused and impatient. Then he said, "But, my son, we are not moths. They are not men."

"But our life and our end seem the same," said young Edward. He was very rebellious. He could not understand why his father's expression was so blank. Heinrich began to blink his eyes, trying to form an answer.

He said, at last, "But, Eddie, there is a meaning in your life and mine. The geniuses."

A grim glow lighted the young Edward's face. Yes, the geniuses. It was worth while to live and to work to bring something bright and vivid to the drabness of life! Something greater, nobler, more passionate, than mere existence. And in that work, itself a satisfying answer, there was a promise of a larger answer. Man was no thoughtless mechanism, breeding more mechanisms for endless generations, for no heroic end greater than materialistic benefits which meant nothing in the face of expanding life, which meant nothing in the face of death. Man, indeed, was no moth. He had a reason for being born; his destiny was not in this world, but in Eternity.

Not in his small animal gratifications, but in God. God gave significance to life; God gave transfiguration to mere physical existence. That was the answer, the promise!

In working, and in hoping, and in labour and deprivation, the young Edward thought, I am contributing to that glory. I am developing something great in my brothers and sister, their genius, which comes from God. And so he nodded his head joyfully at his father, and said, "Of course, the kids! It's kind of—kind of—like offering yourself on an altar." He smiled shyly. "Helping them to help God make the world more beautiful. When you do that, you show the power of God."

"Yes, yes," said Heinrich, without understanding. And then to Edward's astonishment, Heinrich continued, "They will receive honours from men. They will become rich and famous. You and I will stand humbly in the background, unseen, unheard. You and I are nothing. We can only work."

"You began to hate your father, then," said Padraig. "You began to remember that he was exploiting you, for all his conversation about the brotherhood of man. He was depriving you of your dignity as a human being; he had relegated you to an inferior plane, where you had no importance of your own. Equality, the idealism of your father, did not apply to Edward Enger."

Edward looked at the scene of himself and his father. Heinrich was slowly becoming flat and without colour; the parlour was dissolving, the heat was blowing away. Then it was all gone, and the wide and jewelled summer night was all about Edward, and Padraig's face was smiling sadly, and was so young and thoughtful and kind.

"Yes," said Edward. "Now I know. But I know a number of other things, too. How Pa must have suffered. At the end, with all he had worked and dreamed for, he had nothing. He felt useless and without purpose, and unneeded."

"He knows, now, that you have forgiven him," said Padraig. "He is very sorry; he could not be at peace until you forgave him."

Edward said, "I'm glad. I ought to have understood before. Our childhoods are like a library behind us; we have only to open the old books and read."

Padraig continued, "And then, slowly but implacably, you began to hate your brothers and sister. You had many gifts, and intuition. You knew in your heart, as the slow years passed, that their own gifts were meagre. So all your work and sacrifice and planning were coming to nothing. Your brothers and sister were depriving you of the significance of living. And, as the meaning of life, the spirituality of existence, escaped you because of your brothers and sister, you lost the Source of life and turned from Him, losing your own reasons for existence."

Padraig's eyes shone on him with compassion. "You were desperate. Without your conscious knowledge you looked for revenge. They had called themselves geniuses; your parents had declared they were. You knew it was not so, though you still tried to believe it, for life would be intolerable without that belief. You would make them live up to their assumption of genius, not for their sake, no longer for the sake of God, but for your own sake. They would never escape you. They would have to justify your own being. It was not really power you wanted, though you deceived many that it was. You were in mortal error. You had built your meaning of life on men. Deprived at last, you took your vengeance not only for your spiritual damage, but because your family had compelled you to dominate them."

Edward was silent. He looked about him at the radiant trees and grass, at the incandescent light of the moon, at the splendour of the mysteriously looming stars.

Padraig spoke again. "One day a promise was made to you when you were a child. Your hatred and vengeance darkened the vision of it, though it was closer to you than breathing.

"You know now that the things of the world, desirable though they seem, are the things of the earth and its meaningless materialism. Life is nothing, if it does not have a meaning. And its only meaning is God. Life has no verity outside the context of Our Lord. If men live without Him, they will eat the dust of the earth, and it will give them no sustenance, though they have all else. Man must equate his being with God; without that equation his life is a sum that cannot be added, for the numbers of the sum are meaningless. We were born to know Him and love Him, to work with Him on earth, to join Him after the dissolution of our bodies. His is the Truth and the Life and the Light. His is the illumination of our days. He is the answer you sought, and which you never found. Your father, in his terrible ignorance, kept you from the finding."

Edward bent his head. He was silent, and he was broken-hearted. He had lost the promise and the vision for ever. Then he looked at Padraig and said, "It is too late now."

Padraig smiled. "No, it is not too late, God is merciful. Your life has been bitter and full of pain and striving. You have had less joy in it than most men. You have done what you could in your chaos of living; you have been kind to the friendless; you have been just to all save your family. You have been compassionate. Above all things, you have been compassionate. Has not Our Lord said that charity is greater than faith and hope? You may choose even now, for no soul is bound. You are not dead. Your spirit is still in your flesh. You have only to choose. Listen!"

Margaret's wailing and agonised voice filled the warm and scented air. "Ed! Come back, come back! Dear Ed, you are all I have. Please, dear God, don't let him leave me!"

He started to his feet. "I'm coming!" he called to her. "My darling, I'm coming! Wait for me."

He turned his back to Padraig. The winter lay all about him, bleak and cold and lifeless. The snow glistened under a fainting moon, a small and frozen moon. The trees stood over him, stark and black and coated with ice. He took a step, then glanced back at Padraig. But Padraig was gone.

Edward ran over the snow and the wet and broken earth. Then the darkness was all about him, and he could see nothing. He opened his eyes.

He was in his bedroom, warm but with pain. A nurse hovered in the background; he was only just aware of her presence. He remembered everything. His dear Margaret was kneeling beside him, her face drawn and white and anguished. She was murmuring something like a litany.

It was an enormous effort even to whisper. He said, "Margaret? Darling?"

Her head lay like a stone on his pillow. He had her hand, which was as cold as death, and put it against his cheek.

"It's all right," he said, in the faintest of voices. He smiled at her. "It'll be all right—all the days of my life."

She was crying, and kissing his hand. "You've forgotten the rest of it," she said, and she was trembling with her joy; he could see ripples of returning light on her poor face. He waited, and she faltered.

"Surely, goodness and mercy shall follow me all the days of my life—and I will dwell in the House of the Lord for ever."

"Goodness and mercy," he said. "Goodness and mercy."

Chapter Fourteen

"I think, perhaps," said Edward, "that in a way it all clarified when my hen, Betsy, was killed. I suppose that sounds ridiculous, but I think it is true."

He could see the sky beyond his bedroom window; it shone with a patina like pale-blue metal. An elm bough, faintly brown, stretched its arm across the window and the buds on it had become gold with returning life. The spring wind howled softly along the eaves, and the elm bough trembled. The fire on the hearth fluttered in hot tongues among the heaped-up logs. The room was very quiet. Maria sat near Edward, knitting as always, and she listened. She had listened a great deal during these long days. She looked at her son, high on his pillows, at his quiet grey face and his peaceful eyes and his thin hands crossed on the crimson quilt.

"It is said that a pebble can throw a giant," she said.

Edward moved restlessly. "I don't think I was ever a giant. In fact, I think that in many ways I was a pigmy. A strong spirit shouldn't be thrown by a pebble."

"But many pebbles heaped up become a wall, an obstacle," said Maria. She put the knitting in her lap. "I have been guilty of many things, but the worst was that I never told you, my son, that I loved you. I also knew my strength, which was in you. My other children were weak; I wished to use your strength to shelter and guide them. Now I know that no man should be exploited for another. It is a crime against humanity and God. If the strong condescend to charity, out of greatness of heart and by an act of the will, then that is acceptable and most gracious to God. But force used against the strong for the benefit of the weak, who are often greedy, should not be accepted by the strong."

Edward turned his head to her with an effort. "I injured my brothers and sister," he said. "I ruined their lives."

Maria nodded gravely. "It is always so. You narrowed their hearts and their souls, by giving them what they demanded."

Edward was silent. He looked at the bough against the window, and he thought how strong the tree was, because it had to battle the elements for its life, and had to thrust its mighty roots into the earth, striking through stone and clay, in order to wear a crown in the sun. Then Edward said, "I'm not reproaching you, Ma." And he smiled. "But Pa wasn't the only one to blame, when I was a kid."

"Have I not admitted it?" said Maria, calmly. A streak of sun moved across her thick white hair. "Do you think I was, and am, very wise, that I have not committed almost unpardonable crimes? I told you I would never forgive you when your father died, and you would not go to him. I beg your forgiveness, as I have begged it before. I do not think what you have told me was a dream."

"I'd like to think it wasn't," said Edward.

"It was a vision, perhaps. But you were dying; so the doctor told me. He would permit no one in your room but your wife." She paused. "Who knows of the vastness of the human spirit? Is it confined only to flesh; is it concerned only with mundane things? No. Your dream was a vision, and it had a purpose, as you have seen. You have said that perhaps it was only the lucidity of approaching death which gave you an inner glimpse of yourself, of your motives. That is words without meaning. There can be no lucidity without a soul. There can be no soul without God."

A nurse came briskly into the room with a glass of hot milk, and Edward drank it slowly, and thought. He had lain in his bed like this for nearly three weeks. For five days he had been semi-conscious, a life in death filled with nightmares. He said, "I'm fairly well now. I've been wondering why the family hasn't at least come to the door to see me."

Maria compressed her lips, and took up her knitting again. She said, "The doctor advised against it for a few days more. You must not be disturbed too much." She did not tell Edward that Margaret had passionately insisted that Edward must be told this, for she had declared that she would not permit her husband's brothers and sister to see him without her express permission. She had flung this command into their silent faces, and they had obeyed.

"I have a lot to say to them," said Edward.

"And they will have a lot to say to you," replied his mother ambiguously.

"I'm glad that Greg didn't go away after all," said Edward. But his face grew taut. "I want to talk to him."

Maria said, "I think you will be interested in what he'll have to say. He was a fool; he has explained. He has sent his wife away. That must say much to you, that he has driven her away."

Margaret came into the room and stared at Maria coldly. "I think it's time for Ed to rest, Mother Enger," she said. She walked quickly across the floor, and took one of Edward's hands and kissed it with unashamed emotion, and she stood beside the bed as if to protect him. Maria rose ponderously, and she gave Margaret a kind but curious look, long and thoughtful. "Certainly," she said.

"I'm not such an invalid," Edward remarked with a smile. He moved his head to rest it against Margaret's arm. He tried not to show concern for her, for that would worry her. But she was appallingly thin, almost gaunt. The coral had gone from her lips and cheeks, and the brightness of her hair only emphasised her pale and emaciated face, the tense cords in her throat. There was a quiet air of pentness about her, a stiff rigidity, born of the long anguish she had suffered, and the terror that still haunted her nights. She had not been out of the house since the night of Edward's heart attack. "You should have a little faith," he had said to her. "You gave me what faith I had, yet you don't have it now, yourself."

"I remember that you almost left me," she had said, in that intense voice she had acquired lately. "And, according to what you call your dream, you didn't care." It was useless to explain to this poor and quietly frantic creature. Fear was still her twin, breathing with her when she breathed, lying with her when she lay. She did not entirely believe his doctors, that he would live. When she did sleep, under sedatives, it was with her door wide open and her lamp lighted beside her bed, and several times during the night, when he tossed uneasily and woke, it was to see not only the white and nodding cap of his nurse, but Margaret standing beside him in her nightgown.

Maria went to the door, and then stopped there. "I should like you to join me in the living-room in an hour—my daughter," she said. Margaret stared at her harshly and unforgivingly. " I will see," she answered.

Margaret sat beside the bed. There was a constant tic in the fine skin under her cheekbones, and this concerned Edward. " I'm not such an invalid, darling," he repeated. He held her hand ; his was warm, hers cold and dry. " Only this morning, Dr. Bullitt said I could get out of bed for a little while next week, and probably you and I can go abroad in the summer. You mustn't pamper me."

Her pale lips quivered tightly. Edward knew as well as she that his condition was an old and chronic one, and that it had culminated, under stress, in a coronary thrombosis. He would never again be able to drive himself, to work without surcease, to excite and worry himself. Yet, there were all those debts, and the never ending depression, and the need for work, and more even than work—money. Margaret pondered on this. She tried to make up her distracted mind whether it would be more a shock for him to hear the news that had come three days ago, than to let him suffer the anxiety she knew he suffered in spite of the new peace which was strengthening in him each day.

" I wish you wouldn't see William so much," she began cautiously, watching him. " He wears you out, and he comes without the doctor's permission."

" He's only here for half an hour a day," said Edward. " Besides, business must go on. Poor old William. I think I've robbed him of ten years of his life." He patted Margaret's hand, and laughed feebly. " He's running big telephone bills up, always in communication with New York. Dear, do you think it would be better for me to think and wonder what's happening, and exciting myself, than to hear the truth about my affairs, daily?"

So, she could tell him, and her throat swelled with a deep breath. " You don't have to worry any longer, about money," she said rapidly. " Not ever again. And we'll go abroad, as you said, and you'll be able to keep your Green and White Stores out of the hands of that big chain which has been pressing you and trying to gobble you up."

He half-raised himself on his pillows in order to see her better. He wondered if she had finally broken. But she was looking at him with brilliant eyes, though her softened mouth was sad. " I think you can hear the news," she said, and two tears slipped down her cheeks. " It's bad, and good news, at the same time. But first, I'm going to give you one of your pills."

" Damn the pill," he said. Alarm coloured his protruding cheekbones. " Come on. Tell me."

So she said, " Now, you've got to promise me to be calm and sensible." She was really crying now. " In a way even the bad news is good. You remember how poor old George Enreich was suffering; he couldn't get any relief——"

He interrupted quickly. " So, that's it. George is dead." He lay back on his pillows, and Margaret snatched up his wrist and felt his pulse. It was somewhat rapid.

" Listen, listen! " she cried. (Had she done wrong? What if something happened to him?) " I wouldn't have told you now, but his lawyers have been pestering me and your doctors! They've got to have your signature or something. I promised them to tell you when I could."

He was caught up in grief. " I didn't know," he said. " I suppose he wondered why I didn't come." So George was gone; one of the fixtures of his life was gone for ever.

Margaret knelt beside him, her face quivering with fright. " Darling, he knew. He knew right the next day. I sent him word, because his man had called about something. I forget why he called! It didn't matter. Look, you must take your pill. I won't say another word until you swallow it. Here's your glass of water, too."

He took the pill with listless abstraction. " Poor old George," he murmured. " I hadn't seen him for a month. There never seemed to be much time for anything, for anybody. Dear," he said, looking at her and seeing the pallid fear on her face. " I'm all right. Don't worry. Do you know you're the chief cause of my worry these days?"

" Oh, don't bother about me, Ed! What does it matter about me? You've got to listen. George was an old man. He was not far from eighty; you forget. And he had a long and very nice life, for many years. He was never sick a day until he got that arthritis. Do you think people can live for ever?"

He tried to calm her. " Margaret, you must stop tearing yourself to pieces over me. I'm going to get well. Do you hear me? I'm going to get well." But he knew, himself, that he would never have his old strength again, that never again would he be able to work as he had done, and what would happen then? This mortgaged house, the depression that never lifted, the debts, the waiting faces of those who wanted his Green and White Stores.

"You're right about George, poor old man," he said, putting a soothing note into his voice. "I remember the last time I saw him. He said if he had to wait much longer to die he'd just open his liquor cabinet and drink twenty bottles of whisky and get it over with. He was in awful pain all the time. Father Jahle was with him some of the time, wasn't he?"

"Yes," said Margaret. She put her head on his pillow. "The priest wouldn't go away until the doctors said you were out of danger. Such a wonderful person. You don't know, Ed, what a help he was to me. He had a premonition about you; he came the very day you got—sick." A spasm ran over her body and he felt it, and put his hand strongly on the head beside his.

He kept his voice calm. "I suppose Father Jahle—buried—George?"

"Yes. He did. I should have gone to the funeral, but I couldn't. Father Jahle asked me. But I couldn't! I was too afraid to leave you. But I did send flowers," she added, lifting her head and speaking like an earnest child. "In both our names."

He smoothed her fingers, noting again, with sadness, how thin and transparent they were. "That's good," he murmured. He was suddenly very tired. He could not let Margaret see how charged with sorrow he was for George Enreich, in spite of George's deliverance from pain. He thought of the years he had kept himself from his old friend, and he thought, What a waste not to forgive, not to try to understand. So we think we'll all live for ever?

Then he remembered his experience on the night he was dying. His dream—had it been a dream after all? In what he called logical moments he tried to persuade himself that it had been a dream. But then, he remembered things. He had not known that his family was in the living-room, with the lights lit, yet he had heard them, he had seen the lamps. A small verification, but still it was a verification.

If it were true, and he was inclined to believe it was, then George was not dead, but living. Padraig's voice came faintly to him from spaces not to be dreamed of: "For there is nothing but God." So he said, now, and was not so tired,

"I'm sure George is all right, though he's probably trying to organise heaven, if he's there." He laughed for Margaret's sake.

The pill began to act; he felt drowsy and content, and his grief became more bearable. Margaret was watching him with that new intenseness of hers, breathing as he breathed, relaxing as he relaxed. "Is Father Jahle coming later?" he asked.

"Yes, if you're a good boy, and won't get excited again." Margaret kissed his cheek passionately. "You don't know how you worry me! And now I've got to tell you the rest. Hold my hand tight. Tight. You *are* stronger! George Enreich left over ten million dollars. And, Ed, darling, he left you five of them, and the rest to the Church!"

The sedative was a warmth and a heaviness in Edward's shrunken body. He felt only a faint surprise, a faint gratitude, a faint, after a moment, disbelieving jubiliation. His drowsing eyes fixed themselves incredulously on Margaret, who was crying and nodding and smiling all at the same time.

"Five million dollars," she stammered. "He had no relatives; you were all he had. The will was made out ten years ago, the last one. Five million dollars, Ed! And now we can pay off the mortgage, and you can rest, and have no more worries. Oh, Ed!"

Edward closed his eyes. No more debts, no more despair—no more . . . Thanks, George, he said in his deepening drowse. Thanks, and God bless you. . . . He slept.

The nurse came in, with a smile for Margaret. Poor, pretty lady. She would have an "attack" one of these days soon if she didn't relax. She bent over Edward. "Why," she said happily, "we've got quite a nice colour for the first time." She felt Edward's pulse, while Margaret rigidly watched her. "And our pulse is doing fine," said the nurse. "We're going to be well before we know it."

As Margaret reluctantly went downstairs to join Maria, tears still ran down her face. She had not cried since the night that Edward had been stricken; there had been an ice barrier in her, a barrier of fear, behind which she had crouched, tearless and mute. She did not know that she was weeping now, for the tears slid down her cheeks even though her expression had lost its rigidity and tightness, and her mouth was trembling. She met Monsignor Jahle on the stairs and did not see him for a moment. He put his hand on her arm and she started, and looked at him blankly before recognising him. Then she gave a great, wordless sob and smiled at him. "It's all right, Father," she said. "He's so much better. And I told him about George. You were right; he had to know."

He regarded her with deep and paternal tenderness. It was possible that she had forgotten how he had sat with her for hours every day, in her speechless terror and agony. She had certainly not known or heard what he had said to her, over and over, as one speaks to a child. But she put her hand on his shoulder and said, "I'll never forget how much you helped me, Father. Never. I was afraid to listen, but I did. You did not tell me to 'resign' myself to whatever God had willed; you told me that Ed would live. You said that, all the time. If it hadn't been for you I think I would have lost my mind."

The staircase and lower hall were in shadow and silence. Only the voice of the big clock below strode through the quiet, relentless and unhurried, unconcerned with human agony. Margaret still smiled tremulously at the priest, unaware of her steadily falling tears. He took out his own handkerchief and gently dabbed them away and she was surprised. "Am I crying?" she asked, and took a tear from her cheek and looked at it, startled. "I didn't know. I haven't cried for a long time."

The ice barrier was melting in the sun of her release. She leaned against the balustrade and her breath was half-sobbing, half-laughing. "I am being such a fool," she stammered. "But it wasn't until to-day that I knew, for sure, that Ed wasn't going to die."

"I knew it all the time," he said. She nodded soberly, then was embarrassed. "It's strange that all my life, from the very time I could remember," said Margaret, "I had the deepest faith and trust in God, even in the orphanage, even with the Baumers."

Her wet eyes looked into his with shy earnestness. "And that's why I don't understand. When Ed became sick—I didn't trust God any longer. I lost my faith in Him. I—I even hated Him. I was frightened almost to death. He seemed—monstrous—to me. An enemy."

"That is an old story," said the priest, with sadness, but with no reproach. "Even Our Lord cried to the Father, asking why He had forsaken His Son. That was His human nature, calling out in sorrow and pain. Do you think He does not forgive you, dear child? He understands, where no mortal could understand. In return, He asks us to understand others, as best we can." He hesitated. "Mrs. Enger spoke to me a moment or two ago. She and her children are waiting for you downstairs."

Margaret lifted her head and her eyes flashed, then she saw the priest's grave and tender and admonishing expression. "I'll try to—understand," she said, but her voice had hardened slightly. He sighed, smiled. "You must," he said.

He started up the stairs. Margaret said, "Ed's asleep, Father. He'll probably sleep for about an hour; I gave him his sedative. I'd like to think you'll be there when he wakes up. You can tell him about George, too."

He nodded, and continued up the stairs. She saw how old and weary he was; his hand clung to the balustrade, helping him climb. I'll try, I'll try, Father, she said to him, silently. But you mustn't expect too much from me.

As Margaret went slowly downstairs she began to remember, as if in a faint, dark nightmare, filled with one far and echoing voice, the hours Monsignor Jahle had spent with her. She remembered crouching in a chair, but in what room she could not recall. The calm and loving voice had gone on and on, and it had been like a steady hand holding her and preventing her from plunging into some black pit in which she would have been for ever lost. Her children had come to her, Gertrude white and voiceless with grief, and Robert silent and pale, no longer sunny and smiling. They had meant nothing to her then. She could only sit and listen to the priest, without knowing what he said, yet desperately holding to his voice. "He will live, he will live. I have heard God's promise," the priest had murmured, endlessly.

Her steps became slower. Then she stood in the hall, thinking. The hardness did not completely go from her face, but the pale fixity of her mouth relaxed a little. She would, at least, listen to Mother Enger, though she would not be able to look at the others. They had brought Ed to the very edge of death; they were responsible for all his suffering and despair, the loss of his youth, his debts, the burden that had lain on him.

She entered the living-room. Edward's brothers and sister

were there. And David, so worn and thin. It was David who came to her, smiling a little. But, you, too, exploited and deprived him for years, her accusing eyes told him. She brushed by his hand and stood before Maria and said, in an emotionless voice, "Well, I'm here. What is it?"

Did she always knit? Margaret thought, hysterically. She's like those old women who knitted below the guillotine; Suddenly she hated Maria, and her hands clenched at her sides.

"Please sit down, Margaret," said Maria, calmly. David had drawn a chair for Margaret, and without glancing at him she sat down. She resolutely would not look at him or his brothers and sister. There was silence in the huge room; only the splutter of the fire broke it. David, Ralph, and Gregory sat without speaking, scattered over the room; Sylvia was there, stiff and straight. The firelight caught a gleam of silver, a glow of amber glass, a side of a prism hanging from a lamp. The blue spring evening stood at the windows like coloured medieval panels.

Then Maria let her knitting fall into her immense black lap. She regarded her children steadfastly, each in turn. They were no longer young. There was no peace in them, in their middle age. Perhaps it was because of this that she thought of them as children, strengthless and rootless. And frightened. David, forty-eight, lean and elegant and polished, with the patches of white on his narrow temples. Sylvia, so very thin and unfruitful, her painted mouth a magenta slash in her stark and whitely gleaming face, her black straight hair without grey, though she was forty-six. Gregory, his restlessness stilled at last, his body diminished, looking like a weaker and smaller and blurred image of the sick man upstairs. And Ralph, not so ruddy now, not so lusty and assured now, staring down at his knees. Her children.

She thought of how silent they had been since their brother's almost fatal illness, and of how quietly they had crept about his house, hardly speaking to each other, and how their eyes had avoided meeting each other's eyes. The oak had been stricken; the birds who had perched so heedlessly in its branches, taking its shelter for granted, had been tremendously alarmed, terrified and distraught.

"I am an old woman," said Maria, and now her tone was

formidable and commanding. "I am also your mother. I must ask that none of you interrupt me while I speak. To-day, I am the accuser and the judge; I am also the accused."

Her light blue eyes, veined and prominent, moved from one face to the other. Her children did not move, but they looked at their mother, and even Sylvia shrank a little in her chair, before straightening herself again. Then Maria's eyes touched Margaret. "Nor are you innocent, my child," she said.

Margaret flushed, opened her mouth, but Maria lifted her hand. "I must speak without interruption," she said. She picked up her knitting.

"My son lies upstairs," she continued. "It is only three weeks ago that he was struck down, when we were told that he would probably die. Who struck him down? You? Or himself? His wife would say you, and me. I would say all of us and his dead father. And Edward, himself. None of us is without guilt.

"To each man his brother presents a different aspect. Brothers and sisters do not see their brother as their mother sees him, nor does she see him as they see him. To his wife, he is a different person; to his children, he is still another man. To God, he is still another. Which, then, is the true aspect?"

Maria paused. "I would say all of them are true, even the worst, even the most unflattering, even the most superb and selfless and kind. To all of us he presented a different face. And each face was his own. Nevertheless, we are not exonerated."

She laced her great fat fingers together and looked into the distance. "I must ask you a question, Margaret. Did you know that my son was a true artist? A true and authentic genius?"

They all stirred. Margaret said, "I suspected it, a long time ago."

Maria nodded. "It is so," she said. "From the time he was a child I knew. Why, then, did I insist that he sacrifice what he was, what he could have been, to my other children, who were so weak and uncertain and gifted so feebly in what I at first believed was their genius? Because Edward was strong; he had the soul of a giant. And I had pride. It was not enough for me that one of my children achieve greatness. I wished all of them to have a measure of it. By sacrificing the greater I had him as my ally, who would help me develop the gifts of the lesser. Too, I saw he was the only one who could obtain the money necessary, for that developing of his brothers and sister. And money was desperately needed.

"I was not like your father, who believed that the strong should be ravished and even destroyed for the weak, and that they should be punished for their very strength, and be humbled. I did not believe, as he did, that men should be faceless, in a monotonous Eden, controlled by despots. He was never a very intelligent man, and I say this of him, who was his wife. It was a matter of politics to him, but he never, in his simplicity, understood reality. Edward was also a genius in the too little appreciated art of making money. I decided that this art would not only serve all of us, but would also serve him. He had courage, as none of you had courage. He had power in himself, and there was no power or courage in any of you."

Margaret, who was closer to Maria than any of the others, saw that the old woman's eyes had filled with tears, and for a moment there was a softening in her, a pity, for she had never seen tears in Maria's eyes before. But when Maria spoke again to her silent children her voice was as strong as before.

"I know this, that you disappointed your brother, when the gifts you had openly claimed you possessed did not materialise, or showed themselves as the mediocre ones they were. Nevertheless, he had no right to be so disappointed and show it so savagely. He had done a wrong thing; he had built his life on men, and when a man does this he builds his life on a bog which is without stability or fertility. True, he was working very hard, his youth devoured in that work, his lost youth, and he could not reconcile himself that you were what you really were. He believed that you were deliberately frustrating him, that you could be greater than you were, and that out of cruelty and greed you would not be what he thought you should be. And so he revenged himself on you and took from you what small measure of strength and courage you possessed."

Margaret cried out in bitter anger. "How dare you say that of Ed, Ed who gave all his life to these—to these wretches? Ed, who sacrificed himself, and wanted nothing for himself!" Her eyes were blue fire in the dusk.

Maria help up her hand. " I have requested that no one interrupt, please." She looked at her children, but none of them looked at her. They were very silent.

" You were his meaning for living," she said. " But no man should choose another mortal for his reason for existence. That is blasphemous. I am certain that in God's sight you are not held responsible for my son's blasphemy though you are guilty of other things, such as weakness and lack of courage and honesty and pride."

They all looked up quickly at their mother then, startled, then hesitant, and even ashamed.

Maria went on as if she did not see their glances. " Edward turned away from God when he looked for his reason for being not in God, but in you. He turned away from God when he exerted his power over you. This, too, he understands. Yet, you too, are not guiltless. You submitted to his power, and that is a crime against God. There is nothing so depraved as a slave, for a man is not a slave without his will."

She looked down at her clasped hands. " No, no man is ever enslaved without his will. There is always a moment when he can choose, even if the choice is death. In the sight of free men a slave is despicable, for a just reason.

" And now I must tell you that I have known for many years, why you submitted to your brother's power. You had wronged your deepest spirit, because you had no courage. And, knowing this, you revenged yourself on him, by forcing him to exert even more power over you, by forcing him to support you. I have known for many years what you have been doing, without his knowledge." She smiled at David faintly. " You and I have known this, but not the others. My children, look at your brother, David. He is that modern composer, called, in a somewhat vulgar manner, Davey Jones."

Now everyone in the room moved and sat up in astonishment, and Gregory and Ralph smiled and even laughed. They stared at David. Ralph exclaimed, " Why, for God's sake! " And Sylvia's thin red mouth twisted with wry mirth. Margaret said, with a loathing look at David, " So, you're a rich man! And you never once tried to help Ed, who was dying of overwork and debts and worry! "

Maria said sternly, " How little you know, Margaret. David has taken no money from his brother for many years. He did not tell Edward who he really was, because he did not wish to disappoint Edward, who surely would have been furious. Moreover, in 1929, David came to me and begged me to find a way to give his money to Edward. I knew it could not be done, for Edward hated his brother—for many reasons. But I must continue.

"I have known for too long a time that Sylvia is a wealthy designer of ladies' gowns and hats, that Ralph is the engineer who has designed many fine bridges, and was paid impressively for them, that Gregory has written many flippant stories and articles, for which he was amply recompensed, besides the books which so enraged his brother. You seem amazed, my children. But though I am only your mother, and therefore apparently not very intelligent, there is little a mother does not know about her children. There was too much smirking satisfaction about all of you, too much slyness, too much knowingness. And so, I looked for the reasons. I was also helped "—and she paused and smiled to herself—" by a very intelligent young man whom I will not name at present. He does not believe in the surface; he looks for the secrets of others."

All at once her face changed, became condemning and cold, as her eyes again moved from one shame-faced man or woman to another.

"Why did not all of you, when you became wealthy, have the courage to tell your brother, to face his anger and disappointment and humiliation, and leave his house? Because you had betrayed yourselves in your lack of courage. You were also greedy. You wished to keep your money for yourselves. Yet, you were self-betrayed and hated that betrayal, and blamed it all on your brother, to hide your guilt from your own eyes."

Her slow look of denunciation passed over them. "There is one thing I do not understand. You have been kind to each other and loyal to each other, with the exception of my son, my strong son, Edward. You must have known that his home was mortgaged. He never talked to you of business, but you must have known. Yet none of you came to his help, none of you offered, none of you even lied and said, 'I saved the money you gave me, and here it is.' You permitted him to reach the point of dying, without a word."

Then Sylvia broke out in a faint cry. "We wanted him to fail, to be ruined!" she said. And she covered her face with her white and bony hands. She continued in a muffled and trembling voice. "We never really talked about it together. But that is what we meant, and may God forgive us."

"Be sure I won't, and Ed never will," said Margaret in a low tone of hatred.

The medieval colour against the windows drifted into grey and the room darkened. The fire alone lit the room and the figures in it were like shadows, themselves, motionless and mute. Here a cheek was seen, without tint, or the outline of a head, or a fallen hand, or a still foot. Someone moved a heavy boot, as if in pain. A man muttered. Maria nodded to herself, as she listened. "You are not evil, my children," she said. "If you were, I should not have called you here to-day. Stupid and greedy and heartless, yes, blaming Edward when the blame was yours. Hiding yourselves from your own sight. Pettily vengeful, yes. But not evil."

David spoke gently, but with his mother's own sternness. "You knew all the time, Ma. Why didn't you talk to us, years before?"

"A man's salvation comes from God and from himself," she replied. "Had I spoken before this extreme situation it should have been of no use."

She looked at them formidably. "The strong inevitably take their revenge. Yes. But still, that is not the only reason for what my son did to you. Who can know the labyrinths of the human spirit, the devious passages of the mind, the diversification of the soul? We are not actors upon a stage, or puppets, who are motivated by only one emotion, which can be explained. For no man can explain another. A man is known in all his parts only to God."

She turned to Margaret, who was as still as stone and as obdurate. "Margaret," she said, "you too failed your husband, when he needed you. I had hoped that your love for him would have saved and lifted him. It did not."

"Are you speaking of me?" cried Margaret, with outrage and anger. "I would have given my life for my husband!"

"I do not doubt it," said Maria, with sad patience. "But that was not enough. I know now, from my observation, that you never opposed him except once. It was not you who rescued your children from Edward, after all. It was themselves. You would have sacrificed them to his delusion, eventually, had the children not rebelled. Surely there were many times, in many years, when you could have said to my son, 'You are wrong. Your brothers and your sister are not entirely fools and devils. Look at them. But perhaps you could not have said that, for you did not see, yourself. You did not question; you did not doubt. Unquestioning love should be given only to God, and not to any man, not even to a husband. There was no pity in you, because you loved unwisely and blindly. Instead of rescuing my son, you pushed him deeper into his illusions, you stimulated his indignation against his family, you cried injustice. Surely, it was injustice, but there is never a complete injustice. There are occasions when even the deepest love must say, 'nay, nay,' and not 'aye, aye.' For the sake of the loved one, himself."

Margaret was breathing very hard, and loudly, in her rage. She stood up. And then, without warning, she suddenly was struck with the memory of that day in Father Jahle's home, when he had begged her to help Edward. She remembered old Pierre, so long dead, who had spoken to her so oddly, the eve of her wedding. And she was sick and dazed with the glare of her sudden understanding, and she hated herself. But not as much as she hated the others in this room.

"Perhaps I was wrong!" she exclaimed, brokenly. "Yes, I was wrong. But still I feel that if Ed was wrong, too, in lots of things, his family was so much more wrong that his faults were nothing at all." She swung on Sylvia. "I think of them all, that you were the worst! You hated Ed. . . ."

Sylvia stood up as if dragged violently from her chair, and in that increasing dimness there was a wild denial in the shape of her thin body. "Do you think I saved your life, and the lives of your children, just for you, and them? God help me, I didn't know then! But I know now. I saved the three of you for Ed, and so did Dave. Look at our hands! You won't see your blood on them now, but it was there, twenty-two years ago, Margaret!"

"What?" muttered Margaret, and put her hand to her cheek.

"It is so," said Maria. "The doctor could not come. I worked, but I could have done very little alone. Perhaps I could have saved you, or one of the children. But not all of you. It was Sylvia, who after assisting me, cared for your children, and watched them, while David and I continued to struggle to keep you from dying. It was David whose voice you heard and who kept you from death, and not Edward's, though you believed it was. If Edward has his wife and children now he owes them to God and to my children and to myself."

"Oh!" cried Margaret, and her voice was a groan. "Why didn't you tell us?" She began to shiver; she felt as if she had heard the most devastating news and had committed the most dreadful crime. "Why didn't you tell Ed? It would have made such a difference." Shattered by the revelation, which still seemed to her unbelievable, tears dashed down her face.

Maria said, without a rise in her voice, "But your husband knew. I told him on the morning of his return from Cleveland, after you and your children were safe."

Margaret stared at her dumbly, trying to see her in the darkness, which flickered with the crimson of the fire. Then she whispered, "I can't—I can't—believe it. Ed would have . . ." Her forehead was icily wet, and she shivered again.

Maria said inexorably, "He told me he would give his brother and sister extra money."

Margaret pressed her hands hard and suddenly against her cheeks. "Oh, no," she murmured, appalled to her very heart. "Oh, no!" Her throat closed on a sick lump of nausea.

Maria nodded. "Yes, it is so. And that is what you must understand now."

Margaret fell into her chair, and dropped her head to her shoulder and cried desperately. The sound of her weeping filled the room, a tearing and wretched and heart-broken sound of remorse and misery. She remembered the bright and horrible nightmares of her encounter with death. She remembered Edward's voice—but it had been David's—which had called to her valiantly and tenderly, and she remembered the hand which had withdrawn her from the abyss. She cried out in her extremity, "Oh, God forgive me! God forgive—us!"

Sylvia stood up, uncertainly, all the bitter repressions of her life stiffening her body, holding her back. And then they were gone in the first warm flooding of her heart with absolute compassion. It was as if she had been released, made airy, strong and strongly tender, free of resentment, free of fear, free of a long grief. She went to Margaret with the swift movements of a young girl and knelt beside her and took her in her arms, as a sister, and said in a sister's loving voice, "It doesn't matter—darling. We're all stupid, even Ed. Don't cry, dear. I love your children too, remember? I think I love you; I'm sure of it. We were friends for a while, weren't we? We'll be friends again. Don't cry so. You'll tear your heart out." And then Sylvia, who had not wept since Padraig had married Maggie, was weeping with Margaret.

Dave came to them, and he put his hand gently on Margaret's forehead. "What does it matter?" he asked. "We understand now. I think, in spite of our greed and cowardice, in spite of the badness of our objective motives, that we all really love Ed. We loved him even when we hated and were afraid of him. I think, under it all, that we didn't want to disappoint him, or were ashamed of disappointing him."

His hand dropped to her shoulder, and Margaret turned her head to look at it, mournfully. He had seen her as her husband had not seen her, in the dishevelment and abandon of approaching death. This hand had saved her. It had been spattered with her blood. It had smoothed her sweat-soaked hair. It had touched and soothed her body. And in return for his love—and she knew now it was utter love—she had snubbed and insulted him. Humbly, she pressed her lips to his hand.

Finally, as Margaret's sobs slackened, and she let herself collapse in Sylvia's arms, and held David's hand with the desperate clutch of a child, Maria said, "There is an old poem. 'In tragic life, God wot, no villain need be. Passion spins the plot. We are betrayed by what is false within.' And so it was. We were false to the instinctive nobility God instils in every man. We betrayed Him, and ourselves."

She turned to the only one silent in the room, her son, Gregory. "You wished to say something," she said, not questioning, but only stating a fact.

"Yes," he said. "I think I knew what Ed really was. I knew, even when I was a kid, that he was better in every way than myself. Once I read some old notebooks he had; things he'd written when he had a little time in the shop. And he was strong, and I was weak. I envied him. I took my revenge on him by caricaturing him in a magazine. I took my revenge by taking up—things—that I really hated and had contempt for. Because he despised them. That was my revenge, too." He paused. "In one of his notebooks he had written about a Fourth of July, when we were all kids. It was a poem, and a damned good one, too. About what America meant to him. He really loved his country. Later, it was enough for me to try to pull his country down, and destroy it. It was like destroying Ed himself."

His voice had a high shrillness and self-hatred in it. His unseen fist hit the arm of his chair thuddingly. "God damn it," he said, and now his voice deepened. "It's too late for any of us to do anything for Ed. He hates us like poison, and he has reason for it, too."

"I do not think it is too late," said Maria, and for the first time in her children's memory her voice was trembling and changed. "If I had thought you would not respond this way I would have not spoken. Edward is getting well. I suggest that each of you, one by one, go to see him alone, beginning to-morrow, and tell him what you have really accomplished—and what you have accomplished is good in its own right—and offer him all you have. He is a most terribly lonely man."

Margaret lifted her head from Sylvia's shoulder. "But, Mother Enger, he doesn't——"

Maria overrode her voice quickly. She repeated, "You will confess to him, and offer him all you have." And Margaret kept her peace.

She rose ponderously and left the room. She moved heavily into the hall, then into the morning-room, where Gertrude and André and Robert were waiting, where she had asked them to remain. Gertrude was crying, and André's arm was about her. Robert sat in silence, his elbows on his knees, his chin in his palms.

"I was sorry I was late," she said, in her stately fashion, as the young men rose. "But I was detained on important business."

She smiled at André. "I believe your parents will be very happy. I believe that my son, Edward, and his wife, Margaret, will be happy. You will make our Gertrude a very good husband, but not in the way that term is accepted. She will never suffer from boredom. You may tell your father, Gertrude, to-morrow."

Maria was very tired. Sometimes she believed that life was too wearying to be endured.

Chapter Fifteen

Edward sat with Monsignor Jahle, near his opened window. He could see the brilliant tulips trooping through the warm dark earth of spring, and the white and green burst of the trees, and the long green undulations of the new grass. He said to the priest, "It's very strange, but for the first time I can really see the world. It's not because I almost died. It's because there's no hate in me now, and I'm not afraid. Even without George's money, I wouldn't be afraid. Fear drives us to terrible things; I think that's the explanation of all the agony in the world, and all the wars and hatred. All this would be ended if we didn't fear each other. And coming down to it, why should anyone fear anyone else? We're flesh and bone and spirit of every other man; we have the same passions and the same griefs and the same hopes and solitary miseries."

"Yes," said the priest. "But it was said centuries ago by Our Lord. Do you remember what He said, Eddie? 'Little children, love one another.' For, He is our Father."

He looked at Edward's quiet and peaceful face, and, strangely, his younger face, in spite of the suffering, both mental and physical, which he had endured.

Edward said, as if speaking to himself, "I thought, almost all my life, that my family had rejected me. I used to complain to myself that I was never asked to come down to Christmas Eve celebrations, and that I was kept from any religious education. And never wanted. But now I see that it was I, myself, who rejected my family, and rejected God. I'm not going to be maudlin and say it was all my fault, and that no one else had a hand in it. And that I was not exploited. I *was* exploited, by my father, and I knew it, and I took my own revenge on the whole family. I, too, didn't have courage. When even a child knows he is exploited, and he has some courage, he shouldn't allow the exploitation. It's his own shame and fault when he does. And I think I knew it, and hated my family because I despised myself."

"Only God knows all there is to know about a child or a man," said the priest. "He never judges us by men's standards. And, by the way "—and the old man smiled—" I understand that you and your minister are good friends, now. It's too bad about Mr. Yaeger, but you can make it up to him some way, even though he's dead."

Edward laughed. " Poor old Yaeger. I think I used to scare him to death. But I do understand, now, why I helped him through my parents. I was ashamed of myself."

After the priest had gone Edward sat alone in contentment as the blue twilight began to fill the room. He thought of how all his brothers and sister had come to him, one by one, to offer him all they had, to tell him all they had done through those years of dark nightmare. They had spoken simply, and he had listened as simply, without hurt or resentment, but only regret that those years had been wasted and blasted. By all of us, he thought. It would be ridiculous if it weren't so tragic. I'm not far from fifty; half a century! It took me this long to understand, and for them to understand. At that, we're lucky!

When his nurse came in he asked her to call his brother, Gregory. There was something not yet resolved, which must be resolved now.

Gregory arrived almost immediately. He seemed crushed, and much smaller in stature and bulk. " Well, how are we?" he asked. Edward smiled and said, " You saw me this morning. I haven't changed. Sit down, won't you, Greg? I want to talk to you."

Gregory, suddenly nervous, sat down and lit a cigarette. His restless eyes had quieted these weeks, but they had a dull and lost expression. " Give me a cigarette," said Edward, kindly. " Never mind. Damn the doctors. Thanks. That tastes good! I've sent for some drinks, too. I said, never mind!"

A maid brought in whisky and soda, and the two brothers sipped a little while in silence, while the blue at the windows turned to a gentle purple and the wind brought in the fragrance of earth and grass and trees.

Edward spoke, as if idly, " You're a writer, Greg, a damned good writer. Wait a minute; I'm talking now. And so, I want your opinion. Is André—that gay jumping-jack—a writer, too?"

Gregory moved, and exhaled as if in relief. " I can tell you this: I'm a hack compared with him. I never liked him, and

I love your kid, Gertrude, and he'll lead her a hell of a life, but a stimulating one, and I think that'll be good for her. She takes life too seriously, but André makes her laugh, and that's important."

Edward looked thoughtfully at his cigarette. " Margo made you laugh, Greg."

Gregory stirred, as though touched with pain. " Yes, she did," he muttered. " But what does that matter?"

" And you love her," said Edward, and turned his head to look at his brother. " She didn't bring on my attack. I'd had warnings for years, but I wouldn't go to any doctors. I had an idea what was wrong, and what would happen. You see, I was grimly trying to kill myself. I often wanted to. Never mind.

" Let's talk about Margo. She has the earthiness you need, and the common sense. And you love each other. When she jumped on me, and hated me, it was for your sake. She was ' protecting ' and ' helping ' you, because she knew you needed her, and she thought I was frustrating you, which I was, by the way.

" And I think she didn't understand much about the indoctrination you'd been pounding into her all the time you were married."

" No, she didn't." The film was lifting from Gregory's eyes, and the sick dullness from his face.

" So," said Edward, " why don't you go to New York to-night and bring her home? After all, I'm going to build you a house on this land, and you'll need a wife, and Margo refuses to divorce you. Ask her to forgive you. She will."

Gregory stood up in wild agitation. He put his hands on Edward's shoulders and said, huskily, " You mean it? After all we did and said? After everything?"

" Don't be emotional," said Edward. " And give me another cigarette. Why shouldn't I mean it? I'm naturally patriarchal, and I've got to have one member of the family near me. Sylvia'll still be here, with her bread-pudding husband, though they'll spend half their time in New York, and Dave spends most of his time with Billy Russell, down on that Alabama farm, writing their damned popular music. And Ralph and Violette are still batting around the world, with Ralph designing bridges all over the place and forgetting his art.

" Robert is going into the business after he's graduated in

June, and he'll be in New York at least half his time, while I manage things here with the help of old William. Gertrude's marrying André in June, and they insist on that flat at the Clinic, and I hope they get sick of it and decide to come back home! But I don't interfere any longer. Besides, they'll probably end up in New York. What's there for a writer in Waterford?

"So Margaret and Ma and myself will be alone. I'd like to have you near by for masculine company, though you, too, will be with Margo a lot of the time in New York. I'd like to give you a house, on this land, as a reconciliation present. You'll have to have a quiet place to write, you know."

Gregory, buoyant and excited, glanced at his watch. "I can just about make the Empire State Express!" he exclaimed. His broad face flushed. He started for the door, then swung back, and caught Edward's hand.

"I said, don't get emotional." But Edward smiled. "Go on. Pack your bag. And don't come back without Margo. I'll bet she isn't reading the *Daily Worker* any longer."

Gregory ran out of the room, and Edward could hear the rapid pounding of his footsteps, and the sound was the sound of a young man.

Margaret came in, briskly, and kissed him. All the worn anguish of her face had gone, and it was blooming again. Her blue eyes sparkled, and she sank into a chair with a wide gesture of her arms, simulating exhaustion.

"That girl's trousseau," she said. "It's killing me. I bought millions of sheets and other lines to-day. And she'll have only two weeks when she comes home from school to do her personal shopping and get her wedding-dress. This'll be a madhouse. Darling, have you been very lonely while I was away?"

"I'm never lonely any longer," Edward replied, and reached out and took her hand. They gazed at each other with deep happiness and eloquent silence. Then Margaret put the back of Edward's hand against her cheek and held it for a long moment.

"Oh, darling," she whispered at last. "I'm so happy these days. So terribly happy. It scares me."

Her voice caught, and she kissed his hand before releasing it.

"Nothing scares me any longer," said Edward. "By the way, I received our itinerary for our jaunt to Europe to-day.

I want you to look it over. Now, darling, wipe your eyes. We have a lot of planning to do, not only for ourselves, but for the children. We're going to be busy."

Margaret dropped to her knees beside him and put her head on his chest and he held her to him, feeling the trembling in her slight body. She was still fearful for him; she was not getting over her terror, and he knew it. It was wrong that anyone should put a whole life into the keeping of another, and all that he had said to her in these weeks was as nothing to her. She had been stricken too deeply, and now, for the first time since his illness he was afraid for her.

He looked at the deepening sky. A single star pulsed there in pure grandeur. The birds called and wove themselves in melodious patterns in the twilight, busy about life, joyful in life, innocent and delighting in life. But men were not birds, short of existence and memory. They were creatures of grief and despair, inheriting sorrow with soul, anguish with knowledge, torment with immortality. And terror, with God. For his spirit, man paid with blood and tears, and for his happiness he paid with the knowing that happiness in the world was eternally threatened, and must have an end.

Edward prayed. Dear Father, I know now that we are here to know and love and serve You in this life, and that there is nothing but You, and life has no meaning without You, and that we'll join You after the death of our bodies. I know that as a part of You we'll return to You, for it was out of You that we came and nothing can separate You from us.

This I know. But this dear wife of mine has forgotten, because she is afraid. Afraid for me. I don't know the mystery of Your plans, or how long I shall live, or whether or not I shall die to-morrow or a year from now or twenty years from now. So far as I am concerned, I'm content.

His arms tightened about Margaret, who was so very still and tense, and who crouched against him, clutching him as a frightened child will clutch its father. He kissed the bright hair with its streaks of grey, and his heart beat strongly.

He continued his prayer. Yes, I am content, about myself. But I am praying to You now for only one concession.

Permit my wife to die before me, and give assurance to her that I will not leave her, not once, all the days of her life, and mine.

The star flamed more radiantly as the sky darkened, and

now the thin edge of the moon quivered in silver fire as it rose above the trees.

Margaret raised her head from Edward's chest, and her eyes were shining. She drew a deep breath, and smiled peacefully.

"Do you know something, darling?" she asked, and her voice shook. "All at once I'm not afraid any more. Not any more!"

THE END

Taylor Caldwell

One of today's best-selling authors, Taylor Caldwell has created a host of unforgettable characters in her novels of love, hate, drama and intrigue, set against rich period backgrounds.

'Taylor Caldwell is a born storyteller.'

Chicago Tribune

THE BEAUTIFUL IS VANISHED
CAPTAINS AND THE KINGS
TESTIMONY OF TWO MEN
THE EAGLES GATHER
THE FINAL HOUR
THIS SIDE OF INNOCENCE
DYNASTY OF DEATH
CEREMONY OF THE INNOCENT

Rhanna

Christine Marion Fraser

A rich, romantic, Scottish saga set
on the Hebridean island of Rhanna

Rhanna

The poignant story of life on the rugged and tranquil island of Rhanna, and of the close-knit community for whom it is home.

Rhanna at War

Rhanna's lonely beauty is no protection against the horrors of war. But Shona Mackenzie, home on leave, discovers that the fiercest battles are those between lovers.

Children of Rhanna

The four island children, inseparable since childhood, find that growing up also means growing apart.

Return to Rhanna

Shona and Niall Mackenzie come home to find Rhanna unspoilt by the onslaught of tourism. But then tragedy strikes at the heart of their marriage.

Song of Rhanna

Ruth is happily married to Lorn. But the return to Rhanna of her now famous friend Rachel threatens Ruth's happiness.

'Full-blooded romance, a strong, authentic setting'
Scotsman

Catherine Gaskin

'Catherine Gaskin is one of the few big talents now engaged in writing historical romance.'

Daily Express

'A born story-teller.' *Sunday Mirror*

THE SUMMER OF THE SPANISH WOMAN
ALL ELSE IS FOLLY
BLAKE'S REACH
DAUGHTER OF THE HOUSE
EDGE OF GLASS
A FALCON FOR A QUEEN
THE FILE ON DEVLIN
FIONA
THE PROPERTY OF A GENTLEMAN
SARA DANE
THE TILSIT INHERITANCE
FAMILY AFFAIRS
CORPORATION WIFE
I KNOW MY LOVE
THE LYNMARA LEGACY
PROMISES

FONTANA PAPERBACKS